To Yu...
from aut
and

N. Valeoy

CLAY MASK

KATE VALERY

Order this book online at www.trafford.com
or email orders@trafford.com

Most Trafford titles are also available at major online book retailers.

Print information available on the last page.

ISBN: 978-1-6987-1159-1 (sc)
ISBN: 978-1-6987-1158-4 (hc)
ISBN: 978-1-6987-1160-7 (e)

Library of Congress Control Number: 2022905629

Trafford rev. 06/14/2022

www.trafford.com
North America & international
toll-free: 844-688-6899 (USA & Canada)
fax: 812 355 4082

To the memory of
Armenian genius scientist, doctor-psychiatrist,
inventor of the cure for schizophrenia
with the help of a Clay Mask

Acknowledgments

I would like to thank my dear daughter, Inna August, for insisting that I write this book, which was in 2006 just outlined in a few sentences of the main ideas and events. The four of my main characters were barely sketched based on a newspaper's article about a genius scientist in Armenia who invented a cure for schizophrenia with the help of a clay mask. I read this article more than fifty years ago, but the invention itself and the unbelievable story of its creator-psychiatrist shocked me so much that I remembered it for many years.

While thinking about ideas for more new books to write, I jotted a sketch of the novel **Clay Mask**, but it was postponed for fifteen years because of many different circumstances in my life.

Maybe it would sound paradoxical, but I would like to thank the pandemic of COVID for giving me a chance to return to my writings. While sitting locked up at home, I got a huge inspiration, looking through my old notes and wrote my two last novels – **Midget or Symphony of the Ocean** (2020) and **Clay Mask** (2021). If not for COVID, I would have continued traveling around the world, enjoying excursions, concerts, theaters, exhibitions, museums, restaurants, as I did during previous times. But the pandemic stopped everything, so, I found new happiness, joy and fun returning to my creative writing occupation that was neglected for fifteen years.

And again, the biggest thank you to my dear boyfriend, Robert E. Butler, with whom we traveled together before the pandemic, but during this new boring reality of life, found another entertainment – editing. We edited **Midget** in summer 2020, mostly in the forest, in the fresh air.

However, **Clay Mask** took us much longer – summer 2021 in the forest and winter 2021-22 at home. Still, it was an amazing, really enjoyable process while we were laughing, giggling, joking, teasing each other, summarizing Bob's favorite words which he always pushed on me instead of my parasite-words. Sometimes we were even arguing fiercely (but friendly), until finally finding a mutually reasonable decision about grammar or word order.

Huge thank you, my dear Bob, for that enormous amount of time that you dedicated to my works, although you were always thanking me for giving you the opportunity to be first to enjoy my books which you considered page-turning and fascinating.

PART 1
THE BOOK OF POETRY

CHAPTER 1

Doctor Aaron Dispenmore was sitting by the computer in his home office, looking for information about a Psychiatry Scientific Conference in New York, scheduled for December, when he heard a light knock at his door and a sweet voice calling, "Daddy, it's time for a walk."

It was his five-year-old daughter, Laurie.

"I'm coming, sweetie," Aaron answered and closed the lid of his laptop, while glancing at his watch. It was seven o'clock exactly. Laurie never missed a minute of their time together.

He also liked their evening walks very much. They were really refreshing and soothing after his busy work days. The purity and vigor of his sweet child was a huge contrast with the heavy, black energy which he absorbed daily from his patients.

Aaron opened the door of his office and saw Laurie standing in the hallway ready to go. She was wearing a pink floral dress that her grandma, Aaron's mother, Beth, had recently sewn for her. A roomy fabric bag was hanging on Laurie's shoulder.

Aaron knew what was in this bag – small see-through lunch bags and empty plastic containers. During their walks Laurie collected a lot of things: flowers, bugs, snails, rocks, seashells, pine cones. When home, she played with her 'treasures' on the patio or in the backyard, cooking pretend dinners for her barbies. Today, one of the barbies' heads was sticking out from her bag. For their walks Aaron allowed only one doll at a time, so Laurie took them in turns.

It was the middle of June and the weather this summer was unusually hot for Seattle. Aaron was wearing a t-shirt, shorts and sandals, and Laurie wore sandals, too. In the evening the sun was still bright and they both needed sunglasses, as well.

"Look, daddy," Laurie said proudly, showing him her feet, "I have nail polish on my toes."

"Where did you get it?" Aaron asked, surprised.

"Granny gave it to me. We polished our nails together."

"Good for you," Aaron smiled, petting her blond curly hair. "Okay, let's go now."

They circled their house and went down the winding road that twisted between high hills for about a mile and eventually led to a busy street with a bus station and a convenience store. There Laurie would buy ice cream, using her allowance earned by cleaning her room, loading and unloading the dishwasher, and folding clean laundry. Aaron knew that in her big bag there was always a little wallet with money.

They passed by six houses in their fenced neighborhood and then started on an undeveloped part of the road. On the right side was a big field, a former swamp, now a huge construction site. The new townhouses in this area were growing like mushrooms after rain.

On the left side of the road were high hills, covered by a fir forest. The contours of ranch houses above were visible between the big old trees.

Next to their neighborhood was a building on top of the hill. It was hidden deep in the forest, and from the road only a small part of the roof could be noticed. A driveway paved with gravel led from there down to the street. Aaron and Laurie passed this private road every evening and had never paid any attention to it.

However today, Laurie found a dead snail on the street and decided to have a funeral for it. She already knew how to do that. They once had an old cat, who had died last year. They buried it with honor, made a little grave in their backyard and decorated it with flowers.

"Oh, poor snail," Laurie moaned, squatting beside the little sticky spot. She fished a plastic spoon from her bag and started digging a hole in the dusty sand at the edge of the asphalt. Then she placed the dead snail into the hole, spread the soil to cover it and set a little yellow flower on top.

"Rest in peace," she said and pressed her palms to each other, pretending that she was praying. She was so cute that Aaron could not stop smiling while watching her.

"Sir," he suddenly heard a woman's voice from behind and turned around abruptly. From the hill, on the gravel driveway, a young woman, more like a high school girl, was running down and shouting at him, "sir, do you live in the area?"

There was no panic in her voice. She ran probably only because it was more comfortable to move fast down the hill, than to walk slowly with gravel rolling under her feet. The girl stopped in front of him and Laurie, looking at them inquiringly.

"Yes," Aaron answered. "We live in the area. Why?"

"Then you probably know, where a bus stop is?"

"Yes, we do," Laurie stepped in. "There, by the ice cream store." She pointed her little finger in the direction of the big street.

Aaron was surprised by the question. The girl was coming from the house on the hill. It looked like she was living there and should know the area herself. But just to be polite, he said, "Yeah, about a mile. There is a street with a bus station and a convenience store. There are buses with three different numbers. Where do you need to go exactly?"

"Downtown," the girl announced, smiling.

"I think, none of the buses go downtown from there, but they do go to the three different train stations, as I heard. And from there you could easily reach downtown," Aaron explained, attentively eyeing the girl. He had never seen her in the neighborhood before.

She seemed about sixteen, tall, slim, pretty, with long straight blond hair and blue eyes. She wore a light-blue t-shirt and shorts, which showed her slender, well-tanned legs. Sport fabric Chinese slippers were on her feet and a little backpack was on her back – a typical 10th or 11th grade student. There wasn't anything special about her, quite the opposite - she looked very ordinary.

Often, while driving and passing schools at the end of classes, Aaron saw dozens, even hundreds of girls like this. They were walking home from school in groups, laughing, giggling with friends, and having fun. Or they were walking slowly, typing something on their phones, with earphones in their ears, not seeing anything around them, completely immersed into regular teen gossip about each other. They all were young, pretty, fresh, tall, slender, with long hair - so similar and trivial. He would sometimes wonder how the boys who were hitting on them at school found a difference between their girlfriend and others. Professionally, Aaron learned to read people well, but between those average teen girls he could not see any individuality whatsoever.

"Do you live in the area?" he asked.

"No," the girl shook her head. "I have no idea where I am. My parents dropped me here three days ago, but I don't want to stay any longer."

The reasonable question to ask was, why she didn't call her parents to pick her up, but Aaron felt that it wasn't his business to inquire of the perfect stranger, so he didn't say anything else.

Laurie said, instead of him, "Look, here is the grave of a snail. I made it. Someone on the street squashed the poor snail."

"Really?" the girl turned to her. "Where? Show me." She squatted with Laurie together, looking at the ground.

Jeez, there is about a ten-year difference between them, but they both act the same age, Aaron thought, observing a connection between the girls.

"I have a barbie here," Laurie said, pulling her doll from the bag. "I have twelve of them, but daddy does not allow me to take them all for a walk with us. So, they go in turns. Today is her turn."

"What is her name?" the girl asked.

"Tacoma."

"Isn't Tacoma a city?"

"Yes, it is. But I like it as a name, so I am calling her Tacoma," Laurie explained.

"I had seven barbies when I was your age. And I still have them."

"Why don't you go with us? We will see you off at the bus station," Laurie suggested.

"Thank you, it would be very nice of you," the girl agreed.

They stood up and walked together, talking very friendly and socially. Aaron followed them, being quite surprised. Laurie was a nice child, but not so much with complete strangers. It seemed unusual to him. At first, Aaron was listening to what they were talking about, but later, noticing that the subjects were mostly about barbies, he stopped paying attention.

Laurie waved her arms, showing the stranger girl the construction site on the right, ranches on the left, then - flowers from her bag. The girl was smiling, listening, nodding and commenting something nicely and attentively. Then Laurie nodded, agreeing on the girl's suggestion, and they ended up holding hands and walking together like best friends.

Aaron didn't protest because he knew that children usually have good intuition about strangers, almost like dogs, and they can feel if something is wrong or dangerous. According to his observation of Laurie, everything was right and he allowed his little daughter to walk ahead of him with the unknown girl, farther and farther away.

He started thinking about the conference in New York again because the conditions of attendance there were interesting and inspiring professionally. Scientists should make their own personal scientific discovery, and from there, if it would be recognized, they would be eligible to be nominated for the Nobel Prize. It was not easy, but worth a try.

When Aaron approached the busy street with the bus station, the girls had already crossed it and were standing on the other side by the empty buses. As soon as the light turned green he ran across the road to reach them, catching himself on being too reckless for allowing the unfamiliar person to lead Laurie that far ahead.

What was I thinking! he thought, showing a bit of a scowl. As he approached, the stranger girl who was hugging Laurie by the shoulders, said to him, smiling, "Thank you very much, sir. I will take a bus now. I just don't have any money. Would you mind lending me some for a bus pass?"

"I don't have any cash on me," Aaron answered, and it was true. He didn't like carrying cash and always used only credit cards. They weren't accepted on the buses, but, he had never taken a bus in his life.

"I do," Laurie suddenly stepped in, again. She took out her little wallet from her bag. "I have five dollars here. Would it be enough?"

What could Aaron say? His child was nice, helpful and generous. He should be proud of how he raised his daughter. It was impossible at such a moment to say no.

"Where exactly downtown are you going?" he asked, as the girl took the five one-dollar banknotes from Laurie's little hand.

"I don't know," the girl shrugged. "I would like to see my friends."

"I understand, but where are they living? Which part of downtown? I mean, maybe this money wouldn't be enough, if there is another bus after the train. Do you have an exact address?"

The girl shrugged again. "I don't know. I will walk and find them. They live on the streets."

Her answer was so unusual, that Aaron didn't know what to say. The girl was clean, neat and even smelled of strawberry shampoo. It didn't look like she would have any homeless friends.

"Thank you, little one," she said, thrusting the money into her shorts pocket and squatting in front of Laurie. "I am not sure that I will see you again and I may not have a chance to return your money, but... you know what... I can give you something, as well."

She opened her backpack, pulled out a standard size pocketbook and handed it to Aaron's little daughter. "Let's say I sold you this book for five bucks," she suggested and laughed.

"Thank you," Laurie said, taking the book and putting it into her bag. "Daddy will read it to me before sleep."

The girl hugged Laurie, jumped into the bus and paid for the ticket. While Laurie waved a farewell to her, Aaron held his daughter by her hand, just in case, until the bus left. Then they walked into the convenience store and Aaron bought Laurie an ice cream.

"You were so kind, helpful and generous with that girl," he said. "That's how people should always be – helping each other. You really deserve to have your treat. Thank you, my little darling. I am proud of you and incredibly happy to have a daughter like you."

"Thank you, daddy," Laurie smiled. "I like her. She told me a lot about her barbies."

"Did she tell you her name?" Aaron asked.

"No. She told me the names of her barbies. And she said that she likes my Tacoma."

"Did she ask your name?"

"No. She called me - little one. But I like her very much."

"Okay," Aaron agreed, still thinking that the stranger girl was so unremarkable and ordinary, that there was not much to like.

On the way back home, as soon as Laurie finished with the ice cream, she continued picking her different 'treasures' for the barbies' soup and Aaron kept thinking about the conference, so they both were having a good time, as they usually did during their evening walks.

As they approached the gravel driveway that led down the hill, beside where they had met the girl, there was now a police car standing across the road. Another police car was up on the driveway, closer to the house hidden between trees. Two policemen were situated by the car, holding some folders.

"Do you live in the area, sir?" one of them asked, as he saw Aaron and Laurie.

It seemed to Aaron a bit funny – this was the second time during the last hour that he had heard the same question.

"Yes," he nodded.

"While walking around, did you by a chance, meet this young woman?" the policeman inquired, showing the photo, and Aaron was astonished to recognize the girl which they had just seen off on the bus.

"Yes, she walked with us to the bus station. She left on the bus about twenty minutes ago."

"Which bus number?" the police officer glanced at him with interest.

"I really didn't notice. She said she is going downtown. What happened? Is she a runaway? Are you looking for her as a missing person?"

"No," the policeman shook his head. "Not at all. Sorry, I can't give you any information."

"Let me see, let me see," begged Laurie, jumping to catch a glimpse of the photo in his hands. He bowed down and showed her the picture. "Yes, it's her. You know, she has seven barbies. And she has friends who are living on the streets downtown."

"Thank you, sweetie. It's especially useful information," the policeman smiled at Laurie. "Sir, would you mind telling us everything you know about this young lady?"

"Of course, I don't mind," Aaron agreed, "but I have almost nothing to say." He repeated to the policemen everything that the girl had said, included all of his observations, and added, "She mostly walked with my daughter, holding her hand. I didn't hear much of what they were talking about."

"She told me the names of her barbies," Laurie said, really wanting to be involved and helpful, "Rosie, Vally, Anastasia, Ruby, Kiki, Nora and Tobi."

"Did you remember them all?" The policeman looked surprised, no less than Aaron.

"Yes," Laurie reassured, feeling proud that she had a chance to show off her memory. "She said that Rosie is the best, and Tobi is the worst. Tobi is angry. She kills people. But the good thing is that she does not come out very often."

"Actually, sir, it was very reckless of you to allow that," the policeman shook his head in disapproval. "Very-very reckless. Don't let a stranger touch your child... ever."

"Sorry," Aaron uttered confusingly. "I feel that now. At the time, she looked quite nice."

"They all do," the policeman noted.

Aaron talked a bit more with the officers, then exchanged business cards with them, in case something else comes up, and then he and Laurie left. It was getting late and his little daughter's bedtime was approaching.

"What happened, daddy? What happened?" Laurie wondered on the way to their house.

"I don't know, sweetie. They just want to see that girl. Maybe she is lost and her parents are looking for her."

Aaron purposely avoided the truthful answer, trying not to scare his daughter. But the policeman told him clearly that it wasn't the case. The stranger girl was obviously a suspect in something which the police did not want to share.

"But I like her very-very much," Laurie repeated. "She told me a poem about a little birdie."

"What poem?" Aaron asked, expecting to hear a childish rhyme like a *Twinkle, twinkle, little star.*

"I can tell you. I remember," Laurie said confidently. "She wrote this verse for her uncle, just today. Listen." She stopped in the middle of the road and started to recite.

> "Little birdie is banging it's chest on the glass.
> There is a world outside:
>> Yellow houses and purple towers,
>> Green grass and pink flowers.
> I can see it, but I can't reach it.
> Please, give me a chance to live,
>> Open the window for me!"

"Jeez!" Aaron remarked in surprise. It was not childish at all. It was more worrisome, disturbing, and sad; also full of hidden pain and not ordinary at all. "Why did she tell you that?"

"I don't know," Laurie shrugged. "She said her uncle was very kind to her and she wanted to do something nice for him in return."

"Well," Aaron concluded, making a wry face, "actually, it's not our business. We should go home now, sweetie. Grandma is already waiting for us, I am sure."

But this moment left him something to think about later.

At home, Aaron kissed his daughter good night and let his mother, Beth, take Laurie upstairs, prepare her for bed, and read her a book. They usually did that in turns and today was grandma's turn. He went to his office, opened his laptop and continued researching the New York conference. Despite of today's unsettling events, he still had to work.

His mother knocked at his door in about one hour, holding a local newspaper, *The Neighbor.*

"Arie, my dear," she said, "here is an article in our community paper which you should read. It's about that big house on the hill in the forest, next door. Laurie told me the story about that girl you met. Here, in the last issue, there is a warning for the whole neighborhood to be overly cautious.

"This building is a shelter for severely mentally ill youth. Almost like a jail for very sick and troubled young people who committed some heinous crimes and are not criminally responsible because of their illnesses. It includes kidnapping children, rape, robbery, assaults with deadly weapons and even murders.

"It's still not a prison, and security is not very tight. Occasionally some of those teens escape. That is what the warning is all about. I read it yesterday. Sorry, I didn't say anything to you before you went for a walk tonight."

"Wow!" Aaron exclaimed, knitting his brows and shaking his head in disbelief. "Shame on me! It's my profession and I didn't notice anything in her. She looked so ordinary... Actually, until that poem..."

'The ordinary girl' didn't seem that ordinary anymore.

CHAPTER 2

It was already close to midnight, but Aaron still didn't go to sleep. There was a lot of information about the New York conference to read and to study. He would normally be interested in it, but something else was bothering him and taking his attention away from work.

He was very curious about that girl he had met during his walk with Laurie. There were three points in his curiosity. First – what mental illness she had, that wasn't visible, and he, in spite of being a professional, missed? Second – which crime she committed that caused the police to look for her? And, third – what spell did she cast on him that made him so reckless that he almost allowed her to kidnap the treasure of his life – his little daughter? Aaron shuddered imagining that she could easily have jumped into a bus with Laurie and gone, if there had been one leaving at that exact moment.

The chance to satisfy his curiosity was pretty slim. The police would not tell him anything. What else could he do? To visit the mysterious house on the hill trying to find out some information about the girl? But it was also very questionable. Privacy laws did not allow institutions to share any data about their patients.

Then Aaron suddenly remembered that the girl gave Laurie a book. He completely forgot about it, and Laurie obviously had as well. Otherwise his mother would have told him that they had read this new book before his little daughter went to sleep.

Aaron tiptoed to Laurie's bedroom and carefully entered, trying not to make any noise. There was a nightlight on the wall beside her bed, and consequently, the visibility was pretty decent. For a couple of minutes he watched his sleeping child who was lying in bed with her arms wide spread and her beautiful blond curls matted on a pillow. She looked so cozy, cute, innocent and happy, but at the same time very vulnerable.

Aaron shuddered again, thinking that because of his recklessness this bed could be empty now, and he and Beth would be crazily crying somewhere at a police station, begging them to find his daughter. It was too scary of a thought, so he pushed it away, and turned around looking for Laurie's big fabric bag. There it was, hanging on the back of a chair.

He thrust his hand inside and immediately felt the book cover between the lunch bags and plastic boxes full of Laurie's 'treasures'. Taking out the book and walking away from his daughter's bedroom into his own room took Aaron only several seconds. He sat on his bed, turned on a reading lamp, and looked at what he was holding in his hand. It obviously was not a children's book.

"Rosalyn Vivano," Aaron read, "Lightening in Darkness of Soul. Anthology of poetry. Hmm... wow... interesting..."

He didn't have a chance to open the book or even look at the back cover because at that moment his phone rang in his pocket and he answered the call. It was Helen Harrison – a former best friend of his late wife.

"Hey, Arie," she said. "Where the hell are you?"

"At home."

"Why? Didn't you promise to come over tonight?"

"No, I didn't. As I remember, we talked about the weekend, but it is still only Friday."

"Jeez, are you kidding me? The weekend starts in half an hour. What are you doing there?"

"I am reading a book... Before sleep..." he answered.

"You sound like you're not thirty, but seventy. Interesting book?"

"I don't know, yet."

"What is it about?"

"Poetry."

"Since when are you reading such rubbish?"

"Since tonight."

"So, that's what you prefer instead of seeing me?"

"Hmm..." Aaron didn't want to answer. Helen was aggressive and he really didn't like that. He readily would say – yes...

"Why are you always playing such a picky diva, Arie? I am actually doing you a favor by sleeping with you. I am a beautiful woman and it would be enough for me to just whistle and a line of men would be here right away for that."

"Okay," he said, "then whistle..." and hung up.

He was tired of her attacks, knowing that all day on Saturday she would call again and again, and insist that he come over in the evening. And he probably would, after his walk with Laurie.

Aaron lowered his head onto his pillow, put the book aside and started thinking.

His history with Helen was pretty tricky. She had chased him for ten years. It felt funny to him that he couldn't point a finger at who she was now. She was not a girlfriend because they had never dated and he didn't want to go out with her. She was not a friend because, in his opinion, the meaning of friendship was mutual liking, understanding, help, support and shared interests. Aaron didn't like her, nor did she understand him, and, although they had some common professional interests, still it was more fierce competition than help and support. She was also not a lover because he was sure that this word implied the presence of mutual love in a relationship, but he had none. Helen always repeated that she loved him, but he didn't believe it.

So, who the hell is she? Aaron thought. In his mind he gave her the proper status – the best friend of his late wife, with whom now he had sex sometimes because she was very persistent with that.

Aaron and Ally were high-school sweethearts and had been madly in love since they were sixteen. At the age of twenty, they got married and went to college together. During their sophomore year they met Helen Harrison, who was smitten with Aaron at first sight. He noticed right away, how she looked at him and his suspicions were confirmed when she saw his wedding band and exclaimed, "Are you married? At twenty? Are you crazy? You shouldn't be a doctor in psychiatry, you should be a patient!" He and Ally, both considered this as a joke.

Then Helen invited Ally for coffee, then shopping together, then to a hairdresser, and they eventually became good friends, and in time even the best of friends. They were very close and open with each other and Ally excitedly told Helen everything about her husband. Pretty soon, Helen knew all his likes, his habits, his preferences, his attractions, his interests, everywhere, even in bed. In return, she told Ally all the details about her boyfriends, though the value of this information was unequal. But Ally didn't get it.

Aaron was a talented and very advanced outstanding student, compared to both young ladies. He earned his undergraduate university degree in just two years, then obtained his master's degree, then in the following two years - his PhD.

Ally was getting her bachelor's degree, when they decided that it was time to have a child. So, little Laurie was happily conceived, carried and born before Ally got her master's. Her graduation party took place when Laurie was one-month-old. And the same evening became the evening of Ally's death. Aaron was left a twenty-five-year-old widower with a tiny baby in his arms.

Luckily for Aaron, if it is possible to use the word *luck* at all in this situation, his mother, Beth, was there. She had just retired and came from Atlanta, to visit her son's family and to see her newly-born granddaughter. When Aaron and Ally went to the party, she stayed at home with Laurie. Ally was breastfeeding, so there were prepared a few bottles with her milk in the freezer for the grandma to feed Laurie when it was needed. That was it. Nothing more left from Ally.

For the first couple of months after Ally's death, Aaron wasn't capable of doing anything, he simply cried like a baby from the sudden shock, horror, and pain. So, Beth took upon herself to give tiny Laurie all the care she needed.

If it was not for his mother's stay, the tragedy would be doubled for Aaron. There was no chance for him to get any other help with the baby. Ally didn't have any family at all - she was a foster child. It was the reason they got married so early. Aaron wanted to give Ally the possibility to feel and create their own family.

Aaron himself was very lucky with his upbringing – his parents were from the two very different national backgrounds, both European. His mother, Beth, was Greek, dark haired with the brown, almost black eyes, which he inherited, and his father was a tall and blond English man of many generations. They were good, kind and happy people, and Aaron was raised in warmth and love.

In his family, they were not novices for the tragedy of death. Aaron's father, George Dispenmore, died of cancer several years before. However, it was very different.

He was ten years older than Beth, in his seventies, and he had been battling the illness for five years. They were worrying about him, helping him, and supporting him but deep inside their hearts they knew that the end was approaching. They were emotionally prepared for that.

George Dispenmore was a commercial pilot, he was happily married, he raised his son, he lived a long, interesting and successful life which one day would be coming to an end. It was sad, but it was a logical way of life - what life normally was supposed to be.

Ally Dispenmore, on the contrary, was twenty-five, young and healthy. She walked the Earth with the fresh outlook, and her life had just started. She didn't accomplish much yet, but she had a husband who loved her to death; she had borne a child and she just earned her master's degree. Her whole life lay ahead of her and then, oops, she was gone. It was unexpected, not normal, not a regular way of life. It was a complete disaster. It was a bolt from the blue.

The loss of Ally felt for Aaron like a loss of everything - loss of the meaning of his existence. Without her, there was no need, no reason and no interest for him to live. He was absolutely lost and seriously ready to commit suicide. His mother was the one who sobered him.

Beth sat beside him on his bed where he sobbed, digging his face into a pillow. She was petting his head and patting his back.

"Arie," she said quietly, comforting him. "You have to calm down, son. Did you forget that you are not alone? Here is a tiny piece of Ally which she left with you and which will be with you forever – your mutual little daughter. And you should live for her. She does not deserve to become a full orphan and go to foster care after my death. I am not young, Arie. Let's assume I will live ten more years. Then Laurie will be only ten and she could find herself out in the foster system. From Ally, you heard what usually happens with little girls in those stranger's houses. You don't want this for your daughter. She is a creation of your love with Ally, she has yours and Ally's blood together.

"You're a smart boy, Arie, you always were. So, get reasonable, sober up, collect yourself. You have no right to die now. Your mission is to live and to raise your child. I will sell my house in Atlanta. I will move here with you and Laurie. I will try to be the best substitute mother for her, but you have to be the father now. You have to be the man of the house."

Aaron was incredibly thankful to his mother for her support. It looked like she had given him life for a second time now. After his emotional death, he was reborn again, and finally found the inner strength to hold himself in check and surpass his tragedy.

But he was still numb and dead inside. Except for his little family, he had only one interest – to finish his doctorate, and to learn more about science, psychology, psychiatry, finding more different ways of treatment for his patients, and working hard. And yes, maybe one day to make his own scientific discovery and try to get the Nobel Prize. He became increasingly career-oriented and knew for sure that his only love story had completely ended. No women and no love would exist for him from now on.

During that difficult time, Helen somehow distanced herself while knowing perfectly that the way to Aaron's heart was now open. She had no idea that he made for himself a strict decision – he had no heart anymore; it died with Ally. But even if Helen guessed that, she was pretty sure that she would be capable of reviving his heart because of her extensive experience with men. So, she grabbed at this chance like a fierce predator grabbing for prey.

However, for some reason Aaron felt in his gut an extreme resistance to her. For a couple of years after Ally's death he refused to see Helen and avoided talking to her. He prohibited Beth from communicating with Helen as well, and from letting her in, when she tried to come over to express her sympathy and suggest her help.

Beth didn't really understand that because to her this young woman, whom she saw at Ally's funeral, looked nice and friendly. During the years after Ally's death, she tried to touch the subject of Helen with her son a couple of times, but was always unsuccessful. He was adamant about the topic.

"No, mom," Aaron said. "You don't know her. I have a deep feeling that she is malicious and manipulative, and obsessed with power and control. She pretends to be in love with me, but in reality she just wants to suppress, to squash, to own me and I will never allow that. I don't have any evidence, but I feel that she is double-faced, and I won't give her a chance, ever, to take even one step inside my house and to interfere with you or Laurie in any way."

"Oh gosh, Arie," his mother was surprised. "If she is just obsessed with power and control, as you assume, she could choose any other man. Why exactly you? Maybe you're too harsh on her? Maybe she is really in love with you? And there's nothing wrong with that. You're an attractive man."

"Mo-om!" Aaron smirked. "I am - to you, because you are my mother and you love me. It is the only reason why you are overestimating me."

"I don't think I am overestimating you, son," Beth laughed. "But you should think that one day Laurie will need a mother and you will need a woman. You're not a monk and not a saint, you're a normal twenty-eight-year-old man."

"Mo-om!" Aaron blushed. "I don't want to talk about that."

"I think you have to, Arie. Three years have passed since Ally has been gone. You have to move on. Think about that. Maybe, try to give this woman a chance. She is pretty, well educated. You have known her for many years. Now you are colleagues. And she loves you."

Aaron knew that his mother was wise. Usually, he respected her opinion and advice, but this was too private of an issue. However, he started thinking about that and tried to understand what was going on inside his body and soul.

He considered every human as a half of a spiritual person, and a half of an animal. His spiritual part on this scale was full – family, work, memory of Ally that will occupy it forever. But his animal part, what his mother had suspected right, was empty, and, with years, subconsciously he was getting eager to fill this emptiness. He held himself in check sexually only because he was not thinking about that. He prohibited himself from those thoughts, and they evaporated, they were gone.

But the physical nature of a human's body existed objectively and it was impossible just to cancel it and to pretend that it was not there. So, he kind of yielded, and when one day Helen called and, probably already for the hundredth time, invited him for a visit he decided to give it a tentative try.

However, Aaron set the boundaries of their agreement right away: no love, no dates, no friendship, just casual sexual encounters and only when he wanted - maybe once in a couple of weeks. Not as she wanted, almost every day. If she agreed to these conditions, he could stay. If she did not, he would leave right away and forever.

Of course, Helen agreed and was even happy about this arrangement. It was better than nothing. She waited many years for him. And she was also sure that she could turn everything toward her desired direction anyway. She would finally get him and he would belong to her forever.

Actually, it turned out not to be bad for Aaron, much better than he expected. Helen knew him pretty well from Ally's stories.

They continued these casual meetings for two years, but it wasn't going at all in the direction which Helen craved. She obviously overestimated her own power and underestimated Aaron's stubbornness and strong will. He was doing strictly what he wanted, only. It was impossible to influence him.

One time they even fought fiercely. It happened when Helen proved that she knew some very personal, intimate and sacred details about him which she could never know by herself. It became clear to Aaron that she found out these things from Ally, and it made him furious.

Aaron could see now that all her so-called 'friendship' with Ally was fake. It was a plot which she invented to catch him. She collected information, like a professional spy would gather data and then look for a foreign government to whom he could sell it for large sums of money. Helen wanted to sell it to him for the biggest price – his love.

The realization of this made Aaron very angry. He yelled that he hates her, would never see her again, and he stormed out from her condo, slamming the door.

However, Helen found a way to earn his forgiveness. Aaron didn't answer her calls and didn't let her in his house, but, at work, she sneaked into his office. She cried a lot, swearing that her spying was because of her love only - her real true love which made her crazy.

Aaron softened a bit because he could understand that. In his time he was crazily in love with Ally. He knew that this kind of love existed and partially believed that she, maybe, really had experienced that and was forced by that to cheat on Ally, wanting to know everything about him. And also, he thought, *What the hell! I kind of got used to sleeping with her. At least, it worked for a while.* So, one new condition was added to their agreement – Helen should forget what she had learned from Ally and just be herself.

Now, laying on his bed with the book beside him, Aaron sincerely tried to find some feelings for Helen in his heart. Alas, there was none, except for one – a premonition that something was not right. He still distrusted her love, still remained cautious with her and still suspected her of something, not knowing exactly of what. But for sex she was pretty good... Well... His experience with women was quite restricted. What did he know except for Ally and Helen? Practically, nothing...

Aaron took the book, flipped through it casually, then turned it around and there she was – the ordinary girl from their evening walk with Laurie. There was a picture of her on the back cover, the same picture that the policeman had shown him.

She authored the book of poetry?! Jeez! Criminal poetess! Wow! Aaron thought bewildered. Then he read the back cover.

Rosalyn Vivano was born in 1995 in Seattle, WA. She began to write poetry at age 11 on an Internet Poetry site. From the very beginning, her audience was shocked because no one could believe that these poems were written by a child. Since that time, she has won all literature youth competitions in the USA in all categories – fiction, non-fiction and poetry - in all age groups 12-14, 15-17, 18-20.

Rosalyn is really involved in the youth movement *Slam Poetry* and performs her poems on stage in all their events in Seattle and also in New York, Atlanta, San Francisco, Los Angeles, Boston, Philadelphia, Minneapolis and Chicago.

Her poems were published in many respected magazines like *Fiction and Poetry, New Yorker, Poetical Discovery, Young Authors of the West, Literary Orphans, Doll Hospital Journal, Vagabond City,* and *Vine Leaves Literary Journal*. She is also working as poetry editor for those magazines and for two years teaching poetry class in high school *Lord of Scotland* from which she graduated with an honors diploma in 2012. This anthology of poetry by Rosalyn Vivano contains her selected works written at age 15-17.

Aaron dropped the book in complete shock. She was not a teenager as he thought. She was already twenty, though she looked much younger than her age. And she was quite famous in her area. At least, she was extremely far from ordinary... And she was mentally ill... And she was a criminal whom the police were looking for. Unbelievable! It was a big puzzle for him to solve.

He decided for sure, that the first thing in the morning, he would go to the house on the hill to learn more about her. Now he was on the hook of curiosity a hundred times stronger than before.

And then he read the whole night.

CHAPTER 3

This Friday evening a psychiatric nurse, Thomas Spencer, arrived at his night shift at the *Youth Shelter* five minutes earlier than his usual work time seven p.m. He chatted for a while with another nurse whom he would relieve. Then, making sure that his partner was gone home, he walked into a hallway and unlocked one of the doors.

"Hey, kiddo," he said. "How are you doing?"

"I am okay. I am ready," answered a girl who was sitting on her bed with a prepared backpack lying beside her. She had taken a shower, changed into a clean light-blue t-shirt and shorts, combed her hair and made herself look very decent. She even smelled like strawberry shampoo. It was a big difference from the previous nights when Thomas was dealing with strong attacks of her illness.

"Who is here with us today?" he asked.

"Rosie," she smiled

"How about Vally and Nora from yesterday?"

"They are gone, uncle Ashot. For now, I am Rosie. I am absolutely sure. Don't worry about me."

"Okay, Rosie. Here is the address," he gave the girl a little piece of paper and she thrust it into her short's pocket. "And here is money for a bus. I know there is a bus station not far away," he continued. "I am giving you half an hour to find it. Then I will call the police. I have to. Got it?"

"Yes," the girl nodded. She made a step toward him and hugged him strongly. "Thank you so much, uncle Ashot. I, actually, wrote something today, while waiting for you," and she gave him a piece of paper.

He hugged her as well, patting her back. "Okay, kiddo, thank you. I will read it. I have the whole night for that. Good luck!"

"See you tomorrow, uncle Ashot."

"Tell Liam, I will come home a bit later. My relief partner just asked me to stay in the morning for three more hours for him. So, I will leave here only at ten."

"Yes, uncle Ashot, will do," Rosie nodded. "Bye."

They walked together out of the house. Beside the gravel driveway heading down the hill Thomas stopped, unlocked the gate and let the girl run by herself toward the street. Down, where she was heading, he noticed a man standing by and a little girl who was squatting and digging something on the edge of the road. He heard Rosie shouting, "Sir, do you live in the area?"

Good luck, Thomas thought. *Maybe those people will tell her where the bus stop is.* And then he walked into the garden behind the house to water flowers which was a part of his regular duty. He was not just a psychiatric nurse here, but also a security guard, janitor and maintenance worker.

At about nine p.m., when the police finally left after Thomas completed his report about an escaping patient on his watch, he got a phone call from the owner of the shelter who was obviously mad, receiving the incident report from the police. He told Thomas sternly that he was fired because he had neglected his duty by forgetting to lock one of the doors.

It was pretty much expected and Thomas didn't worry about that. He now had far more important things to do, than work here. This would be his last shift.

He prepared a large pot of coffee and comfortably placed his laptop on the desk by the office entrance knowing that it would be a long and difficult night. He was ready to start his experiment – the patient was found; the big part of a puzzle was solved. Only one piece was missing – a doctor. But he should be ready to introduce his materials of a cure to the doctor, once he will choose one. His articles needed to be prepared beforehand. It was time to work on them now.

All information about his twenty experiments in the Psychiatric clinic in the Armenian capital, Yerevan, which he established during 1980–85 and brought to the USA as a microfilm in his pocket, was now deciphered, written down and packed into several folders. They were kept at his home, in a safe, where his husband, Liam, was keeping his Japanese cameras and lenses.

Those were the most important things in their life – his folders and Liam's cameras. Liam Johnson was a professional cameraman in movie productions; Ashot Petrosian, was a medical doctor and scientist in psychiatry.

In spite of the tag on the chest pocket of his nurse uniform displaying his American name – Thomas Spencer – he still asked people around to call him Ashot. He loved his real name and didn't want to part with it. If people wondered why he preferred to be called that strange name, he normally answered that 'Ashot' was a fond nickname which his mother used for him. Everybody believed that explanation and followed.

Now Ashot decided to start his introduction to a doctor, or to the board of judges at the New York Psychiatry Scientific Conference with a simple short biography. With that, he began to write.

... I was born in 1955 in Yerevan, the capital city of Armenia. At that time Armenia wasn't an independent country – it was one of the Kavkaz Mountain Range Republics of the Soviet Union.

After my high school graduation in 1972, I moved to Moscow, the capital of the Soviet Union, where I became a student of the First Medical Institute. I successfully got my master's degree in 1977, and accomplished my PhD study in psychiatry in 1980. Then I returned to Yerevan where I got a high position in the newly opened psychiatric clinic under the roof of The Scientific Research Institute of Psychiatry.

At the same time I got married and had a little daughter, Annush, born on May 17, 1981.

During my five-year work in this clinic, I discovered a very unusual method of treating some patients with severe schizophrenic conditions and completely healed twenty of them. They became 100 percent healthy people.

One of my cured patients was a homosexual man and he fell in love with me. It helped me to understand suddenly that I am gay as well. In the Soviet Union it was a sure ticket to a prison - it was considered a serious crime. However, I confessed my sexuality to my wife because I wanted to be honest with her. She promised not to report me to the police. She wanted me to keep my work with an impressive salary and pay her a good child support. I just moved out and we amicably divorced...

Confused, Ashot stopped writing. He wasn't sure if it was correct to write about that. Here, in the USA, same-sex marriages were approved by law and he and Liam had been already married for three years, but still... It was not related to his business. It was private. His writing now should be a presentation of his work, his finding of the cure, but not a personal life story. However, without providing an explanation, it wouldn't be understandable for Americans.

Then he continued:

... In 1985, expecting that with Gorbachev in power, there would be more freedom and out of the box thinking in the communist society, I decided to introduce my scientific discovery of patients' treatment to the Board of Academicians in Moscow's Academy of Medical Science. I wasn't looking for any fame or money. I just wanted to make my way of the remedy known because it proved to be successful and it could save the health, and even life of many sufferers.

However, it didn't turn out well. The president of the Academic Board suggested approving my invention, which deserved a Nobel Prize in his opinion, if I would put his name on it. He promised that when he received the Nobel Prize for it, he would share the money with me. The discovery was my baby, and the meaning of my life.

It meant everything to me, and just giving it away to a powerful undistinguished bureaucrat was too hurtful and humiliating. I became very angry and boldly refused, though I knew that in the Soviet Union people usually got severe punishment for keeping their dignity and self-respect.

Right away, I was declared as a charlatan who was shaming the status of a 'soviet psychiatrist' and lost all my achievements – my medical master's diploma and my PhD diploma; even my high school diploma and my passport were taken from me. It was prohibited for me to do any medical work. If I did, I would face many years in prison, or get admitted to a special locked psychiatric clinic, where, with the use of strong drugs, I would be turned into a male who completely lost his mind. That was what the communist society usually did with people who went out of the way of their rulings. And Gorbachev's time was, sadly, no different from all previous times.

Together with the loss of work came the loss of salary, causing me the inability to pay child support to my former wife. This made her upset and she decided to report me to the police as a homosexual. To escape my arrest, I was forced to become a fugitive on the loose...

What happened to Ashot in the Soviet Union after that he really did not want to share here. It was a big secret of his survival. Now, he just sat by his computer and kept thinking, and remembering the events that occurred thirty years ago, and trying to choose some pieces of the story which would be safe to reveal to the Americans - if there would be any at all...

...The best way to get lost and escape arrest was to go into a huge city with a population of millions, like Moscow, where one could easily disappear in a crowd, and Ashot did exactly that. Before leaving Yerevan forever, he obtained some money by selling his car and everything he had in his apartment: furniture, dishes, even clothes, leaving himself just a couple of spare sets in a small backpack. He kept money in a pouch, hanging on his neck under a t-shirt, together with the little of what was left of his family treasures: his father's golden ring and his mother's antique golden cross. He knew that he would need to pay somewhere, somehow, for food and shelter. His biggest treasure - the microfilm with the documentation of his discovery and all his patients' files - was in the zipped chest pocket of his jacket all the time.

Ashot was sleeping on a bench in the Moscow train station for a week, not knowing what to do or where to go. He really didn't want to die at the age of thirty, but it seemed as he likely might - to save himself from the horrors of a communist prison. And for what? For being a creative and talented scientist who made a discovery that really was worth the Nobel Prize? What future was in front of him? None. What waited for him ahead? Nothing. He was at the bottom of life at the moment. Was there a way up? He doubted it, but he still had hope. Like a sailor from a sunken ship, holding onto a piece of wood, floating in the middle of the ocean hoping that maybe, just maybe, some other ship will pass by and save him. One chance in a billion... The last straw of life... Please, God help me...

Ashot was raised as an atheist as required for all Soviet Union citizens. Armenian Christianity was one of the oldest in the world, but ancient Armenian churches only allowed visits as museums. He never prayed or even thought about God. As a scientist he believed in the material base of things, although his cure contained a lot of spirituality, but he still found the physical explanation of energy fields and layers of auras that surrounded a human body.

However, now, there was nothing left for him, just to pray, and he did. Somehow the inner craving for faith may have been hidden inside his soul for generations, for hundreds of years of Armenian devotion to Christianity. Ashot wasn't sure where it appeared from or why. Maybe his mother's golden cross hanging on his neck and touching his bare chest spread some special energy into his being?

While laying down on the hard wooden bench in the train station, he just prayed and prayed, even though he didn't know how. Nobody had ever taught him. The prayer subconsciously came out from the deep of his soul.

The train station had a strong odor. The stale smell of dirt, sweat and urine from public toilets was eternal there. It was disgusting and made it difficult to breathe. A break in a stable rainfall finally allowed Ashot to go outside and sit on the bench on the edge of the huge Three Train Stations' Square.

Now, it was a dark and chilly night. The lights of the city were shining around and cars splashed through puddles on the wet asphalt.

Ashot heard a sound of high heels clicking beside him, but he didn't turn his head until someone tapped his shoulder.

"Hey, little man, do you have any spare smokes?" a husky voice asked. He realized that it was Tamara, a train station prostitute, whom he had seen around throughout the duration of the week. She had never approached him before. To her, he didn't look like a potential client. He looked poor.

"Yes, I do," Ashot said and pulled out a pack of cigarettes from his outside pocket and handed them to her. He never smoked himself, however he knew that it was beneficial to have the cigarettes always on him for protection. To refuse such a request on Moscow's streets could leave one severely beaten or even killed.

"Oh, that's generous," Tamara laughed, taking three cigarettes from the pack which she returned to him. "Thanks, little man. Why the hell were you sitting here the whole week? Do you have money? Do you wanna have some fun?"

"No," Ashot shook his head. "I am gay."

"Wow!" she whistled. "What if I call the police? You can be arrested. Aren't you scared to tell me about that?"

He shrugged. "Well, prostitution is a crime as well. I could call the police on you. Aren't you scared?"

"No, silly," she chuckled huskily. "I am paying the cops here. They even pimp me out. I am okay. But don't worry. I won't rat you out. You gave me the cigarettes. It was nice of you. And you look kind of decent, though far from handsome. You have such an eggplant looking nose. Are you Armenian? They usually have big noses..."

"Yes, I am," Ashot said. He wasn't offended. He realized that it was a sort of friendly joke on her part.

"Oh, Armenian!" Tamara smirked and sat beside him on the bench, crossing her full thighs, exposing her black lace leggings.

She lit the cigarette. "I know a lot of anecdotes about Armenians. Like – 'where one Armenian did his business, there is nothing left to do even for two Jews.' And a lot of 'Armenian Radio' jokes. Here is one: To screw a woman wearing a condom is the same as to sniff a rose wearing a gas mask." She neighed loud and sincerely. "Jeez! I love them. They are funny. They, actually, mostly assume that you, Armenians, are crooks and rich thieves. But if you were rich, you would drive a Mercedes, not sleep on the train station bench, wouldn't you? Why the hell are you here?"

"I was a doctor, but I've lost everything," Ashot explained. "My family, work, education, even my passport... everything."

"Well," Tamara shook her head in surprise, "so, you're kind of an outlaw? Nice. Welcome to the underground world, bro."

And then, with difficulty suppressing a spasm of tears, Ashot suddenly told her his whole life story. He didn't know why he started talking. Probably he couldn't stay silent anymore. He had no chance to converse with anybody for a long time. His tragedy just burst out from his soul. Talking was giving him mental relief – he was not alone. Someone was listening with interest, and it didn't matter that it was a train station prostitute. She was a human being sitting beside him and it was all that mattered at that moment.

"Wow!" Tamara said as he finished his story. She lit the second cigarette and smirked. "Actually, it's pretty typical for this damn country. We, my husband and I, are dealing with similar kinds of crap."

"Are you married?" Ashot asked bewildered.

"Yes, I am. My husband is in the hospital now. I am earning money here for our illegal escape over the border. He is a high class boxer, a sportsman. There was a competition and he was told that he should lose because his competitor was the son of a big communist boss. He refused. He is actually a pretty honest dude and has self-respect. So, he won the fight, and after that he, of course, lost his work as a boxing trainer and plus, an assassin was sent to our home. He stabbed my hubby with a knife. It was aimed at the heart, but the knife missed it by one centimeter, so my husband survived. As soon as he leaves the hospital we will escape from this cursed country."

"Do you know how to do that?" Ashot looked at her with interest.

Tamara nodded, inhaling a big cloud of smoke. "I got one client here, Sergey. He is a professional smuggler. He gave me the whole route. I guess, for you, freaking Armenian, would that not be a bad idea too?"

"I never thought about that," Ahsot uttered slowly. "It never crossed my mind... I don't have a passport anymore. How could I go over the border? I can't buy a tourist trip... but... now I have no future and no life here. If I could escape from here... it's probably the only way for me to survive."

"Not just survive," Tamara giggled. "Thrive! That smugger told me how all of his clients are doing there. They are great! In the free world, Russian talents are blossoming. Though, you're not Russian, but anyway... How about your English? Do you know some?"

"Actually, I am not bad at English. When I passed tests for my PhD, I had the foreign language exam on a pretty high level. It was obligatory. I forgot a bit now because it was a few years ago, but I could remember, if needed."

"Good," Tamara said. "I am learning now, and my husband in the hospital is reading a school English workbook. Grade five!" she laughed huskily. "What the heck!"

"Could you take me with you and your husband on that escape trip?" Ashot asked.

"No. It is difficult and people shouldn't go in big groups. Even my hubby and I will go our separate ways and meet each other later. But I can tell you, what you can do, because you were kind to me with those cigarettes. I've never actually met such a nice person here, at the train station, and I feel pity for you. It's not fair what all of us are getting here in this puddle of shit country."

Now, Ashot was sitting by his computer in the office in Seattle and thinking about how this happened. Did God actually hear and send him this strange woman at an even stranger place at the most difficult moment of his life? Just because he begged Him for help?

Just because no one else could help? It was unbelievable! He had difficulty absorbing what had happened to him and how the story of his life turned out.

...Tamara told him the whole route – where to go and how. It was long and complicated, as well as difficult to remember. Ashot suggested writing it down, but she prohibited him from doing so.

"You shouldn't have any paper with the description of the route and names of the people who will be helping you. What if the police catch you? If they get this paper, it will be a dead end for many people who are relying on this, especially for me and my husband because we will go a couple of weeks after you. No way, baby! You should learn it, remember it and repeat it to yourself every hour until it is stuck in your head." And so he did.

Ashot had no way to know if the escape route she gave him was real and she wasn't just joking or playing with him. But he had nothing to lose. There were no other choices left for him, so he decided to go. At least, if it was not successful, he would die trying, not just rotting on the bench at the stinky train station, doing nothing. He needed to be a fighter, and he became one.

He gave Tamara the rest of the cigarettes and even some money, after asking how much she charged for her service, so she didn't lose her income while spending that night talking to him. She was pretty happy about that. They even hugged each other friendly and wished each other good luck, while parting forever. On his way out from the train station Ashot bought another pack of cigarettes for his future protection.

He also talked to God. He thanked Him for the chance to live and begged Him to continue helping. He swore that if his escape was successful and he would survive, he would became a believer. He would pray every day and go to church service on Sundays.

CHAPTER 4

Aaron usually didn't read poetry, except for what was required by the English Literature school program he took many years ago when he was a teenager.

He casually flipped through the book, first, and found out that it was combined from seven chapters and the names of them were... *Jeez!* he thought. *This is turning out to be more and more interesting...* the names which the girl had told Laurie as the names of her barbies: Rosie, Vally, Anastasia, Rubi, Kiki, Nora and Tobi. They were seven different female beings from whose perspective she told the poems.

All those beings were various by character, and all of them obviously were her. So, she had seven different personalities... DID (Dissociative Identity Disorder), based on schizophrenia. With multiple personalities there was only one diagnosis, no question about that. The girl did sincerely talk to Laurie about her illness, just in a very obscure way which made it understandable and acceptable for a child – barbies.

One point of Aaron's curiosity was solved pretty easily.

The quality of the poems was unbelievable, unthinkable, unimaginable! There was a burning fire on each line. It mesmerized the reader, it hurt, it burned, it turned one inside-out and forced them to shake, to shiver, to cry. It was not just human words, it was something from above and beyond; in some characters – from paradise, in others – from hell.

Aaron felt that he was shaking while reading the poems. The feeling of the universal pain enveloped him, reminding him of a time when he was almost insane after Ally's death. This girl, Rosalyn, probably survived something similar, at least very close to what he had survived. A child or a teenager just couldn't create this, invent this, if some great pain hadn't been experienced by her personally. A young person's fantasy wouldn't be capable of imagining this extraordinary emotion for nothing, from nowhere, without a reason.

Normally, a person uses 7–10 percent of their brain. About 90 percent of it is a mystery which is unknown to science, so far. Nobody knows what is hiding there, what kind of potential, or abilities, or talents, or creativity. It looked to Aaron as Rosalyn somehow sneaked into this unknown area of her own brain. She said in one stanza,

"I am a sponge absorbing other people's pain
and then splashing it out together with my own.
Isn't it too much of a burden for my soul?
Ain't I too young for this?"

Was her talent a special quality that came out from this unknown part of the brain? There were billions of people in the world and she could feel and take in all their pain? It was definitely too much. It could turn her insane. And it was what did, as Aaron guessed.

Clearly, she was a genius, but this was not normal. Some geniuses in all areas and forms of art, and even science, in many cases, were mentally ill, and oftentimes mentally ill people were geniuses. Normal was to be the middle person, the ordinary one, the regular one, the not special one. It would be boring, simple, dull, but it would be normal.

Aaron felt like he had a fever - he was very hot and burning inside. His heart was hurting. He pressed his face to his pillow, trying to calm himself down, but he couldn't.

"Girl," he whispered to himself. "What did you see? What did you survive? What happened to you? Why are all your poems about death, blood, burn, hurt, pain? What kind of child are you? Where are you from?"

The personality in the first chapter of the book, Rosie, was the nicest one. There was some love, beauty, peace, but still...

"The sun is shining on the marble of your tombstone
And it is getting scorching hot.
The petals of roses are falling on it and drying out instantly.
They are scattered in ashes like our love."

All of these he could write about Ally, if he was a poet. He couldn't express his feelings in writing, but she could, and to him it looked like she did it for both of them. The girl's poetry was so close to him, so unbelievably ambient, like they had the same soul and the same heart. Like they were spiritually combined into one being - two different bodies, but one soul. It felt like a miracle.

Even with Ally, Aaron wasn't that close. He didn't feel and didn't understand her that deeply, like he had understood this complete stranger, Rosalyn Vivano. And all those poems were written when she was fifteen- to seventeen-years-old, as the book cover said. She was just a child! It was unimaginable!

The second chapter of the book, written by Vally, was a tearful one. Those were tears of an unloved child, feeling loneliness and pain, but not an adult's pain - a true child's pain. What was the difference? Aaron couldn't say, he just knew it, felt it.

The third chapter, Anastasia – oh, she was a queen here, a beauty, an actress on the stage, a triumphal celebrity. She wore fantastically gorgeous dresses and make-up, probably a dream of almost every girl. She had confidence! She was believing in herself, blossoming, flying to the sky in her success.

The fourth chapter, Rubi, was about love with a boy, maybe her first love, Aaron guessed. But still there were several very scary thoughts. One poem especially caught his attention because he couldn't get what she meant and what the answers to those questions could be. He assumed that maybe the peaceful guy here would die first, but why? He decided he would ask her about that when he saw her. There was no question in his mind that he would see her. He would find her and talk to her. It didn't matter if she would be on the Moon.

The name of this poem was **Your Twin.** Why twin? What did she mean – a spiritual twin, poetically imaginable twin, or real twin brother?

Your twin is in a desert,
You are here.
He is running on orange sand, he is breathing dust.
You are running on green grass, you are breathing fresh air.
Guess who could die first?

Your twin is in a battle,
You are by the calm ocean.
Enemies are in front of him, bullets are whistling over his head.
Friends are in front of you, birds are singing above your head.
Guess who will die first

Your twin is at war,
You are at peace.
He has an automatic rifle in his hand, he stops and starts shooting.
You have a bottle of water in your hand, you stop and start drinking.
Guess who died first?

Aaron had no idea, he needed to ask her. He craved to ask her. He knew he wouldn't rest, he wouldn't stop until he asked her about that poem, until he could find her, see her, unravel her mystery...

The fifth chapter, Kiki, was probably the happiest one, with jokes, laughter, teasers, humorous situations. Here he saw a bit of a funny and happy child, a bit of a freshness of youth...

The sixth, Nora, was about her grandmother, full of kindness, warmth, but still very sad and carrying unbearable pain. Why? Rosalyn had probably loved this old woman and she died, but maybe not. Aaron felt something scary and very tense was hidden here as well.

And the final one, Tobi – it was a complete horror: blood, torture, fights, murder, death. The girl herself was Tobi with a knife. She was fighting with murderers and she was killing them herself. She wanted revenge for everyone who was killed in front of her. She fought for fairness and she fought fiercely.

Though, it looked to Aaron that she felt doomed in some poems and lost the fight. She bowed her head and gave up, and just melted away from life.

We Are Family
You are a black pile of soil on the green grass,
I am a white cloud floating in the blue sky.
Our child is bloody-red in between.

He is grabbing you with one hand,
And me with another,
He is trying to hold us and connect.

He is calling, daddy, mommy, stay with me.
Blood is dripping on the ground,
Yours, his and mine.

We're sinking in this crimson blood,
We have no chance to live.
We're together, we are a family of the dead.

Aaron felt that it was her own moral death. It was where and why she became mentally ill. It was the end of her normal life, ordinary life, if she ever had one.

Then, how come she was so nice, calm and quiet, when he met her during the walk with Laurie? How come she looked so average, regular, and normal to him? Now Aaron realized – she was Rosie that evening. Her other personalities were gone at the moment. That's why he didn't notice any abnormality. And his little Laurie didn't feel or see anything bad either. Her intuition told her to trust the strange girl. How many times had Laurie stated that she liked her?

That was the cast that the girl spelled on him. Aaron got it now. Consciously he considered her very unremarkable, but subconsciously he was drawn to her, attracted by her, not even noticing it at first. She enchanted him very well. This realization answered one more question lingering in his mind.

He shuddered, imaging what could have happened, if she turned into Tobi that day. She probably had in her backpack the knife which she mentioned in her poems. Maybe she killed someone the day before, or a couple of days before? That's why the police were there... This thought concluded the last point of his curiosity.

About a couple of hours were left until the reasonable wake up time for Saturday morning arrived. Aaron sensed that it would be not a bad idea to sleep for a while, preventing exhaustion the next day. He honestly tried but there was no way for him to rest and relax. His head was brewing and his thoughts were swirling. That girl with her poetry grabbed his attention, his curiosity, his thoughts, his feelings, his memories, his emotions, his heart, his everything...

Instead of sleeping, Aaron counted minutes until the moment when it would be acceptable to walk into the shelter next door to ask for help to find her.

CHAPTER 5

Ashot was stuck for a while on his biography. He didn't know how to make it short and then to move to the scientific part – the explanation of the core of his invented cure. Probably, he should simply say:

...In 1985 I emigrated to the USA. A few years later I got a college degree as a psychiatric nurse and began working...

It would be appropriate for Americans who were mostly law obedient citizens and didn't like anything illegal. They didn't trust people who partook in illegal things and it was right, if you weren't from a country where surviving legally wasn't possible; from the country where the choice given to an innocent person was – legally die in prison, or illegally run and survive. What would your decision be, you, who were happily born in nice and quiet legal conditions? What would you do?

...The first part of the escape route was very simple and easy. Ashot knew the further he would go, the more difficult it would be, but he had no options.

He was like a soldier on the battlefield; like he was running while bullets were whistling around his head, but he had to keep running. If he stopped – he died; if he laid down, trying to hide - he would be dead; if he kept running ahead, he may be dead, but maybe not. In fighting, in moving, in running - there was a chance to survive. Ashot almost physically felt the touch of death on his throat, but he kept pushing ahead in spite of it.

He was immensely scared of this unbelievable trip, but suppressed his fear because nothing was more awful than being raped to death by hundreds of gangsters in prison who would know for sure that he was a gay. That was the usual way of death for homosexual people in the Soviet Union.

So, the first part was simple.

Ashot waited until morning when the commute started and there would be a huge amount of people on the underground trains, which were called *Metro* in Moscow. He got easily lost in the crowd and went actually only one stop ahead – to Kurskaya, where another big train station was located beside a large square. The railroad from here led toward the south of the country, to the Black Sea.

Here Ashot bought a ticket for the first train to Sukhumi, Republic of Georgia, which was leaving in about one hour. He also bought some food because the trip on the train was expected to be two and a half days long. As for drinks – the conductors on the trains always provided hot tea - very poor quality and taste, but still, hot tea. The bed sheets were also provided by the conductor. They were gray, a bit moist because they weren't dried properly after the laundry, and smelled of cheap soap, but, anyway they were somehow washed and supposedly clean.

The service in the Soviet Union was poor, but, still, it was better than nothing, and much better than it would be in prison. In spite of the service quality, Ashot heard from many acquaintances that they loved and enjoyed the trips on trains, but he never did. It was disgusting, especially the stinky toilets, but he had no choice and no right to be picky.

He could potentially reach Sukhumi on an airplane but for that it would require a passport. There was the procedure of registration of the passengers which he would never pass. His name was probably already on a *Wanted* list. He wasn't sure, but to check would be too risky.

Also Sukhumi was a bit farther than Ashot needed. From there he has to take a train and go a few stations back – to the meeting point with the next person in the smugglers' chain. It would be too messy and complicated. So, Ashot simply boarded the train in Moscow and in two and a half days successfully exited on the Lazarevskaya station near Sochi on the Black Sea coast.

This was where the difficult part of the trip started. He was supposed to meet a Turkish contrabandist, Rassul, on the beach in front of the cafe *Violet*. According to prostitute Tamara, Rassul was selling drugs which he brought from Turkey once every two weeks. On his way back to Turkey, he was taking escapees with him.

Rassul knew the Russian language pretty well because he kept his business running for many years. The coast guards on both sides, Turkish and Soviet, were regularly bribed and turned a blind eye when Rassul approached or departed the coast on his boat using oars, while cautiously trying to be quiet.

As soon as he left coastal waters and reached the neutral territory in the sea, he turned on the motor, and his boat went much faster, almost flying. This way he crossed the Black Sea which was 350 miles wide from Soviet vacation village Lazarevskaya to the Turkish port Samsun on the opposite coast. While approaching the Turkish coastal waters he turned off his engine and used the oars again. Because of the manual parts of his journey, it usually took him three days one way to reach the Soviet Union, three days to stay there selling drugs, then three days on the way back to Turkey and five days to stay at home to collect drugs from dealers – a two-week round trip all together.

The most difficult part of it was to meet Rassul because after arriving at Lazarevskaya beach Ashot had no way to know when Rassul would be coming. Sitting and waiting on the beach would be impossible and dangerous. Ashot would be very noticeable between regular vacationers and beach-goers. They were all well-tanned, almost naked, only wearing bathing suits, all the time laying in the sun on towels, playing volleyball or swimming in the sea.

Ashot couldn't get undressed because the pouch with money and gold hanging under his shirt would be visible. But, while not undressing, he automatically showed beach thieves that he had something on him that was worth hiding. This way it got even more dangerous. He could be beaten, robbed, even possibly killed.

So, Ashot went to a farmers' market. He used his skills as a psychologist and psychiatrist, while talking to some elderly women and one of them agreed to rent him a cot in her backyard to sleep on. It was normal there, even nice. Many people arrived here from other parts of the country to vacation on the beach and everything was rented by locals – houses, apartments, rooms, sheds, tents in the yards, even beds and cots in the back yards, or just blankets on the front lawns. It was the main source of income for the local population. The weather was always hot and dry in summers, so sleeping outside felt even better than inside.

At the beginning Ashot was thinking of going to the market or to the cafe *Violet* to ask about Rassul. But then he realized that he wouldn't get any answers because people would suspect him of being an undercover cop investigating the drug sales around the area. So, he asked his landlady for help again.

She was suspicious at first, too, but Ashot told her his whole story with the reference to Sergey – Tamara's client, the smuggler from the Moscow train station. This really softened the senior woman's heart. She even gave him a discount on the cot in her yard, then went to the cafe *Violet* and found the information that Ashot needed – Rassul would be there in three days.

She also helped Ashot exchange money: rubles to the USA dollars - because starting with Rassul, all payments ahead would be required in free converting currency. God probably really was watching over Ashot because this money exchange procedure was usually a dangerous one. He knew that many people were robbed or killed during that moment, but for him all went surprisingly smoothly.

Rassul was a big, tall and rough-looking man. After Ashot told him that his friend from Moscow, Sergey, sent him here to say hi, Rassul established his charge - $200.00 for delivering him to Turkey. He accepted the golden ring of Ashot's father as payment. It had probably cost much more than that, but was pretty bulky and not comfortable for Ashot to wear it hanging on his neck on a rope. Rassul gave Ashot instructions to be on the beach in three days, at midnight, and to have enough food and bottled water for the three days crossing of the Black Sea.

When Ashot realized that he was on a running motor boat in the middle of the sea with a scary looking perfect stranger, also a Turk, he shuddered. He knew the history of his country well – Turks (Muslims) attacked Armenians (Christians) for hundreds of years, creating a genocide on a religious basis, slaughtering whole villages, including women and children, and even babies. He was quite sure that Rassul recognized him as Armenian. While laying on the bottom of the boat, covered with a blanket which the Turkish smuggler gave him, Ashot expected to be hit on the back of his head and thrown in the dark water after his money and his mother's golden cross were taken.

But that never happened. Rassul was sitting by the steering wheel of his boat, sometimes murmuring something quietly, like prayers, or chants, or songs. He talked to Ashot only once when he showed his passenger how to relieve himself over the board of the boat into the sea, and politely turned his head aside, not to look.

The sea wasn't completely quiet, but not stormy, so the boat wasn't bothered by waves. They arrived in Turkey also at night, paddling with oars again. Samsun was the biggest Turkish port on the Black Sea coast, but Rassul didn't go there. He headed to a separated small harbor slightly farther east, where the fishing boats usually landed their catches, and there he let Ashot out.

"Do you know where to go from here?" Rassul asked.

"I need to find Abu-Ahmed's small spices shop at the market," Ashot said. "He will put me on the big ship to North America."

Rassul nodded. "Ten more bucks and I will drive you there. I know him well. My car is parked not far from that pier. Is it okay with you?"

Ashot agreed. It was much more comfortable than walking by himself at night, in a foreign country that he knew nothing about.

Rassul dropped him in front of the requested shop after a half hour drive and advised him to sit outside and wait until five a.m. when Abu-Ahmed would wake up for the first morning prayer.

"Don't worry," he said, "this old man speaks Russian. Here, at the market, practically everybody does because dozens of their merchants are here in crowds all the time. We have a pretty big business going here with Russians."

"Could I ask you something?" Ashot inquired before parting with Rassul. "Why didn't you kill me while we were at sea? You probably noticed that I am Armenian?"

Rassul chuckled. "Why should I? Who cares who you are? You paid pretty well. I am doing my business and I respect my reputation. Don't say to anybody here anything stupid like that. We're in the 20th century, not in the 18-19th. Who cares about history nowadays?"

He shrugged, patted Ashot's shoulder and left.

It was the year 1985...

Now, as Ashot was sitting in his office during his last night shift in the Seattle *Youth Shelter*, it was 2015.

CHAPTER 6

While thinking at home, Aaron felt very confident about what he would say to officials in the *Youth Shelter* as an explanation of why he was looking for Rosalyn Vivano. However as he walked up the gravel driveway and stopped in front of the big robust metal gate, he lost his self-assurance and realized that he would look and sound strange. But it didn't matter to him. His inner calling was so strong that he knew nothing would stop him from seeing her again and finding answers to all of his disturbing questions. And maybe... He didn't know what... He was just completely smitten with the thought of seeing her again and not thinking about anything further. Just to see... With that he pressed the button on the buzzer.

There was no answer, but Aaron waited patiently and pressed the buzzer a couple more times, until he saw an aged gray-haired man in a dark-blue uniform approaching the fence from the other side.

"How can I help you, sir?" he asked politely. The tag on his chest pocket read: Thomas Spencer, Psychiatric nurse.

"Good morning," Aaron said, stretching his hand with his business card to him through the metal bars. "My name is Dr. Aaron Dispenmore. I am working at the university Psychiatry Department and I am looking for information about one of your patients here."

He noticed that the warder watched him with a bit of surprise, as he took his card. "Hmm... We usually don't have doctors' visits here on weekends," he uttered thoughtfully, but unlocked the gate anyway and ushered Aaron in. "If you don't mind, sir, could you go to the office, please?"

Aaron nodded in agreement.

They circled the big house and Aaron noticed that the surrounding yard looked more like a vacation resort than a prison. There was a swimming pool in the middle, with a hot tub on its side. The big garden around was well tended and full of blooming bushes, trees and flowerbeds. There was also part of the garden where growing vegetables were visible – tomatoes, zucchini, beans, as well as blueberry and raspberry bushes.

However, that whole area of the property was separated with a very high metal net fence with barbed wire on the top. This was the only sign of the real meaning of this facility. A group of teenagers, maybe six or seven girls and boys, were playing in the swimming pool and they had no chance of escaping from there. But it was pretty noisy in the pool. It looked like they were having fun.

Noticing Aaron's glance, the warder explained, "Two hours have passed since the kids had their breakfast, so they are allowed to use the pool now."

"It's okay. I am not a health inspector," Aaron laughed because it was noticeable that the warder still wasn't sure who he was and why he had come.

They entered the lobby of the house. There was a reception desk by the entrance and farther away was a big dining room with a kitchen at the back, where a woman in a white robe was fussing, probably preparing lunch.

"That's all the staff we have on weekends," Thomas Spencer explained. "Missus Cook over there, who is funny, but really our cook, and I am the nurse, security and maintenance person. On working days we also have teachers and a gym trainer because the kids have school here..." he stopped a bit confused, not knowing if Aaron would be interested to hear more about the facility or not. "It's actually not my shift now. I am covering for my partner, but he will be here in half an hour. You can talk to him longer, if needed. I am leaving at ten a.m."

"I don't think I will take a lot of your time, Mr. Spencer," Aaron answered. "I am just looking for information about a girl whose name is Rosalyn Vivano."

The warder knitted his brows. "Sorry," he said, "we don't have a patient with that name here."

"You probably don't have one now because she escaped last night," Aaron objected, "but I saw her in person while I was walking with my little daughter down the street. We helped her to find a bus stop. She gave us her book. And also here, I see that you have it as well," he pointed at the book that was laying on the reception desk. "So you must've known her."

"Hmm," the warder shrugged, looking even more confused. "Sorry, I misunderstood. Rosalyn Vivano is her pen name. Her real name is Rosa Garcia and, yes, she escaped yesterday night because of human error. Somebody accidentally forgot to lock her room. I have reported it to the police."

"As I realized from her book, her diagnosis is schizophrenia," Aaron continued.

"Sorry, I can't disclose that."

"You don't need to confirm that. It's pretty visible on every page."

"Well," the warder shrugged again and looked at Aaron's business card. "What do you want exactly, Dr. Dispenmore?"

"I would like to suggest some treatment for that girl. At our university Psychiatry Department we have larger resources there than elsewhere in regular clinics. Could you help me to find her, or any information...?"

"Why?" the old man looked at him suspiciously, narrowing his eyes. "Don't you have enough patients? I heard that psychiatric departments are usually overloaded."

"You're pretty well informed," Aaron smirked. He had the notion that this person had known much more about the subject than he was revealing. The tone of the conversation made him feel some jealousy on both sides, like two men were fighting over a woman. "I can tell you why. Rosalyn is a very talented young lady and her illness is probably diminishing her talent. If she could get better help and maybe healed, her talent could blossom much more."

After quite a long moment of silence, the warder thoughtfully nodded, "Okay... Sit down, please, Dr. Dispenmore. We need to talk."

He pointed Aaron to a chair by the desk and moved out another one for himself. As Aaron sat, he also noticed the piece of paper on the desk beside the book on which Rosalyn's poem **Little Birdie** was handwritten, exactly the same poem she read to Laurie. However, he didn't say anything, just watched the warder's face attentively.

The man was somewhere about sixty, not tall, stocky, with dark brown eyes, almost as dark as Aaron's, and with a big nose resembling an eggplant shape. There were deep wrinkles on his forehead and cheeks. His skin was very well tanned, almost brownish as an African, although he was obviously of the Caucasian race. His hair was curly, bushy, but with the top of his head starting to get bald. He had a wedding band on his ring finger and a large antique looking golden cross on a chain on his chest. The main impression for Aaron was that he was somewhat kind and a good person who really cared about his young patients here. But he definitely was hiding something.

"What do you want to talk about?" Aaron asked. "I told you everything about my intentions in respect of this Rosa Garcia, if this is who she really is."

"First of all," the old man suggested, "let me introduce myself. My nickname is Ashot and I prefer to be called that."

"Well," Aaron shrugged, "you can call me Aaron, if we continue our acquaintance, but I don't see much reason as to why we should. I just need some information, like her address, or her family doctor's name and then I'll get out of your hair."

"I can give you her home address," Ashot said with an unexpected ease. "You could talk to her parents, but I don't know if she is there. However, you can find this out by yourself."

He took one of the folders out from the drawer of his desk, opened it and jotted the address from there on the little piece of yellow note paper. "But, your suggestion of treatment for Rosa sounds strange to me. As a professional, you know that there is no cure for schizophrenia. However...," he looked at his watch, "my shift is finishing, but I would like to talk to you more, Aaron. I have a really interesting proposition for a doctor about an important scientific discovery which could be presented to the Psychiatry Scientific Conference in New York this December. Did you hear about the conference?"

"Of course, I did," Aaron nodded. "I guess every psychiatrist in the country is excited about it now. Everyone is interested in winning recognition there. But not everyone has an important discovery. I, personally, don't."

"But I do," Ashot said. "And if you will agree to work together, we can go 50/50 with this."

"But you're not a scientist," Aaron objected, knitting his brows, "or a doctor..."

"I, actually, am..."

At that moment the door of the lobby opened and a smiling young man appeared standing in it.

"Hey, Ashot, thank you for covering for me. Jeez, my car is finally fixed. I can take over from here. You can go now."

"Okay," Ashot answered, standing up. "Have a nice day, Jake. I will call you later to report the events of my night shift. Bye."

He took Rosalyn's book from the desk and also the paper with her poem, packed them into his briefcase which, as Aaron noticed, was holding his laptop already and turned to the door, ready to go. Aaron stood up as well and walked outside with him.

When they approached the gate, Ashot said, "I can tell you, Aaron, if you are interested in Rosa, all is said there in her poems. She is turning real life into a poetic image, but still, it is the truth. If you read more attentively, you will know everything about her. Here is one example. Let's take the last poem which she left on my desk before leaving yesterday, *Little Birdie*..."

"I know that poem," Aaron interrupted. "She told it to my daughter when we walked her to the bus stop. And then my daughter repeated it to me."

"Hmm," Ashot paused, looking a bit confused again, but then continued. "I just want you to read her perception of the world – *yellow houses and purple towers, green grass and pink flowers.* Stay for a moment here and take a look down the street. The houses on the other side are white, but when the evening sun is shining, its beams angled a way that colored them bright yellow. And look ahead, far away. Those towers..."

Aaron glanced farther on the horizon. From this top of the hill, where he was standing now by the gate, he could see a hazy view of the ocean gulf and downtown high-rises on the other side. They really looked purple from here.

"Wow!" he said. "Who would notice that?"

"Exactly. Only the poetic soul and mind of that sick girl. Now, look on your right down the hill."

Aaron saw the steep slope covered with bright green grass. Piercing pink petunias were growing on two long flower beds along it.

"See," Ashot smiled at him. "This is green grass and pink flowers. This is a view from the window of Rosa's room. It is all true. So, just read attentively, if you want to know more about that girl."

"And the birdie banging its chest on the glass..."

"This is a poetic image of herself, of course... Just read. Poetry does not require a lot of explanation. It requires feelings. In some cases – extremely deep feelings. So, now, I am sorry that we were interrupted... What do you think? Would you be interested in working together and preparing a really advanced and practically shocking scientific discovery for the conference? I am honestly ready to share it with you because I need a partner for that – a professional American Doctor. I can't do that alone. They wouldn't let me in with only a nursing qualification. Here is my business card. Take it, please, and think about it. Then you can call me and tell me what you've decided."

"It depends," Aaron shrugged with an uncertainty, but took Ashot's business card and thrust it into his pocket. "What is the discovery exactly?"

"I have invented a successful cure for schizophrenia and I completely healed twenty people. Actually, twenty-one already."

"What?!" Aaron looked at him scornfully, realizing that this man was probably as 'crazy' as his teenage patients here. "But you told me yourself some minutes ago that there isn't any cure for schizophrenia."

"There wasn't until I invented and proved one. You told me that you would like to give Rosa a better treatment. Why not make her 100 percent cured and absolutely healthy? She is an amazing kid and really deserves it."

Aaron took a deep breath, closed his eyes for a few seconds and shook his head. "Thank you for your suggestion, sir. I am sorry, but I wouldn't be interested. Seriously, not at all. Ever."

He was sure now that this man was some kind of a crook or scammer, or con artist. A nurse, security and maintenance worker invented something that the best scientists of the world were unsuccessfully searching for many years?! He obviously had no knowledge or qualifications for even thinking about that. Clearly, it was an absurd and a ridiculous joke.

"Well... that's unfortunate," Ashot noted sadly, "but don't hesitate to call me, please, if you change your mind. For now, have a nice day."

"You too," Aaron answered and ran down the gravel driveway toward the street. He had gotten her address and he knew now where to go.

CHAPTER 7

While Aaron was driving to the West Blaine neighborhood of Seattle where Rosa Garcia's parents were supposedly living, Helen had already called him three times. He didn't answer the phone mostly because he didn't know what to say to her yet. Aaron had not decided if he would see her that evening or not. It depended on many factors ahead. He had no idea how the day would unfold and didn't know yet whether he would see Rosa or not.

Aaron tried to remember the small details he heard from the girl during their short conversation last night: "My parents dropped me here three days ago.... I am going downtown... I would like to see my friends... They are living on the streets..." Very scarce information, but here he hoped to find out, at least, why her parents dropped her at the shelter and why she didn't call them to pick her up.

The neighborhood was beautiful, clean and expensive, almost like the one where he lived himself, but there was a privilege here – no special *Youth Shelter* nearby, so it was more safe.

When Aaron parked his silver Mercedes by the house with the proper number, he observed a lovely family dynamic. Three curly, dark haired little boys, ages approximately eight, six and four, were playing Frisbee on the front lawn. A woman was watching them sitting in a rocking chair on the porch and knitting. A large golden retriever was lying down at her feet.

Aaron got out of the car and walked toward the woman on a little trail paved with the red star-shaped bricks. The dog stood up and pranced toward him with his tail wagging.

"Don't worry, sir. Our Oscar is very friendly," the woman said, smiling. "How could I help you?"

"I am not worried," Aaron smiled back and petted the dog's head. "I'm usually good with dogs. Good morning, ma-am. I am Doctor Aaron Dispenmore from the university Psychiatry Department and I am looking for Rosa Garcia. Is this the proper address?" With that he handed the woman his business card.

"Oh," she took a deep breath while accepting his card. "I am actually her mother. I know that Rosie escaped from the facility. The police were here yesterday evening. But she didn't come home, and obviously, she never will. It's not her home anymore. She is twenty and she should be on her own from now on."

"Don't you worry about her well-being?" Aaron wondered, noticing that the woman was very slim, pale, bleak and tired-looking.

"Not anymore," she said sadly and shook her head. "I am exhausted and I am done. I have these three little ones here to worry about."

"Well... We have a special university program which could suggest some treatment for your daughter, if we would be able to find her. Do you have any idea where she might be?"

The woman desperately waved her hand. "I doubt any treatment would work. We have tried everything. It's absolutely hopeless, Doctor. And where might she be? I have no idea."

"We have some information that she probably went downtown. Have you ever heard about any of her friends who live there?" Aaron prompted.

"You know, she has a lot of friends, though some of them are imaginary, just in her mind. Most of her real living friends are from that Poetry Club. Some of them are as mentally ill as she is, and they are really living on the streets because their parents kicked them out. You know, people's patience has boundaries. You can only tolerate so much and then you can't anymore..." fighting the tears, she sighed and sadly shook her head. "Have you ever seen Rosie's book?" she continued.

"Yes, I've got one copy from that shelter," Aaron lied. "I am just wondering why she used a pen name?"

"It is actually our real last name, Ivanov. We have a Bulgarian background. I was Slava Ivanov, when Rosie was born. Then I translated my name into English – Gloria. It is easier to pronounce and to understand for Americans. And Rosie just moved the last letter V to the front of the name, then she got that Vivano. And - Rosalyn? I don't know for sure. Her second name is Lynn. I guess it is how her boyfriend used to call her, combining her both names together. Officially by the passport her first name is Rosa. Her father, my first husband, died in a motorcycle accident when she was six-months old. Mostly my parents raised her. But then my mother died and Rosie ended up in this youth facility for four years, from age eleven to fifteen."

"Why?" Aaron inquired, surprised. "According to their mandate only youths who committed serious crimes should stay there?"

"Sorry, but I don't want to talk about that," Gloria uttered sadly. "Rosie got ill. That's it. They have a good school there. She continued her education successfully, and that is where she started to write her first poems. The English Literature teacher there was really excited about her talent and promoted her to all competitions which she always won, even being in the facility.

"While she was there, I remarried and now have these three little rascals over here. At fifteen, Rosie was acquitted and went to high school from which she has some friends as well. She kept her friendship with them even now. I think Ben's family still considers her almost as a daughter."

"Who is Ben?" Aaron asked.

"Her boyfriend... the black guy who was shot and killed by police while jogging in a park three years ago. It was a big story on TV News. Rosie spent another year in this shelter as a result of that.

Ben's family... they are pretty kind people. Maybe she could go to them. Though they have a bunch of little kids, as we do, and it may not be safe for them to take Rosie in."

"Do you know their address or last name?"

"I don't think so. Let me ask my husband. Maybe he remembers," she stood up, left her knitting on the chair and opened the door into the house lobby. "Miguel, could you come here, please?" she shouted.

"Daddy is in the garage. He is working on the car," one of the boys said. "Do you want us to call him, mommy?"

"Yes, please," the woman nodded and the boys ran around the house, yelling, "Daddy! Daddy, come here!"

A couple of minutes later they ran back followed by a stocky dark-complexioned Mexican man, wearing dirty overalls. On his way he was wiping his hands on a piece of fabric.

"Miguel, this is a Doctor from a Psychiatry Department," Gloria said.

"I could guess what this is about," Miguel laughed. "Our never ending problem! Sorry, Doc, I can't shake your hand, mine are still all greasy. I usually work on my antique cars on weekends. We are having a show in a couple of weeks and three of mine are still not ready. How can I help you?"

"I am looking for your daughter, Rosa," Aaron started, but Miguel interrupted him in the middle of the sentence, "Sorry, these three little ones are mine. Rosa is not my daughter, but my step-daughter, although I adopted her. I also spent huge amounts of money on all her poetry trips and concerts around the country. You know, airplane tickets, hotels, travel insurances, dresses, make ups, food, medications. Jeez! There were thousands and thousands... I did all of this for her success, trying to be a good father. And what do you think? Is she thankful? Not at all. She thinks it should be like that because she is entitled, because she is a genius." Aaron could hear by the tone of his voice that he was really offended and hurt.

"Miguel, please," his wife begged. "The doctor doesn't need to know that. He just needs the last name of Ben's family. Or their address... Do you remember it?"

"Of course not, honey. How could I? They lived in that black district, somewhere beside a park... No, I absolutely don't remember," he shook his head.

"Okay," Aaron changed the subject. "You dropped Rosa at the *Youth Shelter* last Tuesday. I'm just wondering why? To understand that might probably help us to find her."

"Oh, I can show you," Miguel said, agitated. "I really can show you why."

"You don't have to, Miguel!" Rosa's mother exclaimed.

"No, darling. He is a Doctor. If he ever treats Rosa, he should know what he is dealing with."

"The Doctor has other patients with the same diagnosis. He obviously knows," his wife objected.

"No, no, no, he should see this. Come in, Doc, please." Miguel opened the door and waved to Aaron to come in.

They walked up the stairs all together, followed by the boys and the dog, but on the second floor landing Miguel turned to his wife and said, "Honey, please, take this gang back outside. I don't want them in here."

"Okay, okay, let's go boys," Gloria ordered and, going down, she took the two youngest ones by their hands. The older boy and the dog ran ahead.

Miguel opened the door to one of the bedrooms and turned the light on because the window was closed and covered by blinds with a tapestry on top of that.

"Look, Doc," he said. "This is Rosa's room."

There were three big mirrors on the walls which were covered with towels. A lot of garlands of Christmas lights were hanging from the ceiling. The walls were scratched and badly stubbed by a knife which was sticking out from one of the walls – a big butcher's knife. And there was some dry blood on the ivory carpet under it.

"She had a very bad and scary attack on Tuesday. She hallucinated that someone was coming out from the mirrors to get her, so she covered them. Then she tried to fight with that someone with this knife. And she cut herself a bit during this fight. What do you think, Doc? Do you have any children?"

"Yes, I have a five-year-old daughter," Aaron answered.

"Do you want someone like that in the same house, beside your child's bedroom?"

"No, definitely not," Aaron shook his head. "I understand you, Mr. Garcia. Absolutely understand."

"We did call her psychiatrist, Dr. Evelyn Hertz, who has been taking care of Rosa since she was eleven, and the doctor advised us to take her back to that shelter. I don't know what kind of treatment she planned to do there. However, we are sorry, we can't take it anymore in our home. My wife cried every day because of Rosa and it really needs to stop. We won't let that girl back here ever, under any circumstances, Doc."

"I am not blaming you," Aaron uttered thoughtfully. "It is really sad and tragic. Especially considering Rosa's unbelievable talent. But, okay, I will try to do everything that is possible to help you and Rosa, as well. Thank you for sharing."

While Miguel and Gloria were walking him toward his car, Aaron asked, "Last couple of questions, please, before I leave – does Rosa have an uncle?"

"No," Gloria shook her head. "I don't have any siblings at all. And Miguel... he has two sisters, both in Mexico. They are young and not married yet."

"How about her biological father?"

"No, he didn't have any siblings either. Don't forget, we were from a communist country. The people there usually had only one child – it was difficult for them to feed more kids. Also, Rosie doesn't know anything about him. She never asked and I never told her. You know... one more death in the family... I didn't want to let her know and disturb her nerves..."

"Which got disturbed anyway," Miguel interrupted. "But why do you inquire about an uncle? I don't get it."

"She wrote a poem for her uncle..."

"Oh, that poetry again," Miguel sighed. "It's obviously her sick imagination. Nothing else."

"Okay," Aaron nodded and then turned to Gloria. "And the very last question, please – was your mother's name Nora?"

"Yes, of course. Why?"

"In Rosie's book, there is a chapter called 'Nora'. I guessed it was written about her grandma. I just wanted to be sure. Did you read her book?"

"No. I am scared even to touch it. It will break my heart."

"Which is broken by this child anyway," Miguel added sarcastically. "And I didn't read because I don't care about poetry."

"Okay," Aaron said. "Thank you very much for your time. Have a nice weekend."

And with that he left.

CHAPTER 8

Aaron drove a few blocks away from Garcia's house and then parked his car on the side of the street and rested his head on the steering wheel. There was a complete disaster and mess in his mind. In a way he was happy that he made this visit and found some information he was looking for. But, on the other hand, he thought that maybe it would be better if he hadn't come and didn't know the things which he discovered now.

During the years of his work in the Psychiatry Department, he saw, safe to say, hundreds of patients with the same diagnosis as Rosie. He always saw them in his clinic or in psychiatric hospitals, but never at their homes. He couldn't even guess what they did at home and how their families survived.

Luckily for him, no one had an attack of their illness while in his office. Aaron knew the story of one colleague of his, although from another city, who was killed by a patient that came to his appointment with a knife. He always knew that potentially it could happen, but still this was somewhat pretty far away and he never took it too seriously.

Rosie turned his thoughts, his heart, and his soul upside-down and inside-out with her talent and her deeply spiritual creative works. While reading her poems Aaron felt that, by her soul, she was the closest person to him in the whole world. At the same time she was a mystery which now started to unfold, but it would probably be better if it didn't.

Aaron couldn't believe that he met her less than twenty-four hours ago. He felt like he knew her his whole life, the whole past and the whole future — forever. But in reality, it was all his own imagination. Why? What's happening to him? Did he turn crazy as well?

"Hey, buddy, sober up," he told himself aloud. "Think properly, what did you get?"

First of all, the girl wasn't a criminal. She didn't belong now to this shelter and it was probably good that she escaped from there. The police were looking for her only because this old warder, Ashot, reported an event. It gave Aaron a chance to breathe a bit easier.

Second, he obtained from her parents the name of her doctor who had observed her since she was eleven. There was one serious question still left — why was Rosie put in this youth prison for four years right after her grandma's death? Did she kill that old woman? He doubted it because from her poems in Nora's chapter, Aaron knew that she loved her grandma dearly. But illness could do anything. Still, four years was a huge term for an eleven-year-old child. There should be a serious crime taking place for a sentence this long. Dr. Hertz managed Rosie's case then, and it was obvious that everything would be documented in her file.

And then, later, Rosie was given another year in this shelter after her boyfriend was killed. Why?

Aaron decided that on Monday, the first thing in the morning, with the name of the University Psychiatry Department he would request Dr. Evelyn Hertz to send over the complete Rosie's illness history. Then he would know everything. No mystery would be left.

His phone rang. It was Helen again and this time he answered.

"Hey, Arie, where the hell are you?"

"I am not sure. Somewhere on West Blaine Street..."

"Where? Jeez! It's pretty far away. What are you doing there?"

"Some research."

"Why didn't you answer the phone?"

"Driving."

"Wanna go for lunch?"

"No, I'm still busy. But I will come tonight. I promise. Good news... I think... I want you."

"Finally! Oh, gosh! How did I deserve that?" she giggled sarcastically. "Is something happening? Did somebody hit you on the head?"

"Figuratively speaking, yes."

"Say thank you from me to whoever did it. What time?"

"I guess, pretty late, after ten. Today is my turn to put Laurie to bed."

"Why can't your mother do that?"

"She did yesterday and she will do tomorrow. Don't question my parenting. I know what I am doing. You don't know anything about it."

"I do, silly."

Yes, she did in reality. By trade Helen was a child psychiatrist, who worked with mentally ill kids aged from two to twelve. She knew a lot about children, but her statement irritated Aaron. It was her usual demagogy when the words were right but the meaning was completely wrong.

She didn't know anything about parenting in real life, as he did, because she never dealt with healthy children. She also didn't have her own kids whom she could love and understand.

Aaron was sure that she was cold and indifferent inside. He couldn't even imagine how Helen would be capable of loving a child or anybody at all. Her constantly declared love for him was only sexual, as he understood, and did not deserve to be named love. He was deeply convinced that it was the same animal reflex and craving for relaxation as he had toward her.

"Okay," he uttered slowly. "Do you want me to come or not?"

"Of course, I do, my love."

"Ten o'clock then," he hung up.

Aaron hasn't finished summarizing the information he got from Rosie's parents, yet. There still was a lot to comprehend. He liked to solve mysteries. That's why he became a psychiatrist – the conditions of peoples' brains were a huge mystery. He always craved to understand it, to uncover it's secrets and to learn how to change it for a patient. If not a doctor, the second choice of occupation for him would probably be a detective.

One question - why Rosie ended up in this shelter the first time - was on the way to be resolved as soon as Aaron received her file.

Another group of questions were about this boyfriend of hers. What happened? Why was he killed by the police? Was she there at that moment? Was the poem *Your Twin* about him?

She was seventeen at the time. *What a fate this poor child had,* he thought, *at eleven - the loss of her beloved grandma, at seventeen - the loss of her first love, boyfriend!*

How was it different from his own fate? He lost his dearest father; then, some years later, his first love – his wife. Somehow it was similar. Somehow it was connected. In his heart he physically sensed this connection with this girl.

Aaron felt a strange strong urge to talk to her, to share those connections, to ask what she would think about them. It was extremely important to him. He needed it almost to the point of obsession, not knowing and not understanding why. But he knew that if he could talk to Rosie, they would find a way to solve these mysteries. They would discuss them, they would understand them and understand each other. He was deeply sure about that, in spite of her illness. There would be no illness when she would be with him. He would somehow protect her from that illness, somehow cure her with this spiritual connection.

Though, as a doctor, as a practitioner, he knew that in reality there was no cure and understood sadly that all his dreams about those connections were in his imagination only.

So, today's part of Aaron's investigation was finished. Now he needed to drive home and return to his usual life. He would have lunch with his small family - Beth and Laurie. Then he would have a nap for a few hours because he was reading the previous night and didn't sleep. He really needed a good rest to finally relax.

Then he would go for a walk with Laurie and, by the way, show her these images from Rosie's poem **Little Birdie.** He would lead his little daughter up the gravel driveway and, standing by the gate of the *Youth Shelter,* point out to her the yellow houses across the street, purple towers at the other side of the ocean gulf, green grass and pink petunias in the flowerbeds along the driveway.

He knew that Laurie already liked Rosie. Now he extremely and greedily craved for Laurie not just to like, but understand and love Rosie. He needed this. It was important to him to connect them - the two female beings, the closest to his heart and soul.

Then he would put Laurie to bed, read her a book - a children's book, not Rosie's of course. And if she would ask about Rosie's book, he would tell her that she will get to read it sometime later, when she grows up to be as tall as Rosie. And this would happen, if she would always eat well.

And then, finally, he would drive to Helen and try to solve one more puzzle about himself as a man – what he was now, what he was capable of, what he would do, and how he would behave when he would deal with a woman he would love again. He needed to learn this lesson to understand and to evaluate himself because he knew for sure – he wasn't the same person anymore. Something had really changed in him. And he almost shook with anticipation of what was coming...

CHAPTER 9

In his small Tesla Ashot entered the underground parking of their condo building, parked in his usual spot and plugged the car in for charging. Liam's Chrysler wasn't in the parking lot next to him. That meant that Liam had already left for his movie production set. There was no reason to rush home then. Ashot had a chance to sit for a while in his car and think things through.

This morning's visit of that young doctor was pretty disturbing. The man obviously put his eye on Rosie and at some point it was good. It could help the project. But anyway, the doctor refused to work together with him. Ashot was hurt a bit by that, but not so much anymore. He already talked to a minimum of twenty doctors and all of them refused him. So, it was nothing new. He began getting used to this and became indifferent.

Actually, it was their loss, not his. Ashot would do the project anyway, but he wouldn't be able to present it to the Psychiatry Scientific Conference by himself. It was sad. The people who really needed his invention wouldn't be able to get it. But at least Rosie would. And that was his inspiration – to heal this amazing talented kid, to give her a chance at a normal and happy life. Wasn't it why he survived his difficult escape route to the free world of America?

Now it looked so impossible to Ashot that he even asked himself at times – did I really make it? How? Obviously, with the help of

God. Who else helped him to be strong enough to survive that? Even being a scientist, how could he not become a believer after such a certain proof of God's existence? Ashot kept his promise: he always wore his mother's cross, he prayed every morning and evening and he went to church every Sunday. During his thirty years in America he never missed one service.

Even with Liam they got married and had a big wedding in the Anglican Church which accepted same-sex marriages considering that homosexual people are the same creatures of God as all others. How did it all come to that? Ashot leaned his head on the headrest and tried to remember.

...Summer 1985. He was living for a week in the back storage room of Abu-Ahmed's little spice shop at the market in Samsun, waiting for a big ship to Canada. There was a mattress on the floor between shelves with jars of spices. They were closed, but the lids were not really sealed and Ashot enjoyed the amazing smells of the oriental dishes. Some of them reminded him of Armenian cuisine and this filled his heart with pain knowing that he would never see his motherland again.

However, he could expect to meet some Armenians in America. The Armenian diasporas were wide spread everywhere in the world – during hundreds of years of Turkish genocide many people ran away to survive. What Ashot was doing now wasn't historically new. The difference was that he escaped not from the Turks but from the communist's Soviet Union. And, funnily enough, the Turks were the ones actually helping him. What a paradoxical change of history!

When the ship arrived at port, they had about three days to unload Canadian containers and to reload it with Turkish containers that were prepared and waited on the docks. After receiving Ashot's payment for room and board, Abu-Ahmed advised him to get ready.

Ashot was supposed to go to the market and buy two boxes of drinking water - each of thirty-six bottles, a box of apples and a box of crackers. These were nonperishable foods which he expected to consume during the trip. Water could be spread for three or four bottles per day. Also, he had to buy two big plastic containers with sealed lids which should serve him as toilets.

The route of the ship went through the Black Sea, the Mediterranean Sea, across the Atlantic ocean, through the Panama Canal and along the Pacific coast of North America up to Vancouver, Canada. The trip was expected to last for three weeks, if everything went smoothly – no hurricanes or tsunamis on the way. But who could guarantee that? Only God.

After all the purchases were made, Abu-Ahmed introduced Ashot to a sailor, Nadir, who was a member of the smugglers' chain as well. That man walked Ashot to the big port and helped him to load all his stuff into a huge metal container with an old towel on the floor. This container was the only one that had a door which could be locked and unlocked from inside. In that door, there were holes drilled to breathe through. Obviously, it was used many times before.

Ashot only hoped that none of the people died there during previous trips, but Nadir convinced him that it wasn't the case. He took $1,000 for settling Ashot inside and explained to him that his container would be lifted with a crane and placed on the ship first on the lowest level, so Ashot could walk out from it at the end of the journey. The other containers would be placed on top of it, but the container metal was very strong and they weren't supposed to squash Ashot. It was absolutely safe there according to the sailor.

The main challenge was that in Vancouver the custom officers would come the next morning after their arrival and check all the containers. During the night before that happened, Ashot must walk out from his refuge, clean all the stuff from inside and throw them overboard. So during the next morning inspection the container would be empty and clean, like nobody was ever there. Then, it would be considered as an accidental loading mistake and the smugglers' chain wouldn't be jeopardized.

Ashot himself was supposed to jump off the ship onto the pier and walk away. The distance to the pier wasn't really big, about three to five feet, but still, it required quite a strong jump. For that Ashot was advised to exercise during the trip, not to just lay on the towel and sleep, but work out pretty hard to be able to do this jump.

Three weeks in darkness, breathing through the holes, sometimes throwing up into the toilet boxes from sea sickness because, yes, there were storms with big rolling waves... Plus, exercise... with scarce food and drinks... It was possible to survive only at the age of thirty. Now Ashot was scared even to think about that. But he did all that successfully then and walked from the Vancouver port to the city, took a taxi and ordered the driver to deliver him to Zero Avenue in South Surrey beside the border between Canada and the USA.

Jeez, it's looking so funny, Ashot thought seeing it. He saw the border between the Soviet Union and communists countries of Eastern Europe - the friendly ones. There was a fence about ten feet tall with barbed wire on the top, through which ran the highest, deadly level, electrical current. Behind this fence was a line of a graded sand about 150 feet wide. The grading was renewed every day, so steps of offenders can be visible, in case there were any offenders, which was practically impossible. Then, on the other side of the graded sand line was the similar fence with electrical wire again.

Here, in the capitalists' world, the border was a small ditch, covered with grass and wildflowers, with some water running at the bottom of it, and a single metal pole about 3 feet high. On one side of it was written – Canada, on the other – USA.

There were Canadian houses on Zero Avenue. Behind the ditch were American houses. Ashot told the taxi driver the house number which he got from Tamara. He paid for the ride with almost the last of his money. Just $ 200 was left for one night in an American Bed & Breakfast on the other side of the ditch. That would be the end of the journey.

When the taxi driver left, Ashot jumped over the ditch and walked to the American house. He knew the name of its owner – George Riley.

"I have very good references about your Bed & Breakfast," he said. "I would like to spend one night here. And then, would you mind driving me to Seattle, please? All I have is $200, but I hope that would be enough."

Ashot was dirty, disheveled, pale, exhausted, hurt, weak, almost dead, but still alive. He put on the table his pouch with the rest of his money and dropped his small backpack on the floor. Then he fell on a chair, breathing heavily. "I am sorry, sir... I am looking like a hobo, but if you knew what I survived the last few months..."

"Welcome," George answered and patted him on the shoulder. "I know what you survived. You're not the first one here. Let's go, I'll show you to your room. Then you can take a shower, do some laundry and sleep as long as you want. Lunch is in an hour, dinner is at five. You're welcome to any of them you want, or to both. In the evening you will tell me your story and explain where exactly in Seattle you want to go. Tomorrow morning I will drive you there."

"Thank you," Ashot whispered with difficulty suppressing the spasm in his throat. "God bless you, sir."

It all came back to God. During the past thirty years in America, in his daily prayers Ashot always mentioned the prostitute Tamara, her boxer husband, the Turks – drug smuggler Rassul, market merchant Abu-Ahmed, sailor Nadir - and the American B&B owner George Riley. They were all his saviors sent by God and he strongly believed that there was a special plan and a purpose which God meant by saving him.

Ashot saved Liam fifteen years ago from a severe case of schizophrenia. It was his first experiment on American soil and it turned out brilliantly successful. Liam was perfectly healthy after that and fell in love with him, at first, just from gratitude. God rewarded Ashot for the cure by giving him a true love and the best, nicest husband in the world.

Now Ashot felt that he was predestined to save Rosie whom he really loved like a daughter although she called him - uncle. He had anxiety about his own little daughter, Annush, lost forever somewhere behind in Armenia and subconsciously he was replacing her with that ill girl here. He must heal Rosie now, save her and

71

return her to life, like all those people in his past saved him and returned him to life.

Back in 1985, when Ashot told George Riley that he would like to go to a LGBTQ center in Seattle, the man sadly shook his head.

"You know, there is a pandemic of AIDS now," he said. "Really deadly. It's been a very difficult time there for the last couple of years. In King county – known as gay populated area - 1,200 people died just this year. It was in all the newspapers and on TV almost every day."

"I actually could help," Ashot noted readily. "I am a doctor."

"For that you should obtain the American medical license. But first, just simple documents, like a driver's license, or passport. Do you have any?"

"No," Ashot shook his head. "Zero. Everything was taken from me back there, in the Soviet Union. What would be your advice?"

"Okay," George said thoughtfully. "I can give you advice, but only if you listen to it and follow it. Usually people don't. And I don't want to waste time on useless advice which will never be used anyway."

"I promise, I'll listen and follow," Ashot exclaimed desperately. "You, please, understand me. I have nothing here. No documents, no knowledge of life, no work and no money. I am not in a position to be disobedient. If I ignore advice here, I am dead, I guess. And then, what were all my efforts of escaping and surviving for? I could die at home, if I wanted to."

"Okay," George chuckled. "This sounds like a plan. Look, for now, please, forget that you are a gay. Don't even mention this word, don't even pronounce it. Wait until things calm down in your LGBTQ community there, in Seattle. Wait until you will get your documents and medical license. It may take two, three or more years, but be patient, if you want to survive here in this situation. No gay sex ever with anybody at all, for all those years ahead. It will keep you healthy and alive. Any protection wouldn't be as effective, as just not doing it. You got it?"

"Well," Ashot shrugged, confused, smiling bashfully, "I wasn't even thinking about sex at all. It would be the last thing on my 'To do' list. I will be too busy for days, weeks, and months adjusting to my new life. I swear to God, this challenge is accepted. And this advice is taken. I promise to follow it honestly."

"Second piece of advice that will be helpful, I guess – I will drive you tomorrow to an Armenian church. I see that you are wearing this antique cross on a chain. You must be a believer?"

"Yes, it's my mother's," Ashot nodded. "Actually, I am a scientist and I was an atheist until this year. But now I am really turned toward God. I prayed for my survival and He gave it to me. Yes, now I am a really serious and deep believer."

"In the city of Redmond we have an Armenian Church which was opened just three years ago, in 1982, luckily for you. Let's look it up in the Yellow Pages."

George opened the thick yellow book which Ashot was surprised to see, not understanding what it could be. The man flipped the thin pages for a while and then announced, "Here you go! Holy Resurrection Armenian Apostolic Church, Woodinvill Road, Redmond. It is a bit more than 60 miles from here on Interstate Highway Five, which we call here the I-5. Now go to sleep and say your prayers. Tomorrow morning we will go to this church to seek help for you."

"Oh, my God!" Ashot exclaimed. "Could I hug you, George? I swear, it will be a brotherly hug only! Thank you, thank you so much."

"Okay," George laughed and patted Ashot's back while he was hugging him.

The next day Ashot was accepted to live temporarily in a small guest suite in the church basement and given a job as a church janitor for a little cash. He knelt there in front of this beautiful building resembling the architecture of a real old Armenian church and kissed the grassy American soil. He was at home, finally. That was how his American life started.

Ashot was very happy and extremely thankful for everything he got. It was a safe, calm, quiet, beautiful, friendly, decent life. All that he was missing in Armenia, in the Soviet Union. And here, on the Pacific Ocean coast of the North American continent, were

Armenian surroundings – huge snowy mountains, and Armenian people, and the language, and the food. That was where he found himself a real home, where the church was an actual place of worship and not just a museum.

The only thing that Ashot was deeply hiding from anybody was his sexual orientation, but he stored it at the very bottom of his heart. He patiently waited until better days, as he promised to George Riley, to himself and also to God.

CHAPTER 10

On Sunday morning Helen woke up Aaron by bringing him breakfast in bed on a beautiful tray.

"What?" he muttered, still almost asleep. "What are you doing? Why?"

"Because I love you, baby," she smiled. "And because you really deserve it. You worked so hard, like never before in the two years that I've been sleeping with you. Three times! Wow! And also thank you for the sleepover. It was such a nice surprise for me. Usually, you're behaving like a drunk sailor in a cheap brothel in Hong Kong, ten minutes - you are done and gone."

Aaron raised his head and rubbed his eyes, trying to wake up completely. "Well, it was never actually only ten minutes," he grumbled objectively.

"Okay, let's agree on fifteen."

He made a wry face, "Noooo!"

"Twenty, then?"

"Jeez! Stop teasing me. Why the hell did you bring the food here? It's disgusting! I hate it!"

"Look," Helen sat on the edge of the bed. "All of human society considers breakfast in bed as a symbol of love, comfort, care, but you, Aaron Dispenmore, a freaking diva, of course, are not happy about this. Anything I could do for you will always be wrong. It should be considered abuse. You're a damn abuser!"

"You know," Aaron shrugged. "I could turn the tables easily and call you an abuser for this silly food which I don't want and for blaming me for no reason. I am just waking up, I want to stand up, go to the washroom, take a shower, brush my teeth, and shave. Then I will come to the table for breakfast, clean and refreshed. I will enjoy my time sitting with you and having a nice conversation. Instead of that you are holding me here with this stupid tray on my stomach, with a hot coffee and orange juice which are ready to fall down and spill over. It is really irritating. And not letting me go to the washroom could be considered an abuse as well. So, we are even."

"Okay," she took the tray away and stood up, angrily. "Go to the washroom, go to hell, go anywhere you want. I don't care. The less we, women, care about you, idiot men, the better."

"That's my girl!" he laughed, jumped up from the bed and disappeared behind the washroom door.

When half an hour later, with a towel wrapped around his waist, Aaron came to the kitchen, Helen was sitting at the table with breakfast on it. He sat across from her and smiled, "Sorry, Hel. You probably really tried to be nice, but to me... when my father was deadly ill, he was always in bed and we were bringing him food there. It made me think about food in bed as a sign of sickness, weakness, and dying. Normally, healthy people shouldn't eat in bed. Back about your 'all of human society' comment... The human society invented tables and dining rooms for eating. Here, now, I am ready for breakfast."

Helen smiled, shaking her head. "Arie, you are unbelievable! Why did you come here almost naked? Do you want to seduce me again with your well tanned shoulders and six-pack muscles?"

"No," he laughed. "I think it was pretty much enough last night. I just put all my clothes into the washer because I forgot to bring the spare set for today. You know, it was my first sleepover and I didn't think about that. I am not used to such things. So, probably for the next couple of hours you are welcome to enjoy the view of my muscles. Or you can turn around and not stare at me..."

"So, this first sleepover hopefully won't be the last one? I see that as a big step ahead in our relationship, right?" Helen guessed, pouring his coffee in a big cup.

"I don't know," Aaron shrugged. "It depends..."

"Depends on what?"

"On my situation. We, actually, need to talk. I would like to ask you something."

"Go ahead," Helen said anxiously. He was always so tricky, she never knew what to expect.

"You told me many times that you fell in love with me the moment you saw me. I was just wondering, why? What was so attractive in me that you, as a woman, liked?"

"Wow, Arie, you're the whole package. First of all, you're a looker. Do you want me to tell you more compliments?"

"No, I am just trying to understand how I could attract a woman."

"You're tall, handsome, athletic. You have amazing hair, so thick, dark-brown, a little wavy, pretty long. Jeez, it's so sexy. You have big beautiful eyes, dark, piercing. When you are looking at me, I physically feel like you are undressing me."

"Damn, I never did."

"Maybe you didn't but as a woman, I feel like you did. Plus, you're extremely talented, smart, and the last thing, but very important also, you are from a rich family. Women really appreciate that."

"Well, how did you know that when you saw me the first time as a student?"

"I did my homework when I came to the university. I wanted to see who of my fellow students was worth my attention."

"It doesn't look like many genuine feelings were there," Aaron noted with a smirk. "Did your homework show that I was married?"

"Yes, it did, but I knew that I would figure out how to deal with that obstacle."

"And how did you deal?"

"Pretty much successfully. Look at me – I am sleeping with you now. What else could I wish for? But... the question is, why are you wondering now, how you could attract a woman? Did you meet someone you want to attract?"

"I don't know," he shrugged.

"It's a stupid answer, Arie. You know."

"Then, maybe I just don't want to talk about that."

"But you started this conversation. Then, continue. And finish it with an explanation, please."

Aaron sat silently for a while, then he sighed deeply. "This would be a conversation for friends, but you know that we aren't. So, I am sorry. It's better we go to bed and try one more time before my laundry is finished and I can go home."

"Jeez! The fourth time!" Helen exclaimed. "In just one day? Before it took you four months! This woman has probably really turned you on. Am I right?"

"Again, I don't know," he answered, quite irritated. "I don't understand myself. I don't know what's going on with me. I just... damn... do you want it or not?!"

"Of course, I do, my love. But it's kind of hurtful to me to know that you're only using me."

"It was our agreement, first. And, second, you're using me too."

"Well, I love you, Arie, so I agree to everything you want," Helen said with an offended expression on her face, while she took his hand and led him back to the bedroom.

A couple of hours later, when the laundry was also done, Aaron dressed up and was ready to leave, but stopped by the door and asked one more thing. "Hel, if you said I was such a handsome and attractive student at university, how come not one girl ever hit on me? There were many girls, as I remember. They kind of shunned me. Did they all respect Ally so much? Or maybe you are not very objective? Maybe I didn't look that attractive to them? Or what?'

"At the beginning, too many of them were excited about you, almost everyone, but I pushed them all away. I didn't want a lot of competition in my fight for you. I blocked you from anybody."

"How?"

She laughed. "I told them that you have AIDS."

"What?!"

Aaron was so shocked that he didn't know what to say or to do for some seconds. "Why the hell did you do that?" he exploded then. "It's disgusting! It was mean! It was a lie, a dirty lie! Jeez, it would be such a shame for me, if I had known. The university actually did tests every year for all the students. It just couldn't be true. How could someone believe you? It was proven that I didn't have anything like that. I was married!" He squeezed his fists in anger and hurt. "You destroyed my reputation for nothing. You humiliated me in front of our colleagues! And you pretended to be our family friend?! Jeez, I would've killed you, if I'd known then."

"No, you wouldn't," Helen laughed. "You are not the kind of a person who could kill somebody. I love you, Arie, and I wanted you for myself only. Isn't it understandable? It is an old proverb: the goal is to acquire any means."

"It is a Jesuit's proverb. It's mean. You are not a human, really. You're a she-devil, Hel. I don't know... I won't talk to you after that."

"You will, baby," she smirked. "You proved today how much you need me. I put you on a hook of sex addiction, and you will be with me forever."

"What?! Hell! No! No, no addiction!" Aaron slammed the door, much like he had once before during their fight some time ago and ran to his car. While driving home, he beat his fist on the steering wheel and on the next seat in desperate anger and hate for this woman. His first move was to tell his mother about this, so she would be aware of Helen, but then he decided against it. Beth would probably have a heart attack, if she heard that.

Luckily for him, Beth and Laurie weren't home. On Sunday they usually went to church and after that visited some of Beth's friends where Laurie had a chance to play with their grandchildren and have fun. Aaron went to the home gym in the basement and started exercising on machines and on a weightlifting bench, which he used every morning on working days. Now it was just a chance for him to reduce his anger, to let go of steam and to calm himself down.

Aaron was a kind and forgiving person, but how would it be possible to ever forgive that? If Helen was capable of something like that, wouldn't she be capable of more heinous things, like to kill Ally? The police investigation found no evidence of anything, except for an overdose on drugs. But this scary thought had come to him a couple of times before, although he pushed it away as a crazy one. However, maybe it wasn't that crazy at all?

After two hours of heavy exercise, Aaron did a meditation, then went to the bathtub and soaked in foam with perfumed candles burning around. He knew that it was usually a woman's thing to do. Beth always did it when she had some stress and she told him that it worked pretty well, so he tried. And it looked like it worked for him, too. He finally calmed down and went to the patio to barbecue pork ribs for dinner, expecting that Beth and Laurie would be home soon.

When they came home, they had together a nice family dinner on the patio with quiet and warm conversation. Then Aaron went for a walk with Laurie, as usual. His little angel really soothed him. When they passed the *Youth Shelter* on the hill, she suggested they come up on the gravel driveway and to look once more at the *yellow houses and purple towers, green grass and pink flowers* which were visible from there and which he already showed her during their Saturday's night walk.

"I like it, daddy," Laurie said. "Let's come here every day when we go for our walk and see them. I wish this girl would come with us again. She is a bit older than me, but it was so nice to hold her hand and to talk with her about barbies. She likes them a lot. And she understood me so well as if we were the same age. I would like to play with her again."

"Yes, sweetie, we could do that, "Aaron agreed. "There was something very warm and attractive about her, and I would be happy to see her - if she could ever be found..."

He felt now so relaxed and content as if his angry dispute with Helen never happened. He forgave her. He forgot her. All her bad energy was completely gone and evaporated. The soothing calm refilled his soul.

Aaron decided he would read Rosie's book all night again and look for more questions to ask her. He imagined the conversation with her, although he still had no idea when, where and how he could possibly find her. But he knew for sure that he would.

CHAPTER 11

While sitting in his car and remembering his American arrival, Ashot suddenly realized that most of what he had revealed in his biography was wrong. It absolutely shouldn't be written like that for any scientific conference. Nothing private should be in it, just clear and simple professional information.

He took out his laptop and checked the story which he wrote that night.

... I was born in 1955 in Yerevan, the capital city of Armenia. At that time Armenia wasn't an independent country – it was one of the Kavkaz Mountain Range Republics of the former Soviet Union. After high school graduation in 1972, I moved to Moscow, the capital of the Soviet Union, where I became a student of the First Medical Institute. I successfully got my General Medicine Master's degree in 1977, and accomplished my PhD study in Psychiatry in 1980. Then I returned to Yerevan where I got a pretty high position in the newly opened psychiatric clinic under the Science Research Institute of Psychiatry.

During my five-year tenure in this clinic, I discovered a very unusual natural way of treatment for patients with extreme schizophrenic conditions, and completely healed twenty of them. They became 100 percent normal healthy people....

Then he went on writing.

... In 1985, I emigrated to the USA where I wanted to continue my scientific research about the cure of schizophrenia, and treat more patients. I got my professional evaluation on the American level, at first, as a college degree in psychiatric nursing and started working. Using my scientific discovery which was supported and approved by Dr.... (there should be a name of any doctor who would agree to participate), I cured two more people in the USA. All documentation about the treatment procedures of my patients is provided in the following files...

Actually, for now it was only one who was cured – Liam. Rosie expected to be the second one, but it wasn't done yet. It was almost in the process, but there were still some obstacles to overcome before starting the cure. However, the draft of the introduction should be ready now.

This would definitely sound better, Ashot thought, and with this decision he went to his condo, took a shower and lay down on his bed to sleep after a long night shift.

However, the sleep didn't come easily. The memories, awakened by this procedure of writing his biography, still didn't want to go away and bothered him immensely. Here it was again – summer of 1985...

...Ashot was living in the Armenian church basement suite for a while and worked as a janitor, which was excellent and absolutely acceptable for a new immigrant, especially an illegal and undocumented one. But he clearly realized that this couldn't last long. He should move ahead somehow.

First of all, he was a doctor and a scientist who would like to continue with this career. Washing floors and toilets was perfect for some period of time until he could get on his feet, but obviously, not forever.

Second, he was worried that the church authorities who didn't ask him a word about his immigration status and documentation, would do so one day. He would have no answer for them. Then anything could possibly happen, maybe he would be reported as an illegal and deported back to Armenia. That would be a death sentence and the possibility of it was still hovering over his head.

His third concern was also an important one. According to George Riley's advice, Ashot completely removed any sexual thoughts and all 'gay things' from his head, but he knew that this was also only temporary. He was waiting until the AIDS pandemic in Seattle ended and until his life conditions were settled and organized properly. Then, possibly, the time would come to look for serious love and find a sincere good partner for life. To be alone until the end of time would be too difficult and too lonely. Every person needed someone to love and cherish. And in this case, his sexual orientation would be impossible to hide, so Ashot knew that he would need to move away from the Armenian church and to find another place of worship that would accept him. Though, he had no idea if one like that existed.

It looked like there wasn't any time to waste, because all of his tasks were pretty long-term. He should start moving ahead immediately.

For now, the main important points of the way ahead were language and transportation. Ashot decided to eat as little as possible and keep some money as savings under his mattress because he wasn't eligible for opening a bank account yet. The goal of that was to buy a car, however, without a driver's license it would be useless anyway, so the process of collecting money and getting documentation should go hand in hand.

The English language, as much as Ashot knew it, wasn't really enough for living in the USA. It was one thing to know English in Armenia as a foreign language, to pass the PhD exam, but absolutely another thing to live in an English speaking country a regular essential life. To speak, in spite of an accent, wasn't that difficult. To understand what people were saying to you – that was a problem. Ashot dealt with that by watching TV in his free time, and also by reading books from the church's free exchange library located in the same basement as his suite.

He knew that he was supposed to ask someone for advice on how and where it would be possible to buy some official documents, but this obviously would be a crime. Regular law abiding citizens wouldn't give him this advice. They would be indignant if he would ask them something like that and could easily report him to the police. Plus, they of course didn't know where and how it was possible to do so because they had never done it. They were lucky to be born in America and to have everything they needed honestly and legally.

Ashot didn't have an answer for this problem. He guessed that he should ask some criminals for advice, but he didn't know who they were, where to find them, or how to approach them. The criminals in America obviously weren't any better than criminals in the Soviet Union or elsewhere in the world. It was really the same international thing everywhere.

In Moscow, at the train station, prostitute Tamara said to him, "Welcome to the underground world, bro!" Ashot escaped from there because he didn't want to be an underground person any longer. It was not his lifestyle and not in his character. In his heart he was a very honest and law obedient citizen and dreamed to stay that way forever. But here he was, on the other side of the globe, having the same need for help from the underground world. He tried to find a better life, to find the recognition of his scientific discovery, to be a real doctor, a real scientist, helping ill people. But as a result, for now he still was a 'bro' to the underground world much more than for the beautiful legal world above ground.

The only one who could give him some help at the moment was, once again, God, and Ashot began to include in his daily prayers a request to find a way to obtain legal documents. It wasn't answered for a couple of weeks, maybe a month, but then a miracle happened which made Ashot's faith grow even stronger.

From the church library, he read one book, a crime story, where the main character was a man who was chased by the Mafia and was trying to survive. The only way for him to do so was to move far away, to the other end of the country, but before doing that, he was supposed to change his name. And so he did. Otherwise, the Mafia would find him anyway, anywhere.

Ashot wasn't sure if the way he did this was real, as it was described in the book, or if it was a complete fiction, created by the writer's imagination, but he decided to try it. He remembered that he wasn't sure about the authenticity of the route that Tamara gave him in Moscow, but it proved to be alright. Maybe this one would be true as well. In this case, it would be a Godsend, again, and the answer for his prayers.

He exactly followed the steps of the character from the crime book: took the church's Yellow Pages – now he knew what it was for – and jotted down the addresses and phone numbers of all cemeteries in the state of Washington. Then Ashot called those cemeteries and said that he was a historian who was writing a book about the polio epidemic in the beginning of the fifties. For his book he needed information about the dead children buried at their cemetery in the years 1953 -1957. The good thing about Americans was - they never asked for ID or any proof, they just easily believed what you told them. So, in spite of his accent, Ashot sounded believable and he received the information he needed. However, at some cemeteries there weren't any children at all, some had girls only, some had children who died in other years.

Anyway, after a week spent on the phone, Ashot found what he was looking for. Buried in the city of Lynden, WA, there was a boy, named Thomas Charles Spencer, born on May 10, 1954 who died from polio on July 12, 1956. After writing down this information, Ashot thanked God and swore that as soon as he got a car and his driver's license, he would drive to Lynden and place flowers on the little Thomas' grave. They were the family now and 'blood relatives'.

The next phone call Ashot made was to the bureau of statistics. Exactly like the character from the crime book did, using a dead person's name, he said that he was Thomas Charles Spencer, born in Lynden WA on May 10, 1954. He lost his birth certificate in a house fire and he would like to receive a copy. It was accepted because registrations of birth and deaths were in different computer programs, and the officer had no idea that Thomas Spencer was already dead long ago. In a week, Ashot had a new birth certificate in his hands.

He used to have a car at home in Yerevan, so he knew quite well how to drive. Then he asked some friends from the church to drive him to the DMV, where he showed his birth certificate and asked to take a driving test. It was done pretty successfully and in two weeks Ashot received by mail his new driver's license as Thomas Charles Spencer.

The next step was to buy a car. Again, with the help of church people, Ashot found an old car for $500. It was a bit rusty, but still decently movable. He bought it with his under the mattress savings.

With each step up, he was getting more confident and brave, obtaining more self-esteem and self-confidence. Everything went well and showed him that he was on the right track. God was obviously guiding him, watching and helping. Ashot religiously fulfilled his promises as well. In his new car with his new driver's license he drove to Lynden and placed a huge bouquet of roses on Thomas Spencer's grave. He also sat there on the grass for a long moment and prayed for the soul of that little boy in Heaven, now 'reincarnated' in him.

Then, the newly born 'Thomas Spencer' began looking for a serious job. The first level available in medical fields, of course, were nursing homes where usually all the immigrants were working as caregivers. He got this job easily - most of the caregivers were women and there was always a lack of men. The salary wasn't really impressive, but enough to rent a small studio in Seattle, move out from the Armenian church basement and to start living by himself, independently.

Ashot worked really hard, always taking extra hours when it was requested if some of his co-workers went on vacation or got sick. This job also helped him to improve his English because most of his patients were lonely, bored and craved human communication. Sometimes, Ashot even stayed after work to visit with them and to listen to their life stories which they wanted to share. For him, it was perfect practice and free English lessons.

Also, every Sunday morning he kept attending his first home – the Armenian church. After service in Armenian, he stayed at service in English as well, for more language practice.

Now Ashot was able to buy a better car and to finally open a bank account. He tried to accumulate as much money as possible which he needed to pay for his next step – college education that could move him closer to his real profession - psychiatry. It also went well.

In a couple more years he was accepted into a community college. To study there was unbelievably easy: being in reality a PhD Doctor in psychiatry, Ashot only needed to translate his knowledge into English. His level of English was already perfect at that time, and his teachers were always excited about the ease with which he absorbed the contents of each class and knew it right away.

They didn't know that he was an immigrant, highly educated in this area, who just looked at his previous knowledge from an American angle because the base of the profession was practically the same. For them he was an American – Thomas Spencer, former caregiver from a nursing home; now – a college student and a very talented one.

Some of his classmates were even jealous of his success at learning and gossiped that he was so good because he was old. Really, he was thirty-five to forty during the school when all of them were eighteen to twenty-three, but they had no idea about the real reason behind his perfect knowledge. So, in 1995, ten years after his arrival in the USA, Thomas Spencer graduated from the college with an honors diploma and soon after found a job as a nurse in the General Psychiatric Hospital.

There were even some moments when Ashot was thinking about going to university to get a Master's in Psychiatry here, in America, but then he decided against it. It would take all together about ten more years and he really would be too old at that time to start his American Doctor career.

Instead of this, he began hiking every weekend in the mountains, looking for blue clay - the main organic ingredient of his scientific invention, the cure for schizophrenia.

With that Ashot finally fell asleep with thoughts about the mountains – fresh air, spring waterfalls, fir forests, snowy tops and glaciers. They completely relaxed and calmed him, soothing his heart and soul to rest.

CHAPTER 12

On Monday, the first thing in the morning, Aaron made a request to Dr. Evelyn Hertz to send the personal file of Rosa Lynn Garcia to the Psychiatry Department of the university and make a note that this patient should be admitted personally to him. Then he called Dr. Hertz on the phone and talked for a while about this transaction.

"Though the procedure will take three to five business days," Dr. Hertz said, "I am actually happy to transfer this patient to you. It's time. I specialize in children and teenagers, but Rosa is already an adult, so, there you go. I saw her last week at the *Youth Shelter* and prepared all the paperwork to move her to an adult psychiatric facility. It was planned for today. But the shelter notified me that she escaped last Friday night. So, good luck with finding her.

"Just be extremely careful when you do," Dr. Hertz continued. "Rosa has one murder on her, two attempted murders, a bunch of assaults with a knife, and suicide attempts. However, she has a very special ability in telekinesis, thoughts reading and telepathy, and obviously she is a genius in poetry. So, for your university scientific lab research of that 90 percent unknown part of the human brain, she is the perfect material. Maybe, while working with her, you will be able to make the scientific discovery which is required for the conference in New York. I wish you success with that, Dr. Dispenmore," and she laughed.

Aaron didn't see anything funny in this comment. Maybe it was just sarcasm on her part. Addressing the most special woman who he had ever met as 'perfect material' really jarred upon him. He hung up feeling that there was something similar in these women-psychiatrists who specialized in children's psychiatry; Dr. Hertz reminded him of Helen with her cold and unkind tone of discussion.

Last night, while reading Rosie's book again and again, looking for clues of where it would be possible to find her, he suddenly got it on the back cover: **Rosalyn is really involved with the youth movement *Slam Poetry* and performs her poems on stage...**

Aaron opened his computer and looked up *Slum Poetry*. Yes, it was there. Downtown, at the Greenwich Competition Hall, there were concerts of this club every Tuesday at eight p.m. He attentively read the article and found out that this Competition Hall was actually a very good entertainment place that opened the perfect possibility for teenagers to develop their talents.

Every day of the week they had one competition – singing, poetry, dances, acrobatic, circus, stand up comedy and trained animals performance. Each genre was scheduled on it's own day of the week. The stage wasn't big, so the performance requirement was to be solo or in small groups, no more than two-three people, or two-three animals with a trainer. Every seat for the public had a button, connected to the big computer screen above the stage. The people from the audience would vote by pressing the button after the act which they liked the most. The performer who got more votes won the competition and received a monetary prize.

In the Internet article, there were lots of pictures of teens dancing, singing, performing on silks, doing magic, showing trained dogs, or cats, or pigs, or even chicken. And of course, there she was, his Rosie – Anastasia, the star-poetess.

She looked very different than she had last Friday during their walk with Laurie. She was really dressed up in the style of Snow-White, or Sleeping Beauty, or Cinderella - always wearing luxuriant skirts, the blouses with puffed sleeves and, on the top of them - the corsets of different colors, laced up in the front. Her hair was also done in these princesses' style – a bun on the top of the head and three tight locks on each side of her head. She wore a lot of make-up along with huge false eyelashes in some pictures.

But there were also other days, when she was dressed in a denim jacket with patches and pants with holes on the knees. Her hair was dyed black, twisted into a ban, and she wore no make-up at all. Sometimes she was wearing hats or caps turned backwards or sideways. The clothing and hair styles were probably connected to the contents of the poetry which she performed on that given day.

Aaron flipped through the pages of the article, staring greedily at her exalted face as she lifted her hand with the mic in the air. He listened to her poems read by her excited voice, which at times was shaking with tears, and he was unable to tear himself away from the screen. He knew that he was watching his own soul reciting his own words and his own feelings. He was her and she was him. Two bodies and one soul, the spiritual Siamese Twins. They were together from now on. They couldn't be separated, or one of them would die – much like what may happen with Siamese Twins in reality.

It seemed strange to Aaron that he already knew about that connection, but Rosie didn't.

There were also dozens of photos of other teenagers performing their arts but nothing was interesting for him, only that girl, Rosie, whom at first he believed was absolutely ordinary. It was such a blow to his gut. How could he be so blind? How come he didn't get her extraordinaire, her specialty, her spirituality? How did he miss all of these, and let her go, practically not noticing her? Was he crazy then? Or was he crazy now, after repeatedly reading her poems and getting enchanted by them? What was going on with him? Aaron absolutely didn't understand himself. At some moments he felt as if he was going insane.

But all of that was last night, at home. Now, on Monday morning, after the conversation with Dr. Hertz the situation got worse for him, as she mentioned the murder and two attempted murders. That was obviously the reason why Rosie was in that *Youth Shelter,* but Aaron absolutely refused to believe that. He was sure that there was some kind of mistake. It was one more thing which he needed to talk to her about. So, Tuesday then. Tomorrow. At eight p.m. At the Greenwich Competition Hall. That was when and where he would see her, talk to her and never let her go. He decided it once and for all. And if there was any danger, if she would kill him, he would be okay with that. He'd rather die than live without seeing her anymore.

The rest of the first half of his working day, which was usually spent in the research lab, Aaron studied materials about the New York's conference and printed them out. He decided that he needed to bring them home and share them with his mother, to let her know about this important project which could hold a great opportunity for his professional success. Her advice and help would be very much appreciated.

Then, after lunch, the second half of his working day was dedicated, as usual, to the appointments with patients. It wasn't very interesting. Aaron just renewed the prescriptions of their medications and checked their blood test results to see how those medications affected their livers and kidneys. It was important to know if the chemicals in their blood already reached a deadly level or not yet. That work was tedious - the sad attempts to help those people somehow, though he knew it wouldn't help to cure them at all. It just held them temporarily in check to avoid the awful attacks and danger for the public if they go out.

Aaron felt pity for his patients and was ashamed of himself being so practically useless and unable to cure them, to be ineffective to give them a normal life. That's why the main idea of the Psychiatric Scientific Conference – to push all the psychiatrists of the country to look for a cure for this horrible and also mysterious illness – seemed to be very interesting, attractive and also important for all of human society.

At home, before going for a walk with Laurie, Aaron gave his print-outs to Beth and asked her to read them attentively. "I need to talk to you, mom, later, after I put Laurie to bed," he said. "We need to discuss something really serious. Okay?"

"Of course, my dear," Beth nodded, looking at her son a bit suspiciously. She knew and felt him well enough and had already noticed that something strange was going on with him. He had never before involved her into his work decisions or interests.

Laurie pulled him again to the top of the gravel driveway by the *Youth Shelter*. From there they enjoyed watching the yellow houses and purple towers on the horizon once more. Aaron was a bit surprised that she had not forgotten about that already. Usually, children's memories were quite short and some new toys or fun could easily distract them from previous ones. Why did she still remember Rosie and her poem? Was his little girl enchanted as much as he was? To some extent this excited Aaron – it was what he wanted; but at some point it scared him. Was it too much for a child? Was it too heavy a burden on her soul? This was something that he needed to think about.

Then, later that evening, after he petted Laurie's head, quietly sung her a lullaby and watched her fall asleep, Aaron walked downstairs and found Beth sitting on the couch in the living room with his print-outs beside her.

"How do you like those materials, mom?" Aaron asked, while settling in a cozy armchair across from her.

"It appears very interesting and inspiring for you, Arie. So, how could I not like it? I am always supporting your career, and this is a great chance to take a really big step ahead. But... Do you have some discovery in your mind, which is requested here? And how is it related to me? How could I help?"

"Yes, I have something in mind," he answered. "I might be able to find a patient and work on him to make this discovery. But it will be very time consuming. The amount of the experiments in the lab will be increased a lot. For that I need more time as well. For the following two or three months I will be extremely busy. I probably will stay at work very late, mostly at the lab, of course. And that brings up a problem.

"As a father, I want Laurie to know that she is the number one person in my life and the most loved one. It is very important for a child's developing psychology. Many children, even in good families, where they are loved a lot, are feeling neglected and unloved because their parents are spending too much time at work. Being too young, they don't yet know the concept of needing money for their own well-being. They couldn't get that their parents are at work to get more money for them, for their needs, for their future, like a college fund. They are thinking that their parents have gone to work because they don't love them, don't care, and don't want to spend more time with them. Here is my point – I don't want Laurie to think that about me and suffer because she assumes I am 'neglecting' her."

"You are right, Arie," Beth nodded thoughtfully. "Then how could we eliminate those thoughts and feelings in her heart? Do you want me to do something about that?"

"Yes. I have one idea. What if you take her and you go for a trip together, like a vacation somewhere? In this case, it would look to her like she left me for a while to help her grandma during the travel. She would likely have fun and would be happy."

Beth looked at him with a meaningful smile. "Arie, I am your mother and I knew right away, even when you were a child, when you tried to trick me into something. I see now that you're going in circles – importance of your work, care about Laurie's feelings. Don't blah-blah-blah me please. Tell the truth – is there a woman involved? I know that you, men, love your mothers and daughters but when it comes to a woman, you forget everything that was ever valuable to you."

Aaron blushed. "I don't know, mom. There could be a woman involved, but I haven't talked to her yet and I don't know if she'll agree to work with me."

"So, you are turning to work again. But you're really smitten with her, right?"

"Pretty much so," he answered reluctantly, biting his lips. "But I swear, I don't know, mom. Maybe it is just nothing. However, all about my work and about me not wanting to hurt Laurie's feelings - it's all true. Both of these topics are extremely important to me."

"But Laurie is a smart child. She obviously remembered that last year on your vacation we all went to Japan together. And also, the year before, she went with you to Hawaii. Don't you think she would ask, 'why only grandma is going with me'?"

"Yes. It is good for her to know that sometimes she travels with me, sometimes with both of us and sometimes with you. We're taking turns. Tell her that we are like her barbies going for a walk with us – in turns. That's it. She will understand. Could you think of some place to go?"

"So, you seriously decided to get rid of us?"

"Mo-om! Please..."

"Okay, okay," Beth smiled. "Sorry, for teasing you, son. Actually, I was ready to talk to you about this as well. You probably don't remember your father's distant cousin, Erin? But I have a connection with her, we talk on the phone every couple of weeks. She lives in Florida, in a suburb of Miami, right beside a beach, and she has invited all of us to visit. This summer she is watching three of her grandchildren, two girls and a boy, approximately same age as Laurie. It would be good for us to go, but for you obviously there would be no company. That's why I was a bit hesitant to talk to you about it. But if I go just with Laurie, I guess, it would be great. Right?"

"Mom!" Aaron jumped up from his armchair, hugged Beth and kissed her cheek. "You're amazing! Thank you."

"Jeez!" Beth shook her head. "You're really taken by her? Who is she? Not Helen, I guess?"

"No, no, not at all. I don 't want to tell you anything now because I don't know where I am and what's going on with me at this moment. But I will figure it out later. I just need time, mom. Nothing else. Also, tomorrow night I am going to a concert downtown. It starts at eight in the evening. So, I should leave here at seven. Please, make sure that we have dinner at five, as soon as I come from work. Then I will go for a walk with Laurie from six to seven, one hour earlier than usual. And then I will drive downtown."

"Are you going to a concert with this woman?"

"No. Just by myself."

"I don't understand. It's kind of strange. Who goes to a concert alone?"

"I do. Please, mom, don't ask anything else. I swear, I will tell you everything when you come back from Florida in September. I am sure I will know what to say then."

"Well," Beth shrugged, "it looks like I have no choice but to trust your gut, Arie. If it is so important to you, son, then good luck. I love you anyway."

"I love you too, mom," Aaron smiled happily and walked upstairs to sleep, or maybe just to read more of Rosie's book.

CHAPTER 13

Ashot was woken up by a quiet click of his phone on the bedside table – Liam sent a text saying that he would stay longer on the movie set. He suggested he would pick up Ashot at about seven and they would go out for dinner, so there was no reason for Ashot to cook anything at home.

Ashot texted back a short 'okay' and kept laying in his bed still resting. It was actually good luck to be fired from the *Youth Shelter*. He was getting older and working night shifts became more difficult with every year. Now, after each shift, he needed a much longer break for rest than earlier, but it was not available to him. There was a huge and important job ahead which would take all his time – not just the sessions themselves but also preparations before and documentation after.

His memory returned to the days when he first found blue clay in North America. It was a bolt from the blue, happiness, success - the moment when for the first time on American soil he realized that he could be a doctor again and cure people. It was summer as well, but not 1985 which he often remembered as the most life-changing for him. Now it was the summer of the year 2000 – an equally important one.

… After his graduation from college and beginning his work at the General Psychiatric Hospital in 1995, Ashot started hiking in the mountains every weekend. The surroundings of the city of Seattle, WA, gave a great opportunity for that but only during the summer seasons. The other times of the year were hazardous and made it too risky to go out into the wilderness. The Rocky Mountain Range was young on a global scale and still active. It was number one in the world for avalanches, landslides and earthquakes. These mountains were much more dangerous than his home Kavkaz Mountains in Armenia.

However, these movements of the ground also gave a great possibility to find spots where the soil was broken, open and cracked recently and the inner earthly minerals would show up from the depth and become visible. The challenge was just to look around attentively and find them.

The hiking was really good for Ashot. The long walks and agile rock climbing were excellent exercise in the fresh bracing mountain air. They kept him in shape. But those were just the nice and healthy side effects of his main goal.

It took him five years of those summer weekend hikes, until he accidentally bumped into the place he was looking for. It was pretty far away on Highway 20, after the city of Diablo. It was more of a museum than a city, now neglected, because the construction of the dam was completed many years ago – the last section of it was build in1953.

One day, when Ashot drove by the dam that held the lake, a few miles ahead he noticed a small comfortable clearing by the side of the road and decided to park his car there. He didn't know why - something just forced him subconsciously to do so. From there he walked on a mountain trail for about two miles, attentively looking for the cracks in the steep ridges. It was not a developed hiker's trail, but a natural trail probably made by wild animals. Deep in a ravine was a streaming mountain river, Skigit, shallow, seething by rocks. Ashot decided to check the grounds down there, beside the water, where he noticed some blue-gray clods in the cracks between boulders.

He climbed down, sat on the ground, took some of this substance into his fingers and smeared it on the palm of his hand.

He couldn't believe his eyes at first. He sniffed it to make sure that there was a raw smell of the clay, he even licked a tiny bit of it. The smell and taste were the same as clay back in Armenia twenty years ago. Yes, it was a natural deep underground blue clay, the same smooth and glue-like clay that he used before, from 1980 until 1985 in his clinic in Yerevan.

Ashot closed his eyes and began to pray, thanking God for the find. The tears of happiness filled his eyes. It was a life-changing moment, a real move ahead to his main goal. It was a light at the end of the tunnel. Although there was still a big job to do, Ashot felt as if he was on top of the world.

He marked the place, drew a map to make sure that he could find it again, and went home to do preparations to carefully excavate the clay and to carry it to his apartment by in plastic grocery bags. This was another illegal procedure. The whole area of the mountains there was The North Cascade National Park. It was banned to take away anything out – flowers, mushrooms, plants, rocks, and the samples of the water or soil, as well.

Welcome back to the underground world, bro, Ashot thought sadly. *Again! Oh God, how many times! Why is it always this way for me? I am such an honest and law abiding person at heart! When will my life get legal, finally! Please, help me, God, one more time. I am begging you!*

Luckily for him, the place was very secluded. There was a much bigger chance of bumping into a grizzly bear or mountain lion, than the park ranger.

Ashot prepared ten empty large cardboard boxes in a closet of his apartment and started filling them with the clay step by step.

Every Saturday, he took a backpack with a bunch of empty plastic grocery bags, drove on Highway 20 to the animal trail, very well known to him by now, and walked the usual two miles distance. Then he climbed down a very steep rocky slope to the river stream. To reach the substance, he slowly removed the boulders around the crack that contained the blue clay on its bottom.

Ashot filled the plastic bags with the clay using a small metal scoop. Each bag could hold approximately ten pounds of clay. The climb back up to the slope with a heavy bag in hand was the most difficult part. Finally, at the top, Ashot packed the bag with the clay into his backpack which he left there, and then made another trip down and back. With two bags of clay in the backpack, all together now weighing twenty pounds, he returned on the animal trail, walked back to the Highway and loaded his burden into his car. Then he made another trip to the river, then one more, until the car was full at last.

After that, Ashot drove home and emptied the bags into cardboard boxes. On Sunday, after church, he repeated this procedure again. Filling all the boxes in his apartment took him the whole summer, but he knew that now he was ready to cure about ten patients and possibly even more.

Now Ashot could afford to relax a bit and think about finding love and a partner for life. As he promised George Riley - his first American helper from the B&B by the Canadian boarder - he was patiently waiting until better times would come. And finally it actually happened. Ashot was already on his feet – he had his driver's license, college degree in psychiatric nursing, and full-time work in a respected hospital. He easily rented a bigger apartment and bought a much better car. He was already forty-six-year-old. It was time for him to go out and to finally start enjoying life.

At the beginning of the 21st century the pandemic of AIDS in Seattle started to subside gradually. Even some treatment was invented that didn't cure the illness completely, yet, but at least helped infected people to live longer. Medical science made huge progress and the situation in the LGBTQ community calmed down. Now Ashot dared to visit gay pubs, clubs and restaurants in the area.

He made some acquaintances, but was very adamant against casual sexual relationships. He was looking for a very serious life-long partner whom he could really love, but this wasn't easy. Many gay people around him were too promiscuous, so Ashot just kept his distance and maintained some friendship only with a middle-aged lesbian, Teresa, who tended the bar at the Piano Club. She was also an immigrant from Eastern Europe, Czech Republic, so they had something in common. Sometimes they had long heart-to-heart conversations while Ashot was nursing his Martini or Tequila glass, sitting on a high chair by her counter.

However, one day a pianist, whom he never saw before at the club, grabbed Ashot's attention. He was about ten years younger than Ashot, tall, very handsome and sexy looking, with a full head of blond curly hair. And he also played piano like a God. Ashot didn't dare approach him or talk to him because he saw a big difference between their level of attractiveness.

He himself was short, stocky, dark-tanned from his mountain hikes, and had pretty sharp wrinkles on his forehead and cheeks. His black hair was still curly but started getting thin and half-gray. And the main point was his big eggplant looking nose which he couldn't hide anywhere – it was right in the middle of his face and was the first thing which people usually noticed about him.

However, Ashot observed that in spite of the sex-appeal and the relevantly young age of the pianist, he was always alone and it looked like none of the club's visitors weren't interested in him at all. It was quite strange and he decided to ask Teresa about the man.

"Oh, my dear," she laughed. "Don't be fooled by appearance! The guy's name is Liam Johnson, he was a really famous pianist - professionally well known. His career started at a very young age. He toured almost the whole world – Europe, North and South America, Japan, and Russia while he was a gay-teenager. I heard he was a real genius in music. He won the pianists' contests in many countries. I know for sure - in Paris, Madrid, Munich and Moscow, but maybe more. Then, when he was about twenty, he suddenly became insane. I mean, really, crazy. And he couldn't play concerts anymore because attacks of his illness sometimes happened during the performances, even on stage. His parents kicked him out from home as they were fed up with his illness attacks and also not happy about him being gay. You know... fifteen years ago a lot of judge-mentality and stigma was out there. They had many scandals and fights with him. Liam trashed their house several times and almost killed them.

"Now he is playing only here while he is out from a mental institution, but not very often. The last fifteen years he was mostly locked there. Our guys here are pretty much afraid of him. He is a schizophrenic, and a very dangerous one. One day, last year, he had an awful attack of his illness and he almost killed a guy who tried to talk to him nicely. And he trashed the whole bar, broke some wine bottles and furniture. It took a bunch of policemen to restrict him. You couldn't even imagine how scary it was. But in spite of that our owner still invites him to play sometimes because, as you can see, he is unbelievably talented."

Oh, dear God, Ashot prayed in his thoughts, *are You teasing me? Are You playing with me to send me this patient as soon as I found the clay? Is it a coincidence? Or fate? Or Your will? How could I ever thank You enough for everything You are doing for me? Thank You, my dear Lord. Love you forever. Amen.*

"I will talk to him," Ashot suddenly said, gaining confidence after the prayer.

"No, no, no, my dear. I would advise against that!" Teresa exclaimed worriedly. "Believe me, he is unpredictable. As I told you, one guy already tried..."

"I will talk to him differently than that guy did, I am sure," Ashot assured her.

He knew that he had a special talent to talk with schizophrenics even during their very bad and dangerous attacks. It happened many times in Armenia. Even here, in Seattle, just being a nurse but not a doctor in a psychiatric hospital, he was often called for help to calm down and restrain a patient who had lost his head and got wildly aggressive. Ashot knew the timbre of his voice was soothing and he always somehow immediately felt what those poor sufferers wanted to hear and to be told. He was a real 'psychiatrist from God'.

As soon as Liam finished playing, Ashot stood up and approached him. All patrons of the club watched tensely, knowing already pretty well what to expect. Teresa started frantically hiding the bottles of the best wines under the counter to save them from danger.

Ashot took a chair, placed it beside the grand piano and sat, facing Liam, who looked morose and somber, but at the same time confused, lost and helpless.

"Hey," Ashot said very calmly and quietly. "You're playing so amazingly but I am sure that the people here couldn't appreciate it as much as I do. Only we, chosen by arts and music, could save the world and turn it back to life. Don't you agree?"

Liam looked at him silently for some seconds while Ashot attentively stared into his eyes, as a doctor and scientist trying to find a spark of consciousness, and as a gay-man admiring how fantastically beautiful those green eyes were.

"What kind of art are you doing?" Liam quietly asked after a long moment.

"I am a sculptor. I am creating masks from clay, almost like the ceramic. They are magical, believe me. Do you want to see them?" The audience froze, holding their breaths.

"Yes," Liam said and stood up.

"Then let's go," Ashot suggested, standing up as well and they walked to the door together. They were a pretty funny looking couple with about a ten-year-difference of age. However, Liam looked much younger than his age, but Ashot actually looked much older. As a result they appeared almost as a son and a father – tall and short, blond and dark, slim and stocky. At first glance they obviously couldn't be a good match and the whole audience quietly smirked to themselves.

"Wow!" Teresa whispered in shock, pressing her palms to her cheeks.

People couldn't believe their own eyes. Everybody watched silently as the men went out together and headed to Ashot's car through the parking lot. And then excitement burst out in the club – something unbelievable just happened in front of everyone's eyes and everybody started laughing.

After that neither Ashot nor Liam appeared in the Piano Club for more than three months. Teresa and several of their acquaintances thought that they would never see them again. Teresa even secretly looked through the police notes and funeral announcements in local newspapers, expecting that Ashot was probably already killed and Liam locked into a mental institution again, this time forever.

But then, like a bolt from the blue, they suddenly came together to the Christmas party – holding hands, smiling, and glowing with happiness. They sat at the table, ordered dinner and drinks and while serving them Teresa asked, "Where have you guys been? We haven't seen you for a while and were worried about you. How are things going?"

"Things are going great!" Liam laughed and hugged Ashot by the shoulders. "This Doctor cured me." And he placed an affectionate kiss on Ashot's wrinkled cheek.

"Actually, I didn't," Ashot chuckled, beaming. "I didn't do anything. The Clay Mask did everything itself."

"It doesn't matter who did what," Liam continued excitedly. "I am okay now, 100 percent healthy as determined by a board of psychiatrists at the General Psychiatric Hospital. No attacks, no worry. You don't have to hide your bottles anymore, lady. Hey, guys," he shouted, turning around, addressing the patrons of the club, "don't be scared of me. No danger to anything or anybody. I am healthy and very happy now. And a *big thank you* and *deep bow* for this to an amazing person over here, our Doctor Thomas Spencer, nicknamed Ashot."

Everybody applauded, screamed and whistled in approval, but kind of tentatively, not very confident.

"Wow! Congratulations!" Teresa said politely, not really believing what she heard. "Then maybe you could play piano for us again?"

"The funny thing," Liam continued, "I am not playing piano anymore. Really. I don't know how to do that. I can't even touch one key. My ability to play piano is completely gone after the cure."

"But you were a professional..."

"Yes, but my talent got lost. My skills disappeared. Completely! When Ashot told me after the cure that I was a pianist, I didn't believe him at first. But then he showed me videos of me playing piano, the articles in newspapers about me, my CD recordings, programs of my concerts, even my concerts taped on TV... Jeez, he convinced me that I was a well known pianist, but I don't have any memory of it."

"It's pretty sad," Teresa noted.

"No, not sad at all," Liam objected, smiling broadly. "I am healthy and happy now. And I could change my profession easily because some new amazing abilities appeared from nowhere, which I didn't have before. I still have difficulty believing this myself. This fellow is creating miracles, " and he patted Ashot on the shoulder. "Guys, let's get a drink for him, for his success as a Doctor and for my recovery." He lifted his glass. "Please, champagne to everybody, Teresa."

It was Christmas of 2000. Since that time Liam and Ashot had dated for eight years, engaged for four and married for three. They got their marriage certificate in City Hall first, then in 2012 were wedded in an Anglican Church, the only one which recognized same-sex marriages. Liam wasn't religious but he always went with Ashot to Sunday's services supporting his spouse.

Unfortunately, the Armenian Church was left behind. It played it's positive role in Ashot's life, but now, as an open gay, he had no chance to appear there ever.

Ashot and Liam were a very happy loving couple, devoted to each other. Though Liam was younger and much better looking, he fell in love with Ashot as gratitude for the healing at first. However, with time, as he discovered Ashot's kindness, intelligence, life experience, devotion to his work and bright talent as a doctor, Liam appreciated and loved him more and more with every passing year. Knowing his personality, his loving soul and passionate heart, it was impossible not to love Ashot. He was in all meanings a very good man.

During past years they had a lot of fun together – always joined Pride Parades and other gay festivities, went to special gay cruises every year for vacation, visited gay bars and restaurants and made some friends. Those were happy years, also full of interesting and creative work for both of them.

Liam got a new very successful career as a cameraman in TV and Movie Production Studios. A deep knowledge of professional cameras and all kinds of lenses, and his talent and perfect understanding how to work with them suddenly appeared from nowhere after the cure; as his piano talent and skills miraculously disappeared into nowhere at the same time.

Ashot considered this as a will of God, but deep inside his heart he knew the very clear scientific explanations of that. During the treatment, the whole aura of Liam's body was removed, renewed, and his unopened 90 percent of brain were tapped into – the piano talent went there inside and hid; the camera talent came out unexpectedly to replace it.

Using his excellent knowledge of lenses, Liam invented, created and patented special 4D goggles with dark-blue glass. Those goggles allowed the person who wear them to clearly see the aura of the other human. If turned on the other side, like binoculars, they even gave the possibility to see single particles of aura and their movements around the human body. They could be used for Ashot's future cure sessions.

...Now Ashot laid in his bed, smiling happily at these beautiful and sacred memories, but it was time to stand up, get dressed and be ready to go out for dinner. He took another shower, shaved, put on a decent shirt, suit and tie, then went out of his bedroom and knocked at the door of the other bedroom in their condo.

"Hey, kiddo," he said. "Do you want to go for dinner with us? Liam just texted me that he made a reservation for all three of us at the *Old Spaghetti Factory*."

CHAPTER 14

During his lunch break on Tuesday, Aaron decided to call Rosie's mother, Gloria, to check whether she had some news from her daughter.

"Yes, Doctor," Gloria said. "She called me this morning, saying she wants to come to pick up her clothes. I packed two big suitcases and a couple of bags, everything that was left in her room and put them on the front lawn. Miguel does not allow her to come inside the house anymore. Though he was at work, but boys ... you know... kids could say things sometimes. So, I preferred to follow our house rules."

"Did she say something about her upcoming performance at the Poetry Club tonight?" Aaron asked.

"No. But, you know, I was shocked. She came with a man. He drove a beautiful, expensive car. Tall, blond, handsome looking, wearing a leather jacket. About fifty. He didn't say a word, just picked up her luggage and bags, and put them in the trunk. I was stunned − thirty years older than her! And I noticed a wedding band on his hand. He is married! It's unbelievable! She obviously found a Sugar Daddy, a pretty well-off one, judging by his car. It's so awful, so horrible. Miguel always suspected that she would end up like that with all those poetry things.

"I asked Rosie - who is he?" Gloria went on. "She just shrugged - a friend. I asked - where is she living? She shrugged again - with friends. Then she hugged me and the boys, in turns. They were all crying. I was tearing up too, because we were parting forever. You know, the boys really love her. She knew how to talk to them and how to play with them."

Don't I know that! Aaron thought. *She is unbelievably good with children! I saw with my own eyes how she enchanted Laurie.*

"But you couldn't imagine what this man did at that time!" Gloria continued indignantly. "He took a big professional camera from his car and started filming all of this. I screamed that I did not allow that, but Rosie said that it's her idea because she is making a movie now for some special treatment with some special doctor. Her former house and her former family would be needed for that movie. It was all her delirium of course. Then they left really fast.

"I called Miguel and he asked if I remembered the license plate number, brand, make and model of the car, but unfortunately, I did not. So it won't be helpful to call the police. And they already know that she is mentally ill, so they are not much interested. Anyway she isn't criminally responsible for anything that she is doing. And she is twenty, so we couldn't accuse this man of having an affair with an underage girl."

"You don't have to worry, Mrs. Garcia," Aaron tried to calm her down. "She's not doing anything wrong, I am sure. Okay, I will try to find out what doctor and what treatment she was talking about. I will take care of the situation with Rosie, I promise you. Here, at our university we have some special equipment in the labs that can be useful for treating schizophrenic patients. Maybe we can place her in a hospital. I will work on this."

Of course, all of this was a bluff. Aaron needed only to disarm the Garcia family and make sure that they would leave Rosie alone. He already started realizing what the family dynamics were. It did not surprise him anymore that Rosie was ill and didn't get any better. It seemed good to him that she took all her stuff from the house and wouldn't come back. He didn't want her to be the personality of Vally anymore – a child always crying, unloved and unwanted.

But a movie... a Sugar Daddy... It was kind of a disturbing image and made him a bit nervous. There wasn't any reason for him to be jealous, yet, but he still felt that something, like a tiny needle, slightly pinched his heart. However, the situation just added more mysteries which he will discuss with her tonight. He wouldn't give up, no matter what. He would fight for her fiercely with any man in the world.

Sometime later Helen peeped in his office.

"Hey, Arie, still mad at me?" she asked.

"No," he shrugged. "I was mad for a while because you caught me off guard. It was so disgusting and stupid with this AIDS thing that I got angry. But then I thought, well, it had already passed long ago. Who cares! Now I just know better who you are. There's no reason to be angry at you. You can't be mad at the rattlesnake because it is poisonous. It is it's nature. It is what it is - mad or not."

"So, I am rattlesnake to you now?" she laughed.

"Yes," Aaron nodded. "And it's not funny at all. But I still probably will see you in a few days. I am not sure yet, but maybe I will need to ask a few questions and learn more lessons."

"Whatever counts," Helen smiled flippantly and left.

During Aaron's evening walk with Laurie - from six to seven this evening - she was excitedly telling him about the coming trip to Florida with grandma. He realized that his mother, as usual, did a great job to prepare the child - Beth already packed their luggage and got the airplane tickets for a Wednesday noon flight. They also went shopping this morning and bought new bathing suits for both of them, beach towels and a couple of beautiful sundresses and sandals for Laurie.

"Daddy, please, don't cry that you are not going with us," Laurie said. "We will miss you, but it is important that I go with grandma and help her during the trip. She is kind of old and needs my assistance. And you can't do that for her because you are working. Right? You're a doctor and you 're taking care of many ill people who need you, so it is my turn now to take care of grandma. Right?"

"Of course, sweetie, we need to take good care of grandma. She usually takes very good care of us," Aaron smiled. "We will see each other on Skype and talk as often as possible. And you will meet your little cousins and make friends. You will have fun on the beach all together."

However, to his surprise, once again Laurie pulled him to the gravel driveway and up to the gate of the *Youth Shelter*. She broke off three pink petunias from the flowerbeds that were spread along the green grass slope and gave one to Aaron.

"I will take these two flowers with me," Laurie uttered sadly. "One I will put in my pocket and the other into a little pocket on the dress that my Tacoma wears, so we could remember this nice girl. She told me that she likes my Tacoma. And I don't think you will come here for a walk without me, daddy, so you take this flower and put it in your pocket to remember that girl too."

"Thank you. Of course I will, my darling," Aaron answered, putting the flower into his pocket. He couldn't believe his own ears. His precious little one not only remembered Rosie, though she still didn't know her name, but she also wanted to keep these memories. It seemed strange but absolutely fantastic and fulfilled his dream to connect them forever.

This evening, Aaron arrived at the Greenwich Competition Hall earlier than eight. He didn't park his car in the official parking lot at the back, but stopped for a while across from the main entrance, rolled down his car window and watched.

The huge glass door of the building was wide open and a crowd of teenagers was gathering in front of it. The music playing inside was audible on the street and made the event festive, special and fun. It looked to Aaron that the idea to develop these kinds of activities for young people was great, no matter who invented and sponsored it.

He watched attentively, trying to see Rosie but she wasn't here yet. Would she come? Would she perform tonight? He had no clue.

What if she didn't come? Then what chance would there be for him to find her? And where? This place was Aaron's last hope.

Then he suddenly noticed that the crowd by the door was moving and the whispers began spreading around, "Rosalyn! Rosalyn is coming! Here she is! Rosalyn!" and some of the teenagers started to clap.

Aaron turned his head and saw her going down the street wearing an unusual outfit – black leather pants and, on the top of a light blue blouse, a leather jacket with metal studs and chains. A leather cap was sitting backward on her head. Her long blond hair was loose. She didn't have a lot of make up on, just very little, and it made her look like she was sixteen, not older. Exactly, like she looked last Friday night when he met her and was mistaken about her age.

This outfit wasn't in any pictures that Aaron saw in the Internet article last Sunday night. It was something new and different and he just wondered what today's poems would be about.

She walked with two other young ladies and laughed while talking to them. When they approached the clapping crowd at the door, some teens started hugging her and she hugged them back, very sociable and friendly. It was obviously her turf, she was loved and appreciated here, and she was happy. She was a Poetry Queen here – Anastasia, though most of the guys called her Rosalyn.

Aaron didn't notice where she appeared from – got out of a car or walked from behind some corner, but he felt his gut contracting with a nervous spasm as soon as he saw her. There was something in the whole situation that made him lose his mind. For a short moment he dashed, not knowing what to do - go up the street and check the cars parked there, looking for her Sugar Daddy, or approach her and say hi, or just simply go inside the hall and wait until she appeared on stage. Then, finally, he made a huge effort to hold himself in check and relax.

Rosie and her crowd of teenagers disappeared inside the building and Aaron drove around it, parked his car, bought a ticket at the back door and entered the public hall. He chose to sit as far from the stage as possible because he already came up with a plan of his future actions and didn't want Rosie to see him too soon.

The hall was already almost full. Most of the audience consisted of teenagers' parents and grandparents who came to support their loved ones and to admire their talents. Aaron looked attentively through the rows of the audience. He was pretty sure that the Garcia family wouldn't be here, and he was right. Then he located the button on the edge of his chair which he should press to vote for the best performance.

Finally the bell rang and the host of the show appeared on the stage. He talked about the ideas and goals of the poetry evening and explained that there would be twenty people performing tonight. Each artist could read from two to six poems of their own choice. Then he announced the first performer.

It was not Rosie. It was an African–American young man who read three poems and, actually, they were very good. Somehow it cleared in Aaron's head that his Rosie wasn't the sole talented person in the city, and this thought shocked him, being hurtful and disappointing. He was sure that she was the only one in the whole world, not just in Seattle, but alas, it wasn't true.

The next performers were two more girls who read their poems, and then it was her turn.

"Rosalyn Vivano," the host announced and Aaron felt his gut contracted into a knot, again, in anticipation of seeing her.

Rosie came out, smiling. She appeared modest, but not shy at all. Exactly, like she was on Friday during their walk toward the bus stop. The host handed her a mic and walked away.

"My dear friends," she said. "I am very happy to see you again. I am sorry that I missed our Tuesday last week."

Aaron realized now that last Tuesday, instead of coming here, she had this awful attack at home and was taken by her parents to the *Youth Shelter*. He just wondered, could it be that the attack happened because they prohibited her from performing at the weekly concerts anymore?

"Today I would like to read my two new poems on a very different topic which I never touched on before," Rosie continued.

"I am sure it will be a disturbance for some people. For me it is unusual, too, and kind of fresh, but deeply touching. I consider it extremely important for our society if we want to stay human. My first poem today," she lifted the mic and announced solemnly and loud, "*In Their Shoes*." And then she started reciting.

"Hey, a straight man, look around!
What if the world would turn upside-down?
How would you feel
to be considered outlaw and ill?

Imagine yourself being chased and hated
for the purest love in your heart.
How to find the way to protect the man you love?
What would you do to save it?

Don't be too smart! Don't lie!
Try to understand – why?
Be human! Answer the truth.
What would you do in their shoes?"

She ended almost with tears in her voice and Aaron was surprised about why she choose that topic. A gay people? Homosexuality? How come? If she always wrote the truth in her poems, what was that mean? Was she a lesbian? He felt that his palms got sweaty from the horror of this thought. He didn't want to lose her. He barely could press the button with his sweaty shaky fingers.

The audience was silent as well. Then came some applause but not the ovation like it was for the first young man or the previous two girls.

"**The Wedding Bells**" Rosie announced confidently. She didn't look confused at all.

"I would like to be a flower-girl, who
walks ahead of you at your wedding
and spreads the rose petals to your feet
from a little basket.

The old church walls covered with moss and vines
look so beautiful when the sun shines.
You are the ones who protected and saved me
With your love and warmth.

The antique brass bells are ringing in your honor
on the top of the ancient tower.
I would lift my basket and throw the petals
on your heads like a shower.

I'm not scared of anything or anybody,
to talk about you with admiration,
to announce to the world that today
is the happiest day of life – the wedding of men-gay.

I don't care what people are thinking!
What the heck!
I promise my love and care for you always,
Forever – to pay you back."

Rosie bowed, showing to the public that she finished her performance. Then, still holding the mic, she said, "You can see, guys, that my circle of friends has widened recently. I am discovering new people. I am learning more about what life is. Thank you for listening."

There was much more applause now than after her first poem. Some people stood up and began to whistle and scream their approval, and step-by-step the noise from the public formed into an ovation. Aaron wasn't sure if it was related to the poem itself or to her last comment. He just pressed the button.

This poem was eye opening for him. He realized suddenly that the married man who drove her this morning to pick up her stuff was not a Sugar Daddy but just a gay friend. Maybe she had really attended his wedding and was a true flower-girl? She just didn't want to share this with her family because they alienated her. Her family wouldn't comprehend and allow this kind of friendship. She shared it here, at the Poetry Club, with friends, where there were many more possibilities for her to be understood and appreciated, than at her former home.

Jeez! Aaron took a couple of deep breaths to calm himself down. It was such a relief for him. His Rosie was a woman he could admire, worship and love. She was the woman! She was for him. He would not lose her! Ever! Now it was time to see her and to let her know about that. Aaron stood up and walked out from the hall.

CHAPTER 15

From the main entrance of the Greenwich Competition building, there were right and left corridors, enveloping the audience hall from both sides. There were the doors of the dressing rooms in each corridor. The contestants would be sitting there and waiting to be called on stage, or resting after their performance, expecting the results of the voting. All the doors of the dressing rooms were now open – for today's event nobody needed to change their outfits.

Aaron slowly walked along the corridor and peeped into each room, trying to find Rosie. On the right side, he had no success - there were other kids everywhere. He returned to the main entrance and walked to the left corridor. And there, finally, he saw her in the third room. She was sitting on a chair in front of a dressing table with a big mirror on the wall, bent to her phone, and she was texting something. Her cap was on the table beside her. She already braided her hair and it was now resting on her right shoulder.

Aaron stopped beside the door, holding his breath and watching Rosie although she couldn't see him. He was all shaky inside, as if he was in grade five, when he liked one girl in his class and tried to talk to her, but couldn't - being too scared and not knowing what reaction to anticipate from her. He was thirty now, not ten anymore, but his heart was beating a hundred miles a second, almost ready to burst out from his chest. He felt ashamed of himself, of his lack of self-confidence.

Don't be so nervous, man, he thought anxiously. *Where is your assurance? You're an adult man, a Doctor, for God's sake! And you're an extremely attractive one, as Helen said. What the hell is going on with you? Go ahead!*

He didn't know who she was now – Rosie, Anastasia or Rosalyn - and he didn't want to trigger any attacks by using the wrong name, so he just stepped inside the room and said, "Hi..."

Rosie lifted her face from the phone and attentively looked at him.

"Hi," she uttered with an uncertainty. "Should I know you?"

"I guess, yes, if you have a good memory," Aaron answered quietly, suppressing a spasm in his throat. "My daughter and I were walking you to the bus stop last Friday night. I was wearing sunglasses then, so maybe I look a bit different now..."

"Oh," she breathed out and smiled. There was silence for a long moment. Then the girl said, "I like your little one. She is so kind and warm. It sucks that I won't see her again."

Aaron didn't expect to hear that, but this encouraged him to say bravely, "You know, this is a package deal. You could see her, but you have to see me first."

"Oh," Rosie breathed out again, then put her palm on her forehead and slid it down her face. She kept smiling and looking at him silently. She didn't say a word, just her lips moved a tiny bit. But Aaron heard her voice in his head, like she was talking, "Is your wife included in that package deal, as well?"

So, he answered aloud, "No. I don't have a wife."

"Girlfriend?" he heard her voice inside, though she didn't pronounce anything audible at all.

"No. I don't have any girlfriend," he said aloud again.

"Who is watching your little one now?" he got her thought, realizing that she was talking to him telepathically. Her lips still weren't opening, just quivered very slightly, almost not noticeable, but he got it because he was staring at her face as if he was mesmerized.

"My mother," Aaron answered, feeling more confident, because she was talking to him. His uncertainty almost evaporated, so he continued, "I've got your book and I would like to discuss something with you about it. It raised many questions. I need to clarify some things..."

Rosie kept smiling, looking at him silently. "That was the point," Aaron received her telepathic response.

With a deep sigh, she lowered her glance, as if confused, then put her hand on her forehead and slid it down again. It looked to Aaron like she had opened that telepathic door before and now she closed it.

"Would you like to go for a walk?" he asked tentatively.

She glanced at him fast, then opened her phone and started texting. He didn't know what that was supposed to mean, so he only stood there and watched her, not saying anything else.

"Okay," she said, finally closing her phone and putting it into her jacket's pocket. "Sorry about that. I just sent my ride home. Where do you want to go?" Yes, he got it right about her closing the telepathic door. Now she was speaking normally using her voice.

"Anywhere... where we could talk," he answered. "I would like to ask you something... about your book. But I am not sure - do you need to wait until the results of the competition are announced?"

Rosie shrugged. "It's okay. I know that I didn't win today. I am not always first. Sometimes I am in second or third place. It doesn't bother me. The other guys are good too. We're sharing our winning prizes and our success. We are all friends here, not rivals."

Jeez! Aaron thought. *She is so young and so wise!*

"Thank you for the compliment," she blushed. "You should be careful with me. I can read your thoughts. But it's not about wisdom. It's just that we, poets, all are some kind of outlaw and we love and support each other because we don't have anybody else to love and support us."

121

You have me now, Aaron wanted to say, but stopped himself being afraid that she could read this thought again. Damn! It was not easy to deal with her.

Rosie stood up, put her cap on, sideways again, that made her look mischievous and amazingly cute in Aaron's opinion. Then she approached Aaron and extended her hand to him.

"I am ready to go," she said, looking up, straight into his eyes, still smiling. He took her hand and squeezed her fingers. She didn't protest.

While on the street, Rosie suggested, "We can walk to the ridge. There is a park, and from there we can see the whole city. If you remember my poem **Stars Under My Feet,** it came to me there."

"Yes, I remember," Aaron nodded. "I learned most of them. They are in my memory, in my heart, in my soul... everywhere. They are so close to me. It feels like I wrote them."

"That was the point," Rosie whispered once more. "Maybe we better not say anything now. Let's just find a bench, sit and watch."

The ridge wasn't far from Greenwich Hall. About one third of a mile ahead the street flowed into the promenade of the park on the top of the hill. The city of Seattle was laying deep down in the darkness of the night, shining with sparkling lights like a universe full of stars. But unlike the universe, those stars were multi-colored – blue, red, orange, green, although a few were white, as well. Some of them were blinking and changing as the street lights transformed their color every thirty seconds.

Aaron sat on the bench, still holding Rosie's hand. She sat beside him, but distanced by a couple of feet and freed her hand. "Maybe we could talk about the book another time," she offered quietly. "It would be a hurtful subject now. Let's just watch for a while."

"Okay," Aaron whispered anxiously. He wished he could hug her, or at least put his arm on her shoulders, but he didn't dare, not knowing what reaction to expect. The knowledge of his patients with the same diagnosis held him restrained. Any second anything could happen. So he just froze, looking at the lights of the city with admiration, waiting patiently and tensely for what she would do next.

"You know," Rosie said, "it's difficult to live like that – in a place without time. I have a three dimensional time in a holographic universe here," she put her palm on her forehead. "I am in the past, and in the now, and in the future at the same moment. Do you know something about that?"

"I did hear something," Aaron answered very carefully, being cautious with each of his words. Yes, it was damn difficult for him too, like walking on eggshells or on the edge of a razor. She wasn't his patient. She was a very attractive and enigmatic woman with a fragile psyche. He didn't know how to talk to her not to scare her and not to push her away. But this uncertainty only increased his urge to be with her and to solve her mystery.

Rosie took off her cap and put it on the bench, on the other side of her. Then she suddenly turned and lay down on the bench, putting the back of her head on his lap. He rooted on the spot, almost shocked, then took a deep breath, lowered his face and very tenderly touched her cheek with his lips. It was cool because the evening was getting chilly.

And there, Aaron completely lost his mind. He hugged her waist with one arm, put his other hand on her shoulder where her braid was, then slightly moved his lips from her cheek to her lips. Subconsciously he noticed that she parted her lips just a bit, answering him. And he kissed her very carefully, fondly, without any arousal or excitement, just like believers would kiss the holy icons, or holy cross, or the hand of a priest, or lap of Pope's dress. He felt that it was not just a kiss of a woman but a sacred kiss of a holy treasure, pure and worship-like.

This kiss was also full of the deepest, endless happiness which finally was there, with him, in his arms. Aaron imagined that he was an exhausted traveler who walked through a desert, almost dead from thirst, and suddenly found an oasis with amazingly cool, fresh water. He felt like he knelt beside it and started drinking this life-giving water and couldn't stop, couldn't tear himself away from it; like he was drinking and drinking happy that he found it, that he would be able to live now. He knew that he would never let her go anymore. That girl was his oasis water, the core of his life now, the essence of his existence. Nothing would ever stop him!

Rosie extended her hand and held his arm with her fingers, squeezing it tight. Aaron sensed that her waist under his other arm got tense. She was all shaky, reacting to his kiss, but not in the holy and sacred way he felt, but like a real alive woman. He knew that any sexual feelings were extremely dangerous for schizophrenics and could produce an awful attack. This was the only thing that forced him to stop 'drinking' from this oasis. He realized that at any given second everything could explode. It returned him to reality from his dream and he let her lips go and lifted his head.

Rosie took a deep breath and whispered barely audibly, "Why?"

"Because I love you," Aaron said, feeling doomed.

"You can't love me. You don't know me."

"I do know you. Your book told me everything about you. Your soul is my soul, your heart is my heart. We are the one creature, like Siamese twins in a sense - they have two souls in one body. We have two bodies but one soul. And I do love you. I really do. I was thinking about you all the time after I met you. I didn't know, didn't understand what's going on with me. Everything turned upside-down in me when I read your poems."

She kept looking up at him and, in the semi-darkness, the lights of the city reflected in her eyes and sparkled like stars. "That was the point," she whispered the same words she said already twice before.

"I was rushing around, I was tossing," Aaron continued agitated, not even noticing her words. "I couldn't find the place for myself. Sometimes I felt so crazy that I was thinking I was completely losing my mind. I wanted to see you so badly. I was looking for you, I searched, I walked after you almost like a dog sniffing your tracks. It was insanity, it was a nightmare and now it all came out so clear and so simple. It was a process, I was falling in love with you with every step. And now I am here - I love you deeply, endlessly, forever, and that's it."

"There is an old saying - you know, when you know," Rosie whispered. "When did you know?"

"Now. As soon as I touched your lips. It all cleared in my head in a second, like a click."

"You felt like an exhausted traveler who walked through a desert, almost dead from thirst, and suddenly you found an oasis with amazingly cool fresh water. You knelt beside it and started drinking this life-giving water from my lips..."

"How do you know that image?" Aaron asked, dumbfounded.

"I sent it to you. I wanted you to feel this way."

"You're bewitching me," he said smiling. "You're a miracle, a mystery which I'm craving to solve."

"Not much of a mystery. I am a regular girl, but when I was eleven, I survived something that forced my brain somehow to turn a different way and connect to the holographic universe. We will talk about that another time. Now I just feel that a poem is coming to my head. Do you mind if I tell you?"

"Of course not. I am eager for all the poems which I could possibly hear from you. Please..."

"Place out of Time" she whispered and then started the poem.

"There is a holographic universe in my head,
There is three dimensional time in my brain,
The past was just blood and dead.
We escaped into the Now
to survive somehow.

We're on the top of a hill
surrounded by stars under our feet.
Traveler in a desert, full of holy love,
drinks a cold spring water
from the oasis of my lips.

The future is an island with grass and sand,
the whisper of waves where I will love you mad.
Glass tower in the sky,
a rifle in a sniper's hand

sending a bullet into your head.

I have holographic universe in my brain,
I have three dimensional time in my head,
Please, don't love me, I beg.
I don't want to see you dead."

Aaron stayed speechless for a long moment. "Why do you think I could be dead, if I love you?" he quietly inquired then.

"No idea. My grandma, Nora, loved me so much, and she was killed. Then Ben loved me that much, and he was killed as well. I am kind of dangerous. I don't want to see you dead. But I don't know if it's possible to turn everything back and make you stop loving me."

"No," Aaron said confidently, shaking his head. "Absolutely not. Don't even think about it. I will not stop loving you no matter what, under any circumstances. And it will last until the moment I die. It doesn't matter when or at what age. We are now together. I won't ever let you go."

"Thank you," Rosie whispered. "I am so sorry, I can't say this back to you now. I'm not there yet. But you heard the line in the poem – *I will love you mad*. It is in our future, I am seeing that clearly. But not now. I don't know why. Probably because you know me from my book, as you said, but I don't know you absolutely. You're a handsome man, but I need to learn more than that about you. I don't even know what your name is."

"Didn't I tell you? Sorry. I was so overwhelmed with all these feelings that I forgot to be simply polite. My name is Aaron."

She kept silent for a few minutes, then said thoughtfully, "It's a very beautiful name. I love it. Aaron... Aaron... It sounds so strong, and smart, and sexy. Like the name of a real man. Is it from the Bible?"

"Actually, yes. It's an ancient Hebrew name. My mother couldn't have children for many years, and no treatment helped. Then she started to go to a church and gave a promise to God that if she would have a baby, she would name it from the Bible. Then, when she was thirty-six, I was finally born. If you translate it in English, 'Aaron' means exalted, enlightened and also a mountain of strength. Exalted – yes, I am pretty sensitive and spiritual, enlightened – yes, I have a pretty good education. But about strength... I doubt it. Yes, I exercise, I have some muscles, but I consider myself by character a pretty weak person. When my wife died I cried like a little child for many months. I didn't look like a strong man at all."

"It was not a weakness," Rosie objected quietly. "It was a grief. A strong person can mourn too."

"We were together for nine years – from the age of sixteen," Aaron continued. "I was a teenager, almost a child, and I was thinking at the time that she was the biggest love of my life. We were both kind of childish, we didn't have much in common except for school and friends. She actually wasn't really bright, as I discovered later after her death. It was mostly sexual. I was learning what a woman is."

"Sex is included in real love, isn't it?" Rosie murmured with a deep sigh.

"I know. But now, as I am an older and mature man, I feel a big difference. How I love you now, it's not even comparable. It's so much stronger, so much deeper, it's almost like an obsession, like a calling from above, like... I really just don't have words to express it. I am sinking in this love, I am melting in it, I am dying in it."

"Aaron," Rosie whispered, fondly squeezing his arm again. "You are a very strong man, believe me. It requires a huge strength for a man to allow himself to be as vulnerable as you are with me now. You gave me everything. You opened yourself for me. Nobody ever talked to me like that. It is so unusual for a man. I admire you, honestly. Your mother was right giving you that name. Thank you for sharing. I am so sorry that your wife was murdered."

"Murdered? Why?" he asked, astonished, getting tense right away. "The police grilled me a lot. I was the number one suspect, as usual in these types of cases. But then they let me go because it was clear to them that it was just an overdose on drugs, nothing else. Which I don't believe, by the way. And the police understood that

I didn't have any motive. I didn't gain anything, losing her. Quite the opposite – with her I lost everything. Why did you say it was a murder?"

"I know the past. I can't see everything but I see the main point. When Rubi will come to me, we will ask her. She is a pretty smart investigator. She likes it and she is good at it. For now, I just need to hug you to help you relax and forget everything bad."

"Okay," Aaron agreed because he was a bit shaky after her bold statement about Ally's death.

Rosie stood up from the bench, approached him from the other side, sat on his lap, hugged him by the neck as she nestled her head on his chest. He strongly hugged her. She deepened her fingers in his thick hair on the back of his head and slowly caressed it. "Don't think about anything," she whispered tenderly, "let your brain rest. Just feel those stars under our feet, feel the warmth of my hands. I am enjoying your heart beating in my ear. I feel how full of love it is. Let's, please, never cry anymore. And if it ever happens, I will kiss the tears away from your cheeks. I promise." All her words sounded like a poem. It actually was a poem.

They were sitting in this position, silently, for a very long time, enjoying the feeling of calm and warmth of each other, until Aaron noticed that Rosie's fingers stopped caressing his neck. By the evenness of her breath he realized that she was sleeping and it really soothed him. He kissed the top of her head, then put his cheek on it and closed his eyes. After all those sleepless crazy days and nights when he was reading her book, looking for her, trying to understand his feelings, he was finally there, at his goal, at the 'quiet harbor'. Her peace enveloped him and he fell asleep as well.

When they woke up it was after three in the morning.

"I should go home," Rosie whispered.

"Yes," Aaron agreed, sleepily rubbing his eyes. "Thank you for letting me sleep... I would say... Rosie. Is that right? Are you Rosie now?" It was the first time when he dared to pronounce her name, hoping that it would be proper.

"Yes," she smiled at him, stood up and put her cap on her head sideways again. "Thank you for keeping me as Rosie for that long.

It usually does not last so many hours until the other personalities are coming out. Could you drive me home?"

"Of course, Rosie," he laughed. "Finally I could say your beautiful name aloud."

They walked up the quiet night street toward the Greenwich Hall where Aaron's car was still parked alone at the empty parking lot. Rosie told him her full address including the suite number and he inserted it into his GPS. They drove to the other part of the city and stopped in front of the high-rise building with a big marbled lobby. The mirrors on the walls, a fountain in the middle and live plants in huge golden pots were visible through the glass of the main door. It looked beautiful, well tended and expensive.

"Are you living here?" Aaron was surprised. "Could you afford the rent?"

She shrugged, "Friends."

"Is it temporary? Or forever?"

She shrugged again and laughed, "Maybe for some time."

"What do you see in the future here, with your vision?"

"Aaron, please, I don't want to talk about that now. Don't spoil our amazing night."

"Did you like our night?"

She nodded, "Very much so."

"Do you want to see me again?"

She nodded silently, then answered the question with a question, "Didn't you tell me that you'll never let me go?"

"Of course, I just wanted to make sure that we are on the same page."

"How could we not be? You soothed me. You kept me as Rosie for so long. I am yours. I'll be with you always. If you want – forever."

"I do want," he whispered and kissed her hand, smiling too. "Thank you, Rosie."

Then they exchanged their phone numbers, inserting them into each other's phones, and Rosie got out of his car, walked to the big glass door and opened it with her own key. Aaron noticed that she didn't buzz. While entering the door, she looked back and waved to him, smiling. He waved back to her.

Friends? He thought with a tiny drop of jealousy. *She likes this word – friends. It practically means nothing. No direct answer. Who is this friend? A gay? Or a Sugar Daddy? What would be a reason for letting her live in a building of this quality rent free, for as long as she wants and have her own key. There must be something important and serious behind that.*

Aaron didn't want to ask more questions and show her any jealousy or control. He wanted her to belong to him without any force, by her free will and always remain a free woman. But, he still couldn't understand her mysteries and for now that puzzle was left unsolved.

CHAPTER 16

When Aaron got home in the morning, it was already about five o'clock. There was no reason to go to bed. He was actually satisfied with the sleep that he had with Rosie in the park and felt like it was enough. So he just went to the basement and did his usual hour of morning exercise on the treadmill and on the weightlifting bench. Then he took a shower and got ready for work.

When he exited the garage, Beth appeared on the porch and waved him to stop. He rolled the car window down and smiled at her, "Good morning, mom."

"Good morning, Arie," she answered, approaching his car. "Nice to see you finally smiling." Then she added a bit sarcastically, "I guess it was a successful night after going to the concert alone?"

"Mo-om!"

"I heard when you came home," she teased him. "You know, the garage door clicks loud enough to wake me up."

"Sorry about that. We should probably oil it, so I could have more privacy," he teased her back.

"You will have enough privacy, son, as soon as we leave today." Aaron heard a tingle of feeling being rejected in the tone of her voice.

"Mom, please," he opened the car door, got out and hugged her. "I am sorry. I love you and Laurie more than anything in the world, believe me. But it's very serious and very important. It's even crucial for me."

"I know," Beth kissed his cheek. "I wish you could find a woman you could love who will be a good mother for Laurie. Just be careful, please. Don't do anything reckless. Men sometimes lose their heads pretty easily. I lived long enough to observe that many times. Remember - we are talking here not only about you, but about your child as well."

"I know, mom. I am working on that very responsibly, I swear. About your leaving - during my lunch break today I will drive you to the airport. I want to make an appropriate farewell for both of you."

"Okay, Arie. Then we will wait for you here," Beth agreed and patted his shoulder. "Drive carefully, son. Love you."

The first thing Aaron did at the university was to prepare the paperwork in the Human Resource Department for his two weeks vacation starting tomorrow. Then he spent some time at the lab, looking for any research or studies that were done during the past three years on holographic universe and three dimensional time in relation to the unknown part of a human brain.

Actually, there was a lot done: the studies about Neocortex, Cerebrum, Hypothalamus of the brain; about a cognition to move subjects with electrical waves of the brain; about a consciousness of the universe that interested Aaron the most. It was related to the process of creating art, music and (damn, here it was!) – poetry. It was about special people with the ability to connect their unopened parts of the brain to the energy fields of the universe. He started thinking that this abrupt Dr. Evelyn Hertz, in spite of her being too straightforward, was right – Rosie was 'perfect material' for those studies.

Though, Aaron didn't want to include her in any experiment until he understood where their relationship was going. Their ties should be much stronger, closer and deeper first. He was certain about himself but he wasn't sure about her feelings yet. He actually knew that she wasn't confident herself. It was too early to try to involve her in any scientific brain research. But Aaron hoped that after two weeks of their 'hoped vacation together' the proper level of closeness and intimacy would be scoped, at least he would do everything that was in his power to reach it.

Then Aaron reorganized all his appointments with patients that were booked for the following two weeks. The less important ones were just canceled; the most important ones were arranged with other doctors to cover for him and take in some of his patients temporarily.

Aaron also advised the receptionist to make a note that as soon as the file of Rosa Garcia arrives from Dr. Hertz, she should call him so that he could come and get it.

Then he called Helen and said that he would like to see her tonight, sometime after ten.

"Another sleepover?!" she exclaimed victoriously.

"I am not sure," he said, "but probably, yes. We'll see how things go."

The whole morning he was very busy preparing stuff for the following two weeks which were supposed to be the most important weeks in his life. It would determine everything for him, how his life will evolve further - literally, everything. And it all revolved around Rosie. At some moments he thought, *Am I crazy? I found her, I kissed her, I told her that I love her and she accepted it. I should be calm and content that my goal was reached. She is mine, she will be mine, but I still keep dashing like a mad tiger in a cage. Jeez! Why?*

Then Aaron finally called Rosie and asked her out for dinner that night because he realized what all his morning's fuss was about – he craved to see her. He wanted to think about her all the time, to do something that would relate to her even indirectly. He couldn't live, he couldn't breathe if he was not seeing her.

Her voice sounded sad today and it was noticeable that she was crying.

"What happened?" he asked, right away feeling a piercing pity in his heart.

"Nothing," she sniffled. "This morning Vally came and she is missing you. Nobody loves her, just you. Aaron, please, I really need a hug."

It was unexpected and not so easy for him to absorb that this other personality, Vally, was now present in her. Aaron thought they would arrange time to meet for dinner and have a nice date that would be normal, beautiful and happy if she were Rosie.

Loving her, he still refused to accept the reality that she was ill. He still considered her the healthy woman who he wanted her to be, but it wasn't the case. It was a trying moment now when he should make a choice for himself – to accept her as a mentally ill 'love of his life' and agree to take care of her forever, or just give up and let her go.

In spite of being a scientist and knowing well that there wasn't any cure for her condition, Aaron still hoped subconsciously that maybe, just maybe, he would be able somehow to find this miraculous treatment and return her back to a normal life. He wished this so badly that he was absolutely ready to dedicate all his life to her - no matter what it would cost him.

Though, he knew it would cost a lot. He could even possibly lose Laurie: Beth would never allow a child to be endangered by having a severely mentally ill woman in the house. At times Aaron felt himself in the position of Miguel Garcia. Ahead of him lay an impossible choice, which however, was easier for Miguel than it would be for him. Miguel didn't love Rosie, but Aaron did - madly, obsessively, and forever.

"Aaron, say something, please," he heard the begging voice of Vally on the phone.

"Sorry, my love," he pronounced slowly. "I was just thinking of how I could do that. I wish to hug you too. Let's say in about two hours I could stop for a while in front of your building and call you. And you could come out for a hug. I am at work now and I really don't have any other choice."

"Okay," she agreed with a deep sigh. "Just, please, don't forget about me."

"I will never forget you, my love. I swear to God. See you then." He hung up fast being afraid that she would request something else that would be impossible to fulfill. He didn't want to hurt her with a refusal but he still had other important things to do which couldn't be neglected.

Then Aaron left the university, returned home and picked up his mother and Laurie to drive them to the airport. They could take a taxi, of course, or Beth could drive her car and leave it there at the long term parking lot, but Aaron felt that he needed to take care of them himself and to see them off properly, respectfully and lovingly. It was too early for him to make the faithful choice, yet, and they were both still the most valuable and loved people in his life. They were family, his flesh and blood, and nothing in the world could be closer than that.

While he hugged and kissed Laurie at the airport, she whispered in his ear, "Daddy, are you keeping the pink flower which I gave you to remember that girl?"

"Of course, sweetie. It's under my pillow." He really did put the flower into Rosie's book which was always under his pillow. "And you?"

"Yes, it's in my backpack pocket," Laurie murmured conspicuously.

"Why are we whispering?" Aaron asked.

"I don't want grandma to know. It is our secret, right?"

"Okay," Aaron answered, surprised by her sensitivity to the situation. "It's amusing to have a secret, I agree. Let's keep it this way. I love you, sweetie. Have lots of fun with friends."

When he hugged Beth, she also whispered into his ear, "Don't lose your head, Arie. Be rational, please."

"Why are we whispering, mom?"

"I don't want Laurie to be disturbed, seeing that you're troubled."

"Damn, I am not troubled at all. Everything is okay, mom."

"Arie, I can see through you," Beth said and kissed his cheek. "Okay, we will call you when we arrive in Miami."

It was a bit sad to part with them, but Aaron convinced himself that it was the best way for everybody to enjoy this summer.

While driving back to work, he stopped by Rosie's building, though it wasn't on the way at all, and called her. She came downstairs, sat on the passenger seat beside him and leaned against him, putting her head on his shoulder. He hugged her tenderly. She really was Vally now – dressed in sweatpants and a baggy hoodie, wearing no make-up, with matted hair. Her eyes were red and puffy from tears.

Aaron kissed the top of her head and caressed her shoulders, whispering between the kisses, "It's okay, Vally. I love you. I am with you. You see, it's a beautiful sunny day now. I will finish my work in a few hours, and then we will go out for dinner. Where do you want to go? Is there a restaurant you like? Tell me, and I will make a reservation. We will always be together. Everything will be okay. I will take care of you. Please, don't cry anymore. Remember, you promised to kiss away my tears, if I would ever cry. Now, it's my turn to kiss away your tears. Is that okay? Is that what you want?"

"Yes," she whispered and lifted her face to him.

Aaron took her face in his hands and kissed her cheeks and wet eyes. "You know," he smiled, "when I was a little boy and I cried, my mother kissed me on the eyes and told me that there was an old prediction – if you kiss someone on the eyes, you are closely connected with this person forever. You would never separate after that. So, you don't have to worry that you're not loved anymore, right?"

"Yes," she whispered again, then suddenly hugged his neck and kissed him on the lips, and, God, it was not the 'holy oasis in a desert kiss' at all. It was a very passionate kiss, really arousing. Aaron subconsciously answered it while hugging her, though being cautious. He kept in his mind the danger of sexual feelings for a mentally unstable person. However, at the moment her lips were irresistible. Beth had begged him not to lose his head, but it was exactly what he was doing now, less than one hour after her warning.

Then suddenly Aaron felt that the girl started wiggling in his arms, pushing him away and when he let her go, she began beating him with her fists on his chest and shoulders.

"I need to go home," she screamed angrily. "Let me go home."

"Okay, okay," he agreed, trying to be as calm and peaceful as possible. "You can go home of course. Are we still going for dinner?"

"Yes," she yelled, trying to open his car's door.

"So, I pick you up at six?"

"Yes. Damn, open this door!"

He pressed the button and asked, "What restaurant?"

She jumped out of the car and, running to the entrance of the building, shouted, *"Old Spaghetti Factory,"* and disappeared inside, slamming the door.

"Gosh!" Aaron whispered, squeezing his temples with both hands. "Oh my gosh! How will I manage this? What could I do with that?"

He knew that in spite of anything, he would carry this cross forever. He still felt the taste of her lips on his lips and this was worth more than anything in the world. It made him shake to his core. Slowly, he drove back to the university thinking all the way about what had just happened.

While back at work, first, he called the restaurant and made the reservation. He still wanted to follow his plan of the day. Then he continued with his last part of the working day – appointments with patients.

After work, Aaron went home, took a quick shower and changed into a light gray suit with a light blue shirt and dark-blue tie. It didn't matter to him, if she would be dressed in her sweatpants or even pajamas. He wanted to maintain his style and level of decency and to show her that it would continue this way in their relationship no matter what. He still wanted to give her a lesson like a father would give to a rebelling teen-daughter; still refusing to recognize that she was ill; still subconsciously hoping that she would learn something from him and change.

Aaron called her from the car on the way and apologized that he would be about fifteen minutes late.

"It's okay," she said in a quite happy voice. "I am a bit busy now as well. You just wait for me outside." He didn't dare to ask how

Vally was doing, being cautious not to trigger anything unwanted again, but judging by her voice, she was okay.

However, Aaron hated it for himself – feeling like he was walking on thin ice. It was a moral prison to him. He wanted to be free and relaxed in a relationship with a woman, not questioning his every movement and every word before pronouncing it. He wished to marry her and make her a step-mother for Laurie but at the same time realized clearly that it would be impossible to live with this burden in the family. It wouldn't happen, at least until Rosie became completely healthy. Which really meant – never.

At the same time, Aaron knew that he couldn't ever let her go because she was his existence, his breath, his soul, his love forever – she was everything to him.

Finally, he decided to push this dilemma away and just enjoy the moment. *It is a beautiful summer evening, I am going on a date with the woman I love – what the hell could be better than that!? I should be happy now and, damn, I am,* he thought.

Aaron exited his car and stood, leaning against its side, waiting for her. He closed his eyes feeling the warm sunbeams on his face and when he opened them he couldn't believe what he saw.

She exited the building and was walking towards him, shining, dressed like a model. She wore a white mini-dress with one shoulder and arm exposed, black Greek sandals laced up to her knees, and a bunch of black necklaces on her neck. Her hair was made into a high ponytail with a big black sparkling clip. She also had a white purse hanging over her naked shoulder on a long strap. The dress was kind of elastic and enveloped her body tight, showing every curve of it, which was magnetically attractive. And there was a lot of make-up on her eyelashes and eyelids.

She looked so beautiful, happy and sexy that Aaron lost his breath from excitement. This was his love, this was what he lived for. All his previous doubts evaporated in a second. As she approached, they hugged each other and kissed passionately while still standing by the car.

138

The words burst out from his mouth as soon as, with difficulty, he tore his lips away from her, "My gosh, you look amazing. I love you so much."

"We didn't talk about that yet," she laughed mischievously. "Though I know you confessed to Rosie."

"And who are you now? Not Vally, I guess?"

"No. Vally is gone long ago. I am Rubi. Nice to meet you, Aaron."

"Nice to meet you too, Rubi. Jeez, it will never be boring with you," he laughed.

"Yes, I am fun, I am smart, and also I am an investigator. We have a lot to talk about during our dinner."

"Well, okay then," he opened the car's door for her and she sat on the passenger seat. She put her purse on her lap because the dress slid up when she sat and displayed her legs completely.

"It looks like I am dating seven different women, almost like I am a *Bachelor* on the TV show," Aaron said flirtatiously, while he put the key into the ignition and started the car.

"No, just six," Rubi chuckled. "Believe me, you don't want to see Tobi. I know her. You probably won't survive, if you meet her."

Aaron took a deep breath, thinking, *Damn, it came to a delirium again.*

The sharp despair momentarily eliminated his excitement about her beauty. It didn't matter how miraculous and attractive she was, she was still a schizophrenic. This fact was hiding for a few minutes, or hours, or even maybe several days, but then it always came back. Aaron got lost and confused, he didn't know what to say.

"Would you mind, Rubi, if we drive in silence?" he finally uttered sadly. "I need to concentrate on traffic, please. Okay?"

She shrugged and smiled without saying a word.

CHAPTER 17

When they settled in the restaurant across from each other in a booth, the girl put her hand on the table and Aaron covered her palm with his. He wanted to feel her warmth. She was fantastic, she looked very confident and absolutely healthy and he was caught in that allure again considering her normal, craving to touch her and talk to her heart-to-heart. It didn't matter who she was at the moment. Last night he didn't even ask who she was. Why should it matter now?

"Why did you choose this restaurant?" he asked.

"I was here last Saturday, for the first time in my life, and I liked it. Though, I can't compare because I have never been to any other restaurants."

"First time in your life?" Aaron repeated in disbelief. "Who brought you here?"

She shrugged, "Friends."

Same answer again, he noted subconsciously but then said, "Why didn't you go to restaurants with your family before?"

"I was raised by my grandparents. They were old immigrants. They didn't know English. In their home country they never went to restaurants and they didn't even know that it was possible. My grandpa was seriously mentally ill. My grandma worked three jobs.

They still had no money. I was little. I helped my grandma a lot at home. We were busy all the time. Hundreds of reasons…"

"But what about later, when you lived with your mother's family? I visited them while looking for you. It seemed like they had enough money and time."

"I was like Cinderella there. When Miguel and mom went out, I was watching the kids. When they went out with kids, I was supposed to clean the house, do laundry, gardening, and take our dog, Oscar, for grooming. It was a lot to do for a big family. It sounds probably reasonable for a teenager – to help her mother. But they never said thank you, or allowed me to go with them."

"Miguel told me that he took good care of you financially supporting all your travels and concerts in other cities," Aaron noted.

She laughed. "It wasn't a kindness. He paid for everything because he wanted me to go, to be away from the house as much as possible. I was seen as a criminal by them, I just came out after four years in jail."

"The *Youth Shelter* isn't a jail," Aaron objected.

"Well, even worse – I was not just a criminal, but a mentally ill criminal. Then I started dating Ben, and they kicked me out because he was black. They didn't say that openly but it was obvious. I would have been homeless on the streets, if Ben's family didn't take me in. They were not well off and never went to restaurants as well, except for McDonald's. I was living with them in a crowded small house: their mother, Ben and his twin, Alex, and their two little sisters and baby brother. They were kind people and very loving. That's where I learned to understand little girls and play with them, as you noticed…" she smiled bashfully.

"I remember," Aaron nodded, smiling as well. "You were amazing. My little Laurie is still talking about you excitedly all the time."

"I liked her too. I could easily be friends with her, but you said yesterday that I have to see you first. That's what I am doing now."

"Are you doing that for Laurie?" Aaron inquired surprisingly.

"No, I am doing that because Rosie asked me to help you." Then Rubi returned to her story, "Later I was in the *Youth Shelter* for one more year, after what happened with Ben."

"Why? It wasn't your fault..."

"Aaron, please, I will explain some other time," she begged. "I am giving you just facts now."

At this moment a waitress approached to take their orders. Aaron looked through the menu, but Rubi said right away what she wanted. *Probably she is remembering what she liked from her last Saturday with friends here,* he thought with a bit of jealousy.

"Why did you stop doing your travels and concerts of poetry in other cities?" Aaron wondered after their orders were taken.

"I can't go on airplanes anymore. Once I had a very bad attack on the plane and my doctor said that it was because of the air pressure changes. Now I am on a '*No fly*' list."

"My gosh!" Aaron exclaimed. "They really treat you as a criminal or terrorist! It's unbelievable. It shouldn't be like that."

She shrugged. "I am okay with that. I don't want to disturb or hurt people around me. I have a performance on stage every week here. It's enough. Now, please, Aaron, tell me about you. I would like to know what made you - you. I seriously want to know more to be closer to you and understand you better."

"Okay," he smiled, "if you want..." He began telling her everything that he could remember from the earliest moments of his childhood. About his parents, their house in Atlanta where he was raised, went to school, had friends, played soccer and baseball, met Ally and fell in love. How he traveled every summer around the world with his parents, then around Europe with Ally when they were sixteen, seventeen, and eighteen-years-old. How he moved together with Ally to Seattle where they were accepted to the college, then to the university. How they got married at the age of twenty and then kept traveling every summer during their student years – now South America, Canada, Egypt, China, Japan. He really saw a lot of the world and was happy to show it to Ally then.

"I would be happy to show the world to you as well, one day when you are allowed to fly again," Aaron ended up, smiling at her. "Or, for now, we could make road trips here in the state of Washington."

"Thank you, Aaron. I would be happy to see a bit of the world with you together," Rubi agreed.

When their food arrived, Aaron took a little break in his narrative to eat and they just discussed their dishes. Then Rubi said, "I have a request from Rosie. She asked me to listen to the story of how your wife died and to investigate. I am pretty good with that. I did all the investigations for her cases and I found the truth about what happened there. Do you want to know the truth about your case?"

"I guessed the truth, but I am not sure if I was right," Aaron nodded. "I tried not to think about that a lot because it was extremely painful. But now, after five years, it's kind of moved pretty far away from reality for me. It feels like I watched this in a movie or read it in a book. I know the story like an outsider, stranger, observer but not like a character involved. My love for Ally gradually died and the pain of it subsided during the past years and my heart is completely free from it at the moment.

"As you know, I am pretty much obsessed with Rosie now and this is really serious. I am not afraid to say that openly to anyone, to everybody, even to the whole world. Nothing else exists for me. I don't care what someone could say or judge. If Rosie wants this, I can talk about Ally calmly and objectively. If you could add something investigative to the story and say what you think about it, I am ready to tell it to you," he concluded with a deep sigh.

Rubi moved her plate aside and over the table took his hand with both her hands.

"I am with you, Aaron. I am listening," she said fondly, looking him in the eyes. "Please, tell me everything as you remember it."

... Aaron and Ally arrived at her graduation party a bit late. There were too many things that had to be done at home to leave the one-month-old Laurie with grandma Beth who just came from Atlanta and wasn't familiar with their household.

Ally was breastfeeding and had to leave two or even three bottles of her milk because they wanted to stay at the party to the very end, almost the whole night. Laurie should be fed a couple of times during the evening and maybe, in case she woke up, even at night. The milking of the breast was a pretty long procedure, and afterwards it took some time for them to be ready for the party.

This was the first outing of the young parents since Laurie was born. They badly missed the company of their friends, and were very happy finally to go out, have a good time and enjoy themselves.

When they arrived at the restaurant, it was already crowded and the parking lot was full. Aaron circled it a couple of times and, finally, not seeing any empty spot, he parked his car outside the lot, on the grass, beside a small ditch. They walked inside where beautiful slow music was already playing and people were dancing. Right from the door, they started to dance as well. Aaron hugged Ally, she put her head on his shoulder and in a minute he was already kissing her.

They were unbelievably happy. It was the height of their happiness. Practically, all their dreams came true. They had a beautiful family with a newly born child, they both had an education. Aaron was in the middle of his doctorate, but already had a full time job at the university. They traveled around the world a lot. What else could a young couple dream about at the age of twenty-five? Their whole life was ahead of them and the start of it was amazing.

When Aaron kissed Ally at that moment, he couldn't even guess that it would be his last kiss in the next five years...

He never kissed Helen even once. Kissing for him was something holy and sacred, it was an expression of the deepest love imaginable, but Helen was far below that. So, he never kissed a woman again until he met Rosie, but for Rubi he skipped this part of the story. He didn't want her to know about Helen. He was really not proud of this relationship and of himself for being involved in it.

So, Aaron continued the story about what happened at the party after this happy kiss with Ally.

The bar there was open earlier and most of the people had their drinks; some were already a bit tipsy, though it was only the beginning of the evening. All the people around were from their university, even from their course, although Aaron had moved ahead a couple of years ago. Ally and Aaron were a very social couple, so everyone of course knew them. Even during the dances, many people waved to them, and shouted their congratulations for the baby.

Then, through a loudspeaker it was announced that there was an extra parking lot opening behind the building and those who didn't get the room at the front one were welcome to use it. It was also said that security would check the grounds to make sure that nobody was parked on the grass or at the edges of the ditch and, if so, they would issue tickets for violators.

"I should probably go and re-park our car," Aaron said to Ally.

"Okay," she smiled at him. "Then I will get something to drink and maybe go to the restroom to check how my make-up looks."

"I'll be back in a minute," Aaron said, while she gave him a fast good-bye kiss on the cheek.

He went out from the front door with other people, who didn't get the proper parking spots earlier. To re-park the car on the back extra lot took him no more than five minutes. However, as he got out of his car, he saw some friends from his former class, who were also re-parking their cars, and they greeted him. They stopped for a while and talked and laughed together.

It was just a simple friendly conversation of former classmates who hadn't seen each other for a long time: How are you? Where are you now? How are things going? How is Ally? Oh, congratulations for the baby! Did you get a job already? Where? What department? Does Ally plan to work or stay at home with the baby? And so on. They all laughed and teased each other while sharing their news.

The whole conversation took about fifteen minutes and was, luckily for Aaron, taped on the security camera that hung above the back door of the restaurant. It really saved him later from the suspicions of the police.

Then all the young men walked together around the building toward the main entrance, where another camera taped them stopping for a smoke before entering. Though Aaron didn't smoke, he stood with them keeping the conversation going and laughing. He didn't see the guys for two or three years and was really happy to converse with them now. Then they suddenly heard a commotion, noise and screams from inside the restaurant and saw an ambulance approaching on the street with the sirens howling and turning into the front parking lot toward them.

All of the young men realized that something had happened inside the restaurant and ran in ahead of the approaching paramedics. And there was Ally, lying on the floor, surrounded by shards of the glass that fell from her hand and a puddle of coke with chunks of ice that supposedly were in that glass. She was already dead, but Aaron didn't know that at the time.

After that he didn't remember what happened in reality. He had a blackout, was practically unconscious and had no memory of what he did. The rest of the events he knew only from the security tapes which were shown to him later by the police investigators.

That tape showed that Aaron screamed like crazy, ran to Ally, grabbed her, hugged her, shook her, but some other people pulled him away because the paramedics needed room to do their work. They tried to start her heart again, but it was impossible. They pronounced her dead at the scene and took the body to the hospital. Aaron went with the ambulance. The party was finished not only for him and Ally but for everyone. People were in shock and nobody would continue to have fun after such an occurrence.

As the security tapes showed later, while Aaron was outside, Ally walked to the counter and got herself a drink in a tall glass – cola with some ice. She didn't consume any alcohol because of her breastfeeding and, being an extremely devoted mother, she was always cautious about everything that she ate or drank.

Then Ally came to the table, took a couple of sips from her glass, left it at the edge of the table and walked to the restroom. The crowd began dancing again and many figures were moving around, covering the view of her glass. Later some girls who were beside the table ran to the restroom too and the last of them was Ally's best friend, Helen.

The crowd kept dancing for the next ten minutes. Then Ally and Helen appeared from the restroom, hugging each other, and walking to the table together as the other girls followed them. They were all laughing. Ally took her glass, lifted it to her lips and began to drink. She had three big gulps, then staggered and fell on the floor, dropping the glass. Everybody around laughed, thinking that she was probably drunk. Some girls approached and tried to lift her but then noticed that she was not breathing and started screaming for help. Someone called 911.

The police investigators had no doubt that Aaron was outside, but they suspected that he could have hired someone to put drugs into her glass. The test of the pieces of glass and puddle of cola on the floor showed the presence of LSD, meth and a huge amount of fentanyl strong enough to kill a horse. Whoever had placed it in her glass wanted to be really sure that she would be dead. The same drugs were discovered in Ally's blood during the coroner's examination of the body.

Finally, after many hours of questioning, the detectives realized that Aaron wasn't responsible because he had no motive. He was losing practically everything while losing Ally. Their marriage was perfect, his behavior was believable – he was crying like a baby, almost couldn't talk and couldn't breath from his non-stop sobbing. All their friends and classmates were interviewed and all confirmed that Aaron and Ally were very much in love and happy.

However, Ally's best friend Helen, and also some other girls convinced by her, told the police that Ally was an active drug user. Aaron knew that it was a lie. Ally never did any drugs at all, especially while being pregnant and breastfeeding. The tests of her milk left at home in the refrigerator were done and showed no signs of drugs. Even a blood test of tiny Laurie was taken and it came back completely clean as well.

But Helen insisted that Ally missed drugs because she didn't use them during her pregnancy and breastfeeding, and now, at the party, she had decided to use them while her husband went out.

The other girls were positive about that too and confirmed that, yes, they heard that Ally always did it behind Aaron's back to make sure that he didn't know. This way Aaron was acquitted and the case got closed as a regular overdose occurrence.

"I am absolutely sure that Ally never used drugs." Aaron continued persistently. "We talked with her about that a lot and she was always really against drugs. She knew well the story of her parents who died from drug use on the streets. Also, professionally, I know how to recognize the behavior of a druggie. There never were any signs of it in her. So, someone put them into her glass while she was in the restroom. Before she went there, she drank from that glass and everything was okay. It was very silly and reckless of her to leave the glass unattended, but she obviously trusted the crowd – those all were our friends and classmates. That's all I can say." He stopped and took a deep breath, then asked, "So what do you think, Rubi?"

The girl was silent for a long moment, thoughtfully shaking her head.

"Obviously it was a murder," she pronounced slowly. "There was someone who had a motive. Maybe a revenge on Ally or revenge on you, or some other motive. Let's start from number one – the revenge on Ally. Was there any man who hit on her and she refused boldly, hurting his feelings?"

"No, not at all. I am sure," Aaron objected heatedly. "If it had happened, she would've told me, of course. Every guy there knew that we were married. Everybody knew that she was not the best student – so no jealousy about her career. She wasn't even beautiful. I just considered her pretty because I fell in love with her when I was sixteen. She was my first girl, my first woman and I didn't know any better. But I knew that other guys weren't interested in her at all."

"Okay, then the other thing – a revenge on you. Maybe someone was jealous about your career and wanted to hurt you."

"I don't think so. I moved ahead for two courses, then for two more years. Many guys didn't even know where I was gone. And Ally's death didn't change anything about my career. I still finished my doctorate. I am okay career-wise. It doesn't matter for my work, if I am married or widowed."

"Well," Rubi sighed. "Then there should be someone who wants you not to be married anymore. And not to get divorced, and not to pay alimony and child support – someone who wanted you in the whole package."

"Yes, I always suspected that. There was Ally's best friend, Helen. She chased me for ten years!" Aaron exclaimed, agitated. "She openly told me that she loves me and would fight for me, and would remove the obstacle – my marriage - from her way. I had a feeling that she might have done that. It would have been very possible. But there was no evidence. Helen convinced the police about Ally's drug use and they believed her. How could I prove otherwise?"

"A suggestion of a real investigator would be – to talk to her about that, to force her to confess and tape her confession on your phone."

"Wow!" Aaron said. "That would never have come to my mind. Thank you, Rubi. It's very interesting and I will try to do it right away."

"Good luck," she smiled.

For dessert they had an ice cream named *The chocolate madness* which they ate together with the two spoons from one bowl, smiling at each other and looking into each other's eyes.

Later that evening Aaron drove her home and they stopped in front of her building. Rubi thanked him for dinner and he thanked her for the nice evening. Then Aaron asked, "Sorry for my curiosity. I'm just wondering. Here, living with friends rent free, do you help with some household chores as well?"

She shrugged, "Why? I told you, I am like a Cinderella – turned from a maid into a princess. They have a housekeeper here who comes every second day. No need for me to do anything."

"Then, what are you doing all day long?"

"During the school year, when I was living in my mom's house, I was usually teaching a poetry class for grade twelve twice per week. Now it is a summer break for school, so here I am working online for magazines as a poetry editor. If Rosie is here, she is writing new poems."

"Doesn't the illness bother your work? I mean, don't you hear any voices irritating you, demanding to do something?"

"I don't hear any voices, ever, just the police gunshots at Ben," Rubi said, shuddering, "but the other girls do." She hugged Aaron and kissed him goodbye on the cheek as she continued, "Rosie usually hears poems read to her from above. To Vally someone is saying that she is not loved and nobody needs her, so she is crying. Anastasia hears the applause and cheering whistles of the public at the concerts and it makes her self-assured, satisfied and content. Kiki is surrounded by children's laughter and happy shrieks, as they are running around and playing. Nora is always scared to hear her husband's angry threats. And Tobi... oh, she hears harsh orders - take a knife and kill the enemy. And she has to follow them, she has no right to refuse."

CHAPTER 18

When Aaron arrived at Helen's it was already late evening and she met him wearing beautiful black negligee.

"Do you want to eat something or drink?" she asked.

"No. Just had dinner. Look, Hel, I want to do one little experiment and then we could talk."

"Gosh!" she laughed. "I am not only a rattlesnake for you but also a lab's mouse!"

"No. This time I will be a lab's mouse myself."

"Okay, what should I do?" Helen inquired when they came to her bedroom.

"Just lay down, don't say a word, don't do anything. And turn all the lights off. I need to concentrate on myself, on what I can do and what I can't."

"Interesting," she smirked sarcastically, "what could it be that you couldn't do in bed? We'll see. Should I get undressed?"

"No. Keep them on. And I'll keep my clothes on as well."

"Wow! This will be a really one of a kind experiment," she laughed, but did what he requested.

Aaron lay beside her on his left side, propping his head on his hand and closing his eyes, even though the room was already dark.

He expected that during the vacation trip that he planned with Rosie, they would sleep together in hotels. He knew that sex would be off the table – he would never allow himself to endanger her and him as well. But he wanted to see if he would be able to hold himself in check and not to go over the edge. He wasn't sure it would be possible.

Usually, he had pretty wild abrupt sex with Helen but she liked it this way. Aaron even guessed that she was right in her joke about 'a drunk sailor in a cheap Hong Kong brothel'. He didn't care about her at all - exactly like a sailor there wouldn't care about a prostitute.

However, what he felt toward Rosie was a holy, pure, sacred love with a fragile refined angel and for that he should be extremely tender with every touch. He treasured her, he worshiped her. He loved her in the whole deep meaning of the word LOVE. But he wasn't sure if he could manage this kind of loving relationship without finishing it every time with intercourse.

Aaron stretched his right arm and softly touched Helen's forehead, then eyebrows, very lightly slid his fingers along her cheek, outlined her lips, a chin, then caressed her ear and petted her hair flowing down from her head to her shoulder. With his eyes closed he imagined that it was Rosie and he just studied her, like a blind person would tenderly touch someone's face to learn who it was.

He wanted to be sure that this very fond intimacy wouldn't produce any sexual feelings in him and he would be able to caress Rosie this way and then kiss her as a 'holy oasis in a desert'. That kiss he didn't need to train. It was already done on their first night together in the park and he knew that he could do that.

But now, with Helen, just a couple of minutes after he started, Aaron already felt an erection. It was not what he wanted or needed. So he stopped what he was doing and laid quiet, breathing evenly and trying to calm himself down. It worked. He rested for a while, then started caressing Helen's shoulders. This way, after stopping himself four times, he realized that he would be okay. He had learned how to do that. Now he knew that he could manage his relationship with Rosie.

It felt kind of stupid and childish, like he was a twelve-year-old boy in bed with a same age girl for the first time in his life. But it was what he needed for now, until Rosie could be healed, if ever...

"Okay," Aaron said. He turned and sat on the edge of the bed. "Thank you, Hel."

"So? That's it?" she asked, shocked. "What the hell was it that you did, Arie? No sex today?"

She turned the light on and sat on the bed as well, heavily breathing with anger.

"No. I am sorry. I can't."

"Why? What's wrong with me, you freaking diva?"

"Nothing is wrong with you, Hel. It's just me. Let me tell you a story I read long ago. It was discovered by a scientist-translator from some Middle Ages manuscript. It happened during the inquisition times in Spain. There was a group of young men-friends who often went to prostitutes all together. But one of them met a beautiful girl and fell in love with her, really strongly. His friends invited him one day to go to prostitutes again and he went out of respect for his buddies. However, when he tried with a prostitute, he couldn't get an erection, absolutely, boldly, none. It happened because he couldn't stop thinking of his beloved one and these thoughts gave him a psychological barrier.

"With the mentality of the 16th century, he got scared that the girl he loved bewitched him. He went to the inquisition and reported her as a witch. She was arrested, tortured and burnt in fire. Then he jumped into this fire with her because he loved her so madly that he couldn't live without her.

"It's kind of a scary and dirty version of Romeo and Juliet with a political angle. But it showed clearly, that it is true — if a man is really in love with a woman he absolutely can't have an erection with another one. Because of that I will stop seeing you now."

"You are an idiot, Arie! How is this story related to you? You had a perfect erection many times during the last half an hour. You just didn't want to follow through on it. You stopped every time for some reason. What's going on with you? Are you really in love with another woman? Is she a virgin or what? Did you test on me, how to deal with her? Were you imagining her?!" While saying that, Helen was growing agitated more and more, and finally became furious. She jumped up from the bed, yelling, "You're a damn bastard, Arie! You're a villain, nothing else. You've been bullshitting me for ten years. I was hoping that you'd eventually appreciate the woman who is loving you, but you don't!"

Aaron stood up, walked into the living room, sat in an armchair there and put his phone into the chest pocket of his shirt, making sure that it would be ready when it would be needed to start recording.

"Hel," he said, "calm down, please. Let's talk. Yes, I met someone, and I am in love with her."

"Nice to hear," Helen hissed. "Thank you." Then agitated, she demanded, "Where did you meet her?"

Aaron shrugged, "On a street." He already learned from Rosie to give vague answers.

"What the hell? Who could be on a street? A prostitute?"

"No. Quite the opposite."

"A nun, collecting donations for a church?"

"It doesn't matter, Hel. It is not your business, anyway. I just tried to practice a bit to hold myself in check. I wasn't sure that I would be capable of stopping myself when needed. But it was okay. I managed it. Thank you for your help."

"Jeez," she shook her head angrily. "I could guess – you're scared to hurt her, to lose her. For some reason, she is a kind of fragile statuette - am I right?"

"You learned something about psychology, so you could guess..."

"I know your psychology, Arie, during our ten years of acquaintance. You're a really weak man, you're nothing, just a doormat. A strong, independent and self-sufficient woman as I am, is not for you. You need someone exactly like Ally was - anemic, helpless, powerless piece of shit whom you could take care of. It gives you a feeling of being beside her as a muscular powerful man. You want to be a boss, an owner, a 'father' for a new girl, like you were for Ally. It gave you self-esteem and self-respect. And when

Ally was eliminated finally, you found yourself another similar crap. This is what you're designed for."

Aaron put his hand into his pocket and pressed the recording button on his phone.

"I would like to talk about Ally," he said. "I want to know why you lied to the police that she was a drug user? It was a complete lie, and you know that."

"You didn't know Ally as I did," Helen expressed confidently. "She told me everything, literally, everything about her life and her relationship with you. I know much more about both of you than you know about yourself, and her. You were a stupid naive teen full of hormones and you were blind like a mole not seeing anything because she was the first girl in your life who allowed you to sneak into her panties and touch her vagina."

"Jeez, Hel, why is everything you are saying always sounds so dirty?" Aaron exclaimed indignantly. "You are a kind of disgusting monster. I was in love with Ally. It was a really pure first love."

"It sounds dirty to you because I am telling the truth, and the truth is sometimes eye opening and painful to accept. But you have to. If you are breaking up with me now, Arie, as a farewell, I will tell you everything about your so-called 'happy marriage' that you should know.

"Ally was a poor child of druggies from the street and she was looking for a rich man. Her term with her foster family came to an end and she needed to live somewhere. She had no money, she couldn't rent anything, so she was destined to live on the street as her parents had until they died. Then Ally heard from her classmates that you were a boy from a rich family. She approached you and invited you for a walk. Then she kissed you first. You, as a hormonal teen, turned wild and she allowed you to do anything you wanted. She claimed that she loved you. So, am I wrong? Wasn't it like that? Think about it Arie. Remember the details."

Aaron felt with horror that Helen, on her own, had no chance of knowing about their first meeting with Ally. It happened in Atlanta, when they were sixteen. Helen was in Seattle at that time and hadn't met them yet. The only way she could know this story was if Ally told her. He lowered his head and held his forehead with his hands. He made a huge effort to stay put and let her continue because he needed to record what she knew about the death scene and what she would confess. Otherwise, he would have left right away after she pronounced her first words.

"Your Ally also was a very dull person, a C/ D-student," Helen laughed scornfully, "and as you started to sleep with her, you did all her homework for school, even her exams and she was able to graduate as a B-student because of you. You convinced your parents - nice, kind and naive people – to let her live in your house for free. You took her to travel around Europe and of course, paid for everything."

"Jeez, Hel, my father was dying! Ally helped to take care of him!" Aaron yelled outraged. "She was an amazingly kind and helpful caregiver. And she was my girlfriend and later my fiancee – how could I not pay for trips? It's a stupid accusation."

"Your father even left her a pretty big chunk of money according to his will," Helen smirked.

She couldn't know that by herself! It's impossible! Aaron thought in disrepair. *Damn! Ally, why did you tell her all of this?*

"Yes, it was her salary!" he cried out. "And when we got married, she put this money in our family's joint bank account. She, practically, returned it to me. What the hell is the problem with that?! Yes, my parents loved her because I did and because she was an awesome person. She was just silly to tell you all of this. I am sure you manipulated her. It wasn't me who was 'young, naive and too trusting'. She was."

"You could say that I also manipulated her into using drugs and having the threesomes with me and my boyfriend or with other men," Helen chuckled maliciously. "Ha-ha, I bet it is a nice and unexpected discovery for you, right Arie?"

He smirked, shaking his head. "Those are silly things to say. They are based on nothing. I don't believe one word of yours, Miss Rattlesnake. You are creating a story."

"While you were sitting home and doing her homework and assignments for college, she went out with me pretty often. Do you remember that, stupid, naive husband?"

Yes, Aaron remembered that. Ally was really bored when he did all her studying and always asked to go and visit Helen and have some fun with friends. And he let her go because he was really interested not only in his university program, but in hers as well. He loved to learn and to increase his knowledge. It was fun for him. And yes, sometimes she came home late, and moved to sleep on the couch, saying that she didn't feel well. He never suspected anything, didn't even think about anything bad. Could she be tired from drugs or from sex affairs which Helen had pulled her into?

Aaron started feeling really nervous now, though, still not believing any of Helen's words. But it was a fountain of lies falling on his head that made him shaky inside with protest and defense. Everything sacred in his past life was thrown into a dirty puddle and stomped on. He knew that it was just Helen's revenge on him for breaking up with her. But still it was awful to hear.

"Ally suggested having a child at the end of college because she didn't want to work and looked for an excuse to stay as a tick on your neck, sucking your blood. You would work while she would be resting at home, doing nothing, just enjoying herself."

"Many men have wives who stay at home with children," Aaron shrugged, trying to object. "There is nothing wrong with that. It's absolutely normal."

"Yes, but Ally wanted to put the child into a daycare and keep having fun while you are at work. It was her plan which she shared with me. That's why I decided it was time to free you finally from that disgusting parasite. You had no future with Ally. You didn't match. You were people of different society and intellect levels, and, I am sure, you would be divorced a few years later anyway. But it would be more problems, more sufferings for your daughter, as she grew older. There was no other direction ahead of you, Arie, because we, Ally and I, were really fooling around together with drugs and with men as well. If I were you, I would get a DNA test to make sure that Laurie is your child," Helen recommended, with a vile smirk.

Aaron gritted his teeth and squeezed his fists while trying with difficulty to suppress his feelings. He urged to jump up and slap her on the face, but he wouldn't allow himself to ever hit a woman, even if she really deserved it. He was sure that it all was a lie, but a really mean and hurtful one.

"So, how did you free me?" he asked morosely, narrowing his eyes.

"Ally begged me to give her drugs, as soon as you left to re-park your car. I gave her some and she herself put them in her glass." Now Aaron got a convincing corroboration that it was not true - it was not what was shown on the security tape. He saw the tapes, but Helen didn't.

"You are lying again!" he exclaimed agitated. "Neither you or Ally used drugs, ever. This was the first and the last time in her life when you put drugs in her glass.

"I did love you, Arie, and you needed to be taken care of. I couldn't tolerate anymore how she was cheating on you."

"And killing Ally was your act of 'care and humanity' toward me and my child!?" He stood up, all shaky with anger and hate toward her. "Thank you for sharing. Now I will give this thing to the police and ask them to re-open Ally's case." He took his phone out from his pocket and pressed a button to stop recording.

Like a lightning bolt Helen jumped on him, tore out the phone from his hand and smashed it on the floor. She snatched a decorative metal candle holder from a shelf and began beating his phone into smithereens. "Bastard! Villain!" she screamed. "Do you think you're smarter than I, you idiot? Go, and suck it in, you, a happy widower! Enjoy your new love until I annihilate her as well! You'll never be free from me, Mister Aaron Dispenmore!"

In a flash Aaron grabbed his broken phone from the floor, ran to the door and stormed out of her condo again, now for the third time during the last several months. He was so mad and at the same time in such pain that he could barely breathe. He quickly jumped into his car and drove off. Luckily for him the night streets were empty, otherwise, he could have easily crashed into someone and created a deadly accident. His wheels screeched as he turned onto different streets.

At home, he couldn't even enter the garage, just left the car outside and raced into the house through the main door. He jumped up two steps at a time on the stairs, burst into his bedroom and fell down on his bed, face into a pillow. He was absolutely devastated and mentally drained. His whole life was collapsing under his feet.

Aaron always knew that yes, he had tragedy in the past, but he still sensed that it was a base for his life today - a deep strong base. He had his wife, even dead; he had his child; he had his full happiness before and he expected that he would have it again, in the next phase of his life. Yes, Ally wasn't really smart; yes, she didn't read even one book during the nine years he knew her; yes, he did all the schooling for her, but she was his beloved wife. Who should help the wife, if not a husband?

Aaron knew perfectly well that Ally was never unfaithful to him. It was a complete lie which Helen invented to hurt him the most, to smear all the beauty of his happy marriage for one reason only – her envy. Of course, he never would do a DNA test on Laurie. He had no doubt that she was his child. She looked more like Ally, but the soul was obviously his – tender, sensitive, kind, though Ally had actually the same personality, as well. He would never allow even a tiny shadow to darken the clean holy spirit of his dead wife and his beloved child.

Now Aaron clearly realized that it was the biggest mistake of his life – to start this casual relationship with Helen. She was not a woman, not a person - but a real rattlesnake or even much worse – a devil, a monster. Somehow subconsciously he always felt and suspected this. He shouldn't have listened when his mother encouraged him to find someone to love. Or it should be anybody but Helen. Even now, Helen still threatened that he would never be free from her. What the hell! Why? Wasn't there enough men in the world for her? What was so magnetic about him?

It was absolutely clear to Aaron that she murdered Ally and successfully got away with it. And she was agile enough to destroy his phone and to prevent her unmasking as a murderer. Damn, he should have been more careful with the phone. It was another mistake of his.

Aaron felt helpless, desperate, hurt and humiliated to the very bottom of his heart. He lost the battle for justice for a second time. He lost control of his emotions and finally his tears began suffocating him. He couldn't hold them back anymore and let himself sob like a child, hugging his pillow – again, five years after Ally's death. Exactly like then, he felt once more that he didn't want to live. He wanted to die, and this time his mother wasn't with him to straighten him up.

CHAPTER 19

While Aaron kept sobbing in his bed, he subconsciously heard the sound of a car coming into their fenced neighborhood and stopping somewhere close with the motor still running. The car's door slammed. He heard quiet, muffled men's voices, and then the car moved away and was gone. He didn't pay any attention to that. It just reflected automatically in his ears. Sometimes neighbors could return late from work or bars. It often happened and nobody cared.

Aaron was so completely drained and exhausted from the pain in his soul, so confused and lost that didn't know what to do now. How could he live with the sense that Helen got away with murder; that she purposely destroyed his life and left his child motherless? It was unforgivable. But now it was impossible to receive any help or justice anywhere. Then, what?

Suddenly the door of his bedroom slowly opened and he heard some quiet, soft steps coming toward him in the semidarkness. Aaron jumped up from unexpectedness. "What the hell!" he exclaimed and sat on the edge of his bed, noticing subconsciously that the digital clock at his bedside table showed four in the morning.

"Aaron, it's me," the fond voice whispered as the blurred figure approached him.

"What!?" he turned the reading lamp on and stood up, looking at her astonished. "How? Why? My gosh! Rosie! You can't imagine how much I need you now!"

"I knew that," she nodded. She stood in front of him dressed in shorts and a light-blue t-shirt, her hair loose like it was the very first time when he met her. Her eyes were hidden in the shade of the dim light.

Aaron hugged her tight. They stood for a long time in the middle of the room, holding each other and not saying a word. Rosie pressed her face to his chest slowly caressing his back with her fingers. "I promised to kiss your tears away," she murmured several minutes later. "I heard you crying."

"How could you hear that?"

"Here," she put her palm on her forehead.

Aaron stepped back and sat on the bed pulling Rosie with him. She nestled on his lap, hugged his neck and tenderly slid her lips along his cheeks kissing away the wet tracks of the tears which he already wiped.

"You're my miracle, Rosie. You're my angel. You're everything to me. I really didn't want to live anymore. I would probably do something reckless. I was out of my mind from the pain."

"I knew that," she repeated softly. "I am sorry. Rubi and I, we shouldn't have asked you to do that. It was too risky and too hurtful for you to refresh that wound. It was our mistake. There are some people in the world who manage to get away with murder and it is impossible to do anything about that. I spent four years next door for a murder which I didn't commit. But it's okay. The killer always gets his punishment later from there," as she pointed her finger up.

"Do you mean from God?" Aaron asked.

She shrugged. "You could call it God — it is a holographic universe where everything is written in particles."

"Is that how you know the past, the now, and the future? Can you read those writings?"

She nodded while continuing to kiss his cheeks and softly caress them with her lips. Then she said, "You need to forget everything Aaron, to clean your head. Block the past out from your mind. Just feel my warmth and nothing else." Rosie touched his forehead with her lips and held them there. He sensed a strange calming feeling of rest and relaxation enveloping his whole being. It was like his past tragedy was gone, never existed, was just imaginable; like Helen and all her bad energy melted and flew away. "Is it better now, Aaron?" Rosie asked, looking into his eyes. "How does it feel?"

"Like a paradise," he smiled. "Quiet. Calm. Blissful."

"Good," she nodded, looking satisfied with what she had done. "Sorry that I appeared unannounced. I actually tried to phone you, but your phone didn't answer. I felt something was wrong and I knew that you needed me."

"I didn't think about you then. But subconsciously I needed you really bad. It is a surprise to see you."

Rosie just smiled mischievously.

"How did you get here?" he said wonderingly.

She shrugged, "Friends."

"How do you know my address?"

"I spent four years in the prison next door... where we met."

"I remember you shouted, 'Sir, do you live in the area?'" Aaron smiled at the recollection of her first words he ever heard. "But you still didn't know the exact house..."

She shrugged again, "Friends."

"How?"

"I don't know."

"Okay, let's not think about that now," Aaron suggested tenderly. "I want to lay down and hug you and just look at you, and feel you. And nothing else in the world."

"I would like that too," she quietly agreed.

Never in a million years would he guess that the lesson which he practiced with Helen earlier that night would be needed so soon. He expected it could happen only during their future travels with Rosie but not at home, in his house, during the same night. However, everything related to that miraculous girl was unpredictable, unbelievable and unexpected.

They lay down on his bed, still hugging each other.

"I sense my book here - somewhere close..." she whispered.

"It is under my pillow, always. I read it every night."

She smiled bashfully, "That was the point."

"What do you mean by these words? You say them all the time..."

"I hoped you would understand yourself... I'll tell you one day... later."

"Okay," Aaron turned on his left side, propped his head on his hand and with his right hand he carefully touched her hair, moving it away from her forehead. Then he bent and kissed her lips, tentatively, trying to find the recollection of the feeling of his 'cool holy oasis', but not a real woman. He caressed her really gently, just her hair, her face, her shoulders, not daring to cross any dangerous borders, making sure that he stopped himself when it was needed, until he suddenly realized exactly like it was in the park, that she was once again sleeping.

It seemed strange to him. Usually people with her diagnosis had very big problems with falling asleep. Many of his patients didn't sleep for months, even a year and it really worsened their conditions. Chronic severe insomnia was one of the most typical symptoms of schizophrenia. How come Rosie was falling asleep so easily? Aaron was even afraid to think about the possibility that her diagnosis could be wrong. Maybe she could be cured? It was just a tiny spark of hope, but at least it was better than nothing.

He was too tired to comprehend about that now, after all the stress of the night. Rosie's quietness, calmness and relaxation somehow infected him and he fell asleep, hugging her and resting his head on her shoulder.

When Aaron woke up, it was already ten in the morning and Rosie wasn't in bed with him. He looked around a bit confused. Did it really happen? Was she here? Could it be a dream? He was completely dressed and laid on top of the blanket. Beside him, other part of the bed was really crumpled. So, she definitely was there next to him. But how did she enter the house? Had she percolated through the walls like an alien in a movie?

Then Aaron remembered that he was so upset last night storming into the house that he left his car outside the garage entrance, and the house door - both unlocked.

He went downstairs, put the car into the garage, then returned to the house and locked the main door. Now he noticed Rosie's sandals and a bag on the floor beside the entrance. The bag was wide open and some of her clothes were visible inside. She obviously intended to stay here with him, at least for a while. The little arrow of Cupid pinched his heart and made him content.

At the same time he heard Rosie's laugh somewhere behind, in the backyard. Aaron looked through the living room window and finally saw her.

She was wearing shorts and a flowery top, held by thin straps on her naked shoulders. Her hair was done in two ponytails on the sides of her head. She looked like a real child - barefoot, sitting on Laurie's swings and laughing. She seemed to be very happy, singing loud songs and reciting some poems. While looking at her Aaron felt his heart was literally melting from enjoyment. He realized that she was Kiki now – a funny and happy child whom he hadn't met yet.

He opened the glass door and walked on the patio. "Good morning, Kiki," he said, smiling. The girl ran to him and jumped upon him, enveloping his neck with her arms and his hips with her legs. He subconsciously hugged her bottom.

"Aaron! Good morning! Nice to meet you!" she shrieked in excitement, "I am so happy to see you! Are you happy too? Are you okay? Let's play tag!" Then she kissed his cheek, jumped down and ran across the backyard and around Laurie's playground. He couldn't help but chase her.

They ran after each other, bumping into things in the yard, laughing like crazy. It was such fun, pleasure, and relaxation. Aaron played sometimes this way with Laurie and her friends when they came to visit. But here, now, was a big difference. As he caught the hysterically laughing Kiki, he grabbed her into his arms and kissed her affectionately, unceasingly, until she tore herself out from his hands and raced around the yard again.

This game continued until they both fell down on the grass, tired, breathing heavily but still kept laughing almost to tears. Aaron was all sweaty and announced that he needed to take a shower and get himself ready for breakfast.

"I already showered while you slept," the girl said. "You'll see my towel there." They went inside and, as she started looking in the refrigerator and kitchen cupboards for something that could be used for breakfast, he went to his washroom upstairs. When he returned well shaved and fresh, they kept working on breakfast together, giggling and joking. Aaron felt the happiest at this moment of his life - his amazing beloved one looked absolutely healthy. And she was so beautiful now, blossoming like a flower.

They ate their breakfast, sitting across from each other at the table and looking at each other with undisguised admiration. She recited to him a couple of new funny poems and he told her some jokes. It was the perfect beginning of his vacation.

"Look, Kiki," Aaron said finally. "We need to go to the mall now because my phone was broken last night and I need to buy a new one. And then I'll make a reservation – we will go out tonight for dinner at the *SkyCity Restaurant* at the Space Needle. I would like for us to see *'the stars under our feet'* from a much higher location than the park."

"Wow!" she exclaimed. "I've never been there before."

"Even on the Observation Deck?" he asked, surprised. "Jeez, you were born in Seattle!"

"I know," she smiled bashfully. "It's the same story as Rubi told you about restaurants. Mom and Miguel went with their kids on the Space Needle, but they said that I am big enough and it won't be interesting for me. I stayed home and mowed the lawn and did laundry."

"My girl," he moaned sadly, passionately kissing her hands. "I am so sorry. But don't worry. I will show you everything in the world that is worth seeing. I swear to God."

"Okay," she timidly agreed and giggled.

While in the mall Aaron was preoccupied in the *Apple Store*, the girl was waiting for him outside, sitting on a bench near a tall tropical plant in a ceramic pot. From time to time, Aaron glanced at her through the glass wall of the store, to make sure that she was still there. He noticed that she was talking on her phone, but didn't know if she called someone or got a phone call. He really craved to find out whom she was talking to and what about, but he couldn't hear anything.

Also, Aaron was supposed to listen to what the shop assistant explained to him about the new phone and the contract; then he had to concentrate on making a payment. Plus, he knew that to demand explanations from her would be controlling but he didn't want to show her any control. So, he suppressed this urge while finishing with the purchase and discussing with the assistant the possibility to save and transfer some data from the smashed phone.

As Aaron walked out from the store and approached the girl, he heard her saying, "Okay, uncle, don't worry. I promise you. I should go now. Bye." With that she hung up and smiled at Aaron, "Did you get the phone? Is it beautiful? Show me, show me!" She sounded exactly like Laurie.

He sat on the bench beside her, gave her the new phone and noted trying to sound indifferent, "Your mom said that you don't have any uncles, Kiki."

She looked at him worriedly, "Kiki is gone," she whispered. "Please, be quiet. We should go and hide. My husband could be in the mall. I saw him passing by. He could find me and kill me."

Aaron took a deep breath, realizing that the happy morning was finished.

"Who are you?" he asked.

"Nora," she answered quietly and pressed her index finger to her lips. "Shhhh..."

"Did you hear me, Nora?" he repeated his previous statement persistently. "Your mom said that you don't have an uncle."

She shrugged.

"Who was that man on the phone?"

She shrugged again, "A friend."

"What did you promise him?"

"That I won't have sex with you."

Aaron narrowed his eyes. "So, he knows about me? Why is our sex his business?"

"He cares about me. Why are you asking?" She attentively looked him in the eyes. "Are you jealous? Oh, my gosh!" She giggled, then began laughing more and more, almost to tears. But then in an instant her face looked scared. She stood up, grabbed him by his hand and pulled him from the bench. "We should go, Aaron. We have to go. It's not safe here. My husband is looking for me, chasing me. Please, go, Aaron. I am afraid. I am really scared. I don't want to die. Please, help me, Aaron." She was shaking and almost in tears again, this time not from laughter, but from the real horror of her imagination.

Aaron morosely followed, holding her hand, getting nervous and agitated, not quite understanding why these personalities changed again. What triggered it? Was the visit to the mall the reason for it? Or some passer-by reminded her accidentally of her grandma's abusive husband? Or was it the phone call from this so-called 'uncle' whom he had already started to hate?

At the car, Nora wanted to hide, laying down on the back seat but Aaron very strictly said no to that. He insisted that she sit in the passenger seat beside him. He didn't want to give up and become a slave to her illness and fulfill each demand of her crazy personalities. She was so different from his usual patients that subconsciously he still sensed that she might be just a 'rebellious teen' and not a real schizophrenic. And he didn't want her to feel that he would always follow each of her whims.

Finally, she obediently sat beside him, but bent her head and covered it with both her arms. They drove home in silence.

Adding to the sadness and irritation of these personality changes, Aaron felt a burning, insane jealousy for the first time in his life. He squeezed the steering wheel so hard that his knuckles got white and he gritted his teeth to stop a possible scream at the girl from bursting out. He was never jealous about Ally. There was no reason for that. Nobody was interested in her ever and no man was in her life except for him and his father - during the last days of his life.

Aaron never was jealous about Helen either, though he knew that she had other men even while sleeping with him. He didn't care at all, just was extremely cautious not to get an STD from her, but she, herself, took pretty good care about precautions. So, he was safe, but absolutely indifferent to her.

What Aaron felt now for Rosie was enormously contrasting and unusual even for himself. He craved her to belong to him only, he sensed that he would kill any man who would ever touch or kiss her. Her lips were his. They were his 'holy oasis in a desert' and nobody else's in the world. He found her, he discovered her, she was his soul, his core, his existence. They were together to death. How could anyone else decide, if she could have sex with him or not? Whose the hell business was it?

Aaron was offended and shaking with anger. He knew that he would never allow anyone to make this kind of decision for him. So, what should he do now?

"Aaron, please, stop the car," the girl begged suddenly. "I want to tell you something. Please."

It took him several minutes to find a secure place on the edge of the street. He parked the car, unbuckled and turned to her, looking at her questioningly.

"Come here," she said as she unbuckled and turned to him too. He bowed toward her. She hugged his neck and placed her lips on his forehead, exactly like she did last night, and held them there for a long moment. Instinctively, he hugged her back and they sat this way quietly, not moving and not saying a word. He felt that the anger and pain of jealousy in his soul subside. She soothed him once again, gave him a rest and calmness, and returned his confidence as well.

"Please, promise me never think anything bad about this," she fondly whispered. "Jealousy is a very hurtful feeling. It could leave scars on your soul. I don't want you to feel this pain anymore. Trust me, please. I am yours."

"I hate somebody's interference in our relationship," Aaron whispered back, fondly caressing her shoulders. "I already had a very harmful experience with my wife being manipulated by her girl-friend. This man is pulling strings behind your back as a puppet master, and forcing you to do what he wants."

"No, no, no, Aaron. It's quite the opposite – he is doing everything that I ask for. You don't know anything. I am absolutely free and the decision would be mine. It's all up to me."

"What decision?"

She shrugged. "I don't know what to say yet. I'll tell you when the time is right."

"But how does he know about us? You told him…"

"I didn't tell him anything. Remember, when you came to the concert and suggested we go for a walk, I texted and sent him home. He was my ride. That's it. He probably saw us then, I guess. You don't have to worry about that, ever. The uncle is my guardian angel, nothing else. He wants us to be together and to love each other. I know that for sure. And we will because I love you too, Aaron. I love you very-very much, I swear to God."

He heard that from her, finally. His eyes filled with tears but he held them hard. He didn't want to be emotional and let her see more weakness in him.

"Who are you now?" he asked tentatively, already guessing the answer and feeling relaxed. His heart was melting from the endless happiness again.

"Rosie," she answered smiling. "And I have a notion that I will stay as Rosie for a while. You are making me very happy. Thank you, Aaron."

"You are welcome, my love," he answered, wishing to believe that she would stay as Rosie longer. But he still had doubts – during the last twenty-four hours he saw her as Vally, Rubi, Rosie, Kiki, Nora and Rosie again. It was questionable if she had any control of those personalities.

CHAPTER 20

When they arrived home, Aaron suggested Rosie get dressed and ready for dinner at the restaurant, while he talked to his mother and Laurie on Skype. He went to his office and closed the door. It was too early for them to know that he was not alone here and also that he wasn't at work as they expected him to be.

The call lasted about one hour. They were having a big family dinner over there in Florida being three hours ahead of Seattle time. With Beth and Laurie, there was the old aunt, Erin, her two daughters, Nicole and Ashley, with their husbands and three children. Aaron didn't remember any of them. But Erin's daughters, who were his distant cousins, remembered him – they met and played together once during his visit with his parents. Aaron was eight at that time and they were twelve and fourteen.

It was a lot of fun and excitement for those young ladies, and for Aaron as well, to recall stories about their childhood adventures on the beach. Everybody laughed and seemed to be happy.

When little Laurie came to the screen, she assured Aaron that she was elated playing with the kids all day long - to go swimming, to build castles in the sand and to pick up seashells on the beach. They giggled and chuckled together for a while.

At the end Beth arranged with Aaron that he would make these calls to them every morning – for him it would be at the time before work; for them – before they go to the beach. And with that the call ended.

As Aaron exited his office, he couldn't find Rosie at first. He looked everywhere, even started to worry that she would be gone, but her bag still was on the floor beside the entrance door. Finally, he looked into Laurie's bedroom, and there she was, sitting on the floor, her back propped on Laurie's bed.

She had already changed into a black mini-dress with short sleeves, put make-up on and made her hair into a low bun on the back of her head, sitting almost on her neck. The two curled locks were hanging along her face on both sides. There was a string of pearls around her neck and a matched bracelet on her hand. Rosie looked beautiful and ready to go, but her face was thoughtful. And she was holding Laurie's barbies by her chest.

Oh, my God, Aaron moaned in his thoughts with despair. *Did she turn into Kiki again?*

The girl lifted her eyes at him and answered his not pronounced question, "Don't worry Aaron. I am still Rosie. It is just a bit doleful to remember your little one. You know, as Rosie, I have a right to be sad or happy sometimes, the same as everyone else. It doesn't mean that my other personality came out."

"Sorry," Aaron said a bit confused, then approached her and sat on the floor beside her. "Why are you sad about my daughter?" he asked, hugging Rosie's shoulders.

"I feel guilty like I cheated on her. I took her money and gave her my book in exchange, but the book ended up in your hands, and actually, I expected that. That was my point. But she got nothing. I would like to give back her hard earned allowance and I put it here." She nodded toward an envelope that she placed on Laurie's bedside table.

"Thank you," Aaron said. "I am sure she will be happy. But the money wasn't hard to earn, believe me. It's like a game for her to help with little things in the household; more fun than heavy duty. And it is also psychologically good for a child to learn that money doesn't grow on trees, but should be earned. It's entertaining and educational at the same time."

He didn't say anything else, but decided that just in case he would later check what was in the envelope. Rosie smirked, "You're a good parent Aaron. You could check the envelope now. I won't be offended. Don't you remember that I can read your thoughts?"

"Well... okay," he blushed, feeling a bit ashamed that he revealed his distrust to her, but when it was related to his child, he would always be cautious. He learned his lesson from the day when they met and he allowed Laurie to walk with the unknown girl too far away from him. He took the envelope and opened it. There were five single dollar bills in the envelope, and a little note written in big block letters that read, "Hi, Little One. I am a fairy. The stranger girl whom you helped one day with this money, asked me to return it to you with gratitude. Thank you for your kindness."

"Jeez, you are so smart and ethical," Aaron whispered surprised. "You really feel kids."

She nodded, smiling. "I love them very much and enjoy their company. I would like to become a kindergarten teacher one day, after I am cured. Also, I know that you don't want your mother to know about me yet, so, if she sees this note you always could say to her that you wrote it."

"Sorry about that, Rosie. I didn't mean to hurt you by hiding you. I just want our relationship to be safe from any influence and interference for now. It is too fresh and too fragile and I treasure it a lot."

Aaron took her face in his palms and looked her in the eyes. "I promise, I will do everything that is possible to try to cure you," he affirmed, kissing her cheeks. "Then my family will know about you and we will be together openly and forever. And now, it's dinner time, my love. Let's go."

While driving through the city toward the Space Needle, Aaron got a phone call from his receptionist that the requested Rosa Garcia's file from Dr. Evelyn Hertz had arrived. He made a big U-turn and headed to the university to get it immediately.

"Should I wait in the car?" Rosie asked as they parked beside his faculty building.

"No. You can come with me," Aaron suggested. He didn't want her to develop a sense that he is avoiding to show her to people and concealing her all the time, as if he was ashamed of her.

He realized that it was hurtful enough for Rosie while he made this Skype call to his family. He knew she would be happy to see Laurie and to chat with her, but he forced himself to avert that. Aaron knew that Beth read this warning article in the community newspaper and, as a very protective mother and grandma, she would never allow them any contact with Rosie. He couldn't blame his mother for that. She was absolutely right, but his feelings for that girl begged him to find some kind of cunning balance to somehow satisfy everyone involved in this situation.

However, here, at the neutral territory of the university, Aaron felt no need to cover up things and walked with Rosie, holding hands, around the building toward the main entrance of his department. He took the folder from the receptionist, placed it into his briefcase and then a sudden thought came to his head.

"Look, Rosie," he said, "while we're here anyway, let me show you our lab. We are doing there scientific experiments and research studies of different brain possibilities. In practice, we are trying to find treatment for many mental conditions. Maybe one day you would be interested in working with me there for a while?"

"Okay," she agreed peacefully.

Aaron led her through long corridors to the elevator, then to the next floor and finally they arrived at a string of rooms, containing a lot of special equipment and devices that appeared unusual to Rosie. She stood in the middle of the room, looking around a bit confused though curious.

"Wow!" she exclaimed with excitement and interest. "And what exactly is it that you are doing here, lets say, for example, with this machine?"

It was a big black box with two plates on its sides connected to sliding rails. In front of it was a chair for the person who would be involved in this experiment.

"We have some people here with a special ability to move things. To a bystander it appears like they do that with their 'thoughts'," Aaron explained. "In reality, they have just extremely strong electrical current in their brain. We plug the machine in. The person sits on this chair, holds their hands on the sides, closer to these plates, but not touching them. Then he concentrates and orders the plates to begin moving. If he thinks – left, they move left, if he thinks – right, they are moving right."

Rosie gazed at him smiling mischievously.

"Well," she shrugged, "let's try that. But first, I don't need to sit close to the machine. You don't need to plug it in. Just look." She turned to the device, not even approaching it, and stared at the plates for a few seconds from a distance. They slid on the rail from both sides of the machine to the middle, clashed into each other and then moved back where they were.

"What!?" Aaron exclaimed in a complete shock. "Did you really do that?"

She laughed. "Yes, it's actually very easy." And she forced the plates to move and clash once more.

"Jeez! It's unbelievable! You have much more power than our experimenters. You are a miracle, Rosie."

She giggled confusingly. "Do you have some spoons here?"

"I know what you mean," Aaron exclaimed impatiently in anticipation of another fantastic moment. "I will find something." He opened the doors of cabinets holding some other equipment and took out a box full of different small stuff – tea spoons, cigarette lighteners, artificial flowers and so on. He put a plastic spoon on the table.

"Too lightweight," Rosie laughed and a little spoon flew onto the floor like it was blown by the wind. Aaron placed a metal spoon - it moved to the end of the table but not as fast as the previous one. He put a paper flower on the same spot – it flew away exactly like the plastic spoon. Then he set a glass in the middle of the table. Being heavier, it moved slowly, stopped by the edge, then moved back to the middle, then began turning around, like dancing. He watched this with big eyes as Rosie chuckled and clapped her hands, having fun. She even started to sing and move in a rhythm for the glass dance.

"Well, my super girl," Aaron hugged her and kissed her passionately. "As soon as my vacation ends, we will work here together, document all of these, and who knows, maybe we will find a cure for you. What do you think about this idea? Let's discuss it on our way to dinner, otherwise we will be late."

Rosie walked back to the car, silently holding his hand. When in the car, she finally answered his previous question. "Aaron, do you seriously think that this ability I have is related to schizophrenia? Come on now, you should know better than that. It's related to the holographic universe I could connect to, but it is not related to my illness at all. It's different. It's like, medically saying – one patient could have a healthy and strong heart but a very sick liver or kidney. Those are two different things in one body."

"No," he objected. "Everything is connected in a person's body. His heart could be strong for some time, but sick organs would influence it and in years the heart would get worse step by step."

"Okay, you're probably right, but this even makes the idea of my healing more challenging. If everything connected in my brain as well, I could lose all my abilities when cured. You just confirmed that to me and it makes it even more difficult for me to make a final decision."

"Decision about what?"

"If I agree to be cured."

"I am sorry to say that, my love, but there is no cure for schizophrenia, yet."

"You should talk to my uncle, Aaron. He knows how to do miracles and calm me when I have my attacks. He knows many other things as well."

"What?" Aaron remembered how he was calming her down by kissing her wet cheeks and eyes when, as Vally, she was crying... A spasm of jealousy squeezed his gut again. "Is he touching you? Or kissing you?"

"You're silly!" she giggled. "Jeez! Respect yourself and respect me, please. He is just talking, but he knows how to talk and what to say. It's amazing, compared to you – because you sometimes go overboard and say things without thinking properly first. You lose your head easily."

"Because I love you!" Aaron exclaimed, agitated. "Sorry, I know I should be calm and happy because you are with me. But..."

Luckily for both of them, they arrived at the Space Needle. It prevented the continuation of the conversation which was already on the brink of an argument.

The Space Needle looked very different close up, than from a distance. Rosie used to see it everyday as a thin, tall structure far away on the horizon, like a rocket heading into space. Now she was surprised that close up it looked huge, heavy, monumental and stable. They took the speedy elevators to the very top and entered the restaurant from the Observation Deck. Their table was by the window so it was possible to observe the whole city while the room was slowly revolving.

"My God! Thank you, Aaron!" Rosie exclaimed, completely bewildered. "I haven't seen anything more astonishing in my life!"

"You are welcome, my love," he smiled happily, "but I can guarantee that you will see things even more beautiful and exciting during the following weeks as we travel."

"Where?"

"For now just here, around the state of Washington, because you can't fly. It is one of the most gorgeous places in America and I intend to show it to you. You need to know where you were born, where your home is and where you are living. It's very unfortunate that you didn't have a chance to explore this fantastic place before, but now I am going to right this wrong."

During the dinner, which was very special, unusual and unbelievably tasty, they discussed their schedule for the following days. Aaron was completely free. Rosie was free as well, except for the next Tuesday evening – her concert at Greenwich Competition Hall. Also, she suggested that she would go back to her place every evening because she still needed to do some work on the computer for those magazines whom she was working for as a poetry editor.

So, they decided that Aaron would pick her up every day at about ten in the morning and they would go to the beach for a few hours to have a suntan and fresh sea air, and to swim. On some days they would go boating for a while between tiny islands in the sea. After lunch they would drive around the state and visit museums and special places of interest. Then they would have dinners in different restaurants and after that Aaron would bring Rosie back to her place. They both felt safe and secure to spend nights in different houses, being a bit aware what could happen if they would be sleeping together.

Before leaving the Space Needle, they went out to the Observation Deck. It was already twilight and the lights of the city began turning on and shining down there looking like '*the stars under their feet*' from her poem. They stood enchanted by the stunning beauty of it for a long time. Aaron hugged Rosie from behind holding her waist tight. She snuggled her back to him and pressed her cheek to his arm. He slowly kissed the top of her head, her temple, her ear being absolutely unable to keep his hands and his lips away from her. He wanted her so badly that it made him scared. He had no idea what he could do to heal her and to make her a normal healthy woman able for having sex and loving him fully; to make her the ordinary girl that he thought she was when he met her.

Looking at the night beauty of the surrounding world, Rosie whispered, almost not audibly, a poem that came to her from the universe.

"It would be a Hymn of Love," she said while they were already in the elevator. "I will perform it next Tuesday. It is about us, mostly you, Aaron, and it will be our success. I would win first place for that. I know."

When Aaron came home, after dropping her at her friends' place, he took out his briefcase from the trunk of his car and grabbed her file right away. He sat in an armchair in the living room and started reading. And during that process his whole and endless happiness slowly subsided and turned into sadness, despair and finally horror.

Of course the folder was full of medical information – all medications that Rosa Garcia ever took, in doses and other details of prescriptions were there, along with the descriptions of her every appointment. Her every word, move, and look was documented. It didn't matter where the appointments took place - at Dr. Hertz's clinic or at the *Youth Shelter* - it was registered accurately and fully. However, Aaron skipped all those details. He wasn't very much interested in the medical part, he knew and understood it himself well enough. All that he needed were the facts of Rosie's biography and he got them.

Being eleven-years-old, Rosa Lynn Garcia had first very serious attack of her illness during which she slashed the throat of her beloved grandma and killed her. Then she assaulted her grandfather who tried to stop her and left him with seventeen knife wounds, not life threatening, but severely bleeding. So, he survived and was able to call 911. When the police arrived, grandma Nora was dead and grandpa Vasil was screaming in pain, covering his wounds with both hands. Little Rosa was sitting and crying, all soaked in blood, holding the knife in her hand and repeating through her tears, "It's all my fault. It's all because of me. I did it," then she threw the knife and sobbed hysterically.

At first, she was placed into a Juvenile Facility, which was actually a jail for children. But after Dr. Hertz examined the girl and concluded the diagnosis as acute schizophrenia, she was transferred into the *Youth Shelter* where she spent four years – from 2006 until 2010. During those years she received prescription drug treatment and began developing some unusual symptoms, like poetry talent, moving subjects with her thoughts, communicating telepathically with people around her and reading their thoughts. However, no more attacks happened during that period and in 2010 Rosa was acquitted and let out of the shelter in a stable mental condition. She was no danger anymore for herself and the others according to Dr. Hertz confirmation.

For one year Rosa Garcia was living with her mother's family, while attending high school where she did great academically. Then in 2011 she moved with her boyfriend, Benjamin Brown, and lived in his place for another year. In 2012, she successfully graduated from high school with an honors diploma a year ahead of her class.

When Mr. Brown was accidentally shot by the policewoman, Rosa was there and she attacked the policewoman with a knife, almost killing her. At the same time, she attempted suicide, thrusting a knife into her own stomach twice. Being pregnant at the moment, she had a miscarriage right at the crime scene and was taken to the hospital where she attempted suicide one more time by overdosing on opiate pills. After surgery and her physical recovery, Rosa was placed into the same *Youth Shelter* for one year.

And again, during that year in the shelter she was doing good, had no attacks whatsoever, and was released in 2013. She was living with her mother's family in 2013–2015, until suddenly another attack at her home happened on June 16, 2015, and she was returned back to the *Youth Shelter* by her parents, according to Dr. Hertz advice. On June 19, 2015 she escaped from the shelter and disappeared from the doctor's and police radar. Her condition and place of residence was now unknown.

That was it. That was an amazing genius creature, that was the woman he was madly in love with. That was his miracle, that was his angel and his monster in one body. Aaron dropped the folder and covered his face with both hands. He didn't know what to do now.

CHAPTER 21

At first Aaron was lost. Then he went to his bed, took Rosie's book and started reading it from the beginning to the very end. It was a long read and he began feeling gradually that his belief in Rosie returned to him. His confidence that there was something not right in the whole situation got stronger with every page he read.

Whom should I believe and trust? he thought. *The woman I love and who loves me back as well? Or Dr. Hertz — a cold, indifferent stranger who doesn't love Rosie, doesn't care about her, just formally doing the job? The stranger who only collects facts, not always the right ones, and has absolutely no interest in checking them?*

Aaron remembered that Rosie told him, "I spent four years next door for a murder I didn't commit." And he accepted this and trusted her because he loved her. He sensed that there was obviously something wrong with the documentation. And her book confirmed that. It was impossible not to feel that the author's soul was pure, beautiful, fragile, and tender. In any case she didn't have the soul of a murderer.

She was begging him to understand, to believe, to trust, to love. It was all that attracted him from the first time as he opened her book, enchanted him and held him tight as a magnet. There was no need to ask her any questions about her poems. Aaron knew everything now, all was absolutely clear in his mind. She was talking to him from each line.

Most of the poems were disturbing and tragic, but in spite of that the book didn't make him nervous and sad, as it did before. Now it was soothing and calming because he clearly realized the truth. This poor child, Rosie, was in a dramatic situation during her whole life. Her fate and the span of her existence was destroyed by mean people, unfortunate events, unhappy coincidences and false circumstances. These, all together, crushed her mentally and made her ill, and only his endless love could right this wrong, heal her and save her. He would love her, carry her in his arms and take care of her forever, endlessly, until his last breath.

Aaron even asked himself – if he was in the shoes of the guy from the scary inquisition story which he told Helen – what would he do? Of course, he would never report Rosie as a witch, but if someone did and she was to be burned in fire, would he jump in and die with her? "Yes," he said to himself aloud, convincingly. "Yes, yes, a hundred times yes. I wouldn't live without her."

Strangely, but with this decision came not horror but peace and rest. He pressed Rosie's book to his chest, hugged it and finally fell asleep.

And after that their love story evolved as a song – beautiful and full of endless happiness.

Aaron kept his schedule. Every morning, he woke up at six, exercised for one hour in his sports room in the basement, then talked with Beth and Laurie on Skype and then, pretending that he was going to work, he drove to Rosie's place and picked her up to go to the beach.

On the second day of Aaron's vacation, Friday, they were laying on the towels at Lake Washington Madrona Beach, putting sunscreen on each other's backs, enjoying these small touches that were acceptable in public. Then they swam for a while, as far as it was possible; playing tag in the water, hugging and kissing each other every time as one caught the other; laughing and giggling like crazy; having fun as teenagers would do. In spite of the fact that Aaron was ten years older than Rosie, he felt like he was twenty again; like he was a happy and lightheaded teen or even a carefree child.

Then, after lunch at *IHOP,* they went to the *Museum of Glass* in Tacoma and enjoyed amazing works of glass art not just inside of the museum but outside where they were displayed on the ceiling and the walls of the overpass, as well. Those works were a real miracle. It was difficult to believe that human hands were capable of creating such a divine beauty.

Aaron and Rosie also played two xylophones – the standing one and the hanging one - at the yard of the museum and giggled at each other's clumsiness and lack of skills in music.

At the gift shop, Aaron bought for Rosie a little yellow bird, sitting in the wineglass, as a reminder of her poem **Little Birdie**. He also bought her a vase made from sparkling white glass lace with flowers inside it. They looked almost alive, were unbelievably thin and made from hairlike blue and red glass. All together it cost about $1,000 because the Gift shop was extremely expensive but he didn't care.

Rosie tried to protest. "Thank you, Aaron," she said, tenderly hugging him. "I agree that it's a heavenly beauty. Of course I am happy to have it, but I don't want you to spend money on me. I am not used to it. I was raised in poverty and when I was living with Ben's family, we were very far from well off, too. To me it was normal."

He laughed, "Then you better start to develop another lifestyle now. I am not rich but I have enough money to buy things which will stay as a memory about this amazing day that we spent together. I want you to have it and look at it every time when we are not together and feel as if we are."

These fragile gifts were wrapped for them and securely placed into a hard box for a safe delivery home.

Later in the evening they had dinner at the luxury restaurant, *Chophouse,* and Rosie was finally driven home for the night.

The next day, Saturday, was almost the same with a little difference: after leaving Madison Beach at Lake Washington they went for lunch at *Applebee's* in Bellingham and later in the *Boeing*

Museum of Flight. This exhibition made a shocking impression on Rosie. She was laughing and jumping like a little child being happy to use all the entertainment stations that were available for kids. And the last was dinner in the highest class restaurant, *Art of the Table.*

"Aaron, why are you doing this to me?" she begged almost with tears, looking around at the restaurant's decor and at her plate which displayed a fantastically designed beauty of a special dish. "Are you trying to impress me? No need. I love you. It doesn't matter what, where, when. I love you because of your kind, beautiful heart and soul, not because of all of this..." she gestured around her.

He smiled, "I am doing this because I want to make up for your lost years when you were locked up and didn't have anything beautiful. And you know why I am making it up for you – because I love you. Simple and clear. You did have fun during our last two days, didn't you?"

"Of course, I did. I am just a bit scared. You know - like when Cinderella went to the ball – in a carriage with white horses, Chrystal slippers, a beautiful dress... she was happy. She was in love with the prince, but then... the midnight clock rang out... and it all disappeared. Now there were mice instead of horses, a rotten pumpkin instead of a carriage, rags instead of the evening gown, barefoot instead of Crystal slippers. In the wink of an eye she fell back to her poor and unhappy condition. And believe me, the return is much more difficult than to have poverty and unhappiness all the time, not knowing any better."

Aaron never thought about that. Rosie impressed him - this young lady was a child at times, however, she was as mature as a real adult at the other moments. And that was exactly what attracted him the most. It was her unbelievable inner beauty, combined with her poetry talent and all the different mysterious brain abilities.

"Hmm..." he uttered slowly and thoughtfully, "but the prince found her later anyway. Right? And they end up being married and living in a castle...Right?"

"It's a fairy tale, Aaron. In real life it's not happening like that."

"What if it will? The prince found her with the help of the Crystal slipper. I found you, too... but with the help of your book. Would you marry me and live with me in a castle?"

Rosie smirked.

"Aaron, please. You can't be serious. Stop torturing me. Don't you know about my illness? I am dangerous - I can't guarantee what may happen in any minute, nor which personality will come out. You have a child at home. Don't even think about this ever, please. Not for one second.... At least, until I can be completely cured."

"Sorry," he whispered, lowering his eyes. "Sometimes I get carried away."

"You're losing your head too easily. Please, hold yourself in check, I am begging you. Don't make our relationship more painful for me than it is."

He felt at this point like she was ten years older than him and he was a crazy lightheaded boy beside her. "Is it painful?" he inquired, surprised. "I didn't know that. I certainly didn't want that. It wasn't my intention. I only want to make you endlessly happy. Believe me, please. I am not playing games with you, Rosie. I am deadly serious. I will do everything in the world that is possible, I will pull out all the stops to cure you."

She took a deep breath. "Then you should talk to my uncle, Aaron. If you really love me and are really serious about our future, you have to. Please..."

"Okay," he reluctantly agreed. "I will eventually. I promise. But let's finish our vacation first. And please, let me spoil you a bit more for a while. It is such a pleasure for me."

"For me too," she smiled at him lovingly. "I am just a bit scared. That's all."

"Don't be scared, my love. Remember as you said to me – forget everything bad, clear your head. Just allow yourself to be happy and relax in pleasure."

"Jeez, you sound so sexy, Aaron."

"I am. And you will know that. Just promise me that you won't be scared anymore. Trust me, please, Rosie."

She smiled bashfully and didn't say anything more.

The next day, Sunday, they went to Mount Baker Beach at Lake Washington in the morning and then off to Lynden Fair where all agricultural achievements of the region were displayed. The festive celebration was in full swing. Aaron and Rosie had crocodile meat sandwiches for lunch at a food stand. It actually tasted like chicken, and they laughed about that a lot. Then they went to the petting zoo area to pet lamas, horses, lambs, and goat kids. While eating ice cream, they watched an all-day concert on the band stage. Aaron bought two beautiful sundresses for Rosie at the market, and also an African decorative Mask made from black wood. For dinner they had ribs at the same food stand and then drove back to Seattle full of happiness and new found marvelous fun experiences.

On Monday they boated to and around Whidbey Island. Aaron parked the rented boat in a small harbor and they went to explore Fort Casey Historical Park. They walked on the forest trails, holding hands and kissing every time as they looked at each other. Then, they climbed to the top of an old lighthouse and stood there for a long moment enjoying the incredible solemn beauty of the endless water. Later they returned to the boat and floated around small islands in the harbor, under Deception Pass Bridge where the view was absolutely stunning.

"Aaron, could you stop for a minute on this island, please? I want to show you something," Rosie suggested suddenly. He was surprised by that demand because she hadn't been here before and didn't know the area at all. What could she show him there? However, he stopped the boat by the tiny sandy island covered with high grass, taller than a person would be. Aaron looked at her waiting patiently for what she would say.

"Here," she narrowed her eyes and attentively looked at a grassy piece of the ground. Then she said convincingly, "This is the place. Do you hear how the waves are coming and going, touching the sand? It sounds like they are whispering."

"Yeah... I hear that... but sorry, I still didn't get what you mean," Aaron shrugged confused. "This is the place... Place for... what?"

"Do you remember our first night in the park after the concert? A poem appeared in my head which I told you, **Place out of Time.** It was about the past, the now and the future. The paragraph about the future starts, '*The future is an island with grass and sand, the whisper of waves where I will love you mad....*' This is the place of our future. We will have sex here and conceive our son."

"What?!" Aaron exclaimed, shocked. He couldn't believe his own ears. It was so unexpected that he even thought maybe something happened and some new unknown personality appeared in her.

She looked at him mischievously and laughed, getting this thought.

"Don't worry, I am still Rosie. Sorry, if it sounds disturbing to you. It's not my fault. It is what's written in the particles of the holographic universe. Maybe I shouldn't tell you about that. But a couple of days ago you almost proposed to me. So, I decided to check how you would react to this contra-proposal." Then, some seconds later, she added getting more and more wistful with each following word, "Now, seeing your wry and suddenly pale face, I understand that it is not what you want and all these escapades about a prince and Cinderella living together in a castle were just blah-blah-blah. Okay then. Thank you for clarity, Aaron."

"Jeez, Rosie," he hugged her, pressing her to his chest. They stood silently for a long moment feeling the warmth of each other. "Sorry," Aaron finally whispered, barely touching her hair with his lips. "I didn't expect to hear that in a million years. It was like you hit me with a hammer on my head. I never ever thought about having another child. And why here? Why not at home in a beautiful and comfortable bed? And when? When will it happen? How long should I wait for that?"

"I don't know. It feels like it's far away ahead. I guess, it's after I am cured."

"Oh, gosh," he moaned desperately. "It always comes to the same point. Maybe it's better not to think about this now. Let's boat back to the city. It's almost time for dinner, my love. We should go."

She just nodded and moved aside from him.

The way back to Seattle took about one hour during which Rosie was sitting quietly, holding her temples with both hands. She didn't say a word, but as Aaron glanced at her he noticed that she was soundlessly crying. Tears were sliding down her cheeks and dropping on her chest, on the gorgeous sundress which he bought her a day before at the Lynden Fair market.

With a deep breath Aaron stopped the boat, sat beside her and hugged her shoulders.

"What now, my love?" he asked tenderly. "I am sorry if I hurt you unintentionally."

She hugged his neck, snuggled her face against his chest and suddenly sobbed almost hysterically, all shaky in his arms.

"I can't do that anymore, Aaron. We should stop it. I don't want dating like that. I don't want to be with you like that. I can't handle so much fun. I am not designed for fun. I would rather die. I want to die in your arms. I want you to kill me. Please, let me die, I am begging you. I don't want to live."

This was another shock that he never expected to hear after all the happy and beautiful experiences they shared during the past week.

"You don't want to see me anymore?" he asked in an unsteady voice on the brink of tears as well, sensing a painful squeeze in his gut.

She nodded, yes.

"Why? Just tell me why?"

"I can't tolerate it anymore. All these presents, all these restaurants, all this luxury, all this money you are throwing around. What for? Why? It's not me. Other women would be happy about that. It's all alien to me. I love you too much. Too much for fun. Too deep for fun. Please, leave me alone and let me die. Let me kill myself. I won't live without you but I won't live with you either. I want to die, please, Aaron. It is all such a difficult burden to me that I'd rather die."

"Are you Vally?" he asked carefully, being painfully hit by this confession.

"No. I am still Rosie. But I am Rosie from my book, not Kiki from a fun country. You don't understand how much I love you. I am dying in this love and I want to die in it. You don't know. You don't feel it."

"I do feel it, Rosie. I know how much you love me because I love you as much too. I won't live without you too. But I don't see any reason for us to die. Why not live and be together, and be happy? Why not, tell me?"

"Because I don't deserve you. You are a high class handsome accomplished man, but I am just a crazy mentally ill girl."

"No, you are not," Aaron objected passionately. "You are unbelievably talented. You are a genius poetess, successful and accomplished as well. You are a beautiful, miraculous and special woman."

"Only when I am Anastasia."

"In any personality, you are always my Rosie to me and I swear to God, I won't ever let you go."

He was sitting and cuddling her on his lap for quite a long time until he started noticing that she was calming down step-by-step. Some soothing energy was gradually coming from him and began enveloping her.

"Okay, my love," Aaron quietly said, finally. "I promise, we won't have any more luxury, if you don't want it. Let's ask nature for help. Tomorrow morning let's go to the North Cascade Mountains just hiking together for a while."

"Why there?" she requested timidly.

"Because it is the most divine place in the world. You will see and feel it right away, I am sure. Please, don't cry anymore, yes? Rosie?"

"Yes," she whispered with a tentative smile that was carving its way on her face. "While hiking, I will think about my poem for tomorrow's concert and polish it a little bit. It sounds really exciting. Sorry, Aaron. No more tears, I promise. I will try to hold myself in check from now on."

"So, you're still with me?" he asked, smiling. "Are you still dating me?" She nodded. "Then tonight we are not going for dinner in a restaurant. We are going home and will cook something by ourselves and maybe make a small picnic in the backyard, on the grass. How about that, my love?"

"Really?" Rosie laughed happily. "Jeez, Aaron! You're my miracle! Thank you for understanding. It would be more of my style. It is who I am. It would be a dream." And she kissed him on the cheek as he turned the ignition key on and started the boat again.

For the moment peace was restored but Aaron couldn't be sure for how long it would last.

CHAPTER 22

Aaron spread a picnic blanket on the slope of the mountain which smoothly led about ten feet down and then edged to an abyss toward Diablo Lake. He and Rosie sat snuggling with each other and watched, dumbfounded at the stunning eternity that had opened in front of them.

"Do you feel the energy?" he asked in a whisper, fondly touching her hair with his lips. She nodded silently, yes, and pressed her head to his shoulder. It seemed wrong to talk loud here; it would be blasphemy to break this aura of the divine beauty with any noise.

It was not just an amazing view - there were many gorgeous places and landscapes in the Rocky Mountain Range. But, this place wasn't exactly comparable to anything in the world because of its strongest supernatural energy field.

There were four enormous snowy mountain peaks on the sides, holding the sky like pillars. Between them two endless corridors of bottomless ravines crossed each other. A huge dam held a piercing malachite colored lake where a tiny white boat was visible, floating from one end to another. Far down, at the bottom of the abyss, was the dark ghost town of Diablo, neglected and forgotten more than a half century ago. Some gauges were located not far from it, designed to measure underground movements of the earth and notify people about the danger of potentially approaching earthquakes. Those gauges were placed so deep that it felt like they were almost close to the center of the globe.

The name Diablo probably was given to this place not accidentally by the Mexican workers who built the dam. It precisely portrayed the image of something diabolically scary and at the same time breathtaking, miraculous, unearthly in it's mystic beauty.

"How did you find this place?" Rosie whispered, lifting her face and looking Aaron in the eyes.

"Five years ago, after Ally's murder...I didn't want to live. I was completely numb. I was driving meaninglessly, just searching for a place where I could jump down into an abyss. I stopped here, got out of the car, sat on the grass and this energy suddenly hugged me, enveloped me and held me tight. I sensed something. I heard something... I don't know... I am not religious at all. But I heard, I am pretty sure, 'the voice of God' sounded in my ears. It told me to go home. It was like a higher power, I couldn't disobey it. I drove back home, fell on my bed, and started crying for several months. Until, finally, my mother became tired of it, and returned me to my senses, convincing me that I must live for Laurie. Now I keep coming here about once a year, just to sit, and think, and absorb this energy for a while. But I never hear 'the voice of God' anymore."

"Because you don't need it now," Rosie murmured, nodding convincingly. "It was the voice of God. The universe wanted to save you for me. It is all written in the holographic particles there above. I wasn't religious either, especially being raised by grandparents from an atheist communist country. But my uncle changed me. He was an atheist too, but he told me many stories, how God saved his life a number of times and now he is a very deep believer."

"This could be called God. But, from a scientific point of view, it was the energy of this place that realistically saved my life. It did resonate in my ears, as a voice, and prevented me from committing suicide," Aaron uttered quietly and thoughtfully. "I read long ago - it was discovered that everything alive has energy auras; not just people and animals, but also rivers, lakes, mountains, springs, oases – all natural things - especially which is related to water. In some country, about forty years ago, scientists invented a special camera that could take photos of those auras and the energy streams going up to the universe."

"I know," Rosie nodded. "I saw this kind of camera. Just yesterday night, when you brought me home after our picnic in your backyard, I was shown the camera and my picture was taken. Yes, there was an aura, even a multicolored one, a strange one, and a really misshapen one, broken to pieces. By the aura it was clearly visible that I am not normal and really damaged. I held this camera in my hands."

"Sorry, I don't understand. Have you seen this kind of camera? Where? How?" Aaron asked, confused. "The article I read said that it was invented not in America."

"Now it is invented here, as well. He just finished working on it yesterday. He did it on the basis of the goggles which he created some years ago. In the goggles you can just see the auras and its streams up to the universe; with the camera you can take pictures of them."

"Who did it?"

Rosie shrugged, "A friend."

"Your mysterious uncle again?"

She laughed. "No. Not at all. Uncle doesn't know anything about techniques or devices."

"Then who?"

"Liam."

"Who the hell is that?"

She shrugged, "A friend," then begged, "Aaron, please, you can't swear here, in this place with divine energy. It sounds like swearing in a church."

He held his head with both hands, silently trying to stop himself from another outburst of jealousy. Rosie took his hands, removed them from his head and pulled them to her, then kissed them affectionately. "I love you, Aaron," she whispered. "Believe me, you don't have to worry about anything. I belong to you."

"You have strange friends," he moaned. "They drive you to my place at four in the morning, they are inventing unbelievable scientific things, they prohibit us from having sex... Jeez, I don't get it. I am completely messed up."

"I suggested many times you meet them but you are always finding excuses to avoid that."

"I don't know why," Aaron shrugged. "Something holds me back. It really hurts to feel that you have someone in your life who could be closer than me."

She chuckled. "Gosh, Aaron. You have your daughter and your mom. They are obviously closer to you than I. And I am not jealous about that at all because it is normal."

"Mom and Laurie are closer to me very differently. They are family – my flesh and blood; you are my woman – my heart and soul, and body, I hope, soon."

"My friends are my family too. They are not flesh and blood obviously, but they play the role of my parents. They are much older, like a father and grandfather."

"Two men? Are you living with two men?!..."

"Aaron, forget your insecurity, please. They don't need me sexually. They are a married gay couple."

"Oh gosh!" he exclaimed, being hit by the unexpectedness, and then laughed. "That's where these poems came from at the last concert... Now I get it. I heard that gay men could be very good friends with women. Why didn't you tell me about that much earlier? It could have saved me a lot of frustration."

"Because I wanted you to trust me that I love only you without any safe backup. I wanted you to believe in me - in my love, in my honesty, in my devotion to you."

"Sorry if I hurt you. It's just jealousy. I wish to own you. I crave it... subconsciously maybe. Consciously I know it is wrong, but I couldn't suppress it... until now. Thank you for the clarification. But I still feel very strange since I read your book, Rosie. It turned everything in my life upside down. I can't think about anything but you; to have you, to own you, to dissolve myself into you. I am obsessed with you almost to insanity."

"That was the point."

"Why are you saying this again? What does it mean? You promised to explain it to me."

Rosie sighed deeply. "Okay. That Friday night, when I saw you for the first time with your little one on the street, I knew instantly that you are my fate. You were prescribed to me in the universe. I recognized you. I had seen you before in my dreams, in my visions, many times. But you were absolutely indifferent to me at that moment. It felt like you didn't notice me. I was nothing to you. You just ignored me. While walking with your little one, I was thinking how I could get your attention and attract you. I knew that I needed more time. I needed to see you again. But how?

"Sorry, I lied that I didn't have money for the bus. I had the money, but I thought that maybe we could arrange another meeting for me to return money to your daughter. However, I saw on your face that it didn't bother you at all. I was such an absolute nothing to you, that you wouldn't want to meet me again over five bucks. Then I remembered that I had my book with me and I realized that it would be a hook to catch you. That was the point – do you get it now? The book could make it happen because I felt your soul. You were my soulmate, but you didn't know that then. The book was supposed to wake you up and open to you - who you are; to help you understand yourself. And it did."

"So, it was kind of a plot," Aaron smirked, shaking his head.

"Pretty innocent plot of a helpless girl who desperately needed you. Who craved to be with you because you were my saver, my meaning of everything. I was in love with you, before even knowing you. Please, forgive me for that. Don't be angry that I did it."

"How could I be angry if I love you now? By doing this trick, you gave me everything. You gave me meaning to live in full. I couldn't even guess that such a level of happiness was possible. I am not simply existing, I am on fire inside. Before we met, it was just a boring smolder. I considered myself, not to say happy, but at least satisfied with my life. It was calm, quiet, regular - work, family..."

"Sex with the murderer of your wife..." Rosie interrupted, glancing at him askance. "It doesn't sound regular to me, or calm and quiet..."

Aaron blushed. He should expect that she knew about that, if she was able to see everything.

"Sorry," he whispered, lowering his eyes.

"Don't apologize."

"I am not sorry that I did it," he grinned. "I am sorry that you know about that."

She shrugged. "Very typical statement of a man. But it is understandable that you slept with her - you are a man. It was needed. It was good for your physical health, but not for your soul of course."

"I didn't have a soul until I met you, Rosie. I just understood what a soul is when I opened your book."

"Again, that was the point," she smiled. "Now you know what I mean by these words."

"I do. And I have loved you like crazy since, and I want you like crazy."

"Of course," she giggled, "because there is no 'murderer' to use for that anymore..."

"Quite the opposite. I broke up with her because of you. I want you. I want to be with you. I want not just a woman, but exactly you and nobody else in the world. And I know that this is forever. Please, believe me."

"I do." She hugged him and cuddled up to his chest. "Then take me, Aaron," she whispered a bit later. "I am yours. I don't know why you are stopping yourself all the time. Don't you think I noticed that?"

"Look, Rosie," Aaron took a deep breath and, while holding her by the shoulders, moved her aside from him. "I need to tell you something about that. Just listen, please," he kept holding her, looking straight in her eyes. "A couple of years ago I had one patient, a very nice young man. He had acute schizophrenia, but not as many personalities as you have. Just two or three. However, he was in remission for more than a year already. The medications were working pretty good on him. Then he met a young woman, they fell in love and wanted to get married and start a family. His bride insisted on consulting with me as his doctor. They came to an appointment together, holding hands. They looked very happy.

"I told them the truth. The chance was very big that with an active regular sex life - which would likely start on the honeymoon - comes the danger that his illness will return. It could even be doubled, maybe tripled by intensity. The young lady asked me, which percentage was this possibility. I told them − about 90 percent. But she loved him so madly that she said that she wanted to take the 10 percent risk that this would not happen. In her opinion it was worth trying. So, they got married and went on their honeymoon trip. In about two weeks, he had a severe attack and strangled her during a black out. He didn't even know that he killed her. Then, he was placed into a mental institution for life."

Aaron pulled Rosie closer and hugged her tight. They sat silently for a long moment. She just slowly moved her fingers, thoughtfully caressing his chest.

"So, you are afraid that I'll kill you?" she whispered then. "Look at my hands. They are so small and weak that I couldn't strangle you even if I wanted to. And I don't have any weapons here. I can't believe that you are scared of me, Aaron."

"I actually don't care much about my life. I want you so desperately that I am ready to take a risk too. But I never will allow you to end up in a mental institution. Trust me, I know what it is to be there. I visit patients there at times. It is absolutely different from the *Youth Shelter* where you were. The shelter is a paradise for kids, compared to a mental institution for adults. And the treatment there is awfully scary and painful. I don't want to describe it in detail now, but I will never let you go there, I swear. Death is better than to be there, believe me. I am scared not of you, but for you."

"Two weeks..." she murmured, deep in thought. "It happened to him after two weeks... How many times did they have sex in those two weeks? Let's say, three times per day... Then forty-two times. If we do it just once, maybe some more..."

"Jeez," Aaron laughed, trying to turn everything into a joke, "you are pretty good with math, my love. Now you are sounding like a real child. It never is once, or 'some more'. If I take these brakes off, it will probably never stop. I won't be able to stop neither myself, nor you, until we both die."

"Then better we both die. I told you yesterday on the boat – I want you to kill me. I want to die in your arms. I want to die in your love. You didn't get it of course but it was my confession that I want you. Take me, Aaron, I am begging you. Take me, please, right here and right now. We want each other so badly that we are already dying. We are attracted to each other and it should be obeyed finally. I showed you yesterday our island of the future. We have the future. It means nothing bad will happen now, if we make love."

"Shh," he fondly blew some air into her hot face as she lifted it to him. "Please, calm down, Rosie. It couldn't be here and now. This is not the place for that. It would be best to go home."

In despair, she fell face down on the blanket and started rolling from side to side while beating her fists on the ground."I can't, I can't anymore. Help me, Aaron. Please, stop me. Kill me." She wasn't crying but moaning, almost breathless. This outburst was quite dangerous so close to the edge of the abyss. It took Aaron every drop of his willpower to hold himself in check, seeing this. He jumped up, took her in his arms, carried her to the car and buckled her in the passenger seat. Then he took a bottle of cold water from the cooler bag and opened it for her.

"Have a drink, Rosie, and stop it, please," he said in a harsh voice. "That's enough. You should learn how to be reasonable. I know how you feel. It's no less painful for me, believe me. I want you no less than you want me. Okay, I swear, we will have it, we will do it. Tonight, after your concert. And now... you should turn into Anastasia and get ready for your performance. You told me yesterday that you will think about your poem while in the mountains. You said you want to polish it a bit. Your words. 'Forget everything bad' – your words, Rosie. You held your lips on my forehead when you soothed me. Remember? Do you want me now to do that for you?"

"No," she answered quietly and shook her head, "you have no power for that. It won't help. I can do it myself." She slowly slid her palms in front of her face, twice, then took a deep breath and threw her head back on the headset. Aaron watched silently how her tension subsided and the facial expression relaxed gradually. Her lips quivered a bit as she closed her eyes. Now he got it. A poem came from the universe and inside her head she began to recite it not audibly. Her little attack of madness was gone.

Aaron returned to the slope, picked up the picnic blanket on which they sat, put it into the trunk of his car, then sat in the driver seat and turned on the ignition. It was more than a two-hour drive from here to Seattle, and they had barely enough time to have dinner and then get ready for the concert.

CHAPTER 23

During their drive back to Seattle, Rosie completely calmed down, began talking, laughing and feeling content and relaxed. She sounded to Aaron like an absolutely normal young lady to have fun with - happy, loving and friendly. He dreamed that this condition would stay at least for a while.

For dinner before the concert, they decided to have another picnic on the grass in the backyard. Together Aaron and Rosie baked buns from dough they found in the freezer, made sandwiches with them and also cut some tomatoes and pickles that Beth left in the refrigerator. As drinks they used spring water from bottles.

"It feels natural," Rosie was saying happily, lying comfortably on the grass, with the back of her head on Aaron's lap. It was exactly like she did on a bench in the park on their first date the evening after the concert. "We don't need anything else, do we, Aaron? I was raised with the belief that food is to eat and clothes are to wear to warm up and not to be naked. To make an art from these things, like those expensive restaurants do, feels kind of artificial."

"In some points, yes," Aaron agreed thoughtfully, while caressing her hair and winding her blond locks on his fingers, "but there is much more potential in food and clothes. Why not make art with it? Look, people are using paint not only to paint houses, fences and benches. They are creating fine arts – portraits, landscapes. People are using sounds - not just as car's honking or doors slamming – they make music out of them. Words are used not only for talking and swearing at each other, but to write literature and poetry, as you know. Much the same way the luxury restaurants are using food, or fashion designers - clothes."

"I agree, but not everybody likes or understands painting art," Rosie objected, "not everybody likes poetry or reading books at all, not everybody likes or understands different kinds of music. So, I have the right not to like those food arts because they are not making me happy. I came for dinner being hungry and a hamburger would be enough to satisfy my hunger. But I am given only a couple of teaspoons of real edible food in the middle of a big plate, surrounded with a lot of art drawings made by different sauces. It costs a hundred dollars and I left absolutely hungry as a result, though a hamburger for five bucks would do a perfect job. Don't you feel the same hunger when we leave all these places of food art?"

"Kind of," Aaron laughed. "You are so sweet, my love."

"I am just rational."

"You are right from your point of view, but people who are going to those restaurants are usually never hungry. They are going there for fun, for exploring new arts of different cuisines. Or for business meetings."

"Then we are not going there anymore, right, Aaron? It is just wasting money. The same as for people who don't like classical music, paying for a ticket to the opera would be wasting money. Or for a person who doesn't like hockey, to pay for a ticket to the game would be just wasting money. Am I right?"

"You don't have to worry about money, Rosie. Those things are pretty much affordable for me."

"Sorry if I hurt you by that, but I still do worry. I was raised by my grandparents counting every penny, from paycheck to paycheck."

"I am sorry to hear that. I know that you deserve much more than that. You are worth much more. Your value is extremely high.

To me it's like a level of someone from above – an angel, or a goddess. I just wanted to do something very special and unusual for you with those restaurants. But I was probably wrong. However, your position is a bit contradictory here – I noticed that you are wearing some stylish and beautiful clothes at times."

"Just on the stage as Anastasia. And those are all what Miguel bought me, as I told you - not because of his kindness. It was obligatory for my concert travels and he wanted me to go, just to get rid of me."

"But you do like the sundresses from that Lynden Fair market, right?"

"Of course, Aaron. I feel that you bought them sincerely from your heart. They are beautiful, but they are normal and I am happy to wear them. If it would be something from a Fashion Design show, it would probably cost a hundred times more, but I wouldn't like it at all and wouldn't wear it ever because those things usually are not wearable. They are exactly like those art food plates from the expensive restaurants - just to stare at them, but in real life they are useless."

During this conversation Aaron couldn't help, but look askance at Rosie's face and carefully assess her medical state professionally. He didn't see anything wrong with her. He felt a bit guilty for doing that. Officially, she wasn't his patient yet although Dr. Evelyn Hertz did send her file up to him. However, he should get the Psychiatry Department approval first, before he could start working with her. He wasn't supposed to evaluate and diagnose her now, but subconsciously he still had hope that maybe this, her normal condition, would stay longer.

Rosie then went to his master bedroom to get dressed and put her makeup on to get ready for the concert. Aaron, while waiting for her, turned on his computer in his home office. He wanted to review some details on the requirements of submission of a cured patient for the Psychiatry Scientific Conference. He decided to double check the information wondering if it would be possible to involve Rosie into this process somehow.

Suddenly his phone rang. He noticed on the display that it was Helen, so he didn't answer. She left a message, "Hey, Dr. Dispenmore. I am calling you not as a lover, who I am not anymore, but as a colleague. Do you have any ideas for that conference in New York? I remember that you had nothing when we talked about it before. I actually found a pretty good patient who could be a suitable candidate for a cure – a twelve-year-old boy. Maybe you would be interested in working on this project together? We could go 50/50 for a Nobel Prize. Think about that and call me back."

Aaron's first thought was to delete this message and forget about it. But then he decided to postpone the deletion. He knew that in spite of all her morally disgusting qualities, Helen was a brilliant professional, and it was impossible not to recognize that. Maybe it would be worth reconsidering the idea later, if needed.

When Rosie appeared downstairs ready to go, Aaron held his breath. She looked fantastically beautiful in that Ancient Greek style – long white tunic with a golden belt on her waist and golden sandals. Her hair was spread in a middle part and done in a low bun on the back, but the main attraction of it was the golden ribbon tightened around her forehead which made her hairdressing look as a model of Greek statues as well.

"Jeez!" Aaron gasped, hugging her and going into raptures over her look. "You're my Aphrodite today. What is your poem about?"

"Ancient Greek Hymn," she smiled bashfully. "I love you, Aaron and I want the whole world to know that."

"So, it would be a Hymn of Love? I remember you told me that when we were at the Space Needle."

She nodded silently.

When they arrived at the Greenwich Competition Hall and Aaron wanted to go to the cashier to buy a ticket, Rosie said, "I called them and booked a spot for you in the front row. Just tell them your last name and they will give you the proper ticket. You will be in the audience on your own, Aaron. I have to go and sit in the dressing room. Be patient, please, my love. My performance today will be the last one." He noticed that she was already confident and proud like Anastasia was supposed to be as soon as they approached her favorite place, her turf, her area of expertise.

The crowd by the front entrance was once more huge. It was visible, similar to the last time, that many teens knew her very well. They chanted, "Rosalyn! Rosalyn!", applauded, laughed, hugged her, gave her high-fives. The impression for Aaron was exactly the same as it was before the previous concert – she was at home here, she was loved, respected and admired. Her self-esteem skyrocketed. Rosie got her triumphs here many times earlier and she was truly happy to be here today.

To see and feel this her emotional state, made Aaron really proud of her talent, of her achievements, of her modest and at the same time highly elegant behavior. He was absolutely elated, knowing that she deserved this moral award after all that she had survived and suffered before.

He considered it as a miracle - this amazing person he saw now was his love and the woman of his dreams and she was with him. In one week only he did it, he reached his goal, he found her, he found the love of his life. He felt at the moment that his heart was ready to explode from joy. For him, just to look at her, was, in truth, a seventh heaven or a ninth cloud as the proverbs said.

"Okay, I should go and get this ticket," Aaron said, trying to hold his fervor in check. He kissed Rosie on the forehead, quick and simple, and went to the cashier. "Bye, see you soon," she waved to him and then turned her attention back to her friends, merrily jabbering and giggling with them.

The seat that Aaron got was for a VIP – in the front row, right in the middle. He couldn't stop smiling during all other performances, in spite of some poems being quite sad. Today he didn't care. He was waiting for her. He knew that she would open her love to the world and he was almost shaky inside from the anticipation of that.

More than one hour passed until the host of the concert announced at last, "Rosalyn Vivano," and she walked out on the stage. "It is our final performance today," the host said, handing her the mic, and left. She hadn't said a word yet but already got an ovation, not only for her shockingly beautiful Ancient Greek style appearance, but mostly because everyone knew and loved her. Aaron noticed that most of the people around lifted their phones to be ready to record her presentation. However, she was just standing quietly and smiling, while waiting until the reaction of the audience subsided.

"My dear friends," Rosie said then, clear and loud. "I am very happy to be with you again. My poem today will be about a topic which is fresh to me, and I can say – very unusual. I never experienced anything of this level before. I am starting a new life now and I am happy to introduce to you my..." she almost shouted in her exhilaration, *"Ancient Greek Hymn of Love."*

She waved her hand with the mic up, then lowered it to her face and started reciting.

"They were playing their Hymns on kitharas and lyras
And drumming their rhythms on the leather drums.
I don't have any of these.
I am playing my Hymn with my voice and words
But it is no less powerful
Because it is the Hymn of my Love.

They were playing their Hymns for a rich harvest at fall,
For sowing their crops, for breeding their livestock.
I don't have any of these.
I am playing my Hymn for my modern Greek man
But it is no less powerful
Because it is the Hymn of my Love.

They were playing their Hymns for the sun and stars
To shine on them with the beams from the sky.
I have all of these.
My modern Greek man gave them to me with his love
And it is no less powerful
Because it is the Hymn of his Love.

They were playing their Hymns for the Gods on Olympus
Begging to care about them and protect them.

I have all of these.
My modern man is my Greek God, shielding me with his love.
And it is no less powerful
Because it is the Hymn of his love.

They were playing their Hymns for happiness to last
For a length of life of the loving couple.
We have all of these.
We are holding our hands and hugging each other tight
And this is no less powerful
Because it is the Hymn of our Love."

During the reading, Rosie excitedly raised her voice with each stanza and as the poem ended, she yelled out, "I love you, Aaron!", ran some steps to the edge of the stage, jumped down onto the audience floor, ran three more steps to the front row and plopped on his lap, hugging his neck.

The whole hall exploded with applause, the wild screams, whistles and cat-calls of the public. Shocked from the unexpectedness of her bold action, but at the same time unbelievably happy and proud in the deep of his heart, Aaron instinctively hugged Rosie. Then, not even grasping what he was doing, he stood up, lifted her and started going along the stage, carrying her in his arms to the left side of the hall. There were three-stepped stairs that led up to the stage.

Holding Rosie tight, while she snuggled to his chest, Aaron walked to the middle of the stage and lowered Rosie to stand on the floor. Like a referee at the boxing match, he lifted her hand which was still holding the mic, to proclaim the winner. She flung the mic out of her hand and turned to Aaron. They hugged each other and kissed with an undisguised passion, deep, long and unceasing.

"Rosalyn! Rosalyn!" the crowd chanted, applauding like crazy. The phones and the cameras flashed around taking pictures and making videos of their endless kiss on the stage. The numbers on the big screen above the stage kept running up until the loud ring of the bell signaled that the winning number was already reached.

The host returned to the stage and lifted the mic from the floor. "Our today's winner is Rosalyn Vivano," he announced, shouting to be heard through the deafening noise.

Aaron was almost unconscious, not realizing what he was doing and not giving a second thought to his own action. He didn't hear and didn't feel anything except Rosie's lips and her hot, craving body pressed to him and shaking in his hands with a passion. He was in a dream. They both were insane at the moment and it looked like they were stuck in this kiss forever.

The host smiled at them for a while, then began counting loud into his mic, acting as a conductor with the audience as his orchestra. He gestured to the crowd to number the minutes as well. The chanting of Rosie's name changed into the mob's rhythmical counting. "We will probably have a Guinness Record here tonight," the host laughed. "It would be the longest kiss on the stage ever."

The photos and videos of that kiss were already running all over the Internet - on Facebook, Instagram, Twitter and YouTube. Comments and Tweets began flashing all the way around the world.

"What is Rosalyn doing?" "Is she crazy?" "She is crazy." "Didn't you know that?" "Hey, who knows this guy?" "Who the hell is he?" "I know him. He is a doctor at our university." "Doctor? What the hell! He is an idiot!" "I hope she is not his patient, or he could lose his license." "He is probably married." "Could be." "He is from my neighborhood. I saw him there." "Me too. He is always walking with a child." "Omg!" "Maybe divorced?" "Who the hell knows!" "Did Rosalyn have a boyfriend before?" "Not since Ben was killed." "How do you know?" "She said it's fresh. Do you ever listen?" "What will they do next?" "The next concert they would screw on the stage probably?" "Unbelievable!" "It's disgusting!" "They're both obviously mentally ill!" "I am angry about this." "I think what they are doing requires a lot of bravery." "Yeah, I admire them!" "Bravo, Rosalyn!" And so on, so on, so on...

With the modern social media this video was all around the globe even before the kiss had stopped.

In Florida it ended up on the Facebook account of aunt Erin's daughter, Ashley, who forwarded it to her sister, Nicole, right away, even though it was already after midnight.

"Look, this is our cousin Arie," she wrote. "Auntie Beth said he did not come here because he is working late. I am wondering with which part of his body he is working that late! Lol!"

"Does he have a girlfriend? Should we ask Auntie Beth?" Nicole answered.

"Better not. If she knew, she would tell us about that."

"I didn't get it – why did that girl say in the poem that he is a 'modern Greek man'?

"Auntie Beth is Greek by her national background."

"Really? I didn't know that. That girl must be close to him if she already knows our family details."

"What do you think about kissing on stage, in public? Is Arie crazy or what? If Auntie Beth saw him in that video she would probably have a heart attack."

"Yeah, let's keep it away from her. Seniors usually do not use social media."

In the USA military detachment in Afghanistan, with the thirteen hour time difference from Seattle, it was already lunch time of the next day, as Private Alex Brown looked at his phone and exclaimed suddenly, "What the fuck!"

"What? What's happening?" inquired his fellow soldiers at the lunch table in an eatery tent.

"I'm just looking at what Ben's crazy girlfriend is doing," Alex answered, shaking his head in disbelief.

"What? What? Let me look!" The soldiers jumped up from their spots and surrounded Alex, peeking at his phone display.

"Which girlfriend? The one Ben stole from you?"

"He didn't steal. He won. We played heads or tails on her. Though I screwed her once anyway, when he wasn't at home."

The burst of laughter shook the tent. "How was it?"

"You know the saying – crazy in head, crazy in bed," Alex chuckled.

"Did she know it was you, Alex?"

"No way. I said I was Ben. We are from one egg. Even our mom had difficulty telling us apart. I am also guessing that the child she had miscarried when Ben was killed was mine."

"How do you know? DNA tests couldn't prove this. Your DNA with Ben would be the same."

"No, we didn't do any tests of course. I just counted the days. I don't know, maybe I was mistaken."

"She is kissing that guy now! What the hell will you do about that?"

"When I am discharged by Christmas, I will marry her. Ben and I promised each other, that the one of us who survived would marry her. However, of course, we both were thinking that I would be the one who is killed."

"What if she is already married to this guy then?"

Alex waved his hand. "I won't worry about that yet. Something will come up. Everything will be settled by itself. She did love Ben, it means she will love me."

In New York, the English teacher, Mary Oswald, who was Rosie's fan, admirer and promoter, watched the film on YouTube being full of excitement and pride for her beloved student. "I was not mistaken in recognizing her talent," she said to herself. "I knew that she had the potential to become a star. It's so sad that we moved to New York so far away from her and I can't follow her success closely. What a brave girl she is now! Exactly as I taught her to be! She learned how to stand up for herself and her love!"

In Seattle, Helen Harrison, looked at her Facebook account and found the video which was sent to her by one of her friends. "Wow! Arie!" she pronounced wistfully, shaking her head. "I was absolutely right to understand your personality. You're only capable of loving weak teens, like Ally was. The real woman is not for you, you damn idiot! But I still want you and I will get you back at any price because you are as attractive and handsome as a God. This schoolgirl is right – you are the Greek God from the damn Olympus."

Also, in Seattle, Ashot and Liam watched the same video at Liam's Facebook account. "What do you think about the behavior of our little kiddo?" Liam asked.

Ashot nodded a couple of times, like talking silently to himself, then sighed deeply. "I think we are good," he said calmly. "Everything is ready. She came to the proper point. I believe we will start the cure very soon."

CHAPTER 24

An assistant of the show came out to the stage and gave to the host the winning certificate and the envelope with money for Rosie while her kiss with Aaron still wasn't broken.

"Hey, Rosalyn," the host said and tapped her on the shoulder, "you have to accept your award now." She just waved her hand at him as if he was an annoying fly. Then the host turned to Aaron and said quietly without the microphone so nobody in the audience could hear him, "Sir, that's enough. Please, be serious here. Let her go. Now."

Hearing this said in a very strict tone of voice, returned Aaron to his senses. He gently pushed Rosie away by her shoulders. She turned to the host, smiled timidly and did a curtsy toward him and then a couple more curtsies to the public. Then she took her award certificate and envelope, grabbed the mic from the host and said, "Thank you, my friends. I appreciate your acceptance and understanding. I am so much in love that I don't know how else I could express it."

With that she grabbed Aaron's hand and pulled him toward the exit to the back of the stage. The concert was finished, the audience calmed down and began slowly walking out, gradually emptying the hall.

On the street, some friends still waved to her and shouted, "Bye," and "Congrats, Rosalyn!" She waved back to them. Aaron silently watched, keeping his arm on her shoulders, holding her tight and subconsciously trying to show to everybody that she belongs to him, really seriously, forever. So, everyone, keep away from her.

"Let's go sit in the park for a while," Rosie suggested, putting her jacket on because it was already late and night was getting chilly. "It is one week today since our first kiss. We are having a small anniversary. I would like to tell you something before we do what you promised for tonight, 'after the concert'."

"Okay," Aaron nodded, "I would like to talk to you about something too."

They walked to the park on the top of the hill, to the same bench as the week before.

"Look, Rosie," Aaron said as they sat. "I truly want us to spend some time alone, together, just the two of us and nobody else around. I know you are happy, proud and confident as Anastasia in public. I know that you love it, you are living for it, you are blossoming in it. I am happy and proud for you as well, believe me. You are a genius in poetry, you are obviously a talented actress on the stage, you are a social and friendly girl, and you are amazing in what you are doing."

"Thank you, Aaron," she whispered, lifting her face and looking him in the eyes. "I love you too."

He chuckled. "I am saying all of these not because I love you. I am trying to be objective and neutral here. I am just seeing your level and I really appreciate it. But it was kind of stressful and crazy for me tonight. I greedily want you only for me. Just for two or three days. I am not asking for more. I would like to take you to Leavenworth, a three-hour drive from here. It's a tiny German town deep in the mountains behind Stevens Pass. You never were in Europe, but part of it is right here, in Washington state. True, real Europe – Germany, Dutch, a bit of Switzerland. It is a live fairy tale. I swear – no luxury. We will take a modest hotel, drink German beer and eat German sausages with sauerkraut in a simple

German cafe, go to a Dutch bakery, see a Nutcrackers Museum and beautiful snowy mountains around. And there we will make love as much as we want. I will hold you in my hands and caress you endlessly. We will belong to each other and nobody will see or bother us. We will dedicate ourselves, one to another, completely. It will be our full love, happiness, and enjoyment. And then let's see what happens. Maybe everything will be okay. As I see now, we have been together for almost a week since my vacation began and you still are Rosie. You are good, right? Why not continue this for a while more? Tell me, my love? Do you want to try it with me?"

She took a deep breath and didn't answer for a long moment.

"Rosie, please, say that you want it too. This morning, in the Cascade Mountains, you begged me to take you. Remember? I am just suggesting to be more reasonable and comfortable, not a shortcut. And maybe after that we will be together forever."

"Aaron," she said quietly, visibly fighting tears. "Let me tell you something. I didn't tell you all that was happening during this past week. You saw me as Rosie everyday, but when I went home I had these awful attacks every night. It took my uncle hours to return me back to normal. If not for him... I don't know... I would already be in a mental institution or dead, probably. You are seeing me as I want to show myself to you. But you never saw me when I was in bad shape. I can't go with you somewhere for two or three days because I am not sure you will know how to manage me. You know that I love you madly, I want you madly, I want to go with you madly, but we both won't be safe. We both could be in danger and maybe die. It's torture to me. I can't live like this anymore, I want to die. I swear I want to kill myself because I want to be with you and I can't. It would be better, if you kill me. Or dump me and I will kill myself. We have no life together."

She covered her face with both hands, lowered it to her lap and sat motionlessly. Aaron couldn't say if she was crying or not, but he felt such a pity which was almost impossible to tolerate – the physical hurting in his heart and pain of soul combined together. It felt like their relationship was doomed. They practically couldn't do anything together. They couldn't go anywhere far from home, couldn't love each other fully and normally. It was a dead end.

He tenderly pulled Rosie to his chest, hugged her and bit his lips to suppress his tears while she now openly sobbed, hiding her face on his chest. They sat like this for a long time until she finally calmed a bit, sighing deeply several times.

"Look, my love," Aaron said, at last finding the strength to talk without tears in his voice. "I am not giving up on you. Let's work on that together. Do you want to be with me?"

She nodded, still sniffling.

"Do you love me, Rosie?"

She nodded again.

"Okay," Aaron continued. "I love you too. I want to be with you too. Then let's think together. Let's look for a solution. What were those attacks at night? Who were the girls?"

"Vally, another day Nora. A couple of times Rubi... Then Nora again."

"So, no Tobi?"

"No," she shook her head. "But they were very bad too. Listen, Aaron. I have a problem here. To be with you – I need to be cured. Right? I can't find the nerve to make my final decision that I want to be cured. I know that I could be cured completely, 100 percent. But then it's a big chance that I will lose all I have now – my poetry and all my other special abilities. I will lose connection to the universe particles, I will lose knowledge of the future, the way to communicate telepathically, to read thoughts, to move subjects with my thoughts. I will lose everything and become a simple, ordinary, regular woman that would be capable of being a housewife only. It scares me. I don't want it. You won't love me, if I am an ordinary person. You didn't pay any attention to me when you saw me the first time and thought that I was an ordinary girl."

Rosie showed her palms, moving them up and down, as though she was holding the scales, and said, "Look, here it is – 50/50 choice: to be with you as a dull but healthy woman, or to be with my poems, concerts, friends, my creative works and ingenious life.

I have to choose what I want more, what I love more. And I don't know. I can't make this choice. I am holding back because I am scared to lose you or to lose myself. I don't know what I could sacrifice."

"I will love you anyway, even as a 'dull housewife' as you say."

"No, Aaron, I know that you won't. You are just saying it now because you are exhilarated and want me. You are trying to cheat yourself. But you fell in love with me as you read my book, as you felt my soul and my unusual specialties and if all of these would be gone, you will be bored with my regularity, my simpleness and ordinariness, and your love will disappear, too. Though, my uncle swears to God that there would be another talent appear, like it happened with Liam. He is trying to convince me not to be scared of that. But I still am."

"What? Sorry, I didn't get it. Liam? What happened to him? How is your uncle related to all of this?"

"It doesn't matter," she waved her hand. "Sorry, I am confusing you because you don't know the whole story. It's not important yet. Just help me please Aaron. I know it's my decision, you can't make it for me. But give me some advice, give me your opinion. In short – do you want me to be cured or not?"

"Of course, yes. I want you to be cured, my love," he nodded convincingly. "I have no doubt for a second. Remember, you told me about this island with grass and sand. It's our future. It means that we can be together, right? We have a future together, right? Do you believe in yourself? Did you truly see this vision of our future?"

"Yes," Rosie whispered, lifting her face to him and finally smiling. "Yes, yes, yes. I am sorry. I forgot about that. Yes, we do have the future. It means we could fight the illness and we could win. Thank you, Aaron. Now I feel much better. Now I need to go home and talk to my uncle."

"Well, okay," he agreed, still not getting completely what's going on in her head and guessing that she had forgotten about their idea to have sex tonight. He promised it to her in the heat of the moment in the Cascade Mountains but wasn't sure yet if he was ready for that. In his mind's eye, he was still clearly seeing a warning on the story of his former young newlywed patient.

Then they drove to Rosie's building. Aaron stopped his car a bit aside from the main entrance between the bushes of the front garden, just in case they would want to make love. And his guess was right. As soon as they both unbuckled their seat belts, Rosie turned to him and hugged his neck and he couldn't avoid kissing her again.

"Okay," she whispered suddenly, pushing him away. "Let's go to the back. I want you, Aaron. I am scared of the whole night, but here, let's give it a short try and see what happens. Please, I am begging you, my love. I want you like crazy. Please, please."

Aaron nodded silently. He was so aroused from just one touch of her lips that he couldn't even talk. He turned the ignition off, put the car keys in his pocket and got out of the car. Rosie put her purse with the winning prize on the front seat, then hung her jacket on the back of the passenger seat and climbed out of the car as well.

They sat in the back seat, hugged each other and kissed for a few more minutes. Then Aaron very carefully moved her tunic shoulders down and slid his lips to her chin. She threw her head back, all shaky and moaning in his hands, as he kissed her throat. He tenderly pulled up the skirt of her tunic and caressed her legs. Then he unhurriedly moved his lips from her neck down to her shoulders and then, as he came to her breasts, he completely lost control and was really ready to take her right here, in the back seat of his car.

Aaron was so intoxicated by passion that he didn't notice the moment when her ardent moans turned into a growling. She was not shaking from fervid emotions anymore but convulsed strongly, her eyes rolling back, so that only the whites were visible which made them look scary like a monster's. She stretched her right arm down and pulled something from the pocket of her jacket hanging on the back of the front seat. Then he heard a click of some kind and a sharp piercing pain like an arrow slashed his cheek.

Rosie pushed him away with a wild scream and waved a penknife, making another slice wound on his arm, close to his shoulder. "I will not let you take my Aaron from me," she yelled. "Leave him alone, he is mine. Nobody takes him, he is mine. Mine forever. No, no, no! Leave him with me!"

It was so sudden that he was confused, but only for a second. Then, still baffled, he moved back from her, stretched his arm back, opened the car door and jumped out, closing the door behind him. He grabbed the clicker from his pocket and locked the car. Then he touched his wounds to check how bad they were. Actually, luckily for him, they were not deep at all, almost scratches, but very bloody. The sleeve of his light blue evening shirt was cut and blood was oozing from there. On his left cheek blood was already leaking down to his chin and neck. He tried to wipe it with his hand but just got it all smeared.

In a horrific shock, Aaron bent and looked at what was going on inside his car because he kept hearing Rosie's mad screams and growls. She was still fighting with someone who, in her imagination, wanted to take him away from her. Waving her knife, she cut the back seat beside her, where Aaron was sitting a minute ago, the backs of the both front seats, her own jacket, and even the upholstery on the ceiling of the car.

She held the top of the front seat with her left hand and Aaron saw that accidentally she cut her own lower arm with the knife. Her wound was probably much deeper than his because her blood instantly gushed out making the insides of his car look even worse than before. The blood everywhere was really giving the perception of a murder scene. Her white tunic was ruined the same as his car. Everything was ruined – their love, their life. It was the real end – the end of everything sacred and beautiful that they ever had.

Aaron was scared mostly that someone would hear it and call 911. Rosie then would end up in a mental institution for sure. He didn't want that to happen in spite of everything. He wanted to deal with her by himself. Fortunately, the soundproof condition of his car was pretty good and her screams and growls were muffled, so they weren't heard from a distance. It was far after midnight and the street and a little square in front of the building were deserted. Aaron, standing by the car, was the only one who could hear her outburst at the moment. He was appalled and dismayed, not knowing what to do.

Obviously she was Tobi now – the most aggressive and angry one of all her personalities; Tobi, who had not appeared yet during the whole period of their dating, and now was definitely triggered by sexual arousal. It didn't take her forty-two times of sexual interaction to turn into a monster, as she calculated for his former patient – the young man who killed his newlywed wife. It took her maybe only ten minutes of foreplay to turn into Tobi and to have a severe attack of her illness.

It was visible proof that her condition was much worse than those of his previous patient, which Aaron actually suspected. He tried to avoid sex with her as long as it was possible, he expected this horror, he predicted it and he was scared for her now. He had no idea how to stop her, how to take her to the hospital to take care of her wound because otherwise she could bleed to death.

His hands were shaking and a painful spasm squeezed his gut – the love of his life was dying in front of his eyes; he was clearly losing her forever. What was left for him to do? Just pray... but he didn't know how, he never did. "Oh God, help me please!" he moaned in despair. "Help me to save her. Protect her somehow. What should I do with her now?"

A few minutes passed which felt for him as an eternity, until he noticed that Tobi finally dropped her knife on the floor, beat her fists several more times on the backs of the front seats and then fell down from the back seat of the car to the floor, as well. Aaron watched, holding his breath, realizing that at last she lost consciousness. He unlocked the back door of the car, carefully stretched his arm inside and grabbed the knife from almost under her face. He pressed the button and with a light click the bloody blade disappeared inside the holder. He put the knife into his pocket.

Now it was time to act. Aaron lifted the girl from the floor, laid her on the back seat that was cut completely into a bloody mush. He took off his shirt and tried to tear the sleeves off. It wasn't easy to do, so he used her knife to cut them away. With one sleeve he tied her arm above the wound really tight to stop bleeding and with the rest of his shirt he made a sort of a dressing over the wound and secured it, tightening with his second sleeve. Then he thrust his car keys and her folded knife back into his pants pockets.

After that Aaron pulled her out of the car and carried her in his arms - for the second time during the evening. He headed toward the main building door, pressed buttons at the speaker, waited a few seconds and when a man answered, "Hello," he barely pronounced with a husky shaky voice, "I brought Rosie home. Open, please."

The door moved aside with a quiet buzz and Aaron entered the lobby carefully holding his unconscious loved one by his chest. The trace of the blood drops followed him on the light cream marble floor. He came to the elevator and pressed the button with his bloody hand, smearing it too. Then he pressed the button inside for the 3d floor, leaving spots of blood – his and Rosie's - on the golden panel and on the floor of the elevator, as well. The mirror on the elevator wall showed his awful condition – he was disheveled, pale, with matted hair and shaking lips. His face, left arm, both hands and t-shirt were all smeared with blood. As was the once white tunic that Rosie wore, all torn now into pieces; as was her tangled hair which fell from her bun and hung loose.

On the 3d floor Aaron exited the elevator and walked some steps to the suite #302. He didn't need to buzz or knock – the door opened as he approached, and he was hit by one more unexpected shock of the evening: the old warder from the *Youth Shelter,* the psychiatric nurse, Thomas Spencer, was standing in front of him.

"Hello, Dr. Dispenmore," Ashot said, moving the door wider, so Aaron would be able to enter with the burden in his arms. "Welcome to my private psychiatry clinic. I've been waiting for you for so long."

PART 2
THE CURE

CHAPTER 25

As Aaron entered the suite, he saw, behind Ashot, another man, tall and blond, with a big professional camera on his shoulder, filming his entrance. He didn't care. Nothing reflected at the moment in his consciousness. He could walk, move, almost like a zombie, but he wasn't in much better mental condition than Rosie. He couldn't think or understand almost anything that was going on around him.

"Follow me," Ashot said sharply and led Aaron through the spacious hallway toward one of the bedrooms at the far end which was obviously Rosie's room.

As they entered, Ashot opened the door of a closet and took out a lot of medical equipment wrapped in sterile packaging. He opened one of them and spread a plastic sheet over the bed while Aaron was still standing beside him, holding Rosie tight to his chest.

"Put her on the bed," Ashot ordered, "and sit over there." He nodded toward an armchair, seeing that Aaron was not in any condition to make even this kind of a simple decision.

Aaron lowered his unconscious burden onto the bed and sat across from her in the armchair that had been pointed out to him. He put his elbows on his knees and propped his head on his hands. He was shivering so strongly that his teeth chattered. The more time passed from the beginning of this horrific attack, the bigger shock began to affect him.

Ashot glanced back at the line of the blood traces that led from the door of the suite all the way down to Rosie's bed. Unpleasantly shaking his head, he said to the other man, "Darling, would you mind checking the elevator and lobby for blood? We don't want to scare our neighbors. And also, take care of his car, please."

The man stop filming, put his camera on the table, approached Aaron and stretched his arm. "Car keys, please," he requested in soft, dulcet manner of the voice. Aaron looked up at him, not quite understanding. "You car keys," the man repeated, this time much tougher. Aaron mechanically took his keys out from his pocket and passed them to him. The man left right away.

Ashot rolled in a metal surgical table from somewhere, covered it with another sterile sheet, put latex gloves on and started to take out tools from the packages. "You did a pretty good job," he commented sarcastically, while unwrapping pieces of Aaron's destroyed beautiful festive shirt from Rosie's arm and throwing them into a waste bin. "How did she cut herself?"

Aaron couldn't say anything. A strong spasm was still squeezing his throat. He silently pulled out from his other pocket Rosie's folded knife, all covered with blood, and placed it on the coffee table beside his armchair. Ashot looked at it askance. "Oh, Ben's knife. He gave it to her for protection. They were living in a pretty rough neighborhood. I didn't know that she still had it. I didn't allow her to carry knives usually, but she was cunning enough somehow to sneak it behind my back. Poor kiddo."

In spite of his shaky condition, Aaron couldn't help notice with some kind of admiration how Ashot acted. He was calm, serious, collected, rational and reasonable in each of his movements. He obviously knew what he was doing, preparing syringes, tiny bottles with medications, needles, threads, IVs, bandages, tubes, getting ready for surgery on Rosie's arm. He gave her a shot, maybe an anesthetic, to make sure that she didn't wake up during the procedure. Then he turned to Aaron.

"You better go and take a shower," he said in a very strict tone of voice. "Throw all your clothes into the laundry basket. There is a bathrobe you can wear after. And there is a medicine cabinet also.

You should take care of your wounds as well, and you are perfectly capable of doing that yourself."

Normally Aaron wouldn't tolerate this kind of tone, but he was so lost and helpless now that, again, it did not register in his head. He obeyed silently and slowly shuffled to the large bathroom, adjoined to the bedroom. It was visible that it belonged to Rosie because it was full of women's items on the counter beside the sink with a big mirror above it.

There was also a closet with folded towels on shelves and several bathrobes on hangers. A medicine cabinet on the wall was located beside it. Aaron found himself finally inside Rosie's world, with her friends, in her bedroom, in her shower. He craved to know everything about her and here it was in front of him, beside him and around him. But it didn't get him any closer to a solution to her mystery.

He still didn't know which of the men was her 'uncle'? Why was the old warder from the *Youth Shelter* here? Why did she want him to meet them? How could they possibly help with her cure? There were no less questions than before; in this situation - even more. And the worst of them was – how could they be together and love each other with her being in such a dangerous condition? What future could they possibly have together, if any?

Aaron stubbornly refused to believe in this danger before, he had pushed away all these thoughts. He tried to convince himself that maybe Rosie would be okay, maybe it all was just a lie or some sort of misunderstanding in her file from Dr. Hertz. Now he saw it with his own eyes, he felt it in a painful deep scratch on the top of his arm and the light, but bloody one - on his cheek. Their love was doomed. They couldn't be together. They should part forever. Must he give up, finally?

In spite of the despair, Aaron knew that she occupied such a huge part of his being, that he couldn't live without her. He truly believed her words that she couldn't live without him, as well. It was a dead end. The second time in his life he loved a woman deeply, strongly, with all his heart and soul, and for the second time the way of this love was only one – to death. He really didn't know what to do now.

Moving weakly and senselessly, Aaron took a shower, dried his wounds with cotton balls from the medicine cabinet, put the tincture of iodine on them, squeezing his teeth from burning pain, and then covered them with band-aids. Then he slowly walked back into the bedroom, sat in the same armchair and lowered his head on his hands again.

Ashot had already finished with his stitches and Rosie's arm was securely bandaged and wrapped in plastic on top of it. Beside her bed was a prepared IV holder with a bag full of some solution, but it wasn't connected to her vein yet. However, what shocked Aaron the most was that the old man, while sitting beside the bed on a low stool with scissors in his hand, was cutting Rosie's long blond bloody hair and throwing it into a wastebasket.

"Why are you doing that?" Aaron whispered. The shower relaxed him a bit and helped him overcome the spasm in his throat, so he could talk now, though very quiet. "She loved her hair..."

"For the cure she should be shaved anyway," Ashot answered, not looking at him. "Now you need to carry her into a bathtub and wash her. She has to be clean in bed. She can't stay all bloody and she can't take a shower until her wound is healed. While in the bathtub her arm could hang outside." He turned to Aaron and, noticing his confused facial expression, said strongly and convincingly, "You... you, Aaron. You are her lover. You wanted to have sex with her. You can see her naked and take care of her. Neither I nor Liam can do that. She is a daughter for us. So, go ahead and don't waste my time. She really needs to have an IV connected immediately and get her alternative medications for restoration of the blood loss. As you understand, we can't take her to the hospital for blood transfusion because from there she will go straight into a mental institution for life. We need to fix her here and then start her cure as soon as possible."

"What cure?... How?" Aaron inquired, stuttering. "There... is... no cure."

"Okay," Ashot stood up and made a step to him, staring at him with angry narrowed eyes. "If not for your arrogance, Aaron... If you had listened to me that day when you came to the shelter, looking for her, we would now be almost halfway done on her cure, and this poor child wouldn't be suffering so much because of you. I will never forgive you for such an enormous amount of pain that you caused her during this 'happy dating time'.

"You behaved like a selfish bastard. You were entertaining yourself, showering her with gifts, throwing money right and left, enjoying your rich and powerful lifestyle, and pretending that you are doing that for her. You were playing with her feelings, at the time when the poor child needed only one thing – a cure - and nothing else from you. It's unforgivable for a doctor not to see that and not to understand. But you were completely blind and too busy, admiring your own generosity and refusing to see the tragedy she was enduring.

"You could deserve forgiveness for that only if you would listen to me and do what I am saying now without any questions... Of course, if you only really love her, as you claim... This is the moment for you to prove your love, finally, and help to return this amazing child to a normal human life. If it was just blah-blah-blah on your part, like you, straight bastards, are doing with the girls only to get them in bed, then I will kick your sorry ass out of here in a minute. And I kick really harshly, believe me.

"So, take her and go wash her; do what a loving caring partner is supposed to do when his beloved woman is sick, or wounded, or just had a surgery, or gave childbirth. Damn, you're not a baby, Aaron! I shouldn't teach you these things. You had a wife, you had a child, you have enough experience. You're a freaking doctor, for God's sake! Act like a man at least once."

The harsh tone of the old man's voice sobered Aaron.

"Are you a medical doctor? Do you have a cure for schizophrenia?" he asked bewildered, remembering now that every time Rosie was talking about her potential cure, or when he was swearing that he will do anything in the world to cure her, she was saying, "You have to talk to my uncle, Aaron."

"Yes, I am. And yes, I do," Ashot answered sharply. "I told you that when we met in the shelter, but you ignored that. You were sure that I was some kind of crock because you saw my tag as a nurse and heard about my other duties at that place."

"Then why were you a nurse, maintenance and security guy at the *Youth Shelter,* but not a doctor?"

"There are different circumstances in life," Ashot shrugged. "We could talk about that later, if you cooperate now. Go and wash her. I will give you half an hour for that. Then she should be on the IV – blood transfusion alternatives - haemostatic and erythropoiesis agents, at least until the morning. Cut her dress and everything..." he added abruptly, passing Aaron the scissors and walked out of the room.

Aaron took a deep breath. He hated this man for his angry accusations and diminishing of his sincere actions toward Rosie, but he really had no choice. He loved her and she was in danger because of her blood loss. She needed to be treated. And this her damn uncle obviously knew what to do. Maybe he really was a professional doctor? Aaron had no time now to comprehend this.

He knelt beside the bed and, first, unlaced Rosie's sandals and took them off. They were actually clean, somehow no blood ended up on them. Her toes were thin and tender, the nails were polished with a light pink color, almost not visible. She always had this stylish taste in clothes and makeup. Where did she get it from? Who taught her? At what place – in the shelter, in school, at home? He took her feet in his hands, lowered his face to them and kissed them. There wasn't anything sexual in this move, just his pure and sacred 'holy oasis' feeling.

Sadly, her Ancient Greek white tunic was all soaked in blood, as well as torn into rags with that knife. Aaron unbuckled her golden belt, then cut the whole tunic to the top and moved it to the sides. She didn't wear any bra, there was no need for it. Her breasts were strong like apples and were sticking up by themselves, not requiring any extra support. And again, there weren't any sexual feelings. He sensed as if he was watching an Ancient Greek statue where a nude human body was almost divine by its holy beauty and designed only for worshiping in their temples.

The last thing Aaron cut and removed was her panties on which the blood soaked through the tunic. He couldn't help notice that her pubic hair was quite blond as well and neatly trimmed, but still this view didn't excite him at all – he was immersed into a care-giving and a medical approach now much more than in a private personal relationship. Though, Ashot accused him of being 'her lover', in reality Aaron never had sex with her and never saw her naked. However, he did love her. Was it an appropriate use of the word 'lover' or not? He wasn't sure himself.

But what did strike him, were the two big scars on the sides of Rosie's stomach, not fresh, but still a bit pinkish, so, about three years old. That's what was left of her two suicide attempts after Ben's death. She thrust the knife into her stomach, twice, and it was what possibly, on the top of a nervous break down, forced a miscarriage. Now he realized why she always wore a full bathing suit on the beach, not a mini-bikini. After wounds on her stomach were sewn and the knife was taken away from her she attempted another suicide, as Aaron knew from Dr. Hertz file - an overdose on opiate pills in the hospital.

He shuddered once again, imagining what this poor girl had survived, then collected himself, lifted her in his arms and carried her into the bathroom.

Aaron put her inside the tub, washed away the blood and changed the water three times, until it finally ran clear. Then he dried her body with a towel and her short cut hair with a hairdryer. With difficulties he put a bathrobe on her and carried her back to the bedroom. Ashot and the second man were already there. Aaron realized that it was probably Ashot's husband, Liam, whom Rosie had earlier told him about.

The plastic sheet containing all Rosie's bloody destroyed clothes was now removed from her bed. Aaron put her on the clean sheet and covered her with a blanket, as Ashot rolled up the sleeve of her robe and inserted the IV needle into her vein. He secured it with medical tape and put the sleeve down.

"Here are your keys and your phone. You left it in your car," Liam said to Aaron, putting his stuff on the coffee table. "I moved my car into the visitor parking and yours – into my spot, and I covered it with a tarpaulin, so nobody could look inside, see the bloody damage and call the police. I also washed all the traces of blood on the lobby floors and in the elevator. So far, we are safe."

"Thank you," Aaron murmured. He really couldn't imagine what would happen with his car, nor with himself and Rosie. It was a life changing moment and he was still completely lost.

"Okay, now she will be good for several hours," Ashot said, checking the flow from the IV bag. "Then I will measure her temperature and blood pressure, and we will monitor her periodically further from there. It's four in the morning already. We all need to sleep as well. You can lay beside her, Aaron. You need some rest, too."

"Thank you for the permission," Aaron answered sarcastically, trying to suppress his sharp rejection of this man but being unable to hide it in full.

"You are welcome," Ashot uttered through gritted teeth and Aaron felt that his hate was mutual. Liam was just observing silently. Then he took his camera from the table and Ashot grabbed Rosie's knife, and they left.

Aaron laid beside Rosie under her blanket, hugged her and put his head on her shoulder. She was breathing quietly, calmly and rhythmically in her sleep. It was a good sign. As a doctor, he evaluated that all medical care for her was done properly, even perfectly for home conditions.

However, as his shock gradually subsided, Aaron began feeling really hurt emotionally by those unfair accusations he got from this warder, Thomas Spencer, or Ashot, who was her damn 'uncle' as he realized now. Aaron felt humiliated as a professional, as a man and mostly as a loving soul, loyal to that poor girl. He was hurt, confused, lost and helpless at the moment. Emotions were suffocating him and he couldn't hold the tears of his pain inside anymore. He squeezed his teeth as strong as he could, not allowing himself to make a sound which those men could possibly hear, and during the next couple of hours he finally cried himself to sleep.

CHAPTER 26

As he woke up, Aaron couldn't understand, at first, where he was, what happened and how he got there. He laid quietly on the unfamiliar bed, alone, trying to remember.

He took his phone from the bedside table and looked at the time. It was two p.m. He slept almost all day, after he fell asleep at six in the morning and missed his Skype session with Beth and Laurie. They probably were worried about him because when he checked his missed call list, there were three calls from his mother.

Aaron really didn't want to talk to her now, nor to show his face on screen with a wound on the cheek. So, he texted her, "Sorry I missed Skype. Extremely busy. Everything is okay. Love". With that he felt that as a son and father he was done with his duty and now was time to return to reality.

Rosie wasn't in her bed beside him. The IV holder stood there with an empty medication bag and a disconnected needle hanging on it. Where has she gone? To another room or to the hospital?

Aaron saw his clothes on the armchair all clean and neatly folded. As he touched them, he noted they were still warm, just recently taken out from a dryer. Someone took care to do his laundry. In the distance he could hear the sound of a vacuum and realized that there must be a housekeeper working.

He went to the bathroom to discover that all the waste and laundry baskets were empty and everything around the room was fresh. So, it really was the housekeeper who did the cleaning here, while he was sleeping. What did she think, noticing him in Rosie's bed? It didn't really matter, but the thought made him confused. He had never found himself in a situation like this before.

Aaron took a shower, then checked his wounds. The bleeding had stopped, so there was no need for band-aids. He just put some iodine on them once more and left them open to dry and to heal by themselves. He had no shaver here, so he left his face unshaven to look almost like these men in the movies, designed to appear sexier. He decided, for one day, it would be okay.

Then Aaron got dressed. Since his best evening light-blue shirt was torn into bloody pieces, he had an undershirt without sleeves. The wound on the top of his arm was in full view, as was the other one on his cheek. It didn't look good but he had no choice. He also didn't know where his shoes were, so he walked out of the bedroom in socks.

The apartment was huge. It had two living rooms, a dining room, several dens, three bedrooms, a few dressing and storage rooms. Aaron heard the housekeeper working somewhere in the distance but didn't see her. It looked like no one else was at home. He walked around, looking for Rosie. Then he heard her laughing and walked toward her voice.

The glass door to the patio was open and Aaron finally saw her sitting there at the table with the old warder beside her. They both wore simple home clothes, shorts and t-shirts. However, her uncle, Ashot, also had his big antique golden cross on a chain on his chest with which he apparently never parted. They were discussing something while attentively gazing at the bunch of papers in open folders in front of them. Aaron approached the patio door and quietly said, "Hello."

"Aaron!" Rosie exclaimed, jumped from her chair, ran to him and hugged him. "Did you sleep well, my love? I left on purpose so as not to bother you." She glanced up at his face, then at his arm, and her excited voice died off in surprise. "What's happened? Did

I do that? Oh my God! I am so sorry. Look, I cut myself too." She lifted her hand, displaying a thin bandage on it. Her wound was evidently doing better. "I don't know how it was possible. Why? I am so sorry, Aaron." She hid her face in his chest.

He subconsciously placed his arms around her, bowed his head to kiss her hair, but now there was none, so he stopped. Rosie was probably already shaven because she had a bandanna on enveloping her head tightly. She caught his move and smiled bashfully. "Yes, my love. You see? I have no more hair, but it will grow again. Don't worry."

"I don't. I swear," Aaron smiled back and kissed her forehead instead.

"Come here, let me introduce you to my uncle." She grabbed his hand and pulled him to the patio.

It was huge and had a glass enclosure, so it was more of a sun-room, than a patio only. All the windows were wide open now and it felt for Aaron as if he was outside. A light sea breeze tenderly touched his face, bringing the ocean smell of freshness and salt. A big dining table with chairs stood beside the entrance. At the far end were a counter with a coffee maker, the shelves full of cups and wine glasses, and a small refrigerator with a see-through door. Many different drinks were visible inside it.

Aaron noticed on the shelf a wine glass with a little yellow birdie in it and in the corner by the open window - the vase with glass flowers. Those were his gifts from Tacoma's *Glass Museum*.

Above the dining table on the wall hung a black-wood African mask, which Aaron bought for Rosie at the Lynden Fair market. It touched his heart that all his presents were recognized there and used exactly as they were supposed to be.

As Rosie and Aaron stepped over the threshold of the patio, holding hands, she addressed the old man who was still sitting by the table, "Uncle, this is my Aaron. You know I love him, so, please, welcome him to our home."

"We met already, kiddo," Ashot answered morosely, not lifting his eyes from the papers. "And I would be really happy to welcome him into our cure project, if he cares enough about you and is ready to do that for you."

"He told me that he loves me too and he would do anything possible to cure me. Right, my love?" While hugging Aaron, she lifted her face to him and stared, begging, into his eyes. He nodded silently. "Okay," Rosie continued, smiling. "You must be hungry, you missed breakfast and lunch. Sit, please, here. Let me make something for you, probably coffee first?"

Aaron sat beside the table while Rosie intended to run to the counter with a coffee maker but Ashot stopped her.

"Sit, kiddo," he said tensely. "He is perfectly capable of making coffee himself."

Rosie came to a halt and looked confused. She didn't know what to do. Aaron, irritated that this man was talking about him as if he wasn't here, stood up and went silently to the counter to make his coffee. Luckily the machine was the same as he had at home. While the coffee was brewing, he turned to Ashot and asked matter-of-factly, "Why do you hate me so much, Mr. Spencer?"

"Arrogance, egotism, disrespect, distrust. Many 'nice' qualities that you have," the old warder answered, not even turning to look at him.

"You don't know me," Aaron objected.

"I have enough experience to see through people."

"I wasn't in a proper state of mind last night to answer your assertions, but now I can. How could you know about our dates with Rosie? Why could you accuse me of... God knows what? Did she tell you about our dates?" Aaron insisted, returning to the table with a cup of coffee in his hand and sitting in his previous spot. "This is exactly what I was against. I don't want any interruption or influence in our relationship. I have already had a very bad experience with my wife. She was very naive and her friend manipulated her into sharing the details of our life. Then it was used against us, to destroy our relationship, literally - my wife was murdered because of that."

"I have no intention to destroy your relationship," Ashot shrugged, pursing his lips. "My child loves you and I want her to be happy. So, I want you to be together. Rosie didn't tell me anything about you and your dating, but her other personalities did. After each date, she was endlessly crying as Vally, feeling that she didn't deserve you. Or as Nora, who was full of fear and horror to lose you. Or as Rubi, when she was scared of an unknown crime in which one of you, or both, would be killed... You had fun with her, but I had pain with her because of you. Of course, I worked with her all night, I fixed her temporarily – to go and have fun with you again the next day. But it made me angry that you, as a psychiatrist, didn't see that. I wanted your help! I needed your help in my project to cure her. I was really worried that being so much in love she will have sex with you and it could end up badly. And I was right. It was exactly what happened."

"In spite of all your experience that you are so proud of," Aaron protested actively, "you still don't know me. There was no egotism in my actions with Rosie at all. I didn't try to show off. I really did everything for her that I thought was the best. Maybe I was wrong, I don't know. I don't have any experience in dating. I never dated another woman in my life. My wife and I have been together since we were sixteen. We never dated, we went out with a big company of friends – schoolkids and we were living together in my house. There wasn't any dating in the traditional meaning of the word. After her death, I didn't date anyone ever. Rosie was the first woman whom I really wanted to go out with. I wished to show her a beautiful part of life and the world which she didn't have a chance to know before. I did it sincerely for her.

"Rosie told me that you survived a lot of suffering," Aaron continued heatedly, "but you shouldn't be jealous of my 'luxury and privileged American life' which I was born with. I endured probably no less, when my father was slowly and painfully dying in my arms, and when the love of my life was killed right in front of my eyes. And once more, when it almost happened yesterday with another woman whom I love more than anything in the world. It's childish to make a competition as to who lived the worst." Aaron stopped talking for a moment while fighting a nervous spasm in his throat. The tragedies that he survived really taxed his nervous system and made him too sensitive and vulnerable to the outside world, but he didn't want to show it to that stranger.

Finally, he found the inner power to go on. "Also, I refused to work with you after we talked at the shelter, because I was raised here, in the mentality of my country. We believe that everything that people do has to be legit. You should be a licensed doctor to cure people. Of course, it looked suspicious to me when you suggested it. I don't know all the circumstances, I don't know the whole story of your life. Maybe you are a genius doctor and have a real cure for Rosie. It could be, but I have the right to have my doubts. This is not arrogance, not disrespect and not distrust. It's just my confusion and misunderstanding. Instead of hating me and accusing me unfairly, you should explain your situation to me."

During his agitated speech, Rosie came to Aaron, sat on his lap and hugged him. He held her tight. "If not for this girl, I would be long gone and would not even talk to you, Mr. Spencer," Aaron kept on."But I know that in my lab, in my university I don't have any cure for her. I am clutching at your suggestion as the last straw of hope. If she couldn't be cured, there is no way for both of us to continue like that. For us there is only one choice – her cure or death."

"Hmm," Ashot smirked, shaking his head. "It sounds too dramatic and theatrical. But the main point is that the both of you agreed to be involved in my cure project. We talked with Rosie the whole morning about that. I know she is a little scared to lose her talents. However, she decided that she loves you more than everything else and she is ready to take a risk and try. For you, Aaron. Right, kiddo?"

"Yes, uncle," Rosie nodded, "but don't forget, I had one special condition and I would like Aaron to know about that as well. I need to have one last performance at the Poetry Club next Tuesday as a farewell to my friends, my talent, my youth and all my previous life. It's important to me to part with all of them properly and beautifully. Then I could start my new life.

"And one more very serious thing, uncle Ashot," she kept talking, knitting her brows. "I really don't like it when you are hurting Aaron's feelings. He is the nicest, kindest person I ever met and I care about him wholeheartedly. I want you to apologize to him and you both shake hands in agreement for the project of my cure. If you love me, you both will do that, please."

"Okay," Aaron pronounced nonchalantly, standing up and stretching his arm toward Ashot. "Rosie told me that you're a man of God, Mr. Spencer. You should know that love and forgiveness are more important than hate, which is a sin, by the way. I still remember that from my childhood classes at church. I am not as religious now, but I can forgive you for the sake of my love for this girl."

The old man raised as well and shook his hand, although not with a happy face. "Sorry, Aaron, I didn't want to cause you pain," he said sadly and apologetically. "I was a little overprotective of this child because the accident last night wasn't easy for me as well.

"I would just like to explain to you, Aaron, that the cure which we will do here will be a sure ticket for you to that New York Psychiatry Scientific Conference. I will go there with you to represent my discovery as yours, pretending to be your assistant only. My special circumstances force me to do that for one simple reason – I don't have an American doctor diploma nor a license. In reality I am doing that for you. I am sacrificing my scientific invention of the century for you. I am giving you a healthy woman in your bed and the Nobel Prize in your pocket. And I would like this to be respected and appreciated by you."

"It definitely will if it proves to be true," Aaron nodded, having difficulty believing his own ears. Of course, he craved to cure Rosie, but the fraudulence and the illegality of the idea to present this treatment to the conference as his own jarred upon him very much. It was truly confusing to use someone's discovery this way. He felt that it would be kind of shameful because he didn't deserve it. It would feel like he stole something important and sacred from someone's life. But he wasn't a thief, it was not very easy for him to agree to this kind of commitment.

Only for his love of Rosie he would dare to go for the unknown process of a cure. As to the authorship of the scientific part of it... Aaron decided that they will return to this subject later. When and if Rosie would be proven completely healthy, before going to the conference they would discuss it again. Maybe there could be found a possible way for Ashot's paternity of the cure to be established? Aaron would help to do that for him gladly as a gratitude for Rosie's health.

As for now, he asked in an uncertainty, "If it's all for me, as you are saying, then what is it there personally for you, Ashot?"

"I want to make my discovery widely known to society and have it officially recognized. As a result, it would be available for all ill people as a regular treatment – to let them become healthy and return to a normal life. It could only happen, if it is presented by an official, qualified, licensed American doctor, Board Certified Psychiatrist, exactly who you are, Aaron.

"It would be, also, a huge pleasure for me to get the acceptance for the work of my life, doesn't matter whose name is on it. If it would be the name of a man who helped me to cure my kiddo, I am okay with that. And mainly, I want to make this child healthy and happy finally." He nodded toward Rosie. She hugged Ashot and kissed him on the cheek. Then she turned to Aaron and kissed him as well, and hugged him tight.

"Thank you, guys," Rosie said, beaming. "I love you both, though in different ways, but believe me – really, really strongly."

CHAPTER 27

Liam came home at about four p.m. with two full bags of groceries. He peeked through the patio door and made a gesture to silently greet everybody, then asked, "Dinner?"

"Yes!" Rosie jumped up from Aaron's lap and ran to the kitchen to help him cook. Aaron had already noticed that Liam was a man of few words but many actions. He did things unnoticeable but very useful, helpful and mostly silent. These were the nice and likable qualities of his character.

For some time, Aaron and Ashot were left alone at the patio table. "Well, young man," the old doctor said, "before we start to do anything, I need to make an orientation session for you. We will begin the cure in two days, on Saturday."

"But Rosie asked to perform next Tuesday at the concert," Aaron reminded.

"No problem with that. We will administer one treatment on Saturday and the next one - in a week. We will need a break to analyze the results and do the whole paperwork during this week. Liam will be filming a documentary of the whole process of the cure, so he also needs time for the editing of his film. Rosie will rest for a couple of the days and then she will be perfectly ready for her concert.

"You, Aaron, have two days before the first session to familiarize yourself with the process and to understand what to expect, and for that I am giving you all this material to read." He moved to Aaron a pack of folders which they were studying previously with Rosie. "These are twenty folders of my patients whom I cured in Armenia in 1980-85. I brought them to the USA as microfilm in my pocket and then deciphered them and translated them to English. Also here is Liam's file. I cured him here in the year 2000. You, of course, can't use them in your future records of Rosie's cure because of the time difference. When I did my first cases, you weren't even born yet, and in 2000 you were a fifteen-year- old boy.

"So, we will base the description of Rosie's treatment on her individual case only as required for the conference – 'the one single cured patient'. But, you need to know all the previous cases because they show clearly how the discovery was made and worked, and with Liam – how it worked on American soil.

"Here is one separated folder about my research of the human body auras and their connections to the energy fields of the universe," Ashot continued. "It is specifically a scientific part of my discovery. And here is also another isolated folder with the biochemical research of a natural ingredient – the blue clay. Both studies, about auras and clay, were known to scientists before me, but I combined them together which was never done earlier in the history of science by anyone. I proved that the unique quality of the blue clay - to suck in all viruses and bacteria and any kind of radiation, sun's and nuclear - is possible to use to intake the particles of the human auras, as well. This is the core of my discovery. No one knew that before. I guess that no one knows it even now because my discovery has not been published or announced anywhere.

"And the second part of it is related directly to psychiatry. I did a lot of research and found out that schizophrenia is caused by the distortion of a patient's aura and disconnection of it from the universal feed. By fixing this connection - completely annihilating the old broken aura and renewing it - we could cure schizophrenia.

It was just my guess. I tried it with patients who had nothing to lose anyway – they couldn't get worse because they were at the very bottom of their condition. And I got a nice surprise. It worked. I cleaned their auras with the blue clay – and the rest happened by itself, automatically. The new auras appeared as soon as the old ones were flown to the universe at the very end of the cure and the illness was flown away with them. The person got healthy in a blink of an eye.

"The process of cleaning the aura – that's pretty long and not easy, however, it's still possible to do," Ashot went on with his explanation. "I did this twenty times in Armenia to prove for myself that it works. Then I proved it here with Liam – because, you know, I had my doubts about the angle of the positions of the continents, America and Eurasia, toward the universe. I also had my doubts about the probable difference in the quality of the clay. The chemical ingredients of it could be contrary on the other side of the globe. But no – everything was the same. Our mother Earth is the one for all of us living on it's surface. The result of the cure was perfect - same as in Armenia. You see Liam now. He has been absolutely healthy for fifteen years, though his conditions were worse than Rosie's. He had twelve personalities, so it required twelve weeks of work – one week for each. With Rosie, seven weeks will be enough. Although, with one difference. She is a woman and during these seven weeks she will have her period, possibly even twice. During that time we should take a break – the immune system of a woman's body is pretty low at those moments. She needs more rest to be protected from the possibilities of some side effects and complications. You could read about that in my Armenian files – there were eighteen men and two women; and the women's treatment took a bit longer for that reason.

"So, if we give Rosie nine weeks for the whole cure, in the middle of September she would be completely healthy and we could register for admission to the New York conference in December. Perfect timing!"

"Wow!" Aaron said, shaking his head. "It sounds unbelievable, but, honestly – very interesting. Nothing like that would ever come to my mind. And how does this clay work practically? What are you doing with it? Are you putting it on the patient? Are you touching the patient?"

"Not with one finger. Ever. Any touch and approach to the patient could stress the aura, disturb the flow of the particles and destroy the whole cure. I sit about six feet away from the patient and I work as a sculptor. I make a Clay Mask of the patient's face from the clay. This Mask is supposed to suck in all the sick, broken particles of the distorted aura. It is doing practically the whole healing, not me."

"And what does the patient do?"

"Just talk. I am asking questions and the patient answers them and tells me everything they feel and want to tell about their thoughts, senses, ideas, doubts, experiences, sufferings... Anything. But they should tell the truth. Lying wouldn't help because it would activate the wrong parts of the aura and wrong particles. However, I never had any trouble with that. People always tell the truth in these kinds of intimate confessions. There is a little bit of hypnosis involved into this process."

"So, just talking? And that's it?"

"Yes, that's it," Ashot laughed. "Really, honestly, that's it."

"My gosh!" Aaron exclaimed bewildered, grabbing his head with both hands. "So simple! So unbelievably simple and easy! And the whole psychiatrists' society is breaking heads to solve the mystery of schizophrenia! I can't comprehend it!"

Ashot chuckled. "First of all, young man, all ingenious inventions and brilliant discoveries look simple when they are done. It's easy to say, gosh, how simple it is - why didn't we see it before!? When you read these materials, they will reveal to you much more information. You will understand how difficult it was in reality to find all of these, to connect all the parts and ingredients, to think out through all the ideas and links. And when you attend these sessions with Rosie... I actually need to warn you – they will be extremely challenging for you. I guess that I will even need to establish some special precautions to help you to hold yourself in check."

"Me? Why? How will it relate to me? What would be my part in the process?"

"You will sit and watch with a tablet in your hands and take notes about everything that's going on - what she is talking about and how she is feeling. Liam would be there also with a professional camera, making the movie. We will present to the conference a very impressive bundle of the following materials – the healthy patient; the file of the patient's pre existing conditions from her previous psychiatrist; the documentation of the scientific base of the discovery and of the whole cure process in two versions – digital and paperwork; the documentary film of the cure; the album of the printed pictures taken by a special scientific 4D camera that will demonstrate the patient's auras before and after the cure; and the digital version of those photos on a Data Traveler. Also, we will demonstrate there the special goggles that allow us to see aura's particles and the universe particles; and, also, the special 4D camera capable of taking photos of these particles and their flow up to the Clay Mask, and, at the end – up to the universe. Both these devices were created and patented by Laim and they will be used during the cure sessions. So, it will be a group work, and we are welcoming you, Aaron, to our team."

"Thank you," Aaron said, smiling contently. "I am so impressed, that I am sincerely honored and happy to be involved. I couldn't even guess how scientifically serious it would be."

"I assume that our presentation will be astronomical enough to satisfy the board of judges at the conference and we could win the award – the nomination for the Nobel Prize. I don't think the other discoveries, if there are any at all, would be as significant as ours," Ashot proudly concluded. "With that, I think dinner time is coming. I can smell that Liam is barbecuing steaks on the kitchen balcony and kiddo probably made a salad..."

"...and rice," added Rosie, appearing at the patio door. "Dinner is ready. Where do you guys want to eat – here or in the dining room?"

"For me anywhere would be good," Aaron shrugged, feeling happy because he was almost dying from hunger.

"I guess, it's better here," Ashot recommended. "The weather is too nice. It would be a shame to waste such a day inside."

"Well, then move all the folders away, uncle, and I will set the table," Rosie said. "And what about drinks?"

"I would suggest champagne for everybody because it looks like we have a reason to celebrate the birthday of our team," Liam announced entering the patio with a big dish full of fried beef steaks which he carried in his both hands. "However, we better take a non-alcohol bubbly. Would you mind checking the refrigerator for it, Aaron? And I will reach for the glasses while Ashot is taking care of the folders."

Aaron stood up and walked to the refrigerator, once more noticing how ethical and caring Liam was. He didn't say anything that alcohol was not allowed in Rosie's condition so as not to hurt her feelings. He just beautifully turned the situation in the proper direction. Now Aaron began to understand why Rosie was excited about these men so much – they were really, deeply good people who cared about her sincerely, and unconditionally loved her. And also they were intelligent, smart and extremely bright and gifted in areas of their occupations.

Over dinner, in a nice and friendly family atmosphere, they discussed how to organize and prepare everything for the following months of the cure. Liam said that he just made an agreement today with his production director to have a three months break in his work, so he would be free now.

Aaron suggested that he would go to the university tomorrow and arrange a similar agreement for himself. He also had Rosie's file from Dr. Evelyn Hertz at home which was kind of illegal. So, he should make a copy of it to be included into materials for their cure project and immediately return the original to the university. At the same time, he needed to make the request to his psychiatry department for an official assignment of Rosie as his new patient.

But first, Aaron needed his car to be fixed which could take a long time, and he announced that he decided to simply trade it for the new one.

"What happened to your car, Aaron?" Rosie asked, surprised. "Did we have an accident? I don't remember anything like that."

The awkward silence hung above the table. Ashot was the only one who didn't see the car but he knew from Liam about it's state. He made a short nod toward Aaron, warning him not to scare the girl.

"Yeah," Aaron said with a light indifference to his tone. "Nothing serious, just some scratches on the bumper. You don't remember because this was not significant."

"Then why trade it, why not just fix it?"

"Because the repairs will be too long. They have a huge line of customers. We don't have time to waste on waiting," Aaron continued, not looking at her. He had difficulty lying to the woman he loved, especially knowing that she could read his thoughts. But luckily Liam came to his help.

"You know, kiddo," he said, taking away her attention, "we came up with one amazing idea. Aaron should move in here with us for the next three months. We will work all together on our cure project and it will be reasonable for him not to lose time by driving home and back every day. The distance is pretty sizable, as you know. What do you think about that?"

"Really?" Rosie exclaimed happily. "Aren't you joking, guys? Is it true, Aaron?" He silently nodded although he did not hear about that idea earlier. "Jeez, then we don't need to go on dates. We could be together all the time. Oh gosh, I will kiss him all the time."

"Come on, kiddo," Ashot turned her excitement into a joke, "he will be here not for kissing, but for very serious work. He will study all the materials now, and later he will do a lot of the documentation and paperwork with me. You will have all the fun you want in three months when you are completely cured. But, sorry, not yet. Got it, kiddo?"

"Yes, uncle," Rosie nodded, blushing. "I understand. And I promise to be on my best behavior. Okay, Aaron, let's go tomorrow to the dealership to choose a new car. I really would like to see it."

Aaron would be lost again, but now Ashot saved him, "Kiddo, you forgot that we are busy with you tomorrow? We are doing the test of the clay on you to make sure that you don't have any allergy or unexpected reaction to it. Aaron will go by himself to deal with the car, or if he needs some help, Liam will be there for him. You will see the new car when they bring it here."

"And it obviously will be absolutely the same," Aaron added confidently.

After dinner they moved some furniture around and organized a working desk for Aaron in the third bedroom. It had a bed in it and an adjoined washroom with a shower stall, but was designed in their settings to be Ashot's medical facility – the closet and also several cabinets in the room were full of different kinds of medical equipment. The metal surgical table and the tall IV holder were already relocated back here from Rosie's bedroom. All the tools used for the surgery and the empty medicine bag on the IV holder now disappeared.

Laim carried the files from the patio and placed them on the desk so Aaron could begin to study them. Rosie brought her laptop and positioned it beside the folders."I will be working here with Aaron," she said to her elder friends. "I need to finish my poetry editing for magazines and arrange with them a three month leave, same as you guys. I am actually a busy working person too."

The rest of the evening was very nice and quiet. Aaron and Rosie were sitting together, side by side, each working on their own tasks, sometimes touching each other's hands fondly, or placing a short kiss on each other's cheek and smiling, glancing from time to time into each other's eyes. It was exactly what he was so badly missing with Ally – he liked to study, to learn, to research, to read but she wanted only to have fun and, in truth, always went to parties with Helen, leaving him at home to do her college assignments. He usually explained it to himself that she was too young, however, they were of the same age.

Now, with Rosie, who was really ten years younger, the situation appeared to Aaron to be intellectually and spiritually equal. It felt right. They talked, sometimes sharing their thoughts with each other about what he read in Ashot's files, or what she felt was wrong in somebody's poem during her editing. They consulted each other, explained things to each other and both enjoyed this intellectual and emotional closeness. Aaron felt as if they were already married, living together and working jointly, close, warm and happy. He imagined that it would be exactly like this when she will be cured, and his heart filled with a restful calm happiness.

Finally, Aaron was able to relax from the previous stress he had and, with Rosie by his side, deeply immersed into his favorite field – science – though it was again everything for her and about her. It was about their love now and for their love in the future.

CHAPTER 28

Next morning, when Aaron came to the kitchen to make some coffee, Liam had already brewed a big pot for everybody and was now cooking a traditional American breakfast. Ashot was there too, mixing the blue clay with water in a huge plastic pail.

"Good morning," Aaron said and got all the greetings back. "I would like to go home today to pick up some stuff. Also, I usually exercise in my sports room in the basement every morning."

"Oh, there is no problem with that," Liam replied. "We have a fully equipped sports center in the building and a swimming pool with a hot tub. I can show you later where they are located."

"Thank you, it would be good to know. I probably will use them in the following months," Aaron nodded. "But I guess, first, I need to trade my car before I go home. It will look suspicious to appear in my neighborhood in the vehicle in such a damaged condition."

"I'll show you where your car is now in our underground parking," Liam suggested, "and I can go with you to the dealership, if some help is needed there."

"I don't really feel comfortable appearing at a dealership dressed in my undershirt showing fresh wounds," Aaron confessed, confusingly. "I was thinking I need to go home to get some clothes, first. But it's kind of a closed circle. I don't know where to start."

"I can lend you a shirt," Liam proposed readily. "We are about the same size. It will help us to begin with the dealership right after breakfast. How about that?"

"Thank you. It could possibly be a solution," Aaron smiled. Then, not yet knowing how their household routine usually works, he asked, "Should I wake Rosie for breakfast?"

Ashot shook his head. "Let her sleep a bit longer. We worked with her last night on her mood and also on her wound after you went to sleep, Aaron. And she will have a very important task today – to test the clay. It would be better if she is well rested. By the way," he said as he approached Aaron and looked attentively at his wounds, "they are not healing fast enough. When you come back today, we will need to do some healing work on them. You should look good in the taped documentary, Aaron, not wounded."

"Yes, I agree," Aaron smirked. "I am not even talking on Skype with my family now to avoid unwanted questions." This morning he texted Beth again, "Huge work, very busy. Skype in a few days. Love." However, his reason was not only to hide his wounds from her. Aaron also didn't want these strangers to see or hear his conversations with her and Laurie. His family was too dear to him. He was still not familiar enough with these people and not comfortable with opening too much of his life to them.

After breakfast, before heading to the dealership, Liam gave Aaron a tour of the building – sports club, swimming pool, dressing rooms with showers and toilets, party room and guest suites. Finally they walked downstairs to the underground parking and unwrapped the tarpaulin cover from Aaron's car. Outside it seemed to be normal, but if someone would approach and glance through the window, the damage would look shocking and suspicious.

While they drove out from the garage, Liam said, "We need to stop at McDonald's by the way." Aaron didn't understand why - they just had their breakfast. But he didn't say anything, only nodded.

As they stopped in the parking lot of the first McDonald's they saw, Liam got out of the car, noting quickly, "I'll be back in a minute," and walked inside the restaurant. Aaron waited patiently until Liam appeared with a significant brown paper bag and two cups of coffee. Aaron expected that he would give these things to him, but he opened the back door of the car, poured the coffee on the seat, squashed the cups and threw them on the floor. He tore open the paper bag and scattered the fries around - on the seat and also on the floor. Then he broke the hamburgers and buns into pieces and threw them all over inside the car.

"What are you doing?!" Aaron exclaimed perplexed.

"Covering for our kiddo," Liam laughed. He returned to the passenger seat, wiped his hands on the napkin and threw it in the back as well. "When we get to the dealership, the first question will be – what happened with your car, Aaron. The people there could suspect a murder scene, when they see the damage. They could easily report it to the police. We don't need to be involved in long and difficult explanations and put Rosie at risk of ending up in a mental institution. This way, we will tell them that we went to the mountains to have a picnic, left the food on the back seat and didn't even close the door of the car because nobody was around and we felt safe. Then we went for a short walk. During that time a bear came from nowhere, attracted by the food smell, and did all the damage. We will apologize for our mistake and promise to be vigilant for bears next time. Everybody will laugh, no questions asked, believe me."

"Wow!" Aaron uttered, surprised. "Jeez, you are so resourceful. It would never come to my mind to do that."

Liam shrugged. "That's why I came with you."

The car trade procedure went exactly as Liam predicted. It took about three hours, until they finally left the dealership in the new car with all documentation completed and registered. Then they headed to Aaron's house to pick up his personal things and Dr. Hertz's file of Rosie that was supposed to be returned to the university.

At the house, Aaron showed Liam around and then they sat for a while on the patio, having some drinks which had been left in the refrigerator.

"Beautiful house," Liam commented smiling, spreading in a lawn chair and sipping beer.

"You have a very nice condo, as well," Aaron noticed, opening another beer for himself. "It's almost as big as the house, and even probably more expensive because of the location facing the waterfront."

"Yeah," Liam nodded. "It cost a couple of million because it is the third floor only. The top of the building there goes for three million and more. But I am not comfortable living too high in an area with active earthquakes. The condo looks pretty good, although it's not new. I bought it in 2000 after Ashot cured me. Before that, I didn't need a residence, I spent fifteen years in mental institutions." He smiled bashfully, then continued, "I added Ashot to the title in 2012 when we got married."

"Was Rosie a flower girl at your wedding?" Aaron asked cautiously. "I remember her poem..."

"No," Liam laughed. "If you could remember exactly, she said – 'I would like to be a flower girl at your wedding'. 'Would like' – but not 'was'. We didn't know her when we got married. It was May of 2012. Right after that, Ashot left the General Psychiatric Hospital where he worked as a nurse for many years. But we wanted to spend more time together. You know... to get used to married life. Later, he found a job – night shifts at the *Youth Shelter*. In July 2012, after that young black lad was killed by the police, Rosie was placed there. She had severe insomnia then and spent all nights talking with Ashot. He helped her a lot, returning her to the possibility of normal sleep. They told each other their life stories and became pretty close friends.

"Ashot told me that she reminded him of his daughter left behind in Armenia," Liam continued. "It's quite strange because his daughter was short, chubby with black curly hair and black eyes – a sharp contrast from Rosie. But he had a feeling that Rosie was his child somehow, he couldn't understand it himself. Maybe his little Annush died and was reincarnated in Rosie, or something... He didn't even know if his daughter was alive. If she is, she could be about thirty-four. She was only a four-year-old when he lost custody. A gay in a communist country wasn't allowed to raise a child – not to 'influence' it. Extremely stupid and ridiculous but that's what the laws there were. For being gay Ashot was supposed to get prison for life. That was one of the reasons why he ran away from there."

"Wow," Aaron took a deep breath, "I can't imagine that. My daughter is five. If I lost her, I would probably turn crazy. She is everything to me."

"Yeah, it's pretty difficult to lose a family," Liam nodded with a deep breath. "I absolutely get it. I was eighteen when my parents kicked me out, after they discovered that I am gay. I was shocked and devastated so much that this probably forced my mental illness to strike. Luckily I had a lot of money, otherwise I would have ended up homeless on the street."

"At least your parents gave you that money," Aaron concluded. "Not every teen has it."

"No, they didn't give me a penny. It was all my earnings which I got from ten years of touring the world as a pianist. I was a very famous celebrity child for ten years – from eight to eighteen. I started playing piano at three years of age; and at eight I was already doing personal concerts. Later I won many International Pianists' Contests. One day I'll show you the tapes of my concerts. Ashot keeps all of them."

"Really? And... now..." Aaron looked at him confused.

"I lost everything after my cure – all my skills... ability... talent."

"Oh, I got it!" Aaron exclaimed, suddenly remembering. "Rosie told me about that. You got a new gift after... That's what held her back from the cure. She was scared to lose her specialties, but Ashot convinced her that, even if it happened, something new would appear from the unopened part of the brain. Exactly like it was to you."

"Yeah," Liam nodded. "I am pretty happy with what I have now. Actually, working on movies is much more fascinating than playing piano. Touring concerts would be difficult for my family life, as I am married now, and being a piano teacher would be boring. My Ashot is a very intriguing husband. Life with him is unbelievably interesting, always creative and kind of an adventure."

"As I noticed in his files that I read yesterday, he was a very bright scientist in Armenia," Aaron acknowledged. "I can see that in his way of thinking and in his approach to psychiatric problems."

"Much more than just bright, he is a real genius. He is a psychiatrist from God. I absolutely admire him," Liam exclaimed heatedly. "You just need to know him."

"Then why didn't he get a doctor's diploma here?"

"He had a very difficult immigration and came here actually after thirty. By the time he learned English and got used to American life, he was already forty. It was too late to go to university. He did at least what he could – a college for psychiatric nursing. Maybe one day, he will tell you his story. I have no right to do that for him."

"But you know his story?" Aaron guessed.

"Of course, I do."

"And Rosie knows?"

Liam nodded silently while they continued sipping beer.

"And how was your cure procedure?" Aaron asked after some minutes of silence. "Ashot said that it could be very challenging for me to watch. How? I don't get it."

"I actually don't remember anything, honestly," Liam answered thoughtfully. "I remember breaks between sessions as being regular life. Ashot did all the documentation. We went for walks, hiking to the mountains, and dining out at restaurants. I remember my examination in the General Psychiatric Hospital after the cure. The board of doctors who evaluated me was shocked to find me healthy. It was a triumph for both of us. But the sessions themselves – zero. I don't know why. I'm guessing that it was probably the point of the cure. I, the same as you, will see for the first time how the procedure goes with Rosie."

Aaron felt now much more comfortable after this sincere and friendly conversation with Liam. Then, he packed his stuff, locked the house, leaving the lights on in some rooms, and they headed for the university.

There, Aaron made another little tour for Liam, showing him the research labs and his office in the Psychiatry Department. They made copies of Dr. Hertz file, then walked to Human Resources to prepare paperwork for Aaron's three months leave. He wrote that to work on the admission to the Psychiatry Scientific Conference in New York he needed time for research in a private lab. It was a very much respected reason there. For the university it would be an extreme honor, if one of its members won the nomination for the Nobel Prize. Aaron was sure that his petition would be approved.

He also requested the head of his department to assign the new patient, Rosa Lynn Garcia, to him. She was out of the age group of children and teenagers with whom Dr. Hertz worked and should be transferred to an adult psychiatrist anyway. Aaron wrote the explanation that Dr. Hertz chose him specifically and for that reason sent the documentations of Rosie's illness history to him. It sounded rational and was approved by the department right away without any problem.

When Aaron and Liam returned home, they found Rosie sitting on the patio, by the open window, in the sun. She wore shorts and a strapless top. Her shaven head, neck, shoulders and arms were covered with a very thin layer of the blue clay. It had already dried out on her and even started shedding in some places.

"Wow!" Aaron exclaimed, surprised. "You look like you are having a mud bath. I saw that while traveling to Israel some years ago. There is a special healing mud by the Dead Sea and people from the whole world are going there to have mud baths which look similar. But this is our blue clay, I guess, right?"

"Yes," she laughed happily and mischievously, obviously in a good mood. "I think it's already time to take shower. Uncle said that in three hours, when it is all dried in the sun, I can wash it away. Three hours have passed."

"How about your wound?" Aaron inquired. "Is it okay to make it wet now?"

"Yes, I think so. I'll be back soon." She jumped up from her chair to run to the shower, but Liam stopped her.

"Wait a sec, kiddo," he said, "let me film how you look. It is needed to prove that we did check the clay before the cure." He brought his big camera and started filming the girl from all sides and angles. Then he let her go to the shower. When she returned, wrapped into a big towel, Ashot checked her face, shoulders and arms while Liam kept filming. Then Ashot nodded, satisfied, "Very good, kiddo. No allergy at all. I am checking this," he explained to Aaron, who was watching the examination attentively, "because in Armenia I had one patient who got some allergic reaction to this clay."

"But you said that there is no direct contact between the patient and clay during the cure?" Aaron reminded him.

"Yes. But still, I had one woman who got irritation on her skin even from staring at the Clay Mask. I just want to double check that here will be nothing like that. Now, Aaron, look at her wound."

Rosie extended her arm to him. The spot of the wound was just a very thin scar, almost white. It looked like it was at least a year old. Aaron shook his head in disbelief.

"There are a lot of antibacterial and disinfectant ingredients in this clay. Did you read about its components yet?"

"No. I am still studying the patients files," Aaron said. "I am sorry that it's going a bit slow, but we had to do some other things today."

"It's okay," Ashot agreed. "You still have time tonight and the whole day tomorrow for reading. Before sleeping, I will give you a little bowl of clay. Put it on your wounds. Tomorrow morning you can wash it away. It should be enough."

"Thank you," Aaron nodded, still being a bit confused. To put mud found somewhere on the ground on his fresh wounds seemed strange and dangerous. But he had no choice. Rosie's wound looked convincing.

Then she hugged and kissed him, smiling happily and whispering in his ear, "I already created a poem for the next concert, while I was sitting here and drying in the sun."

Aaron kissed her too and nodded his approval, completely giving up, feeling that he would do anything for her – even put a clay on his wounds - just to see her happy face and to feel her lips on his cheek. By his love to her he was bound and bewitched completely.

CHAPTER 29

The rest of the evening Aaron spent reading Ashot's files.

Rosie insisted on staying with him. She moved all the files from his bedroom into the living room and placed them on the coffee table in front of the couch. She convinced him to sit on the couch and laid down beside him, nestling her head on his lap. It was exactly the same setting which they had on the bench in the park the evening they met. Rosie held his left hand tight, pressing it to her face and slowly kissing his fingers. This way Aaron can read, holding pages from the files in his right hand.

This continued for a while, until Aaron finally said, smiling, "Rosie, my love, it's kind of distracting. You are turning me on. I really should concentrate on what I am reading."

"Okay," she let his hand go, "just kiss me once, like our 'holy oasis' and then I will go and find something else to do. You don't understand, Aaron. I miss you so badly. And I need you. I am scared, believe me, I am very-very scared to be cured. I am shaking from uncertainty, not knowing what to expect."

He kissed her tenderly, carefully and then asked, "Did you see the future? How will you feel after the cure?"

"I saw. I know I will be healthy. I know I will be alright."

"Then what's the problem?"

"I don't know. I don't clearly understand myself. I was ill for so long, almost nine years. I kind of got used to my illness and I am somewhat hesitant to part with it. I really don't know how to live a normal life."

"Don't think about that now. I will be with you. We will find out how to live that normal life together. We will help each other, and teach each other, and everything will be great."

"Okay, if you say so," she took a deep breath. "Sorry to bother you, my love. I know you should concentrate. I probably need to go and combine the rest of my poems into more books. You know, my book included poems which I wrote from fifteen to seventeen. Now I would like to do another book – from eleven to fifteen, and one more – from seventeen to twenty. That would be it. After that I won't be able to write more poetry."

"Why are you so sure that you will lose your talent? Liam is the only case of losing talent. And he actually turned out pretty good. He told me that he is much happier with his new profession now. I don't see anything like that in the cases I am reading about.

"I noticed that some of Ashot's former patients, in Armenia, had changes in their marital or relationship status after the cure – two men got divorced, one woman left her husband, one man found a new girlfriend and one, who was a gay, fell in love with Ashot. If we could count Liam who fell in love with him as well, that would be only six cases all together – a pretty small percentage, so it is obviously not related to the cure and not important. It is just what happens with many people in their regular life. However, not one patient of Ashot's in Armenia ever lost any talent."

"I asked uncle about that," Rosie explained. "He said his patients there were not educated and not bright people. In the communist regime mentally ill people were not allowed to get an education. They were taken out of school in grade 8-9-10 because of their illness. They were not allowed to do any sports or art classes, or any other activities; or to go to college or university. If several of them had some talent, it was not developed and nobody knew about it - even themselves. Those were really people who had nothing to lose. That's why uncle felt such a pity toward them and made it his life goal to help them return to a normal life."

"Jeez, it sounds like a pretty scary situation for these poor sufferers in that regime. Luckily, it doesn't exist anymore in the former Soviet Union," Aaron acknowledged what he knew from the TV News.

"It still exists in some parts of the world," Rosie objected. "Can you imagine what would happen with a mentally ill person in North Korea, for example, where even normal people are going to prison forever for saying one wrong word? The ill one would just be shot on the spot. I would have been executed by age eleven, if I was there."

"Oh... let's not talk about that, Rosie," Aaron shuddered. "We, you and I, can't help the unlucky people in those countries anyway. The highest politicians of the world are trying to do that. But we should concentrate on our task, please. It would be good if you get busy, working on your poems and future books. I seriously have to work on Ashot's research because my involvement is truly needed for your cure. Also, it's damn interesting and eye opening to me as the psychiatrist. I am educated very well, but still, I am learning a lot of new information here. Really, a lot!"

Rosie brought a box full of notebooks containing her poems, sat on the couch and they both kept busy for the whole evening, sitting side by side.

Before retiring for the night into his separated bedroom, Aaron put the clay on his wounds and topped it with a band-aid to keep it there until morning. To his unbelievable shock, after showering the next day he discovered that his wounds were practically completely healed, just the two thin light scars were left and they were almost invisible. He just said a simple "Thank you," showing them to Ashot, who came to check on him first thing in the morning. But inside his heart, Aaron was absolutely dumbfounded and ready to bow his head in front of this old strange man from the other part of the globe. However, he preferred not to show that to him openly.

After the friendly breakfast that they had all together, Ashot and Liam decided to go hiking for the whole day and take Rosie with them. They wanted to give Aaron a chance to work seriously, not to be bothered by anyone.

As soon as they all left, the housekeeper came and started working around the condo. Aaron, not wanting to be in her way, went to the sports club on the main floor of the building and exercised there for one hour. Later he swam for a while in the pool.

Then Aaron returned to the condo and called his mother on Skype. While talking with her and Laurie for one more hour, he managed somehow to turn all the conversation to be about them. For himself he mentioned just a lot of work, and nothing else. They, however, had a bunch of exciting experiences, especially Laurie — friends, excursions, learning to ride her new bicycle, activities on the beach, a puppy which they rescued from an animal shelter. When their video session was almost finished, Beth said, "Arie, here is Ashley. She came to pick up her kids. She wants to talk to you, too. We are leaving you with her now. We have to go. Aunt Erin with Laurie's little cousins and puppy are already waiting for us on the beach."

Then Aaron's cousin Ashley appeared on screen. "Hi, Arie," she started, then stopped for a moment. "Let me just check if they are gone." She walked somewhere and then returned to the screen. "Listen, Arie," she said in a conspirator's tone, "Nicole and I, we saw you on YouTube kissing that girl on stage. Does your mom know about that?"

"No," he blushed. "And let's keep it that way. She will know later, when they come back home."

"We guessed that. But you should be more careful. Nowadays nobody can hide anything from social media. I am not sure it was an appropriate thing to do for an adult doctor at a teens' gathering. Are you serious about that girl?"

"Deadly serious. I will marry her in September."

"Wow! But she looks very young for that."

"Listen, Ash, my mom was ten years younger than my dad and, as you know, they had a very happy life and perfect marriage."

"Well, I know, that could happen sometimes. How long have you known her?"

"All my life," Aaron answered confidently.

"Hmm," she hesitated, "but you were married and had a child... How did that girl fit into this setting in the past? She was probably about ten-years-old at that time..."

"Ash, stop it, please. I don't want to talk about that now," he snapped at her, getting irritated. He himself just realized with horror that today was Friday, exactly two weeks from that Friday evening when he met Rosie during his walk with Laurie. He didn't think before that it had been a very short time passed. He really felt like he knew Rosie and loved her his whole life.

"Okay, Arie," his cousin took a deep breath, "just think please, how it could affect your child."

"Laurie knows her and likes her very much. I am pretty sure she would be happy."

"Laurie knows her and your mom – doesn't?" Ashley sounded surprised.

"I don't want to talk about that," he repeated, cutting her off very strictly. "And keep it away from mom, please. I don't want her to get nervous for no reason. Let her have a good vacation."

"But you would invite us to your wedding, at least, wouldn't you, Arie?"

"We will talk about that at the end of September. Bye, Ash, and say Hi from me to your sister. I have to go now."

Aaron turned off his computer and dropped his head in his hands. He was shocked by this eye opening thought – how long he did know Rosie. He survived so much during these two weeks, from highest happiness to deadly horror. He was so emotionally exhausted and drained that it felt like years passed, not just days. However, all of this really helped him to understand himself – the famous 'cognize yourself' idea - as taught in scientific philosophy.

Obviously he was not a slow mover; he had an inflammable, explosive personality. Everything could happen with his feelings in a minute – or never happen at all.

Helen was right reminding him how he fell in love with Ally – just in one day. Ally was a new girl in class. When he brought her home after kissing on a bench in a park, his parents allowed her to stay for a while asking Aaron who she was. He said, "My classmate who needs help."

They guessed by the word *classmate* that he had known her probably for all his eleven years of school. Much later they found out that Aaron knew her for one day only, but it was too late – he was in love, he slept with her every night, and she became a very nice surrogate daughter for them – caregiver for his dad and household helper for his mom. Everybody was happy as a result. Especially, he was very happy for the following nine years until her death - really, deeply happy.

What was the point now that he knew Helen for ten years already? She was a monster and he hated her anyway. Why should the amount of time matter? The question that Ashley asked bothered Aaron for some minutes but then he rejected it boldly. Yes, he knew Rosie for just two weeks but he knew that she was the one. He fell in love with her as soon as he began to read her book and realized that she was his destiny, his soul, his life forever. Aaron didn't care who would say what or think what; he knew what his feelings are. It was only his business and nobody else's. Every cell of his being screamed inside him, "Leave me alone! Mind your own business! I love her!" He didn't want any remarks about his life and his relationships from any relatives anymore and decided that from now on he would just send short texts to Beth instead of making long Skype sessions.

This decision calmed him down and he returned to reading Ashot's materials which should be completely known to him by tomorrow – the memorable day – the beginning of the cure.

Rosie and her friends returned home from their outing pretty late. After hiking they went for dinner at a restaurant.

"Did you eat something Aaron?" she asked, hugging him. "I was worried that you were sitting here alone, hungry."

"No," he laughed. "Don't worry about me. I know how to survive. I ordered pizza."

"Do you have any questions about what you read?" Ashot wanted to know.

"Just a couple. It looks like you did some followup on your first ten patients in Armenia, but there is not a word about what happened later with the others..."

"I had no chance. In 1985, after the last ones, I emigrated to the USA."

"Right away?"

"Yes," Ashot answered coldly. "My situation required that immediately. What else?"

"When, during the cure, the Clay Mask is sucking in the damaged particles of the aura, isn't there any chance that it could give them away, back to the patient? Like the radiation sometimes goes both ways..."

"Not until the Clay Mask is broken into smithereens which is the final moment of the cure. With the Mask in one piece the particles are sitting there inside very tight."

"Are they staying in the Mask even during the breaks between sessions of the cure?"

"It's already your third question," Ashot smirked. "Well, yes. Clay holds everything in it all the time. It's safe. Good night now, Aaron. We need to work here for a while. Tomorrow's wake up time is at eight a.m. The session starts at ten."

During this dialog, Liam began moving furniture in the living room, placing three long folding tables in a line across the empty area. Aaron realized that he was preparing a setting for the cure. They also placed three chairs on one side of the tables and one chair on the other side, at the middle table, about six feet across from the opposite chair.

Ashot brought from somewhere a big plastic tray to put on the table, then a bunch of small terry towels and a pail with the clay soaking in water. He and Liam were working fast and organized, as a well trained team, staging all the needed equipment: cameras – big professional and small scientific 4D, two pairs of 4D goggles, computer, tablet, and, on the floor between the chairs, a few bags full of different things that potentially could be needed during the session.

"Good night," Aaron said to them and walked into Rosie's room to give her a goodnight kiss. She was already in bed, turning into a fetal position under the blanket. He sat on the edge of the bed and hugged her. "How are you coping, my love?" he asked fondly. "Are you a bit anxious?"

"Yes," she looked at him and he saw that her eyes were wet. It was obvious that she was crying. "Aaron, I am scared," she whispered with shaky lips. "I am very-very scared. Please, stay with me. Would you mind sleeping with me tonight? I can't be alone. I am begging you. Be with me, please."

"Yes, of course." He wanted to lay down on the top of the blanket, but she shook her head, no.

"I want you to undress and lay under the covers. I need your warmth. Please, understand. I don't have any knives here or anything like that. You can check under the pillow, under the bed, everywhere. I promise, I won't be dangerous. I need your love so much, Aaron. It's a life changing moment for me. During the cure I should tell my life story to my uncle. He actually knows everything anyway. And Liam knows too. I will tell all to the Clay Mask this time. But you... You wanted to know everything about me. You wanted to talk about my book, when you came to see me for the first time. I refused, remember? In the park I said, *maybe we could talk about the book another time. It would be too hurtful a subject now...* Tomorrow will be *another time.* You will know everything. I won't be a mystery to you anymore. And you won't love me anymore," she covered her face with both hands, being all shaky with sobs.

"Okay," Aaron took a deep breath, undressed quickly and slid under the blanket, hugging her tight and pressing her whole body to him. "Sweet angel, my love," he whispered affectionately, kissing her forehead, her wet eyes and cheeks. "Please, don't be Vally anymore. Please, stay Rosie for me. I will love you always. I know everything about you from your book. And I fell in love with you exactly because of that knowledge. You have nothing to worry about. If you trust your uncle and his cure, just do what he is requesting and what's needed for you to get healthy. It's your gateway from illness into our future which you know will be passionate lovemaking on *the island with grass and sand*. Right, my love?" he smiled, trying to encourage her.

"I don't want to wait for the future," she protested persistently. "I want it now, Aaron. Please, my love. You promised to take me when we were sitting on Diablo mountain before the concert. It was my fault that I spoiled everything with this damn knife, accidentally cutting myself and you. I am very sorry. It will never happen again, I swear."

Aaron didn't want to confess to himself that he was scared too. He had no idea if the lovemaking could affect the cure process the next day or not. Ashot didn't say anything about that. But they insisted that he live here. Wasn't it obvious that he would be close to Rosie all the time? The situation would provoke him. Was it done on purpose, or what? It would be much safer if he was living at home and driving here every day if sex was not allowed, wouldn't it? Or were they so sure that he could hold himself in check? Did they trust him that much while practically not knowing him?

But how could he be that strong, when, all in tears, she was begging him to love her? How, when he hadn't had sex for a pretty long time? How, when he loved her so madly and wanted her almost until insanity? How would it be possible to resist?

Fighting a huge amount of guilt, being deadly afraid to destroy the future cure, Aaron murmured between kisses, almost giving up, "You can't promise, Rosie, that you will be okay. It was not you. It was the illness who did that last attack. You can't guarantee what the illness will do now."

"I can. I will be quiet, I am almost sleeping. Please, love me, Aaron. Now. Please, I am begging you. If you love me, you will do this."

It was absolutely not what he had imagined in his dreams as their first lovemaking. There was no wild passion and no madness that was usual for him. All was really calm and quiet. He slipped his hands under her bottom, lifted it a bit and entered her very solicitously, cautiously, fondly, not to scare her, not to hurt or push her away. He was usually very careless in sex thinking only about himself. He thought about neither Ally, nor Helen at all, ever. But now, for the first time in his life, he thought and really cared about this girl with all the deepness of his heart.

She answered to his rhythm at first but then got more slumberous, just holding his shoulders hard and breathing heavily and in the middle of the act he noticed, surprised, that she weakened and was really sleeping. The pleasure that he had with her was strong, intense, even piercing like lightning through his brain. It was something very special that he never experienced in his life before. It was so unbelievable. He felt that it was worth dying for. That sensation just confirmed for him what he already knew – she was created by God for him and he would never let her go.

As he came, he bit his lips to hold the moan in and not to wake her up and then, relaxing, dropped his head on her shoulder. For a second, an idea flashed in his mind to wake her and send to the shower, but then he decided, "What the hell, she wanted to have a baby anyway. Let it be."

And soon he fell asleep as well, still holding her in his arms.

CHAPTER 30

Aaron woke up when it was still dark. It was difficult to know what time it was, but obviously very early in the morning as there was no daylight, yet. While lying motionlessly, he kept wondering what to do now.

He felt satisfied, relaxed and absolutely happy. But the problem was – he didn't want to show Rosie's friends that he slept with her, not knowing what kind of reaction to expect from Ashot. Would the old man be angry that having sex might affect the cure that was supposed start this morning? Or maybe it wouldn't be a problem at all for their project? Anyway, Aaron didn't care if someone looked at him with a meaningful smirk, as if judging. The intimacy with the women he loved was too private and too sacred for him to show and reveal to anyone. It was his and Rosie's life, business, and feelings but nobody else's.

However, to leave Rosie now and sneak into his bedroom felt like a betrayal of her. She needed him and she begged him to stay with her, not to disappear and hide after the lovemaking. It would be mean and disrespectful and Aaron would never do that to her. So, what should be his decision?

Rosie was peacefully sleeping in his arms. Listening to her calm breathing, he felt such an endless passion for her that he couldn't resist the urge to love her again. Aaron tenderly touched her shoulder with his lips, then her cheek, then found her lips in a semi darkness and kissed her deeply and affectionately. His erection already started and was stronger than he could suppress. He completely forgot about her danger, her illness, about anything that happened before in his car. Last night it was okay and ended up with her sleeping, now it started with it. Her eyes were still closed and it looked like her brain continued to sleep but her body answered him now very actively and ardently. She was convulsing in his hands, moaning and crying, until they finally came together with a strong orgasm.

As he dropped his head on the pillow, breathless, Rosie opened her eyes and whispered astonished, "Aaron?" It sounded strange to him, as if she would expect someone else with her but not him. Then she blinked, rubbed her eyes to wake up completely and smiled, lovingly kissing his shoulder. "Thank you, Aaron," she murmured. "Thank you, my love."

"How do you feel?" he asked, calming down after the first daze.

"Great. Perfect. Light. Like I am ready to fly."

Scientifically he knew that it was a normal reaction of a woman's body for receiving a huge amount of testosterone and estrogen from a man, but spiritually, it made him happy with a realization that he fixed her mood and she would now go for her cure being calm and content.

They went to shower together, laughing and splashing, and caressing each other with a soap foam, playing like kids at first, but in a few minutes it turned more serious. Their smiles disappeared and reverted into heavy breathing and irresistible craving for each other again. They both completely lost control allowing the mad and greedy lovemaking to happen there once more, the third time during this night. And again, nothing bad had occurred. It looked like Rosie wasn't ill at all.

When they eventually returned from the shower to her bedroom, Aaron asked, "Should I go to my room? What do you think? Do you want them to know? Or not?"

"I guess it will be visible in my aura and uncle will know anyway," Rosie said with a mischievous smile, still hugging him and tenderly looking him in the eyes. "But this is only my speculation. I am not a scientist, I don't know. I feel it would be better not to show them so openly what's going on. It feels ethically wrong. It's kind of 'our thing', right? You and I only. Of course, we did display our love to everybody at my concert, but this is different. My uncle and Liam know anyway that we love each other, so I guess there's no need to show them more than that, right? I love you to death, Aaron, but you better go now. We probably could have a couple more hours of sleep." She kissed him goodbye on his cheek and with that he carefully sneaked to his bedroom, fell on his bed and slept soundly, like a baby, until the alarm clock rang exactly at eight a.m.

During breakfast, Ashot made a preparatory speech for his team.

"Eat well now, guys," he said, "because our next meal will only be after the session is finished. We will have just water bottles beside each person, to sip as needed and very short bathroom breaks, no longer than a couple minutes. We can't predict yet how long the first cure would be. It was different with every patient, from a couple of hours until ten, or even twelve hours. We can't stop until the flow of the particles will end by itself. We will see that through the goggles and you, Aaron, will take pictures of it every minute of the flow with the 4D camera. I can't do that myself because my hands will be dirty with clay while forming the Clay Mask. Liam will tape the whole session with his professional camera and the particles won't be visible on his film. For that reason – the pictures are on you, Aaron. Both of us, you and I, will wear goggles all the time to control the view of Rosie's auras. When I see the moment that the picture of aura's condition needs to be taken, I will make you a sign with my hand, like that," he snapped his fingers, "and you'll take it instantly. Are we clear on that?"

Aaron nodded obediently, though the feeling was not nice and a bit humiliating, like he was an apprentice, student, or uneducated child.

"Also, all of us should be dressed in white doctor's robes to make it look on film like we are working in a real clinic," Ashot continued. "As you can see now, we completely changed the scene of our living room and fixed it to look like an official clinic – nothing of home or household items around. And Rosie will wear a hospital gown.

"To prepare an admission for the Psychiatric Conference makes everything much more difficult than I had before. Then, I worked with a patient by myself without any devices or films. And, Aaron, the documentation which you read, I did for myself only. Now we will work with you together the whole week on the materials to be presented to the conference, so it should be serious, responsible and scientific looking. And Liam at that time will be working on the editing of his film. Any questions?"

"Without goggles and a 4D camera, how did you know with your previous patients that the flow of the particles finished and the session could end?" Aaron wanted to know.

"When it's done, the patient will fall asleep at the end. I used a lot of intuition to give it some time. Of course, it was not as exact as it will be now. But it still worked. With all our equipment today, it should be even better."

After breakfast, a short bathroom break and accomplishing the last small details of readiness, everyone settled in their designated spot.

"Aaron," Rosie whispered to him, all shaky from fear, "please, say that you love me and promise that you will be with me all the time." He nodded and soundlessly mouthed back, "I love you," feeling such pity and compassion for her that his heart was about to explode. But he believed that they should do that together - it was their future, love, and happy family life. They both had to be brave and strong. So, he smiled at her and showed her a thumbs-up.

"Okay, is everybody ready to go?" Ashot asked, glancing around the room. "Then, action!" He gestured to Liam like it was a movie set and started his presentation. "We are beginning today the first session of the cure of a patient, Rosa Lynn Garcia, diagnosed in 2006 with acute schizophrenia, based on Dissociative Identity Disorder of seven personalities." Liam's camera went on him, first, then on Rosie and later on Aaron, when it came to his name. "We are using a scientific method of natural organic treatment of this illness, newly discovered by Board Certified Psychiatrist, Doctor Aaron Dispenmore, MD, PhD, of the Psychiatry Department of Washington State University. I am the assistant of Dr. Dispenmore, the Registered Nurse of psychiatry, Thomas Spencer. Under Dr. Dispenmore's supervision I will help with developing the organic material of the treatment – the biologically clean blue clay - into a Clay Mask resembling the patient's face."

With these words Ashot pulled a big chunk of wet softened clay out from the pail on the floor and placed it on a tray in front of him on the table. It was about the size of Rosie's head and neck. He started working on it, squeezing it, rolling, twisting, and petting its surface, making it smooth and glassy. While doing that, he continued talking. "We will clean, first, the damaged and dysfunctional aura's particles of the most important patient's personality - the heaviest one, the most traumatic one, and the most dangerous one which is practically the base of Rosa Garcia's illness as Dr. Dispenmore determined."

Tobi, obviously, Aaron thought. He was not surprised by this statement. He didn't determine anything about Rosie, not even started seeing her as his patient, but, anyway, it was expected that Ashot would turn everything to him during this process. Aaron has no other choice in the situation, just to accept anything that would be said.

Against his expectation, Ashot went on, "This personality was named Nora by the patient."

Wow! Aaron thought. *Was I that much mistaken? Is Nora worse than Tobi? To me she looked scared and abused, but not dangerous at all...*

"The procedure of removing damaged particles of the aura, which are managing this personality, will be carried out with the creation of the Clay Mask, depicting the patient's face," Ashot continued, and then addressed the girl who looked at him with her huge fearful eyes. "Please, tell us about her, Rosie. Who is Nora? How come she impersonated herself in you? When did it happen and why? Anything you know, remember, want and can tell us. It's completely up to you what you wish to share..."

Rosie coughed a little, nervously trying to clean her throat and asked, "Can I close my eyes?"

"Do anything that makes you feel comfortable," Ashot nodded. "And don't be scared. We only have people here who care about you and want the best for you. Okay?"

"Thank you," she whispered, closed her eyes and propped her head on her hands, putting her elbows on the table. "I need to think about what I remember first." Then she coughed a bit more, lifted her head and opened her eyes, looking straight at the back of the clod of clay that stood in front of Ashot. And she began her narrative. "Nora was my grandma. She taught me letters very early. I was a three-year-old child when I started to write my first book. I was sitting on the floor and drawing. Then I wrote some words. Grandpa Vasil came to me and asked what I was doing. I answered, 'I am writing a book'. He was in shock and screamed that I was a genius and should go to Oprah to become famous. He yelled that he would beat Nora until she made me go to Oprah. I didn't understand who Oprah was or why I should go there. I was very scared because I didn't want my grandma to be beaten because of me. I knew that it was my fault because I started writing the letters and that book..."

Rosie stopped, fighting her tears, and took a deep breath. Aaron gritted his teeth, feeling that he was already emotionally hurting. It was unbelievable what this child survived! She was only three while watching those horrors. Question was not why she became ill, the question was – why not? And this was only the beginning. The tablet shook in Aaron's hands and he put it on the table.

"Control yourself," Ashot whispered to him. "I warned you it will be challenging." He snapped his fingers and Aaron got the sign. He took the small camera that was on the table in front of him and took a picture of Rosie's head. Her aura was broken in some spots and deformed before, as he saw through the goggles, but now it began getting black, losing the other colors. Aaron took a picture of it and then took his tablet again to describe the changes of view in connection with Rosie's words.

He understood now why Ashod decided to begin with Nora's personality and considered it the most traumatic and dangerous. Tobi was a reaction to the illness. Nora was the reason and the base of it. To withdraw her first could undermine other personalities and make them easier to be removed. Like breaking the fundamental structure under a building will make it collapse and become easier to demolish.

Damn! Aaron thought with admiration. *This old fox really knows what he is doing.*

Now he just needed to hold himself in check, listening to the continuation of Rosie's — Nora's story — no matter how difficult it would be. He ordered himself to concentrate on the scientific part of the procedure — attentively watch auras, describe Rosie's movements and facial expressions in the tablet, and take pictures of the particle's flow toward the smooth back of the head of the Clay Mask that Ashot had already formed.

CHAPTER 31

Rosie grabbed her bottle with a shaky hand and greedily took a sip of water. Then she put it back on the table while sighing deeply a couple of times before she continued the story.

"When I was very young, I didn't know that my grandpa, Vasil, was a sociopath and malignant narcissist as it was determined by psychiatrists during my case. He also had paranoia. My mom told me that only when I started living with her, after being released from the *Youth Shelter* at age fifteen. Vasil was already dead from a stroke at that time. I knew that Vasil loved me very much and I loved him too when he wasn't malicious and angry. He was really charismatic and I knew that people who didn't know him closely, were considering him charming. He played with me a lot because he wasn't working – he was on a pension and had nothing to do all day.

"Grandma Nora was working three jobs, but those weren't well paid ones. We never had enough money, even for food. What she earned, Vasil usually wasted it right away. He considered himself a big businessman, saying that he is buying stuff to resell to make money. But it was always the opposite. I remember he bought a Japanese tape-recorder for $500, played with it for a couple of days, then sold it to a neighbor for $100. For $1,000 he bought a motor for a car. He hoped that if he ever would have a car and its motor needed to be replaced, it would be useful. But it never happened. This motor was laying on our balcony for years, getting rusty, and then it was finally put out to recycling - we still had no car and the motor wasn't needed.

"One day Vasil took the last $250, went to the jewelers and bought Nora a golden ring with a blue gem. He bought it as an apology after beating her the day before. I remember that she was crying when she got this ring. I asked her why. She said, we have nothing to eat. That was our last money and instead of buying food, he bought the ring which she didn't need and didn't want. She was in such despair that she flushed the ring down the toilet. She didn't know that it was possible to return it to the store and I didn't know either."

"How did you live until her next paycheck?" Ashot asked calmly. He obviously heard the story before, but followed the procedure of the cure precisely.

"I don't know. She found something somewhere. I was too young to understand. I don't remember," Rosie took another sip of water and continued. "Vasil was playing active games with me – tag, ball, soccer and taught me martial arts which he knew quite well. I was often sitting on his neck while he was running with me. He taught me to climb trees and roller skate. He was actually good when he had no attacks and we had a lot of fun together."

"Did he ever hurt you?"

"No. Not at all. I never was molested or raped like other girls. My poem **Poison Ivy** about feelings of the girl who was molested by her grandfather, and my poem **Enemies' Cities** about the girl who was raped by her father – they are about my girlfriends Samantha and Brenda from school, grade four. They were my best friends. They shared their tragedies with me and we cried a lot together. The girls were in immense confusion and troubled mentally. They both loved their grandpa and dad very much and they didn't want to send them to prison. But both of them felt that they had to.

"Also, this resulted in a tragedy of breaking their own families. Their parents and grandparents got divorced after that, and the girls were thinking that this was their fault. The catastrophes were huge for them, and I hugged them, I comforted them and I felt their pain. I told them that everything would be okay, though I knew it wouldn't. But it was a 'holy lie' to soothe them. Those were the first times when I began feeling someone's pain. And I always thought how lucky I was that my grandpa Vasil was different. He was fun, he was playing with me, he was nice with me. He never hurt me physically even a bit, but my soul, my feelings – that was another story.

"When I did something wrong, he always beat Nora, forced me to watch and said, 'Look what will happen with you, if you don't listen'. But he never touched me with even one finger. Never. I was always scared for grandma Nora. I loved her and didn't want her to suffer. I felt very guilty that she was crying and screaming in pain because of me. I was sure it was all my fault and I tried to do my best, to be a very obedient child to protect her. But it didn't help much. She was always scared and I was getting this fear from her. It infected me. I kind of absorbed it. I sensed that I am her. Nora was my second lesson on feeling someone's pain. I wrote about her much later in my poem **Shuddering rain.**

Yes, I remember all these poems, Aaron thought. *I was shocked when I read them not understanding how a child could be so sensitive to someone's pain. I was thinking that it came from an unopened part of her brain, but in reality it came from her awful upbringing. Jeez, my poor love! However, maybe I was right, maybe all those dreadful experiences opened her unknown part of the brain and that's how she began writing poetry and got her special brain ability. That's where her talent came from.*

Aaron would give anything for the possibility to hug her now, but he suppressed this wish and kept doing his work silently, holding himself in check. He now felt ashamed of himself for the comments to Ashot about the cure, *Patient is just talking? So simple! So easy!* It was not easy to listen to this, it was horrible, hurtful, painful almost to tears. Especially because he loved this patient and that tripled the intensity of his feelings.

Aaron glanced at Ashot who had already finished creating the back of the clay head and turned his attention to the ear of the Clay Mask. His hands were sliding fast and agile around this big clod of wet clay, forming it into a proper shape. He looked more like an artist, a sculptor, than a psychiatrist.

Through the goggles Aaron saw the flow of the particles from Rosie's face and body. It smoothly streamed toward the Clay Mask disappearing in the back of it. This unfinished sculpture worked as a magnet. Though some of these particles were black or dark blue, they still shone like sparkles. The other ones were of different colors and were flashing in the flow like multicolored Christmas lights. It would actually be very beautiful to watch, if it wouldn't be so emotionally hurtful. Aaron probably would enjoy watching that interesting scientific phenomenon, if only he could be an indifferent observer.

Gosh! How many particles are there! he thought. *When will they all finish, finally! I can't take it anymore! I can't breathe!*

Rosie was silent for a while, putting her head on the face cloth towel that was laying, folded, in front of her on the table, serving as a small pillow. Then she lifted her head. Her eyes were wet and eyelashes stuck to one another.

"My grandpa Vasil was always saying that he is a great teacher," she said. "One day, when I was probably in grade one, he looked accidentally in my school workbook and noticed that my handwriting was not neat. My letters were crooked and falling down from the lines. He started yelling that he would teach me how to write properly. He forced me to sit at the table, gave me a pen and paper and said, 'write!' He brought Nora, pushed her down on all fours and started beating her back with a belt, saying to me, 'I will beat her until your handwriting will get beautiful'. I tried! I tried so hard! But my hands were shaking and tears were streaming down my face. I almost couldn't see anything I was writing. My letters were getting worse instead of getting better. Nora was screaming in pain. Finally, I threw my pen, covered my face with both hands and began crying and howling like crazy as well.

"Then Vasil tossed the belt and walked away. He didn't ever check my school work after that. It occurred only once, but I was scared all the time that he would check it again. However, it never happened, he just forgot about my handwriting completely. So, in reality he obviously didn't care how I am writing - beautifully or not. He was simply a sadist, as I understand now, and just wanted to have his fun and looked for reasons to beat Nora."

Rosie was shaking while telling that part of the story and Aaron felt that his gut was squeezed with a spasm again from intolerable compassion and pity toward her. In despair, he craved to stop this execution but didn't know how it would be possible to do. *When will those damn particles finally be gone!?* he moaned in his mind.

"Why didn't Nora leave him?" Ashot wanted to know.

"Because she didn't know English. If she left him, she would never find another job. We wouldn't have a place to live. But this caretaker's job gave us an apartment. Also, Vasil all the time repeated that if we left, he would find us and kill me. We both, Nora and I, believed him. He always sounded convincing. Nora tolerated everything and sacrificed herself for me. She was scared to put me in danger."

"Why didn't you call the police and ask for help?" Ashot inquired.

"Vasil always said if the police would be called, he would be an angel in front of them. And when they leave, then he will kill both of us for real. We believed him and we were too scared. And also, if the police would be called, everyone in the building would know. Nora could lose her job. No one wanted to keep a caretaker for their condos, who had scandals in her family, involving the police. We kept quiet about Vasil's deeds, and nobody knew. This way Nora kept her job and provided a place for me to live and money for food. She cared about me a lot. She loved me so much that she was actually living for me, only."

"I was about ten, when I saw my grandpa for the first time using a knife. Just a big kitchen knife. I dropped my school bag and it fell accidentally close to our TV. Vasil started screaming that I could have broken the TV and I needed to be beaten. He pushed me on a bed, gave Nora a belt and ordered her to beat me. She refused. Then he took a knife and held it to her throat. He said he would cut her throat if she didn't beat me. He turned his back toward me, but kept the knife at her throat.

"Nora somehow bowed to me and whispered in my ear, 'Scream, pretend that I am beating you'. And she began to beat the mattress beside me with the belt. I screamed really loud and Vasil believed that she was beating me. It continued for maybe five minutes. Then he let Nora go and said to me, 'What a monster your grandma is, look, Rosie, she was beating you. I never ever beat you, right? It is because I love you and I am a very good grandpa. And Nora is a monster grandma. You should love me always and hate her.' I nodded, pretending that I agreed, but in reality I felt the opposite."

What a double-faced devil this man was, Aaron thought, feeling all shaky with anger. *Not just mentally ill but also a real villain. He was a sick animal! How could it be possible for a child not to get completely mentally crushed after surviving all of this?*

Rosie lowered her head on the towel again and cried soundlessly for a while. Her shoulders were shaking. The flow of the particles got really dark and Ashot gestured to Aaron to take pictures. While doing that, Aaron noticed that the whole stream narrowed and began to shrink. *Maybe it is coming closer to the end?* Aaron thought. *Oh, God! Make it finish finally, please. I can't tolerate it anymore. It is breaking my heart. It's such a torture.*

After giving the girl some time to rest and calm down a bit, Ashot asked, "Do you remember how you ended up in the *Youth Shelter*? Why? What happened?"

Rosie lifted her head and looked straight at the Clay Mask. "It was again because of me," she sniffled, "it was my fault. I killed Nora."

"How? Tell us please." Ashot said to her fondly, then he gestured to Aaron and whispered to him, "Pictures non-stop. Now."

Stuttering from her sobs, Rosie continued the story. "I went to visit my mom for a few days, and when I returned home, I put my bag with my clothes in it on a chair. Then I changed and hung my t-shirt on the back of that chair but not very neatly. It fell down on the floor and I didn't notice. Nora was at work at that time. As she came home, she passed that chair, saw my t-shirt on the floor, picked it up and put it inside my bag that was on the chair. She thought that it belonged in my bag. Such a simple and casual happening. Nothing important in it, right? Just a small every day piece of life. But it was her death verdict. If I had hung my t-shirt more accurately, nothing would have happened. Nora would be alive. I killed her by hanging my t-shirt so recklessly."

She covered her face with both hands, dropped her head on the towel again and stayed in this position for a while, breathing heavily. Aaron concentrated on the pictures and took them every ten seconds. The flow of the particles got even more thin and more dark, like a black string. Other colors completely disappeared.

"Later I started looking for my t-shirt and couldn't find it because I didn't know that Nora put it in my bag. Vasil began screaming at me that I should know where my stuff is. Nora shielded me and said that it was her, who put the t-shirt in my bag without telling me. Vasil snatched a kitchen knife, grabbed Nora by her hair, pulled her head back and slit her throat.

"It happened so fast and unexpectedly that I had no time to even think. Nora fell on the floor, blood gushed around. I ran to her, hugged her, wanted to help her, but I was so shocked that I got lost and didn't know what to do. It didn't even come to my mind to call for an ambulance. She wasn't moving and I realized that she was already dead. I got so mad and angry at Vasil for what he did. I grabbed the knife from the floor where he dropped it, jumped at him and started beating him with that knife. It was the first time when I knew that I was not myself anymore. I was Tobi."

Rosie choked, coughed for a while and then wiped tears from her cheeks. She slid her palm in front of her face a couple of times, like closing a mental door and suddenly turned calm and quiet. She froze for a long moment. Then she continued indifferently, almost like a zombie. "I hurt Vasil badly. He had seventeen wounds, but somehow they were not life threatening, luckily for him. I wanted to kill him. He ran from me to another room, locked the door and called 911, saying that his eleven-year-old granddaughter killed her grandma and tried to kill him. The police were there really fast - within minutes.

"Before they came, Vasil told me, 'Listen, Rosie, you love me, right? I am a good grandpa. You should protect me and say that you killed her. I could go to prison for that but you don't want that for me, right? You are a child. Nobody would arrest you. There is no danger for you. You have to say that you did it and I will support that as a witness'.

"I was in such shock that I absolutely didn't understand what he was talking about. But I was sincerely sure that it was my fault because I didn't hang my t-shirt properly and let it fall down on the floor. I still was holding the knife in my hand as I hugged Nora, put my head on her chest and cried, all covered in her blood. I was sure that my clumsiness with the t-shirt was the reason that Nora was dead. I felt such an unbearable guilt. I was crying hysterically and repeating, 'It is my fault. I did it,' when the police arrived. At that time Tobi was already gone. I was Nora now. I felt that her soul came out of her body and entered into mine." This was the end of her story and everyone froze speechless.

As soon as Rosie finished talking, Ashot stopped his work with the Clay Mask. It was supposed to just stay now uncompleted and keep sucking in the stream of the particles coming from Rosie's head and body.

Suddenly the girl leaped from her seat and the flow of particles instantly got huge and multicolored again. "No, no, no!" she shrieked, beating her fists at the table. "I am scared! I am dying! Aaron help me, please, help me. Hug me! Save me! Hold me, Aaron! I am begging you. Love me! Please, help me!" Then she plopped back on the chair and her head fell on the table again. She was unconscious instantly.

Not even thinking what he was doing, Aaron threw his goggles and his camera on the table, jumped up and made some frantic steps, heading to circle the long table and hug her.

"Stop! Don't approach her! Don't touch her!" Ashot yelled at him, rising as well.

"She needs me! She needs comfort!" Aaron yelled back at him. "I won't allow you to torture her anymore." He came to a halt half way, but just for a second, intending to keep going for her help.

"Stop, you idiot! Don't move!" Ashot screamed, then bowed down and took something from a bag on the floor beside him. "If you make one step closer to her, I will kill you," he growled through his teeth, and Aaron heard a loud click as the old man pointed a gun at him and lifted a cocking device on it. "I am not joking. Go back and sit, you stupid idiot!"

Liam ceased filming, put his camera on the table and sat silently, hugging his head with both arms and swinging from side to side with his eyes closed.

"She is in pain. She is suffering. She needs me!" Aaron cried out, seeing that Rosie was convulsing, but she suddenly quit and lay unconscious again - her head on the towel.

"I am serious! I will kill you! Sit back! Now!" Ashot shouted with ire.

"I don't care. I would die for this woman!" Aaron retorted wrathfully.

"And I would kill for this woman to get healthy. If you approach her, the whole session would be ruined. We will have to do it again tomorrow. I don't want her to go through this pain once more because of you, moron!"

Aaron froze on the spot, squeezing his fists tight and breathing heavily, gazing at Ashot with enormous hate as the old man, exasperated, ordered him, "Go back and sit down! Put the goggles on and take pictures. If you love her, you will do that for her. Don't even dare to destroy her cure. Stop being a crybaby! Be a man finally, for her sake. It's a shame to even consider you as a doctor!" He lowered his gun to the table, noticing that Aaron was slowly giving up and yielding.

It took a huge effort from Aaron to suppress the wild storm brewing in his soul and to hold himself in check finally. Gritting his teeth, he returned to his spot, put the goggles on and took the camera with his shaky hands. Ashot shook his head with a sad expression on his face, showing that he was really disappointed in him.

After dealing with Aaron's mad outburst and interruption, and establishing back his power over the situation, Ashot wiped his hands on a small towel, cleaning them of the clay and took the 4D camera from Aaron.

"I am taking pictures by myself now," he said, calming down a bit, but still in a harsh tone. "Get the tablet and make notes of what is happening with the flow, its size, colors, everything. Keep working, Aaron. Now we are just waiting for the flow to end. That will go on for a while and could take some time. Be patient." Then he turned to Liam, "Thank you, babe, that you stopped filming. Would you mind continuing now, please?"

Liam slowly removed his arms from his head, took a deep breath, stood up and lifted his camera onto his shoulder. Not saying a word he resumed filming.

Aaron saw that the stream of the sparkling particles began getting smaller gradually. He described this on the tablet and marked the time. It took about half an hour until the tiny sparkles turned into a thin line instead of the flow, then they became a dotted line and then – disappeared completely.

"Thank God! Amen!" Ashot said with a sigh of relaxation. He put his goggles down, made a sign of the cross on his chest and forehead, and kissed his golden cross on the chain. "We did it! Our child is now one seventh cured, Liam! Nora is gone and never will come back. This poor girl will never be scared again and won't remember any horrors of abuse and that murder ever. Sorry, Aaron. I was forced to stop you from ruining the process. Maybe I was too tough on you, but I had to do that. For her sake and her future health."

Ashot took the gun from the table and wiped it of the clay residue that was left previously from his dirty hands. "It is actually a replica, a toy but not the real thing," he said, smiling, putting the gun back into his bag on the floor. "Rosie will sleep until tomorrow morning. It's normal after the session. Take her, Aaron, and put her in bed. Now you can do anything you want with her."

"Thank you for the permission," Aaron growled quietly, feeling even more ashamed that the gun was not real. To be scared off with a toy was even more humiliating. He approached Rosie, took her in his arms and carried her to her bedroom barely holding a spasm of tears in his throat while watching her pale and lifeless face. Behind his back he heard as Liam asked Ashot, "Darling, were my sessions similarly horrible nightmares?"

"Yes, babe. Some were even worse," Ashot answered. "But it really was worth it, as you can see your life now, already for fifteen years. It's like a surgery - painful, bloody, but needed to be done to save a patient's life. This is serious mental surgery. So, now we can rest too. Let's cook some dinner, darling." Then he called, "Aaron, if you want, you can join us".

However, Aaron didn't answer anything. He put Rosie on her bed, lay beside her, hugging her, and stayed motionless, almost unconscious as well. Then the sobs began gradually coming out from the deep of his shocked soul, shaking him. He was overwhelmed to the edge, to the core of his existence and so exhausted emotionally that he didn't know how he could live further.

CHAPTER 32

The tender sensation of Rosie's lips on his forehead woke Aaron up.

"My love, how are you feeling?" she whispered fondly, noticing that he had opened his eyes.

There was already daylight in the room, so it was obviously late morning.

"Okay. Why?" he smiled tentatively. It would be reasonable to ask how she was feeling after the cure session yesterday, and he was a bit surprised that she asked him this question instead.

"You weren't sleeping quietly," Rosie explained. "It looked like you had nightmares. You were moaning and thrashing in bed. I felt that you were hurting and I wanted to do the healing. I have been holding my lips to your forehead for a long time. Are you better now, my love?"

"Yes, I am okay, I guess. Thank you, Rosie, and I see, you are well too, right? And you didn't lose your fantastic abilities."

"Did we have my cure session yesterday? I don't remember anything."

"Yes, we did."

"And how was it?"

"Okay, I suppose. You are feeling good and you are healing me. So, everything must be alright. Do you still remember your poem for the next concert?"

"Yes, of course," Rosie smiled happily. "My poetry spirit is still here. And I tried to move your phone a bit on the bedside table, with my mind. It is rather heavy, but it moved anyway. So, I am okay, Aaron!" she giggled happily and clapped her hands. "I am oka-a-ay! But, sadly, all my six personalities are still here as well. I feel that they are kind of 'at home' here," she pressed her palm to her forehead. "That's why I wasn't sure, if we did this cure or not."

"Don't worry, they will go step-by-step," Aaron said, being quite bewildered that she completely forgot about the 'Nora thing' and was sure now that she always had just six personalities. It was a big achievement of Ashot's. That made Aaron believe and trust more in the process of this unusual mysterious cure, which had, by the way, an impressive scientific explanation. However, he wasn't sure, could he tell her about Nora's disappearance or not. It would be better to ask Ashot about that. So Aaron just carefully changed the subject.

"Look, it started to grow," he said, softly petting the spiky hair on her head. "It's looking cute, even kind of more sexy. I like this haircut. Will you go to the concert like that? Or do you want to buy a wig?"

"Yes, a wig, and I will need a special costume. It would not be difficult to get, just some stuff from *Dollar Store* or *Party World*. And, my poem will be about you, Aaron, again."

"Jeez, you make me scared. Should I be ready for something extra special?"

"Yes, super special, my love. Do you want to go to shower now? Together?"

"I don't think so," Aaron objected. "First of all the guys are probably already awake ..."

"Don't worry about them. Today is Sunday. They've gone to church. They always do. I checked earlier. We are absolutely alone and can do what we want."

"I think I need to go to the fitness club downstairs and do my exercise first, then shower. I am not completely out of yesterday's stress yet. I need to let out some more of it. Do you want to go with me?"

"Okay," she nodded. "I will, though I usually don't exercise. Maybe I have to start with you, right, my love? But what do you mean – yesterday's stress?"

Aaron shrugged. "It doesn't matter. Forget it." He didn't want to worry her by telling her how shocking her cure session was for him.

They went to the club and Aaron did his workouts, while Rosie sat and watched and took pictures of him with her phone. "I will be looking at them when you are not with me," she laughed. "For inspiration!"

Then they took showers there before going to the pool, swam for a while and chat with some other residents who came to swim as well. After that Aaron and Rosie took another shower at home, to wash away the pool's chlorine and to love each other. Aaron was a bit wary of that, but Rosie insisted. Everything went smoothly and fondly, without even a hint at her mental condition. It was great again. He was happy beyond belief, and it looked to him like she was blissful as well.

The older men came home, when Rosie and Aaron were in the kitchen making breakfast though it was already past lunch time.

"Guys, do you want to join us?" Rosie asked.

"No. Thanks, kiddo, we had lunch at church, as usual," Liam answered.

"But I would like to do a physical check on you, Rosie," Ashot said.

As soon as she finished her meal, he checked her temperature, blood pressure, pulse, eyes, skin for rashes and smiled, satisfied. "Very well, kiddo. I think we did a good job yesterday. What is your opinion, Aaron?"

Aaron nodded silently. After his nervous breakdown during the cure session he still had difficulty talking to Ashot.

"But I still have all my six personalities, uncle," Rosie reported, putting her palm on her forehead. "Why are they not gone?"

"You did have seven, kiddo," Ashot answered calmly. "One is gone. After the next session another will go. Don't worry about them."

"Which one is gone?"

"Nora."

"Nora?" Rosie lifted her eyebrows in surprise. "Who is Nora?"

"It was your grandma, I guess," Ashot prompted. "Do you remember her?"

"Yes, a little. They raised me, Grandma Nora and Grandpa Vasil. But I was very young when I lived with them. I don't remember much, just that they were nice to me. Grandma always hugged me and grandpa played ball with me. I know that they both died. I have a few very fond memories of them."

"Excellent, kiddo," Ashot smiled. "That's how it should be."

"I would like to go now and buy some things for my concert next Tuesday. Could I go with Aaron?" Rosie requested.

"No, kiddo," Ashot answered before Aaron even had a chance to open his mouth. "I guess Liam could drive you, but Dr. Dispenmore and I need to go somewhere. I want to show him something and we need to talk seriously. Actually very seriously."

Aaron felt humiliated at that moment like he was a third grader and was called to the principal's office for a misbehavior, but he just gritted his teeth and kept silent.

Ashot took the goggles and 4D camera from the table in the living room, placed them in a bag and they all went to the parking garage downstairs. They left the building in their two cars - Liam with Rosie for shopping, Ashot with Aaron – for some unknown destination.

The old man drove to I-5 north and Aaron at first couldn't understand where he was heading. To Canada, or where? But he didn't want to ask anything, so, he sat uncommunicative. Ashot was silent as well. The tension between them in the air was palpable.

However, it surprised Aaron, when Ashot turned right on Hwy 20 toward the North Cascade National Park. It was a route known to him too well - his beloved spiritual place beside the Diablo Lake where he took Rosie last Tuesday before her remarkable concert which ended with their long kiss on stage. *Why is he going there?* Aaron thought. *Did Rosie tell him something about our visit to that place?* But, again, he didn't ask anything, just stayed quiet.

Ashot passed the Diablo dam for a couple of miles, then stopped at the clearing beside the road and turned to Aaron.

"Let's go, son," he uttered calmly. "I will show you something important that you have to know for your future as a doctor." Aaron was really surprised by the change of his tone and the unexpected word 'son' instead of 'stupid idiot' that he heard previously, but again, didn't say anything and followed Ashot wordlessly.

They walked about two miles on an animal trail, then climbed down the river on the steep slope and stopped at the edge of the rocks line almost by the water. Ashot bent and moved some boulders aside.

"Look into this crack," he said. "Do you see it? There is the blue clay. It is the only spot of it that I found. I am thirty years older than you. By the logic of nature I should die first. I want you to know where you could take more clay, if you will continue to cure your coming patients, being a respected doctor who won the Nobel Prize. It is the successful future of your career, son. You shouldn't tell anybody about this place because it is your professional business secret. The map explaining how to find this place is in the folder about my chemical analysis of the clay. You probably saw it there, just didn't know what it was."

"Why are you giving it away to me?" Aaron asked bewildered. "So far, I felt that you hate me."

"At the church this morning I prayed for you. I begged God to help me to understand you and I got my answer. God showed me how to deal with you. I got the spiritual perception of your heart and soul – and of your behavior because of that. You really do love my kiddo, Aaron, don't you?"

Aaron blushed and didn't say anything, feeling uncomfortable to talk about such a personal topic especially with a man who obviously was Rosie's father figure.

"I saw everything in her aura's particles," Ashot continued, completely composed. "After sexual excitement, in yellow layers of auras, orange sparkles appeared. You saw them too in the goggles, but you just didn't know what they meant. Partially, I was angry at you that you didn't manage to hold yourself in check after you knew what an awful onrush happened with her in your car. But then I realized that it won't affect anything in her cure. And, also, there was no danger for now that any outbursts like that could happen again. On the first morning after the attack, while you were sleeping, I worked with her psychologically and calmed Tobi for a while. Rosie will be okay and capable of lovemaking for a few days. But no more than that. Then Tobi will return. So, be careful, please, and think about that before losing your head another time."

Aaron stood silently, dying inside from confusion and shame. Although at the same time he had the feeling that a blessing for his relationship with Rosie was actually given to him. He didn't know what to say. Ashot opened his bag and took out goggles and a 4D camera.

"Now, put the goggles on, Aaron," he said, changing the subject. "And look at the clay in the crack. You could clearly see the stream of particles that are going straight up to the sky, don't you? The clay is not alive, so it doesn't have an aura, and all particles are just white sparkles – the energy, but they are here, right? Now, let's take a picture of them. Then look at the river. Watch the stream of the particles that are rising from the water up to the universe. They are the same white sparkles. It means that the universal energy that exists in water – a fact well known in science - in this blue clay is also similar. That's where the clay's power is. Do you get it?"

Aaron nodded, astonished by the fantastic beauty of the miraculous connections of the Earth with the universe. If he didn't see this with his own eyes, he would be having difficulty believing it.

Then Ashot bent down to move big boulders back to cover the crack in the ground. He started to climb up on the steep slope toward the animal trail. Aaron followed him silently, still bewildered by the discovery he saw. His heart softened a bit toward this old man.

When they reached the car and Ashot did a U-turn to drive back home, Aaron suddenly asked, "Would you mind, please, to stop at the top of the hill above the lake? I would like to show you something as well."

"Okay," Ashot agreed and in a few minutes as they approached the place he parked his car on the side of the road. It was actually very close to the Ashot's animal trail, not farther than a couple of miles. Aaron got out of the car, came to the edge of the abyss and sat on the grass. This time Ashot followed him. They sat for a while speechlessly watching the lake. Then Aaron said, "You revealed to me your sacred place, Ashot. Thank you for sharing and for your trust. Now... this is my sacred place. It has a very special energy here. I guess, like nowhere else even in this mountain range. I don't know exactly, maybe even nowhere in the world. You could feel this energy, I am sure."

Ashot nodded, not saying a word.

"Five years ago," Aaron continued, "I really wanted to jump into this abyss because I didn't want to live without my wife. There were, maybe, a few seconds left for me to live, but suddenly I heard a voice in my ears which said that I shouldn't do that, I should go home. It felt at the moment like the 'voice of God'. I don't know... I am not sure... But I sensed it not just in my ears, but kind of on my skin, as well. I absorbed it. And I had no power to disobey it. I went home and stayed alive since.

"During the years after that, I came here sometimes to sit, to watch the lake, the mountains, to feel this energy, to think about the meaning of my life, the meaning of everything. I brought Rosie here last Tuesday before her concert. Did she tell you about that?"

"No," Ashot shook his head.

"I was physiologically alive all those years, but I was kind of numb in my soul. I was acting almost like a robot or a zombie – work, home, walking with a child, talking nicely with my mother, with friends whom I went golfing occasionally with, with co-workers, with patients. It was all dead and meaningless emotionally.

"Rosie's book woke me up. I opened it, I started reading and I got mesmerized, bewitched, engaged... I don't know how else I can say it. I fell in love with her so much, so deeply, so miraculously... Short to say, I am alive now. I am not that robot anymore. I am a normal human being. And my guess is that all those feelings that I missed for five years - they accumulated somewhere inside me. They collected in my soul like steam in a locomotive and now they are exploding sometimes. For me it wasn't difficult to hold myself in check before. Now it is. Especially when I see that Rosie is in pain. She suffered so much during her young life. I don't want that for her anymore. So, Ashot, I am sorry. I apologize for my outburst yesterday. It was just too much for me to absorb. I hope that other sessions won't be that hurting. I only worry a bit about Tobi."

"Well," Ashot smirked wryly. "Apology accepted. And I apologize for this thing with the gun. You just scared me that everything could be ruined. You should understand, Aaron, that this is the future of this girl. Could you imagine, if during a heart transplant surgery, the surgeon would drop his scalpel and begins hugging the cut open patient, saying, 'Oh, she needs me, she wants a hug'? As much as you love her, you still should force yourself to remain professional. At moments like that, she is not your girlfriend, she is your patient and nothing else.

"Other sessions won't be as harsh as Nora was, but still... there may be a few moments. I probably will do some short sessions with you, Aaron, before each Rosie's cure, to make it easier for you to tolerate. And don't worry about Tobi. I am expecting that if we eliminate all other personalities, Tobi probably will go away by itself. If I am right that she is not really a personality, but only the reaction to extreme emotions. We will see.

"And about your story... I've got it. I believe that it was God who saved you. I had similar experiences several times during my darkest moments. He saved me too. He probably needs us to cure Rosie. We are tools in His hands now. He trusts us and we both should prove that His trust is not in vain. However, thank you for sharing as well, son."

CHAPTER 33

On the way back to Seattle, as soon as they left the mountains and reached a cell connection area in the valley, close to the city of Sedro-Woolley, Ashot's phone clicked announcing a text being received.

"Hmm... Liam was told not to call except for an emergency," Ashot uttered with an unhappy expression on his face while trying to find a place to stop the car to look at the text, "'Vally. Come ASAP.' Damn, not good," he sighed deeply, shaking his head.

"What's happening?" Aaron wanted to know, feeling tense right away,

"Rosie turned into Vally, probably crying like crazy and Liam doesn't know what to do with her. We need to go home quickly to deal with that."

Noting that he kept driving at an officially allowed speed, Aaron asked, "Couldn't you go faster?"

"If I get wild and have an accident, it wouldn't help. Let's not make things worse. You need to learn how to always stay calm, son..."

"Rationally I understand it," Aaron agreed, nervously biting his lips. "It just is so difficult when this happens with Rosie..."

"Learn, son. You still have at least two months to tolerate until she will be completely cured."

Then they drove in silence. Aaron didn't dare to distract Ashot's attention anymore.

At home, in the elevator, the old man said, "Aaron, please, do not approach her. I will take her to the patio and talk to her. You stay inside, beside the door, so she can't see you, but you'll hear everything that is being said. You need to know how to deal with this in future months, when you are together, far away from me.

"You should learn how to be a psychiatrist, son – to do more than just prescribing pills, which, sadly, is everything that they were teaching you at university. I am not talking here about the practice of scientific research in labs that you were taught perfectly. But the main goal of our profession is human contact, the skill to sooth patients, to calm them psychologically through talking. Sorry, I don't want to hurt your feelings, but to be a psychiatrist you have to know how to calm down a mad wild man in his worst episode, not to mention a crying child."

"I already dealt with her as Vally," Aaron shared, "the day after we met. I was hugging, kissing, and soothing her fondly."

"Like a lover, not like a doctor," Ashot smirked. "And did it work for you?"

"Not really. She calmed down for a couple minutes, but then suddenly started screaming at me and beating me."

"Well," Ashot nodded several times, as if agreeing on something that he told himself in his mind. "Okay, just watch patiently, Aaron."

When they entered the condo, Liam, confused, was sitting on the couch in the second living room and Rosie was crying beside him, with her face on his shoulder. A bag with their merchandise was on the floor beside them.

"Hey," Ashot said, approaching them, "Vally, let's go outside, so you can show me what you bought." He took the bag with one hand and Rosie's arm with the other and pulled her to the patio door. Rosie obediently walked with him. Ashot made sure that she sat on the chair at one side of the table and took another chair directly across from her. He put the bag on the table between them.

He acted so fast and confident that there was no room left for any doubts or questions. For the patient there was only one way - to listen and follow orders.

As they settled, Ashot smiled at Rosie, showing her a good mood. "Wow!" he said while taking from the shopping bag a silver lacy fabric with sparkles, then a shiny plastic crown and a blond wig with long hair. "It looks like it's for a princess. Is that what you wish to be at your concert?"

Rosie, still sniffling and smearing tears on her cheeks, probably nodded. Aaron couldn't see it inside the room, but he could hear the sounds. He and Liam both listened attentively. Aaron heard Ashot's voice change in a very smooth, velvety tone, breathing with kindness, calm and a bit of drowsiness.

"He is using hypnosis," Liam whispered into Aaron's ear.

"Yeah, I guessed that," Aaron nodded.

At that time, after giving the girl a moment to sniffle a bit more, Ashot continued, "So, this obviously will be a triumph for Anastasia, right? Why are you crying then? Aren't you happy for her?"

"Because it will be my last time on stage, uncle. Poetry is everything to me. I am very scared that my talent will be lost. I don't want a cure anymore. I refuse the cure..."

Ashot didn't object and stayed silent.

"If I will be normal but without my talent," the girl continued, "Aaron won't love me anymore. I know that, I feel that. He swears that he will love me anyway, but he doesn't understand himself. He doesn't know. I don't want to be healthy. I would rather stay ill and have my poetry and his love."

"Listen, Vally," Ashot finally said calmly, "you're a smart girl and you know that the poetry club is for teens, and you are twenty. They are letting you stay a bit longer because they love you there and they are making an exception for you. But it can't last forever. Very soon the time will come when you leave anyway. You do know that, don't you? We talked about that before. Right, Vally?"

"Yes, uncle," Rosie sniffled again.

"I understand it's sad, but as we live our lives, everything changes, nothing is forever. Look at me. I was such a strong and brave guy, and what now? I am getting old. What do you think I should do? Cry about that? No, I am accepting it and will keep living until God takes me."

"You have love, uncle. Liam loves you and I love you. You can be happy and accept everything."

"You also have love, kiddo. Liam and I, we both love you very much. I am not talking about Aaron who is head over heels for you. Isn't it enough? Damn! You have three men in your life. Tell any other girl about that. She would be jealous like crazy. Right?" he laughed and Rose giggled a bit as well, though still sniffling.

"Vally never was loved," she sadly said then. "She was always crying from pain in her soul."

"Tell her to go, please. Now you are loved a lot. All this love should push Vally away. And you will shine at your concert, as Anastasia, not Vally, right? And then – you never know what God had prepared for you. I am sure it would be something absolutely amazing and you will be much happier than now. Look at Liam. He lost his piano. But isn't he happy with what he is doing now? Did you ask him?"

"Many times," she nodded, "many times, uncle. I know everything will be okay. I am just scared. I don't want to lose Aaron. If I lose him, I die. He is everything to me."

"You just told me a couple minutes ago that poetry is everything to you, kiddo."

"Yes, I love them both, poetry and Aaron, and I don't know how to choose."

"I have a solution," Ashot said convincingly. "You should trust God on it. He will do everything that is the best for you. Look what he did for me? Look what he did for Liam? Look, even what he did for Aaron recently? He sent you to him. You are like a miracle in his life. It is amazing, isn't it? We all are better now than we were some time ago, aren't we? Let's keep doing our cure and don't worry about anything bad. Many good things will happen as a result of it. I promise that to you, kiddo."

There was silence for a long moment on the patio. Then Rosie took a deep breath and whispered, "Uncle, could we go for dinner at the *Old Spaghetti Factory?*"

"Of course, kiddo. The guys are probably already hungry as hell. Let's go and get them," Ashot answered, as she jumped up and ran to the living room, laughing and giggling happily. She plopped on Aaron's lap, hugged his neck and started kissing him right beside Liam. Aaron realized that she was probably Kiki now. It was too childish, maybe even too silly, but anyway much better than the endless tears of Vally.

During their dining out, she calmed down, step by step, and finally changed back to Rosie which was a huge relief for all of them.

Aaron and Rosie sat across from each other in the restaurant. He couldn't help notice that in spite of her red eyes from crying, she was especially pretty now with this short haircut. In his opinion, she looked much better than with long hair. It appeared so alluring and sex-appealing that it made him grin at her significantly all the time. Rosie blushed and smiled back, obviously reading his thoughts. Then she slid her hand in front of her face and answered him telepathically, "I want you too, Aaron. You know, you are a very sexy looking man for my taste."

It was amazing that she didn't lose her telepathic ability after the first cure session. It gave Aaron hope that maybe she won't lose anything ever, except for her illness. It would be the greatest outcome imaginable.

The older men had enough life experience so they could see these flirting games in front of them. They laughed and teased this young couple who were crazily smitten with each other. But the jokes were friendly, so nobody was offended and just had a lot of rosiness on their cheeks.

Gradually, Aaron started feeling at home in this company. Any tension he had before evaporated. He almost got used to these men. If they were Rosie's family now, they would be his family as well, and he finally accepted this.

During dinner, they also made plans for tomorrow. Ashot and Aaron will start working on editing and polishing all of their observations taken during the cure, preparing both versions of the session – digital and paperwork, summarizing all the materials they had. Liam would, first, drive Rosie to visit her friends from the Poetry Club, and then – do the editing of his film. The weekend was finished now and the busy working week was ahead of them all.

While retiring for the night, Aaron openly went with Rosie to her bedroom.

"Aren't you worrying anymore about what guys will think?" she asked hesitantly.

"No," he answered. "This morning, I kind of got a blessing from your uncle. It looks like he, at last, approves our relationship. Sorry, my love, it is a bit awkward to ask, but... aren't you worrying about birth control?"

"No. Why?" Rosie shrugged. "If we have a child, I am okay with that. But I know that you didn't want it. That's why you are asking?"

"It's not that I didn't want it. While on the boat, talking about a child, you just got me off guard. I was caught unexpectedly, then. Now I am already used to the idea. I just want to be sure that you didn't change your mind. I am asking because today I am so much in the mood that I will caress you like crazy... like to death... We won't sleep at all, I swear."

"I am actually in the mood, too," she whispered, hugging his neck and kissing him. "Though, as you know, I was a pretty good sleeper during sex, ain't I?"

"Yeah," he laughed. "It happened a couple of times before. But I'm sure we are already passed it, right, my love?"

CHAPTER 34

The working week started as it was planned and Aaron was happy to get into a regular routine which he really liked. It made him very comfortable and gave him the feeling of being settled, living with a friendly family and almost being 'married'. Emotionally it was finally a rest, a calm; also, there was very interesting, productive professional work which led him to the future of his dreams – as Ashot promised - the healthy woman he loves in his bed and a Nobel Prize in his pocket.

Though the Nobel Prize was still far away on the horizon, the woman he loved was already here, every night with him, in his bed and in his arms. And Aaron caressed her, sometimes wondering if it would ever be enough for him.

On Monday the housekeeper came to work in their condo, as usual, but Ashot closed the door into the first living room, where they did the cure session and asked her not to clean anything in there, and not to even enter that room at all during the next three months.

"You don't want her to see the Clay Mask?" Aaron asked.

"Of course," Ashot nodded. "It's my private laboratory, for patients, co-workers, but not for public view. At the hospital, for example, nobody lets the public enter the operation room, right?"

"I am just curious, how is the Clay Mask doing there?" Aaron asked. "Could you show me?"

"Not much to see," Ashot answered, "but I'll show you. You don't just have the right to look at it, but you must know how it is preserved between sessions. Don't forget, it is your work which in the future you will do by yourself."

In that living room everything stayed as it was left in anticipation of the next session. The unfinished Clay Mask was standing on the same tray, but it was covered now by a huge clear plastic box. Around the Mask, inside the box, were placed several bowls with water which was evaporating under the plastic cover. The drops were hanging on the walls and top of the box. It was obviously a humid environment inside to prevent the clay from drying. It was looking much like a tiny greenhouse for tropical plants, orchids, that grow originally in rainforests.

"The clay needs to be wet all the time," Ashot explained, "so I can keep working on it. If it dried out, it could break, crack, or otherwise get damaged, and then the particles could spread the wrong way at the wrong time. It would be disastrous. So, we should be very careful and protective with it. But it is normal, Aaron. We need to take care of our equipment the same way as surgeons are taking care of their equipment and tools in their operating rooms."

"Yes, "Aaron agreed, "it looks very serious - like you have created a real small private hospital."

"And when we finish with the cure, we will need to have an officially licensed and registered private clinic to present it to the conference in New York as the place where the cure was made. I can't do that, obviously with my nursing qualifications, so it goes again, on you, Aaron. Just think, where would you like to register your clinic? Should we rent or buy a place for it? No rush. We still have a lot of time until that moment."

"Okay, I will think about that," Aaron agreed.

"But no hurry, only after the cure is completely done," Ashot reminded him once more. "Now, let's keep working on the materials of the last session. We still have time for that today."

They continued their work the rest of Monday, however, the next day, on Tuesday, the day of Rosie's stage performance, none of them was working. Aaron left the condo for a couple of hours and drove to a mall to buy some stuff. Liam was busy preparing his camera for filming the concert. Ashot went to get two huge bouquets of roses – red and white ones - and hid them in big pails with some water in the back of his car. It was assumed that Rosie would go to the concert with Aaron in his car, so she wouldn't see the flowers ahead of time. All her men wanted to surprise her.

They also booked a late evening party after the concert in the Space Needle at the *SkyCity Restaurant*. Rosie invited about twenty of her friends from the club and all staff of the Greenwich Competition Hall to celebrate her farewell.

Rosie stayed in her room during the day, editing her poem and working on her stage costume. After finishing with his camera settings, Liam cooked dinner and they ate together, joking, laughing and enjoying the company of each other.

Rosie's performance was booked at the end of the concert, so Ashot and Liam were expected to appear close to this time. But she and Aaron went for the beginning of the concert and left the condo first.

The atmosphere in front of the Greenwich Competition Hall was the same as Aaron saw twice before – crowds, music, laughter and the happy spirit of youth. He genuinely enjoyed it, especially looking at Rosie as she blossomed turning into Anastasia.

She was now wearing one of the beautiful sundresses that Aaron bought her at the Lynden Fair market. But it was not for the stage. Aaron helped her to carry a pretty significant bag with her performance costume. When he settled her in one of the dressing rooms, she hugged him and said, "I booked for you a VIP seat in the front row. You better go now, my love. I should change and concentrate. I need to be alone for a while."

"Promise not to jump down on me this time, okay?" he smiled, kissing her goodbye.

"Okay, I promise. And you promise not to kiss me for that long, if you come to the stage at the end."

"That I can't promise, but I will try," Aaron chuckled, being in an excellent mood. "Good luck, my love. See you soon."

Aaron was dressed for an important event tonight. He wore a new blue festive shirt, which replaced his previous one that he tore into pieces to bandage Rosie's wounds after her awful knife attack in his car. While in the mall this morning, he also bought light-gray pants at the same store as the shirt, to prepare for the biggest day of his life.

As usual, the concert lasted about one hour until the last performance. Then, two men, assistants of the show, pulled on the stage an equipment which was customaryly used for trained animals' actions. It was a high raised small platform with the two step ladders connected on both sides of it. There were ten steps on each side. It stood normally along the stage, so the audience could see how the dogs run up the steps on one side, do some tricks or flips on the platform and then run down the stairs on the other side. Now the assistants turned the platform, so one of the stairs led up from the back of the stage, and the other stairs led down toward the edge of the stage, toward the public.

Aaron was surprised to observe these preparations. Rosie didn't tell him that she planned to use any equipment for her performance. The poets never did. He noticed Liam appeared with his camera at the side of the stage, ready to film. Ashot wasn't visible yet. *He is probably waiting backstage with those flowers,* Aaron guessed.

"Now, our last performance tonight - Rosalyn Vivano," the host announced and Aaron held his breath, not knowing what to expect. Calm beautiful music began, which wasn't common for poetry performances as well. But it was very quiet, so Rosie's words could easily be heard through it. Then she came out, walked up the backstairs and stopped high on the platform, smiling at the audience who greeted her with an exploding ovation.

Rosie was dressed like a fairy. She wore a blond long-haired wig and a silver crown. On her feet were plastic slippers covered with shiny pieces of polished glass pretending to be gems. Her body was wrapped into a lacy fabric with sparkles which looked like a cloak.

As the excitement of the audience subsided, she lifted her microphone and said, "My dear friends, I am so happy to be with you tonight, but sadly it will be my last performance. I am leaving the club where I belonged for five years, to start my new life. So, I want to say my farewell. My poem is **Farewell Anastasia**.

One upon a time there was a poetry fairy named Anastasia.

She lived in a crystal castle in the sky, deep in the universe.

With her angel's wings she flew from star to star, planet to planet,

Spreading shiny drops of spiritual beauty everywhere.

(Rosie spread her arms wide like wings and waved them as if flying.)

She knew the happiness and ecstasy of creating poetry,

But she didn't know what love is.

One day she asked God to show her the human love and He pointed

At a man down on the Earth who loved her, admiring her poems and her talent.

Anastasia felt right away that this man was her destiny

And she fell in love with him instantly. "If you come to Earth," God warned her, "you will be a regular woman, not the fairy anymore.

Your talent would be gone, your poetry spirit would disappear forever."

But Anastasia loved this man so much that she decided to go anyway.

She began walking down the crystal steps from her castle to Earth.

(Now, Rosie started walking slowly down the stairs.)

With each of her steps one of the sparkling white feathers fell off her wings,

Each of her tears turned into diamonds, rolled somewhere lost
in the darkness.
Her wings were getting smaller, lighter and less beautiful,
Her sparkling sky dress turned into ordinary earthy clothes.

(With each step down, Rosie threw away her silver fairy's cloak, then
her crown and finally the wig. Underneath the shiny fabric she wore an
old stretched colorless t-shirt and jeans torn at her knees, so the threads
were hanging untidily.)

She was losing her poetry images and her inspiring words,
She was losing herself and became something that was not her.

(At the end of the stairs, Rosie threw away her slippers and walked
barefoot.)

She touched Earth with her foot and stepped on it, finally.
She fell down on the ground being simple, spiritless and
colorless
In front of this man who loved her as a miraculous fairy, and she
said,
"Take me, I am here for you. I am a soulless, talentless empty
dead doll.
Would you love me now, if I am not your poetry fairy Anastasia
anymore?"

In every following stanza, tears sounded in Rosie's voice more
clearly. She barely could hold them to finish the poem. Then, with
her last words, she sat on the floor, threw away the mic, covered
her head by crossing her arms on the top of it and cried desperately,
shaking with sobs.

It was truly high-level acting as the audience thought, exploding
in a squall of applause, whistles and screams "Bravo! Bravo!" But
Aaron knew those were her real feelings. It was what she gave
away for him, sacrificed for him and sincerely struggled with at the
moment, not being sure, if he will love her without her talent, in
case, if she would lose it in reality.

It was flattering for him that she loved him more than her poetry, that she chose him over her creations and success. However, he knew that this choice cost her a lot. It was an anguish in her soul now, and he absorbed it from her. Her pain was so sharp that he didn't want her to experience it.

Aaron jumped up, ran along the stage to the steps on the left side of it and raced up. He grabbed Rosie, lifted her from the floor, moved her arms aside from her head, picked up the crown that she dropped and placed it back on her head. He also picked up the microphone. Then he lifted Rosie in his arms and, holding her tight, said into the mic, "I will love you always. You are forever my fairy Anastasia, my poetry queen and my true love."

The audience was wailing in ecstasy, clapping crazily; everybody was filming. Rosie sniffled, wiped her tears from her cheeks with her palm and giggled happily, dangling her feet, while she hugged Aaron's neck and kissed him. It was a light, fast kiss, not like at the previous concert at all. He kissed her on her cheek, as well, then had her stand on the floor, lowered himself on one knee in front of her, took a little box with a ring from his pocket and said into the microphone, "I love you, Rosalyn Vivano! Would you marry me?"

Rosie took the mic from his hand and screamed into it, "Yes!!! I would!! I love you, Aaron!" With that he put the beautiful diamond ring on her finger, lifted her in his arms again and walked, carrying her down the small stairs from the stage to the audience floor.

Still carrying her, Aaron walked the middle aisle of the hall to the right side of the audience, then back, and then – to the left side. Then he returned to the stage and repeated this route, right and left, in front of the first row. All the way he let Rosie get high-fives from the people, and give high-fives back to them. Liam's camera followed them all the way.

It was her triumph, and the peak moment of her life. She was boundlessly happy, feeling as real Anastasia now. As if God, seeing her devotion to love, changed His mind and gave her His permission to stay Anastasia on Earth forever, being a beautiful and talented woman though not the fairy anymore.

Then Aaron brought her up on the stage where Ashot was already waiting. The old man handed Rosie the flowers, hugged and kissed her on both cheeks and she kissed him back. She was sinking in the smell and beauty of the fresh roses, hugging the bouquets with her arms. The audience kept applauding and shouting "Bravo, Rosalyn!". Cell phones kept flashing and videos kept popping out on Facebook, Twitter, Instagram and YouTube spreading the moment around the globe. Once more the same people in Seattle, Florida, New York and Afghanistan who saw the previous video of their kiss on stage, now watched Aaron's proposal.

CHAPTER 35

After the concert a big party was thrown at the *SkyCity* restaurant at the top of the Space Needle with music, dancing, and laughter. A lot of poetry sounded there – everyone of Rosie's friends from the Poetry Club read their poems. She recited her **Ancient Greek Hymn of Love.**

At some point it looked like a wedding. Rosie and Aaron were sitting in the middle of a long table with the rose bouquets around them. Ashot and Liam were beside Rosie. Everyone was greeting the young couple's engagement and told stories about Rosie's former performances. They remembered the funny occurrences that happened in the history of the Club during the five years that Rosie was a member.

Guests sat at the small tables that were spread around the room, the food and drinks were served by waiters. The dance floor was available all the time because the music was played non-stop. The DJ just made it quiet for a while when someone was addressing the audience. Sometimes applause started with the screams, "Kiss the bride!" and Aaron passionately kissed Rosie.

At the end, they had danced their 'first wedding waltz'. Liam filmed the whole party.

Aaron wore the same festive pants and shirt as at the concert, and Rosie, after her performance, changed back into her beautiful sundress. So, the only difference with a wedding was that they both didn't wear special outfits. Also, there was no priest, no gifts, no relatives or friends from his side.

At home they placed one rose bouquet in Rosie's bedroom and another one on the dining table at the patio. Then Rosie went to shower and Aaron was ready to enter her bedroom, as Ashot said, "Aaron, can I talk to you for a minute?"

"Yes," he answered, turning to the old man who gestured to him to follow onto the patio.

"Listen," Ashot said quietly, making sure that nobody except for Aaron could hear him. "It was very reckless of you not to consult with me before doing this 'show-off' with a ring on stage. It's too early for an engagement."

"Why should I ask for your permission for everything?" Aaron snapped. "You're not her father."

"Jeez, Aaron. I am not her father, but I am her psychiatrist, which in reality you should be. I am playing this role only because you don't. You were a boyfriend, a lover, now – a fiance. She is not ready for any of these yet. She needs a doctor and the cure, first. You are rushing the process. Be reasonable, please."

"How? I love her. Were you reasonable, when you fell in love with Liam while he was sick and you cured him?"

"Yes, I was. I liked him, but we didn't have anything romantic at all until he was completely cured. It took three whole months. Only after Liam got his evaluation from the General Psychiatric Hospital and it was proven that he was completely healthy, we went out on our first date."

"Well. Everybody is different. He was your story. Rosie is mine," Aaron objected stubbornly. "You told me yourself on Sunday, there, in the Diablo mountains, that you removed Tobi and Rosie is capable of love."

"Yes. But if you remember properly, I said, 'for a while, for a couple of days.' Now, with this engagement – she is overjoyed. We wanted to make a farewell supper for the Poetry Club only, but you turned it almost into a wedding. I am just warning you – please, be very careful with her now. You're walking on the edge of a razor here."

"I will be careful, okay. Thank you for the reminder," Aaron nodded with a very unhappy expression on his face and walked away.

As he entered Rosie's bedroom, she still was in the shower, waiting for him. He quickly undressed and joined her. They were laughing and splashing at the beginning, but, as usual, it ended up with lovemaking again. Then they dried each other with towels and Aaron carried her, hot and pink, to bed. He knew that they will probably have a long break in sexual encounters starting tomorrow. But now it seemed to him that she was still okay to be loved more during the night.

Rosie put on a black lacy negligee and said, giggling, "I want to seduce you, Aaron."

"I am already seduced for the rest of my life," he chuckled as well. "But, anyway, it's very sexy and beautiful. Thank you my love."

"How does the ring look on your fiancee?" she asked, stretching her arm to show off. "Okay?"

"Absolutely amazing!"

Aaron was on the top of the world when she accepted his proposal. Before, at the restaurant, while they were talking about Prince and Cinderella, she boldly refused. She said then, *Don't even think about this ever, please. Not for one second... At least, until I can be completely cured.*

She wasn't completely cured yet, but after the first session, Aaron felt pretty confident that she would be okay with the idea of marrying him. He really wanted to connect to her as tight and strong as possible. He swore that he will not allow himself to lose her, as he lost Ally. He will not allow fate to be repeated.

Aaron felt that he loved Rosie so much that he was turning absolutely insane hugging her in bed, holding her in his arms and taking her again and again. She did not object, appeared very happy as well, and answered him passionately and eagerly.

Then, they finally fell asleep, calm and quiet, like babies, still hugging each other.

It was like a bolt from the blue, when a wild scream woke Aaron up. Rosie wasn't beside him anymore. She was somewhere in the kitchen, screeching and howling, and plates were thrown on the marble floor, breaking with a loud thunderous noise. He jumped up, put on a bathrobe and ran there. She was standing beside the open drawer, holding the big sharp knife which Liam used to cut beef steaks for the BBQ.

As Aaron tried to approach her, she waved the knife at him shouting, "Go away, I hate you! I want my Anastasia back. I won't be with you. I want to be with my poetry. I don't want to live. I will die now!" Rosie had already slashed one of her wrists and blood was on her bathrobe, on the kitchen counter and on the floor. She needed to be stopped and restrained, but Aaron struggled with this. He didn't dare to approach her because he could easily lose his eye or get his face slashed.

He heard Ashot and Liam's bedroom door slammed as they raced out, both in their pajamas. Ashot disappeared in Aaron's bedroom, which was also a medical equipment storage room. Liam rushed in the hallway and entered the kitchen from the other side. He came to Rosie from behind and grabbed her by her both lower arms, squeezing them tight to her sides, so she couldn't wave the knife anymore. Seeing that she was restricted for a while, Aaron stepped in and snatched the knife from her hand.

She was still kicking and jerking, trying to free herself from Liam's hands and almost kicked Aaron in the groin. He barely jumped aside to avoid it. Then Ashot appeared with a syringe in his hand, and thrust the needle into Rosie's thigh. It was probably a very strong sedative because it worked fast. She jerked a couple more times and then went limp and lifeless in Liam's arms.

Ashot pulled off her bloody bathrobe and dropped it on the floor. Rosie was left in her black negligee that she wore underneath of the robe. Then Ashot covered her cut wrist with a kitchen towel and said to Liam, "Carry her to bed, honey."

"I can do that," Aaron protested.

"You did already enough," Ashot answered through his teeth.

Liam dutifully carried Rosie to her bed. Then, a minute later, he went to the third bedroom and rolled out the tall IV holder; and then – the metal table with equipment for surgery, while Ashot was staying with Rosie, probably preparing her wrist for stitches.

After they were gone, Aaron lifted Rosie's bathrobe and put it into the laundry basket in his bathroom. Then he swept up the fragments of the plates from the kitchen floor, took one of the small towels and washed up the blood on the counter and the floor. Tomorrow morning the housekeeper will come and he didn't want her to see that, so he rinsed the towel with cold water to remove any traces of blood. He also washed the knife and placed it back into a drawer.

Then Aaron sat on the stool beside the kitchen counter, put his arms on top of it and lowered his head on his arms. Ashot didn't invite him to Rosie's bedroom to watch the surgery, and he didn't dare interrupt. He still sensed Ashot's anger and felt guilty for his lack of self-control with Rosie. He felt feverish and almost ready to cry, but he gritted his teeth and stubbornly held his tears back not wanting the men to see them. He didn't want to humiliate himself in front of them more than he already was.

About half an hour later Liam walked out from Rosie's bedroom and silently disappeared into his own room. Ashot walked out as well and approached Aaron.

"Thank you for cleaning the kitchen, Doctor Dispenmore," he noted sarcastically. "It was a great help from your side."

"You are welcome," Aaron murmured, not lifting his face from his arms and not looking at him.

"Seriously, Aaron?" Ashot said angrily. "Are you capable of thinking with your brain, but not with your penis, finally? You exhausted her emotionally, you drained her, you broke her. You should realize that your sexual madness is too much for this fragile child!" As the old man headed to his bedroom door, he waved his hand hopelessly and added, "We're done talking here."

"What could I do? I can't stop myself! I love her and I am a man," Aaron exclaimed defensively.

Already holding the door knob, the old man stopped in his tracks and turned to him.

"You're not a man, Aaron," he uttered indignantly. "You're a spoiled brat. You're unbelievably selfish and think only about your own pleasure. I am really ashamed and disappointed in you. You're a doctor. You know all the danger that this amount of sex created for her. Did you ever think about her, at all?

"The MEN are the people who are going to a war, to a battle," he continued with an ire, "who are doing expeditions to the North Pole, to the Amazon Jungle, to deserts; who are going to the cloisters and become monks to serve God; who are driving ships through the oceans; who are flying to the moon; who are drilling tunnels through the mountains... Those are MEN, Aaron, who are sacrificing their sexual pleasure for higher goals during the times when spoiled brats are wasting their lives in brothels."

"I never went there in my life! I love Rosie!" Aaron protested heatedly.

"Sadly, I am not even sure that you know what LOVE is," Ashot went on. "What is your life experience with love? You've got your first wife when you were sixteen, practically a child. You never were emotionally, intellectually and spiritually connected with her, as Rosie told me. She was a sex-toy for you, and when she died you were not grieving like a man, but screaming like a spoiled child from whom his beloved toy was taken away.

"You even did all the school work for your wife - in reality for yourself. You enjoyed studying and you didn't want anyone to know that she is not as bright as you – the superman – deserve to have. It was not a help for her, it was your egotism, your showing off. If you really loved her, you would take your time tutoring her and forcing her to study and improve her brain development. This would be for her."

Aaron froze in shock, hearing unexpectedly a third opinion about his marriage. He knew that he was a loving and devoted husband. Helen told him that he was a weak doormat who loved Ally only because she was even weaker. And now he heard that he didn't love Ally at all but loved only himself. This made him furious.

"Why in a million years do you have the right to judge me?" he yelled.

"It's not a judgment. It's a psychiatric session to heal you, Aaron - to open your core and to help you become a better person. Actually, to help you become a MAN really."

"It's not a psychiatric session! For psychiatric sessions people are coming voluntarily, they are seeking help, they are asking for help. And the main rule is – you never humiliate a patient during the session. I don't need any help, I didn't ask you to help me. You're just having pleasure to hurt me and to humiliate me because you hate me. Don't worry, it's mutual. I hate you too!"

"I do not hate you, at all. I wouldn't waste my time on you, if I did," Ashot smirked. "In reality, I love you as a son, Aaron. And I want you to be a good loving husband for my kiddo, but not a bastard who will use her as a sex-toy, suck out all energy from her, make her almost dead and drive her to a suicide. That's all."

"I love her," Aaron exclaimed in despair. "I connected with her emotionally, and spiritually, and intellectually, more than with anyone in the world. She is not a toy. She is the whole world for me. If you are as smart as you claim, you should see that yourself. What do you want from me, finally? What do you want me to do?"

"I don't want you to do anything. You should feel and understand yourself, what you have to do, when your beloved one is sick. Go and sit beside her and hold her hand the whole night. This is what a MAN would do while a spoiled brat would go to a brothel."

"Stop repeating this all the time! It's disgusting! I already said that I never did this in my life."

"Then you should probably start right now because Rosie will be sick for awhile and you're not capable to control yourself and to live without sex."

"I am perfectly capable. I know how to hold myself in check. I was alone for three years after my wife died! From age of twenty-five until twenty-eight – the best sexual years of every young man. You couldn't understand this because you never knew how to live in abstinence."

Ashot smirked again. "Actually, I lived without sex for sixteen years, son, from my age thirty, as you are now, until forty-six when I met Liam and healed him. It took me sixteen years to settle in this country, to learn the language, to get an education, to find a job, to find the patient to cure, and to find a man whom I love. The whole sixteen years! And I am not complaining. You told me before, Aaron, we shouldn't compare our lives – who survived the worst. I agree. Stop comparing, then. Go, and stay with her, and hold her hand until morning, as a MAN who loves his partner would do, again, while a spoiled brat would go to a brothel. Prove to me and to yourself that you are the first 'ONE', but not the last 'one'."

"I know that I am the man. I don't need to prove anything to anyone. I don't have to, and I won't!" Aaron angrily exclaimed at Ashot's back while the old man entered his bedroom and closed the door behind him. Still breathing heavily and shaking with anger and endless hate toward Ashot, Aaron walked to Rosie's room.

She was sleeping quietly and deeply. Her bandaged hand was stretched aside and connected to an IV. She didn't lose as much blood this time, as during her previous attack in the car. So, alternative agents to replace the blood transfusion weren't needed now. Then, the IV package was probably just a regular solution to wash her up inside and to calm her down, Aaron guessed.

He really wanted to take her and to run together from this home, from these people as far away as he could. But it wasn't possible yet. She still needed her cure, needed to be here.

Aaron noticed that the ring was not on her finger anymore, but on the bedside table. Probably Ashot removed it so as not to damage it accidentally while he was working on the stitching of her left wrist. Or maybe not. Maybe it was on purpose just to hurt him again. He took the ring and placed it back on Rosie's finger. Then he laid on the top of the cover beside her and hugged her.

His head was still boiling and it was difficult to relax in such a condition, but then he took his mental brakes off and let himself cry, squeezing his face to Rosie's shoulder, until he finally fell asleep.

CHAPTER 36

Aaron saw Laurie in his dream. She was running and laughing on a meadow, between grass and flowers, trying to catch butterflies while he was sitting on the ground, watching her. The grass was tall, so only Laurie's head and shoulders were visible. There were a lot of flowers around - clover, dandelions, daisies, blue bells — spreading a smell of honey, attracting bees that were buzzing above them. The sun was shining brightly in Aaron's face. Laurie was happily shrieking, and he was laughing with her.

The energy and the beauty of nature, of the child, of the sun, was so pure, so enchanting and delightful that Aaron felt as if he was floating in the waves of enjoyment and rest. It was calmness, bliss, Heaven. He didn't want to wake up and wished he could stay in this dream forever.

Alas, it finished, finally. He woke up and found himself in bed, still hugging Rosie who kept sleeping full of the sedatives. Knowing that they all went to sleep at three a.m. when the surgery on Rosie's wrist was accomplished, Aaron could guess that it was about four now. It was still dawn and the semi-darkness in the room made him feel gloomy. So, he had slept for no more than one hour, though it felt like he dreamed endlessly, all night long, watching Laurie. In theory he knew that all dreams lasted no more than a few seconds, so the feeling of prolonged time with Laurie probably meant one thing – he missed her.

Aaron realized now how badly he missed her and Beth – his beloved family, the people who sincerely loved him and would never hurt him. They were always kind, treasured and respected him, and never in their life mistreated him.

In this unfamiliar home, he was exhausted, disrespected, emotionally hurt, and completely broken. He was treated like a stupid child and humiliated beyond any boundaries. He reached the edge about which Rosie's mother, Gloria, told him, "You can tolerate only so much, and then you can't anymore." Aaron understood her now. He can't bear this abuse, absolutely can't. The pain in his soul was so horrible and intolerable that it clouded all other feelings completely. He couldn't even say, if he loved Rosie now. It felt like his love had died, being stomped into the ground and buried there by this awful hurting in his soul.

Aaron understood in theory that this man, Ashot, probably, was a real genius in his scientific invention, in his cure of schizophrenia. Deep in his mind Aaron admired and respected that. But he saw that Ashot was also unbelievably rude and disrespectful with him, and Aaron endured this only for Rosie, for his love, for his dreams and hopes for a future life with this woman. Now, the last straw broke the camel's back. He felt absolutely empty inside – no love, no dreams, no hopes – everything was dead, killed by this terrible pain of insult.

Aaron realized that Ashot, practically, doesn't need him for Rosie's cure. The old man was only using him for his license, his diploma, and his qualifications – to get the Nobel Prize. Aaron thought that Ashot was probably jealous of him having all these achievements at a pretty young age. That's why he hated him so much and Aaron can't tolerate this hate anymore. It was killing him, driving him to the edge. It was so disgusting and hurtful, that Aaron didn't want to live here any longer. Not at all, not for a minute. He can't stay in this home, and he won't.

He stood up very quiet, trying not to wake Rosie, and walked to his bedroom. He took his sports bag, with some of his changes of clothes that he had in this condo, and went to the parking garage downstairs where his car was parked in a visitor spot. He got into his car, took the phone from his pocket and called his mother on Skype.

Beth answered his call right away. It was already about eight a.m. in Florida and she had just woken, though Laurie was still sleeping.

"Arie, my dear!" she exclaimed happily, but at the same time a bit worriedly. "It's so nice to hear from you and to see you, finally. I am already tired from all these short texts. But… you are calling in such an unusual time. It must be very early in Seattle. Has something happened? Are you able to talk longer?"

"Mom," he said. "We will talk longer soon. I am heading to the airport now to get a ticket on the first flight out and I need your exact address to take a taxi in Miami. I will be with you for dinner, or if I get lucky, maybe even for lunch."

"Oh, it would be amazing, Arie. Laurie would be very happy to see you, and I am sure, all the family would be as well. So… did you get some vacation from your work?"

"No, I decided to quit, to let it go to hell. I'm tired, mom. I am exhausted. I can't stay here anymore. I need to be with you and Laurie."

"Thank you for your love, Arie," Beth said tentatively. "But wait a sec… What happened?"

Her mother's heart felt something unusual in his outburst, something not normal for him. He was a workaholic and loved his job dearly. He would never drop it, especially such an interesting project for the Psychiatry Scientific Conference on which he worked now, as she knew.

"I am just tired, very tired and overwhelmed. I need a rest. I need to hug you and Laurie," he was almost choking on these words and stopped, biting his lips trying not to cry in front of her.

"Arie, please," Beth begged, "talk to me, first, before you quit your work. I know how important it is to you. You actually would never drop it without a serious reason. I feel that it's not the project that is boring or uninteresting. I feel that you are really hurt. Tell me, darling, please. You know that I will understand."

"I would prefer to talk to you in person," he murmured, sniffling.

"But you can't come here and just leave your work. We need to talk now, my dear. You know that I can help, Arie. Please, tell me what happened, my love... please."

Aaron took a deep breath. He loved his mother so dearly; he was deeply touched how she felt and understood him right away; how she was always there for him.

"Mom," he said finally. "The project is very interesting, it's unbelievable, it's fantastic. It's like an A-bomb in science. But the work environment is very hostile. The partner with whom I work hates me and is extremely rude with me. And it hurts. I can't tolerate it any longer."

"But why, Arie? Why? How is it possible to hate you? You are such an amazing person."

"Sadly, only for you, mom. He is a real genius in science, but he is old, he has some problems with the legalization of the documentation. I guess he is jealous that I am younger and have much more success and official recognition than he has. It's kind of personal."

"But, Arie... If he is a genius, as you said, he should be smart. He should understand that jealousy is a silly thing at work. To reach the best results, you should be together in the project, not against each other. It is so simple. What do you mean by the word - personal? Is there a woman involved? Did his wife fall in love with you, or what... Arie? I feel something there. Before we left for Florida, you told me that you are interested in one woman, but not sure if she would want to work with you. Is she your third working partner now? Is it about her? Tell me please honestly, son."

Aaron took several deep breaths before he suppressed a spasm in his throat and could talk normally.

"Okay, mom. Yes, there is a woman, and yes, she is working with us. And yes, I love her, and she loves me. And everything is okay between us, but this man..."

"Does he love her as well?" Beth asked worriedly. "That's why jealousy is there?"

"He is actually her father. And he hates me because he is thinking that I am hurting her."

"Oh, Arie. He is definitely wrong. How could you hurt the woman you love? You're the kindest person in the world. You wouldn't hurt a fly!"

"He is thinking that I love her too much, that too much love could hurt her."

"I don't quite get it. But, Arie... Just think... You're a father yourself. Imagine that some man is hurting Laurie. What would you do?"

"Oh, I would kill him."

"So... Just try to get into your partner's shoes. He is the father and he thinks that you are hurting his daughter. Maybe he is wrong about you, but it is his perception. Remember, Arie, when you were taking psychology courses at university, you told me about that concept. For each person, the reality is their own perception of the world. It is very interesting and understandable – that's why I remember it for so many years. If something is white but a person is seeing it in his perception as black, for him it is black. For him it is the truth. All religions and faiths are based on this. It's a psychological thing, right, Arie?"

"Jeez, mom, you're turned into a good shrink!" Aaron even smiled. "Thanks to me."

"Yes, thanks to you, my dear. Now, why does this man have a perception that you're hurting his daughter? Love can't hurt. Love can do only good.."

"Mom, the problem is... that girl... she is ill... It is very serious, and it's probably not a proper time for her to be in love. She should be healed first. I understand it, in theory, but I am so crazy about her, I love her so much. I can't wait. I make mistakes. I know that I am losing my head sometimes."

"Is it a terminal illness?" Beth asked disturbed.

"No, it's curable. She is on treatment at the moment. In a couple of months she will be okay."

"And you want to leave her now and come here? Arie... I don't understand. You can't do that to the woman you love. She probably needs you. I am sure that being sick, she needs you even more. Did you ever think about her feelings? Do you really love her? I mean, for 'better or worse'?"

"I do. I want to marry her when she is cured."

"Jeez, Arie, then why aren't you worried about her feelings? Then, how could you even talk about leaving her now – alone, sick, suffering, loving and missing you! It could make her condition worse. Did that ever come to your mind? Did you ever think about her before thinking about yourself? You can't do that to her! You have no moral right! It's impossible. It's not you, Arie. Not my caring, kind and loving son. You're disappointing me, even saying something like that."

"I am tired, mom. I am dead. I am broken inside by fights with that man. I shouldn't allow anyone to talk to me in such a tone. He even pointed a gun at me once. I can't tolerate it anymore. He is pushing me away. I have to leave, and maybe never come back here."

"So, you are considering dumping the love of your life while she is sick because her father was rude to you? Arie... my dear, this sounds shocking to me. How could you do that? It's not you, son, it's not my dear Arie whom I raised."

Now, as Beth took a deep breath, Aaron kept silent, not knowing what to say.

"Arie," his mother continued sadly, "let me tell you something. When your father was dying, it was extremely difficult for me. He was the biggest love of my life. His illness lasted five years. The first two years Ally and you helped a lot, so I was still working. But then you moved to Seattle, for university. I was left alone with your dad. I even left my business and stayed with him. I was taking care of him all by myself.

"It was exhausting physically and emotionally, I was suffering, I was crying every day. I was in pain to see how my love was dying in my arms. But I never left him. Not even for a minute was I thinking of sending him to a hospital, to a nursing home or to a hospice. He was the man I love. He was ill, and I was his wife. I gave my word to be with him always, 'in health and in sickness', 'for better or for worse' and I kept my promise to him and to God.

"That's what you do, Arie, if you really do love someone who is sick. And you do that, it doesn't matter how difficult it is for you, how tired you are. There is no question – I can, or I can't anymore. You can, if you truly love her. And plus, her illness is curable, as you said. So, it's much better than the case with your dad. Your girl will be healthy soon and you will be happily married. I would be very glad to see this. Just be patient, Arie. Stay with her, love her, help her, support her. And God will bless you for that. And I am giving you my blessings, my dear son."

"I understand that, mom," he uttered thoughtfully. "I know how it was with you and dad, I remember that. But nobody was abusing you in this difficult time. Imagine, if my dad would have a father who would be beside you and who would be blaming you, swearing at you, screaming at you, pointing a gun at you and accusing you that dad's illness is your fault. It would add a lot to your exhaustion, wouldn't it? How would you tolerate this? This would cloud your judgment as it did mine. From this pain of mistreatment I can't even think properly."

"You just need to ignore that, Arie. Combine all your will power together. Be strong as much as you can. I know you can do that. You did it after Ally's death. The father of your girl is probably in pain as well because of his daughter's illness. He is worried, maybe, too much about her. But it is understandable. Put mental plugs into your ears. When he does or says something not nice to you, just go to another room, don't listen, don't pay attention, ignore it, never answer or fight back, just block your ears. The abusers really love it when the victim protests and fights back. Their power is established in fight. But if you just ignore them and don't hear them, they kind of lose their power. It gets uninteresting and boring for them."

"Jeez, mom, you are a real shrink," Aaron now laughed.

"No, Arie, I am just an old woman who had a long life and got a lot of life experience, and saw a lot of things around. That's it. And, most importantly, I am your mother who loves you very-very much unconditionally. Even when you show me some signs of being an egoistic jerk. I am sorry to say these words to you, Arie. But you really need to judge your own behavior."

"Okay," he shrugged, "you almost convinced me to stay. I will think about that for a while."

"Don't think. Just go and be with her. Where is she now?"

"At home, sleeping."

"And you are...?"

"In my car, ready to drive to the airport."

"Stop it, Arie. Assess your feelings. If you truly love her, go and stay with her. I am begging you. I want you to have a good wife, who would also be a good mother for Laurie in the future. Is this girl really worth your efforts? Is she a nice person?"

"Yes, she is an angel, mom, and super smart, talented, brilliant. And she loves me madly."

"Oh God, Arie. It sounds amazing. Then go, and be with her, right now, immediately, son. Please, do that for me, for yourself, for Laurie and for that poor ill girl, of course. Heal her with your love."

Aaron slowly shook his head and took a few more deep breaths. "Well," he said, calming down gradually, "you pulled some strings in my heart, mom. You've kind of sobered me up again, like you always did before. I love you, mom. Please, kiss Laurie for me. Tell her that I love her a lot. I will follow your advice and give it one more try to work with this man. But I swear to God, it will be the last one. Then, I should probably go now. Thank you for your support, mom. Love you, as always."

CHAPTER 37

Aaron disconnected the Skype call, lowered his head on the steering wheel and closed his eyes. He shuddered, suddenly realizing what he had done. Pain of humiliation clouded his head so badly, that all thoughts of Rosie were lost at the moment. Now he remembered how he read her book gradually falling in love with her; realizing that she is his soulmate and that not one person in the world is spiritually and emotionally closer to him, than she; how he was looking for her, how he came to see her at the Greenwich Competition Hall that first time.

He remembered how he first kissed her – the unbelievable feeling of this 'holy oasis'; he remembered his oaths that he will love her forever. Then their dates at restaurants, on the boat, her tears, her begging him to dump her so she could kill herself and better to die, than live without him. And he, himself, said to Ashot that if she won't be healed, they will both die because they couldn't live without each other. Even sexually, she gave him much more than Ally or Helen. She gave him complete, deep, unbelievable satisfaction and the greatest happiness imaginable. He was madly in love. He was obsessed with her.

And after all of these? He just ran away, was ready to fly to Florida, to leave her, not saying even bye? All because he really lost his mind under the anguish of Ashot's mistreatment? He gave himself his word that he would fight for her fiercely with any man in the world. And he forgot all of these because some old man was sarcastic with him and reprimanded him as a naughty child?

Jeez, how could I do that? Aaron was shocked and really ashamed of himself.

He left his car, went to the fitness club and worked out for a whole hour, relentlessly, with huge commitments. He was hating himself, wishing to kill himself, hoping his heart would explode from extreme overloading. It wasn't easy. He drove himself to a condition that he almost couldn't breath, but nothing bad happened, just that his muscles got bigger and stronger. As he finished, he finally managed to regain his breath and recouped his consciousness.

Once again, Aaron was thankful to Beth. She really was a great mother. She got him sobered up and opened his eyes at his own behavior, returning him to his senses. Now he got scared - what if Rosie woke up and discovered that he was gone? Without a word, without a trace... After giving her an engagement ring? She will be shocked, she will not know why...

He took his phone and texted her, "My Love, will be back ASAP. Busy now." Then he thought for a while and called Helen.

"Oh," she exclaimed happily, "congrats, Mr. Groom! Seriously? Now you're giving me an extra job — thinking how to free you from a second wife. Lol! And why are you calling so early? It's only seven a.m. You should be in bed, hugging your bride!"

"Shut up!" he said, irritated. "I am calling as a colleague only. You left me a message some time ago, saying that you found a boy to cure for the conference. Is it true?"

"Yes. I am working on it. I kind of found a new approach to schizophrenia."

"What is a new approach? Could you tell me about that? I probably would be interested."

"Well, okay," she agreed peacefully and started telling him about her work, not in detail, of course, just the common aspects. Aaron listened attentively, sometimes asking questions. They talked for about half an hour.

"Okay, Hel," he said finally. "There is some rational seed in what you are telling me. Let me think about it for a while. I still don't have anything yet. If I don't find my own way, maybe I'll join you, as you suggested before."

"Of course, you don't have anything because you were busy with other things, as I know. I saw on the Internet your kiss and your proposal on stage. You turned into kind of an actor now, instead of a scientist."

"It's not your business, really. But maybe I'll give you a call in a couple of weeks."

"A couple of weeks?" she smirked. "Are you crazy? I will be far ahead in my research. But well, still better than nothing from you, my love."

Aaron hung up and went back to the condo.

As he entered, Ashot and Liam were already in the kitchen, cooking breakfast.

"Good morning, Aaron," Ashot said. "Welcome back."

"Good morning," Aaron answered morosely. "I went to exercise."

Ashot smirked, obviously knowing that there was much more than just that.

"How do you like your eggs?" Liam asked calmly and neutrally as usual.

"Sunny side. But I would like to see Rosie, first. Give me some time, please."

He went to his bedroom and left his bag on the floor, then walked to her room.

She was lying in her bed in a fetal position and her engagement ring was on the bedside table again. Aaron knelt beside her bed and lowered his face on the blanket, not saying a word.

"Why did you dump me?" she whispered, putting her hand on his head and petting his hair. "I know I was bad last night. I probably deserved this."

"If you know what happened, then you know why," he mumbled barely audibly. "I didn't dump you. I just need some time alone. I was hurt very much. I lost my head from that pain. I turned crazy."

"I know. I felt your pain and I wanted to heal you, as I always do - to put my lips on your forehead. But you weren't here..."

"I am here now. I love you and I want you to take my ring back. Please, don't put it away anymore."

Aaron took the ring and placed it on her finger, again, and she did not protest. She bowed her head and kissed his forehead.

"We did talk to uncle," Rosie murmured. "Especially Liam. He heard everything.... I know it was my fault. I should know better and say 'no' to sex. But I just love you so much..."

"Same here. I should know better too. And I love you so much, as well."

"Promise, we will behave until I am cured..."

"I swear to God, we will." Aaron took her hands and kissed them. Her IV was already disconnected, and the bandage on her wrist looked big and fat – there was obviously the clay inside, as Aaron realized.

"Did you forgive me?" he asked.

She nodded. "The person who truly loves always forgives, Aaron. And I do."

"Do you want to go for breakfast?" Aaron suggested.

"No, my love. I did have something already. I need to lay here and rest for a while until my wrist heals. Uncle said, maybe two-three more hours. I probably need more sleep. You go for breakfast. The guys are waiting for you."

When Aaron returned to the kitchen and sat at the table, Ashot was silent, but Liam who was still fussing by the stove, acting like nothing happened, asked, "Bacon or sausage, Aaron?"

"Bacon," Aaron answered, admiring once more Liam's ethics, patience, calmness and understanding.

"Babe, go ahead," Liam uttered quietly, tapping Ashot on the shoulder. Then he turned back to the stove and kept working on breakfast.

"Well," Ashot took a deep breath. "I am glad that you come back, Aaron, because our kiddo really needs you. I would like to apologize, but for one thing only – for what I said about your first marriage. I really had no right to talk about that. It's not my business. It was long ago and not related to our project here in any way. I just made an assumption about your character for myself but I didn't need to throw that in your face. It was kind of insensitive on my part. And for that I apologize.

"However, I was very angry that you overloaded Rosie and practically pushed her to suicide attempt. And this is right now. This is my business and for that I am staying on what I said. You have to think about her more than about yourself. I mean – if you truly love her, of course. You have to learn how to hold yourself in check from now on. So, I hope, we'll agree on that, and we're okay now and can continue our work."

He stopped for a moment, giving Aaron time to answer that the apology was accepted, but it didn't happen. Aaron sat silently, not looking at him and not answering.

"Well," Ashot continued then, "I wanted to consult with you, Aaron, on how we proceed with the cure. I would like to hear your opinion about something."

Aaron really wanted to say, *Why do you, genius, need an opinion of a stupid idiot and spoiled brat?* But he bit his tongue on that, remembering what Beth said to him – do not fight. So, he kept silent.

"Breakfast is ready. Here we go, guys," Liam announced with a cheering voice and placed the plates in front of Ashot and Aaron, as well as one for himself.

"Thank you, Liam," Aaron said. He was confused a little bit - to eat with them together was a sign of friendship and he didn't have that feeling at the moment, but, damn, he was really hungry. So, he accepted the breakfast in respect to Liam's sincere attempts to establish some peace.

After they all ate in silence for a few minutes, Ashot went on, "Well, I planned to do the next session on Vally – to finish with Rosie's childhood experiences and finally to stop these rivers of tears forever. And we will do it on Saturday, as planned. But because of what happened... Because the girl was too overloaded with her feelings from the poetry club performance and of the farewell party... Because I can see too much pain in her for parting with this creative business which has a huge importance in her life... Because of all that, I think that we should eliminate Anastasia first to stop this pain. Before Vally. And I would like to do one extra session for Anastasia tomorrow. What do you think, Aaron?"

"So, you think, now, that this suicide attempt was not because of me, overloading her with my proposal and love, but because she didn't want to lose her poetry talent? I agree. In truth, she was screaming, 'I want my Anastasia back!'" Aaron noted sarcastically.

"These two things are going together. She is doing that for you, Aaron. She is risking the loss of her talent for a chance to be healed, which is for you. And I would like to keep it this way. I can't predict, will she lose talent or not. It never happened in my experience with anyone, except for Liam. But, if she does, you need to know, Aaron, that this sacrifice was done for you and respect that."

"Which I do, that's why I proposed marriage. I wanted her to be sure, to see, to understand that I am here for her always, no matter if talent or not."

"And then, you ran away in a couple of hours..."

"Babe," Liam quietly put his palm on Ashot's shoulder, "please..."

"Sorry. I had learned from you, Aaron, probably, to get carried away. I should know better. Thank you, darling, for reminding me," he nodded to Liam. "Okay, what do you think about the extra session, Aaron?"

"I don't have any experience like you, Ashot," Aaron said thoughtfully, "but maybe you are right. If it is painful for her, it would be better to chop it up, like with an ax, once and for all. Especially, because as you said, she should leave the club anyway for age reasons.

"I also want to tell you one thing," Aaron continued. "This morning, I called a colleague of mine at the university who works on the same project for the conference in New York. She is working on a twelve-year-old boy, basing her research on MRI studies of the famous psychiatrist Dr. Amen. She found on the MRI that the boy has a tumor in his brain. Now she is involving a brain surgeon to remove the tumor, which she considers the cause of the boy's illness. It is not cancerous at all, by the way. Kind of a schizophrenia's tumor. I never heard about anything like that. It is kind of an interesting and unusual approach to the problem. So, I am wondering, did we do Rosie's MRI to check for possible things like that?"

"It was done, actually, a couple of months ago. It is in the file of Dr. Evelyn Hertz which you brought to us, Aaron."

"Oh, maybe. I just skipped the medical part of that file. I was interested in her biography facts at the moment. So, how was it?"

"It was okay. No physical changes in her brain, no tumors," Ashot noted. "It looks like a healthy brain, actually, which is strange knowing the intensity of her condition. But for me it is just an exact proof of my theory that her problem is in the damaged aura and it's destroyed particles that lost connection with the universe energy and turned black. It was very visible during Nora's session, as you saw, Aaron."

"But she still has a connection with the holographic universe that gives her a vision of the past, now, and future. Hasn't she? Isn't it through the auras?" Aaron wanted to know.

"As well as poetry, and telepathy, also," Liam added bashfully. "Am I right, babe?"

"You are learning, honey," Ashot smiled at him, then explained, "Different layers of aura and different colors, guys. You will see that when we will do Anastasia, Aaron, through your goggles. And you, Liam, will see that later when we print pictures taken by the 4D camera. So, are we good to go for an extra Anastasia session tomorrow?"

Aaron nodded in agreement. He finally felt friendly, calm and determined for the most important goal – to cure the woman whom he really loved.

CHAPTER 38

The second session the next day started much like the first one.

After everything was settled at the same spot as it was the last time, Ahot asked, glancing around the room, "Okay, is everybody ready to go? Then, action!" He gestured to Liam like it was a movie set and, while beginning his presentation, he removed a big plastic box that covered the unfinished Clay Mask on the tray which was still wet and soft inside. Then he put away bowls with water surrounding it and started working on the Mask again, petting its surface, refreshing it.

"Today we will clean the damaged and dysfunctional aura's particles of the very important patient's personality – the beautiful, confident, inspirational and creative celebrity one, which is the second base of Rosa Garcia's illness as Dr. Dispenmore determined. This personality was named Anastasia by the patient," Ashot went on. "The procedure of removing damaged particles of the aura, which are managing this personality, will be carried out with the continuation of creating the Clay Mask, depicting the patient's face."

Then he addressed the girl who was sitting across from him on her side of the table, looking sad, though there was no fear in her eyes now. "Please, tell us about her, Rosie. Who is Anastasia? How come she impersonated herself in you? When did it happen and why? Anything you know, remember, want and can tell us. It's completely up to you what you wish to share…"

Rosie coughed a little, nervously trying to clean her throat and asked, "Can I close my eyes?"

"Do anything that makes you comfortable," Ashot nodded. "And don't worry. We only have people here who care about you and want the best for you. Okay?"

"Thank you," she whispered, closed her eyes and propped her head on her hands, putting her elbows on the table. "I need to think what I remember first." Then she coughed a bit more, lifted her head and opened her eyes, looking straight at the clearly formed back of the head of the Clay Mask that stood in front of Ashot. And she began her narrative.

"When I was a little girl, I didn't have many friends. There were some kids at school who were nice to me and we played together. Nobody hurt me or bullied me ever. I was comfortable at school. I remember, my teacher in grade one told my Grandma Nora – 'When Rosie enters the classroom, all kids begin to smile. She is our sunshine'.

"But I never invited my school friends home because I was ashamed that Grandpa Vasil would scream or swear. One day I went to visit one girl at her home, and I was surprised how nice her grandparents were with each other. I asked that girl, does her grandpa beat her grandma ever? She was shocked by my question. She probably told her parents or grandparents about that and nobody invited me anymore.

"Other kids communicated with each other after school – birthday parties, family days together, sleepovers… and these events make them closer to each other. I wasn't anywhere there, so, step-by-step, they stopped being friends with me because to play just at school wasn't enough to develop a real friendship. I was left alone, without friends, with just classmates, but it was not the same."

Rosie took a deep breath. Aaron observed attentively her aura through the goggles and described the shapes and colors in his tablet. There weren't many changes yet, except that colors got a little bit dimmer.

"I kind of got used to being mostly alone, but subconsciously, I obviously was missing friends. It wasn't normal for a child not to have any," Rosie continued. "Only when I came to the *Youth Shelter,* I got my first real friend. There was a girl named Hope. She was a bit younger than me. I was eleven when I was placed there, but she just turned ten. She was small, slim, and looked even younger than she was. As soon as I entered the door, she ran to me and hugged me."

At that moment Rosie stopped and smiled. Aaron was surprised. It was the first time he saw her smiling during the sessions. And he made a note, that the colors of all the layers of her auras got brighter and shone again.

"Probably I attracted Hope because I was closer to her age – other kids were much older, like fifteen-sixteen - but maybe not. Probably she just felt the spiritual closeness between us, because it was what I felt instantly toward her. We began talking. She told me that her illness was kleptomania which meant that she was stealing things from stores, and couldn't stop. It was not such a heinous crime, but her parents placed her in the *Youth Shelter* for treatment because it went on non-stop and made their public life very uncomfortable. It was a shame every time when Hope got caught to deal with the police, doctors, and explanations.

"Right away Hope told me that she is writing poetry and suggested we do that together. I told her that I tried to write a book while being very young, but then stopped doing so because of my Grandpa Vasil and his screams about me going on TV with Oprah. I still didn't know who Oprah was and why I should go there. But Hope was from a good family and kind home. She watched a lot of TV with her parents together, so she knew Oprah and she explained to me who she was.

"Hope showed me the poetry site on the Internet where she was very active. It was an adult site where you should be eighteen or older, but she lied about her age and was accepted. I did the same. I wrote my first poem, **Black Lake.** It was very tragic, about my Grandma Nora's murder. Surprisingly, this poem was a triumph on that poetry site. I got a lot of points – stars. Nobody believed that a child wrote this. It was kind of a mature adult subject of death. But it was good for me because it helped me to hide my real age.

"To be on this site, you should choose a screen name. Hope's name was 'Angel'. I said to her that I need to think about that. And it came to me at night when I was sleeping. I saw in my dream a crystal castle deep in the darkness of the universe and the beautiful fairy, Anastasia, who lived there. She flew from planet to planet and from start to star and dropped little diamonds everywhere – words of her poems. In the morning, I told Hope – I found the name. I saw her. She is the poetry fairy Anastasia."

"So, you became Anastasia at that time?" Ashot asked.

"Not always. When I created poems, I was Rosie. They usually came to me during my sleep, but Anastasia was a voice who was saying them to me. I heard her voice. It was calm, and quiet sometimes but very agitated, loud and excited other times, depending on the topic of the poem. And when I recited the poems during the day, I felt that I became Anastasia myself. I even changed my posture, my gait, all my movements. I proudly lifted my head and smiled victoriously when I was Anastasia. I started to look different when I was her. And it was a happy look, a confident look, a brave one, a self-respected one. It was amazing. I felt like I was flying."

Rosie really shone now while talking about these happiest moments and the stream of particles got wide, swirly and really sparkling like stars. Aaron felt happy for her, as if this spirit was infectious. He was just a bit aware that the stream was going so fast into the Clay Mask that it will probably finish soon. Then what? He had no idea what to expect if it happened. He only hoped that Ashot would know what to do in this case..

"How long did this continue?" Ashot asked. "Until now?"

"No," Rosie smiled sadly. "I am not that lucky. My happiness of the first friendship and true spiritual closeness ended pretty soon. Hope was cured and released in six months. We had to part. We both were sitting, hugging, and crying a lot. I wrote a very sad poem – **Please, don't go**. It was an unbelievable feeling of loss, like my heart was torn into pieces. I know that she is alive, she will be okay from now on and she will have a good life with her nice family. But for me it felt like she was dead no less than Grandma Nora. She was taken from me, though she promised to keep in touch on the poetry site. However, when her parents came to pick her up, they tore her from me with difficulty. She was screaming that she loves me and wants me to go with her, though we both knew that it was impossible.

"Her parents were so nice that I read their thoughts that maybe they would adopt me to keep us together to make Hope happy. But then they asked her, why I was in this shelter and she answered truthfully – for a murder. I saw with my own eyes, how her mom's face changed in an instance. They let her hug me and kiss goodbye, but this was the end. Hope was never in touch since, and she even left the poetry site, probably, because her parents forced her to do so. She was gone forever."

Rosie's voice shook like she was reliving that moment now and the stream of the particles turned black. She cried and the tears slid down her cheeks to her chin and then to the hospital gown that she wore for the procedure. Aaron felt sharp pity toward her, but held himself tight, just bit his lips and kept working, taking pictures as Ashot gestured.

"But Anastasia was left with you?" Ashot asked.

"Yes," Rosie continued, after taking a couple of deep breaths and sniffles. "Now, not having anybody to talk heart-to-heart or to hug, I turn to poetry for most of my time that was free from school classes. I started writing poems continuously, like crazy.

"The first time, I discovered that I can read the thoughts of the people when I read Hope's mom thought about me being the murderer. After that, I started practicing and succeeded easily in the readings. Also, I started moving subjects with my thoughts, just for fun, when I got very sad and bored from loneliness. I developed the telekinesis ability to a great level. When Dr. Evelyn Hertz came to assess me, she was surprised about that. She insisted that I should be shown to some other specialists, and I saw many different doctors, but this didn't go anywhere further. Nothing happened after that."

"Did you make any other friends in the shelter?" Ashot inquired quietly.

"Yes. Some months later after Hope was gone, we got a new literature teacher, Mrs. Mary Oswald. She was a kind young woman, about twenty-five, married with a child – a little boy. As soon as she learned about my poetry creations and my involvement on the Internet poetry site, she became very interested in me. She was so excited about my poems that she said that she will never stop, until she makes me, if not famous, at least popular and well known.

"She helped me a lot, sometimes staying after work, even when her family was waiting for her at home. But she was teaching me extra, for free, just because she said it was her calling – not to let my talent die. She taught me to edit poetry and to get involved in poetry contests. She sent my poems everywhere, and when I got the first prizes, she was happy, maybe even more than I. She became my volunteer agent who promoted me.

"Mrs. Oswald also convinced me to write not only poems, but short stories and non-fiction articles. With her advice I wrote my first non-fiction – **The Open Letter to my Grandpa Vasil** - about my childhood and Grandma Nora's death. It became a sensation and was even published in many high level literature magazines. At that moment it looked like I was really getting famous.

"We also became very close friends with Mrs. Oswald and she asked me to call her Mary when we weren't in class. I shared with her everything about myself, my life, my thoughts and feelings, exactly like I did with Hope. She shared with me a lot, too. Like Hope, she had a very nice and happy family, so she shared her blissful experiences: family vacation trips, family gatherings for Christmas and birthdays, or for her wedding; her happiness of being a mother, of being a loving and devoted wife. I learned from her that life can be normal and beautiful, not just a house of horrors as my life was; that there was no need to hide, to be scared all the time. She taught me that a woman should be brave, creative, caring and most importantly – free spirited. Mary was not just a teacher for me, but she became almost a mother or an elder sister which I never had."

"Were you Anastasia with her?" came the next question of Ashot, who already finished one ear of the Clay Mask and started working on its face, forming the nose.

"Mostly, I was Rosie with her, but when we did talk about poetry, about contests and my winnings, I was Anastasia, especially when I recited my new poems to her. Mary also found the Greenwich Competition Hall. She made contacts with the owner and organizers and established that once I am released from the shelter, they will accept me and include me into their group of teens involved in performances. Mary did a lot for me, she opened the world to me.

"However, when I was alone at nights, Nora was always there and I was scared, and crying, and hiding under my bed, and shaking from the horrors of Grandpa Vasil. I always imagined that he would come and slash my throat the same as Nora's. Although, he had already died from a stroke at that time."

The flow of particles became shaky, crooked and darkened again, which Aaron described and memorized in photos right away.

"Also Rubi started coming into me. She was brave and convinced me not to be scared, but to fight for justice and to do an investigation of Vasil's crimes. She was good in remembering the small details, analyzing them, connecting them; she also knew how to comprehend and interpret them. After Anastasia, whom I loved the most, I really loved Rubi, as well. Anastasia was connected to poetry and creative works only, but Rubi became my closest friend in an everyday, non creative life. From all my personalities she was most convincing and independent, exactly like Mary, my real friend, taught me to be."

Aaron took the pictures of particles that got really white now, shiny and sparkly like stars. Yes, they clearly reminded him of Rubi, the strikingly beautiful and self-confident model with whom he went to the *Old Spaghetti Factory* restaurant the first time. Anastasia and Rubi - they were to the highest degree beautiful sides of the girl he loved. It felt kind of sad for him to know that they are

working now to eliminate Anastasia and that such a big happy part
of Rosie's soul would be gone. But probably, Ashot was right. It
needed to be done to make the girl healthy.

"How did your friendship with the teacher Mary continue?"
Ashot asked. "Did it end when you left the shelter?"

"Oh," Rosie took a deep breath and her eyes filled with tears
once more, however she held them and did not cry. "It never ended,
but, again, there came a bolt from the blue a couple of months
before I was out. Mary's husband was transferred to New York
by the company where he worked, and they had to move. I got
separated from her.

"Though, it was better than losing Hope. Mary was an adult
woman and she made decisions for herself about our friendship.
We continued to stay in touch – on Skype, by emails, but the long
distance relationship wasn't the same. She was busy working in a
new school there, then she had a second child. She had her own
life to live and gradually our connection get weaker. We are still
keeping in touch sometimes, just to say a Happy birthday, or a
Merry Christmas. When I was in New York on my concert trip, I
visited their family. They, now four of them, attended my concerts.
But still, it is not the same closeness anymore."

"And what happened with Anastasia when you left the *Youth
Shelter*?"

Rosie smiled broadly and happily. "Anastasia was blossoming.
I was fifteen-years-old, exactly a good time to start to do concerts
in Greenwich Competition Hall. I was winning, practically, all
the time. My poems got published in many magazines and they
invited me to work as a poetry editor for them. I traveled with my
concerts all over the country. Then my book was published. When
I graduated from high school, I was invited to teach a poetry class
there. During this period of time I was Anastasia. She was happy,
she was proud, she was creative, self-confident and beautiful. But
again, only in my creative work. At nights Nora was there, scared;
and Vally was there, crying for being neglected and not loved; and
Rubi was there, as usual encouraging more investigations.

"Kiki and Tobi weren't there yet; but later, once, Tobi appeared in an airplane when I saw a man who reminded me of my Grandpa Vasil, sitting across from me in the next row. After that, I was prohibited to go on airplanes anymore and placed on a *No Fly List,* as if I was a terrorist."

Jeez, poor man, Aaron thought remembering Tobi's attack on him in his car. *He was lucky that she didn't have a knife on the plane. I hope he didn't get a heart attack.*

"To lose the chance to travel was a big blow for Anastasia," Rosie continued. "The concerts in the other cities and states were very important for her and they weren't possible anymore. Though, she was still able to perform here, in Seattle. Her triumphs get small and restricted. The whole country wasn't by her feet anymore, but just the one city. For Anastasia it was a kind of tragedy. Like I told you, Aaron, about Cinderella – better not to have happiness at all, then to have it and lose. I told you that because I experienced it on my own skin. It was Anastasia's pain and she suffered a lot. Then, somehow she accepted it and overcame it because Seattle was such a huge success. Anastasia got hundreds of fans here who loved her and admired her. So, she got used to it. But I can't imagine what could happen to her if she lost her poetry forever. I am shaking even when I think about it. I don't want it. I am scared."

Rosie covered her face with both hands and lowered her head on the towel on the table in front of her.

"Pictures non-stop," Ashot whispered to Aaron because her flow of particles became now wild and deformed.

"I don't want to lose my Anastasia," Rosie sniffled. "I want her back. I want to be with her always."

Then she lifted her head and yelled, "Aaron, please, go away. I don't want you. I hate you. I want to be alone always, with my Anastasia only."

"Quiet," Ashot murmured to Aaron and put his hand on the top of his arm, holding him. "Don't listen to that. Just pictures..."

Rosie jumped up, screaming and yelling, waving her hands, like she was holding a knife. She grabbed her bottle with water and threw it at Aaron, which hit him in his chest, then she threw the little towel that was in front of her, and started beating her fists at the table.

While holding the camera with his shaky hands Aaron kept taking pictures of her aura's which became a crazy hurricane instead of a straight stream as they were before.

Ashot stretched his arms, protecting the Clay Mask, so she couldn't accidentally break it. This outburst was even stronger and scarier than one she had at the end of the Nora session. But, fortunately, it didn't last long. With a wild howl Rosie fell back on her chair, with her head on the table, convulsed a couple of times more and then lost consciousness. The stream of particles straightened up and went big and intensive toward the Clay Mask.

Ashot wiped his hands smeared with clay on the wet towel and took the camera from Aaron.

"Thank you, son," he said. "You did good today. I will take pictures now. Let's wait for about half an hour and see. The flow will subside gradually. Please, keep doing descriptions on the tablet: time - quality of the flow, every minute."

Aaron didn't answer anything but was shaking from the shock of Rosie's desperate hate towards him. He knew it was just an attack of the particles, it was not really true, but it was still very painful to hear. He kept doing his job persistently and accurately. The stream of particles subsided very slowly. It took much longer than at the first session to wait until it turned finally into a thin string, then dots and then melted away all together.

"Well done, guys," Ashot said, with a smile addressing his team. "We did it once again. Two down, five more to go. Thank you God for your help and bless this girl for her bravery." He made a sign of cross on Rosie and then turned to Aaron. "Thank you so much, son. You did a very big job today by overcoming your vulnerability. Now I see the doctor in you and I am very proud of you."

"I really appreciate you saying that," Aaron answered quietly. "Can I put Rosie to bed now?"

"Yes. Please, do that, son, and then we all should go out for dinner to relax a bit."

"Will she be okay staying alone at home?"

"Absolutely. It's guaranteed that she will sleep until tomorrow morning. Plus, we will lock her room."

"Babe, was I the same wild at the end of each session?" Liam asked, putting his camera on the table.

"Pretty much so."

"Did I scream that I hate somebody?"

"Yes, darling. You were really angry at your parents."

"Strange," Liam shrugged. "After my cure was accomplished I didn't feel any hate toward them at all. Everything calmed down. I forgave them and kind of love them from a distance."

"God helped you," Ashot concluded.

Aaron didn't notice and didn't realize this turn of conversation was, again, Liam's ethical tactic to tranquilize and encourage him after those hating screams of Rosie that happened already twice. This was a bit worrisome for them all.

CHAPTER 39

During dinner Ashot summarized the whole experience of the session explaining to Liam and Aaron how the Clay Mask worked on Rosie this time.

"We all are tired now, I guess," he said at the end, "so we should call it a day. Tomorrow Liam and I will work on our last sesion materials. But you, Aaron, will be doing a very big special job – to watch Rosie. This will be a very trying moment because we don't know what will happen when she awakes. Will all talents and special abilities be gone or not? You could observe her from two different angles – as a psychiatrist and as a loving fiance. And tonight you better sleep with her, not to miss a second of her awakening."

"How was it with Liam?" Aaron asked. "When exactly did his piano talent disappear and his new skills come out? Right away? In several days? In a month?"

Ashot and Liam looked at each other and smiled.

"Tell him, babe," Ashot nodded. "You must recall this better than me."

"Hmm, as I remember, we didn't talk about music right away after the cure was completed as I broke my Clay Mask," Liam said thoughtfully. "It was more medical talking – how are you feeling? What is your temperature, blood pressure and so on? Then we

349

concentrated on my assessment in the General Psychiatric Hospital, doing the MRI of my brain, and also dozens of other tests. Nobody was even thinking about piano. About a month passed until it was finally medically proven by the board of the highest level psychiatrists, that I am completely healthy. Then Ashot suggested we celebrate this at our piano club where we met.

"He said, 'Maybe you could play piano there again'. I was surprised. I didn't get why he was saying that. I had no idea how to play piano. It took some time for Ashot to persuade me that I was a pianist before. He played my CDs, showed me my TV records, articles in newspapers and magazines with my photos... Jeez, I was really shocked. It was difficult to believe, but all the material evidence finally convinced me.

"I wasn't sad. I have no memory of it in my heart and, because of the lack of the feelings toward piano and music, the discovery didn't hurt me. I had no remorse. I just thought, 'Oh, what the hell! What job could I do now? It looks like I don't have any profession'."

"And when did these camera skills appear?" Aaron inquired curiously.

"It came up accidentally," Liam answered. "I wasn't thinking about that, of course, and had no idea that I had them now. Ashot just had a camera that broke one day, not long after my cure was accomplished. He wanted to take it to a shop for repair. I said suddenly, 'Let me try to do it'. He was surprised, we disputed it and then, he finally yielded. I fixed it easily, though I never did it in my life before. Then I got curious and I bought a higher level camera for myself. With nothing else to do, I started filming everything around me."

"Then you decided to improve your camera," Ashot laughed, "and added some special features to it."

"Yes, I wanted to do long distance shots, just to entertain myself," Liam nodded. "But I did my camera's improvement successfully. And I realized that I really love to do things with lenses. It felt like fun. One day I went to a TV studio and proposed to fix some broken cameras for them, if they ever have some. They were kind of surprised, then asked me to film a couple of scenes, for fun, again, and said, 'You obviously have a great deal of experience to work as a cameraman'. 'Yes', I answered, laughing inside because my experience in reality was zero. But strangely, I could do better than even many well educated and experienced professionals. So, they offered me a job. I discussed it with Ashot and came to the assumption that because I didn't have this talent and skills before and was never interested in anything like that, they must have appeared after the cure. From this unopened part of my brain, maybe."

"So, the new talent appeared about a month later," Ashot concluded. "I am just praying that our poor kiddo survived this transition easily, like Liam did. You didn't suffer at all, right, darling?"

"No. It was interesting. I was absolutely happy all the time after the cure."

At home, when Aaron was ready to enter Rosie's bedroom for the night, Ashot said to him, "So, son, tomorrow all day will be on you. Take Rosie on some date. Go to the beach or anywhere else, when she can have fun. Behave normally like nothing happened, don't say a word about poetry, Greenwich Hall, her special ability with telepathy or anything else. Just listen and observe what she memorizes, or says, or does. Make sure that she is wearing your ring, envelope her with love.

"I am seriously worrying about that transition from her talents to something else, nobody knows what," he continued. "I will pray that all her talents stay in her, or, if they disappeared, it would go smoothly and harmless for her. God bless you, son."

"Thank you for your trust," Aaron answered. "I promise, I'll do my best."

Ashot was right that Rosie would be safe to sleep alone at home when they went out for dinner. She was still sleeping calm and quiet when Aaron sneaked under covers beside her and hugged her fondly. He was worried too, especially after her screaming twice during the last two days that she hates him. What if it would really happen? How would he live then?

No, he tried to convince himself. *No, we are talking here about talents possibly disappearing but not about love vanishing. No, don't even think about this, ever.*

Aaron barely could sleep, being nervously on guard almost half of the night, until tiredness and exhaustion finally broke him and he fell asleep like a baby, holding Rosie tight.

In the morning, he slept in a bit and missed her awakening. She, instead, woke him kissing his forehead and tenderly lining his eyebrows and his lips with her finger.

"Aaron," she whispered, "wake up. I love you."

Thank God, he thought, opening his eyes and staring at her, smiling happily. She was smiling back. It looked to him like she didn't sense any loss and so far didn't suffer at all.

"Did we do my cure session yesterday?" she asked.

"We did," he nodded. "It was very good, my love." Then he continued cheerfully, not letting her say or even to think about something else. "We will have an amazing date today. Let's get up and get ready. You go to shower first. I will prepare some things for our field trip and a picnic."

"No shower together?" Rosie whined a bit disappointed.

"Not now, my love. We should go really fast - first, to have breakfast at *IHOP* and then we will be boating really far away. I would like to have a lunch-picnic on a desert island."

"Wow! It sounds romantic!" She jumped from the bed and ran to the washroom while Aaron went to the kitchen to make sandwiches. Then he packed a cooler bag with some fruits and vegetables and also with bottled water.

He went to shower while Rosie was putting on her make up and getting dressed in one of her favorite sundresses that he bought her at the Lynden market.

"Should I take a bathing suit?" she shouted to him through the water sound.

"Yes," Aaron shouted back to her from the shower. "There is a beach bag with throw and towels by the door. Add whatever you need."

They left the condo about seven a.m. while Ashot and Liam were still sleeping.

"Show me, please, how your wrist wound is doing," Aaron asked during their breakfast.

"It's okay," Rosie said, lifting a thin bandage displaying a hairlike pink scar. "Uncle pulled out the stitches yesterday morning."

"Perfect," Aaron nodded, once more feeling an admiration toward Ashot. "I am happy for you. Then, you could swim, if we decide to do so."

Their conversation evolved around their previous dates remembering fun they had at the Lynden Fair, in the *Boeing Museum of Flights*, in *Tacoma's Museum of Glass*, on Whidby Island in a historical fort, on all the beaches. So far, Rosie didn't say one word about the Anastasia related experiences and Aaron felt proud of himself for how he managed to distract her from the sensitive topic.

However later, already on the boat when they headed toward Deception Pass Bridge, Rosie suddenly asked, looking at her ring, "Aaron, we are already engaged, right?"

"Yes," he nodded.

"So, you proposed to me. When did it happen and how? Strangely, I don't remember."

"Just a few days ago. Your uncle and Liam had a big party at the Space Needle and I proposed to you there."

"Funny that this didn't register in my head," Rosie laughed. "It should be such an important moment, right?"

"Of course," Aaron laughed as well, trying to turn this conversation into a joke. "You probably were too overwhelmed. The most important thing is that you said – yes."

"How could I not say yes, if I love you, Aaron. I am so happy with you."

"This is my goal – to make you happy."

"And how long did we date?" Rosie continued. "I don't remember, as well."

"Oh, probably forever," he chuckled again. "Not very long but long enough to realize that we love each other and don't want to live without each other."

"And where we met, and how?"

"It was sort of unusual. I was walking on a street with my daughter, Laurie, and you approached us and asked where a bus stop was. We showed it to you. And then we started dating."

"Oh, I remember your little one. She is so cute and kind. She did lend me money for the bus, right?"

"Yes. Then you decided to return it to her. You brought an envelope with a funny note from a fairy who is bringing her money back from Rosie. It was cute and inventive. I liked it very much."

"And you fell in love with me because of that?"

"Yeah, let's say so."

"Okay," Rosie nodded. Aaron didn't know if those answers satisfied her, but she sat quietly and thoughtfully after that and didn't ask anything else.

When they came to the tiny island all covered with tall grass with a sandy beach, Aaron stopped the boat and dropped anchor. "We are here," he pronounced slowly, gazing at Rosie attentively and meaningfully.

"Oh, it would be a nice place for a picnic," she said. "It is very secluded and far away in the ocean. Nobody could see or hear us."

"Do you remember it?" Aaron asked carefully. "We passed it before."

"No," she shook her head. "Maybe it was when we were boating the other day, right?"

"Yes, about two weeks ago. We stopped here for a while. Remember what we were talking about?"

"No! Aaron, you are sounding enigmatically. What were we talking about here? That it would be a great place for a picnic?"

"More important. We decided that it would be a great place to make love."

"Oh," she laughed. "Why here? Why not at home in a comfortable bed?"

"It's exactly what I told you then, but you insisted that here it would be better."

"Really? Why? It's strange. I don't remember."

Aaron dropped their bags on the sand, then jumped out from the boat and gave her his hand, as she jumped out as well. They took their sandals off and walked barefoot into the grass, spreading the tall stems and observing their surroundings curiously.

"It looks very virgin, like nobody was ever here. At least, no garbage which is a sign of wild humans," Rosie giggled. "What are we going to do here all day?"

Aaron spread the throw in the middle of the island and they sat on it. "I guessed that we will love each other, then maybe swim for a while, then have our picnic-dinner," he suggested. "Or you have other ideas?"

"I... I don't know," Rosie blushed. "Did we... did we have sex before?"

"My love, I proposed to you," Aaron smiled. "What do you think?"

"It means, yes?"

"Of course."

"Well. Okay then. I'm just... just a little bit scared. I don't understand why I don't remember anything."

She lay down and put the back of her head on Aaron's lap, as he knew she liked to do. He observed her attentively, trying to make sure, just in case, that she didn't have any weapon – no knife or anything at all that could be dangerous in case of another attack. No, there was nothing of that kind. All her belongings were now on her – the sundress and underwear only.

Then Aaron bent over and kissed her, like the first time, in the park, on the bench. He was excited that nothing changed in her feelings toward him after the last cure session. It looked like probably, all her talents and skills were gone, at least she didn't remember them. But it was not the worst that he could expect. She still loved him. He was happy beyond belief and didn't want to wait anymore. He missed her badly and when he kissed her, this time it was a very passionate kiss. Not a 'holy oasis' at all.

CHAPTER 40

Rosie was a bit hesitant to relax at the beginning. It seemed that she forgot their kisses and lovemaking as well as many other things. But being aflutter, Aaron noticed happily, that she gradually started answering him. That encouraged him and he took all his mental breaks off and let himself sink into mad passion. She was not a fragile crystal statue for him anymore. He sensed her as a real live woman – beautiful, hot and desirable to insanity - the woman who wanted him too.

In a moment their clothes flew away somewhere in the surrounding grass. Aaron completely lost control and affectionately caressed her, frantic, chaotic, not thinking about anything. He just enjoyed the feeling of her smooth tender skin, her hot breasts and nipples that were getting hard like little rocks under his lips.

Rosie proved to be easily excitable. He drove her to one orgasm after another, while she was crying, sobbing or laughing hysterically, threw her head back and convulsing, and shaking in ecstasy in his hands. Aaron enjoyed enormously absorbing her pleasure, watching her trembling eyelashes, quivering lips and her helplessly wiggling hands.

For the first time in his life he practically felt the wisdom of an old proverb that much bigger pleasure is in giving than in receiving.

He gave her a huge delight, not really thinking about himself at all, and this paid him back hundreds of times more.

Within a minute, Aaron was ready to get into her, but held himself to prolong as much as it was only possible, to watch her longer and to savor her climaxes more and more with his eyes. Then, he finally entered her, and, after he was done, they lay motionlessly, almost unconsciously for a while, relaxing and recuperating their breaths. And, probably, in half an hour it started all over again.

Aaron would be surprised that Rosie didn't remember this little island, that she saw it in her vision of the future, if he didn't know about the cure session and it's goal – to eliminate the Anastasia personality from her. This geographical area was in her poem *Place out of Time*, in her words, *The future is an island with grass and sand and the whisper of waves where I will love you mad*. Now, obviously, the poetry and any memory of it were lost and the unusual ability of connection with 3D time and holographic universe was gone along with it.

But it was really interesting that earlier her vision was right. It was a little island, there was grass and sand, there was a very clear hearing of the whispering waves coming and going, lightly touching the sand. She loved him mad right there. As she confessed to him during their first boating, they will conceive their son here, and it was exactly what they were doing right now. She obviously completely forgot about all of that, but Aaron remembered it very clearly.

He felt so endlessly thankful to her for everything – for loving him, giving him so much pleasure, willing to marry him and be with him forever, and willing to have his child. With this beautiful sense of deep thankfulness and endless love, he continued, after short breaks, caressing and arousing her again, and making love to her more and more.

He completely forgot Ashot's warnings about the danger of overjoying her. That thought flashed for a second in his mind, but then flew away momentarily because everything so far looked safe.

Rosie was exhausted but seemed very happy and even begged him not to finish ever, crying that she wants him eternally.

This craziness lasted for about five hours in a row, until they both became completely sated with each other and exhausted so much that they just can't do anymore. They slept for a while, then swam around the island, playing tag. Later, laughing, joking and teasing each other, they had their picnic-dinner. Eventually they packed their bags and boat back to Seattle.

Rosie looked absolutely happy. She was sitting on the edge of the boat, swinging her legs and singing something quietly, smiling and shining. Aaron was happy as well, until he suddenly remembered the continuation of her poem **Place out of Time.** And that made him shudder. *Glass tower in the sky, a rifle in a sniper's hand sending a bullet into your head.*

What the hell was this about? he thought frustrated. *If the first sentence of this stanza about our future — the island with grass and sand - is absolutely true, then this danger could be real as well. Where are those glass towers? Practically, everywhere, in every downtown of every American city. And why would a sniper with a rifle hide there with a purpose to kill me? Why? I didn't do anything bad to anybody. Helen? She is not that angry at me anymore, even suggested working together. I still didn't get it.*

However, maybe it was a poetic image only, Aaron decided later. There was really no reason to put a shadow of a darkness on this happiest day of his life; and he pushed these thoughts aside. He looked at Rosie and absorbed her infectious good mood.

"You know, Aaron," she said, noticing that he is watching her, "I am so delighted that I am ready to fly. My soul even wants to sing."

"Okay," he suggested, "then do it." *A new talent?* he thought excitedly. *Oh, God, it would be amazing if she got a vocal voice and became a singer.*

Rosie coughed for a while, cleaning her throat and started to sing a popular song, but very quiet, a bit husky and with some false notes, that even Aaron, not being a professional musician, noticed right away. Then she stopped and giggled confused. "Oh, it sounds so funny. I have no voice at all. I am squeaking like a mouse. Sorry, Aaron."

"It is nothing to be sorry about, my love," he laughed, too, to support her. "I am not the best singer as well. So, we are a good match."

"Yes. And also we're a perfect match in other things, right?" she hinted, smiling at him significantly.

"Agreed," he nodded, and they kept chuckling all the way home.

When they entered their condo it was already ten p.m. Ashot and Liam were sitting on the couch in the living room watching TV.

"Hey, welcome home!" Ashot exclaimed, turning off the TV and standing up right away, to look at them to assess their appearance. They were holding hands, while carrying bags in the other hands and they were beaming with felicity and bliss.

"Uncle!" Rosie shrieked, dropped her bag on the floor, ran to Ashot and hugged him tight. "Uncle, I am so happy! So happy! You can't imagine how happy I am! Please, don't blame Aaron, I am begging you. It's not his fault. I wanted him even more. I forced him. I seduced him. It's all on me. But I am super happy, so, please, forgive me."

"Okay, okay," Ashot answered surprised, patting her back. "It's okay, kiddo. I am happy too, if you feel good."

Jeez, Aaron thought, astonished by her outburst. He hoped not to show Ashot much of the sexual part of the day, to avoid another scandal, but Rosie, like a little child, sincerely gave everything away not even thinking. Aaron dropped his bag on the floor, as well, then sat in the armchair and propped his forehead on his hands, not daring to look at Ashot and the girl hugging him.

"Uncle, I need to shower," Rosie continued. "You know, we did swim, so I am all salty. Good night. I love you." She kissed Ashot on his cheek, then waved to Liam, "I love you too," and ran to her bedroom.

"Well," Ashot pronounced, slowly turning to Aaron and making a step toward him. "So? What?"

"You can kill me, you can blame me, you can hate me," Aaron said nervously, not lifting his head and not looking at him. "I know what you will say. I know that I am a stupid idiot and a spoiled brat for you. But, Rosie and I, we love each other. We love each other to death, to insanity. I can't stop myself, nor can't she. She told the truth – she wanted me no less than I wanted her. I really can't hold myself in check. You can kick me out, of course..."

"Son," Ashot interrupted, putting his hand on Aaron's shoulder. "Calm down. Didn't you hear what she said? She is super happy. Why should I be angry at you, if you made my child super happy? I know that a couple days ago I hurt you a lot, blaming you unfairly, and I am sorry for that. Now we have passed it. Believe me, I am not that old, I can understand. I still do know what affectionate love is, don't I, babe?" He turned to Liam and winked at him, smiling.

Liam giggled, but didn't say anything aloud.

"Well," Ashot continued, patting Aaron's shoulder. "I only wanted to ask, what about Anastasia? What did you observe?"

"Gone," Aaron answered, taking a deep breath of relief and daring finally to lift his face and look at Ashot as the old man returned to the couch and sat beside Liam. They both gazed at Aron expectantly and questioningly. "Completely gone. Rosie doesn't remember anything about the poetry, the club, her concerts, or about her book. Not even how we met, how we kissed on stage, how I proposed on stage. Nothing. So, I created a completely new story, explaining everything about our relationship. Based on the truth, of course, but I edited out all 'Anastasia things' from it. Also, the telepathy, mind reading, telekinesis, possibilities of seeing 3D time, and so on - all her specialties are practically gone. She is just a regular young woman of her age now, though beautiful, smart and sexy and I still love her, in spite of all these losses."

"No new talent yet?" Liam asked.

"So far, nothing. I am just wondering how you will explain it to her if she finds her book here, or her poems, or her work of editing poetry for magazines on her computer."

"We will tell her the truth, of course," Ashot confirmed, "but later, as I told it to Liam in his time. We will do that when we know that her transition is not going to be hurtful for her. For now, we checked everything at home, hid all the copies of her book, and also her computer. Liam bought her a new laptop today. Tomorrow is the 'Vally' session, but after tomorrow we will give it to her, as a gift for her half way of recovery, or something."

"Okay," Aaron nodded. "So, tomorrow, as usual, wake up time at eight a.m. and the session starts at ten. Right?"

"Yes, and please, sleep with her, son, to keep an eye on her during the night. But probably, enough of sex."

"Really?" Aaron laughed, "I am not a machine. I think I am done for a few days ahead."

"But I still will lock the door of your bedroom," Ashot warned, "to prevent her access to the kitchen knives while you are sleeping because you will sleep like a baby tonight I am sure. But, don't worry, I will unlock the door exactly at eight a.m. Good night."

"Good night," Aaron answered, and with that they all retired into their rooms for the night.

CHAPTER 41

After Rosie slept calm and quiet all night, Aaron realized that her last illness attack and attempt to kill herself by cutting her wrist were triggered not by his marriage proposal and passionate sex. It was initiated by the pain of parting with her poetry club and, potentially, with all her talents. Of course, it was a tragedy to her to lose the things that were her only happiness and refuge for so many years.

And at present, since Anastasia was gone, Aaron made Rosie overjoyed maybe hundred times more on this small island, but she was okay and still happy. So, it was the right motion on Ashot's part to decide to remove Anastasia as soon as possible to soothe the girl. The old man obviously got it now that he was wrong blaming Aaron previously, and apologized for that. With this restored peace it was a good time to start the next cure session – to clean out the poor, little, ever crying Vally.

On Saturday morning their third session started much like the previous ones. Ashot made his introduction and then suggested Rosie to tell them about her personality named Vally. At the same time, he continued his shaping of the Clay Mask. The nose was already done, so he moved down on the clay face to form the lips.

Rosie didn't look very scared, just a bit sad. She thought for a while, then took a couple of deep breaths, drank some water and started her narrative.

"When I was a very young child, I never lived with my mom. She gave me away to my grandparents to raise after my father perished in a motorcycle accident. I didn't know that. She didn't tell me that ever. But when, at age of eleven, I found myself in the *Youth Shelter* and got my ability to see 3D time, I saw the past and found out about it myself.

"I realized that my mom didn't want to hurt me by telling me the story of my father's death because it wasn't beautiful, like if he did a heroic act of some kind. He was dunk and the accident was obviously his fault. Actually, he was a heavy drinker, and she even planned to divorce him, but the accident made their separation faster and easier. As for me, in any situation, I could be end up with my grandparents."

"Did your mother come for visits?" Ashot asked.

"Yes, she did but very seldom, maybe once in two-three months. Sometimes, she took me to stay at her place for a while, like two-three days, but this happened even more rarely, about once a year."

"Didn't your grandmother replace her in your imagination?" the old man wanted to know.

"Not really..." Rosie thought for a while, then continued. "Though, my grandma, Nora, was very nice and loving, but she still wasn't the mother that every child subconsciously needs. Also, she worked a lot and had no time to play with me, or to go for walks. So, I missed my mom badly and always dreamed of seeing her."

"What did you do with your mother together during her visits?" followed the next question.

"Not much. She usually brought some food for us because we almost had none, and maybe a toy, like a small Teddy bear, or a little doll for me. Then we drank tea together. She talked with my grandparents about her life which I didn't understand. I was sitting on her lap by the table, hugging her and feeling very happy. But she would leave pretty soon, and then I began to cry.

"Those were the moments where Vally appeared inside me. I sensed with every cell of my body and every particle of my soul that I am not loved, not needed and not wanted. I was nothing to my mom, just a burden from which she was eager to free herself. It was so painful! So unbearably painful! I cried, howled, screamed for hours after she would be gone. It was very irritating for my grandparents and they suggested she come to see me even less often to avoid my hysterical outbursts."

"So, you probably forgot her?" Ashot inquired. "Didn't you?"

"Actually not. I accidentally found in a magazine a picture of a woman, slim and blonde, that resembled my mom a little bit. My grandma cut it out and placed it on the wall above our dining table. When I wasn't eating well, she pointed to the picture and said, 'Look, Rosie, your mama is watching. She wants you to eat'. Or, she wants you to behave. Or, she wants you to stop crying. It was used like a tool to manage my behavior and it worked. I got scared that if I didn't do what I was supposed to do, my mom never would come again."

So far Aaron observed that the colors of the auras were very dim and bleak, almost gray. *It is probably a sign of sadness,* he guessed, describing that and taking pictures, as Ashot gestured to him. Then the old man asked Rosie, "Did your mom visit you in the *Youth Shelter* during your four years there?"

"No. Not even once," the girl shook her head. "Probably, she didn't want to see me - the murderer, who killed her mother. Or maybe she was just too busy with her life. She recently married Miguel. While I was in shelter, my brother, Fernando, was born in 2007, then a second brother, Enrico, in 2009. And she was already pregnant with my third brother, Alberto, when I was released from the shelter in 2010. Mom was probably very happy and she didn't want to take me in after I left the shelter. She didn't know me and didn't love me. I was a stranger-murderer for her."

"Then how come you ended up living with her?" Ashot asked.

"In 2010, when I was acquitted, both my grandparents were already dead and I had no place to go. The shelter officials called Child Protective Services and they forced mom to take me. The foster system was overloaded, and if a child had a birth parent who was financially up to standards and didn't use any drugs or alcohol, that parent was supposed to take the child by a court order. It doesn't matter if the parent wants it or not."

"Wasn't Miguel against your placement in his house?" was Ashot's next question.

"No, at first he wasn't. He probably loved mom and wanted to show her that he is nice and kind to her unwanted child. He even adopted me and gave me his last name. They also needed help with the babies and household, so a fifteen-year-old girl could be a good maid. That's how I became a Cinderella."

"Was Vally in you, while you were in the shelter?"

Rosie nodded convincingly. "Of course, all the time. In spite of my beautiful friendship with Hope and with my teacher, Mary, in spite of being Anastasia most of the time, and even being Rubi sometimes, Vally was always there. I felt subconsciously that my mom never visited because she never loved me and never will, and I can't prevent Vally from the pain of this and stop her from crying."

"But when you started living with your mother's family, weren't you happier?"

"Not at all," Rosie shook her head vigorously. "I saw how much she loves my brothers and how she tolerates me only because of the court order. She never, ever hugged or kissed me, which was torture for me because I am a very hug-loving person. I can't live without the warmth and touch of a human. But I didn't get this warmheartedness from anybody there."

"How was your relationship with Miguel? Have you ever hugged him?"

"At the beginning I tried. I craved to have a father figure in my life. I missed a man's influence so much. It was a happiness when I could hug Miguel, feeling like he was my daddy. He was okay with that for a while, but then an awful tragedy happened – again, someone else's tragedy, but it affected Miguel a lot, and then it turned on me."

During a short break Rosie took a couple of pretty big gulps from her water bottle. Aaron noticed that her auras completely lost their colors and turned into sparkling black, as it was at the darkest moments of Nora's session.

"Miguel was a very high level computer programmer. He worked in a government office. One day a terrible story happened with one of his co-workers. That man had a step-daughter who was an angry mean girl. She was jealous that her mom loved him a lot. The girl started to hate her mom and decided to take revenge on her. She went to the police and made a complain that her step-father is molesting her, raping her and sexually assaulting her all the time. It was a lie. The man was very nice and decent, he never did anything like that. The investigation did not find any proof of what the girl was complaining about, but the judge decided in her favor. Mostly it was: she said, he said, and in these situations judges always believed a child, assuming that the child would never lie, if there wasn't smoke without a fire...

"So, that man ended up in prison for many years. The mother was so angry and devastated that she kicked the girl out and the girl committed suicide, leaving a note that she is killing herself on purpose, for revenge - to cause her mother more pain. But even with her gone, the man was still staying in prison. He lost his job, he lost his family. His life was completely destroyed for nothing.

"While this dreadful story of his co-worker unfolded, Miguel got really scared of me. Somehow he assumed that I am also that mean and could do something similar to him as well. He never hugged me anymore, never allowed me to sit beside him on the couch or even approach him. He was always screaming at me, 'Don't touch me, don't come close, don't hug the boys'. It sounded like I was some kind of sexual predator. I was accused for nothing, exactly like that poor innocent man who was left in prison. I was left in a moral prison state of unfair treatment and complete, hurtful distrust. Why? Why? What for?"

Rosie choked on her words, beat her fists on the table, and sniffled. Tears were sliding down her cheeks.

"Did this type of handling ever change for you?" Ashot asked compassionately.

"No. Never. It was even getting worse. The only thing left for me to hug and to love was the dog, Oscar. He always felt when I was unhappy and in distress and came to console me. I took him in bed and slept, hugging him. But then Miguel assumed somehow that I am doing some dirty sexual things with the dog and prohibited Oscar to sleep with me."

"Jeez, Aaron thought angrily. *How was it even possible to guess something disgusting about this innocent child? Does Miguel have such a dirty soul to even think about something like that? Or he got madly scared by the stupidity of our justice system with his co-worker?*

"Miguel also thought that it would be best to let me go far away from home for as long as possible. He began insisting that I take every club's suggestions for a concert trip. He was buying me all the beautiful and expensive clothes which were required for my stage performances. Many kids didn't go because their parents did not want them to be out, or because their family didn't have enough money to pay for these trips and outfits, but I always went. Fortunately, this increased my popularity and fame as Anastasia, but, unfortunately, it didn't help Vally. She was always there, always with me at nights and always crying like crazy."

"How long did it last?" The next question followed, as Ashot almost finished working on the Clay Mask lips.

"For about a year."

"How did your mom react to that success of yours? Wasn't she proud of you?"

"I don't know. She didn't say anything about that. But she somehow developed a huge distrust for me as well. I had one very bad altercation with her which drove me almost to suicide. I didn't see any other way to get rid of the pain of her distrust."

"Would you mind telling us about that, Rosie? What happened?"

"I was already in high school. I started dating Ben and didn't want to go on concert trips anymore. Mom and Miguel didn't approve of my boyfriend. They said that this guy would be a bad influence on me, assuming his skin color, I guess. Otherwise, there was no reason for them to think ill of Ben. He was very kind, good and loving, and had excellent marks at school. Noticing my problems at home, he suggested I move in with him. His mother, Keysha, allowed that, feeling pity for me, as well.

"At first, I was a bit hesitant to move in with him, but then one more last straw broke the back of my camel and forced me to move out from my mom's place to Ben's. Just a very simple thing.

"I did my homework in math and needed to give it to my mom to check. She was very good with math, but I wasn't. When she came to my room and asked me to give her my notebook, I somehow couldn't find it. I said to mom that I didn't know where it was. She started to scream at me that I am a liar, that I didn't do my homework. 'I did, I did,' I tried to convince her. 'I just don't remember where I put it. I will find it.' But it was useless. She didn't listen to me, only yelled and yelled how bad I am, what an awful liar I am, how lazy I am and so on.

"When she left my room, slamming the door, I was hurt so much that I didn't want to live anymore. I can't understand why she didn't believe me. Why did they always presum something bad about me? Why didn't they trust me even a bit?"

Rosie dropped her head on a folded towel in front of her on the table and cried hopelessly, pitifully and endlessly, shaking and having difficulty breathing.

Aaron gritted his teeth, barely holding himself in check, wishing to hug and kiss her. "Quiet, son. Pictures!" Ashot whispered gesturing to him. Aaron desperately shook his head in disbelief that the poor child survived, and then kept working persistently.

"I took a belt... climbed on a chair... by the window... and tried to hang myself... on a curtain rod," Rosie continued stuttering through heavy tears. "But it didn't hold my weight. I fell on the floor with the curtains together and lay there, all hurt and bruised, crying the whole night. Nobody even peeked into my room to check what all the noise was about, nobody discovered that the curtain rod was disconnected from the wall until the morning."

"Did you ever find your notebook?" Ashot inquired.

"Yes. While laying on the floor all night, I noticed it under my bed. It must have fallen down somehow the previous night. That's why I couldn't find it. I took it and brought it to my mom in the morning to prove that I am not a liar, and that I really did my math homework. But it turned out even worse."

Aaron bit his lips. He couldn't imagine what else could be worse than that.

"My mom didn't believe me again. She said that I did this homework this morning to cheat on her - it wasn't done last night, it wasn't lost and found again – I am still the liar and she didn't believe a word I was saying. Then Miguel blamed me for breaking the curtain rod. It was a full disaster. So, I packed my clothes and went to Ben's."

"Was Vally there with you?"

"No. Somehow Ben's family had a calm and good influence on me. I didn't cry there the whole year... until Ben's death. Then I was placed in the *Youth Shelter* for a year, once more. At first Vally was with me there, crying non-stop. Then the nurse, Mr. Spencer, came to work there and helped me a lot with my insomnia. I started sleeping well, so Vally was gone again for a while."

Aaron was looking at his beloved with admiration. Even during the cure, under half-hypnosis, she was still very ethical and careful, not calling Ashot – uncle, and keeping the situation official for the documentation.

"In a year I was released and returned to my mom's house. The situation there continued to be the same. I already graduated from high school in the summer of 2012, before Ben's death and before I went to the shelter. So now, living with mom I was free from studying and began working part time - teaching poetry at school and doing some editing for magazines. But 90 percent of my time I was the real maid and worked in our household as hard as possible to imagine. Though, in the first year I still traveled for concerts sometimes. But then, Tobi destroyed my trips and I became a stay at home housekeeper."

"Did your mom and Miguel treat you the same as before, or better?" Ashot asked.

"The same, and some things got even worse, especially distrust. I got used to many things, but distrust I can't tolerate because the hurting of it is absolutely unbearable... intolerable. You feel helpless when you are falsely accused and can't prove the truth. It's despair, it's insanity, it's madness of pain. Vally was back and I cried all the time."

"Would you mind telling us why you ended up in the *Youth Shelter* for the third time?" the old man inquired. "What happened on June 16th this year?" He evidently knew the story because he gestured to Aaron and whispered, "Pictures unceasingly. Buckle up, son."

Aaron remembered the view of Rosie's room that Miguel showed him when he came to their house, looking for her. It was four days after her attack and her placement back to the *Youth Shelter*. Then it shocked him, appearing really scary. But he had no idea what exactly triggered this attack of Tobi with a kitchen knife on her room walls.

"It started from a very simple and common situation," Rosie said nervously, breathing heavily. "There was a big jar of cookies and we all were eating them. I was allowed to have them as well. There were two cookies left at the bottom of the jar and nobody wanted them anymore. So, they stayed there."

She stopped, fighting the tears and Aaron noticed that a stream of the aura's particles turned into a black tornado moving toward the Clay Mask. It was pretty strange because so far nothing fearful and awful was happening in Rosie's story about the cookies. But her soul obviously knew what was coming and the auras reacted at it ahead of time.

"Then, a couple of days later, Miguel opened the jar and wanted to put more cookies in there, but noticed that the last two that were left there previously were now missing. The jar was completely empty. He asked, who ate those cookies. I don't think that the cookies themselves were worrying him. He just wanted everybody to tell the truth, nothing else.

"'No, we didn't take them,' the boys said and ran outside to play. It was obviously the truth because there were three boys and two cookies. If they tried to share them, it would be a fight and screams, and everybody would hear and know. Miguel and mom didn't touch the cookies as well, so they looked at me. 'I didn't', I said but they evidently didn't believe me. 'If not you, who else?' they said. 'We don't have any ghosts in this house'.

"'Why don't you, Rosa, tell us the truth at least once in your life?' Miguel said. 'We're not worried that you ate the cookies, we are worried about you not telling the truth. Lying is an awful thing. Look, where the lie of a girl drove my innocent co-worker – to prison for life. Lying is a real crime. So, tell the truth, please, confess that you ate those cookies, and everything will be okay. Nobody will be upset with you anymore.'"

"But I really didn't eat those cookies," Rosie screamed, beating her fists again on the table. "I didn't! I didn't! I don't know where they went! They wanted me to lie, they wanted me to confess to something that I didn't do! They were against the lie, but forced me to lie! It was a disaster! It was everything upside down in my life. I didn't want to lie that I had the cookies. I was telling the truth!!!"

She covered her face with both hands, dropped her head on the table and sobbed hysterically. Aaron bit his lips, put the camera on the table and squeezed his fists, breathing heavily. It was impossible to see her in such an emotional state.

"Pictures! Pictures, son, please!" Ashot whispered. "We are close to the end." He gave Rosie a few minutes to collect herself a bit, then asked, "Did you find out eventually, what happened with the cookies?"

Rosie nodded silently, sniffling and smearing her tears on her face, then wiped it with a little towel.

"The scandal about cookies was on Monday evening. I went to my room and all night I was crying. I was scared. I saw the monsters coming out from the mirrors and forcing me to confess to something that I didn't do. It was such a torture. I covered the mirrors with towels, to protect myself from those monsters."

Aaron remembered seeing those mirrors in her room, covered with towels. Miguel told him that Rosie did hallucinate that some monsters are coming from there to get her. But he didn't tell Aaron, and maybe didn't have any idea, that those monsters were in reality himself and her mother. Though Aaron guessed even then that the situation in the family was not good for the girl, he just didn't know exactly why. Now he knew.

"Tuesday was the day of my concert and during my sleepless night I created a poem *Monsters of the lie* which I wanted to share with my friends. During the day, Miguel was at work and mom left for a walk with the boys and the dog, so I was alone. I went outside, lay on the grass on the front lawn and kept crying continuously.

"Our neighbor next door, a senior lady, Mrs. Sanders, came out to water her lawn and saw me. She approached me and asked, 'What's going on, my dear?' She said these words so nicely, quietly that they soothed me and I told her the story about the cookies. 'Oh, my God! Rosie, my poor girl!' she exclaimed. 'I ate those cookies. Remember, a couple of the days ago your mama asked me to watch the boys for half an hour? She went to the hairdresser and you went with the dog for grooming. She said that if I would feel hungry or thirsty, I could feel free to take anything I want in the kitchen. While the boys were playing in the backyard I went to the kitchen, looked into a cookie jar and thought, 'oh there almost nothing left. Probably, I can clean it up!' And I ate them. I am so sorry. I will apologize tonight to your parents and replace the cookies, I swear to God!'"

Jeez, Aaron thought, *how such small and unimportant things could destroy or fix someone's life!* He felt thankful to this, unknown to him, old woman who came to Rosie's protection.

"Did Mrs. Sanders do what she promised?" Ashot wanted to know.

"Yes, she did. When Miguel returned home from work and mama was preparing dinner, Mrs. Sanders knocked on our door, holding a pack of cookies and apologized that she forgot to tell my mom afterwards that she ate the two last cookies. But it didn't help me, as I hoped it would. When she left, mom and Miguel began screaming at me that I am a double liar. They assumed that I went to the neighbor to complain about them and that I forced the old lady to come and lie in my favor to protect me, although, in reality, I ate those cookies. Their mind was made up and nothing could change it, even Mrs. Sanders' confession."

Rosie kept talking and crying at the same time. "Then they said that I probably learned to be a liar from my Poetry Club. Miguel was sure that all poets, singers, dancers, band musicians and other creative people are using drugs and alcohol and are liars because of that. In his opinion it was bad company for me and could lead me to using drugs or alcohol, and finally to prostitution. He said he didn't want this influence on his boys. So, I am not going to perform my concert tonight and ever.

"I screamed, grabbed a kitchen knife, and ran to my room, feeling that Tobi is coming. She was there. She was ready to fight for her beloved friend Anastasia, and protect her weak and abused friend Vally. I started beating the walls with that knife in mad rage, feeling an immense pain in my soul. It was all dark in my eyes. I didn't see anything. I just kept thrusting the knife into the walls, imagining that they were Miguel and mom."

She stopped talking, breathing heavily and desperately trying to calm down and collect herself, although those attempts were unsuccessful.

"I stopped only when I cut my finger and felt the physical pain of it. That kind of eliminated my soul pain and I left the knife to stay in the wall in my room. Blood was dripping from my finger to the carpet. I went to the medicine cabinet and put a band-aid on my little wound. Then I sat on the floor in my room and waited to die."

Aaron remembered that view of her room – the knife sticking from the wall and blood on the floor. It shocked him when Miguel showed him that, but he still felt that something was not right. The whole situation seemed wrong. He guessed then that maybe her parents prohibited her to perform at the Poetry Club and this triggered the attack. Today Rosie confirmed his previous suspicions.

"They called Dr. Evelyn Hertz for advice on what to do with me," the girl continued. "She suggested they take me to the *Youth Shelter* for several days. She said that she will come there and evaluate me. Right after this evaluation I will be transferred to an adult mental institution because I am a twenty-year-old woman.

"To the surprise of my parents I agreed to go and they drove me to the shelter without any resistance on my part. I knew that the nurse, Mr. Spencer, would be there. He was my only hope for some help and understanding. If not for him, I would find the way to commit suicide and die. I didn't want to live anymore being accused and distrusted for nothing.

"So, on Tuesday, June 16th 2015, I was accepted to the *Youth Shelter* temporarily. I missed my concert. Anastasia was on hold, but Vally was there in full swing. When Mr. Spencer came on the night shift, he was very much surprised to see me there again. He still remembered me from the years 2012 - 2013 when I was there. Seeing that I was on the edge of suicide, he began to work on me right away. He talked with me for a long time and finally calmed me down."

"We don't really need those details, Rosie," Ashot noted quietly.

"No," she shook her head, "Uncle, I want everybody to know that you are my Guardian Angel, the one who saved my life. Next day Dr. Hertz came and started to do paperwork to transfer me to an adult mental institution for years because of my very unstable conditions and danger for myself and the others. It was planned for next Monday. I told Mr. Spencer about that and we thought together what to do. We came up with a plan that he will cure me himself with a Clay Mask. On Friday night he released me and let me go. Then I ran down the hill from the gate where I bumped into you, Aaron..."

"Thank you, Rosie," Ashot tried to stop her, "that's enough of the story for now."

But she continued, unexpectedly turning back to anger. "I hate my mom and Miguel," she screamed suddenly. "They wanted to imprison me forever. Why? Why did I deserve that? I never lied. I was always nice and kind. I never hurt anybody in my life. Why did they want to do that to me? Why?!!!"

She cried and sobbed, hitting the table with her fists, then she jumped up and kicked the chair on which she was sitting. It fell backwards and turned upside down. Rosie angrily threw her water bottle on the floor. Ashot moved the Clay Mask closer to him and covered it with both hands. Aaron took pictures continuously.

Rosie kept screaming, then fell on the table, her face down and, from there, slid onto the floor and lay there along the table, unconscious.

"Should I lift her?" Aaron asked with shaking lips.

"No, no, no!" Ashot cried out. "Nobody should touch her or approach her. We don't want to disturb the flow of the particles."

"Then, what do we do?" Aaron yelled, jumping up. "The particles are not going to the Clay Mask now. She is on the floor, but the Mask is too high!"

"Calm down, son!" Ashot exclaimed fast and nervously, as well. "Let's take the tray with the Mask and put it on the floor. We need to level it with Rosie's head."

They cautiously took the tray, holding it together by both ends and carried it, slowly walking around the table to Rosie's side. Then they lowered the tray on the floor about six feet away from the girl's head and accurately lined it up at the same angle. They both saw through the goggles that the stream of the particles, after twisting around for a couple of the times, returned to the normal straight line – from Rosie's head to the Clay Mask.

"Thank you, God," Ashot whispered, making the sign of cross over Rosie laying on the floor, and kissed his golden cross that hung on his chest. "Now let's move our chairs closer to this side, so I can keep taking pictures. It will take a while, until the flow ends. Please, keep making notes on your tablet, Aaron."

Liam with the big camera on his shoulder walked to the other side of the room to keep filming the whole situation from the other angle. Now they all were waiting.

CHAPTER 42

This time it took them about three hours to wait until the stream of particles ended. When it finally finished, all the men were exhausted because they couldn't stop doing their work until the flow stopped – Ashot took pictures of the line of the particles, Aaron described it on his tablet while marking every minute of the time, and Liam kept filming the whole procedure.

"Oh my God," Aaron whispered, taking a deep breath of relaxation, and, finally, putting the tablet on the table. "Why was it so long? Can I lift Rosie now?"

"Wait a sec. First, let's take the Clay Mask back on the table and cover it," Ashot answered. "This is priority number one. If it breaks now, it will be a dead end. Rosie will never be cured. We are only half way at this point, and we can't restart everything again from scratch."

They lifted the tray carefully and brought it back to the table. Then Ashot placed the bowls with water around the Clay Mask and covered it safely with a big plastic box, as was done before.

"Now you can carry her to bed," Ashot nodded to Aaron and then turned to Liam, "Babe, you got it, of course, that the last part of her story should be edited a lot. No personal information need be opened to the conference in New York. They shouldn't know about my relationship with Rosie and also Aaron's. It should all be strictly official."

"Of course, darling," Liam laughed, taking his camera away. "It's not my first rodeo."

Aaron carried Rosie to her bed and then returned to the living room. "I want to thank you, Ashot, a hundred times, a million times, for what you did for Rosie," he said heatedly, "You are a real hero and I am bowing my head in front of you for that."

"It wasn't much of a heroism," Ashot smirked. "I just want to prevent this amazing child from being placed into an adult closed mental facility for all the years of her youth. It would be practically a death sentence – the loss of her life from twenty until thirty-five or forty, maybe even forever. Especially, when I know that I could cure her. I just had to let her go to protect her. I had no choice."

"You put your head on a chopping block for her! You lost your job!" Aaron continued excitedly. "If not you, Rosie and I would never have met! Jeez, I can't even express how much I am thankful to you. I owe you a big one! And I am really sorry, if I was sometimes angry with you. I just didn't know. I couldn't imagine what was really happening there. How could I ever thank you for that?!"

"Don't worry about me losing my job," Ashot shrugged indifferently. "It wasn't a big deal. I needed to be free anyway and have more time to concentrate completely on Rosie's cure. We have enough money to live with Liam. And if we could succeed in our project of her cure and get the Nobel Prize with you, it will be enough money to cover our years of work. The best 'Thank you' you could do for me, Aaron, is your involvement in this project. I don't need anything else from you."

"But I still admire you," Aaron insisted. "You are a believer, a man of God, and, in spite of that, you broke all the rules and did something officially illegal for Rosie. It must be very difficult for you to find the courage for that."

"Son," Ashot laughed, shaking his head, "you can't even imagine how many times in my life I broke rules and did illegal things, which I knew were right. I can tell you a little story.

"When I was a boy, about eight-years-old, I had a very religious grandma," he said, tenderly patting the golden cross on his chest. "It's actually her cross. She passed it to my mother, so I knew it later as my mom's cross. One day I asked grandma, 'what is God?' She explained to me very simple, very clear for a child. God is when you do the right things - not by the rules, but by your gut. God gives you the feeling of what is right and what has to be done. So, that you could know later that you did the right thing and your clean conscience allows you to sleep comfortably.

"To save this amazing girl from annihilation in the severe mental institutions system was the right thing to do at that moment. And nothing else existed for me then, no other rules or laws. So, I am grateful for your understanding and appreciation, Aaron, but there is no reason to admire me for that. I am sure, in my shoes you or Liam would do the same. Any decent human being would do the same."

"Okay, back to the cure," Liam said, smiling, being obviously admired by Ashot's story as well. However, he politely and ethically turned the conversation away to avoid the sensitive topic about the legality of Ashot's life. "At the end of Nora's session the flow of the aura's particles to the Clay Mask was a bit more than half an hour. In Anastasia's session it was about an hour. And now, almost three hours. I don't get it. Why was it that long, babe?

"I think, I was wrong when I considered Nora as the most difficult personality," Ashot explained. "Vally had obviously much more damaged particles of the auras, than the others. More dirt – longer time to clean."

"But Nora saw the murder," Aaron objected. "Vally just fought with her mom about a lost notebook and cookies. What is worse? What could potentially cause more damage?"

"Look, son. The murder was only one experience and it last for about one hour. The emotional abuse of this poor child continued for all twenty years of her life. It was not just a fight about a notebook or a cookie, it was an unbelievable hurt of distrust. As they say, if you get hit physically, your bruise will heal in a few days, but if you get hit emotionally, it will take much longer to heal; it will need help. And if you didn't receive any mental and psychological help, the damage could stay in your soul always.

"It was exactly what happened with Rosie. Her soul was bruised hundreds of times and it lasted forever. This Dr. Evelyn Hertz didn't heal her, she just prescribed her medications to hold her in check for a while. So, this emotional pain accumulated in the girl's soul more and more... until now. Today, thank God, we cleaned it out completely. There will be no more tears. She will be an absolutely happy child."

"You are a genius, Ashot," Aaron murmured, shaking his head in disbelief. "I can't forgive myself for being so judgmental and missing it before."

"Well," Ashot smirked timidly. "We fixed that now, didn't we?"

"You are so humble," Liam laughed. "That's why I love you, babe. So, what now, guys? Should we go out for dinner again?"

"Yes," Ashot answered. "We need to relax a bit and make some kind of small celebration. There was an important road mark achieved today."

When they settled for dinner at the *Old Spaghetti Factory*, Aaron asked, "I am just wondering, what will we do next? Eliminate Kiki, or Rubi? Kiki is actually a very happy child. Wouldn't Rosie lose her fun and childish side with it? Or Rubi, who is brave and confident... Wouldn't Rosie lose her bravery and confidence with it? It feels a bit worrisome to me."

"I think Kiki would be easier to do first," Ashot answered. "I don't think, son, that Rosie could lose her happy and childish side, as you are guessing. There is a difference between the features of a character of a normal person and a wrong, ill personality, even a nice one. Being a healthy woman, Rosie still will be happy and childish sometimes, when the mood and situation are proper for that. But Kiki... did you ever see her in this personality, Aaron?"

"Yes," he nodded. "Just once, at my home. She was playing in my daughter's playground and she appeared and behaved like a real five-year-old kid."

"That's exactly what I am talking about. It's not normal for a twenty-year-old. For her age it is normal to be happy, to be in a good mood, but to sincerely impersonate a little kid, live like a kid and behave like one, is not normal. But I expect it wouldn't be that harsh of a session, like it was with her other personalities. It is based on her seeing happy children and craving to be like them. So, the whole mental sphere would be mostly nice and I don't expect she will have any pain in her soul, like it was with Nora, Anastasia and Vally."

"When do you want to do this session, darling?" Liam wanted to know. "We still have a lot of work on materials from the previous ones."

"I know. Let's schedule it the same as we did this week – Kiki on Thursday and Rubi on Saturday. I think it worked not bad. And tomorrow is Sunday. We are going to church, but you, Aaron, take Rosie on a date again. Just do it please in some public place, not on a deserted island anymore."

They all laughed, as Aaron nodded, blushing a bit. "Sorry," he said. "I was just checking on Anastasia – if Rosie remembered her poem about our future on *the island with grass and sand*. It was proven that she doesn't. Okay, I will find some place to go on a little excursion."

Next day when Ashot and Liam left for church, Aaron suggested that he and Rosie would visit a small town, La Conner, not far away, just about one hour drive from home.

"I am still dreaming to show you Europe," he said. "But if you can't go to Leavenworth in the mountains which mimics Germany, a little bit of Denmark and Switzerland, then we can go to La Conner which is by the water and would be resembling the south coast of France. How do you like this idea?"

"Aaron, you don't need to ask," Rosie smiled, tenderly kissing his cheek. "I love any ideas of yours because they are always amazing and always fun."

She slept quietly the whole night after the very heavy Vally session and now seemed pretty happy. She didn't even ask if the cure was done, as she usually wanted to know earlier.

They drove to La Conner, which was a tiny town but it was still possible to find nice things to do there. Aaron walked with Rosie, holding hands, all the way along the promenade. They stopped at every shop, art gallery, cafe, restaurant; took pictures with a giant circle cut of an ancient tree that was growing there hundreds of years ago. After it died and was cut down, a piece of it was displayed on its side to show to the public the significant size of its diameter. When Aaron and Rosie stood beside it, hugging each other and taking selfies, Aaron's head was on the level of the middle of the cut's diameter, though Aaron was 6 feet tall. Rosie was 5 feet 5 inches, and her head barely reached his shoulder. So, the whole tree diameter was probably about 12 feet, as they calculated laughing and teasing each other about that. To see this ancient tree was fun and a very unusual experience.

Then they came to an art gallery where there was a big sign on the door: **We speak French here.** The huge windows displayed beautiful art works from multicolored glass, similar to those they saw at the *Glass Museum* in Tacoma.

"Let's go in and take a look," Rosie suggested. Aaron agreed because it would be a pleasure to see these amazing things once more.

The gallery was not big but full of artifacts, so it was pretty stuffy there and it would be impossible to walk together between shelves, cabinets and tables. So Aaron and Rosie separated for a while. He went on one side of the store and she – on the other. While he chose to buy two tiny glass cherries hanging on the hair-thin V-shaped stems, also glassy, Aaron noticed that Rosie approached the gallery owner, a senior lady, and talked to her.

When Aaron came closer, he heard that they were speaking French, as was advertised on the gallery front door. He still remembered some French that he learned at high school as a foreign language. He was a good student, but didn't use French for many years, since his last trips to Europe; so he could speak a bit of it now, but obviously small talk only. However, nothing more was required for the communication with the gallery owner.

"Yes, my dear, you are right. I am usually buying my things from that *Glass Museum*," the lady answered Rosie's question. "But not from the public display and not from their gift store of course, but from the hot shop where the glass-blowers are working. I want to have different things here, than those that are in their museum."

"Of course," Rosie laughed. "It is good to have your individual style in the gallery. We were in this *Glass Museum* and in this hot shop. It was even scary to watch their work, but absolutely exciting at the same time. Do you remember, Aaron?" she turned to him, as he approached.

He nodded, thinking that she was sounding good in French, obviously she was much better than him. But she graduated from high school just three years ago and he graduated nine years before that and forgot most of it. *That is the reason,* he thought.

Aaron offered to buy the two tiny cherries as a memory of this visit. While he was paying and the old lady packed the cherries into a hard box with soft cottons inside, they all kept a nice French conversation going. The woman wished them all the best, noticing an engagement ring on Rosie's finger.

"When will the wedding be?" she asked, smiling kindly.

"As soon as possible," Aaron answered and Rosie giggled a bit, blushing when the lady added, "I am sure your children will be smart and beautiful."

"Thank you," Aaron nodded, "I am sure about that as well."

"Have a nice day!" Rosie shouted to the lady and waved to her while exiting the gallery.

"Wow, I can see that you were a good student," Aaron noted excitedly. "You got the high school honors diploma not in vain. I am really proud of you. My French started getting rusty since high school. And we were in France with Ally probably ten years ago. It was the only practice I had."

"No, you were still okay," Rosie laughed. "At least this lady understood you, as I saw."

They kept laughing and walking. The next stop was a little boutique on the promenade where Aaron bought Rosie a white Greek style tunic. It was looking similar to her previous one that perished in blood during her knife attack in his car. Rosie tried it, wiggling and dancing in front of a big mirror and got absolutely excited.

"Thank you, my love," she said, kissing Aaron on his cheek. "It would be a good match to my golden Greek sandals and belt. I like this ancient Greek style. There is something mysterious and 'ritual-like' in it. Don't you agree?"

Aaron nodded, as he asked, "Did you have one of these before?" He intended to check if she had any memory of her Anastasia *Ancient Greek Hymn of Love* performance.

"No," she shook her head. "But I always wanted to have one. It looks just great!"

Later, they sat on a bench for some time, enjoying the view of the boats by the pier and a huge bridge, spanning high over the channel. People were walking by and Rosie asked someone to take a picture of her hugging Aaron with this bridge in the background.

Then they saw a couple walking with a child about seven- or eight-years-old. He was lagging a bit behind his parents. Speaking very agitatedly in an unknown language to Aaron, the man told his wife a story, many times repeating and emphasizing the same single word. Then the child shouted a question to them in which Aaron understood just the words, "Mama, Papa....?"

"Oh, my gosh!" exclaimed Rosie and started laughing.

"What?" Aaron wanted to know, astonished by her reaction. "What is so funny?"

"Jeez," she shook her head. "It's unbelievable. That man told his wife about his co-worker, whom he considered very stupid, and he repeated many times this word – stupid, stupid, stupid. The child didn't hear properly what they were talking about, but heard this loud word only, and he asked, 'Mama, Daddy, are you talking about grandma?' It's kind of funny, but it is sad at the same time. They obviously call grandma at home – stupid, which is actually very not nice for a child to know. But this is a typical attitude of Russians. They are usually disrespectful to each other, especially to seniors."

"Did these people speak Russian?" Aaron inquired, a bit surprised that she understood. She nodded.

"Russian is very close to Bulgarian, right?" he asked then.

"Pretty much so. This is the Slavic group of languages: Ukrainian, Russian, Polish, Czech, Bulgarian, Slovenian, Serbian...

They have a lot of similarities and the same words, though they are still different languages."

"But if you know one of them, it is also possible to understand the others, right?"

"Yeah... Sometimes... Maybe... I guess so," Rosie agreed, a bit confused.

Okay, now I got it, Aaron thought. *She lived with her grandparents as a child and they didn't know English. So, they must be speaking Bulgarian at home. She knows Bulgarian, and this is how she got this Russian conversation. Reasonable.*

"Probably, it is time for us to start heading home, my love," he said. "The guys said that they will wait for us for dinner. But maybe, on our way, we could get some coffee? There are many cozy coffee shops around."

"It would be nice," Rosie agreed.

Walking toward their car, they stopped for coffee in a small cafeteria on the pier right above the water. Aaron took just a middle size cup of black coffee, but Rosie ordered a small cappuccino which was served for her in a porcelain cup. A charming white lief was drawn on the top of brown foam which made her admire the barista's drawing talent.

At the next table a young Chinese couple was talking in their language. The woman was laughing infectiously about something the man said. Looking at her, Rosie started to laugh as well.

"Oh, my gosh! It's so funny!" she exclaimed, repeating some words that sounded in her mouth soft like a 'meow-meow.'

"Rosie, darling, it's not polite to make fun of somebody's language," Aaron whispered to her. "Please, don't do that. People's feelings could be hurt."

"I am not making fun of the Mandarin language," she objected, giggling almost to tears. "It is just an unbelievably funny joke about a dragon and a tiger. Look, she is laughing like crazy as well."

"I know, it's catching, if someone is laughing so much beside you," Aaron agreed, smiling and barely holding himself not to giggle loudly, too, "but still... Let's be nice. Did you hear this joke before from some Chinese friends..." he almost said – *at the Poetry*

Club, but bit his tongue and fixed his sentence, "... at school... maybe?"

"I don't know," she shrugged. Noticing her uncertainty, he decided not to force her to answer and changed the subject. "So, what do you think about La Conner? Isn't it beautiful and special, as I told you? To me it really feels like the south France coast. Jeez, I can't wait until we will be going with you to travel Europe."

"Me too," Rosie nodded, as she finally stopped laughing. "Thank you for coffee, my love. Now I am ready to go home." She stood up, picked her bags with presents from the floor and they started walking to their car.

CHAPTER 43

On Monday the intensive work of the whole team continued.

Ashot and Aaron worked together to combine the folder of the photos of the flow of the particles that was shown on each picture. The descriptions of the process, documented on the tablet at every minute of the session, needed to be attached to each photo.

Liam did the editing of his film, but his amount of work was much smaller because not a lot of reduction was required. So, he did some other house chores - buying groceries and cooking – in case they decide not to go out for dinner. He also drove Rosie to see some of her high school friends and to meet Ben's family.

After picking her up at three p.m. from Ben's house, Liam went with her to the beach for a while, just to entertain and occupy her with some fun. Then, at home, Rosie helped him to cook their meal and set the table.

While they all were having dinner on the patio in their condo, Rosie told the men how she visited Ben's family today. Ben's mother, Keysha, was at work, and his three little siblings – the eight-year-old sister, Anika, the middle sister, Tina, six, and a little brother, Dante, three, were watched by the senior neighbor woman. Keysha gave permission to Rosie to take them all for a walk to the park nearby and play with them on the playground. Right away, Rosie turned there into Kiki and really enjoyed her day with the kids. She was missing her little brothers very much lately and was craving children's company, which was always fun and pleasurable to her.

"There were also many other children in the park," she said to the men excitedly. "There was one woman from India with two kids – a boy and a girl. They started playing with my children and communicated easily, though these Indian kids didn't speak English. But kids can always find a way to understand each other. It was lovely to watch. I was sitting on the bench for a while and chatted with their mother. They are new immigrants, just came from India a couple of weeks ago through the family reunion green card program. So, she didn't know a word in English yet, but it is already arranged - she will go soon to the ESL school and learn."

All three men looked at each other significantly. "How did you chat with her, kiddo?" Ashot asked.

Rosie shrugged. "I don't know... Hindu, probably..."

"So... Do you know Hindu?" Aaron inquired carefully.

She shrugged again. "I don't know... We just chat..."

"But you were talking aloud? It was not telepathically, right?" Liam wanted to know.

"Come on, you, guys," Rosie laughed. "What is so confusing to you? Just two women chatting while watching their kids playing. I didn't even notice which language it was. She told me she only speaks Hindu."

"Okay," Ashot changed the topic instantly. "What are your plans for tomorrow, kiddo?"

"I hope Liam could drive me again to Ben's house," Rosie said, looking at him questioningly. "I would like to go to the park with the kids once more. And then, when you pick me up, after three p.m., we could go swimming for a while, like we did today, right, Liam? It was nice, wasn't it?"

Liam glanced at Ashot and the old man slightly nodded.

"Of course, kiddo," Liam answered then in a cheerful voice. "Of course, no problem."

This evening, when Rosie went to shower before sleep, Aaron stayed longer in the living room with the men. "Look, guys, we need to talk," he said quietly to be sure that the girl couldn't hear him. "Did you notice something? I mean about the Hindu language story."

Ashot and Liam both nodded silently.

"I have a suspicion that maybe there is a new talent appearing in her," Aaron continued. "What do you think? It looks like she is not noticing it herself yet, and not paying any attention to it. But if we talk to her about this new talent, we should talk about the loss of the old ones. How could we do that carefully, not to hurt her? Liam, you still haven't given her that new computer yet?"

"No," Liam shook his head, "there was no time for that. She wants to go out and play with kids. She never asked about her old computer, didn't even notice that it was gone. I, personally, don't know how to start. What do you think, babe?"

"Let's observe for a couple days," Ashot suggested. "I would prefer to have that conversation with her after the Kiki session. Just keep your eyes open on these moments. Something could come out from them eventually. Let's just give her a bit more time."

"It was on TV, remember, babe," Liam prompted, "the story of a young man in Australia who got into a car accident and was in a coma for some time. When he woke up, he started to speak Swedish, though he never learned it, never was in Sweden, didn't have Swedish blood or relatives, or even friends — absolutely nothing. Doctors said that after the extreme hit on his head, it came out from an unopened part of his brain. So, there must be languages hiding there. What do you think?"

"I remember the story," Ashot nodded. "But there is a big difference. Our kiddo wasn't hit on the head. We are working on her aura's particles. I guess they could also be responsible for this unopened part of the human brain, after knowing what happened with you, darling," he nodded to Liam. "However, it would be a very new experience for all of us. Nothing about languages was ever in my practice. Let's observe more, especially you, Aaron. Something could appear during her sleep."

When Aaron went to Rosie's bedroom, he vowed himself to avoid sex, making sure that she stayed in a childish funny mood.

She was Kiki during the day, probably because not many of her other personalities had left. However, at night she turned back to Rosie, but a happy one, and they were just laying down, hugging each other and talking in a whisper for a long time.

After eliminating Anastasia, nothing happened that Rosie feared or expected and Aaron had anticipated as well. Obviously she lost her poetry talent – poems weren't flying to her anymore from the universe, recited by a voice of the poetry fairy. She wasn't aware of that yet because Ashot, nor Aaron or Liam told her anything clear about that and her own memory about Anastasia was gone.

But she didn't become soulless, dull, talentless, ordinary and boring as she awaited what a simple regular woman might be. She was still bright, smart, intelligent, well-read and well educated. To talk to her was very interesting to Aaron, and not just because he loved her. They discussed many engrossing topics, exchanged their views and opinions, and built a new deep spiritual and intellectual connection, no less than it was before on the basis of the poetry.

Aaron was studying her, exploring her new brain ability and renewed soul, like she was for him a different woman. However, it still was her, his Rosie, his love, only a little bit revived in a beautiful, positive way. There was less tragedy hidden deep in her now, but more calmness, rationality and spiritual clarity. The many-years-old layers of pain, hurt and abuse shredded away, one by one, with each session, and a healthy, strong, confident, gorgeous personality appeared like the Aphrodite out of the ocean's foam.

It felt as a miracle to Aaron and he realized more and more, what a genius Ashot was. The old doctor truly deserved a Nobel Prize for his invented treatment of schizophrenia and Aaron was determined to help him to get it. He shared with Rosie these thoughts of admiration about her uncle while they were talking heart-to-heart. They were conversing about that a lot, until they finally fell asleep.

Following his regular schedule, Aaron woke up at seven a.m. While Rosie was still sleeping, he went to exercise at the sports club in the building, and then to the swimming pool. After finishing his sports routine he called his mother and Laurie on Skype that he tried to do as regularly as possible.

A few days ago, he told Beth that the problem with his work partner was resolved and they continued working together. So, she was glad to hear that her son listened to her advice.

Now Aaron went to his car at the underground parking to make the call because he didn't want Rosie to hear him, if she woke up. At first, he chatted with Laurie, who was getting well-tanned now, spending so much time on the beach. She showed him her new pet – a crab which was sitting in a small aquarium - and told the story of how the kids caught it.

Then he asked Beth to talk in private and she sent Laurie to the kitchen to have breakfast with her cousins and aunt Erin.

"Mom," Aaron said. "Do you still remember the Greek language?"

"Of course," she laughed, shocked by the question. "Why?"

"Then I will need your help in something. We are doing experiments of learning languages during the patients' sleep. I would like to call you tomorrow on Skype at the same time and introduce you to one young lady. Could you please talk to her in Greek?"

"Is it a young lady you love?" Beth inquired right away.

"It's not the point, mom. Don't ask her anything like that. And don't announce - 'well, we are speaking Greek right now!' No English greetings at all. Just start talking to her in Greek, as if you know that she is a Greek woman herself. Tell her something simple in Greek – about the weather, flowers, kids... I don't know... not private and sensitive subjects, please. I will be right there and I will observe and listen. I need to know if she will understand you and also, if she will answer you in Greek as well. And... very important... Please, make sure that Laurie won't be there. I don't want her to see this woman, yet."

Aaron was aware that Laurie could recognize the girl they met beside the *Youth Shelter* during their memorable evening walk and could reveal this to Beth. It was still too early to open to his mother the truth about Rosie's illness, at least until his beloved would be completely cured.

"So, you don't want Laurie to know that you found the woman, Arie?" his mother asked. "I agree. She could be disturbed and worried, maybe even scared."

"Okay, mom. It's again not the topic now. Just send Laurie to the beach with the others, and talk to my young lady in Greek. Very simple request. Would you do that for me, please?"

"Of course, Arie. Did I ever refuse to help you, my dear?"

"Thank you, mom. Love you. See you tomorrow at the same time, then. Bye."

Aaron turned Skype off, impatiently anticipating how important Beth's conversation with Rosie would be and what will happen when they meet and see each other, even virtually. Then he ran back to the condo, feeling like a boy, expecting to open his Christmas or birthday gifts.

Aaron didn't tell anybody about his plan to check on Rosie's language ability because it included a big private part of his life – to introduce his beloved fiancee to his mother, though still hiding the fact that they were already engaged. Professionally, he also wanted to take some initiative in his hands, not always to be Ashot's apprentice, only. He just told Rosie during their next whispering conversation in bed at night, "My love, when we wake up in the morning, I will call my mom on Skype and I would like you to talk to her for a while."

"Did you finally find the nerve to introduce me?" she asked without any shadow of offense, more teasingly.

"Believe me, Rosie, I know her better. It will be easier for her to accept our love, if she would know, at first, that we are working together. So, I presented you as my co-worker for a start."

"Why should it be uneasy, in the first place, if she loves you and wants you to be happy?"

"Sorry, I probably expressed myself wrongly. Not 'easy'... just, it would be more comfortable for me. To tell the truth, I feel a bit feverish. It's deadly important to me that you like each other. Please, don't say anything sensitive, just chat for a while about nothing, like weather, flowers... I don't know..."

"What if she asks me – do I love you? I don't want to say – no."

"I don't think she will ask something like that knowing that we are working together. Let's try anyway, my love. I think it's time to start moving our relationship in a proper direction. Come on, Rosie, we will be married soon."

"Will we?" she laughed. It was fun for her to flirt with him.

"Okay, I am dialing."

As Beth appeared on the screen, Aaron said, "Good morning, mom! Here is the young lady I told you about." With that he turned the screen toward Rosie, while still sitting beside her and hugging her waist. Now their faces were on the screen together, but then Aaron moved aside.

"Good morning, my dear," Beth said in Greek. "It's so nice to meet you."

"Good morning, Mrs. Dispenmore," Rosie answered in Greek as well to Aaron's deep shock, though he partially anticipated that this could happen. "Nice to meet you too," Rosie continued. "What is the weather like there, in Florida?"

"Very warm, high level of humidity. Everything is blooming. Sorry, but Arie didn't tell me what your name is, my dear?"

"Rosie."

"Oh, it's a beautiful name."

"Thank you, Mrs. Dispenmore," the girl said smiling, trying to be extremely polite.

"By the way, I really like your haircut, Rosie."

"Thank you, Mrs. Dispenmore. Do you think it fits me well?"

"Great, my dear. It makes you look very outstanding, not like the most ordinary girls with long hair. And it displays your beautiful features clearly. You made a good choice of style."

"Thank you, Mrs. Dispenmore. I really appreciate your nice words," Rosie grinned, feeling sincerely flattered and staying overly polite.

"You are welcome, my dear. You know, here, in Florida, we have roses everywhere," Beth continued." They are my favorite flowers. I am kind of obsessed with them."

"Yes, me too," Rosie nodded. "But I am also obsessed with children. I really love to play with them. I feel as a happy child at those moments."

"That's nice to hear," Beth answered. "There is an old proverb – children are the flowers of our life. Have you heard of it?"

"I have, Mrs. Dispenmore. Actually, many times."

"Okay," Aaron said in English, appearing on the screen that he had moved away from Rosie. "It's time for us to go to work. We just wanted to say Good Morning to you, mom."

"Have a good day," Beth uttered, now in English. "Bye Rosie. It was very nice to meet you."

"Bye, Mrs. Dispenmore. Same here," Rosie answered in English as well and waved to Beth, peeping in from the side of the screen again.

Aaron disconnected Skype and hugged Rosie. "Thank you, my love," he whispered, covering her face with passionate kisses. "You were amazing! I am sure you made a perfect impression on my mother."

"Not much of an impression," Rosie chuckled. "We only started the conversation, as you interrupted. Why did you make it so short?"

"Next time it will be longer, I promise, my love. Now, you go to shower first. We should be ready for the day, right?"

"Right," Rosie jumped up and ran to the washroom. "Will you join me?" she shouted already from inside.

"Not today," Aaron shouted back. "Too busy a day ahead, baby." As he heard Rosie turn on the water, he called Beth on the phone.

"Thank you, mom," he said. "Thank you so much. You did a great job. How was her language?"

"Is she Greek by nationality?" Beth asked.

"No. Not at all."

"Are you sure, Arie?"

"Absolutely."

"She doesn't have any accent as every new learner normally would do. And I used purposely very uncommon words," Beth explained, "like - humidity, obsessed, proverb, favorite, ordinary, features, outstanding... A person who just started learning a foreign language usually doesn't know these sorts of words. Did you understand what we were talking about with her?"

"No. Not a word."

"Shame on you, Arie. You never were interested in learning some Greek. When you were five-six- year-old I tried even to bribe you into learning it. I paid you 10 cents for each learned Greek word. You did learn about twenty of them, bought yourself an ice cream, and on that the story had finished. Do you remember at least some of those words?"

"No, mom, of course not," he laughed. "I didn't feel the inner need to learn Greek. I communicated perfectly with you in English. No offense, please, but what was the reason to waste time?"

"None taken, Arie. Just knowing more languages makes you better educated."

"Come on, mom. I am educated enough."

"Maybe, my stubborn boy," Beth chuckled, shaking her head. "But I can tell you that this young lady, Rosie, is a very good student. How long did your team teach her during her sleep? And why exactly Greek? Did you plan to involve me to check the success of your study?"

"Mom, I am sorry, I don't have time to answer all these questions now. Shortcut - it's not just Greek. There will be many languages. I just remembered accidentally that you were born in the USA in a Greek family. I only wanted to try. Okay, mom, huge thank you. I have to run. I'll call you tomorrow. Bye."

Feeling happy that Beth seemed to like Rosie, and proud of himself for coming up with the idea of such an experiment, Aaron went to the sports club downstairs to exercise before another day of hard work awaited for him.

Jeez, he wondered a little bit unsettled, *what did we do with this cure? What is happening here? French, Russian, Mandarin, Hindu, Greek... Is it a new talent or new madness and insanity?Help me, God! Let her be healthy, please! I am not letting her go! I will marry her, or I will die!*

CHAPTER 44

Before the Kiki session of the cure, Aaron didn't say anything to anybody about his experiment with Rosie about the Greek language. He thought it was still too early to come to a conclusion and to share his ideas with Ashot. Also, Ashot was obviously busy and worried about something and Aaron didn't want to escalate the situation.

Later, finishing his mutual work with Aaron on materials of the previous sessions, the old man started digging in his old files of the other patients, reading something attentively. Then he began flipping through Dr. Evelyn Hertz's file of Rosie's medical history, made some notes in his notebook, checked a few things on his computer. Something was evidently bothering him, but he didn't say anything to Aaron either.

After dinner, Ashot suddenly announced, "I am not sure if we will do the Kiki session tomorrow. Kiddo, let's talk for a while." He asked Rosie to follow him to his den and closed the door.

"What is it about?" Aaron asked Liam who was sitting on the couch with him watching TV, but the guy just shrugged and stayed silent. When Rosie and Ashot came out about thirty minutes later, she ran to Aaron, plopped on his lap and hugged his neck passionately.

"Is everything okay, my love?" he asked anxiously.

"Yes," she smiled and waved her hand. "It's nothing. Uncle is just overprotective as usual."

"So, are we doing Kiki tomorrow?" Aaron asked, addressing Ashot who came out from his den, following Rosie, and sat on the couch in the living room as well.

"Yes," he answered and then turned to Liam, "Would you like to go for a walk, darling?"

Liam nodded silently and they left. It was noticeable that Ashot wants to talk to Liam in private too. Aaron, as always, was the only one who was left in the dark and this felt uneasy to him again.

Damn! he thought. *Are we a team or not? Am I still a stranger and a stupid idiot to him? Or what?*

"Aaron, come on, it's nothing wrong. Forget it. I love you," Rosie whispered, seeing his unhappy face. She tenderly kissed him on the cheek and winked conspiratorially. "While they are gone, it's the perfect time for us to go to the shower, finally, and to make love. Almost a week has passed after our day on the deserted island. I don't know how you're coping so patiently. I am missing you like crazy. Please..."

This really disarmed him. "It would be difficult to disagree, my love," Aaron laughed and they went to Rosie's bedroom holding hands. This time it was not the night of the heart-to-heart sharing, but the night of the deep, hot, endless love.

The next morning the Kiki session began at ten, like the previous ones. When everybody settled in their places, Ashot made the same introduction as he did for every session and then asked Rosie what she wanted to say about her personality named Kiki. She thought a couple of minutes and started her narrative, smiling, looking straight at the back of the Clay Mask's head. Ashot continued his work on the Mask where it was stopped after the last session — its lips that were half done.

"As I mentioned already, being a child, I didn't have many friends but I really wanted to have them," Rosie said very calmly and relaxed. "When I saw little kids playing in the park where I went with my grandpa Vasil, I always envied them — how happy they were, how they were laughing, giggling, shrieking delightfully while running around. Somehow, I never played with them. I usually sat and watched them. I wished to be like them, feel happy like them, enjoy life like them. I tried to sense inside me what they are feeling and get the same joy. When I came home after seeing the kids, I practiced to be like them – ran around the room, jumped, laughed loudly, screamed happily, and waved my arms. I played tag and hide-and-seek with myself. I felt excited and happy at those moments and tried to keep them going for as long as possible."

"Why didn't you play with kids in the park?" Ashot asked. "Was there some kind of language barrier because you were talking Bulgarian at home with your grandparents and didn't know English at that time?"

Cunning fox! Aaron thought. *He turned his question toward the language now! While working on Kiki he is making his research on the possibility of her new talent at the same time. It's resourceful!*

"No," Rosie laughed. "Not at all. I knew English from birth. We never talked Bulgarian at home and I didn't know that language, not a word. Grandpa Vasil prohibited that. He said we should talk in English only because we are Americans now and we have to learn it. And it was kind of a positive thing. I was watching TV all the time. There were amazing children's shows like Teletabis, Little Bear, Dora the Explorer, Barnie and Friends. At age two, I already spoke perfect English and knew all the letters because of these shows. They were my friends and my teachers."

Aaron saw in his goggles that all layers of the particles flowing toward the Clay Mask were multicolored, bright and shiny because the story was nice and happy so far.

Damn! I was wrong, he thought. *But if she didn't know Bulgarian, how did she understand those Russians speaking in La Conner? I was sure it was because of the similarity of the Slavic languages. So...a new talent... really?*

Ashot pronounced aloud almost the same question that Aaron thought, "But you told us before, Rosie, that your grandparents didn't know English. Do you remember that? We guessed that in this case you would speak Bulgarian at home?"

"Sorry. When I said that I probably didn't express myself clear enough," Rosie smiled apologetically. "Of course, they knew a bit of English, otherwise, how could they get a job as a caretakers? They had to understand the residents' requests and demands. I meant that their level of English was very low. They knew the simplest words only and they had awful accents, so it was almost impossible to understand them. That's why grandpa Vasil insisted for all of us to practice English. At age three or four, sometimes I worked as a translator for them – from English to English, if someone didn't understand them, I clarified. It was fun. I laughed a lot and it helped me to be Kiki."

"So what was the problem, then?" Ashot wanted to know. "What was holding you back from playing with kids in the park?" He already added the last touches on the Clay Mask's lips and turned the whole thing a bit to the right side to form the second ear.

"Grandpa Vasil prohibited me from playing with children because he was scared that I would get infections from them – the cold, flu or measles. He was sure that all the people around us were sick. He had severe paranoia, but I didn't know that as a child. I had to listen to him and obey, otherwise, you know what would happen – he would hit Nora. So, I just sat and watched how kids were enjoying their lives, pretending inside my soul to be the same."

"Was Kiki with you when you were in the *Youth Shelter* for four years?" the next question followed.

"No," Rosie took a deep breath. "Sadly, no. There weren't any younger kids in the shelter. My friend Hope and I were the youngest ones there. Most guys were teens, of course, because the shelter was designed for them. I was very busy there - being 'shaking by horror Nora', 'crying Vally', 'fighting for my confidence Rubi', and 'blossoming with poetry Anastasia'. No room was left for Kiki. I never felt as a happy child there."

Rosie thought for a long moment, like trying to remember something but still kept silent. Aaron saw that the colors of her aura got really messed up with each other into a strange looking cocktail, however, the stream kept going to the Clay Mask, so everything seemed to be in order. Ashot didn't even gesture for him to take pictures, so he just described those mixed colors in his tablet dairy.

"Yeah," Rosie said, finally remembering something. "I also was very busy in the shelter doing my school work. I craved to be the best student and always to have good marks. I had some feeling that the better educated I will be, the better my personalities will love and respect me. So, I tried to do my best."

"So, you were good at studying a foreign language at your shelter school?" Ashot inquired.

"Yes. I learned Spanish and I was brilliant at it. When I was moved to my mom's house, I even talked with Miguel in Spanish only. He was excited about that and this was probably the reason why he was nice to me from the beginning and even adopted me."

Jeez! I was wrong again, Aaron thought frustrated. *I learned French at school and just assumed that she did too. Then when did she learn French? Maybe later, somewhere... Or really, a new talent... It's very confusing. Damn!*

"Miguel even asked me to speak Spanish with the boys while he was at work and to tutor mama a bit," Rosie continued. She placed her elbows on the table in front of her and rested her cheeks on her fists, smiling. She looked very happy, even enjoyed the nice memories that were so scarce in her life. "Kiki was back there. I played with my brothers a lot and felt myself on the same level as them – one, three and five-year-old. Until the tragedy with Miguel's falsely accused co-worker happened, everything was good at home. I had happy moments there and Kiki was blossoming."

"Pictures!" Ashot whispered to Aaron, making a gesture with his hand. "We need some good ones for a change." Aaron grabbed the camera from the table and started taking pictures of the particles that were beautiful and shiny. However, there was some black background visible under the sparkles. It was kind of unusual, and, obviously, important to document in photos. *Damn! This guy feels and sniffs everything like a dog!* Aaron thought about Ashot with an inner admiration.

It was true because the next question the old man asked was exactly what Aaron thought a minute ago, "Didn't you learn some other languages for your concert trips? Like French for New Orleans, for example? Were any classes available for that in Greenwich Hall?"

"No. Why?" Rosie laughed sincerely. "All concerts were in English only. And I never was in New Orleans. Also, the Greenwich Hall is not a school, it's a competitive concerts club. You are asking funny questions, sir!"

She took her water bottle and started drinking. As she finished and put the bottle away, her story continued. "When I was living with Ben, Kiki was happy to be with his little siblings. I felt at home, playing barbies with the girls. At that time, they were four and two-years-old only, and Dante was a baby. I liked to carry him in my arms whenever we went for walks. He was so cute and laughed all the time, and Kiki laughed with him."

"Then, the second time you were in the shelter, there was no Kiki again?" Ashot inquired.

"Right. When I was released for the second time from the shelter and returned to mom's house, Kiki returned for a while. There I played with my brothers again. But in general, Kiki was my less appearing personality throughout my life. That's why she was not really developed like the others. I decided once that if I would ever be cured, I would go to a college and become a kindergarten teacher, to be more with kids and to compensate for Kiki. I was thinking about that a lot. I knew that poetry would be my part time job only, but full time I wanted to be with kids, to teach them and play with them."

Rosie paused, took a deep breath and suddenly her face became sad and frustrated.

"That's why it is so upsetting now that it will never happen!" she raised her shaking voice with tears. "I lost my chance to attend college, I lost my dream to be a teacher. I lost everything and everything is finished for me!" She covered her face with her hands and lowered it on the table, crying pitifully.

Aaron couldn't understand what happened so suddenly and why her mood changed unexpectedly. He just saw that the stream of the particles toward the Clay Mask became dim, thin and it looked like it was almost ending. Rosie's cry and sniffles stopped in a couple of minutes. It was not clear if she lost consciousness or fell asleep. The dotted line of sparkles from her head to the Mask continued, but no more than ten minutes, then ended completely.

"Okay," Ashot said with a deep breath of relief, made a sign of cross on Rosie and kissed his golden cross on his chest. "We are done for today."

"So fast?" Liam asked, putting his camera on his table. "It's unusual."

"Kiki didn't contain a lot of damage," Ashot answered. "It was quick to clean. Take her to bed, Aaron, and come back right away. We need to talk."

"Okay," Aaron stood up to go around the table to pick up Rosie, while he asked, "I just didn't get it, why was she screaming that everything is lost and she can't go to a college?"

"Because she is pregnant," Ashot smirked sarcastically. "Another big achievement of yours Dr. Dispenmore. Another time you are destroying everything for this poor kiddo. And another time I am the one who needs to work hard to fix your mess."

CHAPTER 45

Aaron grabbed Rosie, pressed her tight to his chest and ran to the bedroom, slamming the door behind him. He put her to bed, covered her with a blanket and raced back to the living room. He was so furious that he was shaking with anger.

"Why in the hell is my fiancee pregnant with my child and I am the last person in the house to know that?!" he yelled.

Ashot already put the bowls with water around the Clay Mask and covered it with a plastic box. He turned to Aaron and said calmly, "Let's go to the patio to talk. I don't want any more scandals around the Clay Mask even when it is under concealment." With that he walked out from the room. Liam followed carrying his big camera and then disappeared into his own den, not saying a word, as usual.

"Why in the hell did she tell you about that first?" Aaron kept shouting while walking behind Ashot to the patio. "Women normally say such things to the most important person in their life, to their partner, to the man who is the father!!!"

Ashot sat on a chair beside the table and looked at him scornfully. "Calm down and shut up, you idiot!" he uttered with emotional arousal as well. "Did you ever listen to yourself, Aaron?! It is your egotism again. You are screaming not because you are worrying about her, about the baby, about potential danger and collapse of her cure. You are screaming because you are not the first one to know.

"What the hell is this?" the old man continued. "Your arrogance, nothing else. You want to be the first? The only one? That is what this is all about. And also some kind of jealousy toward me - you're scared that she is closer to me than to you. Believe me, she is not. You and I are in very different dimensions in the relationship with her. She didn't tell me anything. You are not the last one in the house to know. Kiddo doesn't know about that yet."

"Then how do you know?" Aaron asked, breathing heavily, trying to hold back his frustration.

"Sit down and listen carefully. That's what you are supposed to do before you start screaming at the people around you."

Aaron gritted his teeth and silently sat on another chair across from the old man who went on, "I told you before that we should take a break in the cure for a while when a woman has her period. Rosie knows that she was supposed to warn me, when it happened, so we could postpone the cure sessions. Now, already more than a month has passed and I didn't hear anything about that from her. I checked Rosie's medical folder of Dr. Hertz that determined when her last period was and it worried me because she is obviously late now.

"So, I talked to her and she assured me that she is always very regular, never late in her life, except for the one time when she was pregnant with Ben's child. So, I gave her a little bowl and suggested that there needs to be a urine test done in the morning. She didn't get it that it was for the pregnancy check. She was sure I needed it for some other medical reasons, as most of the tests I usually do.

"While we went for a walk with Liam last night, I bought two pregnancy tests from a pharmacy. So, this morning, before the session, she brought me the bowl with the urine and I tested it while she was gone. I didn't tell anything to anybody, so, be happy, you are actually the first one to know... if this is what is important to you," Ashot smirked and moved a little long box to Aaron with a test stick in it. "It is a very sensitive test, high quality, newly developed. She is one week pregnant."

Aaron looked at the test, put his elbows on the table and rested his forehead propping it on his hands. "So, it must have been after that deserted *island with grass and sand*," he pronounced slowly with a deep sigh. "She knew that. She told me that our son will be conceived there while she still had her vision of 3D time – the future. It was in her poem ***Place out of Time.***"

"If you knew that, you should have used protection, Aaron. You should think about her, as I told you many times," Ashot uttered quietly.

"No," Aaron shook his head. "It wouldn't change anything. It is our future. It is our destiny. I believed that she could see the future then. It is what's written in the particles of the holographic universe fields. Rosie had the ability to read them. She knew."

"I realize that you trusted her fantastic abilities at the time," Ashot continued. "But now we have a serious problem here. I know that you are young, you are in love, you want to create a family, marry Rosie, have children with her. It is all normal and understandable. But you need to give her time to be cured before all of these happen.

"You're rushing like crazy. You are undermining the whole process of her way to recovery. Your kiss on the stage cost her a lot – she almost killed you and herself in your car after that. Your marriage proposal on the stage cost her no less – she attempted suicide, here in the kitchen that night. Your conception of a child... I don't know... I am even scared to think what could happen with our project of her cure now. I don't have experience with this. None of my patients was ever pregnant during the cure sessions.

"I can't guarantee now what will happen with her or with the baby," the old man went on sadly. "How will the change of the aura of her body affect her pregnancy? Will she have another miscarriage? Will the baby be born healthy, or ill, or deformed? Science doesn't know anything about that. I don't know that either. My cure was 100 percent guaranteed before. Now, it will be experimental only. And, as you know yourself as a scientist, not all experiments are successful. Some of them fail, some of them even turn out deadly.

"You can't imagine, Aaron, how much I want to scream at you and even to kill you... seriously," Ashot shook his head in despair. "But I learned during my long life to hold myself in check because I know, rationally, that anger won't help here. We can't turn anything back. We should think a lot together to find a decision what to do now. To continue the cure, or to leave it like that - unfinished. We have two of the most difficult, scary and aggressive personalities left to eliminate – Rubi and Tobi. Rubi is planned for this Saturday, after tomorrow..."

"Rubi is actually pretty nice. I saw her a couple of times," Aaron objected. "She is beautiful, sexy and very smart."

Ashot smirked. "Just wait for it, and you will see. I worked with Rubi almost every night of your 'happy vacation dating'. You don't know what it cost me to sooth her.

"However, if the cure is not finished properly," he went on, "if Rosie will not break the Clay Mask to let all the damaged particles of her aura to fly up to the universe, they will still be here. All that we have done until now will be in vain, all her sufferings and efforts will be in jeopardy. And then – no happy ending. You can't marry a dangerously mentally ill woman. You can't bring her home to your mother and little daughter, if she stays in her unstable unpredictable condition. The tragedy will continue for all of us. Is that what you wanted, Aaron? I am sure you didn't but it is what you did with your uncontrollable mad passion which I still have difficulty to name LOVE."

Aaron stayed silent. He didn't know what to say. He felt guilty beyond immensity, also completely lost and confused.

"It is love," he finally murmured tentatively. "I just... Rosie said she wants to have a child. I didn't care much at first and she was hurt. She was crying because I didn't show any excitement about this idea. So, I kept thinking about that and got used to the thought. Yes, if we will be married soon, why not have a child? It will compensate for her craving to be with children – not at work as a teacher, but at home: our son, and my little Laurie. I know that she and Laurie - they will be okay, they will love each other. They were attracted to each other very much when they met."

"Aaron, wake up," Ashot barked at him angrily. "It's not a time to worry about your future family relationship. It's time to think about the cure. How should we continue? Do you realize the risk for a child and for her? Can you think, again, about someone else except yourself, damn it!?"

Aaron looked up at him as disoriented like he was really suddenly awakened. "Okay," he inquired, "if she doesn't know about her pregnancy yet, then explain to me why you said that she is devastated to lose her chance to go to a college because she is pregnant?"

"She has a gut feeling that something is not right with her; that for some reason her dream to get an education as a teacher can't go ahead, at least for now. You saw yourself, Aaron, the difference in the flow of the particles during today's session in comparison to previous ones. Something changed and it was obviously because of the pregnancy."

"But actually the whole Kiki session went not bad at all," Aaron commented. "It was short, mostly quiet, calm, except for the last outburst only. And even it wasn't so brutal for Rosie, just a bit sad. Maybe this pregnancy will not be as bad as you expect? Would everything be turned to the best because of that?"

"It could, if God wish. I will pray for that," Ashot nodded. "I'm just saying that now I can't predict the result of the cure for sure and I can't guarantee anything. It makes me worried. I am used to working with certainty."

"But when you started with your first patients, you didn't know for sure what would happen. You were experimenting and it came out just great," Aaron objected.

"I was experimenting on people who had nothing to lose, who were doomed. They didn't have anything in front of them except death. I knew that my experiments were giving them a chance to be saved and it turned out as a nice surprise for me and for them, when they got healthy. For kiddo – she has a lot to lose. She is young, bright, and it looks like a new talent began to appear in her. She has a life ahead of her, she has a man who loves her, she could have a family, children, everything... We will walk here on the thin ice. Do you want to take that risk, Aaron?"

"Actually, I do!" Aaron exclaimed convincingly. "I need her to be healthy, I want her to be healthy! If we stop now, it will never happen. No... No, we need to continue the cure no matter what."

"Okay," Ashot nodded. "I was inclined to that direction as well. But, we should ask Rosie. She must know and make her own decision about her future with you and with this child of yours. So, tomorrow morning, as soon as she wakes up, you will give her this second pregnancy test and ask her to do it. Or maybe stay with her... I don't know what will be more comfortable for both of you. But she has to do that herself to find out first. Don't reveal to her that we already know that. It has to be her discovery and then we need to have this conversation, all together, friendly, nicely, maybe during breakfast. Not to underline that this is a life decision, just to make it easy and not scary for her. Right? What do you think?"

"I agree, of course. But also I would like to suggest talking to her about the appearance of her new talent. It could make her more excited and to wish more persistently to continue the cure."

"Okay," Ashot uttered with an interest. "Is it something about knowledge of the foreign languages? During the session today I tried to get more information from her about this topic. But I found out practically nothing. Tell me what you had noticed, on top of this Hindu story that she told us."

"While we were in La Conner, she spoke with a woman for about fifteen minutes in French absolutely fluently. I guessed that she learned it at school, but – wrong, she learned Spanish there. Then she translated to me what some Russians were talking about. I guess it was because she knew Bulgarian and the Slavic languages have a lot of similarity – wrong. You found through the Kiki session that she didn't know Bulgarian.

"Then she laughed at Chinese people telling jokes. She somehow understood the meaning of the joke. I was confused how she could know Mandarin, but something distracted me from asking her. I was thinking about that all night. Then I decided to do my own research. I called my mother, who is a Greek woman, and asked her to talk to Rosie in this language. She did and even thought that Rosie is Greek by nationality, so good and fluent she was in Greek.

"So, for now we got: French, Spanish, Russian, Mandarin, Hindu and Greek. It's already six languages which she understands and potentially can speak some of them fluently. It's kind of a miracle. And I am not sure, how many more there could be?" Aaron ended his narrative.

"Hmm," Ashot shook his head thoughtfully. "Interesting discovery. Thank you, Aaron, you did a great job on this. I could suggest one more experiment on the topic. You know that I am Armenian, but I was raised and educated in the Soviet Union where the official legal language was Russian."

Aaron was surprised that Ashot started to open to him his life story which was completely blocked for him before as he was considered a stranger. He felt elated that he finally deserved Ashot's trust and closeness somehow. Did the old man appreciate his research of Rosie's new talent, or was he softened a bit toward Aaron, realizing that he will soon be a grandfather of Aaron's child?

"I talked with my parents at home and also got my school education in my home city of Yerevan in the Armenian language, of course," Ashot continued his tale, "but we learned Russian at school a lot. Later, I studied at the Medical Institute in Moscow as a doctor for five years and then three more years for my Psychiatry PhD – all in Russian, only. So, Armenian and Russian to me are like my two birth languages. I will do my own test on her later.

"However, tomorrow we need to discuss with Rosie her pregnancy, first. Let's not confuse her with the two different topics. The most important problem now is to make a decision, if we will do the Rubi session on Saturday or not? If we move ahead with the cure, I suggest we finish it as fast as possible, while the pregnancy is not fully developed. Let's do Rubi on Saturday and Tobi on Monday. Then we are left with only one personality – Rosie. I am not sure if we need to do anything about that. But we will think this through later.

"After the cure is done and she breaks the Clay Mask, then, the following day, I will talk to her in Russian, at first, and if she will be okay, then – in Armenian. Russian is kind of widespread in many parts of the world, but Armenian is very much localized and uncommon. Nobody learns it and speaks it, if you are not an Armenian by nationality.

"I will double check your assumption about her knowing the Russian language, Aaron, which is very possible, but if she will get Armenian... I don't know... It will be shocking... It will mean that she now knows almost any language on Earth. It's very extraordinary... a super rare new talent and an even more impressive one, than Liam's. And I couldn't even guess what we will do about that and how she will live with that dumbfounding ability – which is even more unbelievable than ones she had before."

CHAPTER 46

Next day Aaron woke up feeling some light touches on his forehead, eyebrows, cheeks, lips. As he opened his eyes, he saw Rosie beside him, smiling and tracing her finger on his face.

"Good morning, my love," she whispered. "I am looking at you and trying to remember everything about us – how we met, how we dated, how we fell in love. I am studying you, learning who you are, but I can't remember anything before that fantastic love day on a little deserted island. I know that you told me how we met, I remember your story, but I don't remember the fact itself. It is strange, isn't it?"

"It's okay," Aaron said, kissing her hand and the finger that was touching him. "We will create our new life story. Let's agree that our past will be just this day on the tiny island, but our future is ahead. By the way... about the future... We need to check something."

"What?"

"You always liked to take showers together, Rosie. Let's go now..."

"Okay," she jumped off the bed and ran to the bathroom.

"Wait!" Aaron jumped up as well and ran after her. "Wait," he said as he entered the washroom. "I would like to show you something, first."

He opened a little box with the pregnancy test that he placed on the edge of the sink last night, and gave Rosie a stick. "I'll go to shower and you test it, please, and then join me. Okay, my love?"

She looked at the stick astonished. "Why?"

"Just in case, if we will have a baby. It is nice to know, isn't it? I remember that you wanted to have a child, right?"

She shrugged. "I don't know. I don't remember. I never thought about it. Maybe I am too young for that? We are not married yet... Do you think I could be pregnant?"

"It's always a possibility for a healthy woman in love," Aaron laughed. "I would be happy to have a child with you."

"Okay," she shrugged again with an expression of uncertainty on her face, "but... anyway, I love children. I just don't know how good a mother I might be. I don't feel mature enough."

"You will be a great mother and you will have a father of the child beside you, who is mature enough and experienced enough. Right?" he chuckled, patting himself on his chest. With that Aaron sneaked behind the shower curtain and turned the water on, leaving Rosie to do her test in private.

She joined him in a minute.

"Are you already done?" he asked surprised. "So fast? Shouldn't you wait for a while for the result?"

"I did it, but I didn't wait for a result. I am scared, Aaron. I left it on the sink. I want to look at it, holding your hand. I want to be with you. I can't do that alone. Could you please love me now, before we look at the result?"

"Of course," he agreed momentarily, hugging her tight and covering her wet face with passionate kisses.

As they exited the shower afterwards and put their bathrobes on, they approached the sink, holding hands, to look at the stick. Yes, it was what Aaron already knew it would be – one-two weeks pregnant.

"Wow," Rosie sniffled and hugged him, hiding her face on his chest. "I don't know, Aaron, should I be happy, or sad, or excited, or scared, or what...? Tell me, please. I am confused. I don't know anything now. I actually don't feel anything inside me, like I am pregnant."

"It's too early to feel anything, my love," Aaron whispered, tenderly kissing the top of her head. "But I think we both should be happy and for that – let's go right after breakfast to City Hall and get married. Just get our marriage certificate first. Then we could prepare a wedding. What do you think?"

"Yes," she murmured, looking up at him with a shiny smile but still with tears in her eyes. "I just... just don't have a proper dress..."

Aaron giggled, realizing how young, naive and childish she still was. "My love," he said, "don't worry about that. We will find a dress, I am sure. Let's go now and have breakfast with the guys and let them know our news."

During breakfast, Ashot and Liam played a great game pretending to be really surprised and excited about the news. They hugged and kissed Rosie in turns, congratulating her, and also shook Aaron's hand, complimenting him as a future father. Rosie blushed, looking a bit baffled.

Then Ashot said, "Kiddo, you know that we're now doing your cure sessions? That we're eliminating your extra personality one by one, right?"

"Yes," she nodded.

"We're not finished yet. Two sessions still left to do. I don't know how it could affect your baby. Do you want to continue the cure, or stop it until the baby is born?"

A tense silence hung over the table. All three men gazed at Rosie expectantly. She shrugged, shook her head thoughtfully, then looked up at Ashot. "What personalities are still left, uncle?" she asked.

"Rubi and Tobi."

"I love Rubi," she whispered. "She is my best friend. Even my only friend now... if I don't have any other personalities anymore..."

"No, kiddo. She is an imaginable friend, but you now have real live friends, all three of us here. You don't need imaginary friends any longer. They helped you when you were extremely lonely. Now, look at us – we are a pretty big company of friends who really love you, care about you, and are always ready to help you, to entertain you, to have fun together. Or, to solve some serious problems with you together, if needed. We are here for you, Rosie. Does everyone agree, guys?"

"Of course," Aaron and Liam confirmed, smiling.

"Okay," Rosie took a deep breath. "Rubi always tends to solve crimes. She is investigative and smart, but kind of... It makes me scared to always think about crime. Maybe it would be better to let her go. What do you think, uncle?"

"I agree, kiddo. It would be much healthier for you to live without any thoughts about bad things, especially during pregnancy."

"And Tobi..." Rosie continued. "I don't like her. She is fair, she wants to fight and protect, but it is sometimes too much. Look, she even wounded me," she extended her left arm to show the two thin white scars on her wrist and on the lower arm. "Tobi really could accidentally kill me or Aaron, or even the baby, later. Yes, I think she should go too, uncle. I don't want to postpone the cure, not for a day. No, no, no. You know, Aaron and I - we will go to City Hall to get married today. I need to be healthy to be Aaron's wife. I know that for sure."

Ashot and Liam glanced at each other. "Where did this idea come from, kiddo?" the old man asked.

"Aaron suggested and I agreed. I am pregnant. We need to be married. We love each other. We don't want to wait, right, Aaron? So, you, uncle, and Liam, please, go with us together to be our witnesses."

"Gosh! You're rushing like hell," Ashot, in displeasure, shook his head looking at Aaron. "If you decided this, kiddo, you must now go to your closet and find a dress for the occasion. And you, darling, help her to choose," he nodded to Liam.

"Okay, let's go Rosie," Liam jumped up. "It will be fun!"

As they left, Ashot turned to Aaron, who already expected another bunch of angry accusations and exclaimed, not giving the old man a chance to open his mouth, "I know, I know what you will say. But you should understand. I am scared more than anything in the world to lose her. I want to fasten her to myself somehow, as much as possible, as soon as possible. I need it to assure myself that she is mine and I can sleep quietly."

"Does an official piece of paper do this job for you?" Ashot smirked. "Why such insecurity, Aaron? She loves you. Now, having your child, she will certainly be with you. Why are you rushing like crazy?"

"I don't know. I just can't stop myself. Something inside is telling me that I have to do that. Also, Ashot, I noticed that you kind of tricked her to continue the cure. You mentioned in passing that you don't know how it could affect the baby and she probably doesn't even notice that. Do you think it is fair?"

"Aaron, you, as a father, agreed to put the baby at risk. I, as her doctor, agreed with that as well. Who is more important to you – Rosie or baby?"

"Of course, she is. If something happens to the baby, I could easily do a dozen new ones," Aaron laughed. "But if I lose her, it will be a dead end. No other woman exists in the world who is like her, and who could replace her, ever."

"Okay," Ashot nodded. "It is your egoism talking again, Aaron, but I agree, too, that kiddo is an unbelievably special creature of God. Also, there is one rule in medicine. If there are difficulties during childbirth and one could die – mother or baby - otherwise it's absolutely impossible to separate them, doctors will choose whom to save, who will live. And, in most instances, the woman would be chosen. She is already a person, she has people who love her, who need her, maybe other little kids. She is grown up, useful and known to society, she could later have other babies. A baby is not a developed person yet, and nobody knows if it will be healthy or sick, who will die soon, anyway.

"I can tell you one true story in my own family. It happened in the 19th century. My great-grandma had nine children and at age thirty-five she was pregnant with the tenth child. Her heart got very weak at that time and the doctor said that she won't survive a childbirth and suggested an abortion. My great-grandfather was very religious and didn't agree. He said, 'I will not allow anyone to kill a human soul'. Okay, she gave birth and she died in the process. The baby died a few days later, nine children ages from three to fifteen were left motherless. I couldn't hear this story without shaking from anger. This idiot did not allow the death of one soul, but he easily killed the two of them and left nine more souls to suffer. What could be more stupid than what he did? It is very sad that nobody asked the woman's opinion at that time. She was not a person – just a thing which a husband possessed. Damn it! Disgusting times!

"So, we asked Rosie's opinion," Ashot continued. "There is nothing wrong with the process now, if she said that she chooses to continue the cure, Aaron. She herself wants to get rid of her extra personalities, especially rough ones. And we, you and I, chose Rosie's wellbeing over some unknown danger to the baby – maybe actually, none. However, I still don't understand why you are so obsessed with the fear of losing her?"

"Before we started the cure, you gave me the files of your first patients from Armenia to read," Aaron explained. "I noticed that five of them changed their relationship after the cure, including the one, who fell in love with you. If we count Liam, it would be six. So, six of twenty-one is a pretty significant percentage, about 28 percent. I asked you, if you followed up the others and you said – 'no, I have no time because I emigrated to the USA.' I have kept thinking about that since. What if the feelings are always changing with the change of the person's aura? What if she will not love me anymore after she gets healthy?"

"So, if you get married, it doesn't help," Ashot laughed. "She could divorce you, anyway, if this would be the case. Come on, Aaron, don't be a child. You are really worried about nothing. Okay, probably, to calm you down, son, I will try to find some of those people through social media. Liam is pretty good at it. When we finish Rosie's cure, we will work on that, I promise. Actually, I am curious myself, not about their marital statuses, but how they feel in general now, health-wise, thirty to thirty-five years later. It would be useful to know to reassure ourselves that everything will be good with Liam in fifteen more years and with our kiddo - thirty more years from today."

"Hey, guys, I am ready to go," Rosie exclaimed happily, entering the room with Liam in tow. "Look at me? How do you like my dress?"

She was wearing the new white Greek tunic that Aaron bought her in La Conner. It was tightened with a golden belt under her breasts and the golden Greek sandals on her feet laced up to her knees. The belt and sandals were the two things that survived Tobi's attack with the knife in Aaron's car; two things that were left after her performance of the **Ancient Greek Hymn of Love** and the Guinness record kiss on the stage in Greenwich Hall. And now she was wearing them to get married. It looked symbolic to Aaron. It was a continuation of their love story and one more step on the way to their happy future.

CHAPTER 47

On the way to City Hall, they stopped at the jewelry store and Aaron bought wedding bands for himself and Rosie. They chose the rings together – in a pink gold, fretted and inserted with tiny white gold pieces. Rosie liked them so much that she jumped and giggled happily all the way to their destination.

At City Hall they went to the registration office, signed in, and were told that waiting will take about a couple of hours. Not to waste time they decided to go out for lunch at a small cozy restaurant around the corner.

While they settled in a booth, Ashot noticed that their server was a Philippine fellow. The old man excused himself from their company, pretending that he was going to a restroom, but went to the kitchen instead. He approached the waiter as he was exiting the kitchen and asked, "Excuse me, sir, do you speak a Philippine language?"

"Yes," the waiter answered, surprised. "Not perfect because I was born here, but I know Tagalog. We spoke it at home in my childhood and even now I am speaking with my mother."

"Then I have one request," Ashot continued confidentially. "Would you mind, please, while taking our orders, to speak Tagalog with the young lady at our table? Just her. The other three of us can speak only English. And please, do not underline that you're talking to her in another language. Just do it naturally, as if you see a real Philippine woman in front of you. And then move straight to English with the rest of us. It would be greatly appreciated."

Seeing that waiter looked at him bewildered, Ashot explained. "It's nothing special, just personal. We would like to check if she knows the Philippine language or not. I am a teacher and I am giving her a test."

"Okay," the man laughed. "I will try, sir. It's kind of interesting. While working here with the public, I see many different unusual moments sometimes."

As they all were ready to order, the server came to their table and addressed Rosie in a language unknown to the rest of them. "I guess, we should start with the lady first," he said, smiling. "What dish did you choose, Miss?"

"The New York steak. Please, be sure that it is well done. I don't like raw meat," she answered to the deep astonishment of Aaron, Ashot and Liam who didn't understand a word.

"What would you like for a side – French fries, mashed potatoes, rice or vegetables?" the waiter continued while the men listened almost with their mouths open.

"Mashed potatoes and some veggies, please, especially carrots, if it is possible. I am crazy about carrots," Rosie continued and laughed.

"Of course, Miss. How about a drink?"

"Cola with no ice," she said. "I don't like it too cold."

"Done deal, Miss," the waiter said, finishing to jot her order in his notebook and then turned to Ashot. "Your choice, sir?" he asked in English now.

When their orders were taken and the waiter was gone, Ashot suddenly tapped his palm on his forehead, "Oh, damn, I forgot to add something to my chicken." With that he stood up and almost ran behind the waiter to the kitchen.

"Thank you, sir," he said, giving a significant tip to the server. "You did just great. What do you think about her language?"

"If you are a teacher and she is a student, give her the best mark," the man laughed. "She is good. If I didn't see her face, I would be sure that I am speaking with a Philippine woman. She was effortless and practically, has no accent. So, what now? Do you want me to continue when I bring your food?"

"No, thank you, sir. Now we can turn back to English," Ashot smiled as well. "Test is done. She passed."

Nor Aaron, neither Liam asked anything, when Ashot came back to the table. They got the game. Just later, when Rosie went to the restroom, Aaron guessed quietly, "So, the seventh language? Right?"

"My God... so far. It was the Philippine Tagalog," Ashot took a deep breath and squeezed his head with his hands. "I don't know where this is going. I don't know if we should be glad or cry? Not a word, guys, please. We will discuss it with her later. Let's just enjoy our meal for now." Everyone nodded in agreement, smiling.

Back in the City Hall building they passed the lobby where a small counter with refreshments was located. Together with a few tables it created a little cafeteria for people who were waiting in the lines, so they could spend their time in a more pleasant way, having coffee.

Suddenly they heard a girl's voice shouting from behind, "Hey, Rosalyn! Hey! It's so nice to see you!" They all stopped and turned around abruptly. The teenage girl from behind the counter, with curly brown hair, wearing a black apron on the top of her floral dress waved to Rosie. Then she came out from the counter, ran to Rosie and hugged her. "Jeez, it's so nice," she happily shrieked, as Rosie patted her back as well. "Why didn't you come to the last concert on Tuesday, Rosalyn? We were sure that you'll always come to watch us. You know, Tommy won last time with his poem **Welcome Home** about soldiers coming back from Afghanistan. It was shocking. Many were crying in the audience. It was a triumph. It reminded me about your performances which were usually as striking."

She let Rosie go from her hug and pointed at the African-American guy who was also behind the cafeteria counter, serving some people. "We have a summer job here with Tommy," the girl continued. "Say Hi to him."

Rosie obediently waved to the young fellow and shouted, "Hi, Tommy. Congrats for your win!" Though, the expression on her face was blank, like she followed the request automatically, not knowing in reality what she was talking about.

"Thank you, Rosalyn," the guy shouted back. "Sorry, I am too busy here right now and can't talk to you." It was true - the line of customers was never ending.

"By the way, you look great, Rosalyn," the girl continued to jabber away. "I remember this dress from your *Ancient Greek Hymn of Love.* You looked like an Aphrodite in this Greek style. However, the long hair with that golden ribbon on your forehead was much more Greek. But don't regret that. This haircut looks good on you, too. I remember, when I saw it at first, I was shocked as you threw away your wig in the *Farewell Anastasia,* while walking down the stairs."

Ashot attentively observed Rosie's face, not saying a word. It was a trying moment when the name Anastasia was pronounced aloud, but to his deep relief, she didn't react to it at all.

"This dress is new. We just bought it a couple of days ago," Rosie objected instead. "I am wearing it for the first time. Nobody saw it yet."

"Oh, maybe I am mistaken," the girl laughed and then turned to Aaron, "Hi, Dr. Dispenmore."

"Should I know you?" Aaron asked, surprised.

"Of course not. But I know you. I am Jessa Green. I am studying Comparative Literature in the English Department at the university. Our main auditorium is on the same floor right across the hallway from your research labs. I saw you many times there, but you, of course, don't remember me because of the hundreds of the students around. I am also Rosalyn's best friend from the Poetry Club, right, girl?" she winked at Rosie. "We are the besties. Would you come next Tuesday, Rosalyn? I will perform a new poem about a butterfly. I'm sure you will like it."

Rosie still looked at her confused. "I am pregnant," she whispered suddenly.

"Wow! Congrats!" Jessa exclaimed and clapped her hands. "We all actually expected it would happen after your last two concerts."

"We're getting married," Rosie uttered softly, leaning closer to Aaron, like seeking protection from him and he tenderly put his arm on her shoulders.

"Oh, yeah! That too. Everybody was sure about that after this proposal on stage. Congrats, Rosalyn. And you too, Dr. Dispenmore. Please, phone me, Rosalyn, or text me. We probably can go to the beach one day. Some girls told me that they saw you on the beach with your dad."

"Yes, I am the dad," Liam interrupted suddenly. "Sorry, Miss, we should go. Our time in line is approaching."

"Jessa, come back, please," Tommy shouted from behind the counter as the line of customers was growing. "I need you here."

"Sorry, sorry, I am coming," she yelled, turning to him. "Phone me, Rosalyn, and come to the concert. Everyone would be so happy to see you." She quickly hugged Rosie once more and ran to her work.

"That was unexpected," Ashot said, gesturing to them all to go toward the registration office.

"Who is this girl?" Rosie asked. "I see her for the first time. And why does she call me Rosalyn? Maybe she is mistaking me for someone else? I absolutely didn't get what she was talking about. Poems... Poetry Club... the stage... concert... Do you know, Aaron, what is it all about?"

"Okay," Ashot announced solemnly, taking away from Aaron any chance to answer. "We are going to do what we decided to do now. Then, kiddo, after you get married, we will go home and discuss that, okay? Let's not mess things up and do everything step-by-step. For now, to get a marriage certificate is the goal why we all came here. Let's follow this direction. Then, later, we will celebrate your commitment with a beautiful dinner. Where do you want to go, kiddo?"

"*Old Spaghetti Factory,*" Rosie announced happily.

"Did you seriously fall in love with that place?" Liam teased her, supporting Ashot.

"Yes!" she exclaimed. "It was the first restaurant in my life, as I told Aaron, when I was with him there as Rubi. Right, Aaron?"

"Yeah!" Aaron seconded their attempts to take Rosie's attention from an unforeseen bumping into that girl, Jessa, from the Poetry Club.

They approached the office right in time. A secretary came out and called, "Mr. Aaron Dispenmore and Miss Rosa Garcia." Holding hands Aaron and Rosie entered the wedding hall with their witnesses in tow, in happy anticipation that they will come out some time later as a husband and wife.

CHAPTER 48

When the newlyweds, accompanied by Ashot and Liam, arrived back at their building, Liam stopped the car in front of the main door on Aaron's request and waited as the young couple got out. Then the older men drove to the underground garage to park Liam's Chrysler. Aaron took Rosie in his arms and carried her through the main door, lobby, and elevator to their condo on the 3d floor.

He remembered how he was carrying her through the same route the first time, about a month ago - unconscious, almost dead and bloody. She was dressed in a similar white Greek tunic then, just torn into pieces and soaked in blood.

He recollected seeing himself in the mirror on the elevator wall - he was then disheveled, pale, with matted hair, shaking from shock. His face, left arm, both hands holding Rosie were all smeared with blood - the blood of both of them; their blood combined together in horror and tragedy.

And now Aaron walked through the lobby, holding his beautiful, happy and shiny young wife in his arms. She was smiling, laughing and hugging his neck affectionately and kissing his face while he carried her. She was blossoming in delight and she had their combined blood inside her – their baby.

In the elevator mirror he saw now how strikingly beautiful and spectacularly happy they were together and his heart filled with the endless gratitude toward Ashot – their real Guardian Angel, as Rosie once called him. What a transformation this old man did for them during a short period of time! He helped them to create their new beautiful life together! Without him it would never have happened!

Even at the halfway point of Rosie's cure everything dramatically changed for the better. Just a few weeks left to finish the last two sessions, then let Clay Mask dry for sometime, and then Rosie will break it and get completely healthy.

There will still be a lot of work with her official evaluation at the General Psychiatric Hospital, preparation of all the materials for the conference in New York, then Rosie's introduction to Aaron's mother and Laurie when they return home from Florida, then their huge wedding with all of Aaron's family in attendance... It was a lot to do, but it was a giant shiny light at the end of the tunnel of hard work, which never was possible before and never would have happened without Ashot.

When Aaron brought Rosie to their suite, Ashot opened the door for him, the same as he did before on that most tragic day. Aaron let his young wife stand on the floor and they both hugged the old man.

"Uncle, thank you for everything!" Rosie exclaimed cheerfully, kissing Ashot's wrinkled cheeks. "I owe you my life! I owe you my happiness! I am in debt to you forever! We love you, uncle!"

"Thank you a million times, Ashot," Aaron said, patting the old man's back. "I can't even imagine how I could thank you enough for saving my beautiful wife for me, for giving this happiness to both of us."

"Okay, okay, kids," Ashot laughed, freeing himself from their hugs. "You don't need to thank me a lot. I am doing this for you, kiddo, because I love you as a daughter and I know that you love me back as your uncle. As for you, Aaron, you confessed many times that you are hating me. It's okay. I accept that. You can keep hating me, just work with me on the project. It would be your very best Thank you. I don't need and don't expect anything else. We both want Rosie healthy, but I also want hundreds of other sufferers healthy too. We are working for this beautiful girl, but we are working for all of human society as I said already many times. And I really appreciate your help, Aaron."

"I don't hate you," Aaron answered feeling really confused and ashamed of himself. "I just sometimes misunderstood you, but now I realize clearly what you did for us. You gave us life, you gave us everything and for that I love you as my uncle with my wife together."

"Well," Ashot chuckled, "if we all agree finally that everybody here loves everybody, we should continue our work. Let's all settle comfortably around the table on the patio and start the next important faze of our project. Babe, please, bring all the stuff to the table," he nodded at Liam, "including your films. We need to talk seriously here, guys."

Liam brought from somewhere Rosie's book, a few folders, her old computer, her cell phone, the new computer which was still in a package and also his big camera. He organized all the items on the table. Aaron knew already what was coming and sat beside Rosie, hugging her tight, just in case. She looked at the preparations with interest, like she was seeing all of these things for the first time.

"This is a new computer which we are giving you as a wedding gift," Liam said, moving the package aside. "We will organize and set it up with you together later, kiddo."

"Thank you, guys," Rosie answered, smiling. "It's always great to have a new computer. I actually don't remember, if I ever had one? Obviously, I should. No one lives today without their computer or phone, right?"

"Yes, kiddo," Liam nodded and then suggested to Ashot, "You take it from here, babe."

"Okay," the old man took a deep breath and asked, "Do you remember, kiddo, that you had many personalities before?"

She nodded, silently.

"Do you remember how many?"

"Not exactly... mmm... no, I can't say, uncle. I know that there are two left now."

KATE VALERY

"In reality, there are three left. Two that we need to remove, Rubi and Tobi, and one more which is the real you, Rosie, and she must stay. You have to be Rosie always because this is who you are. The other personalities were interfering into your being and disturbing you. That's why we removed them and said goodbye to them.

"So, back to the personalities that are gone now. Two of them, Nora and Vally, were sad but the two others, Kiki and Anastasia, were nice and fun. But still, they had to go because they were part of the illness. We don't want illness to stay in you. We want you to be healthy, right?"

She nodded again and took Aaron's hand, visibly needing support and reassurance from him. He tenderly caressed her fingers.

"I wanted to postpone this conversation until all sessions of the cure were accomplished, but because we accidentally met that girl, Jessa, today at City Hall, you had questions about her, kiddo. So, we need to answer them now. Before we do that, I just want to remind you of one thing – the story of Liam here."

"Yeah, I know," Rosie chuckled. "I heard that many times how he lost his talent as a pianist, but got one as a super cameraman now."

"Not exactly 'super'," Liam giggled, "but... decent enough to have a job."

"So... did I lose something as well? Some talent?" Rosie asked, looking at each of them in turns. "I guess this is where you all are going with that, right, guys?"

"Yes," Ashot confirmed.

"Then say that straight," she laughed. "Why are you talking in circles, like preparing me for something drastic? I am not a fragile baby. I am a serious adult married woman, for God sake, you guys!"

"We are happy to hear that," Ashot smiled, obviously liking this attitude. It sounded like the confidence of a healthy person. "Then take this book, kiddo, and turn it to read the back cover."

Rosie took her book and glanced at her photo on the back cover.

"Wow!" she exclaimed. "It's me! Am I an author?" Then she read the text and shook her head thoughtfully. "Oh, now I am getting this, why the girl at City Hall said about poetry and concerts, and club, and that the boy, Tommy, won the prize... all of these. So, I probably knew her while I was there. She said we were 'besties'. It must be offensive to her that I didn't recognize her."

"I don't think she noticed that, my love," Aaron said. "You didn't tell her much and you shouted 'Congrats' to the boy, Tommy, as she suggested. You still could be friends. You could call her and go to the beach together. You could have your phone back now, I guess," he added, glancing at Ashot for confirmation and the old man gestured to slide Rosie's phone toward her. "I saw that many guys at that club loved you a lot. They would be glad to continue a friendship with you, I am sure," Aaron went on. "You can call them and renew your connections. And we could attend the concerts all together in the future, right, guys?"

Ashot and Liam nodded.

"How do you know that they love me, Aaron?" Rosie inquired.

"I went to the concerts three times. I saw your success with my own eyes. I saw how all your friends greeted you, hugged you, cheered you and recorded your appearances on the stage. I was really involved in that with you, my love."

"We will show you the videos of your performances and Aaron's involvements a bit later," Ashot stepped in. "Now tell me, kiddo, how do you feel about that?"

Rosie shrugged. "I don't know. Interesting. Curious. I don't remember any of that. So, why do you think that I lost this talent? Maybe I can still create poems?"

"Could be," Ashot agreed. "You can try later. But I assume that it wouldn't be possible because your personality, Anastasia, who revealed poems to you while flying in the universe, is gone. It was a beautiful, great talent, but it was also not normal, kiddo. Normally, healthy people don't hear voices, reading poems to them. And our task was to make you healthy. Also this Poetry Club is for teenagers and you have outgrown it and would be excluded from their performances anyway soon. So, it is time for you to move ahead with your life.

"However, if you are still be interested, there is some work to do with these poetry materials," Ashot moved two folders closer to Rosie. "Here are your poems which were not included in your book by date. You combined them into two manuscripts – from your age eleven to fourteen, the beginner ones; and from age eighteen to twenty, the last ones. You could work on publishing these two books, and you could visit the concerts, and you could meet your friends from this club, even simply for socializing and hanging out together. So, not much lost - your creative life could continue."

"And I probably could work on translating my poems to some other languages," Rosie suggested tentatively, looking at all of them in turns. "Right, guys?"

They all nodded, silently, while exchanging mutually understanding glances when it came to the topic of the foreign languages.

"And I could publish my two new books here, and then all three books in other countries!" she continued excitedly, laughed and clapped her hands. "Wow! Even, if I don't write any new poems, it will still be fun! Great! Thank you, guys. I love you all." She kissed Aaron on his cheek, then jumped up, ran around the table and kissed Ashot and Liam on their cheeks as well.

All three men were unexpectedly surprised by the happy turn of this event which they worried so much about. They guessed that she would cry, or scream, or get angry about her loss, but it wasn't happening because the base of her main personality, Rosie, was getting healthy enough to have a normal reaction to unforeseen news. Now the men all realized that they were overprotective because they didn't expect that the cure would work as good and as fast as it did in reality.

Then they all settled comfortably in the living room and watched Rosie's performances on YouTube, Facebook and on Liam's films. It included her kiss with Aaron on stage, Aaron's proposal on stage and the film of the **Farewell Anastasia** party of the poetry club in the *SkyCity* Restaurant at the Space Needle, which looked almost like a wedding party.

Rosie watched her own performances bewildered. "I actually did pretty good on stage," she noted. "I am not scared or confused to appear in public. Though, I don't think I could be an actress. I am not interested in immersing myself in a character of someone who is not me. I prefer to always be myself. But I have a gut feeling that I will find some kind of other job that will be in the public eye as well, and it will be fun. Seeing these films I am feeling braver and more confident, guys. Thank you all so much. Love you!"

Later, when it was time to leave home for dinner at the *Old Spaghetti Factory,* Rosie went to her bedroom and changed into the white elastic dress with one sleeve that she wore during her date with Aaron at this restaurant. She put on a bunch of black necklaces of different sizes and shapes, as she did last time, but she couldn't do that pony tale with a sparkling clip because of a very short haircut that she had now. She put black shiny earrings on her ears instead and put the same white purse on the long strap to hang on her naked shoulder. On her feet she wore the same black Greek sandals laced to her knees. Also, she applied lots of makeup and looked like a model, as Aaron determined then. With this short hair she had even more stylishly striking visage now.

"Wow!" exclaimed the men who were waiting for her in the living room as she appeared from her bedroom. "You look stunning, Rosie," Liam commented.

"Hello, guys," she said, smiling happily. "I know that it is easy for you to mess up. We are twins. Rosie is gone. I am Rubi and I am ready to go to celebrate my marriage with Aaron."

"Damn it!" Aaron whispered to himself barely audible but Ashot heard him and murmured back, "I told you, son, it's too early to relax yet."

CHAPTER 49

During their dinner at the *Old Spaghetti Factory* Rubi was the dominant person at the table. She was smart, intelligent, witty, teased everybody, laughed and shone. Her company was in truth pleasurable and they all enjoyed the evening especially Aaron who couldn't tear his eyes from her.

Once, Rubi winked at him and then said turning to Ashot, "Uncle, I have one request for you. We got our marriage license from City Hall, but I kind of feel that it is not enough. I want much more for us. I would like to have a wedding at a church."

"We will have it, my love," Aaron answered instead of Ashot. "We talked about that already. When your cure will be finished and my mother and Laurie come back home, we will do that."

"I know," the girl nodded, "it will be our big wedding then, but I want a small wedding now. Look, uncle, at what I am suggesting. Would you mind, please, calling the minister of your church and ask him to marry us this Sunday? After your morning service ends, we could come in and he could wed us. You could walk me down the aisle as my father. Wouldn't it be cool?"

"I don't know, kiddo, if it would be possible on such short notice," Ashot doubted. "They had a schedule there for weddings and other special events. It should be booked."

"Then call right now and book it," Rubi insisted. "We don't need to complicate things. It's all very simple. Look... imagine this picture. Service ends and the minister announces, 'Please, don't go home for a while, stay for another fifteen minutes for a wedding'. Then Aaron comes out and stands beside him with a couple of best men. Then you are walking me down the aisle with a couple of bridesmaids in tow and Liam is filming all of these. The whole congregation will be our guests. You bring me to the minister, give me to Aaron and the minister weds us – we give our vows and kiss. Then everybody goes to lunch at the church basement as you all usually do. That's it - fast and simple, and comfortable for everybody."

"At first, it sounds crazy, but there is a reasonable seed in it," Liam chuckled. "I am okay with that. What do you think, babe?" Ashot shook his head and didn't say anything.

"Don't you want a wedding dress and veil?" Aaron asked, surprised.

"Sunday morning, while uncle and Liam will be at the church service, you and I will go to the store and buy these things and then come straight to the church from there."

"It is possible if you are not picky," Aaron giggled, remembering how Ally dealt with her dress. "Some brides are choosing and adjusting their wedding dresses for months. But I know that you are special, Rubi – for you the point itself is more important than the frills and I absolutely agree with that. Nothing else counts except for our love. I am just wondering where you'll find these best men and bridesmaids so soon?"

"I'll call my 'besty', Jessa, because you guys suggested to renew our friendship, and ask her to organize boys and girls from this Poetry Club. If they all love me, as you, Aaron said, they could come for the service as our guests and some of them could be our best men and bridesmaids during the wedding. They don't need special dresses and suits, just something nice and respectable. I am sure your minister would be happy if about twenty new youngsters appeared in his church for morning service. Churches always like to attract new people, especially young ones."

"Jeez, Rubi," Aaron shook his head in disbelief, "you could work as a wedding planner or a manager of a big business. You are so resourceful and so inventive! You are shocking me, though in a good way."

"Why shocking? It's something wrong? You, my love, don't need a special groom's suit as well. Just a regular decent suit of a dark color will be okay. This simplicity with the outfits will make things much easier for everybody. This all sounds like a perfectly organized event as I planned it. Right, uncle?"

Ashot shrugged. "I don't know, kiddo. However, I think that this probably would be good for our cure project. Let me think about it for a while, and then I'll call our minister tonight. I promise."

When they returned home and were ready to retire for the night, Ashot pulled Aaron aside and said very quietly, making sure that the girl couldn't hear him, "Be vigilant, son. While she is in shower, check everything in the room for knives or any other dangerous things. I will lock your room, so she can't reach the kitchen knives while you are sleeping."

"Do you think Tobi could come?" Aaron asked, getting a bit tense right away.

Ashot shrugged. "It is always a possibility, especially if not so many other choices are left. Rubi is very sexy and you know what could happen because of that."

"Would you really make this call to your minister?" Aaron wanted to know.

"It sounds crazy, but I will. I think this sort of a small wedding will give her a sense of security, calm her down and soothe her. It will be very good for the cure. I am sure that subconsciously she is a bit scared because of this pregnancy. You are not the only one who wants to secure her to yourself stronger. She struggles with this insecurity too."

When Aaron entered the bedroom, Rubi was sitting on her bed, talking on her phone and laughing. He didn't ask anything, just sat in the armchair and waited. He realized that she was talking to Jessa, discussing the details of the small wedding on Sunday.

Together they were making a plan on how to organize it better with other boys and girls from the Poetry Club.

The mood and attitude of his beloved new wife made Aaron excited. It was unbelievably interesting and beautiful to see how fast, almost momentarily, she adjusted to the fact of her lost poetry talent without any regrets and how she instantly accepted his idea to keep her friendship with her fellow club members – young poets and poetesses.

That girl was extremely easygoing, a quick learner, fast, bright, eager to live, to move ahead, to discover, to find, to learn, to know. She lost her poetry talent and obviously other special brain abilities but it was replaced by the great healthy talent of living life in full.

As she finished her conversation on the phone, Aaron suggested for her to take a shower, saying that he will join her soon. While she was in the shower, he attentively checked everything and everywhere in the room for knives, scissors, tools, even pens and pencils. None of these were there, so it looked like a safe place for him to make love for the first time to his wife as her husband, although he married Rosie and didn't really want her to be Rubi at this moment.

When Aaron joined her in the shower, hugged her and kissed her, she answered very passionately and moaned between kisses, "It would be fun. I am having sex with my best friend's husband! You just married Rosie and you are already cheating on her! Jeez, who could expect that! It's okay. We're twins. We can sleep with the same man."

This sounded so unexpected, stupid and disgusting to him that he froze momentarily, took her strongly by the shoulders and looking straight in her eyes said strictly, "Stop it, please, and never say that again, girl. I am married to Rosie and I love her and never want to cheat on her. If you don't feel like Rosie now, then we will wait until you do. That's it."

With that Aaron turned the water off, took a towel, wrapped her in it, then lifted her in his arms, stood her on the floor and continued, "Put a bathrobe on and go to bed. I'll finish washing up and come to you. Then we will talk about that."

"You don't want me?" she whispered in shock, looking at him with huge eyes.

"Go to bed," he repeated rigorously, closed the curtain and turned the water on again.

When he came to the bedroom in about ten minutes, his wife - he didn't know, Rosie or Rubi - was lying in a fetal position, wrapped in her bathrobe and a blanket and she was crying soundlessly. Aaron laid beside her, hugged her and uttered apologetically, kissing the back of her head, "I am sorry, my love. Maybe I was too harsh. I guess you were only joking and I didn't get it properly. I don't know. I just love Rosie so much that for me this kind of joke sounded offensive. Our relationship with Rosie is so pure, so holy, so sacred that even a tiny hint of indecency really hurts. Let's wait for a while, until Rosie comes back, then I will love you madly, with all my heart, soul, and body, and … everything. Okay, my love? Please…"

Gradually, the girl's crying calmed down but she didn't answer anything and didn't turn to him. Aaron continued kissing the back of her head and petting her shoulders, until finally felt that she was sleeping. Then he sighed with relief and fell asleep as well.

He was woken up in the middle of the night by a wild scream. Rubi or Tobi, he had no time to realize who exactly - was beating him on his chest and on his head, yelling, "I hate you. You don't want me. I won't live like that. I won't be with you. I'll kill myself. You don't want Rubi, that's okay. I love her. I will go with her. I will leave you for her. I hate you!"

She jumped out of bed and ran to the door, trying to open it, but it was locked. Aaron stood up as well and wanted to approach her to restrict her somehow, maybe to hug her. She pushed him away and banged on the door for a while, screaming. Then, realizing that the door was locked, she ran to the window, opened it wide and jumped up on the window sill. It would be just seconds until she'd jump down outside, but Aaron was fast enough to grab her from behind and pull her back into the room.

They were on the third floor with huge blooming rhododendron bushes down below in the garden, so a jump from the window probably wouldn't be fatal, but dangerous enough to cause serious injury. However, about thirty feet away from the building was an edge of the hill and a steep rocky slope down to the ocean, and to end up there could be lethal.

"Calm down, Rubi," Aaron begged her, squeezing her tight while she fought and kicked him trying to free herself. "Do you want to talk to your uncle? He will help you to quiet down."

"Go to hell!" she yelled. "Why do I need uncle? I need to have sex with Aaron. I want Aaron. I love Aaron. Let me go!"

Maybe she was Tobi already, he couldn't comprehend. It was obviously a complete mess in her head. But, luckily for Aaron, he heard that the door unlocked and Ashot rushed in with a syringe in his hand. He inserted the shot into the girl's arm, while Liam ran in behind him heading straight to the window and closed it immediately.

Aaron felt his wife weaken in his arms and got soft and helpless like a doll. He lifted her, placed her in bed and sat on the edge beside her holding his temples with his hands.

"I can't anymore," he moaned in despair. "I can't, I can't. I don't know what to do!"

"Jeez, I hope the neighbors didn't hear and didn't call the police," Liam said, still breathing heavily from the unexpected wake up and run. "Luckily our building is air-conditioned and all windows are closed, otherwise we're in trouble."

"What happened?" Ashot asked Aaron. "Too much sex again?"

"No, quite the opposite. I refused because she said some stupid things, like she is Rubi and I am cheating on Rosie with her," Aaron explained, shaking his head in disbelief of himself. "I didn't want to hear that. It was so stupid and made me angry."

"Son," Ashot said, sitting down beside him on the edge of the bed. "You're the doctor. You should know better than confronting your patient. Just nod in agreement to what your patient is saying to you, even if it sounds like delirium."

"I know that," Aaron uttered sadly, "but I still have difficulty considering her as my patient. She is a woman to me, my love, my wife. Subconsciously I am perceiving her as a normal person. And when we are making love, to me it is not only my body involved in the process but my heart and soul as well. We are making LOVE! I am not just screwing a prostitute... like a drunk sailor in a cheap brothel in Hong Kong," he added, remembering Helen's witty comparison and emitting a short chuckle.

"It's too early to consider her a normal person, son, until she breaks the Clay Mask," Ashot noted, smiling at Aaron's last words. "We are not finished with the cure yet. So, I hope she will be sleeping quietly until the morning and then at ten a.m. we will start the work on Rubi's elimination. We're heading there. Give the process a couple of more weeks and kiddo will be completely okay. Please, be patient for a while more.

"And, by the way, I did call my minister. We had a long conversation. He knows that I am doing the cure for Rosie. I told him the story before. He will find some time on Sunday for your small wedding. They already have someones' wedding booked at three p.m., so right after the morning service ends, at noon, it will be okay to do it before the other people come to decorate the church for their big wedding. The minister could dedicate a half an hour to us. Do you still want it, Aaron?"

"Yes," Aaron nodded with a deep breath. "You know, I am kind of doomed. I can hardly find the power to bear her attacks and mood changes. It drives me crazy. I am really on edge to break down. But you are my last hope. I really trust you, Ashot, that she will get completely healthy pretty soon. That's why I am still here, hoping and trusting your judgment."

"Thank you for your trust, son," Ashot noted calmly. "I appreciate this. I just will pray a lot so her pregnancy doesn't destroy the cure. And I hope that God will answer."

CHAPTER 50

Aaron barely could sleep from the stress of the last attack. One bruise on his chest was hurting. One more was on his head, under his hair, so it wasn't visible, but it was painful as well and gave him a headache. He could tolerate physical pain, but it was even more hurtful and humiliating because it was his newlywed beloved wife who caused it.

He had never been beaten by anybody before. Even being a boy, he never fought at school, never was bullied or abused by anyone. He was used to a happy life where everybody loved him and was friendly to him, and he was always friendly back. The only arguments in his life before were the ones he had with Helen but those were just verbal, not physical fights. Even when she snatched his phone from his hand, he had no injury from it, only a wound in his soul.

Here his pain was doubled – it was physical and emotional as well. Aaron tried to reason himself that Rosie would never do that to him. It was her illness that did it. And the illness would finish soon - it will end. It would be cured and everything would be okay after that – 'happily ever after'... But still, subconsciously, he was offended and furious.

At six a.m. he went to the sports club downstairs to exercise and to let out the steam of his frustration. He worked out fiercely for the whole hour, then swam in the pool for some time and then called Beth and Laurie on Skype, sitting in his car at the underground parking. They chatted for a while, nicely, happily, lovingly as usual and, finally, this conversation really soothed him.

Then Aaron came to their condo where Rosie was already at the breakfast table with Ashot and Liam. As he entered the suite, she ran to him and hugged him.

"Good morning, my love," she exclaimed excitedly and kissed him on the cheek. He took her face in his palms and looked attentively in her eyes.

"Good morning, Rosie," he said. "Are you really Rosie now?"

"Yes, I am," she giggled, "of course. Who else could I be? I am Rosie, I am your wife and I love you. Right?"

"Okay, then," he uttered, kissing her on her cheek as well. "In this case we have some unfinished business from yesterday night. I guess you already ate your breakfast. Let's go and have some dessert."

Aaron lifted her in his arms and carried her to the bedroom as Liam glanced at Ashot questioningly.

"It's okay," the old man nodded. "It would be best for both of them. Especially for Aaron. I am worrying about him more than about kiddo this time because the session today would be extremely difficult for him. He needs to be really relaxed to survive it."

At exactly ten a.m. everybody was settled at their spots beside the Clay Mask for the next session of the cure. Ashot made his usual starting presentation and lifted the cover box from the Mask to make it ready for the continuation of his work on it. The big part of the sculpture was already done. He should keep working on its eyes now.

"We will eliminate today the personality named Rubi with the help of this Clay Mask," he said, watering the clay head to refresh it a bit. "Please, Rosie, tell us who Rubi is and how she appeared in your life and why she impersonated herself in you?"

Rosie took a deep breath, put her elbows on the table in front of her and squeezed her palms together, intertwining her fingers. "Well," she started her narrative looking straight at the Clay Mask,

"I guess I told you already, Madam Mask, that Rubi appeared while I was in the *Youth Shelter* for four years. My English teacher and friend, Mary, taught me to be a brave, confident, and an active girl with a high level of self-esteem. It's exactly who Rubi was.

"Being in the shelter, I was connected a lot with Anastasia. She dictated to me the poems from her 'castle in the universe'. But I felt that I am kind of nothing, nobody, who didn't deserve Anastasia's attention and friendship. Then unexpectedly came Rubi and convinced me otherwise. She told me that I am the recipient and I am getting those poems and making them alive. Without me Anastasia wouldn't be known to anyone and wouldn't be successful. So, I am the most important person. I am the boss. I am a creator of my own life and fate, and I believed her. I loved Rubi and I confided in her about everything that I was feeling, thinking, creating... everything. She was my very closest friend."

"Did Rubi stay with you, when you left the shelter and moved to your mother's place?" Ashot asked.

"Not a lot. There were mostly Vally – for crying at home, Anastasia - for travel with the concerts, Kiki – for playing with my little brothers and Rosie - for doing household duties. Even Nora and Tobi appeared once during my flight on the airplane that made me attack a stranger passenger. I am very sorry about that, by the way. But Rubi was there very seldom, mostly with Anastasia when I was preparing for the concerts. She encouraged me and supported us both – me and Anastasia – during the performances."

"Did Rubi become a dominant person in you ever?" followed the next question while Ashot intensively worked on forming the right eye and eyebrow on the Clay Mask.

"Yes, it happened when I moved in with Ben. In his home I was mostly Rubi, though sometimes Kiki because there were three very young children around me. Sometimes I also was Rosie as the atmosphere in the house was nice and loving. I was very thankful to this family that they allowed me to live with them rent free, so I tried to help their mother, Keysha, as much as I could with the household chores."

So far, through his goggles, Aaron saw that the stream of particles from Rosie's head toward the Clay Mask was smooth, level, multicolored and beautiful. Nothing bad happened yet and he really enjoyed observing and documenting this calm, nice procedure on his tablet. He didn't see any changes or problems created by her pregnancy. It looked like it would not affect the process of the cure at all, at least for now.

Ashot seemed calm and elated as well, as he asked his next question, "Where and how did you meet Ben?"

Rosie smiled. Aaron noticed that it was obviously a nice memory for her.

"We were classmates at school. When I was released from the shelter and moved in with mom, I started to attend a high school, grade eleven and twelve. I was a bit ahead of my class because the school at shelter was very good and I was studying fiercely to be the best student. So, when I got into the *Lord of Scotland* high school, my classmates were one year older than me.

"On my first school day, grade twelve, one boy approached me and suggested we go for a walk during the lunch break. His name was Alex. He was an African-American, and he had a twin brother in our class, Ben. I agreed gladly. First of all, he was unbelievably handsome. To my taste, he was as handsome as a movie star or a man-model and I looked at him with admiration. Second, I was very curious because I never had any prior contacts with black people in my life. When I lived with my grandparents as a child, everyone in their high-rise condo building where they worked as caretakers, was white. Then, in mom's place and neighborhood everybody was white as well. Even in the *Youth Shelter* for mentally ill dangerous teens, everybody was white. So, it was very interesting to see these people, new to me, to learn something about their culture, their traditions and their lifestyle. I actually craved to immerse myself into their life and I was very happy."

Aaron bit his lips. It was something unexpected for him. He knew that her boyfriend was Ben, but now something unforeseen began to open to him what he never expected. He wasn't jealous yet, just a bit tense, getting aware of what was coming. But according to the flow of the aura's particles everything still was okay and happy for Rosie. So, he kept working intensively, not looking at her, just immersing into his tablet screen.

"So, you started dating this boy?" Ashot asked.

"Yes," she nodded. "I was very happy and actually fell in love. Although, it was impossible to tell those twins apart. They were completely identical, they only wore t-shirts of different colors. Ben always had red ones, but Alex changed different colors, like yellow, gray, blue, black, white, except for red. This way they decided between themselves they would keep their appearance to be recognized separately. But I knew that they were sometimes cheating at school during exams. Ben was a much better student. He usually had very high marks and when there was a difficult test coming, he exchanged t-shirts with Alex and passed the exam for him as well."

"Was this first love of yours mutual?" Ashot inquired.

"Yes," Rosie smiled, "but it was kind of funny. They both fell in love with me very hard. They were really jealous of each other, but they never fought because they loved each other very much. One day we all went together for a walk in the park. We sat on a bench and they said 'Rosalyn, we need to talk. You should choose which of us will be your boyfriend.' I couldn't because they were both the same and I love them both equally."

Aaron realized suddenly that yesterday's outburst of Rubi, that twins could both sleep with the same person, really started making sense now. This was very unexpected for him - kind of shocking and hurtful. He even fidgeted on his chair, gritting his teeth, as Ashot whispered to him barely audible, "Buckle up, son. We need to clean this out." Then the old man addressed the girl, "So, how did you make your choice, Rosie?"

"Openly, I didn't," she laughed. "They threw a coin for heads or tails and Ben won. They were sure that fate made this choice for them, but it was me. I turned the coin with my thoughts this way and I was kind of glad about that. In spite of their physical similarity, they were very different personalities, as I already noticed. I was the only one who could clearly recognize them apart because of my special abilities to read thoughts. I knew Alex was stronger, faster, braver, but also more lazy with schooling and less intellectual. Ben was kind and very smart. He was actually the best student not only in our class, but at the whole school and everybody was saying that he will get a scholarship for college because of his success in physics and math. He helped me a lot with my schooling, though I was okay but he tried to make me as perfect as he was."

"Did Alex get angry or frustrated when he lost you?" was the next question.

"I don't know. At that time, as I read his thoughts, I was sure that he was devastated, maybe even ready to cry. But he sat on the bench, rested his forehead on his hands and sat silently for quite a long time. Then he said, 'Well, okay, I will go and sign up for the army and volunteer overseas. I don't want to be in your way, guys.' And he hugged both of us together. After that he never talked to me and never approached me at all. I was dating only Ben and I was very happy, in spite of my situation at mom's house that worsened every day."

"So, Ben became your first real boyfriend?" Ashot asked. "Did you have sex?"

Rosie blushed a bit, "Yes, actually we did."

"Was it later or before you moved into his house?"

"Of course, before. The first time it happened after we cleared our relationship with Alex and he kind of gave us his blessing. He was working at McDonald's after school. Their mom was at work too and the kids went to daycare. So, Ben and I were the only ones who came home and did our school work together. I was always brave and confident with him. I was always Rubi. He made me somehow feel this way. Probably, it was because of how he treated me – like a very independent girl with very high self-esteem - lovingly and respectfully. He was in truth an absolutely amazing guy. Then it happened, kind of accidentally. We began kissing at first. He asked, if I wanted to really love him and I said yes. It was truly how I felt. I loved him and I wanted him like crazy. I wanted to marry him, to have children and to be with him forever."

Aaron took a deep breath and lowered his head on his hands. *Hold yourself in check, idiot,* he thought. *Don't be stupid! You were with Ally for nine years and married for five of them. You had sex much more that she, thousands times more, actually. This poor guy is dead, the same as Ally. Don't create a problem for yourself out of nothing.*

This thought somehow sobered Aaron and removed any hint of jealousy. He continued his work, convincing himself that the past was water under the bridge and to be jealous of a dead person was both silly and disrespectful.

"How long did your relationship continue until you moved into his house?" Ashot inquired.

"Maybe about a couple of weeks. Then the scandal with my mom occurred and I packed my stuff and moved immediately. Ben drove his mom's car to pick me up from my place. He and Alex already had their driver's licenses but, of course, they couldn't afford more than one car for the household. Even their mom's car was pretty old and often broke down."

"When you moved in, did you sleep in the same room with Ben?" was the following question.

"Yes. It was a small three-bedroom bungalow. They had one room for the twins, but when I moved in, Alex went to sleep on the couch in the living room. In our bedroom were two single beds, but we moved them together so it was okay. The two little sisters had the second bedroom and their mom with the baby had the third one. It was crowded, but everybody was nice to each other and there was always a lot of laughter, jokes, games and fun."

"So, did Rubi blend into this setting well?" Ashot asked, smiling.

"Rubi was there almost all the time – blossomed with confidence, happiness and love. She liked to make little shows for the whole family sometimes – talking telepathically, moving objects with her thoughts, reading people's thoughts. Occasionally their neighbors gathered for these shows, even the whole street, sometimes. Alex, who organized that, charged people some coins for the entrance, and afterwards we went with the whole family to McDonald's for an ice cream. I loved their hot chocolate fudge! Those were really the happiest days of my life."

So far, Aaron didn't see any changes in the flow of the aura's particles from Rosie to the Clay Mask. *The last session of Kiki wasn't bad,* he thought. *This one looks even better now. God, I just hope that it is really the pregnancy that makes everything better.*

"You told us before that Rubi was a good investigator," the next question came from Ashot. "Were these, her detective skills, noticeable at that time when you lived with Ben?"

"Yes, she came at night to talk to me while Ben was sleeping. We talked a lot about my case of Nora's murder for which I spent four years at the shelter. I still didn't clearly understand what happened there with my grandparents, but Rubi analyzed every second of it and explained to me that it was not my fault. She helped me to feel better about myself and to be confident that I am innocent. I was..."

There Rosie stopped suddenly in the middle of a sentence and froze silent. Aaron saw that the colors of the particles became dimmer, almost turning gray.

"What's happening?" he whispered to Ashot.

"How do you feel, Rosie?" Ashot asked, getting visibly worried because her face was getting pale.

"I am tired. I would like to sleep for a while," she murmured and lowered her head on the table.

"Okay, then, have a rest," the old man agreed, gesturing to Aaron, "Pictures!"

Aaron grabbed the camera with shaking hands and began snapping the shots of the stream of the particles which was colorless now, but still pretty wide and strong. Rosie closed her eyes, took a deep breath of relaxation and then it became clear that she was sleeping.

"What the hell just happened?" Aaron exclaimed bewildered.

"I don't know," Ashot shrugged and lifted his hands in quandary. "Normally the patient sleeps at the end of the session. Now we are barely in the middle. It never happened before in my experience. I don't know... if the stream of particles will end, as it should at the end of the session, then our session will be broken in half. What does that mean? Will it be invalid? Should we repeat it again from the beginning? Need we continue as soon as she wakes up? Or the next day? Or ever?"

"So, what do I do now?" Aaron inquired desperately.

"Let's continue for a while and see," Ashot said, turning the Clay Mask a bit and moving his hands off it. "After a short break I'll keep working on the Mask. You, son, please, take about ten pictures, then just watch the flow and describe everything on the tablet. Then ten pictures again. And continue this way. I don't know how long this sleep of hers will last in this situation."

He wiped his hands from the clay, took his golden cross from his chest and kissed it. "Help us, God!" he whispered. "Help this poor child! Save her and her baby, please." Then he closed his eyes and began to pray.

CHAPTER 51

The tense waiting lasted for about fifteen minutes as none of the participants knew what to do and what could happen next. Then Aaron noticed suddenly that the colors began returning to the flow of the particles of Rosie's aura. She took a deep breath, blinked her eyes and opened them. Then she lifted her head from the table and looked around a bit surprised.

"Oh, you are here, guys," she mumbled. "Sorry. Did I sleep for a while? It was a very nice rest and now I feel comfortable. Were we talking about something with you, Madam Clay Mask?"

"Yes," Ashot answered, suppressing his happy smile of content, trying to be professional for filming. "We talked about Rubi - how she came to you at night to discuss the crime investigations."

"Oh, yeah," Rosie nodded. "She did that. It was important to me to realize that I am innocent and can move ahead with my life. We made plans with Ben. We decided that after our school graduation we will go to college together, then in a year, when I will be eighteen and he will be nineteen we will get married and have a child."

"Wouldn't marriage and parenthood interfere with your schooling?" Ashot asked curiously. "Who will watch the child while you are in class during the day and doing your homework at the evenings?"

"Don't think please, Madam Clay Mask, that we were careless teens," she giggled. "We thought out everything. We talked about that with Ben's mother. Her three kids were going to daycare a couple of days a week and she agreed to add our child to the group. Other days they were watched by a senior neighbor. Keysha didn't have money to pay for that, but she had a deal – she did laundry for that lady and cleaned her house once a week, and the boys, Ben and Alex, mowed her lawn. While living with them I participated in those activities as well, just for fun, because I had a great deal of experience in housekeeping from my life with mom's family."

"So, Ben's mother approved all your plans?"

"Not really. She warned us about the difficulties of an interracial marriage. She asked both of us to sit together and said,'You guys could expect problems with other people about your love. My boyfriend was white, but as soon as he found out that I am pregnant, especially with the twins, he said that his family won't accept that, and he just disappeared forever'.

"Ben and I, we both disagreed and said, 'Millions of men in the world do the same thing to women, even being the same color of skin with them. It's not a racial thing, it's a men's thing.' It looked like we convinced her about that part. Then Keysha asked if I expected that my family would accept Ben. 'No, they won't, I said, but they don't accept me in the first place, so I consider myself an orphan without any family whatsoever. I don't care what they think at all'.

"'Okay, Keysha said, then... are you sure, Rosalyn, that our community will accept you? You probably don't know that the racial thing goes both ways'. 'I guess that everybody here loves me, I said, because the whole street is coming to my performances and people look excited.' She shook her head sadly and noted, 'But then they came to me and said, 'why do you allow this white trash girl to seduce your nice boys? They are amazing boys and they easily could find a good girl in our community, without bringing to your home this stranger which doesn't belong here.'"

Rosie took a deep breath, and drank some water from her bottle. It was visible that the subject was painful for her and she needed a moment to collect herself.

"It was like a blow to my gut," she continued then. "I was shocked to hear that because I couldn't expect that in a million years and I started crying. Keysha hugged me and patted my head, trying to console me. I knew that she truly loved me. Ben got very angry. 'Tell me who said that, mom, he demanded, and I will deal with them. It's not their freaking business! It's our home! It's our family! And it's my life!'

"'We can't separate ourselves from our community', his mom objected. 'We are all connected here, we belong here. And, at this point, I see difficulty for you, kids. You should find some place to live with a highly developed diversity, where people of all different colors and nationalities will surround you, so you could blend in together. Of course, I will take care of your baby, because I am very proud that you both want to get an education. It will be your wild card for a good future, but just think about a place where you could move after college'. 'New York, I said confidently, the most diverse and democratic place on the Earth. I have a good friend there, my teacher, Mary. I will consult with her.'

"Rubi put on a brave face," Rosie continued with a deep breath, "however, in reality I was hurt a lot. I trusted those neighbors, I loved them, I was thankful to them for accepting me and loving me. But at that moment I realized that it was not a sincere love from their side. I was crying all night. It was not a cry of Vally – weak, helpless and scared. It was Rubi who was crying – angry, confident and determined to show those people that I will live here in spite of what they are thinking and saying. I wanted to show that I belong here and never will go away at any price."

Now Aaron could see that it was Rubi talking – she lifted her head and even her whole posture became straight and strong. The stream of particles got big, wide and piercingly bright. She was proud of herself and persistent in her attitude.

"Although Ben hugged me, consoled me," she went on, "and promised that he and Alex will deal together with that problem,

Rubi was very adamant to meet this situation head-on by herself. Next day, when nobody was at home, I went to McDonald's alone and decided to show myself off and buy an ice cream. The restaurant was located in the middle of an African-American community, and all the workers and patrons there were black. I was the only one white person in the room.

"The line was pretty big, about twenty people. I stood at the end of it and moved with the flow toward the counter. When my turn came, I ordered the ice cream, paid for it, was given a number and moved aside to wait. I stood there and waited for a very long time, but my ice cream wasn't coming. I noticed that all the people who were behind me in the line already got their orders and left. More people were coming, more numbers were announced, but not mine. I patiently waited for more than half an hour, then approached the counter and asked politely, 'Excuse me, where is my ice cream?' and showed my receipt and my number.

"The cashier looked at me in surprise like I was speaking not English but some other language, then said, 'Sorry, it will be here soon.' I stood there waiting, offended, shaking inside, but nothing changed, until one old man at the end of the line finally felt pity for me and shouted, 'Hey, you, what are you doing? She is Ben Brown's girlfriend for God sake. Give her that ice cream finally, you damn pranksters!' After that I got my ice cream right away. I went outside, sat on the cement steps in front of the building, put my ice cream on the ground and began to cry."

Rosie stopped for a while, sniffled a bit, barely holding her tears even now, about four years after the occasion. The flow of the particles got dim and misshapen again, as Aaron marked in his notes and then took a picture of it.

"Was it hurtful because they did not accept you in their community?" Ashot asked carefully.

"No. Not that at all," Rosie vigorously shook her head. "There were many different feelings at the moment. I experienced on my own skin for the first time in my life what 'racial discrimination' is. I was in their shoes. I got what they all feel on an everyday basis. I understood how hurtful it was for them to live in this condition all the time. So, I felt pity for them - no offense and anger at all - but pity, sympathy and compassion.

"And I could see the past, as you know. Then, I saw in my mind, what all their ancestors survived long ago during slavery. We learned that at school, so I knew the facts formally. But sitting there I physically felt how they were delivered from Africa in the 17th and 18th century in the holds of ships, with no food or water, in chains. When the ships arrived and holds were open - out of hundreds of people there only a few were still alive. Then I saw in my mind how they were sold – not like humans, but like things, like furniture or something... It was all printed in the particles of the holographic universe forever. It stayed there and will stay eternally. I could see that, I could read that. I felt inside my heart and my body as if it happened to me. It was so scary, so malicious and so horrible that I can't stop my tears of compassion. Together with these people I sensed their pain. At that moment my poem was born:

> I am a sponge absorbing other people's pain
> and then splash it out together with my own.
> Isn't it too much of a burden for my soul?
> Ain't I too young for that?"

Aaron clearly remembered how he read this poem in the Rubi chapter of her book and was wondering what she was talking about. Who were the people whose pain she felt?

"I realized that those guys in McDonald's taught me a history lesson and opened my eyes," Rosie continued. "They educated me, changed me. In one hour I grew many years older. I was not a teen girl anymore, but an adult, maybe even an old woman in my heart. I felt extremely guilty for my white ancestors, even though those who did this to Africans weren't really my ancestors – mine were Slavic in Europe and weren't related to American slavery history in any way, but still... My ice cream melted and I threw it into the waste, but I kept sitting there, on McDonald's porch, covering my face with my hands, thinking, shaking and crying..."

"So, it was a spiritual catharsis experience for you as a result, but not the establishment of your position in the area, as Rubi planned?" Ashot suggested.

"Yeah, it was a moment of my spiritual growth and improvement," she nodded slowly. "But then very 'not spiritual things' came. A group of black teens appeared from nowhere, surrounded me and began to scream profanity, all words in the book, and touch me and pull my hair. So, I jumped up and ran. They ran after me and I read their thoughts. I knew that it could be bad – if they catch me I would be raped by the gang for sure. So, I stopped for a moment and sent to them telepathically a feeling of a rope across the street. They all stumbled against it and fell down. Some of them hurt their feet or knees pretty badly. It gave me a chance to run away and escape into Ben's house.

"I told him and Alex what happened and they both went out and confronted those guys. There was a very big altercation, even a fight. Later that day, Ben gave me a penknife and said that I should not hesitate to use it, if some guy from that gang approaches me. 'Even if you kill someone, he said, the police will not do anything to you. This is a dangerous gang well known to them. It would be considered self-defense of a white girl against a black guy who wanted to sexually assault her. You should use your white privilege here.'

"Rubi was upset about this. 'I don't want any privilege, I said angrily. I love you, I live with you. I want everybody to be equal and live here peacefully and friendly'. 'You are a dreamer, Rosalyn, Ben answered. I love you too and I will be with you forever. So, I want you to be safe. Keep the knife and be brave to use it if needed'."

"Did you use it, really?" Ashot asked curiously.

"I did... later... but not against that gang. They were probably warned by Ben and Alex that I am armed now and they stayed away from me since. So, this way – with the knife - Rubi established her position in the area. It's the answer to what you asked before, Madam Clay Mask," Rosie finished this part of her story and looked at Ashot questioningly, wondering where he woulded turn the conversation next.

"As I see, Alex was very helpful and really cared for you and Ben," Ashot stated carefully. "Wasn't he jealous about your relationship?"

"I don't know. He didn't ever say anything. He was dating many girls, but short term, no more than a month. Then he dumped the girl and found another one. I asked him once, why he is doing that? 'Don't you love any of them?' I inquired. He made a wry face and laughed, 'I am practicing to gain experience in sex.' 'But how about love?' I insisted. He shrugged, 'My love is gone forever. Leave me alone, please, Rosalyn. It's not your business'."

"So, you practically didn't have any interactions with him during the time when you lived in their house?"

"I guess, I did once. A day before Alex left for the army he had to work his last shift at McDonald's. Ben wasn't home. I was alone, sitting and doing homework at the dining room table. Then he entered the room, wearing Ben's red t-shirt, but I felt right away that it was Alex. He walked in too swiftly for Ben, and then he grabbed me and started kissing me, again, not in Ben's style – too passionate, too mad. 'Are you Ben?' I asked. He laughed, 'Of course, I am Ben. Don't say stupid things' and then he pulled me to bedroom."

Aaron felt that something was coming that he didn't want to hear or to know.

"Did it end up with sex?" the old man asked, as Aaron growled to him in whisper, "Why are you doing that? We don't need that."

"We do," Ashot nodded as he whispered back. "Buckle up, son. It's extremely important."

"Yeah," Rosie smiled a bit bashfully. "Actually, when we started to have sex with Ben, at the beginning of our relationship, we both were virgins and we didn't have any experience at all. We practically didn't know what to do, especially me. I was only sixteen and my senses weren't much developed sexually. While I didn't really know what sex is, I wanted to do that to became a woman. I loved Ben, I liked to kiss, to hug, to cuddle, to walk holding hands. It was amazing, but when it came to intercourse itself, I was scared of it. I knew that I had to do that. It was a part of having a boyfriend, so it was kind of obligatory. At the beginning it was just painful, nothing else. Then, when I healed, I still tolerated it, no more than that. I never experienced any pleasure from that at all, it was just my duty..." she loudly changed her breath and took more gulps of water from her bottle.

"Maybe partially it was because Ben was very cautious and always used protection," Rosie went on then. "He didn't want me to get pregnant before we finished at least one year of college. But this time which I am talking about, I was Rubi and I wasn't sure if the boy was Ben or Alex. I knew that Alex should be at work at that time, but he behaved differently than Ben usually, so I had my suspicions. Also, my vision told me that this was Alex. But Rubi, always being brave and confident, decided, 'what the hell – if men can do that with many women, why can't I try it at least once with the other twin. They are practically the same person anyway'. And I kind of yielded because his kisses made me so damn hot, that I couldn't protest."

Aaron gritted his teeth and made a wry face barely holding himself in check.

"Pictures, son," Ashot gestured to him and turned the Clay Mask angle to work on its second eyebrow.

"This time everything was very different," Rosie continued her story while her voice was a bit shaky. "I felt something unbelievable, unusual. I felt like some higher power from the universe was involved and did this to me. I was jumping, wiggling, twisting, crying, moaning, screaming like I got insane, and, what was scary for me - I couldn't stop being like that. It was as though some devil's spirit was inserted into me. I was laughing and crying hysterically, like never before in my life. There was an exhausting pleasure which wasn't ending but went up and up, and up, until I couldn't tolerate it anymore. I screamed at the top of my lungs because I felt extremely hot inside, and I probably just lost consciousness, because I don't remember anything after that. When I came to, I was covered with a blanket and he was sitting on the edge of the bed, completely dressed, wearing Ben's red t-shirt and looking at me attentively. His dark eyes were like magnets that were sucking in my facial features, like he was absorbing me. As I opened my eyes, he tenderly kissed me on my forehead and said, 'Thank you, Rosalyn. I'll remember that forever.' And with that he left."

Aaron made a huge effort to hold the camera with his shaky hands and take pictures of the stream of particles that was beautiful, multicolored and moved like a big wave toward the Clay Mask. He realized that his wife was describing her first orgasm in her life which happened with another man and he could barely breathe because of his tense nerves. He knew that it was pretty much the same as she experienced with him and it felt as painful to him as if there was a knife in his heart.

"I kept lying in my bed for a while, as the whole my body rang like a string with the waves of pleasure gradually dying down. I felt so light like I lost 100 pounds and was ready to fly. Then Ben came into the room and asked, 'Are you already sleeping, Rosalyn? It's only nine o'clock.' 'Where were you?' I asked. 'I worked at McDonald's to cover Alex's shift. He ask me to do that because he needs to pack his stuff. He is leaving at five in the morning.' I realized with horror that Alex tricked him on purpose to say bye to me in this crazy way. It would be extremely offensive for Ben because they usually trusted each other and were very protective and helpful toward each other. They love each other a lot, but, probably only once in their whole life Alex tricked him to get me because it was very important for him to have me before he left. I guessed it meant a lot to him because he really loved me, but sacrificed his feelings for his brother whom he loved as well. As Rubi, I swear to myself that Ben will never find out about that. I didn't want him to be hurt."

Damn, does anybody care if I am hurt? Aaron thought angrily. *I don't even know now if she loves me or not!*

Then Rosie stopped and suddenly said, "I am sorry, I am tired again and want to sleep more. Is it okay with you, Madam Clay Mask?"

"Of course, Rosie, you can have your rest," Ashot answered. It seemed very interesting and unusual to him that she began addressing the Clay Mask but not him. Probably it happened because the Clay Mask was almost developed now and started looking like a woman's face.

Aaron noticed that too, but he didn't care. He was obsessed with jealousy at the moment and also displeased and upset with Ashot for forcing his wife to share such private things for public knowledge. This all had to be included in the materials for the New York Psychiatry Conference and he didn't feel comfortable with that.

Rosie put her head on the table, closed her eyes and in a minute she was sleeping calm and quiet, breathing evenly. The flow of the particles from her aura to the Clay Mask dimmed again, but this time it wasn't worrisome for them.

CHAPTER 52

"I need a break," Liam said, putting his big camera on his table and left the room.

Making sure that Rosie was sleeping, Aaron turned to Ashot.

"I promised that I won't hate you anymore, but how can I not?" he exclaimed with his voice almost shaking with emotion. "Why are you doing this to me? What the hell is useful in there for her treatment? Why do you force her to say such things that no one should know except me? Those are our private sacred moments. It's only between her and me, and no one else. I repeat – no one! - should put their nose into it. I don't want to know what she felt with other men and no one has to know that. Do you plan to leave it on the film? Do you want to show it at the conference to get your Nobel Prize? But at what price? For humiliating her and me, as her husband?" He squeezed his temples with his palms. "How? How can it help her? I don't understand you. I don't! I don't!"

Aaron held back angry tears, biting his lips and feasting his hands. Ashot sat silently until this outburst ended.

"Are you done yelling?" he asked quietly. "Thank you, then. Now listen to me, please, son. I know that it was hurtful for you to hear. You would probably be surprised but I did it not only for her, but mainly for you – for your safety, your well-being and your happiness. You know that after every session Rosie completely forgets what she was talking about. It is all gone now, straight to here," he carefully tapped on the forehead of the Clay Mask. "So, I want her to forget her first love, first experiences in sex, first feelings. It should be eliminated completely, if you want to have a good life with her, have a family and be happy. If you want to be the only man in her life. Do you get it?"

"Not entirely," Aaron shrugged. "I remember my first wife. I know that I loved her, but this doesn't prevent me from loving Rosie. I know that Ally doesn't exist. Just some memories left... So what? What's wrong if she will remember this dead guy - her first love? This memory won't bother anybody."

"Don't forget that the second guy, who woke her up sexually, is still alive. And she loved him too. He is somewhere on the other side of the globe now, but he could come back any day. You don't want to be married, have a wife, children, and then one day, someone knocks on your door and your wife gets excited. You don't want to be stabbed in the back, Aaron, do you?"

"Do you think it could happen?" Aaron knitted his eyebrows attentively looking at the old man.

"It could happen, if she remembers that. If we erase these memories from her brain completely, she will never react, even if someone 'knocked on your door'. She will say, sorry, wrong address. I love my husband, my kids, and I don't know who you are, sir, so bye-bye."

"You should know, son," Ashot continued, "that the most painful thing in the world is to be stabbed at your back by someone you love. I experienced that once. I know what it is. I did that to my wife when I confessed to her that I am gay. But it had to be done. We couldn't go on together with our life in lies. I needed to be honest with her, although it was painful for both of us. Then she shocked me when she reported me to the authorities to be arrested for my sexual orientation and to die in prison. I was forced to escape my country to survive. I know that I hurt her extremely and she paid me back the same way. It is a tragedy when things like that are happening in a family and I sincerely do not wish you nor Rosie endure something similar to that disaster."

"I didn't know your story," Aaron whispered, looking at the old man with big eyes. "You never told me. I am very sorry to hear that. And, thank you for your care for us. You see - it's nice when you explain things to me, so we don't have to fight."

Ashot smirked. "I still think that after we finish with Rosie's cure, I need to do a couple of the sessions with you, son. Your nerves aren't really firm. You were damaged badly by your wife's murder and didn't get any help or cure at the time. You just overcame it by yourself as best as you could. This needs to be addressed to make you more level headed, calm and stable."

"Okay, we will do that," Aaron agreed. "I hope it will help me to get emotionally stronger and hold myself in check better. I know that you're capable of helping. I trust you now, Ashot. But Rosie's past is too sensitive a subject anyway. How would you feel if Liam described to you all the details of his sex with another partner? Would you be calm and quiet listening to that?"

"Whoa, whoa, whoa!" Liam exclaimed upon hearing the last words when he returned to the room, "Please, don't involve me into your business, guys. I am just a cameraman here." He laughed.

"Yes, I would be calm and quiet," Ashot answered, ignoring Liam's comment, "if it was needed for his healing. I would do anything for him to be healthy, and I did in my time, believe me. We did eliminate all his past experiences during our sessions and he is healthy now. The same for you, son - you were very happy recently when you got married and you felt then like Rosie is completely healthy. Wasn't it an amazing feeling to realize that? But we're not entirely finished with her cure yet. However, believe me, if you tolerate a bit more, all will end soon and she will be alright and happy as a result."

At that moment Rosie lifted her head, looked at them, smiling and continued talking as if she never stopped and slept, "The whole night Ben and Alex were sitting on the porch outside and talking in a whisper," she uttered, and Ashot gestured to Aaron, 'Pictures!' grabbing some fresh wet clay from the pail and starting to work on the Clay Mask hair, putting some locks above its forehead.

Rosie caught them all off guard. They were too involved in their conversation and didn't notice when the flow of her aura's particles became multicolored and alive again which was a sign of her awakening.

"It was their farewell, as Alex was leaving to join the army in Afghanistan," she went on with the story. "Keysha and the kids were there as well, but later they went to sleep after hugging and kissing Alex many times. 'Do you want to say bye to Rosalyn?' Ben asked. 'No, I already did, Alex answered, don't bother, let her sleep.' They didn't know that I wasn't sleeping. I was listening, though I couldn't hear much but I read their thoughts. Alex tried convincing Ben to stop using condoms and to have a baby as soon as possible. It was another trick because he probably expected that I could get pregnant and didn't want Ben to suspect anything. 'We never know what could happen in life, he said. I may go straight to a possible death and I am okay with that. But here could also be car accidents, shooting on the streets, earthquakes... We should leave someone in this world before we die. Let's swear to each other that the one of us who survives will marry her.' Ben agreed and obviously followed Alex's advice. In two weeks my period didn't come as it should and a month later I knew for sure that I was pregnant."

"Was Ben happy about that?" Ashot asked.

"I wouldn't say extremely happy, but he accepted this and his mom did too. But I felt very happy. I forgot to tell you that during the ten months period of our relationship with Ben we usually did a lot of activities together, like skateboarding, roller skating, jogging in the park across from their house. He also always drove me to all my concerts in Greenwich Hall, and all my friends from the Poetry Club knew him, loved him, and some guys were friends with him even more than with me.

"One day we went jogging. We were running side by side, but then I suggested we play tag. I was Rubi on that day. I was brave and confident and ran ahead. Ben was supposed to catch me, but he stopped for a while to drink water from his bottle, so he was far behind me. I felt so happy that I lifted my arms up to the sky and screamed 'Aeeeh!' at the top of my lungs while running. I was thanking the sun and the sky for my happiness. Ben finally got to me, caught me and hugged me. And that was it..." Rosie stopped while choking on her words. Everyone waited already knowing what was coming.

"What happened there next can only be described as the worst case scenario – a police car was accidentally passing by," the girl continued with tears in her voice. "They saw me running and screaming and a black guy chasing after me and, then, grabbing me. They thought that I was screaming for help and he was assaulting me. They jumped out of the car and a police woman started shooting. Ben fell on the grass, his blood gushed on me. I froze in shock from unexpectedness, then I wailed like crazy, grabbed my knife from my pocket and jumped at the policewoman.

"She didn't expect that from a 'girl-victim' and I even knocked the gun out from her hand. I pushed her so hard that she fell on the ground, although she was much stronger than I and obviously well-trained. But I was already Tobi then, and the shock gave me unbelievable strength. I kept stabbing and stabbing her until her partner grabbed me from behind. That was what Ben called 'white privilege'. If I was black, the second policeman would have shot me dead as well, but for a 'white girl-victim' he couldn't do that.

"However, I was so strong from anger at the moment that I even pushed the other policeman away. Seeing that Ben is already dead, I didn't want to live without him. So, I thrust the knife into my stomach, twice, on both sides. The pain was so unbearable that I passed out right there and, probably, fell on the ground as well."

Everybody was silent, as Rosie covered her face with her hands and lowered her head on the table, crying weakly, softly, helplessly. The flow of the particles turned into a black tornado and twisted around the almost finished head of the Clay Mask. Aaron took pictures non-stop.

"What do you remember next?" Ashot inquired after giving her some time to collect herself.

"I came to at the hospital, after surgery. I knew what happened, I remembered everything clearly. After Nora's murder, I had some doubts about it being my fault. But this time I was 100 percent sure that everything happened because of me. I shouldn't have run ahead of Ben, I should have stayed with him while he was drinking. I shouldn't scream like crazy from happiness. I made a false impression to the police that he was chasing me and assaulting me. They just did their job to protect and save me. They were right. I was too careless and silly, behaving like that in the black district of the city. It was very stupid of me and it was my fault that Ben died - not theirs, just mine, only mine." She sniffled and shook her head. "I didn't want to live. I have no right to live, especially when doctors told me in hospital that our baby was gone, miscarried and dead. There my poem came to me **We Are Family.** We really were a family of the dead – Ben, baby and I. I should be with them – really, we were family. So, I swallowed the whole bottle of opiate pills to go with my family."

Aaron clearly remembered this poem and now fully understood, at least, what it was about and how it was created, although he guessed that before, after reading Dr. Hertz's file.

"In this hospital, they saved me again from an overdose on those pills. Luckily for me, the policewoman didn't die after my stabbing. Her wounds, surprisingly, were not life threatening and she healed pretty fast. In a month she was already back on duty. This saved me from 'prison for life'. My mental condition was known to the police and Dr. Hertz actually helped me a lot by insisting on placing me back into the *Youth Shelter* instead of a state prison - which would be required for an 'assault with a deadly weapon on the police officer on duty'.

"The policewoman even came to visit me once because she was in the same hospital as I. She apologized for her mistake and we even hugged and cried together. She was actually, maybe a few years only older than me and said that as a teen she was a victim of a sexual assault on a street and that forced her to became a police officer – the wish to protect other girls. We forgave each other and she refused to press charges on me. So, as the result, I spent just one year at the shelter. Rubi became a vivid crime investigator probably by this policewoman's influence. She was always brave before, but since Ben's murder Rubi became very scared of gunshots, really scared. She heard them often in her sleep and she was woken by them many times.

"So, I had difficulty sleeping. While being in the shelter I didn't sleep at all, until the psychiatric nurse, Mr. Thomas Spencer, started his work there and helped me to successfully overcome my insomnia. And I am very thankful to you for that, uncle. Love you," Rosie smiled, which was kind of unexpected at the end of such a troubling session.

The stream of the particles got calmer, straighter and more stable in the colors. Rosie took a couple of deep breaths, put her head on the table and fell asleep once more. This time it was the end of the session, as Ashot announced in a whisper after making a cross sign on himself and Rosie, and kissing his golden cross.

"I don't know what is causing these sleep breaks and calmness," he said, "but I guess that it could be the pregnancy. Baby got tired and wants to sleep and she follows that feeling. Let's wait until that stream ends. We are probably getting very lucky with this ending of the session, thank God."

This time the flow of particles was over in less than ten minutes. Probably, not that much damage and dirt was left in Rosie's aura after the month-long cure.

Later on, Aaron carried her to bed as usual and returned to the living room. "So, what about Tobi?" he asked Ashot. "Will we do a session on her?"

The old man shrugged. "Let's think about that on Monday," he suggested. "Tomorrow is your wedding at the church, Aaron. We should be ready to survive that, first. But, as you see, my work on the Clay Mask is practically completed. Just a little hair needs to be added to the back of its head, and then – to polish it all a bit... I guess that at the end of next week it will be dry enough for Rosie to break it. That should be it. Our girl should be absolutely, completely healthy."

CHAPTER 53

Next morning, when Aaron went to exercise at the fitness club downstairs, Rosie was at the breakfast table with Ashot and Liam, but mostly on the phone. Usually, it wasn't allowed by the house rules, but today an exception was made – she discussed with Jessa all the wedding preparations at their Anglican church.

Actually, everything was going successfully. Jessa excitedly told her that she and Rosie's other 'bestie', Layla, whom Rosie didn't remember as well, were ready to be bridesmaids and had already chosen from their closets similar looking light-blue dresses which could serve for that purpose. Also, Jessa's boyfriend, Tommy, whom Rosie saw at City Hall serving in the cafeteria, and another guy from the Poetry Club, Dustin, agreed to be the best men for Aaron. About twenty other teens from the Club will come to the church service as guests of the wedding. So, Jessa proved to be an excellent organizer and Rosie sincerely thanked her.

"It's okay," Jessa answered. "You don't need to thank me a lot because I am sure you would do the same for me, right, Rosalyn? I am already engaged to Tommy and next year we will get married, so you will be my maid of honor. And we, Tommy and I, will be the same beautiful mix-race couple as you were with Ben."

Rosie didn't say anything, except, "Thank you, Jessa. See you at the wedding." But as she hung up, she looked at Ashot, puzzled, and asked, "Uncle, who is Ben? She said we were a mix-race couple with him."

"He was one of the friends who died long ago," Ashot answered, being caught a bit off guard.

"From the same Poetry Club?"

"Yes."

"Why did he die?"

"I don't know for sure. Some kind of accident, I believe. You don't need to ask the guys from the Club about that. It was many years ago."

"But Jessa said I was a couple with him?"

"She is probably messed up with something. Don't worry about that, kiddo. It was before your second term in the shelter and before you and I met."

Rosie took a deep breath. "It is so difficult to live like that, uncle," she said. "I don't remember anything about my previous life and I feel like an idiot when people say something to me about that."

"Then you should probably establish the boundaries in your relationship with these girls and say to them that you are having a new life now and don't want to hear anything about the old one. If they want to keep friendship with you, they should accept that. If they won't accept that, you will just find new friends."

"Yeah," Rosie nodded. "I guess it would be the best. I am not actually interested in this poetry thing and this group of teens anymore. They were, maybe, my friends, but now... what do we have in common? Nothing. I think that after my wedding I will say goodbye to all of them."

"In your future life," Ashot continued convincingly, "you will get a new profession, to study or to work. You will meet people with interests close to yours, and they will be your new friends. Everything is ahead of you, and I am absolutely sure that you will be okay. Take me as an example – I left my whole life behind: my work, family, friends, home, country, language, and my hundreds of years old culture... everything. And look, now in my new country, I have work, family, love, even a new child – you... You can make these changes without moving to the other side of the globe, as I did. You can make them right here, at home. It would be much easier for you than it was for me. So, you shouldn't worry about that now. Let's have your wedding first and then, tomorrow, our last session of the cure for Tobi. These are the main goals at present. Let's do one step at a time and not force the events."

Aaron joined them for breakfast later and heard just the last part of the conversation, which appeared to be reasonable to him and he thankfully nodded to Ashot.

Before leaving for the church morning service with Ashot, Liam ordered caterers to deliver a lunch to the church basement for thirty more guests. Then they all left the house at the same time - Aaron and Rosie drove to a wedding store to buy her dress. On the way they first stopped at Aaron's house so he could change into a black evening suit which he had for special occasions, like Banquets or Christmas parties at the university.

"Is this your house?" Rosie asked surprised as he parked his car outside the garage. "It's a very nice looking one."

"You were there a couple of times," he said tentatively.

"I was?"

Aaron just nodded, not wanting even to begin the conversation and to touch the topic of her lost memory of practically everything that had happened before. He was tense and afraid that she wouldn't remember who he was and change her mind about the church wedding that was supposed to start in two hours. But for now, it seemed to be okay – Rosie smiled at him, hugged him and kissed him on the cheek.

While he was changing, she was walking around the house and studying everything.

"Oh, this is your little daughter's room!" she exclaimed happily, opening the door into Laurie's bedroom. "Oh, there is my envelope with five bucks and my letter on her bedside table! Yes, I remember her."

"Excellent," Aaron answered, feeling content that at least these important moments were still left in place. It was a relief for him. "I am ready, my love. We should go fast now because putting on your dress will take some time."

"Okay," she peacefully agreed and followed obediently as he pulled her outside to the car.

At the wedding store Rosie wasn't picky. She chose a dress right away – the one with open shoulders and arms, outlined with a string of small ivory and pink roses on the top, on her waist, and on the rim of the long skirt. It was strikingly gorgeous, but, surprisingly, not expensive – only $800 - because the fabric was acrylic. The other dresses at the store were done from cotton or silk and ranged from $5,000 to $20,000.

With the dress of her choice came the long white gloves covering her elbows and a short veil also outlined by similar roses all the way around. To finish the package deal there were white high heel sandals. Aaron insisted on adding diamond stud earrings and a diamond necklace, to which Rosie agreed, but was a bit confused that they were too expensive. However, they were so beautiful that it would be impossible to resist.

"How do you like it, Aaron?" Rosie asked, glancing at him flirtatiously, as she appeared from the fitting room.

"Wow! No words, my love. I am speechless. There hasn't been a more beautiful bride than you," he said smiling, hugging and kissing her. "Do you want to keep all of this for our big wedding with my family in September, as well?"

"Of course," she laughed. "It's very beautiful and in my taste. Nothing could be better, I am sure. I hope that your mom and Laurie will love it. Would you like Laurie to be our flower girl then?"

"No question about that. Absolutely sure," Aaron nodded. "So, can we go now? I think we will be just in time for the church."

Rosie asked the shop assistant to pack her previous clothes and walked to the car already dressed for the wedding. Aaron opened the door for her and helped her to put the luxuriant skirt of the dress inside the car.

They arrived at the church at quarter to noon, entered the main door and waited beside the entrance to the huge worship hall until the service ended. Then Ashot and Liam came out with the Reverend, introduced the newlyweds to him. Aaron went inside with him. Liam handed Rosie a bouquet of the white roses which he bought on their way to the church. Standing behind Ashot and Rosie he prepared his camera for filming.

"I love you, uncle," she whispered, kissing Ashot's wrinkled cheek and took him under his arm.

"I love you too, kiddo," he answered, beaming, being probably even more happy than Rosie herself, as he saw the results of his hard work beside him, blossoming in success. Then the bridesmaids came out and joined Rosie and Ashot. They were excited as they saw how she looked in this wedding outfit.

Inside the hall, the best men settled beside Aaron and the Reverend. Someone pressed a button on their phone to start the wedding music and Ashot and Rosie slowly walked in, followed by the bridesmaids. The procedure began.

As Aaron and Rosie said their vows, many teens were making videos and taking photos. It was done exactly as it happened in the Greenwich Competition Hall at the end of the concerts, when Rosie and Aaron made their Guinness Record of the longest kiss, and when Aaron proposed on stage. Now, these videos and photos of their wedding were posted on Facebook, Twitter, YouTube, Instagram and anywhere else where it was only possible on the Internet, the same way as the previous ones; and in a few minutes they spread around the globe...

In Florida it was three p.m. and, while lying down on the beach, aunt Erin's daughter, Ashly, looked at her Facebook page, saw the video and the pictures of that wedding and sent them immediately to her sister, Nicole. "Look," she wrote, "this bastard Arie didn't invite us for his wedding. Not only us, but his own mother and daughter! This is so rude of him. Is he completely crazy or what?"

"Please, make sure that Auntie Beth didn't see that," Nicole answered. "She would certainly have a heart attack. Let him explain this to her by himself. He is an idiot!"

"But the girl is pretty, and the dress is gorgeous," Ashly noted in spite of her being upset.

"Come on, everyone could be pretty in a wedding dress, even the last ugly pig! I don't care. I am angry at him," Nicole concluded.

In Seattle, Helen Harrison saw the video and shook her head, "Wow! Arie! This is how you are working on the project for the Psychiatry Scientific Conference? You mentioned that you're working on a schizophrenic patient in a private research clinic. Is this new wife of yours a co-worker, a clinic owner or a patient? I am just wondering..."

In New York, Rosie's teacher and friend, Mary Oswald, full of excitement watched the wedding and wanted to call Rosie and congratulate her this evening. But, surprised, she discovered that her beloved former student blocked her phone number as well as contacts on all the social media platforms. *Why?* she thought sadly. *I don't understand what happened? She always loved me so much and was so thankful for my support...*

In Afghanistan, with thirteen hours difference in time zone, it was now almost two a.m. the next day. Private Alex Brown was sleeping and didn't see this video. One of his soldier-friends showed it to him several days later.

CHAPTER 54

Ashot suggested having a picnic at the edge of the abyss above the Diablo Lake to make it a wedding dinner.

"I guess that would be beneficial for you, kiddo," he said, "to start your real married life by absorbing more of the fresh mountain air along with the divine fantastic energy. What the Clay Mask already cleaned, God could clean double. At least, it will not hurt anything."

Everybody agreed. They all changed from their sophisticated wedding outfits into simple jeans, t-shirts and sneakers, took the coolers with food and water and went for the trip. It seemed kind of unusual for a dinner after a wedding. But they already had the big celebrating dinner before, with the Poetry Club members - at Rosie's farewell as Anastasia - in the restaurant at the Space Needle, although she didn't remember it.

Also, today they had a big lunch with her Poetry Club friends and with the church parish which could be considered as a wedding reception. And they all felt that it was quite enough of the festivities. Now it was time to rest in nature and relax, enjoying its quiet beauty.

Rosie was very happy about the outing in the mountains, reminding Aaron one more time that this is exactly her lifestyle which is the opposite from the fancy restaurants with their culinary arts. He noticed, surprised, that after 90 percent of the cure had been accomplished, this point still didn't change in her, as many other things had.

So their evening in the mountains went nice and was full of the family closeness and warmth combined with a real feeling of the divine nature and its recuperating energy. And then Rosie and Aaron had a beautiful, exciting, endless first night of their official Honeymoon as husband and wife. It seemed to Aaron that a half of his dream, formulated by Ashot, came true. He had an almost - 99 percent - healthy woman in his bed, and the time approached to start working next week on the preparation materials for the conference – another half of the dream – the Nobel Prize. Although, somewhere deep in his subconscious he remembered Ashot's warning – 'you are rushing, son, you are forcing everything to go ahead too fast. Slow down, give yourself and her some time...'

I understand that we both, Rosie and I, need to heal and to calm down before starting the family, Aaron thought, *but it is too late to talk about that. We're already married, we're having our baby, the family has already started. All done. And I don't know, absolutely don't know, if it was done too fast or not? What will happen with us next?*

But he chose to stop thinking about that at present. It was his happy night full of love and it would be blasphemy not to be glad, content and thankful to Fate, to God and to Ashot about the current situation.

The next morning the Tobi session started, as regular, exactly at ten a.m. All the men were feeling a bit uneasy to meet Tobi, knowing pretty well how angry and unpredictable she usually was. But Rosie looked very confident and calm before the beginning of the session and her good mood gave hope to everyone.

Ashot did his usual starting representation and then turned the Clay Mask to face Rosie. He needed to work on some hair on the back of its head. Otherwise, his work on the sculpture was practically over.

"Please, tell us, Rosie, who is Tobi?" he asked. "When did she come to you and why?"

Rosie looked at the Clay Mask's face attentively and then smiled. That was very unexpected in the situation where the conversation should be about the mad angry monster inside her.

"Madam Clay Mask," she began, "I am sorry but I have almost nothing to tell you about that. You should know from our previous conversations that it has already been covered. But just to refresh your memories, I could remind you once more - in reality Tobi is my fierce and loyal protector. She is fair. She is fighting for the truth against everything that is bad in the world. She loved my other personalities like sisters, she cared about them and she heard a voice from above which always said to her – 'protect!' At some point she was like a trained protective dog of universal eternal fairness: she would get a command and she would run to act immediately. That's it. Very simple."

"When did Tobi come to your protection for the first time?" the old man inquired.

"When my grandpa Vasil killed my grandma Nora. I already told you that, Madam Clay Mask."

"Yes. Sorry," Ashot confirmed. "I am just wondering why she didn't come before that, when he did many other abusive things."

"Because these other things weren't as extreme as the murder. I probably needed to be protected from them too, but not on the level where Tobi operates. Her level was the highest one, the utmost one."

"Okay, thank you for the clarification, Rosie," Ashot agreed. "Now, when was the second time Tobi got activated?"

"I already told this as well," she giggled. "Tobi never came during my four years in the *Youth Shelter*. Next time she appeared on an airplane, on my concert trip, when one passenger reminded me of grandpa Vasil. From the distance he looked like him – the same hair and also he wore a similar jacket. I am very sorry that I hurt this innocent bystander, but it was a mistake. Tobi confused him as Nora's murderer. I already apologized for that."

"So, it was about five years later than Tobi's first appearance," Ashot concluded. "She must be called very seldom by the universal protective power."

"Exactly. The next time Tobi attacked the policewoman who shot Ben. It was, again, murder, and Tobi couldn't leave it just like that, without revenge."

"But there weren't any murders, when Tobi appeared later. How come she was still present?"

"Another time I became Tobi in my mom's house, when mom and Miguel prohibited me from performing in my poetry concerts. To me it was the murder of my soul and my creative work that was my true soul expression. And mom and Miguel, both, were monsters whom Tobi protected my soul from – not to let me be spiritually murdered. Very clear. I told you about that, Madam Clay Mask. You have to remember."

"Yes, I do. Thank you," Ashot agreed. "Then tell us, please, about the last time Tobi appeared and almost killed Aaron when he started making up with you on your own request. That moment we didn't cover yet in our sessions about the other personalities."

Aaron was surprised that during the whole conversation, the stream of the particles of Rosie's aura toward the Clay Mask was straight, calm, evenly multicolored, just with tiny black sparkles. It was obvious that very little dirt was left in her aura and these leftover crumbs now were leaving permanently. It was very visible and understandable that her mentality was getting better and healthier with every following second. He started taking pictures of this without Ashot reminding him, and received an approving smile and nod from the old man.

But with Ashot's last question, Aaron felt that a dangerous moment approached – the story of her mad attack in his car.

Rosie took her water bottle and had a couple of big gulps, then took a deep breath and answered, "At that time our relationship came to a point when I had to choose between Aaron and my creative life of poetry. I had to be healthy for him. But I could potentially lose my talent during the cure. To make this choice was difficult for me: very painful to lose one or the other. I wanted him so much that I was scared to lose him. I guess my sexual feelings made me greedy for Aaron. I felt as if someone was taking him from me and I didn't want to give him away. So, Tobi came to help – to keep him and to fight the monsters that wanted to take him. Actually, again, it is simple and understandable. You are smart enough, Madam Clay Mask, you should realize that yourself."

"I do," Ashot nodded, "but I wanted to hear that from you, to be sure. Thank you for sharing, Rosie."

"You're welcome," she smiled at the Mask, then whispered, "Sorry, now I am tired and need to sleep. I am parting with you, Madam Clay Mask, for a long time. Probably forever." She dropped her head on the little towel on the table and closed her eyes.

Ashot wet his hands more in the pail of the water with the clay that stood on the floor beside him and began slowly smoothing the surface of the Clay Mask, making it more fine-textured and glassy. Aaron kept taking pictures of the flow of the particles that got thinner with every minute and finally, after five minutes, disappeared completely.

"It looks like we made it," Ashot uttered slowly, while wiping his hands on a small towel and making the sign of the cross over Rosie. "Thank you, God. Thank you, Madam Clay Mask," he smirked, mimicking Rosie's address. "Thank you for filming, Liam. And especially - thank you, Aaron. You did great today. You proved to me that you finally understood and learned how the procedure works. I would be happy to know that you could cure the next patient by yourself, without me. I will just make a couple of sculptor's procedure classes for you to work with the clay and then you will be good to go. Congratulations, son!"

It was interesting that the Tobi session came up as the shortest one and calmest one out of them all. No one could have expected and predicted that and they all feel relieved now.

"What will we do next?" Aaron asked after he carried Rosie to bed and tucked her to sleep quietly until the following morning, though it wasn't even noon yet. The session lasted less than two hours.

"We need to move the Clay Mask into my den now," Ashot explained. "We will open the window, turn on a fan and lock the door, so nobody enters there for a few days. The clay should dry completely to become fragile and breakable. Then we all will go onto the roof of our building and Rosie will crash the Mask. All damaged particles, combined and held inside the Clay Mask during the sessions will fly up to the universe. They will be gone forever. There is no chance that they will return nor that she could become ill again. She be always healthy and clean. Guaranteed. I did it with my twenty-one previous patients.

"However, I would like to talk with you guys about some important things that should be done during this time." Ashot turned to Liam. "First of all, darling, how much time do you need for editing your film to make it ready to be shown to the conference judges?"

"Hmm... not so much, actually," Liam answered thoughtfully. "If I work on it every day for a couple of hours during the time while the Clay Mask is drying, it should be done pretty soon. I will edit out just a few moments that should be removed from the tapes. But also, I will review all the sessions to double check that nothing undesirable comes to the attention of the judges. I understand that some things they don't need to know. Some are private, and some are your business secrets, babe, right?"

"Of course," Ashot nodded, "and just make sure, please, that it is emphasized that I am doing what Dr. Dispenmore instructed me. He taught me what to do, how to use his scientific discovery of the cure and I am working for him as his assistant only. It should be very clear for the judges that Aaron is the mastermind behind the scientific base of the cure. It's our main point, guys. Are we clear on that?"

Aaron and Liam both nodded.

"So, babe, if you are expecting to be busy a couple of hours everyday, then you will be free from editing by noon," Ashot continued. "Then it will be on you to occupy the kiddo. Keep filming her if you go to the beach, go for a walk, talking about the plans for her future life, about her love for her husband, about her coming baby... Something beautiful and normal that an average healthy woman will think and talk about. Your film must now show her behavior as a very healthy person because during some sessions her outbursts clearly demonstrated her illness. The judges have to see the difference.

"I am asking you, darling, to do that," Ashot continued, "because Aaron and I will be busy working on the materials – printing all the pictures and printing all of Aaron's notes, then attaching every note of explanation to every picture. We started to do that after the first session, but the other things took our attention away from this job. Now it's time to continue. It will be tedious and long work. We will be occupied with it from ten in the morning until ten at night. So, Aaron will see his wife in bed only, and maybe at dinners. And it will last about a month because the amount of the pictures taken is enormous. For the judges, to understand what they are seeing on every picture, they need to read all the explanations attached. But it has to be done if we want to get their approval and win the nomination for the Nobel Prize at the conference.

"Also, Aaron is supposed to learn my file about the scientific research of the clay, the chemistry of it and so on; and to re-write it himself, again, to prove that he discovered it. It will be extra work for him. As for all medical files about schizophrenia, I am sure, Aaron knows them pretty well from his education as a psychiatrist. So, the specification of your scientific discovery was what, son?" Ashot asked, looking at Aaron with a cunning smirk."

"The blue clay was well known to science, as was schizophrenia. My discovery was to combine them together – to use the ability of the clay to suck in the damaged aura's particles for the cure of the illness."

"Excellent! Perfect student!" Ashot giggled. "You just need to read more about that in my files, so you could make a confident speech about that at the conference. And, of course, we will work on your speech together. But," he continued, "there is one more important thing that needs to be done, in which you, Liam, with kiddo together could help us. I would like to find all my previously healed patients in Armenia and to learn how they are doing now, thirty to thirty-five-years after their cure. It could be done through some social media, I guess. I am not good at it, but I know that you,

Liam, are perfect in this. Also our young generation kiddo is good at it, as well. This is one more fun thing which you both could do with Rosie together using her new computer, by the way. I will give you, daring, files of my old patients and you will find their names, ages, addresses, and my clinic name and address, although it could have changed over the years, but still it should be a good point to start with."

"Sounds like fun and an adventure," Liam smiled. "I am sure Rosie would like the idea. Of course, babe, we will work on it and also on my filming of her at the beaches and in the parks, as well. I suspect she will like it too. The girls usually love modeling. So, what are we doing now, while she is sleeping all day long?"

"Now we are going for lunch somewhere and then starting our work," Aaron suggested, glancing at Ashot for approval.

"Exactly. Sounds like a plan," the old man nodded, smiling.

CHAPTER 55

The next week was evolving according to Ashot's plan and everything was moving ahead fast and smoothly. The obligatory meetings for the whole team were arranged during dinners, to share the news about what was accomplished that day and what they all plan to do for the following twenty-four hours.

Everyday after editing a portion of his film, Liam drove Rosie to some entertainment outings. They went to beaches, took a Whale Watching Tour on a small vessel, spent one day rock climbing and even visited the gay piano bar where Liam used to work as a pianist long ago and where he meet Ashot. Liam introduced Rosie to some acquaintances there as his daughter and everyone was surprised by this unexpected statement. Right away many people were asking, if she is a married lesbian as they noticed her wedding band. But she just laughed, saying that she is married to a straight man and expecting a baby. So, she came here only out of respect for her daddy and to see his past place of employment.

Liam also took her one day to a movie set to show her how movie production works and introduced her to some actors and directors. Another time Liam brought Rosie to a TV station to let her know how the news programs are looking from inside while journalists are still working on them. This way, their trips were not just simply fun, but also unexpectedly educational to Rosie and she felt very happy and thankful to Liam for doing that for her.

So, Liam and Rosie had a lot of good times together and developed a close friendship that wasn't there before. Usually, everything that Liam did for her was by Ashot's requests only. Now he took the initiative in his own hands and proved to be very inventive and creative.

After dinners, at home, Liam set up the new computer for Rosie and together they began searching social media, looking for connections with Armenia, especially the city of Yerevan, and precisely The Armenian National Scientific Institute of Psychiatry which was the new name today for the former psychiatric clinic where Ashot worked years ago and made his discovery of the cure for schizophrenia. They were also googling names of Ashot's previous patients to see what might come up.

Aaron and Ashot were also very busy during that week, and Aaron really had no time to see his wife. They only have sex before sleep and in the mornings, in the shower, as she liked. Everything seemed to be okay and the newlyweds' passion was blossoming as it was supposed to be during a Honeymoon of a young couple. Aaron felt that his sexual desire for Rosie's body was very strong. Physically he was satisfied a great deal, but, still, sometimes he couldn't sleep after sex and was thinking almost all night that something was amiss.

His deeply spiritual love, his amazing feeling of 'the holy oasis in a desert', his mad attraction to Rosie's poetry, talent, shining on the stage – all of these were gone and didn't exist anymore. Her specialty, individuality, and uniqueness was gone. His relationship with Rosie changed drastically. From being spiritual Siamese Twins – two bodies and one soul – it turned to the sexual satisfaction only, and this was disturbing and hurtful for him to realize.

One day, as he entered the bedroom, he saw Rosie moving to the door a big box that seemed to be pretty heavy.

"Let me help you, my love," he said. "Where do you want to move this box?"

She shrugged. "There is a storage room beside Liam's den. You can put it there."

"What is in the box?" Aaron asked.

"All my old stuff which I don't need. I wanted to throw them into the garbage bin, but uncle suggested I put it in the storage for now."

"Can I take a look?"

She shrugged again. "Of course, if you want."

Aaron opened the box and was shocked to see a few copies of Rosie's book and folders with her manuscripts of the two other books that she wanted to publish. There also was her old computer, full of her poems, pictures and videos of her performances, and her poetry editing works for magazines. It was all her beautiful creative past, sad, tragic but breathing with talent and spirituality. And she was ready to throw that all into the garbage bin?! He was so shocked that he stayed speechless, not knowing what to say. He only whispered, "Why?"

"It takes so much room, and anyway I will never use those things anymore."

"But you told us that you want to publish two more books of poetry that weren't included into your book by timing – the earliest and the latest."

"Aaron, really? Who needs them? Who is actually reading poetry?"

"Many young people do as you know from your former Poetry Club."

"But I overgrew those teen entertainments. I am a married woman now. I will be a mother soon. I don't know how to do that anymore. And I am not interested."

"At first, as we told you about your loss of that talent, you said that you will try to translate your poems into other languages. You agreed that we will all go to the teens' concerts. You wanted to keep friendship with them!" Aaron exclaimed, dumbfounded by that 180 degree change of her attitude.

Rosie shrugged once more. "I may have said that in the heat of the moment, but then I thought, why bother. It is really not interesting for me any longer."

"Then what is interesting for you?"

"I don't know. I haven't figure it out yet. But I know something will be. Just give me some time, please. Liam found his new interest after a month. I am not finished with my cure completely, yet. The Clay Mask is still drying. Please, Aaron, don't push me. I am begging you."

"Sorry," he uttered, hugging her and tenderly pressing her to his chest. "Sorry, my love. I will wait. I won't push you, I swear."

He had said that so as to not hurt her feelings. But he himself was hurt beyond belief. It seemed to him that some indifference and coldness started appearing in Rosie which he never saw in her before and it was getting unpleasant to him.

A few days later, when Ashot was busy with Liam and Rosie together connecting on Skype with some of his former patients they had found in Armenia, Aaron took a break and drove to his house. He told his team that he needs to take home his evening suit which he used for the church wedding, but in reality, he just wanted to have some time alone to think through some of his feelings and to evaluate his situation.

At home, he went to his bedroom, sat on the bed and took Rosie's book from under his pillow. The dry pink petunia flower was still there, between pages. He pressed the book to his face, feeling the glossy texture of the cover, its smell, the attraction of its energy, and then he dropped the book and broke into sobs, falling with his face to the pillow. It was his love, his Rosie for whom he fell madly, and now she didn't exist anymore. She died exactly like Ally did. He was married today to another woman, absolutely healthy, precisely different, and alien. He didn't love this stranger, didn't know her and didn't want her. He wanted his Rosie – miraculous, fragile, full of hidden pain, strange, unpredictable, reading his thoughts, creating poems and making a glass to dance on the table like crazy; his Rosie with whom he fell in love forever and whom he knew he would love forever... and now she was gone.

The second time in his life the woman he loved disappeared from him, leaving him with the sexual partner only, as Helen was after Ally. This time it turned out that Rosie became that partner after his dead love – Rosalyn-Anastasia. It was even worse than it was with Helen. He felt free to dump Helen at any time, no strings attached, but with Rosie now he was married and expected to have a baby. He expected her to be a step-mother for Laurie and a daughter-in-law for Beth. And he knew that she would be the good one, that Laurie and Beth will love her and will be happy and she will love them back, too. She still had a nice, sincere, open, honest, kind character and was an attractive person to be with. Beth will love to do gardening, cooking and sewing with her, Laurie will love to play barbies with her. They will love to go shopping all together. So, he did it for them? Did he marry for them? But what was in it for himself?

On the day when Aaron and Laurie met Rosie the first time, he saw her as an ordinary girl and practically didn't notice her. He just fell in love while reading her book. What was left now? To stay in love with the book only?

She told him on the bench in the park - after their famous kiss on the stage - that she was scared to be cured because if her talent was gone, he won't love her anymore. He swore to God then that he will always love her even as a 'dull housewife' as she named it herself.

He swore to God during his proposal on stage that he will love her forever and she will be his 'fairy Anastasia' always, after she performed her poem **Farewell Anastasia** at the last concert at the Poetry Club. Was he lying then? No, he was sincere, and excited, and aroused, and was sure that it would last eternally. But she knew better. She was, obviously, smarter than him, even being ten years younger and ten times less educated. Or maybe she wasn't smarter? She just had the ability to see the future.

What was Aaron supposed to do now? Live his whole life ahead with the woman he didn't love only to make his mother, daughter and future baby happy? Only to keep his family going? It would be a spiritual death for him. He didn't want that. He dreamed, wanted, craved to be happy!

Aaron was in such despair that he felt only one wish at the moment - to die. The situation seemed to him otherwise hopeless. Again, he was clutching at a last straw – Ashot. Maybe this damn genius-psychiatrist could help somehow, could do something to restore his love for Rosie – his new, healthy, but perfect stranger wife?

Aaron was lying on his bed for a long time, thinking, comprehending the situation he was in until he finally fell asleep.

When he returned to their building it was two a.m. and he expected that everybody would be sleeping. He quietly opened the door of the condo, and suddenly saw Ashot in his pajamas in the den with the door open.

"Oh, where have you been, son?" the old man asked, surprised to see him entering. His question just popped out subconsciously. Then, not waiting for an answer because he didn't want to show too much control, he continued, "I decided to check on the Clay Mask. It's actually dried pretty well. I guess tomorrow we could break it. Come here, son, and touch it. I would like you to remember how it should feel when it is completely ready to be broken."

Aaron approached and tentatively patted the forehead of the Clay Mask. It felt very dry, a little bit rough and scratchy on his fingers, and the clay was even hot.

"You see?" Ashot continued. "You have to know that because for your next patient you will check it yourself."

"Okay," Aaron whispered nonchalantly. "I feel that. Thank you."

Ashot attentively looked at his face. "What's going on, son?" he asked kindly. "It looks like you have something on your plate. Did something happen? I mean... with kiddo... Did you have a fight?"

"Not really. But I need to talk to you," Aaron uttered with a deep breath barely holding himself in check.

"Okay then, let's go to the patio," Ashot suggested in a calm, caring tone of voice, like he was expecting this.

When they entered the patio, Ashot closed the door to the condo to make sure that they will not bother anyone sleeping. Aaron sat on the chair at the table and lowered his head on his hands.

"I don't know..." he whispered. "I am turning insane. I just really want to die and nothing else. Help me, uncle. Please, help me somehow..."

Ashot was surprised to hear that for the first time since they knew each other, Aaron called him 'uncle.' This clued him that something must be seriously bothering his partner in business and son-in-law. "Okay, son," he said quietly and compassionately, "I am listening."

And then Aaron told him everything that he was thinking and feeling, while at home, hugging Rosie's book and crying in his bed. The despair, helplessness, impression of the end of his love - a tragedy that felt to him as the end of the world – all came out now from his worn out soul.

Ashot listened silently, not interrupting, not saying a word. When Aaron finally finished talking and dropped his head on his crossed arms at the table, the old man moved his chair closer to him and put his hand on Aaron's shoulder.

"I know this love story cost you a lot, son," he said calmly. "But let me tell you something. When you marry the partner you love, you say 'I do' kind of swearing to God that you love this person so much that you will care about them in health and sickness, in rich and poverty and so on. Right? But you should expect that during your life together your partner will change.

"When you get married at a young age, you are not thinking about that. Let's talk about your first wife. What if during your nine years together, she became handicapped? Would you still love her and care about her, even if it would be impossible to have sex with her because of her health condition?"

"Of course," Aaron sniffled. "Of course I would... because her soul will be the same, her personality will be the same. You are talking about the physical changes, and this is not related to Rosie and I. I am having problems because her soul has changed, her character, her personality..." he continued passionately. "I don't know who she is anymore. But I know definitely that she is not the woman I love. The woman I love is gone. I am sleeping with a stranger now!!! Our sex is good, she is an amazing and desirable woman, but she is not my Rosie. I am married to a woman I don't even know..."

"Okay," Ashot nodded. "I was heading to that. She is a new woman with whom you have sex without love. I get it. For you it feels strange. You don't know her soul, yet... But you will, step-by-step. You are rushing crazily, son. I told you that many times. Give her time to go through the change from being a severe schizophrenic to a normal healthy person. Her talent and her mysterious abilities were the part of her illness. Are you saying now that you loved not the girl, not the person, not the woman herself but her illness? Think about that – it is not her personality that is gone, it is her illness that is gone. She is returning now to her normal existence, she is becoming herself finally - the person who she was born to be. Don't you get it?

"Maybe you are considering your marriage to her as a mistake now, but at the same time you are recognizing that she is a perfect match for your family. You're not married for your mom, daughter and future baby, as you are saying. You're married for yourself because if your mom, and daughter, and baby are happy, you will see that, and that will make you happy as well. Nothing is better in life than a happy family, believe me. I am the man who lost it and appreciated its value all my life afterward.

"For now, son, my advice is – meet this new stranger woman, embrace her, consider her your new date who is sexually attractive. Start to know her, to learn who she is spiritually. Try to study her soul, unknown to you yet, make her your new friend and new love. Believe me, she is a good girl, even without her poetry. I am sure that a new special talent will come out soon. We haven't finished exploring this strange thing about some foreign languages that have already begun to appear. There will be something very interesting, fresh and attractive to your heart, no less than the poetry was.

"And if these, her books, are still seeming as such a treasure to you, you could take them yourself and find a publisher for them one day. That's why I suggested to her not to throw all these manuscripts and the old computer away, but store them for a while. Believe me, Aaron, everything will be settled very well. Just be patient, give her and yourself more time.

"Then, if you finally, in some prolonged time, still don't feel in love with your wife, you could divorce her one day. But not now, not soon, not until our project is completely accomplished and you have this Nobel Prize at the end; not until my invention - my cure - would be officially recognized and approved for use anywhere, at any psychiatric clinic in America, maybe even at the clinics of the whole world. It needs to be done, Aaron, because, remember, we are working here not only for Rosie's happiness and your happiness - we are working here for all severely mentally ill schizophrenics to get them cured, to give them a normal and beautiful life. We are working for all of human society and you absolutely have no moral right to drop this project for any personal reason and to destroy our path to the Psychiatry Scientific Conference in New York.

"You are a decent man, Aaron, not a villain. You won't betray millions of people's hopes, dreams and expectations because your wife changed her attitude about her poetry hobby. Think globally, think about others, not only about yourself as I told you many times. Now, go to bed and hug her. She was crying the whole evening after you left and didn't return for a long time."

"Thank you," Aaron said quietly, standing up and heading to the bedroom.

He appreciated Ashot's opinion but his intuition told him that the old man had something on his mind that he didn't reveal completely, something that worried and bothered him a lot as well. Aaron suspected that it was the true reason why Ashot didn't sleep and obviously waited for him to come home – otherwise he could easily check the dryness of the Clay Mask at any other time.

CHAPTER 56

When Aaron entered their bedroom he was surprised to see that Rosie wasn't sleeping but sitting on the edge of the bed. It looked to him like not only Ashot was waiting for him to come back, but she as well. In the semidarkness he couldn't see her face clearly and couldn't say if she was crying or not. He sat beside her and hugged her by the shoulders.

"Aaron," she whispered, turning to him and looking him in the eyes. "I am scared."

"Why?" he asked, realizing that she wasn't crying although was a bit confused and shaky. "Did someone return – Nora, or Vally?"

"No," she smirked. "I am scared as any normal person might be sometimes. I am your wife, Rosie, who is afraid of tomorrow."

"Why?" he repeated and kissed her hair on the top of her head. "I am with you. Tell me why, my love."

Aaron sincerely called her 'my love' feeling at the moment the tenderness for her weakness and vulnerability. She was his beloved former Rosie at the moment – defenseless, begging him for help and protection. Was it really him, his personality – to be attracted to some weak and helpless women, as Helen determined? When Rosie was a healthy, confident new person, he sensed that his love was gone, that she became a stranger. But when she was scared and confused he felt such a huge urge to hug and protect her, and his heart started filling with deep tender love again. Was this feeling returned forever? Or just temporarily - because of the moment of her weakness? He didn't have an answer.

"Uncle said that the Clay Mask is dry enough and tomorrow I could break it," Rosie answered quietly. "It needs to be done to complete my cure. And I am scared to be healthy. I was ill for so long. I got used to it. To have only one personality is kind of boring, too simple, too dull, too plain. I am worried that you won't love me anymore. I am scared to lose you, Aaron. I love you madly. I love you to death."

"Darling," he smiled, "we talked about that already several times. We watched your last performance at the Poetry Club when you read the poem *Farewell Anastasia.* It was exactly about that. The poem even ends with those words. And you saw that I swore there, on the stage, that I will love you always, even being plain and simple, and I proposed to you there."

"So... you still love me," she smiled with obvious relief. "You will be with me while I am breaking the Clay Mask?"

"Of course. We all will be there – your uncle and Liam, and I. It is the last session of your cure. We will document it the same way as we did all the prior sessions and Liam will film it. And also - good news - we are already half done with our work on the materials for the conference. As soon as we finish it, you and I will move from this condo to my house. It will be our house then. And my mom and Laurie will come home from Florida soon after that, and we will be a family. The family with one daughter and a bit later with a son as well. How about that?"

"It's okay," she nodded obediently. "I would like to be a mother for your little one. I miss her."

"I know that this family life would be very different from what you ever had before," Aaron continued, "and even different than I had before. But we will work on it and we will build it – our own family. It will be our new beginning. So, don't be scared. Be excited and happy."

With that he began kissing her and finally the consolation ended up with another lovemaking and then with a calm sleep, hugging each other until the morning.

Next day after breakfast Ashot made the last orientation session, explaining to everyone how the procedure on the roof will work.

"After we will finish there," he completed his explanation, "you two, Liam and Aaron, please, take all the stuff back home, and kiddo and I will stay there for some time. I will talk to her for a while, to check how she is feeling and maybe to adjust her a little bit for the new life."

It took them two trips on the elevator, carrying the Clay Mask on the tray, covered with the plastic box and also the equipment that was used for the cure sessions. Plus Rosie brought a plastic pail, broom and tray to clean the broken pieces of the clay afterward.

On the roof of their high-rise building was a concrete helicopter pad and also a small garden where some bushes in bloom and trees surrounded a couple of the benches. It was a quiet place for residents to sit, rest and enjoy the stunning view of snowy mountains on the horizon behind the ocean gulf. There was also a small kitchen, and restroom, because sometimes people were partying there.

Ashot lifted the box and took the Clay Mask from the tray, placing it in the middle of the helicopter pad. He invited Rosie to stand in front of it. Liam with his big camera on his shoulder was advised to stay at one corner of the square; Aaron, wearing goggles and holding the tablet in his hands – at the other corner. Ashot himself, also wearing goggles and holding a small 4D camera in his hands, stood at the third corner.

When everybody was ready, Ashot commanded, as usual at each session, "Action!" and Liam started filming as Ashot began his last presentation.

"We are performing today the final session of the cure of the patient, Rosa Lynn Garcia, diagnosed in 2006 with acute schizophrenia, based on Dissociative Identity Disorder of seven personalities." Liam's camera went on him, first, then on Rosie and later on Aaron when it came to his name. "During the six cure sessions we used a scientific method of natural treatment for this illness, newly discovered by a Board Certified Psychiatrist, Doctor Aaron Dispenmore, MD, PhD, of the Psychiatry Department of Washington State University.

"I am Doctor Dispenmore's assistant, the Registered Nurse of psychiatry, Thomas Spencer. Under Dr. Dispenmore's supervision I helped with developing the organic material of the treatment – the biologically clean blue clay - into the Clay Mask resembling the patient's face.

"During the previous six cure sessions we cleaned out the damaged and dysfunctional aura's particles of the six different patient's personalities which were the basis of Rosa Garcia's illness as Dr. Dispenmore determined. The procedure of removing damaged particles of the aura, which are managing these personalities, was carried on with the creation of the Clay Mask, depicting the patient's face, from the organic blue clay," Ashot continued. "Now, all these deformed particles are combined inside the Clay Mask, being sucked in by the power of the blue clay. The patient should break the Clay Mask, to let those particles fly up to the sky and join the holographic universe energy fields forever. They will never return to Earth and the patient will never be mentally ill again. Her aura will always stay bright and clean.

"After the Clay Mask will be broken, we will pick up the pieces of the clay and send them to the university lab for analyzing how the chemical ingredients of the blue clay had changed. The result of this analysis will be available for judges of the Psychiatry Scientific Conference to compare the components of the blue clay before and after treatment. This will demonstrate which ingredients exactly have gone to the universe, carrying the damaged particles of the patient's aura – which ingredients precisely served as medicine for the cure of schizophrenia.

"Now, Rosie, please, take the Clay Mask, lift it, and smash it on the concrete. And move aside from the fractures momentarily, so the damaged particles don't touch you while flying up. Please, do that. We, the medical team, have completed our part of the cure. At present, everything is in your hands."

Aaron saw, through his goggles, that Rosie's body was enveloped into a beautiful white-sparkling cloud as she made a step toward the Clay Mask. It was obviously some kind of positive energy that he marked in his tablet notes. She took the Clay Mask, elevated it and exclaimed excitedly, "Sorry, Madam Clay Mask that I am supposed to hurt you. Thank you for your help. Bye!" And with that she smashed the sculpture on the concrete floor with all her power and instantly jumped back.

There was a loud thud and the dry clay pieces scattered around like smithereens. Aaron saw that a big flow of black sparkling particles funneled up to the the sky and Rosie's white cloud followed them, like being sucked into the same stream. It lasted only three minutes and then everything was finished.

Rosie stood quietly, waiting, covering her face with her palms. She probably felt somehow that the procedure ended and removed her hands, lifted her face up to the sun, to the sky, raised her arms and yelled, "All done! I am healthy! I am happy! I am feeling great!"

"Thank you God, we did it!" Ashot said, smiling. He made a sign of cross toward her and kissed his golden cross. Then he took a broom, a tray and swept the pieces of the clay into the pail.

"Thank you everyone," he announced, as he sat on the bench in the small roof garden. "Aaron and Liam, you could go now, guys. I will take it from here. See you downstairs in a while."

Liam, holding his camera with one hand, took a pail with the clay in his other hand and walked toward the elevator, silently as usual. Aaron put his tablet, small camera and both goggles into a big plastic box where the Clay Mask was before, closed the lid and, carrying it, followed Liam. He suppressed his wish to go to Rosie, to hug her, to kiss her, to congratulate her. He didn't even look at her, feeling kind of uneasy, not understanding why. But he trusted Ashot and was sure that the old man knew what is better to do now and how to proceed.

As soon as the elevator door closed behind Liam and Aaron, Rosie approached Ashot.

"Thank you, uncle," she said, hugging him. "Thank you for everything. It feels great. I am so light, I am ready to fly. And everything looks kind of more sunny; as if before I stared at the world through a dirty window, and now, suddenly, this window is washed, clean, shiny. I can see and feel everything closer and brighter. And, who were those men, uncle?"

"Liam is my husband, your adoptive father," Ashot answered. "We didn't adopt you officially, on paper, because you are already an adult, but by the love of our hearts you're our daughter, though you are calling me 'uncle'. But you called Liam 'dad' a couple of times."

"Oh! Yes, I remember that now. Yes, Liam is my daddy and my friend. We had such a good time with him last week. Yes, and we did search for your patients from Armenia as well. It was fun. I loved it," she laughed happily and clapped her hands. "I remember, we found a lot!"

"Yes, you even found a bit too much. You did a great job," Ashot answered. "Then, after knowing what happened in Armenia with my patients, I expected something similar could happen here. And this was exactly what was bothering me in the last few days."

"Why?" Rosie inquired a bit confused.

"I was sincerely worrying about Aaron. I really, deeply care about him."

"Who is Aaron? Is he that other man who was here? Who is he? Your son?" Rosie stretched her arm and looked at her finger with an engagement diamond ring and wedding band on it. "It looks like I am married, am I? To whom? I don't remember anything like that. Please, tell me, uncle."

"You are married," Ashot nodded. "Aaron is your husband. He is actually a very nice man and a highly educated doctor-psychiatrist. Yes, to me he is like a son. We're partners in the business. He did this project of your cure with me together. He loves you very-very much and he wants you to be healthy. You're also pregnant with his child."

"What?!" Rosie exclaimed with an expression of dismay on her face and looked at the old man with huge eyes. "Am I pregnant? Why?! Oh, my gosh! How is it possible? Did I have sex with him? Why? It is so crazy!" She pressed her palms to her cheeks, shaking her head in disbelief. "No, no, no! It's disgusting! I don't understand how it could happen? Why did I marry him? I don't know him! He is a perfect stranger! I don't love him at all. Absolutely! Not even a bit! I don't want to have a husband whom I don't love! I don't want to have his baby! Why should I? What the hell happened to me! Why? What should I do now, uncle? Oh, God, help me, please!" She covered her face with her palms and cried terrified, helpless, all shaking and choking on her tears.

Seeing that she was close to hysteria, Ashot patted the bench beside him and said in a very strict voice, "Okay, kiddo. Stop it! That's enough. Collect yourself. Now, come here and sit down. We need to talk very seriously there."

PART 3
THE CONFERENCE

CHAPTER 57

Aaron and Liam were waiting for Ashot and Rosie's return to their condo for quite a long time.

Not knowing what to expect, Aaron was nervously pacing the living room, until Liam got tired of watching him and said, "I better go to my den and work on the editing of today's film. There is nothing worse than just sitting and waiting."

Good idea, Aaron thought. He went to Ashot's den where all the materials were and started reading.

In truth, the work was unbelievably interesting. He was thrilled with it. Aaron loved his profession and was a workaholic all his life when it came to science. This cure procedure was something shockingly new, unknown, not researched, not studied before. It was really the scientific discovery of a genius and it made the whole process fascinating.

During the cure sessions and between them Aaron was too carried away with his love for Rosie, with his excitement of their engagement and marriage. He was shocked and hurt by her confessions to the Clay Mask, he was absorbing and feeling her pain, he was suffering with her together. As a result all these emotions clouded his perception of the significance of science itself.

Now, because the main goal was reached, the sensual part calmed down – Rosie became his healthy wife - his admiration of the science came forward making the work more interesting with every step. Aaron got so excited and enthusiastic by it that he didn't notice how much time had passed until Liam politely knocked at his door.

"What?" Aaron asked, still attentively looking at the screen of his tablet. "Are they back?"

"No," Liam shook his head. "And three hours has already gone by. It must be a serious talk there."

"Maybe they left the building and went somewhere for lunch?" Aaron guessed turning to him.

"No, I don't think so. There is a service kitchen and a restroom on the roof for people who are having parties sometimes. There is coffee usually…"

"Do you want me to go up and check on them?"

"No. Ashot told me not to bother. He always knows what he is doing. I mean… he is probably rebuilding kiddo's whole life."

"Do you think there could be some consequences that need to be rebuilt after the cure is completed?" Aaron looked at Liam questioningly, then closed his computer and stood up. "Do you know something that I don't know?"

"Maybe. I am not sure. Could be…" Liam uttered slowly and nonchalantly. "Obviously, there is something about these foreign languages. Maybe Ashot adjusted her to that new talent."

"There were more languages?" Aaron inquired. "I felt by intuition that Ashot was worried about something these last days."

Liam shrugged, "I can tell you what I know if you want."

As Liam's story unfolded, Aaron realized that his intuition was right – Ashot was worried and disturbed because some new information came from Liam's and Rosie's research of social media.

In the first days they found his gay-patient who fell in love with him thirty years ago. His name was Patrick Sumbatian. He was healthy and feeling well since his cure was accomplished. He got an evaluation of his psychiatric condition by the authorities at the psychiatry hospital in Yerevan and got permission to get an education which was not allowed for mentally ill people in the

Soviet Union. Then Patrick successfully got his master's degree in engineering and was working for many years at an optical plant.

He was married to a woman-lesbian. They had an original deal – her girlfriend was married to Patrick's partner as well. They bought two condos on the same floor and were living now as neighbors – Patrick and his partner in one suit and his wife and her girlfriend in the next one. This way it was safe. Even if someone suspected something, on paper it was proven that they are just the two straight couples – friends and neighbors.

"So, there has not been much change over those thirty years?" Ashot concluded sadly. "No way out from the closet for us."

"No, Doctor Petrosian," Patrick confirmed. "You are much better in the USA to be legally married to your loved one. It's so nice to see your husband and to know that you are happy. When you disappeared, we were sure that you were arrested and died somewhere in Siberia. I will tell our guys that you are alive and doing just great. They will be glad to hear that."

They were talking in the Armenian language and Rosie, sitting behind with Liam, translated to him in whisper what the conversation was about.

"I didn't openly show any surprise by her sudden knowledge of this rare language," Liam continued his story, "but in reality I paid more attention to her new ability than to the contents of the Ashot's communication. However, Patrick agreed to help find other patients of Ashot's. It was not really difficult to do locally in Yerevan as the Yellow and the White Pages existed now in both forms – paper and digital and Facebook was also popular there.

"Waiting for the results of Patrick's search, Ashot continued talking to him on Skype every evening. In Armenia, with the time zone difference, it was early morning – the time before Patrick went to work.

"Five days later, Ashot already had the full list of his patients," Liam went on. "About the first five people cured in 1981-82 he had information in his file here. He followed up on them himself. They were included in his microfilm which he brought to America.

But for the other fifteen cured between 1983–85... Let me show something to you, Aaron..."

Liam approached the desk, took several pages from one of the files and handed them to Aaron.

"Look, here is the list. Only now Ashot had found out that after the cure... look at this, read it..."

"Okay," Aaron took the paper from him and read, "...five of them got divorced, three – broke their relationship, three died (a woman from cancer, a man in a car crash, a man in mountain climbing accident), one man fell in love with Ashot's receptionist at the clinic, three men immigrated (one – legally to England where he found a girlfriend, one - illegally to France, but got married there right away and got status, and one – married to a Jewish woman and immigrated with her to the USA). The last one's name is Levon Ovanesian. He got an American education as a lawyer and has now his own law firm in New York."

"Patrick even laughed," Liam continued, "and said 'So, doctor Petrosian, if you ever would need a lawyer, you always could have one easily. I talked to Levon yesterday. He remembers you and is very happy that you are found. I can give you his contacts.' Ashot thanked him and promised to keep that in mind. But what worried him was that practically all of his twenty-one cured patients had their feelings changed after the cure and that changed their relationship status and their personal love stories."

"Yes, I know," Aaron nodded in agreement. "Before Ashot wasn't thinking about that at all. He didn't care about patients' personal life and marital status, considering this as not related to their illness or health after cure. Then I brought to his attention that about 28 percent of his cured patients changed their feelings and marital status. However, in my opinion it was not a significant number of cases. I was sure that there was nothing to worry about. But I was evidently mistaken."

Aaron took a deep breath feeling visibly nervous, then went on, "Now it's very clear that feelings have changed for all of Ashot's former patients. Those who were in a relationship - broke up; those who were single - found their love very soon. It is quite obvious that the changes in the aura of their bodies created the modification of their feelings, and affected them seriously. So, what will happen with us now? Could Rosie lose her love to me?"

"We discussed this chance with Ashot," Liam answered calmly. "He didn't want to say anything about that to Rosie or to you, Aaron. He didn't want to influence the way of events and didn't want to hurt you ahead of time – maybe nothing like that will happen. But he was on guard and anxious to see the results of the cure afterwards."

"Why are you telling that to me now?" Aaron inquired a bit suspiciously.

"Ashot recommended to do so, in case his conversation with kiddo will be too long, to prepare you that there could be a problem. He didn't want you to experience a bolt from the blue," Liam answered compassionately. "Your love and your life together with Rosie as a family is extremely important for the success of his cure project. You need to be together at least until the Nobel Prize will be in your pocket and the cure would be officially recognized. Otherwise, your break up with Rosie could destroy the whole project as well."

"Yeah... I got it," Aaron took a deep breath again. "You know, Liam, the last few days I was in trouble too. I wasn't sure what I feel about Rosie as she became healthy. Of course, I care about her... but I don't know. I loved her madly when she was ill. Possibly, I loved not her but her illness... as Ashot guessed... Because now... with the illness gone, my feelings are almost gone as well.

"Yesterday Ashot convinced me to date Rosie as a new woman in hope of falling in love again," Aaron continued sadly as he shrugged and shook his head. "Maybe now he is spending such a long time with her, convincing her to stay with me, for the sake of the project? But I don't know what to do now. I am completely messed up and lost."

"Let's just wait," Liam suggested. "Ashot will explain everything. I am sure, he will help. He knows how sensitive you are, Aaron, and how much you were hurt before. That's why he was worried about you. Believe me, he loves you as his own son."

CHAPTER 58

When Ashot and Rosie finally returned home, she approached Aaron, hugged him and quickly pecked his cheek.

"Hi," she said shyly.

"Hi," he answered, kissing her hair on the top of her head. "Congratulations, my healthy woman!"

"Okay, let's have some lunch, guys," Ashot suggested. "Kiddo, please, set the table on the patio."

"I will help," Laim grabbed Rosie's hand and pulled her to the kitchen.

Aaron looked at Ashot questioningly as the old man nodded to him and gestured toward his den. They went in and closed the door.

"Listen, son," Ashot said. "Tomorrow we will continue our work on the materials. We need them to be ready when we go with kiddo for her evaluation at the General Psychiatric Hospital. I'll show you all the steps of the evaluation I did for Liam. I know that the procedure is still the same. I think it could be done next week. We will present you as a doctor who cured her."

"Yes, the university Psychiatry Department approved her as my new patient before we started the cure," Aaron noted. "It will be absolutely legal and official."

"Great," Ashot nodded. "But today you will go on a date with her. I told you yesterday to start dating her as a new woman. It goes both ways now. She will start dating you as a new man. You both will begin from ground zero to re-build your new marital life. Please, give it a try and be serious about that."

"Okay, I will try to do my best," Aaron answered with a deep sigh. Then he turned the conversation away from the painful subject of his relationship with Rosie. "You know, Ashot, I went today through our materials more attentively and kind of got excited about our chances at the conference. While I was waiting for you I looked at everything from another point of view and your discovery captivated me deeply. Your whole project of cure is so fascinating. It feels like we very possibly could get a nomination for the Nobel Prize. I am seriously craving to do more of this job and to get it ready as soon as we can."

"Well, I am happy that you finally started immersing yourself into this work and feel like it's your own," the old man smiled. "It really is important. Okay, let's go to the patio and we will discuss with the guys our future proceedings. They probably already fixed some lunch."

During lunch, Ashot shared with his team his plan of the next steps. It was huge. First, they will need to finish working on the preparation of all materials of the cure sessions for the conference – minimum one week. Second, take Rosie to the General Psychiatric Hospital for evaluation – it will take one more week because there should be a lot of appointments and different tests to be done. Third, Aaron needs to register his own private psychiatry clinic and get his license for it. It will explain to the conference where his scientific discovery was made and where the process of the cure of the patient was evolved – one more month.

Fourth, they should do research on the other psychiatrists who will present their patients for the conference – to determine the level of the competition. Fifth, Ashot and Aaron need to write Aaron's speech for the conference in which he will introduce his scientific discovery, his patient and his process of the cure. Sixth, they have to do a serious research about Rosie's new abilities for some foreign languages and find out exactly how many of them she knows. Seventh, Rosie and Aaron need to develop a new serious relationship and move to Aaron's house to start their family life.

Eighth, the contact with homeland security should be done to make sure that Rosie, on the basis of her health evaluation from the General Psychiatric Hospital, will be removed from the *No Fly List*. It was necessary because on the last day of November all three of them – Ashot, Aaron and Rosie - will fly to New York to attend the conference.

All these tasks should be done before Liam's and Aaron's leave of absence expires and they both will return to their places of official employment and will be completely busy with their work.

Everybody listened attentively, not asking any questions because Ashot's presentation was clear and understandable. Once more Aaron appreciated that the old man obviously knew what he was doing. It made him confident that with Ashot's unbelievable, absolutely new scientific way of the cure, they possibly have a serious chance to win at the conference. And it felt great.

After lunch was consumed, Aaron turned to his wife, smiling, "Okay, let's get ready for our date, Rosie. Right?" She silently nodded and went to her room to change. Five minutes later she appeared wearing the beautiful sundress that he bought her at the Lynden fair market.

"Oh, the memorable dress," he said cheerfully, trying to keep both of them in a good mood. "You look amazing!"

"Thank you," she answered indifferently. "That dress is pretty simple, but it feels good to wear it on such a hot day. Very reasonable."

"Do you remember where you got it?" he inquired tentatively.

"Yes, I do, of course," she nodded. "I remember everything, Aaron, even my illness although it's completely gone. I am a normal person now. Stop worrying about me, please."

"Good to know," he laughed a bit tense, feeling irritation in her tone. "Let's go then."

Aaron noticed that Ashot and Liam very attentively observed their communication, evaluating how they interact together.

When they were in his car, Aaron asked, "Do you want to go and see my house?"

"Why?" she shrugged. "I saw it already. I know where I am forced to live."

He swallowed that silently, just some minutes later asked, "Where do you want to go then?"

"No idea," she shrugged again. "I don't really care. Maybe to some quiet place, in a park, where we could sit. I need to think a lot."

"About what?"

"About my future," Rosie answered irritably again. "I am starting my life now. You know, I graduated from high school in 2012 with an honors diploma. I was supposed to go to a good college or university. But I wasted three years and didn't move ahead anywhere."

"You moved ahead a lot," Aaron objected. "First of all, you got the cure and you are healthy. This is the main point. Plus, you published a book, and with your concerts you became famous as a poetess. You got married and you are pregnant. It's a lot in three years."

"But all of these are bullshit, except for the cure of course. In these three years I could have graduated from a college, being such a talented student as I was. I could've started an important career, not ending up as a stupid pregnant housewife."

"Okay," Aaron said through his teeth, "if we are talking like this, I need to stop driving because otherwise I will crash into something and kill us both. Let's keep quiet, please, until we get to the park." His wife shrugged silently.

Subconsciously still trying to fix their relationship, Aaron drove to the Greenwich Competition Hall and parked at the back of the building. Then he asked Rosie to walk to the park on the top of the hill where they had sat on a bench after he finally found her at her concert, where he kissed her for the first time and confessed his love to her. She followed him not saying a word. When they sat at the same bench, he asked in a shaky voice, "Do you remember this place?"

"Yes, I do," she answered calmly. "I know that here our love story started. But, look, Aaron, I need to get an education and find a profession before I get married and have a child. I also need to take a driving course, get a license, buy a car, so I could be independent and go any time anywhere as needed, but not to beg you or my parents to drive me here and there. All of you are busy enough and have no time to serve as my chauffeurs. Doesn't it sound reasonable?"

He nodded silently.

"I don't really understand how I got married to you," Rosie continued. "You're kind of a handsome guy, but you are much older than me. I was seriously mentally ill. I probably didn't understand anything that I was doing. You manipulated me to marry you and you made me pregnant without even asking for my consent."

"No!" he exclaimed heatedly. "I loved you. I loved you madly. I loved you more that anything in the world and I was sure that I will always love you, illness or not. Why should I manipulate you into a marriage? What's the reason? What advantage could I have from this marriage? You are not a Hollywood star, not a daughter of a billionaire, not a princess. You were just a simple ill girl, but so unbelievably special, so deeply spiritual and so talented, that I admired you. I worshiped you. I loved you sincerely and forever."

She shrugged again and pursed her lips.

"And this pregnancy happened because you wanted it," he continued agitated. "It was not only consensual – you begged for it. You liked children. You wanted to be a mother for my Laurie and you wanted to have a son. You said that it was prescribed for us in the holographic universe. You had a vision of the little island with grass and sand where we will make our child. You lived in three-dimensional time and you saw it as our future."

"Aaron," she smirked. "Listen to yourself! How does it sounds?! If I really did tell you that, it was complete delirium because I was a schizophrenic. Who, normally, could see the future? Who could convince you about connections with the holographic universe? Only a mentally ill person. All that I said and did at that time - all my special abilities, all my poetry talent – it all was my illness and delirium. You are a doctor-psychiatrist. How could you not see and not understand that?"

"I fell in love with you because of that," he growled, squeezing his fists. "I was blinded by emotions. I knew that you were special, that you were my soul. Nobody in the world was ever closer spiritually and emotionally to me than you."

"I got it - all the shows I did for you sounded so unusual and romantic. You fell for it like a teenage boy. I had sincere feelings for you at that time too. But it was not me, it was my illness that loved you. And for you - all you fell in love with was only my illness, nothing else. And now, with the illness gone, we need to apply more common sense to our relationship.

"We both are left now with a loss of our feelings, right?" Rosie continued. "It is probably painful and sad – not to be in love anymore, but we should keep going. We should at least stay friends, not to destroy my uncle's cure project. He is my guardian angel. He is an amazing person and an absolute genius. He really deserves to get this Nobel Prize because he dedicated all his life to this invention of the cure and worked hard for it."

"Yes, I agree with that," Aaron nodded, "but also, Ashot suggested that we should have a date. Maybe we, as a new couple now, could fall in love again. What do you think?"

Rosie shrugged. "We could try... for my uncle only. Otherwise I have no interest. I don't need any love stories, I need an education. And about this pregnancy... it is not too late to have an abortion because I don't want to have a child."

"No!" Aaron stubbornly shook his head. "Never! You don't want this child... I wasn't sure if I wanted it at the beginning as well, but my love, my Rosalyn-Anastasia, convinced me that she wanted this child. And he should live because of that. It is our child – mine and hers."

"So, I am kind of a surrogate mother for you and your beloved Miss Illness whom you call Rosalyn-Anastasia? It's a big difficult job. I knew some girls before who worked as surrogates at a cost of thirty thousand dollars."

"Don't worry about that," Aaron smirked. "I will pay for your college and university of your choice. It will be much more than that."

"Yes?" She looked at him with interest. "Even for Harvard?"

"Yes, even for Harvard. I swear to God, I will," Aaron nodded. "Just if you swear to God as well that you will keep my child alive. It is the only thing that is left for me as a memory of my love. It is the biggest treasure for me. I don't have anything else as dear in my life."

"Come on," Rosie laughed. "Don't be so dramatic! You have your daughter, your mother, your work, your career – and you will have the Nobel Prize soon. Okay, let's make a deal. I think I can do that because I am feeling quite good. I don't have any side effects of the pregnancy as some other women do. My mom didn't have any problems, as I remember, while she was carrying my three brothers. I read once that this is hereditary for many women. I also didn't have any problems when I was pregnant with my first child from Ben. So, it looks like I will be okay and will be capable to work now on the applications for the colleges. Great!" She clapped her hands happily, exactly like his former Rosie did sometimes, Aaron noticed.

"Okay, do you want to go somewhere for dinner?" he asked then. "I think a decent date should end up with that, right?"

"A decent date should end up with sex," she giggled and glanced at him flirtatiously.

"Maybe," he smirked. "We will think about that when we come home."

Aaron purposely took her to the highest class restaurant *Art of the Table* which she resented before, to see what will happen now. Rosie looked around with admiration and got especially excited when she tried the food. The plate covered with flowers drawn by different multicolored sauces almost shocked her. "Wow!" she exclaimed. "It's fantastic! Did we come here before?"

"Yes, we did," Aaron answered sadly. It was extremely painful to realize the difference between the former Rosie, Love of His Life - and this new healthy wife of his.

"Oh, now I could understand why I married you," she laughed. "Not everyone could afford that, right?"

"Right. But you didn't marry me because of that. You didn't like it here before. It felt too luxurious for you. You said that you love me not because of that but in spite of that. We talked about Cinderella and about the pain of losing something special, what you gain as a miracle, and suddenly it's lost. It was a very deep spiritual conversation which I can fully appreciate only now, as all our spirituality is gone."

Rosie looked at him, slowly shaking her head. "Jeez, Aaron. It was my illness talking, again. Who could not like this quality of a restaurant? Really, only a severely mentally ill person."

"Listen," Aaron demanded strictly and angrily, "stop saying that, please. I don't want to hear anything disrespectful and rude about the sacred moments of my life with the woman I love...Yes, I still love her and I will love her forever. And you have to accept that if you want to be my friend at least for some time."

"It is rude and disrespectful of you as well," she objected, agitated, "while having dinner with me to talk about your love to another woman."

"This other woman was actually you!"

"It was not me. It was Miss Schizophrenia. And she is gone, she is dead. Forget about her. Or, at least not mention her when you should try to renew a relationship with me and to revive new feelings toward me."

"I don't think it's possible," he sadly shook his head.

"So, then you want us to be enemies? We must tolerate each other for the sake of the cure project, for my uncle's sake. We are still working together and we are going to the conference together. Remember that, Aaron. And, please, try to be nice. We need to be friends, maybe even friends with benefits until your child is born."

"And then what?"

"Then I give him to you and leave for Harvard. You will be a single father with a baby for the second time, and a man whose beloved wife, this time Miss Mental Illness, died. But it was your choice. I suggested an abortion."

Aaron gritted his teeth and kept silent. He really wanted to kill her now but still held himself in check. Never in a million years did he expect that the greatest love story of his life would turn into this.

When they returned home, he went silently into the third bedroom and closed the door. He needed to be alone.

CHAPTER 59

Aaron woke up in the middle of the night feeling someone's presence. Rosie was sitting on the edge of his bed and held her palm on his forehead.

"Sorry, Aaron," she whispered, noticing that he opened his eyes. "I shouldn't have told you what I said last night during that dinner. It was rude and insensitive of me. I was very angry that you were talking about your love that is gone. It hurt me a lot."

"Why?" he whispered back. "You don't love me anymore. You shouldn't care."

"Maybe I don't love you like crazy, with a mad passion as it was before, but I still like you as a friend. I know that you're a nice and kind person. And also, your little one... I feel pity for her to be raised without a mother. I understand that. I was raised without my mother as well. I was thinking... She will start school in September and see other kids come with moms and dads. It could be uneasy for her."

"So, you want to pretend to be her mother to make a show for people at her school?" he asked sarcastically. "Is it just that simple for you?"

"You're being impolite again, Aaron. Yes, I want to give it a try. I apologize for last night. If you could forgive me, I will do everything that is needed for our project, for my uncle, for your daughter and for our future child. I will even move in with you as your wife and will take care of the whole family. I promise."

"Hmm," he was surprised. "What changed your mind?"

"I was just thinking. Until recently, I loved you madly and I feel that I should respect those memories, and respect you, and myself as well. You did so much for me and how did I pay you back – with crudeness?"

"Well... what about throwing our child at me and leaving for Harvard?"

"We will think about that later, when our child is born. We still have about eight months to find out how to manage this. Maybe I could take some college here, while he is very young and postpone Harvard for a while, if I ever will be accepted there in the first place. It is a solvable problem, if we will stay friends. Let's promise not to hurt each other anymore. Okay?"

"Hmm," he made a wry face. "Should I trust you? I am not sure. I don't know... My family is too sacred for me. After our parting yesterday, I swore to myself that you will never see them or come to my house. But I still care a little bit about the new healthy Rosie, as you said, maybe just as a friend."

He turned and sat on the edge of the bed beside her, as he continued, "It sounded to me yesterday kind of disgusting to make this agreement as I am paying you with education for being a surrogate mother. It's awful! How could we even talk about something like that? You are my wife! Of course I will pay for your education if you decide to get it. There's no question about that. It's a normal way of family life. Don't you agree?"

"Sorry, Aaron," she murmured tenderly. "I am just as shocked and hurt by the change of my feelings as you are. All that I said was unfair and stupid. I wasted three years not because of you, but because Ben was killed, because my illness forced me to be in the *Youth Shelter* again, because I was returned to my mom's house afterwards and was busy with the household there. This is not related to you at all, but I kind of vented my anger on you. Now, as I calmed down, I feel ashamed of myself. And I am very-very sorry." With that Rosie shifted aside farther from him, laid on her back and put her head on his lap.

"That's my girl," he laughed. "You always did it before. Do you want me to kiss you?"

"Yes," she answered quietly. "And not as your 'holy oasis in a desert' which belongs to your dead love. Please kiss me as a woman now. As a new woman whom you just met and with whom you want to be friends... I mean friends with benefits."

What the hell, Aaron thought. *Fortunately I have experience of having sex with the woman I don't love.* And he just kissed her passionately, not saying a word.

In the morning Aaron went to exercise at the fitness club downstairs and later talked on Skype with his mother and Laurie from his car, as he usually did. When he returned to the condo, Rosie was at the breakfast table with Ashot and Liam. They all were in a good mood, talking and laughing.

"Good morning, Aaron. How are you feeling?" Ashot asked.

Aaron stopped by the door and shrugged, "Kind of strange. It feels like for a months I was watching a movie on a multicolored TV and then suddenly all the colors disappeared and it turned into so called black and white. Which is actually not really black and white, but mostly different shades of gray. I feel dull... Stupid... Empty..."

"But you still could finish watching your movie, right?

"If it is really interesting and worth the effort... I don't know. It's not easy for me to force myself..." he choked on his words, turned abruptly and went to his bedroom, closing the door.

"Jeez, what's his problem?" Rosie said irritably. "I just had sex with him. What else does he want? It looks like he is always ready to cry. It's disgusting for a man."

"Kiddo, don't be cynical," Ashot stopped her. "He is a very kind and sensitive person. To be cynical is not his style, his soul couldn't accept it. He loved you like no one else in the world never did and never will. To lose this love is a huge trauma for him. Especially because he had the same trauma already once before. Try to be more sensitive, please, and more polite with him. He deserves it."

"But, uncle," she objected, "you had a big tragedy and trauma in your life but you never cry."

"I am kind of hardy," Ashot smiled sadly. "To survive in the Soviet Union you should be hardy. A man like Aaron wouldn't last long there. In my former country I cried only once, while I was telling my story to the woman, Tamara, at the Moscow train station. I was pretty much choking on my tears and it was very difficult to talk. Here, in America, I had tears of happiness once as well, when I found the blue clay in the mountains."

"But, uncle, in Moscow you were thirty then and in pain," Rosie tried to justify her opinion.

"Kiddo," Liam interrupted, "Aaron is thirty and in pain. Don't you know that?"

"Okay, daddy," she turned to him. "But you never cry too."

Liam lifted his palms and chuckled. "No reason. I am absolutely happy now. However, when I was ill, before I met Ashot, I was crying a lot, believe me. And I was thirty- to thirty-five-years of age at that time."

"You mean, if Ashot left you now, you would cry?" Rosie asked with curiosity.

"I don't think I will cry," Liam giggled. "I would just die."

"Come on, it will never happen!" Ashot laughed as well. "Forget it, kiddo, and don't say stupid things. You're smart enough to be above that. Okay, now, guys, you do your things, but I have to take care of Aaron. He needs to talk for a while with the Clay Mask. Before we return to our business, I will make several sessions with him to clean his aura."

With all in agreement, Liam went to his den to edit more of his film. Rosie disappeared to her room, to study the book of driving rules for her driver's license exam, while Ashot knocked on Aaron's door and walked in.

Aaron was lying on his bed, face in the pillow, lost and gloomy. Ashot approached and sat on the edge of the bed beside him. "Son," he said, patting Aaron's shoulder. "Listen, please. I get it, it hurts. But we can't continue our work like this; you can't come to the conference and have your speech in this condition; you even shouldn't meet your family and show them this pain when they return home. To keep functioning productively, you need to be cured. Let's make several sessions with the Clay Mask before we continue to do other things. You know how the procedure works. It wouldn't be as complicated a process as it was with Rosie because we won't document anything and we won't film anything. It will be just between you, me and the Clay Mask."

Aaron lifted his face and looked at him surprised. "Do you think I am a schizophrenic as well?" he asked.

"Of course not. But you have anxiety and trauma, and obviously Post-Traumatic Stress Disorder after your first wife's murder. It was neglected for many years. And now, with one more emotional blow, it is getting much worse. As for me, I would like to move my research further and cure not only schizophrenia but many mental conditions with the Clay Mask. I am pretty sure it will work. You saw through the goggles how Rosie's aura cleansed and in my opinion it will be helpful for other illnesses besides schizophrenia.

"Also, for you as a doctor and scientist it will be beneficial to experience this process of cure not only from outside, as an observer, but from inside, as a patient, as well. You know that many scientists and researchers did experiments on themselves, first, to feel, to sense, to experience how it works. We need to do that, son. For you personally, and for others as well. You know that there are millions of sufferers from different mental illnesses. Why not to help you and many of them?"

"How could we do that?" Aaron asked, feeling convinced, however, an ironic smile started to appear on his face. "Who will carry me to bed after each session, as I carried Rosie?"

"We will do that in a very simple way as I did with my patients in Armenia. I'll bring into your room a small folding table and pail with the clay. You will sit on your bed and I will sit across from you at the other side of the table and make your Clay Mask. At the end of the session you will just fall on your side on the pillow and sleep until tomorrow. That's it. While you are sleeping, I will keep working on Rosie's materials for the conference. The next day we will do another session with you, and so on. I guess three or four will be enough. First, we will remove the trauma and grief of your father's death, then - of your first wife's death, then..."

"I think I need one more session – to eliminate memories of a very bad and hurtful relationship with a woman that I had during the last couple of years before I met Rosie," Aaron interrupted. "Would it be possible?"

"Of course, son. You can tell the Clay Mask anything you want to be removed from your soul. And at last, we will do a session, or maybe even two, about your love story with Rosie. It damaged your heart a lot and I am sure it damaged your aura no less. So, it needs to be cleaned up. What do you think about that suggestion?"

"I think... yes... thank you, uncle," Aaron answered thoughtfully. "I know that I won't be able to overcome these things by myself and move on. But I need to move on. I have to – for our project's sake and for my family's sake I need to be rational, reasonable, level headed and absolutely calm. I trust you with that, uncle. I trust you with my life and my future." And he sincerely hugged the old man.

CHAPTER 60

During the week in the middle of the day while Ashot was working on Aaron's cure with the Clay Mask, Liam and Rosie went to discover her foreign languages ability.

"We could probably go to different cultural centers in Seattle," Liam said to her one day, "and talk to people of many backgrounds who know their languages of birth. But I am sure that many of them, after years in America, are more adapted to English. And also, we don't know how literate they were in their language before. They may not be as good as someone who could properly appreciate your ability and your level. It should be a language professional. I know one place where we could check about fifty languages. Let's go there."

The place was a TV station – a learning channel of foreign languages. Liam knew that programs there were created with sophisticated modern technology and combined from lectures on TV and online communication classes with a teacher native to each language. To start, he called his friend, a producer from a news channel, Tami, and invited her for lunch. They met at a restaurant where he introduced Rosie to her as his daughter.

"Oh, I remember your charming daughter, Liam," she said. "A couple of weeks ago you brought her for an excursion to our station. I was extremely busy then, but I saw from a distance both of you walking with our guys. Nice to see you again, Rosie."

During lunch Liam explained that he would like to check Rosie's languages ability compering it to professional learning programs. Tami looked fascinated because she never knew anyone who was able to speak more than two-three languages. The possibility that Rosie might already know about eight of them was very unusual and really needed to be confirmed.

After lunch, they went together to the TV station. Tami found an assistant producer from the department of learning programs, Gary, and introduced her guests to him. Gary was intrigued as well and suggested that Rosie could, at first, listen to a one hour program of a language of her choice. It would give her a chance to see if she could understand what was being said and also, she could talk with the teacher on the screen. There were only two hours left before she and Liam should be at home to share their achievements of the day with Ashot. So, Rosie chose for now two languages – French and German.

It went well. She understood everything, could speak fluently and translate to and from English as a professional simultaneous interpreter. Liam made notes on his phone while she was doing that experiment. Then Liam and Rosie got reassurance from Gary that it will be possible for her to come every day and look at other language learning programs which were available at their studio.

So, these visits to the TV station became their daily routine and in one and a half weeks it was discovered that Rosie had the knowledge of twenty-five languages aside from English. They were: French, Spanish, Italian, Greek, Portuguese, German, Dutch, Sweden, Polish, Czech, Bulgarian, Hungarian, Russian, Ukrainian, Romanian, Armenian, Georgian, Tagalog (Philippine), Mandarin (China), Hindu (India), Japanese, Arabic, Farsi (Iran), Afghani and Urdu (Pakistan).

There were another twenty-five languages in the Learning channel programs catalog, but they were out of Rosie's reach. She didn't know them at all. Still, it was unbelievable and sensational. Gary ran around the TV station spreading the news of discovering a super special girl. Tami came right away and suggested that she will make a two minutes segment on the News about Rosie.

Liam called Ashot to discuss her proposition. They thought it through together and instructed Rosie not to say a word about her former mental illness, her former lost talents, her cure, Ashot's discovery - about practically anything that was supposed to go to the Psychiatry Scientific Conference in New York only, and shouldn't be disclosed publicly beforehand.

"You have to say, kiddo, that you decided to try some hypnosis sessions just for fun," Ashot explained to her very seriously, "and, after a couple of the sessions, you suddenly noticed that you began to understand and speak some languages that you never learned. You asked your daddy to help check your ability, and here you are. Be very cautious not to say anything else – not our relationship with you, not with Aaron, not your marriage, not your pregnancy. Nothing at all, kiddo. All the time, keep in mind that our project for the conference is more important than your five minutes of fame and fun."

"I know, uncle!" Rosie exclaimed in a crying voice. She was so shaken from excitement that she could barely talk normally. "I know everything. I love you so much. I will never betray your project, even involuntarily. I will be cautious with every word, I swear to God!"

Ashot and Liam were a little bit worried but they didn't want to prohibit Rosie to do that segment with Tami. It was time for their kiddo to get involved into real life, to start getting independent, to learn and to experience something new and unusual. There also was a chance to increase her possibility to get accepted to a good college, maybe to get a profession as a languages teacher, or something else of that sort.

They also were confident that she would do well on camera because she had a great deal of experience on stage with her poetry. Rosie didn't remember that fact but the experience itself was obviously there, in her head and in her heart. And they weren't wrong. The little segment interview went perfect.

Tami just introduced the young lady as Mrs. Rosie Dispenmore and then asked, if she was born in America – yes; how old is she – twenty; what foreign language she did learn at school – Spanish; did she learn other languages ever – no; how come this knowledge of twenty-five languages was discovered – after a hypnosis session which I did for fun; does she plan to continue her languages education in college – yes; does she want to become a language teacher in the future – yes. Simple and clear and at the same time - very vague. Many words were pronounced, but, practically, nothing was said at all.

Then Tami made her short summary and journalistic conclusion about the unbelievable abilities that were hiding in a human brain and sometimes are coming out unexpectedly, and that was it. Liam and Rosie thanked everybody in the studio and left. There wasn't any need for them to come again. They headed home where Ashot was waiting for them with a bouquet of roses for Rosie and a bottle of champagne on ice for all of them.

The only one who wasn't involved in this success story was Aaron who was peacefully sleeping after his last cure session with the Clay Mask. Rosie woke him up in the morning.

"Hey," she said, climbing under his cover and hugging him. "You have no idea, baby, I discovered that I know twenty-five languages. I can speak, understand absolutely everything and translate instantly like I am speaking my own language. I just don't know letters in some languages, like Chinese, Japanese, Hindu. Arabic, Urdu, Farsi but it's okay. I will go to college to learn letters, grammar and other linguistic details."

"Wow!" he breathed out and kissed her. "Ashot told you, and I told you – you will be great. Congratulations on the new talent!"

Aaron said that just to be polite. In reality the knowledge of the foreign languages didn't excite him at all. He didn't care much about this knowledge and didn't see anything spiritual in it, like it was in her poetry, in her seeing 3D time, knowing past, now and the future; like her doing the telekinesis or reading thoughts and talking telepathically – all her lost fantastic ability and talents. Those things were close to his heart, they attracted him to Rosie, they created his love; he felt them, he understood them. She was his girl, his love, his woman, his wife then.

Now... Languages... well... It was interesting, unusual but not inspiring and attractive. Zero... he felt nothing. Even with this new ability and knowledge, Rosie was still a perfect stranger to him.

His Clay Mask was still drying in Ashot's den. Aaron knew that it will take three to four days until he will break it, but he already was pretty much level headed and cold. His aura has changed. His soul has changed. He wasn't an extra sensitive, spiritual and intellectual person, disturbed and hurt by PTSD anymore. He was healthy, normal and a regular dude for whom to be 'friends with benefits' with a woman was good enough. He didn't need anything else from his new wife. Maybe it was a really healthy way of life? He didn't know and, actually, he really didn't care at all.

"Aaron," Rosie uttered slowly, pressing her whole body to him, "you know, darling, I came to get my benefit. I really deserve it because I had an exciting day. I got a small interview segment which will be on the 6 o'clock News on TV. Isn't it amazing? I am very happy. So, please, baby, I want you."

"Well," he agreed, smiling, "I am just waking up. Let's go to shower then, right?"

"Right!" she jumped from his bed and ran to the washroom.

It is still exactly the same as she acted before, Aaron noticed following her. He knew that until the cure with the Clay Mask he would already have tears because of these memories. Now, he just smiled. Probably his life really turned from constant tragedy into calmness and fun? Likely his nerves were in truth healed? Could it be in all probability that the new life had started for him and Rosie?

CHAPTER 61

Rosie's interview segment was aired, as Tami promised, on the six o'clock News next day, then repeated on the night News. And then, at another day – on the noon News. After that, although Ashot's team was watching the TV News daily trying to get a glimpse of it, it wasn't repeated anymore.

Now, all the news channels were buzzing about a different sensation, much more important for the United States – one of the most dangerous terrorists' leaders, Abu-Mirvan al-Shababi, was killed in Afghanistan.

The story revealed that a bus with twelve American troopers was kidnapped by a Taliban group and to rescue them would be almost an impossible mission. American General, George Simon, interviewed by the TV correspondent in Kabul said that he can't even order his troops to go to this rescue mission because the chance that it will be successful was probably less than 10 percent. When he asked for volunteers, one of his Privates suggested that he will try to do this alone. While not revealing any details of the operation, the General said that the soldier succeeded not only to return the bus with his comrades, but also to kill Abu-Mirvan al-Shababi who was hiding at the location of the kidnapped bus.

Each day the media disclosed more details of the story. It was already known that the soldier himself was severely wounded during the operation and transported to the Landstuhl Regional Medical Center – the largest American Military Hospital in Germany. He was expected to survive but the healing process will require several surgeries.

Of course, compared to the significance of these events, a young lady speaking some languages wasn't equally important. However, she was still unusual and got more attention from the media.

A few days later, Tami called Liam and asked him to bring Rosie to the studio again because someone wants to meet her. At the moment of this call, Liam and Rosie were in the DMV office and she was sitting at a computer doing her driving rules test. So, Liam gave her time to finish the test and when she was done and told that she is qualified now for her driving Learner's Permit, he broke the news from Tami.

"Oh, my gosh!" Rosie exclaimed happily. "They want another interview. I am getting famous, am I?"

"Not so fast, kiddo," Liam cooled her enthusiasm. "Let's go there right now and find out what they really want."

However, Rosie was almost right. Tami informed Liam that the host of the popular TV show, Johnny Holiday, invited the extra-ordinary young lady to be a guest on his daily evening appearance. His show was always held with a live audience, live music and customarily contained interviews of two very different, sometimes opposite, guests.

At first, Rosie agreed to be on the Holiday's show and Liam supported her, but when they came home and discussed the idea with Ashot, he had some doubts.

The problem was that Johnny Holiday prepared each of his segments very seriously, making a thorough research about the topics. He obviously would invite some people of different nationalities from his staff to test Rosie's ability to speak with them. It would be okay and she could do that easily. But with him the vague mention of some hypnosis session, as a burst of her talent, would not work. He would insist on meeting the hypnotist in person and ask him how often such or any similar occurrences happen in his practice and experience.

"You can go with me, uncle, and say that you are my hypnotist," Rosie begged in a crying voice. "Please, uncle."

"Officially, I am not the one," Ashot objected. "You know that, kiddo. And Mr. Holiday is not a person who will do sloppy work. He will check everything in detail. According to my documentation I am qualified as a psychiatric nurse only and that's it."

"Okay then, maybe we can tell him that the hypnotist refuses to be on the show?" Rosie suggested.

"It will sound suspicious to the host and he may not do this segment of yours."

"Guys," Liam interrupted, "let's wait for kiddo's meeting with the producers of the show. Maybe Johnny will not ask about the hypnotist at all. Maybe it would be convincing enough for him that kiddo is not cheating because we were working on this language research in their TV studio which is a trustworthy resource for him."

With that it was decided that Rosie will work with the producers of the Johnny Holiday Evening Show and see what happens. If he cancels for some reason, so be it. But, maybe it will be okay.

While Rosie went to the studio, for the prep-interview with the Holiday Show producers, she was told that she will be the second guest on the show. Her segment will not be that long as the performance of the music band will take some time from her part of the show. The first part will be about today's topical hero-soldier and it will be much longer because several people will be interviewed. It will be his family, friends and neighbors in person, all from Seattle, and through a poly-cam from Afghanistan – his army comrades and his General.

"I am so happy! It's amazing!" Rosie excitedly told her family during their usual news sharing time at dinner. "This popular segment about the soldier will make the whole show strikingly famous and I will be accidentally involved in this and I will be famous too!"

"Why are you so eager to become famous?" Aaron laughed. "It's just a short term of popularity that means nothing. A week later another event happens and this one will be forgotten."

"I like it," Rosie shrugged. "It's fun!" All the men understood that it was a subconscious leftover of her stage performances at the Poetry Club, but didn't say anything, just exchanged significant looks.

"Aaron is right, kiddo," Ashot said, shaking his head disapprovingly. "Don't think about fame or popularity. Those are shallow things. Better to think deeper – what will you say, if Mr. Holiday asks you what you did for three years after you graduated from high school. There shouldn't be anything about your illness, about Ben's murder, about your year spent at the *Youth Shelter,* even about your life with your mother's family. All of these could open a big can of worms. In this case he may want to interview your mother, or someone from the shelter, or Dr. Evelyn Hertz, or police about Ben's case which was very well known on TV a few years ago. We really don't need all of these now."

"I think you could say that you got married very early and spent three years after high school as a housewife," Aaron suggested. "Especially because you are known to Tami with my last name as Mrs. Rosie Dispenmore. It will answer the question – where did you work or study after school? It sounds quite neutral and says practically nothing. This may be a good way to hide the things which need to be hidden until the conference, right, uncle?"

"Good idea," Ashot nodded. "It could work because you were known as Rosa Garcia while you were working - teaching poetry class in your high school, or as Rosalyn Vivano when you were editing poems for magazines and doing your concert performances. It will prevent the host from connecting two and two, I hope."

"And nobody will check the date on your marriage certificate, I am sure," Liam supported his thought. "This way you will kind of separate yourself from your very tense and unusual real life story and present a calm, quiet and regular life of a simple family woman. It is quite ordinary and not really interesting and will not force more questions, except for your language ability. It should work."

Finally, this decision was accepted at the family council.

During the time when Rosie was preparing for the show and went every day to the TV station with Liam, Ashot and Aaron finished their work on the materials of her cure and made them ready for the evaluation at the General Psychiatry Hospital. It would be their next step. Rosie couldn't get her driver's license until she was evaluated as a mentally healthy person.

Not wasting any time, every late evening Liam took her to the empty parking lot of the nearest Walmart and taught her to drive his car. She was a pretty good student and it was visible that she won't need to take classes at the official driving school to pass the exam.

Meanwhile, Aaron's Clay Mask was dry enough to be broken and one morning Aaron and Ashot carried it up to the roof. Ashot put on the goggles and took their 4D camera.

"I will take some pictures," he explained. "I want you to see them later to compare with Rosie's pictures of the final moment of the cure. For now, I had noticed the same nice white thin cloud of your aura enveloping your body, exactly like it was with Rosie. It would be interesting to observe, if it will go or stay. Sadly I didn't have this kind of technology with Liam, and obviously not in Armenia."

"I am just a bit concerned," Aaron said. "I could potentially lose my feelings toward my mother and my daughter, couldn't I?"

"No," Ashot shook his head. "Don't worry about that. Those feelings are in different layers of the aura. Look, Rosie didn't lose her daughterly love to me or Liam, although at the first moment she even didn't recognize him. But she remembered him soon. I guess - this white cloud is patient's feeling for the sexual partner only."

"Yeah," Aaron smirked, "I have almost nothing to lose. It is mostly gone anyway. What the hell!"

"Then, don't worry. Go ahead, son."

Aaron lifted the Clay Mask and repeated what Rosie had said before, "Sorry, Mister Clay Mask that I should hurt you. Thank you for your help. Bye!" He smashed the statue on the hard cement helicopter pad, jumped back from the pile of fragments and closed his eyes. A few minutes passed until he heard Ashot saying, "Okay, the black particles are flown up. It finished. We are done, son. Congratulations!"

Aaron opened his eyes and was surprised that the world – the sky and the sun - was now looking much clearer and brighter. The huge feeling of eternal happiness was filling his heart. It was not bursting, funny, crazy happiness; it was serene, and quiet, and endless like it would be in paradise, in heaven where your soul will finally find the rest – all clean, clear, calm and holy.

"Thank you, uncle," Aaron said, approaching Ashot and hugging him. "Never in my life have I felt so good and peaceful - blissful emotionally."

"Well," Ashot laughed, patting his back. He freed himself from the big hug, made a sign of cross at Aaron and at himself and kissed his golden cross on the chain saying, "Thank you, God! Now, I think you will be able to work more productively, son. We still have a huge job ahead to open your new business – your own Psychiatry Clinic; then to write your speech for the conference, and so on. It's an enormous amount of work! I am very happy that you are keen on it and ready for it now, Aaron.

"When your past traumatic experiences are not bothering you, you are a good man and good scientist. I was always sure about that but I was trying not to show you my appreciation of your knowledge and talent. I wanted to make you a better person without any arrogance and egotism, capable of being selfless and thinking about others before yourself. And here we are! I respect you very much, son, and I am sure you deserve big success in life and I am very happy to help you get it."

CHAPTER 62

A few minutes before the beginning of the Johnny Holiday Show, Rosie and Liam entered the back room of the studio to wait until she was invited on stage. They were surprised to see that the room was full of people and all of them were African-Americans. There were two senior men, two young men and a young lady of Rosie's age, and a woman with three children. Rosie didn't recognize them, but Liam obviously did because he uttered to himself quietly, "Oh, gosh!"

To Rosie's even bigger surprise, the kids ran to her and hugged her, screaming, "Rosalyn! Hi, Rosalyn!" She squatted and hugged them back, not wanting to hurt their feelings by showing that she doesn't remember them. She knew that they must be from her past.

Ashot explained to her that these awkward situations will probably happen many times - she might meet people from her previous life and not know who they are. But, with the passage of time, these inconvenient moments will happen less frequently. The old acquaintances will gradually forget her and new relationships will emerge in her present everyday life.

While Rosie was hugging the kids, the woman, who was obviously their mother, approached and hugged her as well. "Hi, Rosalyn," she said. "They didn't tell me that they invited you too."

Liam clearly remembered that the woman and kids were family of Rosie's boyfriend, Ben, because he drove her to their house and picked her up from there a few days in a row before the Kiki session of her cure. She went there to see kids and to walk in a park with them and it was where she talked Hindu with the other mother. At the first instance, Liam thought that the presence of these people here was kind of related to her language ability.

But then the young lady almost jumped at Rosie, yelling agitated, "Stop hugging her, Keysha! I don't understand why you are doing that. She is the reason that one of your boys was killed and another one almost killed. She shouldn't be here. I was Alex's girlfriend. And I still am! He loves me. I have been talking to him on Skype everyday. You, Rosalyn, shouldn't be invited to this show. You are married to this older man!" she angrily pointed at Liam.

"He is my father," Rosie answered, confused.

"As I remember, you didn't have a father, Rosalyn," Keysha noted, surprised as well.

"I was adopted," Rosie tried to explain. Luckily for her one of the producers, attracted by the noise and screams entered the room.

"Hey, guys, calm down," the producer said. "Stop shouting! Be nice, quiet and polite now, please. It's your time. You're going to the stage. Follow me."

The group started moving to the exit immediately.

The angry young lady went with the two youngsters who were evidently her friends; then Keysha followed holding her two girls by the hands and one of the older men walked, carrying Keysha's little boy in his arms. Finally, the last old man headed toward the door. He stopped for a few seconds while passing Rosie and said quietly, "Sorry for Leticia's behavior, Rosalyn. You look confused. You probably don't remember me – I am your math teacher from high school, Barry Goodwin. I know your and Ben's story."

"Hi, Mr. Goodwin," Rosie smiled suddenly with relief. "Yes, now I remember you. Thank you for the explanation."

"You stay here, Rosie, until I call you." the producer said and left with the participants of the first segment of the show.

Rosie and Liam sat in armchairs in front of a big screen on the wall on which they could see the stage where the host, Johnny Holiday, made his introduction of the first segment of his show.

"What just happened, daddy?" Rosie asked, looking at Liam helplessly.

"Well," he took a deep breath. "Clearly, the shit hit the fan. The worst case scenario! I guess that... ta-duh... this hero-soldier is Alex, the twin brother of your Ben."

"Oh," Rosie breathed out, "how do you know if Ben had a brother?"

"You told us during the Rubi session."

"Who is Rubi?"

"It was one of your ill personalities. She dominated you mostly at the time when you lived with Ben's family for a year."

"Oh, I messed up. I remember some facts only, that I had a boyfriend, that his name was Ben and that he was killed by the police. Nothing else. And the woman with kids...?"

"She is the mother of the twins, Ben and Alex. By the way, you wrote a poem about them, **Your Twin.** It is in your book. Before the third session of your cure, I drove you two days in a row to their house. You wanted to see the kids and play with them. When I dropped you there, I saw the mother and her children from my car," Liam explained. "The family obviously loves you. But those teens here... I am not so sure... they must be your classmates from high school, or their neighbors. And the older men... one of them was your teacher, as he said. Another one is probably one of their relatives."

"Why was Leticia so rude and angry at me?"

"I would guess that she is jealous about these boys, Ben and Alex. But you should not think about that, kiddo. It is not important for us now. Do you remember why we are here? To announce to the world your language abilities in hope that it will help to start your career and success in your new life. That's it. Nothing else matters. Now, let's be quiet and watch the first segment."

"Okay," Rosie said obediently, moved closer to Liam and put her head on his shoulder. "I am not confident and a bit scared. Could you hug me, please, daddy?"

"Well," Liam laughed and put his arm around her shoulders. "Is it better now?"

"Yes," she nodded.

The interviews that Johnny Holiday did were regular and quite simple. He asked the family and friends, as was usual in these sorts of cases, what could they say about Private Alex Brown. How Alex was as a son, as a friend, as a boyfriend, as a student, as a neighbor? How was he recognized in their community, at the church, at his work at McDonald's? Was he especially brave or strong, or something that could make people think beforehand that he would be a hero?

Everyone said excellent things, of course, as would be expected in similar situations. Johnny Holiday obviously did his homework and already knew things that nobody mentioned. He learned that Alex was not the best student, changed girls like socks, sometimes missed his shifts at McDonald's, fought a lot with the local gang, smoked weed, refused to go to church, even cheated on his own twin-brother with his girlfriend. All of these details were not important right now – nobody is perfect, anyway, so the host of the show purposely avoided them.

What counted today was Alex's bravery and readiness to sacrifice himself for the higher goal, for his comrades, for his country. Those were qualities of a real hero and this was exactly what Johnny Holiday stressed in his conclusion after these interviews with Alex's loved ones.

He also announced that the Ministry of Defense provided a special airplane to deliver the family of the hero to Germany, and a hotel for them to stay there for two weeks to visit with him at the hospital.

Then he added as well that it is already known that Private Alex Brown will get the highest award for military men who distinguished themselves by acts of valor – The Medal of Honor that was usually handed in person by the President of the United States and followed by a higher military ranking.

That was met with a huge squall of approving applause from the audience.

Then the band played Alex's favorite song as Leticia requested, noting that they had danced it at their prom where she and Alex attended as a couple.

At last, the conversation came to the military part. General Simon was talking from Kabul through the poly-cam and explained that he can't say anything about the operation itself because the topic is top secret. But he said that Alex was quite a regular soldier and he absolutely didn't expect him to volunteer for such a dangerous and important mission.

"But... well... in extreme situations sometimes the extreme qualities appear in people," the General concluded. "I am very proud of Private Alex Brown and sincerely happy that he succeeded in this operation."

The last guy on the poly-cam was Alex's closest army comrade, Tyler, who subconsciously wanted to be involved in Alex's heroic act and show to everybody that he influenced it. He wished to feel important and because of that he revealed what he shouldn't probably say but it was too late to change anything.

"Alex wasn't that brave, or crazy, to go on this mission," Tyler said. "It's actually my fault that he did. I showed him on YouTube the film of the wedding of the girl he had a deadly crush on. She was marrying an older man. Alex didn't show much emotions usually because he was kind of a reserved person. So, he didn't say anything to me. He just sat holding his head with his hands for a while. But later that evening he said 'I'll volunteer for this mission that was announced today, Ty. I have nothing to do in this life anymore, but I am a coward. I will never find the nerve to kill myself.'"

"You are lying!" Leticia screamed jumping up from her chair. "I never married anybody! I'm waiting for him!"

"I am sure it was another girl," Tyler smirked, confused. "Kind of... I am sorry... a... white one. I didn't want to hurt you but that is what really happened. Why should I lie?"

"Okay, okay, thank you, Tyler," the host interrupted and disconnected the poly-cam right away. "Of course, my friends, many things are related in life and, as a result, unexpected outcomes could happen. Alex was obviously too modest and humble to say about himself that he is a coward. He said this clearly at the heat of the moment, privately to his friend. We all know that love can move mountains. If in this case it did, we don't know for sure yet. But it was a great end to the story anyway. The twelve American soldiers were saved. One of the worst world's terrorists was annihilated. And the young man who greatly represented his country became our hero and got our pride, respect and admiration.

"Thank you so much to everyone who was willing to come here to talk about Alex Brown and let the country know more about our really brave hero."

Then the band started playing *God Bless America.* The audience stood up and sang together with the musicians. While Alex's family and friends were leaving the stage and were shown by the producer to the main door along the aisle of the hall, the audience greeted them, waved and gave them high-fives. It was such a touching and beautiful ending of the first segment of the show. Many have tears in their eyes, including Rosie and Liam watching from the back room.

"Okay, kiddo," Liam sniffled, wiping his eyes. "You see, sometimes I can be close to tears too," and he laughed. It was a big relief for him to notice that Rosie absolutely didn't connect the story told by Tyler to herself and her relationship with Alex. She clearly did not remember that, which was exactly what Ashot wanted.

"Now you are going ahead by yourself," Liam continued. "I will wait here for you. Do you remember what to say or not to say?"

"Yes," she nodded and pecked him on the cheek. "Thank you, daddy."

"Your turn, Rosie," the producer said, appearing at the door. "Are you ready?"

"Yes, I am," she stood up and went with the producer, confidently holding her head up and Liam couldn't help feel really proud of his special daughter.

CHAPTER 63

Ashot and Aaron watched the Holiday's show at home and both realized right away what happened in the first segment.

"Damn!" Aaron uttered slowly. "Quite an unwanted coincidence!"

"Yes," Ashot shook his head. "Sadly, most of the coincidences in life are usually unlucky and unwanted".

"This guy must have had a serious crush on her, really."

"Yes," Ashot laughed. "She is that kind of a girl. You know that better than anyone in the world."

"But I loved her as my Rosalyn! When she was a special miraculous poetess and a creature from some kind of another world."

"Exactly," Ashot agreed, "and he did too, three years ago. He is just keeping those memories in his heart, maybe forever. You, however, are freed from them with the help of the Clay Mask. If he ever returns home, he will be a good candidate for the cure with the Clay Mask in your new clinic, especially because we will need to start the business going, and the military will obviously pay for the cure of his PTSD."

"Jeez," Aaron shrugged. "You are only concerned about the business..."

"What else should I be concerned about? I warned you that this could happen. I protected your wife from unwanted memories. I am sure that she didn't connect the story to herself in any way. If you want to be sure, let's call Liam and ask if he noticed any reaction from her."

"No need to bother him," Aaron waved his hand. "We will ask him when they return home. Let's watch now. Rosie is already on stage..."

She appeared on the TV screen and Aaron was surprised how much her behavior was similar to her performances at the Poetry Club. She walked out holding herself confident, proud but at the same time humble. She looked elegant in her small black dress with a string of white pearls around her neck and pearl studs in her ears. The black Greek sandals on her feet, laced to her knees, and her short haircut made her visage stunning.

Rosie knew that she looked great. She realized and appreciated her own value as Anastasia before and she obviously felt it now even though Anastasia wasn't in her anymore. But her inner feeling of herself didn't change after the cure. Aaron got a bit attracted to her again, especially because her outfit was exactly the one that she wore with him at their first dinner at the Space Needle a couple of months ago when he loved her madly. Now, she was a new, different woman but definitely attractive, sexy and worthy of his attention.

"Wow!" he said. "She is on her turf there again..."

Johnny Holiday introduced her as Mrs. Rosie Dispenmore and announced that this segment of the show will be very different from the previous one, but at some point similar. It will confirm for the audience what outstanding and special young people America has and what a great future they could expect for the country with this amazing generation.

He started from the same simple questions that were asked at Tami's segment of the News. Then he suggested to Rosie to tell the story how she realized that she has the unusual abilities of knowing foreign languages that she never learned.

"I guess it happened accidentally," she answered calmly and clearly. "I just wanted to remember some of my family history, but all my ancestors have already passed away. So I had no one to ask. I decided to do a couple of hypnosis sessions with the hope to re-new my childhood memories, to remember my grandparents and so on. Very simple. A few days later my husband took me for an excursion to La Conner and there some strange things began to happen."

Rosie told the story about her first languages experiences in La Conner, then - about her session with her Greek mother-in-law on Skype, then - about the conversation in Hindu with an East Indian woman in a park while their kids were playing.

"When I spoke those languages I didn't have a feeling that I was translating something in my mind. Not at all. I didn't even notice that at first because it was very natural, organic; a person started talking to me in another language and I understood them. I answered them naturally, not thinking about pronunciation of the words, or grammar, just conveying my thoughts. It was the same feeling as I have now, answering you in English – easily, smoothly, like a fish in water. So we decided to check what's going on. My adoptive father brought me to this station into the Department of the Learning Programs and we compared my abilities to the professional foreign language classes and we discovered that I know twenty-five languages on top of English."

This statement was met by a big and long applause from the audience.

"Would you mind speaking now with some of my staff members, who are Americans from different national backgrounds and still have their birth languages, Mrs. Dispenmore?" the host suggested.

"No problem. Always happy to prove myself," Rosie laughed.

The three producers appeared on the stage and Johnny Holiday introduced them. "This is Lee Chan who speaks Chinese, this is Alfredo Verdi who is from an Italian family and this is our beautiful Zdenka Milova. She immigrated some years ago from the Czech Republic. They all will tell you their stories in their birth language and you interpret them, please, into English for our audience."

After they all shook their hands with Rosie, smiling at each other, the performance started and went absolutely flawless. The producers were visibly amazed by Rosie's translations and confirmed that it was done right.

Then the host asked to do a reverse exercise – Rosie would tell her story about visiting La Conner with her husband and discovering her language ability, that she already told him in English, but to each of the producers in their native languages – Mandarin, Italian and Czech. They would comment on the quality of her language in this narrative. She did it easily, without any effort or tense and all three producers confirmed that her language was proper, natural, easygoing and even without any English accent – exactly as if it was her native language at birth. They were astonished and shocked by these skills.

"Okay," Johnny Holiday said finally. "It's fantastic! I am bowing my head in front of you, young lady. I barely could speak some words in French that I had learned at school." That statement made the audience laugh and shout the confirmations of the same level of many of them, as well. "Now, as we end our show today, I would like to repeat the song **God Bless America,**" Johnny continued, "and you, Rosie, please sing it with our band together but in a language of the audience's choice. Suggestions, you, guys, please?"

The public started yelling different languages and the host counted them, "Spanish, Russian, Hindu, German, Portuguese, Polish, Arabic... Okay, guys, that's enough. Let me write these proposals and make a small lottery." An assistant brought him little pieces of paper, a pen and a bowl and he jotted down the languages, placed the papers into the bowl and shook it. "Now, please, take one from here, Rosie. It will determine which language you will use singing **God Bless America.**"

She smiled, gracefully approached the bowl he held, took one piece of the paper from it and handed it to him. "Polish!" he read aloud, and the big part of the audience excitedly screamed Hurray! and applauded.

Rosie came closer to the band and said a bit confusingly in her microphone, "I am sorry, I am not a good singer. I apologize for the quality of my singing, but I hope that you forgive me for that because my voice is not the point now. The point is how I will translate the song into Polish. I am ready," she smiled at the musicians and they began to play.

Rosie sang quietly but clearly because the mic really helped to increase her weak voice and the band tried not to play loud to give the audience a chance to hear her singing. But, really, the task was to sing in Polish, and it was done well because the Polish part of the audience stoop up and joined her singing, excitedly waving their arms high. This way the second segment of the show ended as triumphantly and solemnly as the first one.

"This Holiday guy is a good host. He knows how to do his job," Ashot laughed at the TV in their condo's living room.

"Yeah, that's why he is so popular," Aaron agreed.

"This coincidence in timing with the soldier's story turned out very lucky for us, actually," Ashot concluded. "It took away Holiday's attention from the scientific side of Rosie's brain abilities, from a discussion with a hypnotist, which we expected he would do. He turned Rosie's talent to the topic of the greatness of the young people in America and the patriotic endings of the segments. It was beautiful, touching, and didn't raise any unwanted questions. Well done. I am very glad about this outcome."

When Rosie and Liam returned home, she was as happy as a child, running around the suite, jumping, clapping her hands, screaming, hugging and kissing them all in turn. "I love you, guys," she exclaimed all the time. "It was so good, so nice to be there. I was a bit scared and uneasy at first, while in the waiting room, but later, as I came on stage, it felt so much at home and I calmed down absolutely. Talking with Johnny was as comfortable as I am talking with you, guys, now."

"So, now you would like to become a TV host?" Aaron asked with a tingle of sarcasm.

"No. I noticed today, that Johnny turned the spotlights on his guests more than on himself. I don't want to be in his position. I would like to have a spotlight on me."

"Gosh!" Aaron laughed. "You have skyrocketing self-esteem and big goals! But how? You don't have a talent or interest to be an actress and you have no voice for a singer. You are not doing any sports or dances, or anything like arts or music in which you potentially could become a star..."

"I don't know, yet, but I am sure I will figure that out," Rosie answered confidently.

"And well..." Ashot approvingly smiled at her, "there is a wise Russian proverb – only a bad soldier doesn't want to become a General."

CHAPTER 64

Ashot and Aaron hired a lawyer to prepare all documentation required for opening a new private Psychiatry Clinic in Aaron's name. The lawyer was also supposed to find a Real Estate agent for them who will help to purchase a building for the clinic at a good location and, if needed, to hire a construction company to make renovations for this commercial enterprise.

They decided to buy the property as three owners – Aaron, Ashot and Liam – that made the deal financially easier for each of them. To own the building sounded more stable, than just to rent a room for the clinic in some strip mall. Aaron would be the main doctor and owner of the business; Ashot would be his assistant, nurse and co-owner of the clinic. Rosie would be the secretary and receptionist. Liam would be the third co-owner and an investor. The chosen name of the business was *Clay Mask*. **The Psychiatry Clinic of Dr. Aaron Dispenmore.**

After passing this part of the work from their shoulders to the lawyer's, Aaron and Ashot spent the next week going to appointments at the General Psychiatric Hospital with Rosie to process her official evaluation by the board of the certified psychiatrists. The documentation proving that she was now mentally healthy was accomplished after all the tests were finished, and it was added to Aaron's folders with materials for the New York conference.

It was done. The cure was invented. The patient was cured and all the evidence of that was combined, organized and copies were ready to be submitted to the board of judges in New York. Only a Cover Letter that will be transformed later into Aaron's speech at the conference wasn't done yet, and Aaron and Ashot were still working on it.

All those documents were also provided to the Department of Homeland Security and Rosie was removed from the *No Fly List* and got her permission to travel on the airplane to New York in December for the conference, or anytime, anywhere she wanted and needed. In addition, with the documents verifying her perfect mental health condition, she passed her driving test and got her driver's license.

Right away, the men bought Rosie a car. At first, they couldn't decide who should pay for it – her parents or her husband. But after long discussions the decision was finally found – they shared the cost of the car three ways, the same as the expenses to buy the building for the clinic. The car was a used one because rookie drivers were always expected to make a lot of scratches and bumper to bumper damages on it during the first year of their experience. But still, it was drivable, and in a pretty good condition.

Finally, Rosie's dream came true - she became an independent person, ready to make her applications to colleges and to drive by herself to different interviews and appointments.

Now she also made her first appointment to an obstetrician to confirm her pregnancy and to check on the condition of the baby. Everything was proven to be good and developing properly, however, noticing that she came alone the doctor asked her to bring her husband next time.

"He knows everything," Rosie laughed. "He already had a wife and a baby before, and he is a doctor himself. He is extremely busy now, so I don't want to bother him with my problems." The obstetrician was surprised with this answer, guessing that she could be pregnant from a married man, but ethically didn't ask anything else to remain professional.

But Rosie craved to be self-directed, to do things by herself. For so long she was guarded and protected by Ashot, Liam and Aaron. She was thankful for their help, care and love, but now was her time to fly free from the nest. She couldn't move out yet because she still didn't have a job or acceptance to a college with a student loan, and a room in a dorm, but she tried to explore her freedom as much as she could.

Aaron was confused and unsure about their future together feeling her acute desire for freedom. He wasn't certain where his relationship with Rosie was now. In a week his mother and daughter would return home from Florida and Laurie would be getting ready for school – kindergarten. Should he ask Rosie to move in with him and his family or not? Would she become a good step-mother for Laurie, as she recently promised?

Being preoccupied with the work they both were doing separately, Aaron and Rosie drifted further and futher apart from each other with every single day. Practically, they had nothing in common anymore even what was required to be 'friends with benefits'. She wasn't interested in his work and business at all. Although she knew that she should go to the conference in New York with him and Ashot to be presented as a cured patient and to help them to win a nomination for the Nobel Prize. But mostly she intended to do that just to pay her debt to them for her cure; just to be an honest, thankful and kind person.

Aaron wasn't interested in her TV shows, interviews, languages, and college applications. He tolerated all of these as respect for their past love and – the same as she – just to be an honest, thankful and kind person. Even sexually, they became estranged from each other because both of them were very spiritual and deeply emotional, and not really interested in sex without love.

With Helen, Aaron had this experience. But he hated Helen and was careless, sometimes even wild and rude with her. In contrast to that, he still liked Rosie as a person, cherished the memories of their love and was nice and tender with her, although his soul was now empty. And this emptiness pushed him away.

One day Aaron finally found the nerve to talk to her about that problem. "I don't want to bring you home and introduce you to Laurie," he said. "She really fell in love with you as the girl we met on the street, as the girl with seven barbies, as the girl who wrote the poem **Little Birdie.** Now you are not the one. How could I explain that to her? And what is your role now in my home? A wife? I doubt it. For that we should sleep together, and at least show some love and affection in public. I assume it would be very awkward for both of us. And a big wedding with all my extended family...? Jeez! It sounds absurd now."

"I don't know what to say," Rosie took a deep breath. "We were in love, we were crazy, we lived in a dream, we were in a hurry. Uncle warned us not to rush until my cure would be finished, but we didn't listen. We were blind from passion and both acted childish. You insisted on marrying at City Hall. I insisted on a church wedding. I agree that we don't need to hurt Laurie with our mistakes. It would be inhuman to harm the child.

"I said to you, while apologizing, at the heat of the moment, that I will move in with you," she continued, "and I will be a mother and even stay with our baby for maybe a year. But it was, again, too stupid and too fast for me to say that. I don't want to be a wife and a mother now. I want to have a career. I promised to postpone it for our baby. But now I am thinking it was wrong. My career after high school was already postponed for three years. I don't want to waste anymore time. You have a lot of experience to be a single father. If you insist so much on having the baby, I guess, it would be okay if I leave him with you and your mom. What do you think, Aaron? Where are we now?"

"Where are we now?" he repeated her question sadly, with a deep sigh. "Maybe, let's give it a small try. When my mother and Laurie returned and settled at home, I will invite you and your parents for dinner in our house and introduce you all as my working team and co-owners in my new business – the Clay Mask Clinic. And we will see how the situation will develop from there.

Maybe you will change your mind and decide to move in with us. But there will be no obligations because for now I won't tell my family that you are my wife. They don't need to know that, yet, because everything is so uncertain and hanging in the air."

"Okay," Rosie agreed nonchalantly. "I am so sorry, Aaron," and she raised her tiptoes, hugged his neck and apologetically kissed his cheek. "Partially I regret that we lost our love. It was fantastically beautiful. Sincerely, I was super happy with you. But to date again, to re-new it... I really have no time for that now. I need to move on..."

Aaron knew that if not for his cure with the Clay Mask, he would already have tears in his eyes, but now he just shrugged indifferently.

The one last thing not accomplished yet for the Psychiatry Scientific Conference was to find out how many other applications were sent to New York and contact those psychiatrists, exchanging information with them. It was required by the rules of the conference. Each participant should know the others and their cure suggestions and determine how his program is different from theirs. This determination should be included into an introductory speech of each candidate.

While Liam was free now from driving Rosie, Ashot asked him to do some research on the Internet to find the information about this topic. And Aaron called Helen.

"Damn, Arie," she exclaimed. "Where have you been? You told me that you would call in a couple of weeks, but now a couple of months have passed. All my research is done, and my boy is ready for the last step - the surgery to remove his tumor which is scheduled in two days. Then he will be completely cured. What do you want now?"

"Did you make an application for the conference?" he asked.

"Of course, I did. You?"

"Yes, I did too. I would like to come with my assistant to your lab, so we could exchange our ideas of the cure. You are still at the same office at the university in our Psychiatry Department, right?

Sorry, I can't invite you here because my clinic is not open yet, we're in the process to start the business."

"Okay," Helen laughed. "Who is the assistant? This teenage wife of yours?"

"No. It's a man."

"A man? Oh, then I am interested." While they were arranging the meeting, Aaron smirked imagining how let down she would be to see his senior business partner.

During that time, Liam discovered that only five applications were submitted from the whole country: two from Seattle (Aaron and Helen), one from Boston, one from Los Angeles and one from Oklahoma City. Ashot and Aaron contacted three other doctors on Skype and mutually exchanged with them the plans of the cure. Their ideas of the cure were different and none of their patients had accomplished a cure program, yet. They were on the final stage, same as Helen, but not done completely.

One of the doctors was working on the cure by changing the electrical balance in the patient's brain; another one invested his whole attention into the psychological and spiritual aspect like hypnosis and meditations; and the last one invented his own, a very new and unusual combination of chemical ingredients in the previously well-known medications. All of them were shaking their heads and smirking when Aaron told them that he invented an organic cure with the help of a Clay Mask. They thought it was not serious and absolutely laughable.

"It's okay," Ashot said calmly. "You don't have to worry about that, son. Let them laugh. It's good because nobody is jealous. The envy between creative people and scientists often could be huge, even deadly. But I know for sure that none of their ways will work. I tried all of them in Armenia. You will see – not one of them will present a cured patient at the end. The only engrossing theory is the one of your colleague, Dr. Helen Harrison. I guess, a tumor could be a possible cause of the illness... potentially. It would be interesting to know the results of her work."

When Aaron and Ashot arrived at Helen's office, she was disappointed that Aaron's assistant, introduced as a psychiatry nurse

Thomas Spencer, was old and not handsome at all. However, she could recognize that he was knowledgeable and a bit bossy toward Aaron. And that surprised her. They discussed the MRI's of her boy-patient and some of her research papers which she presented to them. In return, Aaron told about his invention of the possibilities of organic clay to clean the human auras and cure the illness. In contrast to the other doctors, Helen didn't laugh but seemed very intrigued.

Then, they all drove to the hospital where the boy was already admitted to be prepared for the coming surgery. Helen introduced Aaron and Ashot to the surgeon who would operate on the boy. They discussed the potential success and possible consequences of the procedure. Luckily for them the patient was sedated now and sleeping quietly. Otherwise, he was very angry, wild and not manageable, as the surgeon explained.

Ashot took out from his briefcase the two pairs of the goggles and suggested he and Aaron look at the boy's aura through them.

"Do you see the black, very crooked spots in the aura at the side of his head?" he asked Aaron. "This is obviously where the tumor is located. If it were me, before I do a surgery, I would try to clean the aura with the Clay Mask and do another MRI after that – to see if the tumor would dissolve by itself. But, again, we don't know for sure yet if it is the cause of schizophrenia in this case."

"I am sure I know," Helen answered confidently. "I worked on this research for months. By the way, can I try your goggles? It is an unusual device. I never saw anything like that."

Aaron passed his goggles to her.

"Wow!" she exclaimed, looking at her patient attentively. "Yes, I see what you mean, Mr. Spencer, about the damaged part of the aura in connection to the tumor. The picture of the damage is absolutely clear. You know, the boy was hit once on his head very badly, and after that his mental illness started. In my opinion, it is connected."

"Well," Ashot shrugged, "he is your patient. Good luck, Dr. Harrison. I sincerely wish this poor child becomes healthy. If for some reason this doesn't happen, Dr. Dispenmore and I would be happy to work with him in our clinic using the method of the cure invented by Dr. Dispenmore. Just keep it in mind because I feel such a pity for that child."

"The child will be perfect," Helen laughed, returning the goggles to Aaron. "Where did you get this device, Dr. Dispenmore?"

"We have its inventor on our team," Aaron answered. "He also invented a 4D camera to take pictures of the aura's particles which we are submitting in our materials for the conference."

"Good for you," Helen smiled politely. She stayed with her patient while Aaron and Ashot left and returned to their car.

Ashot started to drive out from the hospital's parking lot, when Aaron got the call from Helen on his cell. She didn't know that he put her on speaker, and said angrily, "Arie... you damn idiot! Do you think you could win at the conference? Only over my dead body! Remember that, you bastard!"

Aaron disconnected the call instantly. "Wow!" Ashot noted, sadly shaking his head. "During one of your cure sessions with the Clay Mask you talked about a woman who murdered your wife and with whom you had an affair. Now I can connect two and two. Why didn't you warn me, son, that it is her? Big mistake!"

CHAPTER 65

A few days later, on a nice summer afternoon, Rosie was in her room getting ready to go out. She wanted to deliver her applications at two more colleges. She preferred to do this in person than online, if they were in Seattle or in a nearby area. Ashot and Aaron just finished their work on the last thing for the conference – Aaron's speech. They were sitting on the patio and discussing with Liam where better to go for dinner, when Liam's phone rang.

"Sorry, guys," he said, glancing at the display. "I need to answer that... Hi Tami, what's up?"

The News producer talked fast and Aaron who was sitting beside Liam couldn't hear her words. He just realized that she sounded anxious and worried, and winked to Ashot, meaning – *another interview at the TV station for your kiddo.* Ashot smiled contently and shrugged, "Probably."

Liam was listening attentively, just reacting from time to time, "Oh... oh my gosh... Who?... Seriously?... Oh, my gosh... I'm so sorry... Jeez... Oh... When? ... In one hour? Are you kidding me? Okay, let me check if she is available."

At that moment Rosie appeared at the door wearing jeans and t-shirt, with a bag over her shoulder, looking like a student and ready to go out. She heard his last words and shook her head. "I am not available, I am leaving, guys," she said.

"Okay," Liam waved at her to shut up. "Yes, of course, she is available. You know, she is already driving by herself, but now I will drive her there. What is the exact address? Okay, Tami, inform them not to worry, please. We will be there as soon as we can, in less than one hour, I hope."

"Dad!" Rosie exclaimed indignantly. "I am busy. You shouldn't make decisions for me! I am a grown up..."

"Kiddo, it's an emergency," Liam interrupted her, which usually wasn't his style, but obviously he was too excited about something exceptional. "You got a job, kiddo. Our Senator, Stephanie Mane, called Johnny Holiday's show and asked about you. She must've seen you in that remarkable performance. Somehow his producers can't find your phone number and they called Tami.

"In one hour the delegation of the eight countries from Eastern Europe will arrive for a conference and dinner with the Senator. None of them speaks English, but they all speak German or French. Her personal German and French translator got into a car accident on his way there and he is in a hospital now. The Senator is panicking because the conference is extremely politically important and she didn't want to cancel it."

"Yeeah!" Rosie screamed like a child and jumped to hug Liam. "What countries, daddy? Which countries?"

"If I remember properly – Poland, Czech, Russia, Hungary, Romania, Bulgaria, Ukraine, and Germany. It's kind of the former communist block that is now free from these regimes and wanted to tighten their connections with the USA. That's why it is so important."

"Yeeah!" Rosie kept screaming and dancing around the room. "I don't even need the middle languages. I know all them. I would be in the spotlight there! I am so excited, guys! Love you!"

"Then run and get dressed into something appropriate for the occasion. It's a government dinner, for God's sake! We are leaving right away," Liam ordered fast. "I will not go in there, of course. I will wait in the car. But to get to the Government building in Olympia in one hour - you will need a very experienced driver. So, chop-chop, kiddo."

Ashot grabbed a couple of sandwiches and a bottle of water from the refrigerator and put them into a bag.

"Take this, babe," he said. "It will be your dinner in the car tonight." And they all laughed.

In a few minutes Rosie appeared from her room wearing a gray English suit with a light blue blouse and black flats on her feet. The diamond studs in her ears and engagement diamond ring beside the wedding band on her hand were the only jewelry. Aaron couldn't help notice once more how great her sense of style was. Nothing better could have been chosen for the official government meeting. Liam was already at the door and they both ran out momentarily.

"Wow! That was a surprise," Ashot uttered, shaking his head, still in disbelief. "She is obviously moving ahead. I am getting proud of my work. Don't you agree, son?"

"Yes, you did a great job for her," Aaron nodded thoughtfully, biting his lips.

"So, we are left alone for dinner today. I guess we should go out and celebrate our final completion of your speech and full readiness for the conference," the old man suggested.

"I am kind of not hungry," Aaron said sadly. "You know, Ashot, I have the feeling that I am not needed here anymore. Our work is done. For my wife evidently I don't exist. My mom and daughter are returning home after tomorrow, and I need to move back into my house and prepare everything to meet them properly.

"We will proceed to establish the clinic with you," he continued, "but for that I will come from my home to meet you there. And we will communicate on the phone all the time. Also, I would like to introduce all of you to my family because I feel that we became pretty close during this time together - like you and Liam are my family as well, my two uncles and friends. Next weekend I will organize a dinner party in my house for all of us - as you said, correctly, to celebrate our final accomplishments. I guess it will be the last time I will see Rosie before we all go to New York in December. And that would be it. I will return to my work at the university after that."

"Well," Ashot sighed deeply. "I see, son, that the Clay Mask has helped you somewhat, but not completely. It works 100 percent successfully for schizophrenia, but for your PTSD you are still having flashes of some sadness in your soul. I am sorry about that. When we start work in our clinic we need to consider that. And maybe we could develop the program of the cure for the other mental conditions a bit differently than for schizophrenia. For now, Aaron, you have to understand that it will pass with time. I promise you that. And I will always pray for you. Thank you for everything, son."

With that they hugged each other as a farewell and then Aaron loaded his bag with clothes into his car. He also took the box with Rosie's books, manuscripts and her old computer – all memorable stuff from her poetry life. It was the treasure that he wanted to save forever.

"Say bye from me to Liam, please," he said to Ashot, who went downstairs to the parking lot to see him off. "Sorry that I can't accompany you for dinner tonight. I just really need to be alone for a while."

Aaron didn't drive home right away. He headed downtown and stopped n the parking lot behind the Greenwich Competition Hall. From there he walked to the park on the top of the hill and sat on the bench where he was three times with Rosie. The twilight was already approaching and the multicolored lights of the city began to turn on, one by one. Looking at them he quietly whispered the poem **Stars Under My Feet** which he knew Rosie created here. It was a holy place for him, a divine view of the eternal beauty of the imaginable stars shining below, and the sacred memory of their perished love.

They kissed here, they hugged here, they cried together here. She slept here sitting on his lap, caressing his hair on the back of his head. She held her lips on his forehead, comforting him, promising to kiss away his tears, if they ever came. Now there were no tears anymore - the Clay Mask really strengthened his nerves.

Aaron just felt so lost and empty inside that at the moment he desired only to die, nothing else. Then he remembered as Ashot told him, *I wanted to make you a better person without any arrogance and egotism, capable of being selfless and thinking about others before yourself. And here we are!* Ashot was right, he changed him. The Clay Mask did it. Aaron knew that he, in truth, was now a better person capable of thinking about others first.

It would be possible to drive to Diablo Lake and jump into the abyss there. Or it would be possible right here to jump down the hill to the rocky edge of the ocean gulf. Even if it eased his pain instantly, Aaron knew that he had no right to do that. He should think about his mother and Laurie – how they will feel returning home to find him dead? He should think about Ashot – how the old scientist would feel without him losing the possibility to get the Nobel Prize which he deserved for the years of his hard work? He should think about his future baby whom he insisted on giving a life – how will he grow up without his single father? Those were people he loved and cared about and he can't betray them simply by suddenly leaving them.

For Aaron it felt strange at the moment, that he even thought about this hero-soldier, Alex – the guy who obviously loved Rosie so much that he was ready to die knowing that she got married and was lost to him. He went on this suicide-mission and he did it for others and he survived. He was overcoming his pain now – actually both: physical pain from his wounds and pain in heart from his lost love.

Aaron even smirked wryly, thinking, maybe it was worth to writing a letter to this Alex guy, to tell him that he will divorce Rosie as soon as the child is born, so she will be free and available. Maybe this information will inspire him to heal faster. Then he thought – it would be kind of childish and stupid. He shouldn't send inspiration to this guy, he should take inspiration from him.

I should be a hero as well, Aaron thought. *Hell with the pain! I will I go on my mission – to live for Laurie, for mom, for my unborn yet baby-son, for Ashot, for my future patients whom I will cure with the Clay Mask and give a healthy life. Ashot is right, everything will pass.*

Aaron knew that he would never come again into this area of the city. If he ever needs to drive through it, he will avoid it as much as possible by changing his route. It was his farewell with his disappeared love, a heartbreaking and difficult farewell.

He still felt the taste of Rosie's lips on his lips, sensed the warmth of her body on his palms, and remembered the touch of her skin on his fingers. He will never forget these feelings because they were the best that he experienced in his life. Nothing was more worship-like, beautiful and pleasureble.

Aaron thought what he would say professionally to a patient who would suffer from the death of his beloved one. It would be a clear standard statement from the book – don't suffer that she is gone; celebrate the happiness that she was with you; cherish your beautiful moments together! And it was exactly what he was doing now – in his heart he celebrated their life together, just two short unbelievable months of fantastic life. With all their ups and downs, with all the tragic moments, blood and tears, it still was the highest level of happiness imaginable. Such a level which not everyone had a chance to experience during their whole life. But he had. He was blessed with it and he was really thankful for that treasure given to him from above. He murmured a short sincere grace for that to God or to Fate, he wasn't sure to whom exactly, just to a Higher Universal Power.

Now my farewell is done, he thought after that. *I just needed to be free from these memories and from this completely strange career-minded woman who Rosie became. So, I am moving on.*

He took off his wedding band from his ring finger and balanced it in his palm for a while, thinking about throwing it into shrubs that covered the steep slope toward the water below. Then, he changed his mind and put the ring into his pocket. It should not be wasted. It should be buried in a grave along with his love.

This final conclusion calmed Aaron down. Completely collected, he drove home, brought the box with Rosie's books upstairs to his bedroom and put it into his closet. Then he took her book from under his pillow, opened the page where the dry pink petunia was, placed the wedding band beside it and added the book into the box. It was done, finished, ended, cooked, burned, annihilated, disappeared...

Now, he was supposed to wait for what his little Laurie would decide. The voice of an innocent child will serve as a voice of God or voice of Fate for him. Laurie's decision will determine what he will do with these things in the box later.

CHAPTER 66

Being left alone for the evening, Ashot felt a bit lonely. During his life with Liam he used to be alone many times, when his husband traveled with his crew for filming in the other parts of the country, or even sometimes overseas. It could be days, weeks, or months. But at that time he was busy working, deciphering his Armenian microfilms, translating them to English, or just sleeping after his night work shifts.

However, during the last few months their condo was very crowded. An active life brewed there. Something was always happening, and now it felt strangely quiet. Ashot was mutually sad parting with Aaron – he really cared about this bright and sensitive young man whom he loved dearly as a newfound son.

Ashot knew that for himself everything would be okay, even if Rosie, as well, would leave their home soon. He will work with Aaron in their new clinic. On weekdays, Aaron will be mostly occupied with his work at the university and would be available for the clinic just a couple of evenings and also a few hours on Saturdays. But Ashot will be there full time. It will be, practically, his own private clinic, although it will be registered in Aaron's name.

They will hire a receptionist for their clinic because it was really doubtful that Rosie will work there, as they originally planned. She obviously will be somewhere on the path with those languages business. Anyway, for Ashot the future seemed to be very interesting and full of serious work, but just tonight it still felt somewhat lonely.

Ashot cooked dinner for himself, then watched the TV News. There was a very short segment, maybe only thirty seconds, about the delegation's arrival from Europe. It showed a big group of people walking up to the main entrance of the Government building and then Senator Stephanie Mane greeting them at a dias stand. Here Ashot caught a glimpse of Rosie, standing to the side, a bit behind the Senator, with a mic in her hand, but that was it. He knew that the segment would be much longer, maybe even a couple of minutes, at eleven p.m. News, and he really looked forward to watching it. At least, seeing this shortcut, Ashot was glad that Liam and Rosie arrived at the capital Olympia safely, although evidently it was a really high speed race to get there on time.

Then he got a text from Liam that they will be home very late because, after the conference and dinner, the Senator decided to entertain her guests and ordered an excursion to the Space Needle, to show them the fantastic view of Seattle at night, and Rosie has to be there as well.

Kiddo will be happy, Ashot thought. *She probably will tell them her poem **Stars Under My Feet,** if she still remembers it and translate it to all their languages. It would be fun for the guests.*

He sat, relaxing, into an armchair in the living room and thought how different Rosie was now after his cure, compared to the days when he just met her.

It was the year 2012, a couple months after his wedding with Liam, when Ashot started working at the shelter for dangerous mentally ill youth. Rosie grabbed his attention right away because unlike the other children, she was in extremely bad shape. She couldn't sleep and she couldn't eat - the strong nerve spasms held her stomach squeezed all the time. She lost a huge amount of weight and looked like a skeleton. She also was dirty, with matted hair and refused to shower and take care about her hygiene. And she just came from the hospital after a miscarriage and the surgery that stitched her stomach knife wounds – her suicide attempts. Her condition was critical.

Ashot felt pity for that child, especially knowing the story of Ben's murder from the TV News, as everyone in the city knew. He started working on her with hypnosis, at evenings, after the other staff were gone and he and Rosie were the only two people who didn't sleep at nights. First, he returned her abilities to sleep properly, calmly, long hours, and easily fell asleep. Then he managed her self-care and hygiene, then – her eating, so she started gaining weight to the proper level. Then he worked on her PTSD after the murder scene where she was involved watching her fatally unlucky boyfriend die.

In about a month the girl changed dramatically although her seven personalities were still in her brain and her schizophrenia diagnosis was in place and active. But these things Ashot didn't touch then, knowing that it would be a long term project. At first he just fixed what was extreme and necessary for physical survival. But in his mind, he selected the girl for the future cure with the Clay Mask because he felt in her something very special.

Talking everyday for hours they got close and became good friends. They developed full trust in each other and told each other their life stories in detail. Everything Rosie confessed during the cure sessions with the Clay Mask later, Ashot already knew for three years.

Now, looking at the result of his work on Rosie, Ashot felt very proud of her, but also of himself. She was healthy, beautiful, shining with the new talent, brave, confident and moved fast to become a self-sufficient successful woman. He won this battle with schizophrenia and returned the girl to a normal life.

But the most important attraction for him in this child was that he sensed somehow that she was his daughter, re-incarnated little Annush, whom he saw last time in 1985 when she just turned four. He even comprehended sometimes: Rosie was born in 1995, Annush would be at that time already fourteen. Could it be possible that Annush died and her soul reincarnated into Rosie, as the

Hindu religion believes? This question that he asked himself stayed unanswered for a long time.

Now he thought about Annush again. If it was possible to find his cured patients in Armenia, maybe would it be possible to find her as well? With that question in his mind, Ashot called Patrick on Skype because in Yerevan it was already morning. It was their regular time to converse occasionally.

As Ashot voiced his request and promised to send $1,000 for expenses that would be needed, Patrick said, "Well... Annush could be thirty-four now, so she could be already married and possibly changed her last name. But I can try to check the Department of Citizen's Conditions and see what is there about registered marriages or deaths. Of course, it would be a bit illegal without a Power of Attorney, but you know, Dr. Petrosian, money can open any door. Hopefully, I can give you some information when we talk next time."

Rosie and Liam returned home pretty late, and she was excited beyond belief.

"It was great, uncle! It was fantastic!" she exclaimed, happily jumping around and hugging Ashot. "It was a success! I was translating the Senator's speech for everybody in French and then in German paragraph by paragraph. But when we had dinner I was sitting with the guests and changed seats, talking to them in turns in their languages. They were surprised.

"Stephanie, I mean Senator, hinted that it would be good if I make an impression on them that most Americans are as smart, talented and educated as I am. It was fun! And actually, Stephanie is a pretty nice woman. She is quite humble and friendly. She even hugged me when I was leaving and requested that I come tomorrow again. She wants to make more excursions." In her exhilaration Rosie was jabbering non-stop. "And... you wouldn't believe, uncle! They paid me! Her assistant came and handed me a check... guess for how much? A thousand dollars! Can you imagine? For an amazing evening of fun I've got a grant! It's unbelievable! You take it, uncle. Put it in your bank. I kind of owe you a lot, and also I don't have a bank account yet, anyway."

"Okay, we will open a bank account for you as soon as possible," Ashot smiled, taking her check and shaking his head in disbelief while looking at it.

"Yeah, you will need an account, for sure," Liam confirmed. "I know at some movie festivals simultaneous translators earn about $20,000 per week. This job requires a very high level of language education, even if they only know one or two foreign languages. You're so lucky, kiddo - without any education you get twenty-five of them. It's a real miracle! Ashot would probably say 'from God' but I think that this is a secret of an unopened part of the human brain, right, babe?" he winked at his husband and laughed.

"Yes," Ashot agreed, "it is what Aaron and his university team are working on in their lab, trying to find out what is hidden there. But we found it at home, without using special technique or special equipment."

"Come on! You have special equipment!" Liam grinned. "My goggles and my 4D camera!"

"Yes, I do," Ashot teased him back, "but you invented it only after I opened your hidden part of the brain. Otherwise, you still would be playing piano in our bar."

"Okay, thank you, babe. I appreciate it," Liam laughed and kissed Ashot's cheek.

"Stephanie asked if I have some ideas where to bring our guests," Rosie continued smiling at their teasing exchange, "and I gave her the whole list: *Glass Museum* in Tacoma, *Boeing Flight* Museum, Fort Casey Historical Park on Whidbey Island, a ride on the boat across Diablo Lake, promenade at La Conner. We could also go to the beaches on Washington Lake, and to restaurants, like *Art of Table* for example. Lynden Fair finished long ago, but another Fair in Puyallup is coming pretty soon."

"How do you know all these places?" Ashot asked purposely, testing her.

"Why not? I was born here."

"No offense, kiddo, but from when you were born, you only saw the home of your poor grandparents as an abused child, the *Youth Shelter* as a prisoner and your mom's household as a maid,"

Ashot objected. "All the sightly places you mentioned, you learned thanks to Aaron. He took you there while you were dating. He wanted to show you the beautiful sides of life. He opened the world for you."

"So, what?" She stopped, confused. "Why does it matter? What do you want me to do?"

"Go to his room and tell your husband about your success, kiddo," Liam suggested. "Share it with him."

"Actually, Aaron left," Ashot said, "and asked me to say bye to you, darling, but did not even mention Rosie. It looks to me, kiddo, like your relationship with him is completely toasted?"

"I don't know," she shrugged. "He should move back home. His mom and daughter are returning soon. Why are you worrying about that, uncle?"

"Because now, when you are raising up and doing good, I don't want you to become arrogant and ungraceful toward him, even if you don't love him anymore. You tamed him, you forced him to fall in love with you purposely giving him your book. And, remember the *Little Prince* by Saint-Exupery the famous quote: 'You become responsible, forever, for those you tamed'."

"I don't know. I didn't read this book."

"Then go and read it. It can be easily found on the Internet. I want you not just to be a better person by your health and success, I want you to be a better person by your heart and soul as well. You were sensitive and compassionate while you were ill, but I probably accidentally removed something very tender from your aura and over-cleaned it. Now we need to fix this little mistake and add a few corrections to your new healthy personality - kindness and sympathy. Believe me, this book could do that."

"Well," Rosie sighed, "I could read for a while, I guess. Stephanie asked me to come about noon tomorrow. I could sleep in a bit in the morning."

Then she approached Ashot and hugged him. "Don't be upset with me, uncle, when I am so happy and excited about my achievements. I don't want to feel guilty about Aaron. It wasn't my fault that my love was gone. I didn't want it to happen. It was a side effect of my cure because it is just experimental. You should work on it more, so this doesn't happen with your future patients."

"Of course, I will," Ashot answered, patting her back. "But Aaron will work with me. He will always be there and I want you to be nice and friendly with him. Please, don't hurt him, more that he is already hurt. Now, kiddo, go and read this book. Good night."

CHAPTER 67

When Aaron met his mother and daughter at the airport, they were looking so exuberant that it was difficult to recognize them. They both were well-tanned to a caramel level, with shiny white hair because Laurie's blond curls faded in the sun and became almost as white as Beth's. Plus, Laurie grew up about four inches and even lost her slight leftover baby fat, looking like a real school girl now.

Seeing Aaron, she shrieked happily, "Daddy!", ran to him and jumped into his arms, hugging his neck and pressing herself to his chest. He held her on one arm and hugged Beth with the other one, and kissed them both, feeling happy, content and, deep inside, some kind of protected and safe. Now his beloved family was finally with him.

At home, Laurie ran upstairs to check her bedroom and unpack her barbie, Tacoma, and many other 'treasures', such as seashells and dried out crabs in plastic containers. It was a huge surprise for her to find Rosie's envelope with five dollars and a letter from the fairy.

"Wow! Daddy, did you see that?" she yelled running downstairs, jumping down two steps at the time, waving the envelope. "A fairy brought it to me!"

"No, I didn't see that," Aaron answered, smiling. "She probably came at night, while I was sleeping. Fairies are usually flying in the darkness when only the moon and stars are shining."

Beth pursed her lips and glanced at Aaron suspiciously. She thought exactly, as Rosie predicted, that Aaron did this letter from the fairy himself as a welcome home surprise for his daughter.

Their first days at home were busy settling and organizing their life the way it was before. Laurie's bicycle and puppy were left behind in Florida as presents for her little cousins whom she spent such a great time with and became best friends. So, now Aaron took her shopping for a new bicycle and some stuff that was required for school. Also they went to the ASPCA to adopt a kitten. Aaron explained to Laurie that Seattle is not Miami, there could be a lot of rain, cold, even snow in winter and to walk a puppy could be difficult. A kitten in their situation would be much easier to manage at home and she agreed, still remembering her old cat that she loved dearly.

Aaron ordered a catering dinner to be delivered from a Greek restaurant for the coming Saturday. "I would like to make a small party to welcome you home, mom," he said to Beth when they were sitting in the living room after Laurie was already sleeping. "I want to introduce my working team to you, so you know them, know what I am working on and with whom. They are very remarkable people. Now this couple of married gay-men became my good friends. We made a scientific discovery together, we cured a patient successfully and we will go to the Psychiatry Scientific Conference in New York to try to win a nomination for the Nobel Prize."

"It's amazing, Arie," Beth said. "I am so happy for you, son. I always knew that you are talented and smart, but to find a great team is extremely important for success. You can't do anything alone. Your dad, as pilot, treasured having a good crew. I, as well, usually had a good staff in my dressmaking and tailoring establishment when I owned it.

"But there were some problems with an old man as I remember. You even wanted to run away to Florida from him. Then, you told me, it was fixed..."

"Yes, it was, mom. More than that, he is like an uncle to me now and we are opening a private clinic together as business partners. I trust him completely."

"Good for you, Arie. I am proud of you that you were capable of managing the conflict properly. And how about the woman you liked? Was she his daughter, as I remember...? The one who spoke to me in Greek? You hinted that it could be something very serious..."

"Sorry, mom," Aaron took a deep breath, "but it is not happening. I don't want to say anything now. Let's have this party first. After you see all of them, I would like to hear your opinion, and then, probably, I will tell you the whole story."

During this week before the party many things were accomplished by Aaron's team – all contracts were signed, the building for the clinic was purchased and the renovation of it was started, the business was officially registered, insured and bonded, and the license was issued. All of these required Aaron's attendance at meetings with Ashot, Liam, lawyer, real estate agent, insurance agent and construction company owner.

At that time Rosie was not around but Aaron never asked where she was – and he sincerely didn't care.

In spite of being busy, he found the time every evening to go for walks with Laurie, however, they never went to the road that passed the *Youth Shelter* where they met Rosie. Aaron told Laurie that it would be more fun to ride her bike at another place, and they drove to the *Olympic Sculpture Park* that had a lot of comfortable trails for the young rider.

Mostly Laurie rode her bike and Aaron walked behind or was sitting on a bench. But sometimes they locked the bike and walked together because Laurie still collected her 'treasures' for her barbies' soups while Aaron was thinking about the conference in New York, or about his new clinic. Also, they were playing ball on the lawn, or tag, or Aaron lifted the girl on his shoulders and ran with her, or taught her a bit of karate that he still remembered from classes he took as a teenager.

He and Beth also continued their tradition – in turns putting Laurie to bed and reading her books or telling stories. Once she asked, "Daddy, did you ever meet that girl again, the one we saw off to the bus during our walk? The girl who had seven barbies and told me a poem about a little birdie?"

Aaron dreaded to hear this question, although he expected it and prepared the answer beforehand. "You know, sweetie," he said, "let's not talk about that now. Let's wait until the weekend when we will have a few guests in our house. And later we will talk with you about that. Okay?"

"Why?" Laurie wondered.

"Because you probably will see someone then, and that will be a surprise for you."

"Will she come?" his little daughter almost jumped on her bed.

"I am not sure. We will see. Please, just be patient. Okay?"

"Okay," she agreed with a deep sigh and settled back on her pillow. "I'll be patient. I promise, daddy."

On Saturday, when the guests arrived, it was a trying moment. While Aaron opened the door for them, Beth and Laurie stood in a hallway in anticipation to greet the visitors. Ashot entered first, holding a bouquet of roses which he handed to Beth, shaking her hand and introducing himself. Behind him Rosie and Liam entered side by side.

"Yeah!" Laurie shrieked, ran to Rosie and hugged her legs. "It's you! It's you!" she exclaimed, laughing happily. Rosie squatted in front of the girl hugging her too.

"Good afternoon, little one," she said smiling. "It's good to see you again. How is your Tacoma doing? Still remember me?"

Laurie looked attentively at Rosie's face and moved aside from her, not answering. Then the girl stepped back toward Aaron, pressed herself to his side and hugged his legs, hiding behind him, confused. There were a few awkward and tense seconds, until Beth fixed the situation, approaching Rosie and shaking her hand.

"It's nice to see you in person, my dear," she said in Greek. "You look even more beautiful in real life."

"Thank you, Mrs. Dispenmore. Same here," Rosie answered politely in Greek as well.

"Did you have any other chances to speak Greek after our conversation on Skype?"

"Greek? No," Rosie smiled while continuing in Greek, "but I was using the other nine or ten languages from twenty-five that I know. I am working as a personal translator for our Senator Stephanie Mane now."

"Wow!" Beth exclaimed in Greek. "Arie obviously did a great job during his experiments to make you learn so many languages. It's such a rare talent! Unbelievable! Good for you, my dear." Then she turned to Ashot and Liam and said now in English, "Nice to meet you finally, gentlemen. Welcome to our home. I had heard a lot from Arie how great his team is."

Ashot and Rosie followed Beth to the living room and settled on the couch with her. Liam gave a bottle of champagne to Aaron and said, winking, "Kiddo is our designated driver today, so we could relax a bit. Do you mind putting it on ice, partner?" And he patted Aaron on his shoulder.

Then Liam squatted in front of Laurie. "Hello, young lady," he said, extending his hand to her. "I am Grandpa Liam, and you are Laurie, as I've heard. Right?"

"Right," the girl answered and shook his hand to Aaron's surprise, not being scared or confused at all.

"I've got something for you," Liam continued and handed her a flat box. "Have you ever played chess?"

"No," she shook her head.

"It's a nice game, very intellectual and interesting. I started playing chess when I was five. Are you five already?"

"I am five and a half and I am going to school!" Laurie exclaimed indignantly.

"My apology. I didn't know that," Liam smiled. "But if you are already five and a half, you are definitely capable of playing chess. Do you want to try?"

"Yes," Laurie agreed, taking the box. "Thank you, Grandpa Liam."

She walked to the coffee table, gesturing for Liam to follow.

"Okay," Liam turned to Aaron, "what is the agenda of the host? Could we play now, or dinner first?"

"Dinner is ready," Aaron answered, nodding toward a long table on which the caterers placed several big steel bowls with dome-shaped lids and little candles burning under each bowl to keep it hot. "But we could wait for fifteen minutes, maybe, to get used to each other a bit first."

"So, fifteen minutes it is," Liam clapped his hands and went to the coffee table to help Laurie to open the box of chess.

While he unfolded the board and placed the figures on it, Laurie ran to Aaron who was putting the champagne bottle into the freezer. She pulled his pants. "Daddy, daddy," she forced him to bow down and whispered to his ear, "Who is this lady?"

"I thought you recognized her," Aaron answered. "She is this girl we walked with a couple months ago to the bus stop, the girl who told you about her barbies and taught you a poem *Little Birdie.*"

"No, she is not, "Laurie shook her head. "She looks like that girl, except for her haircut, but it is not her."

"Okay," Aaron squatted and hugged his daughter, surprised how sensitive she was to feel the difference in Rosie before and now. "Okay, I was joking, sweetie. She is not that girl, of course. She is her twin-sister. Her name is Rosie. Our girl that you and I loved was Rosalyn-Anastasia. You got it? Just twin-sister, that's it."

"Yes," Lairie nodded and ran to Liam who already settled the board of chess ready to play. But before he started to explain to her about the chess pieces and the way they should move, she ran back to Aaron and whispered once more, "I don't like this twin-sister, daddy. Where is our Rosalyn-Anastasia?"

"I will tell you about that tonight," Aaron promised in a whisper as well, petting her head. "Go, sweetie, play for a while with Grandpa Liam. He is waiting for you."

CHAPTER 68

Dinner was organized in a buffet style. Everyone was supposed to fill their plates and then sit at the table in the dining room. Laurie sat beside Liam and explained to him all she knew from her grandma about the Greek dishes. She was so cute in her efforts to attract Liam's attention that it made everybody smile. Beth commented a bit on her culinary knowledge, but mostly was involved in discussion with Ashot about different approaches of science and religion on human brain development. Aaron and Rosie were the only people who kept silent.

After dinner and before dessert, Laurie pulled Liam outside to the patio where she had brought all her twelve barbies. She introduced them all to him by name, then showed him how she usually cooks her soups from ingredients which she collected during her evening walks with her father. Then, Laurie brought her kitten that was quietly sleeping in her room on her bed and gave him to Liam to play for a while. After that, she pulled Liam to the swings and they swung in turns, and they also swung her barbies in groups, and swung the kitten. Finally, she suggested playing tag. Liam was a little tired from all these activities, but it was visible that he enjoyed the child's company. He and Laurie laughed non-stop and looked very happy.

Ashot and Beth moved to the patio as well and settled on the armchairs continuing an active conversation – now about the difference of political regimes in America and Armenia during the time when Ashot was born and raised there. Mostly it was an obvious and well-known topic but Ashot, as a live witness, could add some insights which Beth would be interested in knowing about.

Aaron went to the kitchen to serve ice cream for everyone. He passed Rosie who was sitting alone on the couch in the living room. Seeing him, she stood up and came closer. "Do you want a hand?" she asked.

"Probably," he shrugged. "Six bowls don't fit on one tray. If you could take the second tray, it would be faster." Not saying anything she took another tray, put three bowls on it and moved to him, so he could fill them with scoops of ice cream. Then she started decorating the filled bowls with cut strawberries and chocolate chips. While they worked together it was possible to think that they were still friends, but only they could feel the tension that floated in the air.

Then Aaron and Rosie carried the trays outside, handed a bowl to each person and sat on the patio steps side by side with their bowls as well. Beth observed them, trying to understand their relationship. She found Rosie very likable, especially for her perfect Greek language. She would be glad if her son would have a relationship with that woman. But she sensed that something was amiss...

After everybody was finished with the ice cream, Aaron collected the bowls and trays, carried them inside to the kitchen, loaded the dishwasher and sat on the couch in the living room. It was easier for him to be alone than to see Rosie. The whole week he was feeling quite good doing business with the men while she wasn't around. He organized this party only for a final test that needed to be done – the test with Laurie - and it already cleared everything for him completely.

Then Rosie suddenly returned to the living room from the patio. Everybody outside noticed her leaving but pretended that they hadn't, wishing to give the young couple a chance to talk in private.

"Hey," Rosie said quietly, approaching Aaron, "how are you coping? Last week I didn't see you for a while."

"Mutually," he shrugged. "I am okay. I am not asking how you are. I know that you are perfect."

"Actually, yes," she smiled. "You know, I am working full time now. The Senator hired me as her personal translator, at least until her previous guy returns from his sick leave."

"So, no college is needed," he commented sarcastically. "No Harvard?"

"Not for now. On Monday we are leaving for two months on a government tour around Asia – China, Japan, India, Pakistan, Afghanistan, Iran, Iraq, Egypt, Algeria, Morocco and Spain at the end. From Spain we're flying home. Steph will be involved in important political talks there and visit our military detachments in some of those countries."

"Steph?" Aaron smirked. "You're talking about the Senator as if she is your school friend."

"She is very friendly and humble. Actually, an amazing person. And brilliantly smart. She invited me for coffee a couple of times after work. She asked me to call her Steph, of course, only in private."

"Good for you," Aaron said with a wry smile.

"Aaron, please, don't be so bitter," Rosie said tenderly, while settling on the armchair across from him. "I know that I hurt you. I shouldn't be that cold and selfish with you. Uncle is trying to inflict me with the feeling of guilt because he really cares about you. Some days ago he forced me to read *Little Prince* by Saint-Exupery, pushing on me that famous quote that we are responsible for those we tamed. I was even crying while I read it."

"I know," Aaron responded thoughtfully, "I read it as a teen and was crying as well. It's one of the psychologically wisest books in the world."

"Yeah, but why push it on me!" Rosie exclaimed indignantly. "Uncle says I made you fall in love with me on purpose, haunting you with my poetry, so now I have to be with you. What an old bugger! I really loved you! It is not my fault that the particles of my love to you evaporated from my aura. In truth, it was his fault. He didn't study his cure and it's consequences deep enough to foresee that."

"Well," Aaron shrugged. "I know that it is not your fault. And don't feel guilty. My love died too, and actually because he cured my PTSD with Clay Mask as well. And also because my Rosalyn-Anastasia died. But I am not blaming Ashot. He did what was the best for you."

"While we're dating you always said that you will do everything possible to cure me, to make me healthy," Rosie continued. "I am just wondering... if you knew that it would be the dead end of our love, that you would lose me because of the cure, would you have agreed with that? Or would you keep me mentally ill, but loving you madly?"

Aaron uncertainly shook his head. "At that time I loved you as you were. I didn't need you to be healthy. You were amazing in these personalities. I was obsessed. I craved to own you and I wanted you for myself only. But we were thinking about the future together, to get married, to live as a family with Laurie and have more children. And for that you needed to be healthy. That's why we both dreamed about you to be cured. I know that you were scared to lose your poetry talent, but you never were scared to lose your love. We were both sure that it was impossible and it would never happen.

"Now, I changed a lot," Aaron went on. "The two months of close socializing with Ashot influenced me greatly and the sessions with the Clay Mask transformed me into a better man. I am really a different person today. If you would be ill now, I would still agree to cure you even knowing that I would lose you. I would want you to be healthy for you. Not for me. Because the real true love is to wish and to do the best for the one you love. It doesn't matter what it costs me. No selfishness. Now I would agree to any pain and any suffering of losing you, just to make you healthy at any price."

"Thank you, Aaron," Rosie whispered gracefully. "I always knew that you are an amazing man, and I am so sorry that it all turned out this way."

For a while they sat silently. Then Aaron said, "I want to ask you something... could you, please, return my rings?"

Rosie looked attentively at his eyes, removed her engagement ring and the wedding band from her finger and placed them on his palm, squeezing his fingers around the rings. "Do you want the diamond earrings and necklace too?" she inquired quietly.

"No. You can keep them. They are just jewelry and mean nothing. The rings mean everything."

"So, you're kind of divorcing me right now?"

He nodded. "I want you to be free with no obligations. As soon as the baby is born we will divorce next day. I just want him to have my last name. This is the only reason I am not doing the paperwork for divorce now. Mingling inside these high circles, like government, TV people, international travels, you will shine like a star and could meet someone. Don't hesitate and go for it. Remember, you're a free woman."

Rosie giggled. "We actually go on this trip – three of us: Steph, her secretary, Gabi, and me. Gabi is a man, and a very flirty one. But I don't like him. He is not my taste."

"Was I in your taste before?" Aaron smirked.

"Yes, you were. That's why I gave you my book, trying to catch you, Aaron. You are an absolutely awesome man, probably the best one in the world, and I am sure you will find another love."

"Okay, I am not talking about that now," he interrupted abruptly. "I am not thinking about that. I will be working two jobs and have two children. It is more than enough for me. Forever."

"You never know," she whispered, then stood up, came closer and quickly kissed his cheek. "Bye, Aaron. We should go now. It is Laurie's time to sleep soon. Right?"

When the guests were leaving, Liam pulled Aaron aside and handed him a computer 'thumb drive'. "I almost forgot," he whispered that no one in the hallway could hear. "This is what you requested. Your kiss on stage from YouTube and three of my films – your proposal on stage, the farewell party with the Poetry Club in the Space Needle and your wedding at the church."

"Thank you," Aaron answered and hugged him.

As they returned to the hallway, Ashot hugged Aaron as well.

"It was a great evening, son," he said. "Thank you so much for introducing us to your nice family. I would like to thank you, Mrs. Dispenmore, for how you raised this perfect young man. You can be very proud of him. And you, little one, would you mind giving a hug to Grandpa Ashot?"

Laurie, who was standing beside Liam, hugging his legs, went to the old man who was squatting for her and hugged his neck. "Bye, Grandpa Ashot," she said. "Could you, please, leave Grandpa Liam with us?"

"Oh, no!" Liam exclaimed. "I love you, Laurie, but I can't stay. Grandpa Ashot will be crying without me, right, Grandpa Ashot?" and he winked at his husband. "Let's do this another way," he continued then, squatting before Laurie as well and hugging her. "One day I will take you and your Grandma Beth for an excursion to a movie set and you will learn how a movie is produced, maybe meet some actors. It would be fun! But for now each of us should stay in our own houses. Okay?"

Laurie took a deep breath. "Okay," she agreed sadly, "but promise that you will come again."

"I promise," Liam chuckled. "How can I not come, as we did not finish our chess game yet?"

Rosie was the only one who was standing silently by the door, waiting while all these hugs and farewells would end. Nothing was visible on her indifferent face.

When Aaron put Laurie to sleep, he sat on the edge of her bed and asked, "Do you want me to read a book or to tell a story?"

"The story. About the girl Rosalyn-Anastasia and her twin-sister Rosie. I think grandma read me fairy tales about two sisters before. One was nice and one was mean. I remember."

"Yes. It is quite a popular fairy tale topic, many versions of it," Aaron agreed. "But here we have not a fairy tale but a true story.

Rosalyn-Anastasia was an amazing girl, as you know. You loved her and I loved her very much too. But, sadly, she died."

He was worried expecting that Laurie would cry, but this did not happen. She lifted her head from the pillow, rested it on her hand and looked at Aaron seriously. "So, where is she now?" the girl asked. "In Heaven? Like my Mommy?"

"Yes," Aaron sighed with relief. "She is in Heaven because she was an Angel, exactly like your Mommy. And tomorrow I want you and I to hold a funeral for her."

"Where? At the cemetery? With my Mommy?"

"No, just here, in our backyard."

"Beside my cat? Oh, it would be cute. My cat won't be so lonely there. It would be great, daddy."

Aaron felt that the child couldn't take in the concept of death as a tragedy of loss forever. It settled in her brain more like a game, like the funeral for her cat, for the snail on the road when they met Rosie. But it was okay. He was glad that the whole situation didn't cause her any grief or pain.

"We will make a grave for her and plant a rosebush on the top of it. What color roses do you want?" he asked.

"I like yellow roses, a little bit pinkish," Laurie's eyes shone in anticipation of the game. "Can I go with you to a greenhouse to choose the roses?"

"Of course, sweetie. We can do this together. We met this girl together and we will say goodbye to her together."

"I just don't know, daddy, why did you invite this twin-sister Rosie to come here? Oh... you probably mistook her with the good sister, as I did at first. Right?"

"No. I invited her because she is the daughter of Grandpa Liam and Grandpa Ashot. I am friends with them, so she comes as a family with them. You know, like if someone invited me for dinner and I took with me you and Grandma Beth because you're my family. The same. Do you get it?"

"Yes," Laurie nodded. "But she is not as nice as the grandpas. She doesn't feel like a family. She feels like a stranger. And you know what, daddy?" she turned into a whisper. "Can I tell you a secret? I think I fell in love with Grandpa Liam. He is the best. I love him so much! I decided to name my kitten – Liam - after him. When I grow up I would like to marry him."

Aaron giggled confusingly, not being quite sure how to explain this.

"No, sweetie," he said. "Grandpa Liam is already married to Grandpa Ashot. He can't marry twice."

"But what if Grandpa Ashot dies?"

"I don't think he will die," Aaron laughed. "He is pretty healthy and will live long, I am sure. Let's talk about that when you really grow up, okay?"

"Okay," Laurie sighed sadly. "I don't want to talk anymore, daddy. You better sing me a lullaby in a whisper." She turned away from Aaron and hid her face in her pillow. He tenderly petted her shoulders, guessing that she was probably crying soundlessly.

Even for a child, the rejection of love is more hurtful than death, he thought wistfully.

When Laurie fell asleep, Aaron returned to the living room where Beth was sitting on the couch, with the kitten curled on her lap. She was pretending that she was knitting, but obviously was just waiting for him.

"Well, son," she said strictly, lifting her eyes at him. "Now tell me the whole story, please. I want to know the truth."

CHAPTER 69

From the box in his closet, Aaron brought Rosie's book, and put it beside him on the couch along with his laptop computer. "Mom, I am really sorry that sometimes I hide things from you," he said. "I didn't lie. I just deflected a few moments that could make you nervous and worried. You are... mm... kind of... mm... not very young and your heart is not really healthy. I didn't want you to worry and get a heart attack or worse about things that are not of your making.

"I swear to God, it is true that I sent you and Laurie away because I had to work hard. And you know, I did. Ashot told you a bit about the cure of a patient that we successfully accomplished for the conference. We are in one of the best positions between all psychiatrists in the country now. But, I didn't tell you one thing – the patient that we cured from schizophrenia was Rosie."

"Oh," Beth breathed out surprised. "You had told me that you're teaching her some languages in her sleep..."

"Her sudden knowledge of twenty-five languages was a side effect of her cure. Don't worry, she is not a schizophrenic anymore, otherwise I wouldn't invite her to my home and let her meet you and Laurie. She is completely healthy now. If you have any doubts, I can show you the report from the board of certified psychiatrists from the General Psychiatric Hospital, who did her evaluation."

"No need. I believe you, son. I just remember that you told me before that there is no cure for schizophrenia."

"There wasn't. But we invented it – Ashot and I together. And it is proven that it works. This is what we will present to the conference in New York. Rosie will go with us there because we have to introduce a cured patient to them. She is our living proof that our cure works."

"Wow! Then you must be geniuses!" Beth exclaimed excitedly.

"Yes, Ashot is. I... actually... was kind of his apprentice. I was learning a lot from him. And now that we are opening a new clinic, we will be working side by side. I will have my own patients whom I will cure by myself. To start this work we just need the approval of the cure from the conference. That's it."

"This is all great, Arie," Beth smiled. "But I already knew some of that from the earlier conversations with you. And, I talked with Ashot during their visit today, as well. But... Arie... you're still cunningly avoiding my question about your private life. You told me that there was a woman you were very serious about. I am guessing it was Rosie. But to me it looks like no affection or even interest exists from both sides. Why? What's happening?"

Aaron took a deep breath. It was obvious for Beth that the next part of the story was not easy for him to convey, but he wanted to be sincere with his mother as they had been during their life.

"Well... you remember, probably, when Laurie told you that we met a girl while walking one evening and saw her off at the bus station? You brought me this newspaper about dangerous mentally ill teens who were sometimes escaping the shelter next door. That girl was Rosie..."

"Oh," Beth breathed out in surprise again. "I was wondering when I noticed Laurie's reaction tonight. It looked at the first moment like she knew her... Was Rosie so dangerous that she was placed into this shelter? Laurie told me that the police looked for that girl. Why?"

"She wasn't dangerous. It was all a coincidence. She was an angel in reality, but a very sick angel, and she was a poetess. She gave us her book of poetry. I will give it to you to read, so you could determine yourself the level of her talent."

"Laurie didn't tell me anything about the book..."

"She probably forgot. She was too excited because she liked the ill Rosie very much."

"...but she told me a poem about a little birdie that this girl on the street taught her," Beth continued. "And you were hiding that book from me?! Jeez, you're such a conspirator, Arie!"

"At first, I read it out of curiosity, and then... It's kind of strange. It is difficult to believe... This book... It seemed to me like it was my own soul on each line, like I wrote it. It was like a bullet in my heart." Aaron choked on his words. It took him several seconds to collect himself. "Sorry, mom... For a man, some things are very difficult to tell his mother..."

"You fell in love with her," Beth established a fact which was obvious to her.

"Hmm," Aaron blushed a bit confused, "yeah... I got obsessed. I found her and we dated for some time. But then her illness got worse and... a long story short... I met Ashot and we began to cure her. We decided to kill two birds with one shot: to make her healthy and to secure the cured patient for the conference in New York. It took two months. And now she is healthy, but she lost her poetry talent and got a new one – those languages. That's it."

"So, what happened with your love? I still didn't get any clarity about that, Arie."

"Ashot repeated many times... I am quoting... that he 'will give me a healthy woman in my bed and a Nobel Prize in my pocket'. I agreed with that. The project was extremely interesting scientifically and also, I loved her... I thought sometimes I was insane myself. I couldn't guess before that this level of feelings was even possible..." Aaron suppressed a spasm in his throat and dropped his forehead on his hands.

"What happened, my dear?" Beth repeated sympathetically.

"As a side effect of the cure, her love for me evaporated together with her poetry talent," he uttered quietly, a bit huskily. "She became a different person... a stranger. And I don't love her anymore as well," he lifted his head and looked straight at Beth, now raising his voice, "...because I loved my poetess, my mysterious woman... and today's Rosie is not her. You probably noticed – Laurie felt that right away and stepped back from her. Ashot thinks that I loved not her, but her illness because all her talents and fantastic abilities were the illness. Maybe he is right... I don't know."

"It is strange," Beth shook her head, absorbing his words with difficulty.

"I can show you something, mom, that could help you to understand. First of all, I want to show you at the Poetry Club website, how she was looking when I met her. Then – here is her book to read. When you finish it, I will show you a few films... about us."

"I hope it's not something sexy," Beth glanced at him suspiciously.

"Don't worry," Aaron chuckled. "I will never show you anything you don't need to see. There probably are some sexy moments, like a kiss maybe, but no more than that. But as they say – better one time to see than a hundred times to hear. You will get everything from those films. By the way, Liam filmed most of them."

"Liam? So, it wasn't in private?"

"No, those moments were all in public, at her concerts, at her Poetry Club, at their church. It was beautiful to tears," Aaron stopped for a moment, and coughed, again collecting himself. "I wouldn't talk to you now as calmly as I do. I would have sobbed exactly like after Ally's death if Ashot had not cured my nerves as well. He cured my PTSD, helped me to get over all my past tragedies including this one today."

"So, I see that Ashot was the main figure in all this story," Beth commented matter-of-factly. "It looks like he is holding the whole situation in his hands. He is really an interesting man, one of a kind. And Liam... I would never expect that a gay-man would be as great with a child as he was with Laurie. They usually are good friends with women because of the absence of the sexual tense between the sides. But kids... Jeez, I am learning something new even at my age," she sighed. "Okay, Arie, of course... I am ready. Turn your computer on, please, and let me see this poetry website. And I will be glad to read Rosie's book and watch the films later. I am just wondering... It all ended so sad... What's your plan, son? What are you going to do with this relationship now?"

"Actually, there is no relationship." He shrugged. "But there is one important leftover of it... We will talk about that after you see the films. My plan is – tomorrow Laurie and I will do the funeral of that girl that we met on the street, walked to the bus stop and both fell in love with. She does not exist anymore. She is dead and the funeral will be good to put a definite period on this story and help me to move on. Don't say, please, that it would be silly and childish. I feel deep inside that I need it. It will give me closure."

Aaron stood up, placed his laptop on the coffee table in front of Beth and turned the Slam Poetry website on. "Press here, mom, to go to the next page," he explained. "And when it finishes just turn off right there. And I am going to sleep now. Good night." He kissed her cheek and, before she started to watch, he left fast not wanting to catch even a glimpse of those computer pages.

"Jeez," Beth whispered, pressing her palms to her cheeks, wistfully looking how Aaron ran upstairs, jumping two steps at the time."My poor boy..."

The next day was Sunday and Beth and Laurie went to church, as usual. In anticipation to see their friends whom they were missing during their vacation trip to Florida they were excited. But Aaron insisted that today for Laurie there will be no visiting with Beth's friends' grandchildren. He promised to pick her up right after the service as they have some business to do together.

Aaron drove his little daughter to a greenhouse, where Laurie chose a yellow rose bush with pinkish tingles at the edge of each petal. When they returned home he took Rosie's book, the one where the dry pink petunia and his wedding band were hidden between the pages. He added the two rings that he got from Rosie yesterday - the engagement diamond ring and her wedding band. After that he wrapped the book with plastic carefully, using the whole roll of the wrap.

He didn't invite Beth to attend, feeling that this was only his and Laurie's business. But the old woman curiously peeked through the corner of the curtain from her upper bedroom at what they were doing in the backyard.

Aaron took a shovel, lifted a pretty big square of the lawn and dug a hole where he put the wrapped book after he and Laurie kissed it goodbye. Then, while singing *Amazing Grace* together, he and Laurie in turns threw handfuls of soil on it until it was completely covered. Beth couldn't even hold her tears, looking at her little granddaughter. She was feeling happy and proud that she taught the girl to sing at the church and to be a spiritual human being.

Aaron is not bad too, she thought. *He is not going to church but to make this funeral was his spiritual idea. His soul and heart are obviously at the right place although he is performing this funeral as a game for Laurie. It is a very sad game but probably he really needs it for closure and for the child not to ask any more questions about that Rosie-girl. Or now Rosie-woman...? I don't know exactly.*

On the top of the buried book, Aaron placed the rosebush, added the rest of the soil and circled this flower bed with the extra pieces of lawn. Laurie brought a small pitcher of water and they watered the bush, in turns, as well. After that each of them put their palms together under their chins and said a silent prayer. Amen! It was done.

"Oh, God! Please, help my dear boy to overcome this pain," Beth whispered, after saying a prayer in her room as well. "Please, let him be happy finally!"

After that, this Sunday evening they prepared Laurie for school that will start on Monday. Now, instead of their usual lunch, Beth's church friends with their grandchildren came to visit and to congratulate Laurie. Aaron bought a big ice cream cake, and when it was eaten, he played with Laurie and the other kids in the backyard. They were running tag, swinging on the swings, climbing on monkey bars, sliding from a slide into an inflatable pool with water. It was a lot of fun, exactly like it was in Aaron's life before... before he met Rosie and his whole world turned upside down.

But now he was free from those memories – they were buried under the rosebush at the corner of the backyard. Now he and his little daughter are moving on. Tomorrow morning Laurie will start her school and Aaron will be back to work at the university. Life will be regular and normal again.

CHAPTER 70

As soon as Aaron appeared at the university he was overpowered by the huge amount of work that accumulated there, especially at the labs, while he was absent. His patients who were watched by other doctors were all back to him as well. One of them was Rosa Garcia who was evaluated by the board of the General Psychiatric Hospital as completely cured from schizophrenia by him, although she existed in his office only as a folder.

Immediately, Aaron went to the president of the university and requested the recommendation letter to the Psychiatry Scientific Conference in New York. It was supposed to verify that the unique cure was invented here, in a psychiatric clinic under the roof of their university, by the doctor of their Psychiatry Department, Aaron Adam Dispenmore. The president of university gladly wrote it because such an invention was extremely prestigious for his establishment and potentially led to a chance to get one more Nobel Prize laureate among his staff.

However, he mentioned that he already did a similar letter for Dr. Helen Harrison because she reported her patient cured and brought the evaluation documents from the same General Psychiatric Hospital a few days earlier. "Don't feel upset about that, Dr. Dispenmore," the president said. "It's a big honor for us that we raised in our university two such geniuses as you and Dr. Harrison."

Aaron wasn't upset at all but just curious. He made a mental note to visit Helen's office and check how her twelve-year-old boy-patient is doing.

Then Aaron sorted and organized his schedule for the following weeks, in which he included golfing with a group of his buddies on Sundays. He did it occasionally, a couple times per month while he lived his regular life, before he met Rosie. Now it was time to restore the day-to-day routine, so he called one of the buddies.

"Wow! Dude, where have you been?" the buddy exclaimed. "I hadn't heard from you for ages! We have so many changes in our golf club. They built a new restaurant there and hired a bunch of charming chics. I know you weren't interested, but..."

"I am now," Aaron interrupted, laughing. "I was very busy, working in a private lab, getting ready for a conference. Also, I got married, and now I'm getting divorced."

"So soon?"

"Yeah, my married life lasted about a month," Aaron smirked.

"So, you had enough of it," the buddy giggled. "Welcome on board, dude. I am sure everyone in the club will be happy to see you next Sunday."

When Aaron peeked into Helen's office, she didn't look happy.

"Hey," he said. "I've heard you did a successful cure. Congrats! How is the boy doing?"

"Not very well," she uttered anxiously. "Mentally he was okay after the surgery, although he was very weak, but he still passed evaluation. But then he has complications with his heart which I didn't expect for a child. And now he is in the ICU hooked on machines. I hope he will survive. But... who knows. You have to be happy to hear that, Arie."

"Not at all," he sighed. "I am not obsessed with the competition. I actually feel pity for that child. But at least we know that your idea to remove the tumor was right and the schizophrenia was cured. So, you still have a chance at the conference. However, I disagree with one thing – not every schizophrenic has a brain tumor. This boy is kind of the exception, not a rule. I wouldn't recommend it as a regular cure for all psychiatry clinics."

"Well, you're not a boss, Arie. The judges at the conference will decide this, not you."

"I know. Sorry. In my thinking every schizophrenic, actually, as every person in the world, has the auras. My theory of the cure - to clean these auras - seems more common and possible for widespread use."

"You will not win, Arie. I told you," she laughed. "You're with me, or you're against me. No other choices. By the way, how is your patient doing after the cure?"

"Pretty good. Having a normal happy life. Doing business."

"Any complications?"

"There are a few... like the loss of some feelings. But we will work on it in our private clinic in the future and will find the possibilities to eliminate it, so it doesn't happen with other patients later."

"You still plan to work with that old fart?"

"Yes, for sure."

"Who the hell is he? I noticed that he is bossing you around like you're some kind of an apprentice."

Aaron shrugged. "It's okay. He has a huge experience and I am glad that he is sharing it with me. I am absolutely satisfied to work with him."

"Well, when will you come for the next sleepover?" Helen smiled meaningfully and winked at him. "I see you are not wearing your wedding band. In a month? Already? Don't lie that you've accidentally lost it."

He shrugged confusingly. "I am not lying. We are separated. My wife moved pretty far away."

"Jeez!" she laughed loudly, throwing her head back. "Oh, my gosh! You're an idiot, Arie. Why the hell did you marry this teen? You could sleep with her, but marriage... It's too serious!"

Aaron made a wry face. "She is pregnant. We struck a bargain – she will leave the baby with me and go free. We will divorce."

"What kind of woman would make this bargain? Is she crazy?"

"She was, but now she is not. She is my cured patient, actually."

"Whaaaat!?" Helen laughed even louder. "You hooked up your cured patient?! You're not just an idiot, Arie, but a double or triple idiot! Where is your professional ethics?"

"We dated long before she became my patient."

"But when she became your patient, you should have stopped. Wasn't there enough women around when you had wood?"

"Hel," he objected. "I told you already – everything you're saying always sounds dirty and disgusting. And this is not because you're telling a truth, as you claimed, but because you have a dead soul. You don't understand what love is. You never knew it and never will. You just couldn't get it. It's out of your reach. Your heart is only a muscle pumping blood but not a spiritual part of a human being."

"Well, I still love you, idiot! I have feelings, but I also have a brain, and you're thinking with your prick and calling it love. It's not love. It's stupidity. The love is what I have for you – to tolerate your idiotic behavior for more than ten years and still want you in spite of everything. This is love, Arie!"

He smirked. "We have different opinions on this topic, Hel. I better go now. I thought for a moment about this sleepover that you suggested because you noticed right - I want a woman. I didn't have sex for some time already. But then I remembered as we parted, everything that you lied to me about Ally, about my child, about my life. No, I can't... I'll never forget it and never forgive you for that. And with that being said, bye Hel. Good luck with the survival of your boy-patient. See you at the conference."

Helen didn't answer, just watched angrily how the door closed behind him and then started to google something fast on her computer. "This teen has triple value, compared to his silly Ally," she whispered to herself. "She is his wife, she is carrying his baby and she is his cured patient for the Nobel Prize. So, her annihilation is three times more important and should be done much faster. Where is this damn DarkWeb to hire a hitman? Jeez, they are hiding themselves pretty deep, but it's okay, I will find them eventually. I worked to remove Ally for five years. This girl should be removed in three months, before the conference. Then we will see who is the winner, Dr. Dispenmore!"

Walking back to his office, Aaron pushed away his appalling feelings towards Helen. He had no time to think about her anymore. After seeing all his patients, who had appointments booked for today, he kept working on re-organizing his personal schedule a bit.

He decided that he will work with Ashot on finishing the last touches at their clinic on Tuesday and Thursday evenings. This way he could put Laurie to bed on Mondays, Wednesdays and Fridays. On Saturdays he will be in the clinic with Ashot between lunch and dinner. All Saturday evenings and all Sundays will be his 'me time'. He will play golf and go out with women that exist only in his mind yet.

According to this new schedule, Beth will be responsible to put Laurie to bed four evenings a week. He also decided that their housekeeper, Mary, who came usually once weekly to clean the house, should be coming from now on three times per week for the whole day to help Beth with different household chores. He noticed that his mother is getting older, needs more help, and he, being busy with two jobs now, won't be able to help her as much as before.

That evening at home, Aaron discussed this project with Beth and she gladly accepted, same as Mary who was happy to earn more money. So, everything seemed to settle pretty well.

In his own private plans for entertainment Aaron became more rational and cynical after his cure with the Clay Mask, as the first step down. Then, after the funeral of Rosie's book and their rings - funeral of his Love – there was a second step down. All the purity of his soul died and evaporated completely.

He convinced himself that his sensitive and pure heart turned back to the one of a regular man; the man who he was before he met Rosie and had two months of madly loving relationship with her. He knew once and for all that there never would be another love in his life. He had enough of giving the whole of himself to a woman; of giving her all his life, thoughts and feelings; and then losing her painfully and shockingly.

He swore to God that he will never experience this struggle again. Just fun, entertainment, enjoyment of light casual dates without any emotions and any obligations – that was how he determined his lifestyle from now on and forever.

CHAPTER 71

Beth read Rosie's book much longer than Aaron expected. She was thinking a lot after each poem, comparing the feeling it created in her heart with the image of today's Rosie that she still saw in front of her eyes. She tried to understand what in these poems captivated her son and forced him to fall in love. What was it that he buried in their backyard under the rosebush? What did he reject in the new healthy Rosie now?

When one evening she told Aaron that she finished the book, he brought his laptop into the living room, inserted the 'thumb drive' and suggested Beth watch the films.

"Would you watch with me?" she asked. "Just in case, if I don't understand something."

"It is all very clear, mom. You will be good by yourself. I just can't watch them anymore. Sorry," Aaron said quickly and left, but not to his room, but to his car, and drove away.

Beth shook her head sadly. It was obvious to her that the events unfolding in the films were still very hurtful to him, even after the funeral of the book. In the films she expected to see him walking with Rosie, maybe have some hugs and kisses, beautiful and sweet like in the Hallmark movies. But what she saw shocked her.

First, it was a YouTube video done by some of the teenagers in the Greenwich Competition Hall. It showed Rosie's performance of the **Ancient Greek Hymn of Love**, her bold jump from the stage into Aaron's arms and then their kiss on stage that continued for seventeen minutes with an ecstatic reaction from the audience.

My poor boy acted insanely, but she visibly forced him, Beth thought, shaking her head with displeasure. *However, it could be understandable - she was seriously mentally ill.*

Then, there were three of Liam's films. One - Rosie's last performance of the **Farewell Anastasia** that followed Aaron's proposal on the stage. Second – the farewell party with the friends from the Poetry Club at the *SkyCity* restaurant in the Space Needle, where Aaron and Rosie danced their first wedding waltz.

My God, Beth thought, *it looks almost like a wedding! She just trapped him like a hunter!*

The third film was their wedding at the church and it was not 'almost'... it was a real official wedding performed by a minister.

Oh, my God! Arie is married to her! Beth realized. *And now what? With their love gone, will they divorce? Why was he hiding all of these from me? Why didn't he ask for advice before going for that? If not me, he could have asked at least Ashot. I am sure the old man would be against that rush. Oh, God! Where are my blood pressure pills?*

Aaron returned home late when it was already dark. He entered the living room, where Beth was still sitting on the couch with the lights off. Her dark silhouette was visible in the dim lights of the security lamps, penetrating through the blinds from the backyard. Aaron approached and sat on the couch beside her.

"Where have you been, Arie?" Beth asked quietly.

He shrugged. "Just drove around the city. I needed to be alone for a while."

They were sitting silently for a long moment. Then his mother moved closer and hugged him. "I am not asking anything, son," she said. "You're right. Everything is clear enough. I understand you completely. She was a star. A brilliant, but very ill star. You loved her very much. But what was the rush? Why not wait until we return home and then plan a wedding?"

"We did plan to do the big wedding with all my family when you returned home," Aaron uttered sadly. "But the idea perished from a shocking side effect of the cure which broke everything. And the rush was because she is pregnant, mom."

"My God!" Beth pressed her palms to her cheeks. "But now... love or no love... you can't leave the woman who is pregnant with your child."

"I am not leaving her. I agreed to live together as friends, just for the child's sake. She doesn't want that. She is obsessed with her career. She wanted to get rid of the child. I begged her... I convinced her finally, when my son is born, give him to me, and then go free."

"How do you know it is a boy? Did you do an ultrasound already?"

"No. It's too early for that. But she knows. She had a vision of the future when she was ill."

"Jeez, Arie. Maybe it was just a hallucination?"

"No. It is scientifically proven that some people could have a connection with a holographic universe and see the 3D time. She knew for sure."

Beth took a deep breath. "Well... you are the scientist. You probably know better. So... you will be a single father with two kids now? When are you expecting this child?"

"Some time at the end of April next year."

"Did you ever think that I am getting older and couldn't be a good helper as I was with Laurie when she was a baby?"

"Yes, of course. After the baby is born, our housekeeper, Mary, will work full time and also, I will hire a live-in nanny. You will be just a manager, mom."

Beth smiled. "You are so rational when you are talking to me, Arie. But when you were with a woman, you lose your head. Very typical for men, I told you that."

"What can I do?" Aaron smiled back. "I know in theory that these are obviously hormones. I can't get rid of them, but from now on I will manage them differently. No love, no feelings, ever. I have had enough of it."

"You can't guarantee that, son," Beth now laughed.

"At least, I will try," he laughed as well. "Let's go to sleep, mom. I have a busy day tomorrow."

The cloud of sadness passed and Aaron was glad that his mother calmed down after knowing his story and accepted all the circumstances. The big burden fell off his shoulders. Trust and peace in the family were restored completely.

While seeing Ashot at their clinic, Aaron never asked him how Rosie is doing on her trip around the world with Senator Stephanie Mane, although the old man mentioned that he is talking with her on Skype frequently. He also told Aaron that he requested his former patient-lover, Patrick, to look for his biological daughter, Annush, in Yerevan, if it would be possible.

"I feel kind of lonely without you, guys, hanging in my home all the time," Ashot said. "Liam is back to work. Here, at the clinic, we are practically all done and ready to go. I am just waiting for the conference to pass and to start working here in full swing in January. You will understand this loneliness, son, probably only when Laurie will leave for college."

"I had experienced it even when she left for vacation," Aaron laughed. "So, is there some success with your search for Annush? What did Patrick say?"

"He found a lot. But not much success, actually. Six years after I disappeared from Yerevan, my wife passed away. Annush was placed into an Orphanage Residential School at the age of ten because there weren't any other relatives to take care of her."

"Was it... not good?" Aaron asked, seeing that Ashot's face got gloomy.

"Yes. Those orphanages were bad. But that was not the end of the horrors. It was 1991. The Soviet Union collapsed, Mafia blossomed and made millions on human trafficking. I read about that on the Internet, but Patrick witnessed all of these first hand. The young women were sold to Europe to become prostitutes. The local prostitutes for large sums of money became wives of old European men. The young Russian men were hired by the Mafia as killers. Also, young men, women and children were sold to be cut for organs for use in transplanting. Often Mafiosi grabbed and stole kids from the streets for that purpose, but their first choice were orphanages from where they could sell the children who didn't belong to anybody. They called it – 'an adoption'.

"Patrick found that Annush was adopted but nobody knows exactly what that meant. He said there were three choices that were carried out at this time. First, the healthy kids were taken to be cut for their organs. Second, the pretty kids went for sex slavery, and third, the ugly, sick or handicapped children went for the real adoption by childless families to the USA. You know, people here are warmhearted. They gladly adopted handicapped kids and handicapped animals. The Mafia used this kindness to get the big money from them for the so-called 'under-standardized' children."

"With that being said, how pretty and healthy was Annush?" Aaron asked carefully.

"I don't think she grew pretty. Even at four, when I saw her last time, her nose was much bigger for a child of that age. She obviously inherited that eggplant looking nose from me. And she was stocky and chubby like a little balloon."

"Come on," Aaron objected. "All kids are short and chubby at the age of four. She could grow tall and slim later. You never know. Laurie grew four inches during the last couple of months."

"I doubt it. My wife was short and chubby, and look at me, I am not tall and rather stocky."

"You never know," Aaron shrugged. "And what about her health?"

"At the time I saw her, she was a kid without any health problems. But at the orphanage Patrick was able to find her file which said that she got scarlet fever. They forced her to go to classes, even being very sick with a fever F105.8 degrees. Because of that there were complications to her heart – cardio rheumatism. She spent a year in bed at the hospital. And right after that she was adopted."

"At least, we can be sure that her heart wasn't good enough to be used as a transplant organ. That is already something," Aaron tried to be supportive.

"Yeah," Ashot took a deep breath. "Something... I called my former patient, Levon Ovanesian, our Armenian lawyer in New York, and asked if it is possible to find the information about children adopted from Armenia in 1992-93. He promised to look. But he also said that Annush could be named differently, if she is alive – Annie Smith, Ann Thompson and so on. At least I gave him her date of birth. But he said that he can't promise anything.

"I, by myself, tried to do something as well," Ashot continued. "I went to the Armenian church here, in Redmond WA, where I worked and lived during my first years in America, and they promised to do a search in all Armenian diasporas and churches which exist in this country. We, Armenians, have a special tradition – an extreme, mad love of our children. If someone adopted sick kids from Armenia, it would be Armenian families, and our churches would know about that and have some information."

"Good luck, uncle," Aaron said and hugged him. He felt sympathy for the old man. He couldn't even imagine what he would do if Laurie went missing. But he was sure that as soon as Rosie returns from her two-months-long tour, Ashot will be much happier. His sadness and loneliness seemed to be fixable soon. Compared to this, Aaron's emptiness and disappointment were much worse and he invested all his time and power into the work at the research labs to occupy his head and not think about anything else.

CHAPTER 72

In the middle of September Aaron received from the university's Chemistry Department lab the results of the comparison analyses of the fresh blue clay before cure and dry fragments of the Clay Mask broken at the end of Rosie's cure. They were shocking because all the organic and chemical ingredients from the fresh blue clay were gone – funneled to the universe. Practically nothing was left, just dry soil powder that even turned from a gray-blue into a dirty-brownish color of simple regular top ground clay.

The detailed study was so interesting that Aaron decided to read and think it through before he gave it to Ashot tonight, during the upcoming meeting at their clinic. Then Ashot was supposed to send it via FedEx to the conference to be added to their already submitted copy of the 'Cure Package'. It was the last part of the process.

Aaron was so excited that he couldn't put his tablet down even when lunch time approached. Being concentrated on this job, he brought the tablet to the lunchroom to keep reading the materials while eating.

He didn't pay much attention to the active life around him in the cafeteria which was crowded by students and university staff. He was sitting alone at a small table with almost no room for anybody else to join him. However, suddenly he noticed from the corner of his eye that some figure approached his table, holding a tray.

"Hi, Dr. Dispenmore," he heard a woman's voice and glanced up. "Could I sit with you? Sorry to bother, but there are no free tables anywhere," a girl said smiling. She was obviously a student – very young, chubby, with dark brown curly shoulder length hair, dark eyes, wearing jeans and a top with thin shoulder straps. She looked familiar, but he couldn't point a finger at where he saw her and how she knew his name.

While Aaron's glance openly slid over her naked shoulders, neck and arms, the thought automatically flashed through his mind, *Not my type, not my style, not my taste...* She was not attractive at all.

"Of course, please, take a seat," he answered just to be polite and moved his tray closer to give the girl more space.

"How is Rosalyn doing?" she asked, making herself comfortable at the table across from him. "I don't understand what happened to her. She blocked my phone number, and also unfriended me on Facebook and everywhere. And not just me, but all of us, her friends – Layla, Tommy, Dustin... everyone..."

Then noticing Aaron's confused facial expression, the girl laughed. "It seems that you don't remember me, Dr. Dispenmore? I am Jessa Green, Rosalyn's bestie... I mean, not now, but a former bestie... You met me at City Hall while you were marrying Rosalyn, and then I arranged with our guys to be the guests for your wedding at the church. Layla and I were the bridesmaids. I don't know...," she continued almost with tears in her voice, "is Rosalyn offended that I did something wrong for her wedding? Did she tell you something? What happened? Why? It is so hurtful. After five years of close friendship! Actually, four years, if we could subtract her year in the shelter after Ben's murder. But even there, I visited her many times..."

"Sorry, Jessa," Aaron said with sympathy realizing that he was not the only one hurt by his cured, now healthy wife. "Please, don't take it personally. Rosie just started her new life and she cut off all her past completely. She is now somewhere in South Asia, for business."

"She left?" the girl exclaimed and Aaron noticed that she quickly glanced at his left hand in which he held a cup of coffee. He saw in her eyes that she recognized the absence of his wedding band and this recognition shocked her. "Did she leave you?!"

"I am clearly a part of her past," Aaron nodded, making a wry face.

"Wow!" Jessa cried out, staring at him with big eyes. "It's unbelievable! After that kiss on stage! I was actually the one who recorded it and placed it on YouTube. We all thought that you're such an amazing man. All the girls were talking about you. If someone had so much passion and bravery to announce his love so openly to the whole world, he must be a fantastic man, very sensitive and sexy, we thought. We all were envying Rosalyn..."

"Okay, let's not talk about that," Aaron interrupted. "I don't want to hear anything about her anymore."

"Then what could we talk about?"

"About you, probably..." he suggested shyly.

"Me? Okay," she smiled. "I am starting my second year here, at the Comparative Literature Department. I noticed you about a year ago, and watched you with a kind of admiration because you're such an attractive man. But I couldn't find the nerve to talk to you because you didn't see me, didn't notice me ever, like I am not existing." She blushed, as Aaron laughed.

Well, he thought. *Not my type, not my taste, but why not, if she is practically suggesting...*

"Do you have a boyfriend, Jessa?" he asked.

"I did. If you remember, at City Hall, there was Tommy, the black guy whom we were working with in the cafeteria? We were even engaged. But we broke up now because he was accepted to Harvard Law School and he left for Massachusetts to live on campus. He asked me to go with him, but, gosh, how could I leave Seattle? I am here in university, here are my parents, all my family, friends, my Poetry Club. I asked him to stay and go to the university here, but he said that Harvard is a once of a lifetime opportunity. He dropped everything and just left."

Aaron listened with a half of an ear, trying to determine if she was of a legal age to have sex because she looked very young. She probably sensed his thoughts and blushed even more.

"How old are you, Jessa?" he inquired.

"I am nineteen, and in a couple of months I will be twenty," she answered, as she fished from her pocket her student card and placed it on the table. "I know I look younger. Here, if you don't believe me."

Aaron glanced at the card. Her date of birth was December 30, 1995. The same year as Rosie, but Rosie's birthday was in April...

"So, you are supposed to leave the Poetry Club soon anyway," he said, trying to hide the reason why he was interested in her age, but she got it anyway.

"Dr. Dispenmore, would you like to go out with me for a cup of coffee?" she asked, lowering her eyes and looking at her plate.

Got it, he smirked and said, "By the way, you can call me Aaron. Hmm... Let me think... We're in different faculties. I am not a professor, not teaching anything. You're not my student. I guess, yes, I could accept the invitation, but I have some conditions."

"I am listening," Jessa smiled, lifting her glance from the plate.

"First, you should promise me to never mention one word about your former bestie, Rosalyn, your Poetry Club, your performances, your poems and so on. This topic must be dead. Second, you'll never ask anything about me and my life. Third – we will never talk about love and not mention any feelings at all. If you agree, I will have coffee with you."

The girl bravely looked him straight in the eyes, beaming, "You're such a handsome man, Aaron, that these conditions are a very small price to pay for the honor to be with you."

"Thank you," he chuckled, passing his phone to her. "Well, then... Give me an address where I can pick you up tonight at ten."

"Coffee so late?" she noted sarcastically, while inserting her address and phone number into his phone.

"Yes," he nodded. "I know one perfect place where they are serving coffee 24/7."

The previous weekend Aaron spent on a golf course with his buddies and they mentioned that the Fairmont Hotel had an around the clock cafeteria. He also learned a lot from them about their dates with women.

Aaron never was interested in this topic before and avoided traditional men's discussions which were mostly dirty gossips about their sex affairs. His experience with Ally was too sacred and too tragic for him to share it with a giggling group of dudes. His other experience with Helen could be of that level, but he considered those relationships too shameful and didn't want to talk about it with anybody ever. So, he usually wasn't involved in their fun storytelling.

Now, the time came when Aaron really needed something to occupy his empty and numb soul. Professionally, he knew too well what damage drugs and alcohol were capable of doing to people's brains. They certainly could do the job of reducing pain, but he strictly rejected any abuse of those substances. Sex was a 'better medication' because there wasn't any danger, except to have a heart attack from extensive use of it. But that didn't matter. He didn't care if he died.

So, he told his buddies that he is interested, but would like to increase his experience in theory at first. They gladly suggested their advice.

There is a lot of danger when you're chasing chics, they told Aaron, but it is easily doable, if you are cautious and know how to navigate these waters. The first, of course, is to use a condom to prevent STD and pregnancies. But this is a lesson from a book for teens.

Nowadays there are new risks.

Women started their movement 'Me too' with the goal to destroy us, men, and to squeeze as much money from us as possible. Look, how many politicians, singers, movie and sport stars are sued, arrested and destroyed financially and lost their reputation. Knowing that the guy became a Senator, Supreme Court Judge, Mayor, Movie or Fashion Mogul, or General, females are creating criminal cases lying that he assaulted them thirty-forty years ago, while he was a teenager, which is absolutely ridiculous because there is no evidence at all. Not one woman ever sued a homeless hobo or low-income worker for sexual misconduct, right? Because there is nothing to gain from them.

So, the main point for all of these women is not justice, but stealing your money. They will take your house, your car, empty your bank, and, if they can't do that for some reason, they will take revenge on you, put you in prison for many years and destroy your life completely. Practically, all the women are thieves.

That point of view, summarizing the whole female population of the world, jarred upon Aaron because he knew for sure that his mother wasn't a thief, his daughter never will be a thief when she grows up, Ally wasn't a thief and Rosie wasn't as well. Even Helen wasn't - financially. She wanted to steal him from Ally, but it was all about her feelings, not a material gain. But there was no reason to object to the guys, so he just kept listening.

Also, nowadays many girls at the age fourteen, fifteen, sixteen are looking as if they are twenty or older, was the next lesson. They all want to have sex with you and they would lie to you about their age. And then, you will be accused of having sex with an underage child which is a 'statuary rape' by definition, and you will go to prison for years, as well. To protect yourself, always ask to check their IDs and never even move your finger toward a girl before you do that.

This is reasonable. Will do, Aaron thought, feeling like a naive schoolboy compared to the other men's ruses.

Next point is, the buddies continued, many of these chics would come into a room with you. They would attack you, seduce you, beg you to have sex with them and then they would say that you raped them, that they were screaming 'no' but you didn't stop which would be a lie. It's a serious crime and you would have a huge prison sentence for what you didn't do. To prevent that from happening, always record on your phone her saying that she wants you and she agrees to sleep with you. This record would be your evidence in case of future lawsuits. Copy those records and keep them somewhere safe because angry chics could destroy your phone.

CLAY MASK

Good advice, Aaron thought remembering how Helen smashed his phone when he recorded her confession in Ally's murder. *But, Jeez, it's a game with so many rules! That all sounds somewhat disgusting and misogynistic, like we are enemies in a war with women. I can't even imagine makeing love to someone after all these precautions and preparations. Is it even human? Sounds like some kind of a computer game – calculate and rationalize your every word, movement, and step. I am not sure after all that it would be even possible to sustain an erection. Not to mention having fun and happiness. However, 90 percent of all men in the world live like that. I was always far behind. I was a sensitive dreamer. But I learned my lesson of a bold life that slapped me in the face, twice. No feelings anymore. Better to start late than never.*

With those lessons in mind Aaron asked Jessa now about her age, and was surprised when she showed him her ID card. Why? He didn't ask for that. Maybe she knew the rules and was much more experienced than he could imagine?

The next important step would be to record her agreement for sex during their meeting in the cafeteria this evening. Aaron wasn't exactly sure how he could do that. It would be too bold a question to ask straight out. But then he decided that he will somehow figure this out during the date before going to the hotel room which he already booked. With that he plunged himself into dissipation, hoping that this would help him to replace the slightest leftovers of memories about Rosie and to find, if not happiness, then at least relaxation and fun.

CHAPTER 73

To Aaron's surprise, his relationship with Jessa turned out very good. The situation in his life returned to the times before he met Rosie – calm, quiet, regular, content, and in these settings Jessa replaced Helen, but she was much better. Not only younger, but also kind, happy, funny, absolutely without any trace of anger. And she was - no less than Helen - smart, bright and resourceful.

At their first date at the Fairmont Hotel cafeteria, when Aaron put his phone on the table and hesitated, not knowing how to record her consent for sex, how to even ask for it or hint at it, she solved his reluctance easily.

"Do you want me to record a small agreement video, to prevent me from suing you for rape?" she asked, giggling. Aaron was so ashamed of his intent to record her, that he blushed and remained silent, biting his lips. "Don't worry," she continued. "I am not offended by distrust. It's kind of a new normal. Most men are doing that nowadays after seeing all those sensational accusation dramas on TV News. Of course, you don't know me at all. How could you know that I am not a gold digger?"

Jessa kept laughing while she took his phone and pressed the record button. "I am Jessa Green," she announced clear and loud. "I am a nineteen-year-old woman who 100 percent agrees to sleep with Aaron Dispenmore because I..." she stopped for some seconds, remembering that he had prohibited her to talk about any feelings, "because I watched him from a distance for more than a year and I wanted him madly."

She returned the phone to him and they both laughed.

"You are not serious," he said, smirking.

"No, I am deadly serious. I didn't expect that you were single when I approached you. I just wanted to ask about... you know... But since you're single, it is nothing wrong if we get to know each other closer. And it's true, I wanted you already for about a year. Jeez! And you probably want me too because you invited me here."

"Yes," he nodded, although he wanted not her exactly, but just sex itself. *Not my type, not my taste* – at the moment it didn't matter.

However, it evolved excellent because she turned sex into a merry game. There was no angry fight, like with Helen; no drama, sufferings and tears, like with Rosie. They were just playing, entertaining each other, having a good time and enjoying the company of each other – having fun. It was absolutely perfect and exactly what Aaron liked and needed in his life now – a lightness and an amazing absence of 'deep dramatic feelings'.

At first they arranged these meetings on weekends, but then both agreed that it would be nice to pass a bit more time together. Aaron suggested that he could come to Fairmont for a sleepover every Tuesday and Thursday after meeting with Ashot at their clinic in the evenings. This way, he and Jessa could spend four nights a week in the hotel, after dinner at the restaurant, or a room service meal in their room.

Every morning, around five, Aaron drove Jessa home, then returned to his house, exercised in his basement sports room and went to work. He wasn't even sure if Beth knew that he wasn't home at night. At least she didn't say anything, and Laurie obviously had no idea about his absence.

Aaron and Jessa never met at the university for lunch anymore and didn't go out anywhere, so everything was like it was with Helen, hidden, casual and comfortable for Aaron. The girl asked him only once, if he would like to go out, for a concert, or baseball game, or just a simple walk in a park, but he strictly said, "No. I am sorry, Jess, but we're not dating."

"Then what is it that we're doing?" she wanted to know.

"Having fun."

"Can fun ever be somewhere else, other than in bed?"

"You mean, in the car?" he teased.

"You know what I mean," she chuckled and threw a pillow at him.

"Sorry, we're not there yet," giggling, he threw the pillow back at her. "You are amazing, Jess. Just be patient."

"Okay," she agreed and threw the two pillows at him at once, laughing almost to tears. After that they never touched this topic again. She was smart enough to understand that if she pushed him more, she could easily lose even what she had now. And their relationship continued this way for two whole months.

On a couple of Sundays Aaron went golfing and bragged to his buddies that he hooked a girl, using their lessons. They encouraged him that he could do more, and pushed him toward a pretty waitress who was openly flirting with him while serving their dinner at the club's restaurant. He sincerely tried. He flirted back with her, even asked for her phone number which he was given right away.

But then... Aaron never called her, feeling very uncomfortable with the fact that he was still seeing Jessa. It was not his character, not his personality – to cheat on a woman whom he was with. He absolutely couldn't force himself to do that, subconsciously knowing that Jessa was enough for now. He felt completely satisfied and didn't need anybody else.

After that, Aaron even stopped going golfing, to avoid curious questioning from his buddies. He just continued his relationship with Jessa and was happy until the middle of November, when Rosie returned home from her tour with Senator Mane. Now it was time to get ready for the trip to New York for the conference.

It was a remarkable day when many things happened at once. In the morning, Helen came to Aaron's office to share her bad news. Her patient, the boy, died from complications with his heart that occurred after his brain surgery.

"Arie, I don't know what to do," Helen said wistfully, sitting on a chair beside his desk and covering her face with both palms. "I am lost. All this huge work I had done is in vain." She looked so weak and vulnerable at the moment that Aaron felt pity for her, but then realized that he still should be careful – when a rattlesnake is lying quietly, it still is a poisonous creature which could jump up and bite you deadly at any moment.

"Come on, Hel," Aaron tried to encourage her. "You did all your diagnosis right. Your cure was right, the boy passed evaluation. Mentally he became healthy. He was cured. He died not because of a mistake in your treatment, but because of his underlying pre-existing heart condition. It is not related to schizophrenia. He still could be considered your cured patient. And you have all the documentation to support this."

"I know. I will go to the conference, of course, but it is so sad. I never lost a patient before."

Aaron suspected that it was only a show. He knew that Helen wasn't capable of feeling sympathy or compassion to anybody ever. He didn't say anything but he remembered clearly that in the rules of the conference was a requirement – you should bring a live cured patient. And he had an inner feeling that Helen remembered this as well. It was pretty obvious to him that now she will not win. Knowing her character, he felt uncomfortable about that. She will never sink alone. If it comes to this point, she will drown him with her.

A thought flashed in his mind that she probably could try to kill Rosie, to leave him in a losing position for the conference as well, and he felt content that Rosie was far away, somewhere in Asia or the Middle East and was not reachable, at least for now.

However, in the evening, at the clinic, he met Ashot who was blooming with happiness.

"What happened?" Aaron asked. "Good news about Annush?"

"No. Sadly, not at all," the old man answered. "My lawyer, Levon, found out that not one child was adopted in the USA from Armenia. And my acquaintances from the Armenian church confirmed that too. So, practically, a dead end with that. But my kiddo came back home," he announced smiling. "She had great success over there, in Asia and the Middle East, and I would like to celebrate this somehow. It would be nice to get all of us together again. I will discuss it with Liam and we will invite you, your mom and Laurie for dinner."

"Thank you, uncle," Aaron said, taking a deep breath. He was curious to see Rosie now, but at the same time very reluctant, not knowing how the meeting would go. But, anyway, they will travel to New York together very soon. The conference was scheduled to start on December 1, 2015, but all the participants and guests were supposed to arrive and register earlier. Their three rooms in a hotel were already booked for three weeks starting November 30th.

Ashot and Liam did a lot of research and found a child friendly restaurant with live music because Rosie said that she would like to dance for a while after their family dinner, although this request surprised them.

"What?" Rosie laughed looking at Ashot's questioning face. "Uncle, don't give me that kind of look. I got used to an adult's beautiful lifestyle during our trip. I understand that you want to entertain Aaron's daughter, but it is because you are old. You're the grandpas - she calls you right. But sorry, I am still young."

Next day, at about six p.m. they all gathered at the restaurant for dinner. Rosie was dressed very stylish in a short red evening dress with a diamond necklace and earrings which Aaron gave her for their wedding. He glanced at the jewelry askance thinking that it was not very ethical for her to wear them knowing that she will meet him there. But he chose not to say a word.

On her once shaved head the hair grew now, already covering the back of her neck and long bangs were almost reaching her eyes. It looked fashionable with a sense of chic. And her manner changed a lot. Her bearing was confident, but not humble anymore like it was on stage as Anastasia. She became visibly arrogant and for Aaron it felt repellent.

Rosie, Ashot and Liam sat at one side of the table and Aaron, Beth and Laurie across from them. However, Laurie right away changed sides, exclaiming, "I would like to sit with Grandpa Liam."

"Well, okay," Liam chuckled, "if your dad and grandma agree with that. Please, ask them first, sweetie."

When the permission was received, Laurie cozily nestled beside Liam. "I actually have something for you," he said, giving her a small box of play-dough. "We could mold something from it, like grandpa Ashot is doing his Clay Masks. We could do the masks for all of us. Or have you any other ideas?"

"I would like to make your mask, grandpa Liam," Laurie agreed. She was also given a coloring sheet and pencils by a waitress, and Laurie and Liam both started working on it right away, discussing each picture and laughing.

"How was your trip, my dear?" Beth asked Rosie meanwhile, after their orders were taken.

"Oh, it was absolutely great, Mrs. Dispenmore," Rosie answered with a happy smile. "The experience was huge. Our delegation consisted of three senators: our Steph, and a couple of men, from Texas and Alaska, with their staff members as well. We were introduced to a president, or prime minister, or king in each country. I sat right beside them at dinners and translated continuously. They all were excited about my abilities and considered me as a miracle. Their company was amazing. I felt like a fish in water. I had an inner feeling that I belonged there. It was my level. So, I finally found what I was destined for." She turned to Aaron continuing, "You asked me many times what interests me, what I want to become. I told you, Aaron, not to push me, give me time to figure it out. And here I am finally. I found my destiny and my calling – I will go into politics, become a senator, at first, then probably try for president."

"Wow!" Beth shook her head in disbelief. "But it's very serious work and not easy. Huge responsibilities are there."

"I am okay with that. I am a determined hard working woman and I learned from Steph a lot. She taught me her experience on how she became a senator. I am best friends with her now."

"I see that... you even look like you matured a lot during this trip," Beth continued. "But doesn't this job require some special education? Many politicians are lawyers or...?"

"About education, Mrs. Dispenmore... We stayed in each country for three to five days. Everywhere they gave me a language teacher who taught me their specific letters, grammar, reading and writing to add to my speaking and understanding skills. You know, many of those languages have a special alphabet. But it was not difficult to remember. I always was a fast learner, and I still am now. It was a better education than any university could give, and much faster.

"Also," Rosie went on, "in Kabul at the party in our embassy we met General George Simon and he recognized me from the TV show which we both were a part of. I was surprised. I didn't know that Johnny Holiday sent him a recording of the whole show, including my second segment. George danced with me the whole evening. I can tell he was absolutely smitten. But, alas, he is old, fifty, exactly like my daddy Liam," she giggled, being visibly flattered by the memory of that moment. "He also said that he has very close connections in the Pentagon and he will recommend me as a personal translator to the Minister of Defense. I think, when we return home, after the Psychiatry Conference in New York, I will apply for this position and move to Washington, DC."

Everybody was speechless for a minute, until Ashot broke the tension. "What could we do, Mrs. Dispenmore?" he said, lifting his palms. "Our children are growing up and leaving the nest. Sad, but it is a normal way of life."

"Yes, of course," Beth agreed in spite of the visible displeasure on her face. "I only worry about the baby. Isn't it too many activities for a pregnant woman?"

"I am feeling okay," Rosie smiled. "No morning sickness, anything... My mom was exactly like that, so I am not concerned about the baby."

"However..." Beth started, but Aaron placed his palm on her hand. "Mom, please," was his first word that he pronounced during the whole evening. "Not a good time..."

"Okay. Sorry, Arie," she answered a bit confused. And then their food arrived.

CHAPTER 74

After dinner the musicians appeared on stage and started to play. It was not a bar, or pub, but a high quality restaurant, so the music was quiet, beautiful and relaxing. Noticing that some people started to dance, Laurie begged, "Grandpa Liam, I want to dance with you, please, please..."

Liam glanced questioningly at Aaron, seeking permission, and Aaron nodded in agreement. It would be nothing wrong, quite the opposite – cute and charming. Liam led Laurie to the dance floor holding her hand. There he lifted the girl hugging her waist with his left arm, and in the right hand took her left hand and stretched them to the side.

"You see, sweetie," he explained, "this is the proper position for a dance with a partner."

"Okay," she agreed happily and hugged his neck with her right arm.

"No," Liam fixed it momentarily. "The proper position for your right arm is to be placed on the top of my shoulder. Okay, this is better. You're doing good, Laurie. Now we can start dancing."

"Mrs. Dispenmore, would you mind, please, honoring me with a dance?" Ashot asked Beth, smiling, while standing up from the table and she readily agreed, realizing that he is inviting her to dance on purpose to give Aaron and Rosie a chance to talk in private or to dance as well. In a few seconds the younger couple was left alone sitting across the table.

After a long tense moment, Rosie noted, "You're not really talkative today."

Aaron shrugged silently.

"Are you angry with me?" she asked.

He shrugged again, "Why should I be?"

"I traveled the world, but you were sitting at home. Aren't you envious?"

"I was already in most of those countries. And I wasn't 'sitting at home'. I was working."

"Hmm," she smirked. "Seeing someone?"

"Actually, yes," he smirked as well.

"Back to your wife's murderer?"

"No, not at all. Why are you sounding like you hate me?" he wanted to know.

"Because you're not talking to me. I have to pull each word from you as if I'm using pliers. I remember that you used to talk to me for hours."

"I loved you then."

"So, now you love someone else?"

He shrugged once more.

"Are you jealous of General Simon?" Rosie chuckled.

"Why should I be? I told you, you're a free woman."

"Uncle said that he booked three separate rooms for us in a hotel in New York. Don't you want to sleep with me there at least?"

"You know," Aaron objected more actively, "actually, I have no right. You will be a sensation there, the winning cured patient. The media possibly could follow you, or both of us. They shouldn't know about our relationship because it would jeopardize the whole project. You will go as a patient with your maiden last name. It is announced in all the materials and in films. Liam edited every record and all was attentively checked."

"Okay then," she smiled at him. "Maybe we could dance for a while? I am kind of used to it. We have dances there after dinner every evening."

"Sorry, I am not the General," Aaron said while they were walking to the dance floor.

"No need to be sarcastic. You're a high ranking doctor and pretty soon, a Nobel Prize Laureate," she answered no less sarcastically, hinting that all his future success would be earned by Ashot in reality. It was kind of a blow under the belt. Aaron from the beginning knew that and this thought alone was hurtful enough.

"Do you want me to refuse?" he answered morosely. "I can do that at any moment. I am not as career obsessed as you are, Miss Future President. I don't need this damn Nobel Prize. I am doing that for your uncle, and he did it for you, for God's sake. Could you at least be thankful and respectful for that?"

"I know that and I am thankful enough. But I just shared my life goal and my dream, considering everyone at our table to be my friends who understands and supports me, and would be happy for me. I forgot that there is one enemy among us now who hates me for my success."

"I do not hate you," Aaron took a deep breath, trying to calm himself down. "I am just mourning my soulmate, my angel, the pure person who you were and whom I loved."

"I was a psycho, nothing else. And, of course, as a psychiatrist you could only understand and love psychos, not normal healthy people."

"Would you, please, shut up?" he whispered. "Give me the last chance to feel something."

"Okay," Rosie whispered back, "I would like to feel something too. Unlike you, I didn't have sex for a long time and I miss it." She hugged his neck and pressed her whole body to him, slowly moving along with the music. Aaron closed his eyes, put his hands on her waist line and sensed the warmth of her skin through the tender fabric of her dress. Then he moved his hands a bit down to her low back and at that moment the sensation pierced him like lightning. That was it. It was her, his Rosie in his arms. He shuddered, then pushed her away by the shoulders.

"No," he uttered through his teeth, "no, no, I can't do that. No!" He turned to look where his mother was with Ashot and stepped toward them. "I am leaving, mom. We should go. Now!"

Beth looked at him surprised, guessing that he wants to leave with Rosie.

"No, daddy, please, I am not going home yet," Laurie whined, hugging Liam's neck. "I want to stay with grandpa Liam. Please, daddy, please."

"Okay, son," Ashot said quietly. "You can go. We will drive your family home. Don't worry."

"Thank you, uncle," Aaron said abruptly and almost ran out of the room, down the stairs, to the lobby and to the parking lot. All their group looked bewildered that Rosie didn't leave with him. She returned to the table and sat alone, propping her forehead on her hands.

Right away a man from the neighboring table approached her. "Would you be interested to dance with me, Miss?" he asked politely, bowing his head. "I noticed your partner just left..."

"Well, he is not a partner," Rosie giggled, looking up at the stranger and giving him her hand. "He is my ex-husband."

"How long were you married?" the gentleman asked, leading her to the dance floor.

"About four months... but we were separated for three of them," Rosie made a wry face. "Please, let's not talk about that, sir. I like to look ahead, not back."

She was already dancing, smiling, chatting and having a good time, when Aaron burst into his car. He grabbed his phone with shaky hands and pressed the call button to Jessa.

"Get out to the driveway," he almost yelled as she answered the phone. "I will be there in five minutes."

"Okay," she said, realizing that there was no time for questions. It was Friday, not their usual day of encounters and she knew right away that something must have happened.

To reach her house it took Aaron about thirty minutes, not five, which he had expressed figuratively. Jessa was standing on the sidewalk, waiting patiently. He jumped out from the car, grabbed her and started kissing her wildly, crazily, all shaky with passion.

"Okay, okay," she whispered breathlessly between the kisses. "Let's move somewhere. I don't want my parents to see us through the window."

Aaron pushed her in the back seat of his car, drove a block ahead, turned to a cul-de-sac with big bushes on the corner and stopped there. Then he joined her in the back seat.

"What happened?" she whispered while he hastily undressed her.

"Not now," he growled. "Don't talk. I just want you. I need you."

It was the first time during their relationship when he made love to her pretty mad, even rude, but she wasn't offended. She knew that there must be a reason for that and she accepted it, answering him with a loving smile, as she usually did. After he was done, it took a long time for him to calm down. Jessa patiently waited, slowly caressing his hair and tenderly kissing his cheek. Each of her movements was caring, as if she was a mother, soothing her troubled child.

"She is back," Aaron whispered then.

"I kind of figured it out," Jessa nodded slowly

"Could you think back, Jess, when we met at City Hall that day? You asked 'Rosalyn, would you come next Tuesday to the concert? I will perform a new poem about a butterfly'..."

"Oh, gosh! Do you recall my exact words, Aaron?" the girl asked, surprised. "I was such a nothing - an unimportant person for you at that moment, but you remembered?"

"Maybe it's funny, but, yes. Do you still know this poem? The butterfly?"

"Of course, I do," she laughed. "We, poets, are crazy. We keep our poems in our hearts forever."

"Could you tell it to me right now? Please, Jess..."

Absolutely shocked by this request, after his ban of all poetry things, she hugged his neck tight and murmured into his ear,

"A butterfly is spreading it's wings from a cocoon,
and they are sparkling in the sun.
'It's a happy day', she screams,
I would never believe
that I ever was
a caterpillar."

"And then – a reverse," Jessa continued:

"A caterpillar wraps itself by a silky thread into
a cocoon, which is getting dim.
She is dreaming sleepily,
I wouldn't believe that
I was a butterfly
ever."

"Thank you," Aaron whispered and kissed her, now calmly and fondly. "It's amazing. It's what I needed and wanted."

"You know, it's actually not a very good poem," Jessa laughed. "It should be a 'Nonet', the French poetry style, but I messed up with the amount of syllables and I didn't do it properly. And butterflies and caterpillars, they shouldn't be named – she. I should say – it. Although in some lines I did. There are a lot of mistakes. I didn't get anything for this poem. You're smiling, Aaron. Why? Do you like it?"

"Yes, of course, I do. I don't care about syllables. It's a very deep spiritual understanding of life. In small things, like a tiny caterpillar or a fragile butterfly you see the meaning of the whole universe. You're such a smart girl, Jess."

"Thank you, Aaron. Very flattering. You make me happy," she giggled. "Since you automatically canceled your ban to talk about poetry, maybe this cancellation is for a ban of feelings as well? Now, could I have your permission to say that I love you?"

"You can say that. Thank you," he chuckled. "I am sure I don't deserve it, especially today. Sorry, for my craziness. I just needed to stop the pain of the moment. But, good news, Jess. We are probably heading there."

"Didn't you even notice that you forgot to use a condom today?" she uttered more seriously now.

"Sorry. I just didn't have one. I didn't expect this to happen. It was quite spontaneous after the fight with my ex-wife. I hope it's not your dangerous day, Jess?"

"What if it is?" she asked thoughtfully.

"Okay, let's talk about it a bit later, after I return from New York. Then I will know clearly where I stand after the conference. And if you will read me more poems..."

"I will, if you want to hear them, Aaron. Of course I will. Sadly, I am not even near as talented as Rosalyn. I performed at each concert, but never in five years did I win from her. Ever!"

"Well," he whispered, caressing her shoulder with his lips. "You did win from her today."

CHAPTER 75

The last few days before leaving for New York were pretty hectic for all three participants of the trip. The conference was expected to last for three weeks and their return tickets were bought for December 23, the perfect timing to be home for Christmas.

Rosie did some translation paperwork in Senator Mane's office that will be needed for the month ahead when she will be absent. Ashot, at the clinic, was working on copying all the materials that they will bring with them and provide at the conference in person as originals. They had already submitted the full copy ahead of time, as required. But now he wanted to leave one more copy at home for security reasons. Aaron was busy at the university to arrange the transfer of his patients again to other doctors and to also finalize some research studies in the lab.

At home, Aaron decided to spend more time with Laurie. He walked with her every day, or played chess and board-games if it was cold and rainy. He also put her to bed every evening and in addition to reading her books and singing lullabies, he talked with her a lot in a whisper. Beth noticed this when she peeked once in Laurie's bedroom but didn't ask Aaron anything. She asked Laurie instead, "What is daddy talking to you about for so long every evening?"

"It is our secret," Laurie answered very seriously. "I promised to keep it."

"Okay, then you have to keep this secret," Beth nodded approvingly and didn't dare to ask anything more respecting their father-child privacy. She guessed that it must be something about preparing presents for Christmas for her when Aaron will be away.

After Laurie went to sleep, he spent every night in the hotel with Jessa, not hiding that from Beth anymore. He openly told her that he sees a woman with whom he wanted to make a proper farewell for the next three weeks. And Beth, again, had no choice, but to accept this by not asking any questions. She knew only that it was not Rosie and felt quite content about that.

Jessa was also very happy. But being led by a woman's intuition, she noted once, "I doubt that you're so crazy about me, Aaron. It feels like you trying to put in a lot of sexual satisfaction before your trip because you're afraid to be too close to Rosalyn for three weeks. Am I right?"

"Okay, Jess, we canceled my ban to talk about poetry and your feelings, but the third part of our agreement – the ban to talk about me – is still in place," he answered, smirking wryly. "I am with you now. What else do you want?"

"I am just trying to understand why."

"Obviously because I want it and I need it. What else?"

"You're a stubborn guy, Aaron," she laughed.

"Well... what can I do about that? It's my character, how I was born. But, still... sorry, Jess, it's about me again and we're not talking about that. It's better to say that I will be back for Christmas, I'll bring a lot of presents and, probably will invite you for Christmas dinner to introduce you to my mom and daughter. Is it enough?"

"My God," she whispered, pressing her palms to her cheeks. "It would be a dream come true, Aaron. Then I could introduce you to my parents on New Year's eve."

"Deal!" he chuckled and gave her a high-five.

At the university, Helen visited Aaron in his office once more.

"Is your wife back from her business trip?" she asked, pretending to sound friendly.

"So..." he looked at her attentively.

"What day are you leaving for New York?"

"Before the conference, as required. What do you want?"

"Just curious, what flight are you taking?"

"Why? Do you want to put a bomb in it?"

"Don't be stupid!" she giggled. "What am I now, not just a rattlesnake but also a terrorist for you? I am a Doctor, for God's sake!"

He shrugged.

"What hotel will you stay in, Arie?"

"Jeez, Hel! You know that all the participants and guests of the conference are booked at the same hotel."

"Yes, I know," she chuckled. "I just want to be sure that I will see you with your wife at the restaurant for breakfast every morning."

"So you could put drugs in her glass as you did with Ally?" he asked angrily.

"You're intolerable, Arie! I didn't do anything to Ally, and I also won't do anything to your wife now. But... your cured patient... It's another story. If they will not recognize my cured boy, then we should both lose at this conference."

"Do you want me to report this to the police?" he asked morosely.

"There is nothing to report. It's just a blah-blah-blah friendly teasing each other, as usually old friends do. We have been friends for ten years - almost eleven now, Arie, haven't we? So, good luck, and have a nice trip. See you in New York."

These hints made Aaron a bit nervous, but he guessed that this was Helen's real goal – to get to him, to irritate him, to hurt him. He thought that if her dead boy won't be accepted as a cured patient by the board of judges at the conference, she will try to expose his marriage to Rosie to make his achievement not valid as well, or something of this sort, as she did in her student years – mean politics, intrigues and plots. He wasn't sure that she, in truth, wouldn't be really dangerous for Rosie, but, just in case, he shared his suspicions with Ashot.

The old man took it much more seriously. "You know, son," he said, "I was born and raised in a country where to kill a competitor was normal. So, I learned how to take some lifesaving precautions. I don't think, this woman is a murderer herself, but what she easily could do – is to steal our original materials for the conference, and then, with only the copies, they won't accept our submission. It is very possible.

"So, I have a very significant experience in hiding things from thieves – a pouch on my chest under my clothes. The materials will never be packed into a briefcase - mine or yours. We will carry old newspapers there, making a show for thieves and attracting them to a wrong location. All original paperwork will be in that pouch, and all digital – on a dozen 'thumb drives' - in my chest and pants' pockets.

"You and Rosie shouldn't have any materials on you because you will be in the public eye and serve as a main attraction for the media, and for thieves as well," Ashot continued. "I am a background person, not remarkable at all, practically nobody, and this is exactly good."

"Paperwork is pretty sizable," Aaron noted, laughing. "Three large photo albums and the manuscript with descriptions of all the sessions... It will look like you have a huge beer belly."

"It's okay. Let them think so... I even would wear Liam's leather jacket which is a much bigger size than I am. All materials, serving as my huge belly, will be covered by a long sweater and the jacket on top of it. And it has all zipped pockets for thumb drives. Just perfect!"

"Jeez," Aaron giggled. "Are you serious? It all sounds like a game or joke to me."

"If I didn't do this 'game or joke' hiding money in a pouch on my chest thirty years ago, I wouldn't have been able to reach America and I would have been dead long before," Ashot objected. "It sounds funny for people who never had a need to do so to survive.

"Also, about those breakfasts in the hotel... You are absolutely right that this woman could try to put something into Rosie's glass, especially because you are sure that she did that with your first wife. We will just never appear there and go for breakfast somewhere else outside the hotel.

"Plus, our sleeping arrangements... I actually was thinking about this Dr. Helen Harrison, even before you shared with me your suspicions, Aaron. All guests for the conference will be in the same hotel. I understand it will be comfortable for the organizers if they will need to send a shuttle bus to drive guests for excursions, or something of this sort. It's good for them, but not good for us – Dr. Harrison will be there as well and will know what room you are in. For that reason I booked three separated rooms for all of us. But in reality we all will sleep in one room - mine, again. She could hire a hitman and send him into your room or into Rosie's room, but not in mine. And I will take with me this gun with which I scared you off, son. Sorry about that, but it is a very high quality replica. It's impossible to tell it apart from a real thing. There could be some moments when it could help us."

"Gosh, uncle," Aaron shook his head. "You sound like we're going not to a scientific conference but to some underground meeting of the Columbia drug cartel in a movie. It's crazy. I can't believe that there could be any real danger. Helen is just trying to irritate me and get on my nerves, maybe to play some small dirty tricks on me."

"Aaron, if there is only one-percent risk, we still have no right to take it. It's better to be overprotected than unprotected. Like you, Americans, are saying, 'better safe than sorry'."

"Okay," Aaron agreed, still smiling. "But how could you imagine all of us sleeping together?"

"There are two queen-size beds in each room plus a sofa-bed. I am sure we will be okay. I guess not you, nor kiddo are in a mood for sex nowadays, and none of us is snoring. So, for the purpose of survival and to successfully win at the conference, we should tolerate some temporary discomfort. At least we will be sure that if someone sneaks into your or Rosie's room at night, they will find them empty."

"But then, they logically will think that it would be reasonable to look into your room," Aaron objected.

"Possible. But I know how to prop the door with a chair, what we used to do in my birth country, also I will have my gun, and also, there will be three of us, in case we need to call 911. I can't guarantee that it will be completely safe, but at least, much safer than if each of us would be alone."

"Gosh, uncle!" Aaron laughed. "I love you, but you could be a really good writer of crime stories. Would Rosie agree to sleep in one room with us? She is used to pretty luxurious conditions during her travels with Senator Mane."

"She will have no say in it," Ashot shook his head. "I know how to manage her."

"You knew when she was ill, I agree. But she is another person now."

The old man smirked. "I am not as soft as you, Aaron. It will be an order."

"Wow!" Aaron laughed. "Then good luck with that."

"Of course, I won't tell her anything about that right now but only when it is needed, if it actually will be..." Ashot smiled confidently. "We will see how things are developing, one step at a time."

On the evening of their departure, Aaron said bye to Laurie while preparing her to sleep, but Beth stayed with him longer. Their flight was departing at four a.m., so they should be at the airport at two a.m. and for that leave Aaron's house about midnight. Liam was driving Ashot and Rosie from their place to pick up Aaron and deliver all of them to SeaTac airport for their six-hours-long flight.

After a farewell hug with her son, and barely holding her tears, Beth came out to the driveway and all of them, even Rosie, hugged her as well.

"Don't worry, Aaron, I will take good care of your family," Liam said. "And you, Mrs. Dispenmore, please, don't hesitate to call me if anything is needed. Literally... anything."

"Thank you, thank you so much," Beth repeated, stepping slowly backward to the house while she waved at the car. "Please, take care of my Arie, guys! Love you all! Good trip! Good luck! I am waiting for you to come back with great success, my dear ones!"

CHAPTER 76

In the airplane Rosie sat by the window texting something on her phone and giggled. Ashot was in the middle seat, snoozing; and Aaron sprawled in an aisle seat, with his eyes closed, trying to concentrate and think about his speech at the conference.

"Kiddo," Ashot said finally, "would you mind stop texting, please? It's irritating. I am an old man and need some sleep. A little respect, please."

"Sorry, uncle," she chuckled. "It's George. He is so funny, sending me jokes. Jeez, he still couldn't let me go. For God's sake, he is a fifty-year-old married General! I told him that I am married and pregnant, but he said, it's just friendly chat, nothing else. But he won't let me go!"

"Just stop it, kiddo. Don't answer," Ashot muttered.

"I don't want to be impolite."

"Say that you need to sleep. That's it. And respect that your husband is sitting right there."

"Come on, uncle! Aaron repeated many times that I am a free woman and I can do what I want."

"It doesn't matter what he repeated. You have to understand that he is a live person and has feelings. Jeez, I obviously should overthink my cure procedure because the Clay Mask took something very important from your soul -- sympathy and

637

compassion. You were such a sensitive girl, you even wrote the poem, "I am a sponge absorbing other people's pain

and then splash it out together with my own.

Isn't it too much of a burden for my soul?

Ain't I too young for that?"

"You still remember my poems, uncle?" Rosie asked, surprised. "I don't."

"Yes. It's exactly what I am talking about. Since your own pain is gone, you became arrogant, selfish and insensitive that you never were before. Absolutely never!"

"Then, it's clearly your fault, uncle. Blame yourself, not me, please."

"Leave it, Ashot. Let her be," Aaron uttered sadly. "It's a waste of time. I don't care."

"Yes, son. I see that now. However, for our future patients in the clinic, we should do a whole review of the cure really seriously. It will be a big job for us right after the New Year."

"Of course. I agree," Aaron nodded. "However, to review the whole cure is a long process. While we're doing that, we could already start to work with Clay Mask on selected patients who are completely single – have no partner, no relationship, no love at all. In this case, it could happen the opposite, like it was in Armenia with Patrick and some other patients of yours. And how it happened here with Liam – they will find love pretty soon after. This way there will be no tragedies, no sufferings. Win-win for everybody."

"Very bright idea, son," Ashot said, showing him thumbs up.

"If I knew about the Clay Mask years earlier, I could have saved many lives," Aaron continued, "like one poor newlywed guy who strangled his wife. If I cured him with the Clay Mask and he lost his feelings, they could just divorce, but she could still be alive."

"Then he would probably kill himself from the pain of losing his love," Rosie interrupted suddenly and both men turned to her abruptly.

"Is it how you feel, kiddo?" Ashot asked with concern.

"Sometimes," she smirked.

"But you're always saying that you're happy, always laughing, flirting, giggling, enjoying your new life, new friends, new talents... And you're not only saying that - you're clearly behaving like this is true."

"It is true, but sometimes... when you're nagging me... Okay, okay, that's enough of this, you, guys. I was just commenting on your discussion, nothing else. And I already texted George that I am going to sleep," Rosie noted irritably and put her phone into her pocket. "Let's have some sleep now, please."

Aaron already noticed that Rosie started arguing with Ashot almost all the time. Even at Sea-Tac while boarding the airplane, they had a disagreement about her winter coat that she decided to take to New York. It was a long beige mink fur coat with a hood that cost $20,000. She bought it when she returned from her Asian trip with Senator Mane and was really proud of herself that she can afford it now with her own earned money.

She insisted that she wanted to look decent at the conference, but Ashot was strongly against it.

"Kiddo," he tried to convince her. "You are not a movie star and not going there to shine. You're going there as a product of our work to be presented to judges. Nothing else. You were a simple ill girl with a high school education, shy and weak after five years of mental institutions. You have to keep this image of a nice humble person after the cure as well. Jeans, running shoes, a sweater and a winter jacket from Walmart would be good enough.

"This fur coat is too much," he continued, "the same as your suede boots that are reaching above your knees. And that wool mini-dress or sweater - I even can't say what it is exactly - is perfect for dinner in embassies with Generals and Senators, but not for scientists. Those are people of another level. They live for science, for intellectual life and they respect very simple and humble styles of clothing. All clean, all modern, but simple, pale colors, not eye breaking or striking. It doesn't matter that you are earning so much now that you can afford all of these celebrities' things. You don't need to force it into scientists' eyes because it could make a very wrong impression on them."

"Okay, uncle," Rosie agreed nonchalantly, making a wry face. "I do have these 'Walmart things' in my luggage. But at least on the airplane, could I enjoy a bit of how I look and how I feel wearing all of these? Or in New York, when we will go for excursions, or just walk around? I am a woman, for God's sake! You can't understand me. When I feel the touch of beautiful clothes on my body, my soul begans to sing, to blossom. I feel happy. Don't take that from me, please."

Aaron again, just kept silent, thinking that he absolutely didn't care. But he was surprised that Rosie argued now not only with him, but with Ashot, as well. He guessed that after the conference she would really move to Washington, DC, and leave them all for good.

He knew that after giving him his baby she wouldn't be in touch with him anymore. Or will be in touch only if she decides to go to university and expect him to pay for it as he promised in exchange for his baby's life.

But would she be in touch with Ashot and Liam, still being thankful for them? Aaron remembered her performance that he saw his first time at the Poetry Club before he started talking to her. The last lines of her poem *Wedding Bells* were:

"I promise my love and care for you always,

Forever – to pay you back."

Maybe she said that in the heat of the moment? Just being thankful for them that they gave her a place to live in their condo and saved her from homelessness and from an adult mental institution for years? Their help was priceless, lifesaving! Does she remember that? Aaron really wasn't sure now.

As a contrast to Seattle, New York met them with snow, cold and a strong wind. Even Aaron, walking to the taxi, put the hood of his downy parka on. Ashot, who wore Liam's leather jacket without a hood, pulled his knitted ski hat low on his forehead and wrapped the fluffy scarf across his face.

"You see, uncle," Rosie smirked, putting the hood of her fur coat on. "I was right. I was in New York before. I knew it would be cold. Without this coat I would be dead!"

"Okay, okay, you're always right," Ashot muttered trying to be conciliatory.

But in the hotel the atmosphere was warm by temperature and by the spirit of the crowds of the arriving guests and participants of the conference. Life was brewing. Everybody was excited and happy in anticipation of this very unusual and interesting event. While registering at the front desk, Aaron and his team were given card-keys for their rooms and also a whole package of fliers with information about the conference.

"Good morning, Dr. Dispenmore," they heard suddenly a voice from behind and all turned around abruptly. Helen Harrison was approaching them with two pretty rough looking men in tow – an elder one and a teenager. "Oh, Mrs. Dispenmore, it's nice to meet you finally," she said, stretching her hand to Rosie suggesting a handshake.

In a second, before Aaron or Ashot could object, Rosie gladly smiled and shook her hand, as she used to do during her government tour. She learned now the people of that level, according to their protocol, should always be nice with the public and give them smiles and greetings back. Mingling with the Senator for two months, Rosie was in the spotlight. She felt comfortable, especially because the man behind Helen was looking like a paparazzo. He was holding a camera, similar to one of Liam's cameras, and filming their greeting.

"What an amazing coat!" Helen continued, shining. "Your husband obviously loves you so much that he follows the rule – a diamond must always be in a golden frame. You look gorgeous!"

"Thank you, Ms..." Rosie answered happily.

"My name is Dr. Helen Harrison, a colleague and a very close friend of Dr. Dispenmore for many years. Let me introduce to you my fiance, Dr. Thompson, and his son, Arthur, who are guests at the conference."

"Stop it, Hel," Aaron said sharply and stood in front of Rosie. "I will not allow you to film my wife."

"Sorry," the thug giggled, turned off the camera and put it down. "I was actually filming Helen. This conference is a very memorable event for our future family. We're getting married on Christmas Eve."

"Oh, Arie, you're still the same – controlling and rude," Helen laughed. "But I forgive you. For a genius scientist everything is forgivable."

"Sorry, ma-am, we have to go," Ashot interrupted, pushing Rosie and Aaron aside.

"See you soon," Helen smiled, nicely waving her hand.

"Why? Aaron? Uncle? Why were you so impolite?" Rosie inquired all the way to the elevator and to their room on the eleventh floor.

"We will talk about that later, kiddo," Ashot stopped her sharply.

After Aaron and Rosie settled in their rooms, where their luggage was already delivered, Ashot invited them to his room for a serious conversation.

Aaron explained to Rosie, who Helen was and told her the whole story of their relationship including Ally's murder. "You knew all of these before, as Rubi and as Rosie," he concluded. "I told you everything in detail, but now, since your memory of the past is gone, you forgot all about that. Helen is double-faced and envious, also malicious and angry. She is a bright scientist and capable of doing a great job. But now she has had bad luck – her cured patient for the conference died. She probably will lose because of that. And she threatened to make me equal. It means – to kill you."

"Why?" Rosie laughed. "Why not just kill you?"

"Because she is in love with me. She wants me alive, but humiliated as a loser. She hopes that this will push me back to her," Aaron explained heatedly. "But it will never happen anyway, under any circumstances."

"But she is getting married," Rosie objected.

"It's bullshit, kiddo. You saw those men," Ashot reminded her, taking his turn in the conversation. "They are obviously a couple of hired thugs, nothing else. We should be very cautious from now on."

He told her the whole plan of their defense which they thought out with Aaron at home before the trip – all sleeping in one room, eating breakfast in different places outside the hotel, and him carrying all the original materials in a pouch on his chest. To their surprise, Rosie listened attentively and accepted everything without any argument. It feels to them that she was convinced and became scared of the situation.

"Maybe we should report this to the police and ask them to place a couple of guards beside our door at night?" she suggested quietly.

"We will think about that," Aaron agreed. "Now, let's go for lunch somewhere in the city and watch carefully. If we notice that someone is following us, or something of that sort, then we will go to the police right away."

"Give me a few minutes to unpack my luggage and fill up my pouch with materials," Ashot requested. "I will not leave them in the room without our attendance even for one second."

While the men organized everything, Rosie took a shower, changed into simpler clothes and refreshed her make-up, getting ready for lunch. "Do they have an *Old Spaghetti Factory* here in New York?" she asked.

"Let me check on my phone," Aaron laughed. "Damn, you're a different person now, but in some preferences you are still the same."

However, the lunch and a short walk later in Central Park evolved calmly and normally. Nobody followed them and nothing bad had happened. For now, there was no reason to go to the police – zero concerns to report. They did not stay outside for long because the cold moist wind was unusual for them, irritating, and made the walk unpleasant. All together they finally returned to the hotel to have some rest and to read and discuss the fliers they received at the front desk.

The advertising materials contained daily and hourly schedules of the conference, the topics of expected speeches, the names of the speakers and also the names of the auditoriums or halls where these speeches will be held. It was supposed to take place in the huge Science World Building, a few blocks away from the hotel.

About five hundred guests and participants from eighty countries of the world were expected to attend the conference. The first day, December 1, was fixed for the Opening ceremony; the last day, December 22 was the Closing ceremony where the name of the winner of the competition would be announced and the nomination for the Nobel Prize would be confirmed. For those – first and last - days any guests could sign in for their short speeches, not longer than five minutes each.

For the competition, the cured patients were submitted from ten doctors – five from the USA, two from Germany, and one from each of the United Kingdom, Japan and India. The presentation of each couple - doctor and patient - was scheduled every second day, with the following day of debate and discussion of their cure by the Board of Judges. The deliberation was supposed to take place in public, so the audience will be involved as well and have a chance to voice their opinions.

Dr. Aaron Dispenmore with his cured patient, Rosa Garcia, were scheduled last – on December 20, giving one final day for deliberation before the Closing Ceremony.

"Why?!" Aaron exclaimed, surprised. "Why are we at the end? Wouldn't they already know who is the best by that day?"

"They already know, son," Ashot answered, smiling. "It's a good sign. They received copies of all the materials in September and worked on them for three months. They already likely have formed their opinion. And it looks like a TV show or a concert – the best act or performance is always the final one. Simple logic!"

"Well... This is kind of encouraging," Aaron smiled for the first time since their departure from Seattle. "So, what is on our schedule for now?"

"Next is a dinner for all the participants of the competition – doctors and their cured patients – in the hotel's restaurant and then your meeting with the media in the Oak Room," Ashot read in the flier. "Live TV broadcasting! The importance of this conference is unbelievable! I guess that you guys are going there without me.

At dinner make sure that you're staying as far as possible from this Helen. But, don't worry, I will be sticking around and watching out for you like a hawk."

"Okay!" Rosie clapped her hands. "Then I can finally wear an evening dress!"

She went to her room to change and when she returned she had on the same red evening dress that she wore in Seattle at their last family dinner with dances at the restaurant. However, now she placed around her waist a thin see-through black scarf with sparkles.

"Wow!" Ashot said, surprised, while Aaron kept silent. "It is a new touch of beauty! You look great, kiddo."

"I don't know if it is in good taste," she said with a wry face. "But I have to use it because this damn tummy started sticking out lately and I don't want to show the people here that I was impregnated by my doctor who was supposed to cure me."

"No need to be sarcastic, kiddo," Ashot noted in a fatherly tone.

"You started turning into the same mean person as Helen," Aaron objected, barely hiding his indignation. "Everything that you're saying about the happiest and most sacred moments of my life sounds dirty and disgusting as you are pronouncing it."

Rosie just smirked, not saying anything back.

"Kids, would you please stop bickering finally? You're not in high school, for God's sake!" the old man exclaimed. "Be a bigger man, Aaron. She is just a silly child!"

"No," Rosie objected. "I am an adult woman, clever, bright and talented!"

"Then behave like one," Ashot muttered while he put his pouch on with the sweater and a leather jacket on top of it. And with that they left the room, heading to the restaurant on the main floor.

CHAPTER 77

In the restaurant the group of the competitive doctors with their patients were seated with the organizers of the conference in a special section divided from the rest of the room by a fretted wooden fence. So, Aaron and Rosie were ushered into this area but Ashot went to the big common area of the restaurant for the other guests. However, he chose a table closest to the fence so he could keep his eyes on them all the time.

Helen was already there, but she sat at the farthest end of the long table with the young Arthur, whom she introduced to Rosie as her fiance's son. It looks like he was playing a special role here.

Jeez, she wants to pretend that this is her patient, Aaron realized right away. *She probably purchased a bogus ID for this teen. But how could she fake brain surgery – there should be a scar on his head for that...*

He looked attentively and saw that the side of the boy's head was shaved. It was covered with a cap he wore even at the table, but part of it still was visible, obviously, on purpose. Helen noticed by Aaron's facial expression that he grasped her game. As soon as he and Rosie entered and were seated, she stood up and walked as if to the restroom. While passing Aaron she smiled broadly and bent to whisper into his ear.

"Keep quiet about my boy, Arie. Then I will keep quiet about your wife. Got it?"

"Nice to see you as well, Dr. Harrison," Aaron smiled back pretending to answer her greeting.

He really hated the situation, but felt some kind of relief realizing that Helen found a way which would be not as dangerous, as if she would kill Rosie. More of a fraud than a murder. He was sure that his understanding was true, knowing her life and business style.

However, Aaron blushed, feeling that in his position he was not much better morally than Helen – he can't present his own wife as a cured patient; it would be a conflict of interest. Also, he agreed to pretend that Ashot's invention was his, which was also a fraud and, practically, a crime.

It really didn't matter that Aaron did it out of respect to hard work of Ashot's life and to his genius talent in science; that he did it as gratitude for the old man healing Rosie; and he did it as a dream to help millions of mentally ill people become cured and healthy. Aaron swore to himself that if he received the Nobel Prize for Ashot's invention, he would give the old man all the money to the last penny. But still, it felt uncomfortable. He had a noble goal, highly respectful, morally pure, but, alas, still illegal. This made Aaron feel uneasy, guilty and ashamed of himself.

At that moment, how could he judge Helen? Of course, her goal was only fame and victory over him, but even with his clean intentions, he sensed that he was not much better than her and silently accepted her suggestion to keep quiet.

Sitting at Aaron's right side, Rosie, on the contrary, felt very happy in her habitual environment. On her other side sat a Japanese doctor with whom she started right away speaking in Japanese. The doctor knew English perfectly and didn't need a translator, but he was excited that this young charming lady knew his language and he answered her, smiling with admiration.

At Aaron's left was a senior woman – a cured patient from Germany. She didn't know English, so they couldn't converse, but it was okay with Aaron – anyway he was not in a mood to talk to anybody now.

The dinner was great; with excellent food served by waiters, along with warm conversations and greetings from the organizers of the conference – the two Academicians, a man and a woman, both Nobel Prize Laureates, board members of the American Psychiatric Association and the Academy of Psychoanalysis and Dynamic Psychiatry.

After that everybody moved next door into the Oak Room where TV cameras were set up and a significant number of journalists with their mics were waiting for the participants of the competition. As the broadcast started, the organizers of the conference talked about it's goal and the importance of it in today's society where the numbers of mentally ill people, sadly, gradually increased and the finding of the cure was of huge importance.

Then they introduced to the media all the doctors and their cured patients by name and let the journalists ask questions. Aaron tried to avoid talking too much and questions he re-addressed to Helen. She glanced at him thankfully for that and gave an active and excited speech about their psychiatric research at the Washington state university. However, Rosie who sat beside him whispered to his ear, "I would like to speak about my new languages abilities. I think it would be interesting to everyone."

"No," he whispered back. "You don't want your friend, Senator Steph, knowing about your former illness, cured or not. And if you want to keep attracting Generals and look for a job at the Pentagon, and a career in politics, then you should keep quiet."

Rosie made a wry face, but obeyed, feeling that he sounded reasonable. And when a journalist asked her how she was feeling being cured, she just shyly answered, "Thank you. I feel great and happy." And that was it. Aaron thankfully squeezed her hand – her answer was vague, polite and exactly what was needed now.

Once the event was finished, they returned to Ashot's room where he was already waiting for them. Aaron enlightened him about the media presentation and his short exchange of words with Helen.

"Good," the old man said. "You did well, guys. I spent the last hour very productive as well. I called my former patient,

Levon Ovanesian, who is now a lawyer here in New York and he invited all of us for dinner this Friday at four p.m. Then his wife, Sarah, took the phone and explained to me that it would be their traditional Jewish Sabbath dinner which they usually do before the beginning of Saturday – their religious celebration day. There would be a lot of Jewish food which is absolutely great by taste. I know, I tried it a couple of times in my life. I hope you will agree to go."

"Of course," Rosie and Aaron both nodded. None of them had traditional Jewish food before but they were open to new experiences that were expected to be interesting.

"Now, let's get ready for the night," Ashot said. He took a chair and propped it to the door the way that the top of its back slid under the doorknob. "It's what we did at home in my childhood," he explained. "Even if someone clicked the card from outside and the lock opened, the doorknob would not move and it would be impossible to open the door. Plus, it would be loud enough to wake us up. And the angle of the chair doesn't give it a chance to open, even if it would be hit strongly from outside."

"Jeez, uncle, you are so funny," Rosie laughed.

"I told you, Ashot, that Helen wants to be fraudulent with her patient. There is no danger for Rosie," Aaron smiled. "But, it's okay. As they said, better safe than sorry. Now, I would like to sit for a while on the balcony and have a glass of wine." With that being said, he opened the refrigerator and took out a bottle of red wine.

"Is there some juice?" Rosie asked, taking the wine glasses from a shelf. "I would like to sit there with you Aaron."

"Okay," he nodded.

"Well, kids, I will say my prayers now and go to sleep," the old man suggested. "Open the sofa-bed, Aaron, before you go. I don't want the noise to wake me up in the middle of the night. And no loud bickering please."

On the balcony, there were a couple of chairs and a small table where they placed the bottles and glasses. Rosie put on her fur coat and Aaron - his parka, because it was pretty chilly, but not as cold as it was when they arrived. The wind stopped, the sky cleared and was covered with stars now. The view of the city wasn't really visible because a lot of huge tall buildings were standing pretty close to each other, blocking the panorama. *No **Stars Under My Feet** here, as it was in Seattle,* Aaron thought wistfully.

"I would like to talk to you about something, Aaron," Rosie uttered while he poured juice for her and wine for himself.

He shrugged. "Okay. I just want to say first - thank you that you're respecting my baby and not drinking alcohol. It is nice of you. Some women could be reckless and wouldn't care."

"I am a nice person," she giggled. "I am happy that you at least recognize that."

"What do you want to talk about?" he asked.

"I just think that we should be friends. Uncle is right. We don't need bickering all the time, trying to hurt each other and showing that we are enjoying each other's pain. It's mean, and it's not who we are. Right?"

He shrugged again. "What do you want, really?"

"Tell me, please, about the woman you're seeing now?"

"Why?"

"I genuinely want to be your friend for our child's sake. And I would like to know who would live with you and raise my child."

"Your child?" Aaron smirked. "As I remember, we decided that it will be my child only. Why do you care?"

"I care as your family friend. Tell me as a friend, please... Do you love her?"

He took his glass, slowly sipped the wine, then put it back on the table and shrugged again.

"No, I don't," he answered finally.

"So, there is nothing serious?"

"Actually, there is. I don't love her as I loved you, but I like her. She is a good friend, nice, kind, warm, devoted, and loving. She obviously would be a great wife and great mother. To be with her is light and easy, and always fun. She loves poetry, as I do..."

"Is she mentally ill?" Rosie interrupted.

"Come on!" Aaron exclaimed defensively. "Millions of people in the world love poetry. Don't be mean again!"

"Sorry. I just thought... Please, continue," Rosie smiled apologetically.

"She satisfies me sexually a great deal, still keeping it all effortless and fun, as a game. I absolutely like it. You know, I imagined a life with her. When I will work my two jobs, I will come home tired and she will hug me. We will sit and play on the rug and pillows in front of the fireplace with Laurie and Eric, and everybody will be happy, elated and enjoy each other's company. It would be rest and relaxation. It will be happiness, as I understand it."

"Who is Eric?"

"My future son."

"You already chose the name for him?"

"Yes, I like this name. I had a good friend at school, Eric, when I was raised in Atlanta."

"And you didn't ask me?"

"Of course not. You have no say on it."

Rosie slowly sipped her juice without saying a word. It was visible that the conversation wasn't easy for her. Aaron didn't even understand why she started it in the first place.

"Well," she continued finally, "you will marry her..."

"Not yet of course, since we are not divorced yet. But in the future, maybe. At least, for now I want to invite her for Christmas dinner and introduce her to mom and Laurie as my girlfriend. And then we will see if it goes further from there."

"You're lucky, Aaron," Rosie took a deep breath. "For me it is much more difficult. You kind of easily forgot our love..."

"I will never forget our love," he interrupted. "It was a once in a life thing. I'll cherish that memory forever. But, to tell the truth, we actually couldn't be living together as a family because it was too much, too intense, too insane, too mad. It was a fire that was burning us both. We both would probably die in each other's arms. It would not be a normal regular life which I want with this girl – family, children, fun, calmness and rest."

"I know," Rosie nodded. "I felt exactly the same way about us. I was brave enough to publicly jump from the stage to your lap. I was brave enough to kiss you for seventeen minutes in front of the whole world. I was brave enough to choose you over my poetry talent which was the meaning of my life. That's how I loved you – more than my life. I was dying in this fire as well. It was sad and uneasy for me when it was gone so suddenly. It was a shock. I was scared. I panicked. Uncle spent three hours with me to calm me down and convince me to date you again..."

She took a deep breath, then continued, "But, I am still not sure, if I will be capable now to love anyone ever. Uncle is guessing that I need another big shock which could return these particles of my aura that are responsible for emotions. I hope that as a genius scientist he is right about that. But what a shock? Should I jump with a parachute from a plane or from the highest tower? Or what? I don't know."

Aaron didn't know either what to answer for that. They sat in silence for a long moment, just sipping their drinks. "I think it is time to go to sleep," he said finally. "Tomorrow the Opening Ceremony starts at ten. We could walk a couple of blocks from here to the Science World Building, but it will take some time to get ready in the morning."

Rosie didn't answer anything, just walked inside and got ready for bed.

It was very early in the morning, maybe about three, when she tapped Aaron's shoulder to wake him up while he was sleeping on the sofa-bed.

"Aaron," she whispered, "come here, please. I'll show you something."

"What? Where?" he muttered rubbing his eyes to chase the sleep away. "What do you want, Rosie?"

She forced him to stand up and pulled him toward her bed.

"No," he said. "I won't..."

"Shut up," she whispered. "Just sit here on the edge."

She lay down on her bed, took his hand and put it on her abdomen.

"I don't..." he tried to object.

"Quiet. Just hold your palm here and feel it," she murmured. "It's your Eric. He starts moving. He is alive. He is not just a piece of meat, but a person now..."

"Is it already four and a half months?" Aaron asked.

"I guess so. I never counted, but he knows better. The soul entered his tiny body, the soul that came down – uncle would say from Heaven - but I could say from the holographic energy fields of the universe. Right?"

"Yes," Aaron nodded, holding his breath. He sensed some movements under his palm, slow, soft, then suddenly pretty abrupt, as a kick; then slow again. An amazing feeling of some deep, eternal happiness filled his heart. It was exactly what he felt when Laurie began moving the first time - the sacred holiness of LIFE. The new life, eternal life, his son's life...

"Thank you, Rosie," he whispered, then lied down on top of the covers and hugged her with one arm, still keeping the other one on her abdomen to feel more of the baby's movements. "Now we could sleep for a while as a family. I don't know about you, but I am sincerely happy. Really happy, eternally happy."

"Me too," Rosie answered and tenderly kissed his shoulder.

CHAPTER 78

Aaron was woken up by Ashot's quiet voice. It was dark in the room, only some light from the street lamps penetrated through the big balcony window making the old man's figure visible as he knelt beside his bed, praying.

Aaron realized that he was in Rosie's bed, hugging her while she was still peacefully sleeping. He waited until Ashot whispered, "Amen", then he asked in a whisper as well, "What time is it, uncle?"

"Six in the morning," Ashot answered. "Seriously, son?"

"No, uncle, no. It's not what you are thinking." Aaron carefully climbed out from the bed, walked to Ashot and sat on the floor beside him. "She just showed me that our baby has started moving."

"Already? That's good. It means everything is okay. We were so preoccupied with this conference that we didn't give any time for the baby. Shame on us," Ashot murmured. "But then... you kept staying with her..."

"She insisted," Aaron tried to justify the situation.

"The girls are always insisting," Ashot smirked. "I remember when I was a teen, in high school, in spite of my big, not good-looking nose, the girls always were chasing me. I wasn't interested at all. Maybe I already subconsciously felt that I am gay. Then I got married only because my wife insisted, and also – tradition.

655

Everybody is married to have kids. We, Armenians, are crazy about that."

"Did your first love, Patrick, also insist?" Aaron asked, smiling.

"Oh, very much so. I was kind of hesitant because I still wasn't sure who I was, and I was married... but, here we are. You never know what could happen in life. All is in God's hands."

"Nothing happened here," Aaron smiled. "I only slept on top of the covers to comfort her. That's it."

"I am not blaming you. I was just surprised. It's actually my dream that the two of you will get back together."

Aaron shrugged and took a deep breath. Then, he just changed the subject, "Okay, uncle. Would you mind, please, to undo your barricade by the door so I could go exercise in the fitness club? And maybe to swim for a while in the pool?"

Ashot cautiously removed the chair from under the doorknob and Aaron went to his own room next door, where his luggage was. He changed into a jersey and went downstairs to do his usual work out. He returned in about one hour and found Ashot and Rosie sitting on the edge of the bed and laughing, as she tried to show the old man her baby's motions. But the attempt wasn't successful – the baby probably was sleeping now and did not move.

Ashot had already showered. Now was Aaron's turn - he needed to wash away the chlorine from the pool. He didn't know why he didn't go to his own room to do so. He was kind of used to the idea that they all are living together in Ashot's room. It was comfortable for him. Their own rooms – his and Rosie's – serving them as wardrobes only, to keep the luggage.

While Aaron was in the shower, Rosie winked at Ashot, ran to the bathroom, got undressed and sneaked under the shower curtain behind Aaron's back.

"Jeez, I should remember that you loved that," he muttered as she hugged him from behind and pressed her whole body to his back. "In a shower - is your favorite thing. But I don't want it now."

"Aaron, please," she begged, passionately caressing his tummy. "I didn't have sex for more then three months. I know, you did, but

I didn't. I am suffering. I am still your wife, aren't I? As you said at night – we are still family..."

He really didn't want this. He was scared that everything could burst and flare up again. When you are burned in fire, you are careful while dealing with it afterwards. If you are cut with a knife, you learn how to be cautious next time to avoid injury again. His love was dead, buried under the ashes, but maybe there was a tiny spark, a morsel of a hot coal hiding under its layer. Even when the conscious memories were gone, the memories of the body stayed forever.

When Aaron tried to dance with Rosie at the restaurant in Seattle, when he just touched her waist, and felt her warmth through the fabric of her dress, those memories burst so madly that he was forced to run away and block his body's memory by a wild encounter with Jessa. He closed this door forever, he cut this experience off to avoid an emotional injury once more.

But it was absolutely impossible to refuse her right now and he just simply gave up, closing his eyes and blocking all the thoughts – concentrating on the sensations only.

When everything was finished, Aaron carried his wife, wrapped into a bathrobe, back to the bedroom. He loved carrying her, he always did. That gave him a sense of his physical strength combined with the strength of his emotions. He felt himself as a confident man in power at those moments and he was happy.

Ashot was there, sitting on his bed watching TV extremely loudly.

"Well, guys, it was bold," he said, smiling, reducing the TV sound to a quieter level. "Couldn't you both use the shower in any other room out of our three?"

"If it would be in any other room," Rosie giggled, "we would probably be late for the conference or wouldn't go at all, and stay there forever."

"Okay, just get dressed fast because we don't have time for breakfast outside. We should now go downstairs to eat. Get ready quickly, please. And we should watch out for this Helen-woman."

But it was a big relief for them to see that Helen wasn't at the restaurant. Although the crowd appeared thick, everybody was nice, quiet and friendly. At the table Aaron gazed at Rosie who sat across from him, trying to understand what he was feeling after their sex outburst in the shower. To his surprise and ease, he didn't feel a lot of excitement. He even thought that with Jessa it was actually better. Was it an inner confirmation for him that his love for Rosie was finally completely gone? He couldn't say for sure, but there was no time to think about that now.

Then Aaron called Beth on Skype from his phone. It was only six a.m. in Seattle, but she was already awake, preparing breakfast for Laurie and packing her school lunch.

"Good morning, Arie," Beth said, smiling happily. "I guess you're doing great. I saw you yesterday on TV, but you were kind of hesitant to talk. Why, darling?"

"Mom, it's okay. It was ethically needed to be managed that way. Is Laurie still sleeping?"

"Yes. She really wanted to watch you last night, so she could brag in school that her dad was on TV. But it was very late here – the show lasted from ten to midnight with the time difference. So, I let her watch for just several minutes, but she saw you and even jumped from happiness."

However, Laurie heard her grandma talking on Skype and ran downstairs in her pajamas leaping two steps at once.

"Daddy, daddy," she yelled, excited, "you know, this is the last week of school. We have Christmas break next week. And Grandpa Liam said he will take us to a movie set for an excursion! I will meet some famous actors in real life!"

"It's amazing, sweetie," Aaron answered, smiling. "I am sure you will have a great time there. You know, I am working hard here, so I will be busy for a few more days. Then I will call you again and you can tell me all about that. Love you very much."

"I love you too," Laurie said, sending him an air kiss.

After saying bye to his family, Aaron asked, "Aren't you calling Liam, uncle?"

"No, I don't want to wake him up. He told me yesterday night that he will watch your media presentation until the very end, so, he will call me when he awakes."

"Okay, then we should probably go," Aaron suggested. "Before the conference we need to register at the switchboard in the lobby of the Science World Building and give them all the original materials. It will take some time."

"Yeah," Ashot laughed and patted his big tummy under his sweater and jacket where the materials were hidden. "But as for registration, I did it yesterday night online for all three of us while you were at that media encounter in the Oak Room. So, it's already done."

The Science World Building was just three blocks away from the hotel. The walk promised to be nice and refreshing because the weather changed to a much warmer and clearer one. The sun shone, but Rosie refused to leave her fur coat at home saying that if it was too warm, she could always unbutton it. And she did it – the laps of her coat flapped while she walked holding Aaron under his left arm.

In his right arm he was carrying his briefcase with some fliers which were put there for camouflage. He didn't put his parka's hood on because for him it was warm enough as well. Ashot walked on Aaron's right, close to the edge of the sidewalk, carrying his briefcase, loaded with the same trash, in his right hand.

The street was crowded because most of the five-hundred participants and guests of the conference walked in the same direction – from the hotel to the Science Word Building. The distance was so close that there was no reason for anyone to take a taxi especially on such an amazing fresh morning.

As they approached the main entrance, Aaron accidentally lifted his head as something pushed him. He saw on the other side of the street a very tall glass tower. It caught his eye that one of the windows on either the 5 or the 6th floor was open a bit and a long barrel of a sniper's rifle was sticking out from there. And that was it. He subconsciously shuddered recognizing the tower instantly. He already knew. In a moment, in a second, in a flash…The thought, as lightning, zipped through his mind – the last part of Rosie's poem about their future - **Place out of Time:**

"Glass tower in the sky,
a rifle in a sniper's hand
sending a bullet into your head..."

He had no time to say something to his team or even finish the thought, as with a loud whoosh a bullet went right beside his ear and Rosie screamed and fell on the ground, letting his arm go. Aaron glanced at her and saw blood appearing on the fur of her coat. She didn't move and it was impossible to say if she was alive or not.

The shots continued and more bullets were flying. Aaron dropped his briefcase and fell down on the top of her, hugging her and covering her with his body.

Then he sensed a very strong hit, like somebody beat him at the back of his head with a baseball bat. The piercing bright sparkles flashed in his eyes and everything darkened. He heard just Rosie's voice in the darkness, soft and tender, like coming from the sky, as she kept telling the final stanza of this poem.

"I have holographic universe in my brain,
I have three dimensional time in my head,
Please, don't love me, I beg.
I don't want to see you dead."

Jeez, what's happening? was Aaron's last thought. *Am I dying? Why? It shouldn't be if I don't love her anymore. I don't... I stopped loving her... I did... Or didn't I?...*

Meanwhile, Ashot sensed a hard push at his back. His knees buckled and he dropped down on the sidewalk behind Aaron. A light slim figure in dark clothes with a black ski-mask covering the face snatched the briefcase from his hand and Aaron's briefcase from the ground and disappeared in the crowds.

It was sheer panic on the street – people were running for their lives in any direction and screaming like crazy. But some of them were brave enough to pull out their phones, call 911 and take videos or photos of the open window at the glass tower and the barrel of the rifle which was sticking out. However, this view didn't last long – the rifle disappeared and the window closed.

Laying on the sidewalk, Ashot saw in front of his eyes the back of Aaron's head and blood oozing between the locks of his dark-brown wavy hair. In spite of the shock, the old man clearly realized what was happening and began to pray, mixing his whisper with his sobs, "Oh Lord almighty! Please, save my kids, please, don't let them die. If you need to take someone, take me. Just let them live, please, please, I am begging you, my dear Lord. Take me, take me instead of them."

Time stopped for him. He didn't hear sirens of the police cars coming one after another, surrounding the main entrance of the Science World Building. He didn't hear the sounds of the ambulances or fire trucks. He didn't hear and didn't notice that his phone was ringing in his pocket. It was Liam calling to say Hi and Congratulations at the beginning of the conference.

CHAPTER 79

"Are you okay, sir?" were the first words heard by Ashot from an unknown voice as he finally returned to his senses. Someone's hands helped him to stand up. There were two policemen holding him under his arms, as paramedics were working on Aaron and Rosie.

"Are they alive? Are they alive?" Ashot repeated through his chattering teeth, mechanically, numbly, as a zombie. "Tell me, are they alive?" But nobody answered him, everybody around him was extremely preoccupied doing their job, fast and well organized. Aaron and Rosie both were put on the stretchers of the ambulances that left with piercing sirens heading to a hospital.

In Ashot's eyes it reflected as a complete mess on the street and hundreds of people were fussing around meaninglessly. He didn't understand what they were doing, only heard through the loud speaker that the Opening Ceremony of the conference was postponed until three p.m. Normally it would be already finished at that time.

Bewildered, Ashot stared at his hands smeared in Aaron's blood. He got it probably from the hood of Aaron's parka which he was holding while laying on the ground behind the young man. Some drops of blood obviously splashed onto Ashot's face as well. He felt that his gut was squeezed in a painful spasm, not knowing what happened to Rosie. Was she alive or not? Seeing the blood exuding from a wound on the back of Aaron's head he already guessed the worst. It was like the end of the world for him, but he had no right to give up on the conference. He must go ahead at any price, at any cost, no matter what.

Being pretty much shaky, Ashot finally found an inner power to suppress the sobs that were suffocating him and held himself in check strong enough to talk, although stuttering a bit.

"I will tell you... what happened... I know... what it was ... and who did it," Ashot exclaimed desperately, grabbing the policeman's sleeve. "I will tell you the whole story, just... Please, let me in the building. I need to give the materials to the conference's representative. These materials," he patted his big pouch on his chest. "Please, sir, these are materials of Dr. Dispenmore's cure. Those thugs were hunting us to steal them. I will tell you all about those people. I took a photo of one of them yesterday night during dinner. But, first, these materials need to be delivered to the conference before ten a.m. If it is late, this doctor is out of the competition. Millions of ill people won't receive their cure. You have to understand the importance of it for all of human society, sir. Please, believe me. I am begging you, officer."

God was watching over Ashot again, otherwise he couldn't understand how the policeman agreed to his request. Usually they were very restrictive in their rules.

"I guess, your doctor is out of the competition anyway," the policeman said, shaking his head with compassion. "But okay, we will let you into the building," he nodded to his partner who held Ashot under his other arm and they walked the old man out from the crime scene. It was already surrounded by yellow police tape and forensics were working on it. Some of them were taking photos and putting small yellow markers on the spots of the evidence. When Ashot with two policemen approached the main entrance of the Science World Building, the huge glass doors were closed and guarded by policemen but they let in their fellow officers holding Ashot.

Inside the lobby the organizers of the conference stood at the counter of the switchboard with a group of the building's security guards, policemen and probably detectives. There was also a long table prepared for collecting materials of the competitors and two women were sitting behind it.

"Here are the original materials of Dr. Dispenmore's cure," Ashot shouted to them. "I am his assistant, Registered Nurse Thomas Spencer. I am delivering them."

"Please, come here, sir," one of the women answered, glancing at the big clock on the wall above the counter. "It is two minutes to ten. You came last, but just in time before the official beginning of the conference was supposed to be. All other participants have already submitted their originals."

The two policemen approached the table still holding Ashot. They were a bit confused, not seeing any bag or briefcase of his where the materials could be.

"Please, let me take them out," the old man begged. "They are on my chest. Help me please, officers."

The policemen let him go but stayed very close to him, and were surprised when he took off his leather jacket, then a sweater and asked one of the policemen to hold these clothes. Then Ashot took a pouch from his neck with his shaky hands. He let the policemen open it and unload the three photo albums and manuscript on the table. Next, he asked the policeman to unzip the pockets of his jacket and take out all the twelve thumb-drives. And finally, he asked another policeman to fish out ten more thumb-drives from his pants pockets. He didn't do that himself because he didn't want them to think that he was taking out some firearm from his pockets and could be a danger to anyone. Luckily, his replica gun was left in his luggage at his hotel room.

When all required materials that Ashot kept on him were on the table, the woman counted them, filled the form − a list of contents - and wrote a receipt that she gave to Ashot. "You are the last one," she repeated, "but you are lucky to get here in time in spite of the shooting on the street. Something awful is happening there. Oh, my gosh! I just noticed! Your face and hands have some blood on, sir. Were you injured?"

"No, thank God," he said, making the sign of the cross on his forehead and kissing the golden cross on his chest. "It's the blood of Doctor Dispenmore. I am praying that he could make it. Now, I am all yours, officers. You can take me to the station or anywhere you want. I will help as much as I can and I will tell you everything that I know."

The stars were shining in the dark sky much as down, below the slope, the city lights shone, blinking, appearing as stars as well. ***Stars under my Feet...*** Rosie was laying on the bench, her head on Aaron's lap. She looked up but couldn't see him clearly, just a dim silhouette as he bowed his head and touched her cheek with his lips. And then he kissed her very carefully, fondly, without any arousal or excitement, just like believers would kiss the holy icons, or holy cross, or the hand of a priest, or lap of Pope's dress. It felt to her that he was not kissing the woman in her but a sacred holy treasure - so pure and worship-like this kiss was.

She sensed a light cool air on her lips – not a touch of a man's lips but a touch of a ghost, a spirit that came to say goodbye forever. The touch of his soul. She knew that it would happen. She saw that before in the vision of their future.

"I have holographic universe in my brain,
I have three dimensional time in my head,
Please, don't love me, I beg.
I don't want to see you dead."

She remembered that Aaron stayed soundless for a long moment after she told him that poem ***Place out of Time*** at their first night on the bench in the park in Seattle.

"Why do you think I could be dead, if I love you?" he inquired then.

"No idea... But I don't know if it's possible to turn everything back and make you stop loving me."

"No," Aaron said confidently, shaking his head. "Absolutely not. Don't even think about it, ever. I will not stop loving you no matter what, under any circumstances. And it will last until the moment I die. It doesn't matter when or at what age."

He didn't stop loving her. He saved her, he covered her. The first bullet aimed in her heart missed because of the destruction - her fluffy fur coat laps were flapping - and it got into her left upper arm. The second bullet would have been in her head, if he hadn't fallen down on top of her and protected her with his body. Protected her and his son. Maybe only his son? Maybe only her? He didn't know, he had no time to think, he didn't have time to understand. He was pronounced dead in the ambulance on the way to the hospital. And now his soul came to say goodbye to her and gave her his 'holy oasis kiss' for the last time before flying up to the holographic fields of the universe; to stay there and to wait until the moment of reincarnation happens.

Rosie felt the farewell tears streaming down her cheeks. She was crying soundlessly even before she came to. Then, as she opened her eyes there was a dark sky covered with stars behind the window of her room. It was already late evening. Ashot was sitting on a chair beside her hospital bed, his forehead propped on his hands.

"Uncle, is he dead?" she whispered.

Ashot silently nodded, biting his lips.

"I felt he just kissed me to say goodbye. I knew that. How did it happen? Why?"

"Those thugs... hired obviously by Helen. One of them shot from the tower window and the young one pushed me and grabbed our briefcases. So, I guessed right. My trap with briefcases worked. But Aaron..." he choked on the tears and stopped for a moment to collect himself. "Aaron was their accidental mistake. They were hired to kill you, kiddo."

"I am in shock, uncle," Rosie moaned. "Look at my hands, they are shaking. What will happen with us now?"

"I attended the Opening Ceremony today, from three to eight p.m. They announced that Dr. Aaron Dispenmore was shot in front of the entrance of the Science World Building and took a moment of silence to honor his memory. They also promised that his cure project and his cured patient will stay in the competition which is allowed posthumously by their rules – opposite to the rule that the patient should be alive. Starting tomorrow the conference will go according to their regular schedule."

"Will those people try to kill me again?" Rosie asked tentatively. "I am scared, uncle. I am very scared."

"The police placed an armed guard outside your door for now, until those thugs are caught. It must help. I am sure the detectives will come to talk to you soon. We both are the main witnesses. I was taken to the police station after that shooting and questioned there until two p.m. I told them about those thugs, about Helen's threats, gave them a photo of the young thug which I took at the restaurant during your dinner where he played the role of her cured boy. The police have a lot of information. Many witnesses were on the street. Some took photos of the window of the tower, some made a video of the whole event. It was already on the TV News at six o'clock. I called Liam. He saw it. He is in shock. He doesn't know how to tell Aaron's family. I don't know either. I am worrying if Beth will survive it. She has a pretty weak heart, and had a heart attack some years ago. I guess that the police will notify her, but Liam will try to be there for her as much as possible."

Rosie took a deep breath and wiped her cheeks. "What happened to me, uncle? Was I shot as well?" she wanted to know. "I see that my arm and shoulder are bandaged and it is kind of painful to move. And this IV is here..."

"You had surgery and they removed a bullet. I talked to the doctor. He said they could keep you here for about a week to observe. They want to be cautious because of your pregnancy, especially since you have a history of miscarriage when Ben was shot."

"Oh, gosh! Uncle," Rosie sniffled and began crying again. "What the hell is happening to me? Why? The same situation twice! It's unbelievable. It feels like I am cursed and can't have a normal love and normal family ever?"

Ashot sat on the edge of her bed and took her hand.

"Kiddo, please, don't say that. You are an amazing girl. You are not cursed, don't even think that or say those words ever." He took his golden cross and holding it in his hand made a sign of cross with it over her. "You have love. You are blessed. I love you and Liam loves you. Your friend Senator loves you. Even this damn General Simon in Kabul is smitten by you. Even this soldier, Ben's brother, loves you and went on a death mission for you, and survived. So, you see, not everybody who loves you died. Many people who love you are still alive and will keep loving you. I am pretty sure that your baby, Aaron's son, will love you too."

"Oh, my gosh! This baby!" she sobbed again covering her face with her healthy right hand. "What will I do with him now? I need to take care of my career and concentrate on that only. I can't keep this baby. I don't want him. I was supposed to give him to Aaron..."

"Stop it, kiddo!" Ashot exclaimed strictly. "Don't pretend to be worse than you are. Don't say these mean and heartless things, for God's sake. I can guarantee you that Aaron's mother would be happy to take this baby. It would be what is left of her son. It would be her holy memory of Aaron. Or, in the worst case scenario, if she won't be able, I swear to God that Liam and I, we will be happy to adopt him. I loved Aaron and considered him my son, the same as you - my daughter. This little boy will be my only grandson."

CHAPTER 80

The chaos in front of the Science World Building continued. The main door was still locked because the police had not finished processing the crime scene yet. But, in spite of that, the conference Opening Ceremony started exactly as it was announced – at three p.m. So the participants and the guests of the conference were let in through a small service door at the side of the structure which created a huge line and a delay to usher five hundred people inside.

During his questioning at NYPD station, Ashot told the police about Helen's threats and her hired thugs. It was considered a serious lead and they bugged her hotel room while she was attending the Opening Ceremony. It was a right move that gave them a lot of useful data.

When at the Ceremony it was announced that Dr. Aaron Dispenmore was shot in front of the entrance of the Science World Building and pronounced dead on the way to the hospital, a minute of silence was held in his memory. Shocked by this announcement Helen left the conference hall and returned to her hotel room.

At the front desk of the hotel she picked up the briefcases that her thugs left for her. While opening them in her room, she was struck by another impact – they were filled with fliers and old newspapers. Materials of Aaron's cure weren't there and Helen could only guess that the thugs stole them to sell to some other scientists for more money.

For a few hours she was sitting in her room, crying, which sounded normal to the police, but if Aaron would be able to see and hear her he would be really surprised. He was always sure that Helen had no feelings except for anger and control. But it seemed by her sobs, bewails and laments that she really loved him for all those years.

Plus to despair that she lost Aaron forever by this tragic accident, Helen was extremely angry at herself for hiring the stupid and – that was now proven – not really professional hit men. They not only killed the wrong person but also stole all the materials from Aaron's and his assistant's briefcases.

She paid them $1,000 deposit, and their oral contract stated that she will pay another $9,000 after successful completion of their task. It made her explode when they called her cell phone from an untraceable disposable phone and demanded the rest of the money.

"You, bastards! You, idiots!" Helen screamed in the madness of ire. "What did you do? Why did you shoot him? You should have eliminated her only!"

"Shut up, you, bitch!" the older thug shouted back. "Who could expect that he would cover her – it was his fault, not mine."

"When he fell to cover her, you had to stop shooting, idiot!"

"Then she would be alive and you would not be happy. I needed to finish the job."

"She is probably alive anyway, and I won't pay you a penny more because of your stupidity. Plus, you stole all the briefcases' contents. I am not forgiving. I will report you to the police."

"You're smart enough not to do so, lady!" the thug giggled. "They will arrest you first. We're coming in five minutes, so make sure that you have the money. Otherwise, you will regret being greedy and will follow your damn lover to his grave."

Although the police recording gave them the possibility to hear only one side of the conversation that Helen yelled loud, they got the information. It was clear to them that she will try to escape from the thugs. They expected that beforehand and were ready, waiting by all of the building's exits to arrest her and the killers all together. But they were a little bit late.

As soon as Helen frantically packed her luggage and opened the door to exit her room, the thugs who were waiting for her in the hallway, forced her back into the room, locked the door from inside and demanded money. She finally gave them the last amount but in spite of that they strangled her with a guitar string, so as not to make any extra noise. The police were already by the door and broke in. It was a serious fight – shots were fired and the older thug was killed by the police, while the young one tried to climb down from the balcony to the floor below. In a hurry, he made a wrong step and fell from the eighth floor right to the street. As an outcome, no one was arrested as a suspect in the murder of Dr. Dispenmore and attempted murder of his cured patient Rosa Garcia. The second deadly crime scene on the same street was now surrounded by yellow tape and being processed.

This all happened late at night and the next morning all TV and radio stations were buzzing with breaking news. For the media it looked like the Psychiatry Scientific Conference was becoming a dangerous event adding a huge amount of work for the NYPD.

After attending the second day of the conference, Ashot came to visit Rosie and noticed that the police officer wasn't at the door of her room.

"Where is your guard?" the old man asked.

"The policeman said that he was notified to leave the post," she explained. "There is no danger for me anymore. What do you think, uncle? Why? I guess it will probably be explained on the six o'clock News. Maybe I should go to the patients' lounge to watch TV to make sure that it is true?"

"Well, I heard on the radio in the taxi while riding here, that one more scientist at the conference was killed," Ashot said. "They didn't give the name yet, but I guess that it could be Helen and her cunning plot to eliminate you finally bit her in the ass. If it was really her, she got what she deserved. I will never forgive her for Aaron's death. In spite of God teaching us to forgive. But... Never! And both her thugs were killed while the police tried to arrest them. The policemen actually did a great job. I hope that the information I gave them was helpful. At least, it could help to get justice for Aaron. However, I am sure that the investigation will take a long time. Hey... what is this, kiddo?" he pointed at the big bouquet of the red roses on her bedside table.

"Check the card," she answered. "It's George. I texted him what happened, and he sent me flowers."

"Hmm," Ashot smirked, taking the beautiful card that was sticking between the roses. "'Get well soon. My sincere condolences about your husband.' Well, he sounds decent at least."

"Don't worry, uncle. He is just a friend."

"It's kind of a strange friendship with such an age difference and distance," Ashot shook his head. "He should have forgotten about you long ago, right after you left."

"I am probably unforgettable," Rosie smiled sadly. "Come on, uncle! I was friends with you and Liam before you decided to adopt me. Our age gap with you is much bigger!"

"It's not comparable, kiddo. We're married gays."

"George is married too."

"But he is not a gay – it's a huge difference."

Rosie made a wry face and shrugged. "Please, don't spoil my mood, uncle," she begged. "My stress just started to subside a bit. I need some positive emotions to heal faster. You need me in two weeks to be healthy at the conference as a cured patient. Are you still going ahead with your project without Aaron?"

"Yes," Ashot nodded. "I have to. It's my duty for human society. And now, my duty for Aaron's memory as well. I will read his speech as his assistant who was helping him in the process of your cure. Make sure that you remember that, kiddo, when the judges evaluate you in person."

"I do, uncle. I am not an ungraceful being. I love you and I will do everything that needed to help you."

"Thank you, kiddo," Ashot said and hugged her. "At least, I see that you started smiling a bit."

"I am trying to get over it as much as possible. And it is actually helpful that my love evaporated after the cure. Otherwise, I would probably be dead from grief. But during the last months Aaron was for me like a neighbor or distant acquaintance. His death is sad, shocking, scary but not as painful and personal."

"Wow! A distant acquaintance... However, you just had sex with him about one hour before his death. And you're carrying his baby. Oh, kiddo," Ashot disapprovingly shook his head, then sighed, "Well, maybe it was that shock you needed to get some of your aura's particles back. Maybe it will do something positive for your soul. I sincerely hope so."

Then Ashot changed the subject and continued, "You know, kiddo, at the Science World Building they have a big Notice Board on the wall in the lobby. All the participants of the competition are presented on it. There are photos of each doctor, his patient and his assistant, if he has one. Beside the photos is a flier with a short description of their cure, and a plastic pocket under it - all the guests could put their notes, questions or opinions into it. And you know, many-many people put their notes of condolences into our pocket. I took out about thirty today. People are so kind and compassionate. I took those notes into my room, and I was sitting and couldn't hold my tears while reading them. I don't know, if you would like to see them?"

"Why, uncle? Are you crazy? Do you want to make me cry again?" Rosie exclaimed indignantly.

"I am still trying to wake your feelings up, kiddo. I know that you are a good person and I am sure that it will return. You're just kind of numb now and don't feel any big pain. But for me this loss is extremely painful. I truly loved Aaron as a son I never had. And what it will do for Beth, I can't even imagine. I am not sure she will survive it. I will go to call Liam now - to find out how things are going in Seattle. Stay safe, kiddo. Love you."

After they hugged and kissed each other's cheeks, Ashot left, and Rosie decided to go for a walk in the hallway. She felt confident and much safer now, knowing that there is no danger for her anymore. She put on a brave face while talking with Ashot but in reality her soul was still paralyzed by the impact, although she didn't get it emotionally in full yet.

On the left side of the hallway was a big door with a sign – Rehabilitation Center; farther at the end of a long corridor was a lounge separated by a glass door where patients who weren't bedridden were allowed to watch TV and to socialize.

Rosie entered this room intending to watch the TV News to find out more information about her story, but there was a group of people watching a comedy. Two young men, patients, sprawled in the armchairs and three female nurses - who were probably on a break - were flirting with them, joking and laughing loudly. One of the nurses was even sitting on the edge of the chair, trying to hug a man's neck which seemed not really professional on her part, but Rosie didn't care.

She sat for a while as far from the group as possible and tried to watch TV but comedy wasn't at all what she was in the mood for. She felt tears coming from her eyes, so she covered her face with both hands and sat for a few minutes, sniffling. Then she stood up and abruptly left the lounge.

In the hallway she stopped by a window, put her elbows on the window sill and kept crying burying her face in her palms. She didn't think about Aaron, nor the shooting or the horrors. Her head felt empty, there weren't any thoughts. It was just a feeling of sadness, of an endless, eternal sorrow pouring out from her eyes with those tears. It was an ocean of emotions, the vast infinite ocean, and she was sinking in it deeper and deeper with every second.

Then some unclear images and pictures began floating through her mind, some people she knew in her past – her first little friend, Hope, who inspired her to write poetry; her supporting and devoted teacher in the *Youth Shelter* school, Mary Oswald; her 'besties' from the Poetry Club, Jessa Green and Layla; her little brothers, Fernando, Enrico and Alberto, whom she loved dearly; the dog, Oscar... Then there was Ben, her first love, first boyfriend; his family – his twin-brother, Alex, their mother, Keysha, three little siblings, Anika, Tina and Dante; her math teacher from high school, Barry Goodwin... Then Aaron – the lost love of her life, her vivid admirer, her devoted husband, and his little daughter, Laurie;

her first psychiatrist, Dr. Evelyn Hertz; her uncle Ashot and Liam, as she at first met them three years ago; many-many people were coming closer and closer step-by-step.

The ocean of sadness - where she forgot her past, mislaid all those people, wasted the feelings toward them - was evaporating gradually now. It started feeling to Rosie, as she was waking up, as her memory was returning; but not the horrors, not the abuse and sufferings. The clear, bright, kind, beautiful memories began penetrating from a fog, the sensitive, tender, good feelings reincarnated, and refilled her heart.

She continued crying, but now these were the tears of happiness, tears of relief that she was coming back to herself, finding herself again.

"You need a big shock, kiddo," Ashot had told her. "It could return the lost particles of your aura that are responsible for your feelings and memories."

And it happened now as her beloved uncle predicted. The shock of Aaron's death and of her own bullet wound was huge, enormous, striking. It was so strong that it worked as a magnet toward the energy fields of the universe. It attracted and returned a white sparkling cloud of feelings to her aura - the cloud that flew up to the universe together with the black damaged particles of her aura when she broke the Clay Mask.

Was it returning forever? Or just temporarily? Just for a few days? She didn't know, she wasn't sure... But at the moment it felt calming and comforting.

Rosie heard subconsciously that the door of the lounge had been opened and nurses ran through the hallway to their station – their break probably ended. Then the men walked out as well and headed to the door of the Rehabilitation Center – one of them was on crutches and another one had a cane which clicked on the tile floor. They were talking loud and laughing but then saw Rosie and stopped. The man on crutches disappeared behind the Rehabilitation Center's door but another one approached Rosie. She didn't see that but heard that clicking sound of his cane coming closer. Then she felt that he very carefully tapped her shoulder.

"Hey, Miss," he said."Do you need some help? What's happening? Are you hurt?"

She turned and looked at him bewildered, sniffling and wiping her eyes. "Gosh!" he said, shaking his head in disbelief. "What the hell! Rosalyn? Is it really you? Why did you cut your hair?"

CHAPTER 81

"Is it you?...You... Alex?... Why? How?" Rosie stuttered through her tears. "I don't understand! I can't believe it! I can't believe it!" She looked confusedly at his face, smiling, and shaking, and crying all together. She touched his tight spring locks hanging above his forehead trying to recognize, to absorb, to be sure. "Alex... You..." She attempted to lift her arms to hug him but squinted from pain in her upper left arm, "Ouch! I can't... sorry, I can't lift this arm. It hurts." She hugged him then with her right arm and snuggled her face to his shoulder barely breathing.

He was careful not to touch her wounded arm, while enveloping her waist and pressing her to his chest. "Rosalyn! It's unbelievable! Why are you here?"

"I was shot on the street."

"No, I mean, why are you in New York? You should be in Seattle!"

Overwhelmed by the unexpectedness of the moment, she didn't answer craving just to feel his warmth. They stood silently for a while as Alex slowly caressed with his lips the hair on the top of her head. "It's funny to see you with short hair," he whispered finally. "I never imagined you would cut it. But it's okay. I love it any way it looks. So many memories..."

"I don't understand... why are you here?" she uttered at last lifting her face and looking him in the eyes, beaming. "You should be in Germany as I remember from the TV show."

"What show?" he smiled. "I didn't see any shows. I was in Germany for three and half months. Four surgeries on my lungs and stomach, and leg. They removed bullets..."

"Oh God," she whispered, "you have these scars..." She fondly traced her finger on the scar on his left cheek under his eye. Then – another one on the side of his neck that went down to the collarbone.

"Those are just the cuts from the broken bus window," Alex smirked. "The scars I have on my chest and stomach, and on the leg as well are from the bullets. They zipped me on the left side with automatic guns while I was driving the bus. It was kind of a miracle that I survived. I fell down on the bus floor from the steering wheel. Then another guy, one of the kidnapped ones whom I uncuffed earlier, got into my place and drove to the city," he took a deep breath before continuing. "They sent me to this hospital for rehabilitation. I have been here for two weeks already, but, you see, I am still walking with the cane. Maybe it's forever. I don't know. They are still trying to fix it. Next week I will be discharged and can go home. But... why are you here?"

"I came for a conference with my uncle and my husband," she sniffled, barely holding her tears. "There was shooting on the street. My husband was killed and I was wounded. It was such a horror. Didn't you see that on the TV News?"

"No," he shook his head. "I am sorry for your loss. Sincerely... so-so sorry."

"Thank you," she whispered. "It's a big loss, but... we were separated already for three months anyway. However, it's still sad and painful."

"It must be very hurtful for you, I can imagine," he noted, compassionately petting her healthy shoulder. "I am really sorry to hear that, Rosalyn. But I didn't know about that. I never watch the News."

"Why?" Rosie asked, surprised.

"I watched once, and they called me a 'hero'. It made me so angry. I was almost dying in the hospital. I knew that I was a stupid idiot who just wanted to be killed, not the damn 'hero' at all. After that I stopped watching the News. I don't want to know what else they say about me. I don't want to know all the horrors that are going on in the world. I like to watch comedies now – to laugh and forget about everything."

"Oh... I understand," she murmured and pressed her face to his shoulder again.

"Could we go and sit somewhere?" Alex asked after a few minutes of silence. "I am actually kind of handicapped now with this damn leg. I can't stand on it for very long."

"Of course," Rosie nodded. "Sorry, I wasn't thinking. Is it okay if we go back to that lounge?"

They slowly walked along the hallway, holding hands, then sat in the lounge on a couch and hugged each other as he put his cane beside him.

"We need to talk so much," Rosie whispered. "All these three years... It was so long... So many things happened."

"Why didn't you call me after Ben's death?" Alex asked sadly. "Mom knew how to contact me on Skype."

"I was arrested, ordered in the shelter for a year."

"I know. Mom told me. But after you were out? I was waiting for you. I needed to keep my promise to Ben. I wanted to marry you, but you were just gone."

"I was in a mental and emotional prison," Rosie shook her head. "I was living with my mom's family again, and it was hell. Believe me, a real hell."

"Then why didn't you come to my mom? She loved you. She would accept you."

"I don't know. I felt guilty about Ben. Guilty in front of her and your whole community. It was my fault, you know. I didn't behave properly on the street. I kind of deluded the police. Even a year later, after I was acquitted from the shelter, I still felt guilty. I was scared that your mom would blame me and refuse to talk to me. And I was still ill, had hallucinations. I just... just waited for...

I don't know what for... And then I had a very severe attack of my illness and was placed into the shelter again, for the third time."

Alex took a deep breath. "Probably it wouldn't have happened if you went to live with my mom instead of the hostile environment of your damn family. And how did you end up married? I saw the video of your kiss on stage. I thought at first that this was kind of a joke. I didn't consider it as something serious. But then came another video on YouTube – your engagement on stage. And then one more – your wedding at the church... It was kind of a blow after blow. I realized that you are lost for me, just gone... It was shocking. I knew you loved me. I expected that you would wait for me to come home. I remember how you were reacting... there... before I left. You were crying... screaming, I was afraid... thought you will die... while... that..."

"We didn't talk about anything!" Rosie exclaimed heatedly, blushing. "You didn't even want me to know that it was you. You were pretending to be Ben!"

"But you knew it was me anyway?"

"Of course, I knew.."

"And I knew that you knew... And you didn't protest. I got it that you wanted me no less than I wanted you. I got it that you loved me. I knew you belonged to Ben, but after he was killed, I thought that you would wait for me."

"I am sorry, if I hurt you by not waiting," Rosie sniffled, almost ready to cry again.

"Hurt me? No... Please, I hate talking about my feelings," Alex took her face in both hands and kissed her passionately and she answered to his kisses readily. Then, he finally let her face go and sighed deeply, "Okay, no feelings... I am just saying the facts that I know - you got married."

"I got married because I found the man of my dreams," Rosie continued sadly. "I fell in love. But I was still seriously mentally ill and I had attacks almost every day."

"What about your illness now?" he wanted to know.

"I am okay. I am cured, I am completely healthy. I met my uncle. He is a doctor and he cured me. Also, between my cure sessions I finally dared to visit your mom. She allowed me to take the kids for a walk in the park, even twice. It looked to me as if she forgave me."

"I know. She told me. We talked with her about you a lot. So, where are we now? You're a healthy widow. I am handicapped as a result of everything – a coward-idiot who just wanted to be killed."

"No, no, no," Rosie protested, vigorously shaking her head. "You are not a coward. You're not an idiot, Alex. Stop saying that. This sounds childish. Please... If you wanted to be killed only, you would have gone and stood in front of the Taliban. They would have shot you, and that would be the end. But you were brave... you fought. You saved the kidnapped soldiers in the bus. You killed that terrorist."

"It was an accident," Alex smirked bitterly. "I didn't know who he was. They were just standing beside the bus, the group of them, and I subconsciously started shooting with an automatic gun. I only needed to get into the bus. I knew that the guys were in there and still alive, handcuffed to the seats, and they had to be rescued. How do you know all of this?"

"From the TV News."

"You see! It's exactly what I was talking about. I don't want to watch all of these things. I want to forget."

"You know, Alex, my uncle could help you to forget. He is very good at healing things like that. Not only this... actually, everything."

"I don't know if I will stay here that long," he shrugged. "I will go home next week, I really miss mom and kids. I will be with them for Christmas, and then, in January I will leave home again. I have to go to Washington DC. There will be a ceremony held to see President Obama. I probably will have no time for any healing."

"You can do that later, when you come back to Seattle after the ceremony. I want you to be as okay as I am," Rosie insisted. She took his hand and held it tight with both her hands. "Please... Alex."

"Do you still want to be with me?" he whispered, looking her straight in the eyes, dreading in anticipation of her answer. "In spite of the fact I am handicapped? Tell me."

"I... I do," she whispered back a bit confused, tenderly caressing his fingers. "You were actually my first love... even before Ben. You started talking to me first. I went to the park with you first."

"And I kissed you first, as well... before Ben."

"Yes," Rosie nodded, smiling. "I am having butterflies even looking at you, not to mention touching your hand. And... I really need you right now. Emotionally, mentally... I need help after all those horrors. I need a shoulder to cry on. It's a miracle that we met here. I really, really need you, Alex... If you want, I can actually go with you to Washington, DC for your award ceremony," she suggested suddenly. "There is another coincidence – I will go for an interview at the Pentagon at the beginning of January anyway. I am applying for work there."

"What? Work there as who?" he asked surprised.

"As a personal simultaneous translator for the Minister of Defense."

"Wow!" Alex smirked. "What could you translate?"

"I don't know. Maybe some documents. Maybe some of his meetings with a foreign countries' officials."

"Are you kidding me, Rosalyn?" he giggled. "Are you that good in Spanish? I remember from school that you were not bad, but on the level they require there... hmm..."

"I know twenty-five foreign languages now. They came to me as a side effect of my cure."

"Seriously? It's impossible! It's funny. I really can't believe it," he shook his head, laughing.

"I am telling you – you have to see my uncle. He could do miracles. That's how he made me know these languages. He could cure you too," Rosie said confidently. "If you would be in Seattle for Christmas, it's okay for a cure. My uncle and I are returning home on December 23 as well."

"Are you suggesting I see your uncle in Seattle? Or here? I have to think about that," Alex answered thoughtfully. "I don't know if

I am ready to do anything like treatment now. In truth – I want to come home and hug my mom. And that's it."

"I am not forcing you," Rosie shrugged. "I am just telling you that I was cured by my uncle."

"Okay. If my leg will be better in a week, they will let me go for walks outside for a while, before they discharge me completely. Then we could probably go together and you will introduce me to your uncle. Is it okay? What do you think?"

"There is no need to go outside to meet him. He is visiting me here every day," she said, happily looking at him. "Gosh, Alex, you're looking so sexy. These scars are even making you more attractive, like... kind of a pirate in a movie... Yes, I remember that all... what I felt... what you did... as a farewell before you left for the army... Oh, gosh! It's so annoying that we're both wounded now and can't..." Then she suddenly stood up, bent and took his face in her palms, as he did before to her, and kissed him passionately.

"But, we will be healed in a while... and then can... Right?" he whispered between the kisses and pulled her back to sit on the couch. And they continued sitting there and kissing for a long time.

CHAPTER 82

Liam tried to establish a time with the Seattle Police Department when they will notify Beth about Aaron's death because he wanted to be there for her at that moment. In spite of feeling sad and uneasy with the task, he sensed that it was his duty in respect to Aaron's memory.

Being more distanced from Aaron than Ashot and Rosie, Liam somehow, during the summer, got befriended the guy and began considering him almost as a son. At least as a very close friend, and this closeness increased his shock and pain of the sudden tragedy.

Also, Liam felt very attached to Aaron's little Laurie, sincerely cared about this charming child and had difficulty imagining how she would live without having her father. *What if Beth couldn't survive this blow of fate?* he wondered with frustration. *Who else in the world does this poor child have?*

However, Liam's arrangement with the Police Department somehow didn't work out. When he came to Aaron's house Wednesday morning it was too late. He found only their housekeeper, Mary, all in tears, and she told him what happened there a half an hour ago.

Beth just dropped Laurie at school and came home for a minute to give Mary some instructions of what to do while she goes grocery shopping. She was already leaving when the policewoman knocked on the door.

"At first, Mrs. Dispenmore didn't believe it," Mary revealed, sobbing. "She thought it was some kind of mistake. She said it's impossible, she just talked on Skype with Dr. Dispenmore yesterday morning, right before the conference started. But the policewoman confirmed that he was killed fifteen minutes after that conversation. And then, Mrs. Dispenmore simply collapsed!" Mary exclaimed and hugged Liam, crying on his chest. "I know you're a family friend, sir. Maybe you could help somehow? I am lost. I don't know what to do."

Liam carefully patted her back, trying to calm her down.

"The policewoman called for an ambulance," Mary continued talking while sniffling, "and Mrs. Dispenmore was taken to the hospital. I don't know what I should do now. Laurie is at school. I can't pick her up at two-thirty p.m. because I am going to my second job this afternoon straight from here. And in the evening, I have three of my own children to take care of."

"Okay," Liam said. "I took the day off today because I expected something like this would happen. I can manage the situation for now, but we will need to figure out what's next. Which hospital? And which school?"

Mary named the school and the hospital, then gave him a spare set of keys of the house and with that he left, driving to see Beth first.

When Ashot called in the evening, Liam told him how his day evolved.

"You know, babe, I was surprised how strong Beth is," he said. "She, the mother, was stronger than I, a stranger. A very steadfast woman. Of course, they pumped a lot of medication into her body, but her character... personality... She is just amazingly determined and ready to suppress any grief for the sake of her little Laurie. She needs to live for the child and she bravely held herself in check."

"Or maybe psychologically she still doesn't get that her son is gone," Ashot suggested. "She knows that in theory of course, but hasn't yet accepted it with her heart and soul. The information hasn't sunk in. She will get it later when the first shock subsides. So, what now?"

"Beth decided that she will fly to New York as soon as she is discharged from the hospital, which the doctor said will be the next day. They kind of secured her heart condition for now. So, I booked her airplane ticket for tomorrow evening. You have to meet her at the airport there. She wants to see her son and bring him home. The funeral will be here. The police have already notified the university. Then Beth called the school and arranged that they will release Laurie to me. I went to the school, picked up Laurie and brought her to the hospital to see her grandma."

"What did you tell the girl?" Ashot inquired.

"Not much. I said that grandma felt sick and is in the hospital, and we need to visit her. That's it. The rest was on Beth. She explained to the girl that her daddy is sick as well and placed in a hospital in New York, and she will fly there tomorrow to see him. But Laurie should stay here with me, go to school the last days before the Christmas break and wait until Beth brings daddy home. The little one agreed and was even happy because, as you know... she likes me.

"Then we went with Laurie to their house, cooked dinner together, played chess, watched some cartoons and played with the kitten. I put her to bed, read her a book, kissed her forehead and she is sleeping now. That's it. I am sitting here, in their living room, talking to you. I will sleep here tonight – the housekeeper prepared Aaron's room for me."

"Did Laurie ask about her dad?"

"Yeah, kind of interesting. She asked if I was thinking he would be okay. I said I don't know, I just hope that he will be okay. Then she whispered to me secretly, 'If daddy dies, I promised him that I will put his heart and soul into his grave with him.' I was dumbfounded to hear such a thing from a child. Look, she 'promised him'... It means he talked to her about the possibility of his death. I didn't get it. Did he know what would happen there before going to the conference? Or what? Why even touch on such a subject with a child?"

"Let me think about that," Ashot suggested, "and also I'll ask kiddo. Maybe it is something about their relationship. Or he was really worried about Helen's threats. I'll try to find out. So, what's your plan for tomorrow?"

"Jeez," Liam smirked, "I am turning into an Uber driver here. I am driving Laurie to school in the morning. Then I go to work - I need to find someone who will cover the afternoon shooting for me. Then, I'll pick up Laurie from school, then - pick up Beth from the hospital, bring them home. Beth will pack her luggage and we will drive her to the airport. Then - back home with Laurie, dinner, games, good night time... I feel I am turning crazy. And this even while they have a housekeeper for home chores! I never thought how busy and difficult the life of a housewife is, even with one child, but if she has two, three and more... It's an unbelievably huge job that not many appreciate. Everybody is thinking that she is just 'sitting at home'! I am... darn happy... that I am not a woman."

"You know, babe," Ashot laughed, "I read in some historical book about different religions that in Judaism there was an old prayer – a man was supposed to thank God that He did not create him as a woman. Sounds a bit funny nowadays, but still very true."

"Yeah, especially today when many women are working outside the home plus everything else. Just in one day I felt on my own skin how huge this burden is. But what is worst for me, babe - I don't know what I will do on Friday. I already talked to the guys on the set, everybody is busy. Nobody can cover my shift, but I can't skip it. It is a very important part of the film."

"Maybe take Laurie with you on set," Ashot suggested. "You promised her an excursion."

"I was thinking about that, but for the excursion, for showing her around, I need to be free. I planned to do that on my free day. But, on Friday I will work, and really, babe, it will be a very serious shooting and very important. I know that."

"Please, darling, you're a smart guy," the old man begged. "You'll figure out something. The murder of a friend is not like an everyday occurrence."

Next day, Liam expressed to Beth how busy his working day on Friday is expected to be and she proved herself as a great organizer again. Before leaving for New York, she called some of her church friends, told them what happened with her son and asked for help. Everyone was in shock and agreed wholeheartedly to watch Laurie. They developed a flexible schedule according to which the housekeeper, Mary, will drive Laurie to school in the morning, the church people will pick her up after school and make a play-day with their children. This way, Liam was assigned only to the late evening and night on Friday. It could allow him to work on set without any worries.

Ashot met Beth at the JFK International airport in New York. They had a very sad and sensitive meeting with hugs and tears, then took a taxi to the hotel where Ashot settled her in Aaron's room. For a while he sat and talked to her quietly – from her perspective. But, in reality, he professionally did a hypnosis session on her trying to calm her down and to help her survive her unimaginable loss. Beth was still numb and seemed to hold herself in check pretty well, but he wanted to be sure that she would have the possibility to sleep at night which was important for her heart condition.

On Friday morning Ashot was supposed to attend the conference as usual, so he arranged with his former patient, now a friend, lawyer, Levon Ovanesian, to help Beth with the police business, then – organize the cremation and all other sad but obligatory prep-funeral routine things.

Coming to the Science World Building Ashot stopped first at the Notice Board in the lobby. From the plastic pocket under their photos, names and a flier with a very brief description of their cure he took once again a bunch of condolence notes from guests of the conference. He thought about showing them to Beth, but decided to think more about that. He had some doubts. It would be nice for her to know that so many people were expressing sympathy and respect for her son, but it would once more emphasize the fact that he was gone forever and this reminder could be heavy for her.

Looking through the notes, Ashot found a beautiful sympathy card from one of the local psychiatrists in which a business card was enclosed. It stated:

Dr. H. A. Michelson, MD, PhD, Private Psychiatry Clinic *ARARAT*.

On the back of it was handwritten, "Mr. Spencer, I would be interested to talk to you in person about the Clay Mask cure of Dr. Dispenmore. I have something important to add to the topic. Please, call me."

Wow! Ashot thought. *This doctor obviously read our flier attentively. Who could add anything to the topic of the Clay Mask? Not one person in the world knows about my invention. Sounds strange, a bit disturbing. I should think about that... However, ARARAT...*

He knew that it was a real Armenian name. Mount Ararat was a classical symbol of Armenia, same as mount Kilimanjaro - of Africa, or mount Fujiyama - of Japan, or mount Everest - of Himalayas.

Could it be one more of my former patients from Yerevan? Ashot wondered. *In this case, yes, he would have known about Clay Mask of course. But... the Jewish last name... I didn't ever have any Jewish patients there...*

During the lunch break he called the Clinic *ARARAT* phone but, as he expected, the receptionist answered, "Dr. Michelson is at the conference. Please, try the cell number." It would be impossible to find someone between hundreds of the people attending the conference, even with the tags on their chests. As Ashot called the second number on the business card, there was an automatic answering machine suggesting to leave a message which he did. *Of course, this doctor turned the phone off during the conference,* Ashot realized. *I will try in the evening.*

The invitation to the traditional Sabbath dinner at four p.m. on Friday at Levon and Sarah's house was still valid. It was very wistful that instead of the celebration and fun with Aaron and Rosie, Ashot arrived there alone. However, Levon and Beth were already there. Levon enlightened him about how their day was and how all the procedures worked.

His wife, Sarah, did a very good job during that time trying to take Beth's attention away from her tragedy to the kitchen, dishes, quality of the ingredients and food recipes. Dinner went well and the whole family atmosphere that Levon and Sarah created for Beth was very caring, warm and loving.

Then Ashot took the stranger's business card out from his pocket and asked, "Look, Levon, the name Ararat... could it be something else than our beloved mount in Armenia?"

"Never!" Levon exclaimed and laughed. "What is it? Where did you get it?"

"Some doctor left his card for me. He wants to talk about Clay Mask. Dr. H. A. Michelson... Have you ever heard about this clinic here?"

"No," Levon shook his head. "As you know I am not interested in the psychiatry field at all since you cured me. As a lawyer I am doing only Real Estate deals, nothing else."

"Let me see," Sarah asked, taking the card from Ashot. "You know... we have a senior couple, David and Lisa Michelson, in our Synagogue. I talked to them a couple of times during lunch after service. They are also immigrants from the Soviet Union, as we are. We all are not very religious after our atheist upbringing, so we're going to the Temple Beth Shalom which is not as traditional and restricted as the Orthodox Synagogues. It is more as a family, as a home for us and I love it as a club of our culture and history, more than a place of worship. Practically, all our Jewish immigrants from Russia are there. The locals even call us 'Russians' which is ironic."

"Very much so," Levon laughed. "I remember, darling, you dreamed so much to become 'Russian' in this damn country of abuse, but it was impossible. Then we finally immigrated to the USA, and here you go! You are a 'Russian' for the Americans. And I was considered there as an 'Armenian crock' which was associated in Russia only with jokes about 'Armenian Radio' and indecent anecdotes. But here we are Americans, and that's it. Nobody cares about the national backgrounds, even though everyone here has a background."

"Yes," Beth nodded, finally getting involved into the conversation. "I have a Greek background and my husband was English. But still, I gave my son an ancient Hebrew name from the Bible. If you don't mind, could we say a prayer in his memory?"

"Of course," everybody agreed and, holding hands, all four of them, members of different churches - Anglican, Armenian Apostolic, Greek Orthodox and Jewish Beth Shalom - whispered their own prayers addressed to the same Lord, unified for all humans. Then the moment of silence in Aaron's memory followed.

Finally Ashot took a deep breath and said carefully, "Back to Dr. Michelson... I plan to call him tomorrow."

"Not tomorrow," Sara suggested. "It is the Sabbath. You don't know for sure, but he could be a very religious Orthodox Jew and this business call could be offensive to him. Better to call on Sunday."

"Our conference is working here without taking any weekends off - three weeks in a row," Ashot explained. "If this is the case, as you're saying, Sarah, he won't be at the conference tomorrow, right?"

"Could be... But, let me think about our Michelson's. They told me that they have a daughter and she is a doctor of some kind. I don't remember for sure. I never saw her. She doesn't go to synagogue with them because she is not religious at all. And she is married to some... I don't know... some... I guess an Iranian guy of a very strange new religion... it is called Baha'i... or something... Sorry, I forgot the details. By the way, I will see Dave and Lisa tomorrow at the service and I will ask them."

With this being said, Ashot and Beth thanked the owners of the house for a nice dinner and left – it was already almost six o'clock and Sabbath was about to begin in a few minutes, so Sarah barely had time to clean the table. Any kind of work was prohibited by the Jewish law during the Sabbath which in reality was a very reasonable tradition because it forced people to drop everything they were doing and have a good rest. Levon, as the one not Jewish person in the household, was now responsible to load and unload the dishwasher.

In the hotel, Ashot stayed for a while with Beth in her room and made one more hypnosis session for her, that she, again, didn't even notice. However, it calmed her down more and gave her a good chance to sleep well for another night.

In his room, when Ashot was ready for bed and knelt to say his evening prayers, his phone suddenly rang. It was a Private Number, but he answered it anyway having an inner feeling that it was important.

"Good evening, Mr. Spencer," he heard a pleasant woman's voice. "I am Doctor Hannah Michelson. Sorry, I am calling so late. I just had a very busy day. You left me a message today. Thank you so much. I would like to meet you tomorrow after the conference. Maybe we could go for coffee. Let's meet in the Science World Building by the Notice Board in the lobby in three in the afternoon."

"Okay," Ashot mumbled surprised – it was already Sabbath now but she did a business call... "Are you working tomorrow, Dr. Michelson?" he asked.

"Of course," she laughed. "Why not?"

"Then, maybe we could talk now," he really liked her voice, deep, beautiful, almost like the voice of an opera singer.

"No," she answered. "We need to talk in person. It would be a very long and confidential conversation. Good night, Mr. Spencer."

CHAPTER 83

At first, Ashot felt uneasy about this call. The stranger doctor turned out to be a woman, not religious, not keeping Jewish traditions. Maybe she really was a daughter of those Michelson's that Sarah mentioned – the immigrants from the Soviet Union. It could kind of connect the situation somehow to Armenia – mount Ararat then – because Armenia was at those times a Republic of the Soviet Union, although it felt to Ashot barely possible. And anyway, it didn't feel safe for him.

During all his years in the USA he tried to avoid the recent immigrants from his former motherland as much as he could. But then between Rosie's cure sessions he asked her and Liam to do some research on the Internet, to find his former patients from Yerevan, and it somehow probably opened a big can of worms.

It helped him to understand a side effect of the Clay Mask cure – the change of patients' feelings towards their life partners. It was also pleasant to see Patrick on Skype and to find Levon in New York. It revived nice memories, but at the same time it reminded him about the horrors of the regime.

Even now, when Russia pretended to be a democratic country, the danger of it was still subconsciously sitting somewhere deep in Ashot's bones and will never go away. *The Russian president is a former KGB agent. These kinds of people never change, ever! What kind of freedom could you expect with a ruler like that? It would be silly to even think about any kind of democracy,* he always thought before.

And why would someone with these possible connections want to meet me and to talk about the Clay Mask? he thought now. *Does she work for a new Russian KGB that just has a different name? Does she work for the Mafia? Does she want to buy my invention? Does she want to steal my cure? Is she another competitive doctor, as Helen was?* The thoughts were so disturbing, even paranoid, that Ashot couldn't sleep for a long time because the questions kept stirring in his head.

Then he returned to his best friend and saver – God. He began to pray finally, and this helped as always. God calmed him down, gave him the answer of what to do, how to behave, and how to live. He thanked God, sent his deep love to Him, and at last calmly fell asleep.

On Saturday morning at the conference it was announced that Dr. Helen Harrison was killed by her cured patient, Arthur Smith, who committed a suicide afterwards by jumping out from the hotel window. This was a vague version the police shared with the media and with the organizers of the conference. It was obvious for the professional audience that the patient wasn't cured enough and wasn't healthy if the attack of his illness forced him to strangle his doctor and then kill himself.

So, this couple – doctor-patient – was out of the competition. Now two days of the conference that were scheduled for Helen's presentation and the judges debates were free. The organizers suggested the guests should take a break, rest and go for many different bus tours and excursions – to become acquainted with New York's attractions. It was approved with a big round of applause from the audience.

When Ashot approached the Notice Board in the lobby of the Science World Building after the session ended, he found a middle-aged woman waiting for him. She was short, chubby, with coal-black curly hair, wore big designer glasses, and was dressed very expensive and stylish, as Jewish women traditionally were supposed to be.

"Dr. Michelson?" he asked.

"Yes," she smiled and extended her hand to him for a handshake. "Nice to meet you, Mr. Spencer."

"Sorry, if I am a bit late."

"No, you're not late," she laughed. "It's me. I always like to come everywhere a bit earlier... you know... to feel safe that I am not missing anything. Would you mind if we go to the cafeteria?"

"Of course, not," Ashot nodded and they walked to the other side of the lobby where a restaurant and a small coffee shop were located.

"I invited you - my treat," she said, bringing to the table two porcelain cups of the cappuccino with a beautiful white leaf drawn on the top of a brown foam.

"Thank you, Dr. Michelson," Ashot nodded, smiling, noticing that it was very typical for an accomplished and independent American woman. However, he gallantly moved a chair for her from under the table and she accepted it with a grateful smile. There wasn't any tension between them. He felt kind of easy and at home with her.

"You can call me Hannah, sir," she suggested.

"Okay," he agreed, "and you can call me Ashot."

She glanced at him, surprised. "Armenian?"

"Yes," he confirmed. "My American name is Thomas Spencer, but I am an Armenian by my national background."

"It's funny," she giggled. "My Jewish name is Hannah Michelson, but I am an Armenian too."

"Oh... that's where the name *Ararat* of your clinic came from," he realized.

"Exactly. What a nice coincidence! I never met any Armenians here before. I hope it will help us to understand each other better."

"How many years have you been in the USA?" Ashot inquired. "Or were you born here?"

"Let's talk about the business first," Hannah suggested. "It is much more important than my personal biography. First of all, I am very sorry for your loss of your business partner Dr. Dispenmore. Very sorry. I can't even imagine how sad and painful this loss is for you."

"Thank you," Ashot answered quietly.

"I came to the Notice Board to put a condolence card into the pocket there, then I read your flier and the words 'Clay Mask' grabbed my attention. I would like to ask, how long did you work with Dr. Dispenmore?"

"Hmm..." Ashot thought for a while, wondering if he should tell the truth in this case or not. "Long enough," he said vaguely.

"How long ago exactly did he invent the cure with the Clay Mask?"

"Hmm... Some years ago."

"How many patients did he cure of schizophrenia using the Clay Mask?"

"Well... several... But for the competition at the conference it only requires one cured patient which he provided. The last one is Miss Rosa Garcia."

"Yes, I know that. But then... he was murdered. And today they announced that Dr. Harrison from the same university of Washington state was murdered as well. It is a strange and dangerous coincidence, isn't it? It sounds a bit suspicious."

"Sorry, Hannah, are you a detective, or what?" Ashot started to feel uneasy and irritated.

"No, I am only a doctor-psychiatrist. But these two doctors were killed... It is something curious and unusual. I have attended many Psychiatry Scientific Conferences during my years of practice, many in the USA and in other countries, even oversea, and in Asia. And I never heard of any scientists killed at one of them."

"Sorry, but this is our American reality – shootings on the streets are happening almost every day and hundreds of people are killed this way every year," Ashot lifted his palms. "We can't do anything about that. And Dr. Harrison – she was killed by her schizophrenic patient. Sadly, this is happening in this profession as well. Not so often, but I saw a few cases on the TV News or read about it several times in newspapers."

"Okay," Hannah took a deep breath. "It is true. You almost convinced me. But still... I heard the words 'Clay Mask' before. Did you know Dr. Dispenmore well? Was he an honest person? Could he steal someone's invention?"

"Absolutely not!" Ashot exclaimed indignantly. "He was an amazing man, genuine, sincere, bright, talented, a real genius. We were partners. We were very close friends. He was like a son to me. We opened the Private Psychiatry Clinic together. We planned to work the rest of our lives together!"

Her guess was like a blow under the belt for him. He was already angry at himself that he even agreed to this meeting and conversation. This woman's suspicions made Ashot enraged, but also scared and worried that the whole project of his life could be ruined. At least it was better that she started to talk with him about that rather than just go to the police.

"Well," he said finally, a bit calmer. "It is impossible what you're guessing at, Hannah - absolutely impossible! Where did you hear the words 'Clay Mask'? When? How? Under what circumstances? Please, tell me. I am sure there will be another explanation of this than you are suspecting."

"Okay," she agreed peacefully. "I am sorry about those speculations, especially because they were said about the late person. Of course, there could be another explanation. It was too long ago. I was a child. I could mess up something... Here we come to the topic of the biography now as you wanted.

"I was born and raised in Yerevan by a single mother. I never had a father. When I was ten, my mom was diagnosed with leukemia. In those years there wasn't any treatment for it, as they have now. When she was dying, I asked her about my dad. I craved to have any information, at least something. She told me that he was a doctor-psychiatrist, a scientist, a genius who invented the cure for schizophrenia with a Clay Mask and cured twenty people..."

Ashot felt that he was getting dizzy and grabbed the edges of the table with both hands so as not to collapse.

"That was it," the woman continued. "These words – Clay Mask - sounded very interesting and unusual for a child and I remembered them forever. I decided that when I grow up, I will become a psychiatrist like my dad. Then, my mom said that my father did something bad, very-very bad, and committed a serious crime which was impossible for her to forgive. She reported him to the police and he was arrested and died somewhere in prison. So, I should forget about him because it is a shame to be the daughter of a criminal. And I tried to do so, but I couldn't completely forget it."

Ashot, stupefied, was staring at the table, at his cup, thinking only about his crazily jumping heart. *Please, God, don't let me get a heart attack. Please, Lord, help me to survive that. I need to survive for my project. I have to survive for Aaron's sake, for his memory, for Liam, for Rosie... I must survive even for this my little girl...*

"After my mom died," Hannah went on, "I was placed in an orphanage where I got sick, then – in a hospital, and then I was adopted by a childless Jewish couple from Moscow. They were planning to emigrate to Israel and wanted to adopt a child which could match them, so nobody could guess that I was adopted. All Russian kids were blond and blue-eyed, but no Jewish kids were available. If a Jewish child became an orphan, there were always some relatives who would like to take care of them. So, they hired a lawyer, who found me in Armenia. I looked similar to a Jewish child and they liked me. I actually liked them as well – they were kind people.

"We emigrated to Haifa as a family when I was twelve. There I was converted into Judaism, had my Bat-mitzvah, for which I learned a lot of religious writings and Talmud, although it didn't make me a religious person. But then my 'teen years' approached and I was supposed to serve in the army like all other Israeli girls. My parents were worried that I could be killed in a battle because there still were many military conflicts with Arabs. So, they applied for immigration to the USA. At that time America allowed new immigrants only as a family reunion, but my dad, David, has a sister here, so it was good luck – she sponsored us. Otherwise, who knows, I could be killed as a soldier during a war and not talk here with you now. Are you okay, sir?" she stopped noticing Ashot's almost dead facial expression. "You're so pale. Sorry, does it sound disturbing for you what I am saying about the danger of that war?"

He swallowed hard and lowered his face propping it on his hands.

"What was your Armenian name?" he mumbled quietly with a husky voice.

"Annush Petrosian. My mom was Eva and my father was doctor Ashot Petrosian... oh... what?" she choked on the words, bewildered. "Do you think...what? You said... your name is Ashot... right?"

"When is your birthday, Annush?"

"May 17, 1981."

"Yes," he lifted his face and looked at her attentively, finding the strength to smile finally, however, barely holding the tears in his eyes. "Yes, May 17, 1985 - it was the day when I saw you for the last time when you turned four," he said in a shaky voice. "Welcome to your birth family, Annush. I am your father. I am alive and I am not a criminal. I am the scientist and the inventor of the cure with the Clay Mask which I shared - voluntarily and gladly - with my beloved son, Dr. Aaron Dispenmore."

"Do... wwwe... need... to do a... DNA test?" she whispered, stuttering, astonished, looking at him with huge eyes.

"No need for that. It's guaranteed. The only thing confusing me is your small beautiful nose... I expected it would be like mine – almost eggplant shaped. It was pretty big even when I saw you last time as a four-year-old child..."

"I had plastic surgery when I was twenty-five," Annush confirmed, taking a couple of deep breaths, but beaming, with her eyes full of tears as well. "Oh my gosh! It's unbelievable! I am still in shock. However, it's a happy shock! I am almost ready to cry. I am looking at your hands. See," still shaking, she placed her palm on the table beside Ashot's hand, "the shape is absolutely the same. Look, each nail, each wrinkle... Wow! And your eyebrows... the line of hair above your forehead... Jeez! It's like I am looking in the mirror. Yes, you're my father! Yes, I could see that clearly!" She put her glasses on the table and laughed, and cried at the same time, holding her face with both hands, and couldn't stop her emotional outburst.

"Yes, I am your father," Ashot nodded, "and I didn't commit any crime, believe me. Now, I guess, we need to call Liam, my husband, which is my only 'crime' from the Soviet Union perspective. And, sadly, your mom accepted this mean and stupid law as her own opinion. I hope you can understand that as a modern American woman and as a professional psychiatrist. And then we need to go to the hospital to visit my adopted daughter, Rosie. She should know that she now has a sister."

"And I need to call my husband and my parents!" Annush exclaimed, stood up from her chair, walked around the table to Ashot and hugged him tightly. "They all need to know that they have a much more extended family here now. Gosh, what a happy day! I can't believe it! I still can't believe it! You know, dad, I secretly dreamed for years that it would happen one day. That we, you and I, would be sitting one day like this in a cafeteria, and talking, and drinking coffee, and holding hands. It was my inner vision for a long-long time, since my childhood."

"And I prayed for years that I would be able to find you, although not knowing if you were alive," he nodded and kissed his golden cross on the chain. "You know, Annush, I brought this cross from Armenia. It belonged to my mom – your grandmother – and it was with me on my escape journey all the time. It turned me, the atheist scientist, into a deep believer. And look, God answered my prayers finally and sent you back to me."

CHAPTER 84

On Saturday Liam took Laurie to the *Boeing Museum of Flight* where she excitedly flew, rode and drove on each of the entertaining play-stations for kids.

Later in the evening while the girl was sleeping, he got a frantic call from Ashot who was crazily fevered, even screaming from happiness, that he found his little daughter, Annush, now a thirty-four-year-old American doctor. Who could believe it! In New York! They talked on the phone for a couple of hours. Liam was happy and a bit shaky about this news as well. He even had difficulty sleeping at night overwhelmed by the contradictory emotions – the grief of Aaron's death still overshadowed the joy.

On Sunday Liam dropped Laurie to her church and, again, Beth's friends took her into their homes later for lunch and a play day with their kids.

There was no reason for Liam to attend the morning service at their Anglican church without Ashot, thus Sunday was a free day for him. He finally found the time to drive to his condo and return to Aaron's house with his personal stuff that he needed for his future life with Laurie for the next couple of weeks. And starting the following Monday, as school finished, he began taking Laurie to the movie set with him everyday. Finally the new unusual settings of their life calmed down after the huge shocking mental 'earthquake' and slowly became a normal routine.

However, Laurie still didn't know a thing about her father's death. It was up to Beth when and how to tell her, but it hasn't happened yet.

While working on the set, Liam had no time to watch Laurie, but he found a way – he asked the producer assistant, Nancy, who was a student on practice from the Cinema faculty of Cincinnati University, to show Laurie around and to make sure that the girl felt comfortable. Nancy proved to be a very child-loving young woman and gladly did that favor for him. She and Laurie had a lot of fun together walking around, watching the filming at the different set areas, talking with a few actors and producers, climbing on stairs and even trees that were used as a natural decor in some scenes.

One day, Nancy led the girl to the main office building to get some chocolate from a vending machine that was located in the lobby. The room was full of people. A big line - parents with their children - snaked from outside into the open doors. Inside, the people were sitting on chairs or standing around. The whole lobby was crowded.

Laurie gestured to Nancy to bow down, then asked in a whisper, "What are these people doing here?"

"I think they came for an audition," Nancy answered. "I saw an ad a few days ago that our crew is looking for a little girl for a future movie production. Well... Let's give it a try. Just for fun, right? Do you want to become an actress, Laurie?"

"Yeah!" the girl exclaimed and they laughed and gave each other a high-five, both knowing that it was only a joke.

Nancy said that she knows the assistant who manages the audition line. She approached the woman and introduced Laurie to her as Liam Johnson's granddaughter.

"Jeez, what's happening with Liam?" the assistant winked to Nancy and giggled. "Last summer, I remember, he brought a daughter, which appeared from nowhere... now a granddaughter... He is kind of reproducing way too fast for a gay!" They both laughed which Laurie didn't understand. But then the assistant ushered them through a door inside without having to wait in line.

The room was almost empty, only three people – who seemed to Laurie very old – were sitting behind the table at the far end of it. One man was bald, one had gray bushy hair and a woman wore very big glasses. But they didn't look scary. They smiled nicely and Laurie felt quite confident in front of them.

"Go, stand in the middle," Nancy whispered to the girl and lightly pushed her in the back, staying at the entrance by herself.

"Good afternoon, little one," the bald man said. "What is your name?"

"Laurie Dispenmore," the girl answered, smiling as well.

"Do you know some poems, Laurie? Could you recite something for us, please?"

Laurie nodded and started to read aloud Rosie's **Little Birdie,** almost with tears in her eyes.

"Wow!" the bald man exclaimed as she finished. "It's kind of tragic. Why did you choose this poem, Laurie?"

"Because I love this poetess, Rosalyn-Anastasia. She is dead now. But I will love and remember her always. My dad and I, we had a funeral for her and we sung that song." She placed her palms under her chin and began to sing *Amazing Grace*, so tenderly and clearly that judges exitedly looked at each other, not saying anything but being surprised by the unexpected beauty of her voice – pretty strong for a child of her age.

"Thank you, Laurie," the judge-woman said as the girl finished the song. "I am sorry to hear that the poetess died. It's okay to be sad sometimes. However, do you know something funny? I would like you to make us laugh..."

Laurie told some fun-stories that they learned at school and also a few jokes. Then she was asked to dance and she performed Sirtaki - the popular Greek dance that Beth taught her. She also saw it many times while attending several Greek weddings of Beth's and Aaron's friends. Laurie spread her arms wide, pretending that she is holding the shoulders of her imaginable dance partners. She started moving slowly, as it was required for Sirtaki, accompanying herself by singing the world-famous melody that was getting gradually faster and faster. It was so exciting and funny to watch that the judges began clapping in rhythm and singing with her.

Finally it got so fast, that Laurie couldn't stand it anymore and plopped on her bum on the floor, breathing heavily and laughing at the same time. The judges applauded and laughed together with her.

The last dare was, "Could you remember something sad, Laurie, and cry?"

The girl thought for a while, then covered her face with her palms, sniffled a couple of times and then cried so naturally and sincerely that everybody was absolutely astonished.

"It's okay," the gray-haired judge said. "You did well, Laurie. Thank you. You can stop now, please." But she didn't stop and kept sobbing more and more desperately, stuttering between sobs, "My daddy died... I know that... They didn't tell me anything... but I know... He was sick... he was in hospital... he came to me in my sleep... he told me that he died. He told me that he is in Heaven with my Mommy..."

Nancy came closer to her and hugged her tight.

"It's okay, it's okay, Laurie," she repeated fondly, patting the girl's back. "Your daddy is okay. He is happy in Heaven. He is watching after you, I am sure." She gestured to the judges that they needed to go and everybody nodded in agreement.

Outside, Nancy finally calmed the girl down, bought her a chocolate from the vending machine which was their initial goal when they came here. And then, they returned to the movie set.

Later that day when Beth called on Skype to talk to Laurie, the girl said that she knows already about her daddy's death by intuition, by her dream, by the deep spiritual love connection she had with her father. And Beth had no choice but to confess the truth and apologize that she didn't tell her earlier. They cried for a while, then sang *Amazing Grace* together. Beth promised that she will bring Aaron home and they will have a funeral for him at the same big beautiful cemetery where Ally was placed to rest. Finally they sent air kisses to each other and parted peacefully.

"Grandpa Liam," Laurie said seriously after the call ended. "I promised daddy that I will not cry if he dies, and I will take care of his grave. He told me that he wants to be buried with my mommy, but he also wants me to put his heart and soul with him together there."

"Heart and soul?" Liam repeated surprised. "And how could you do that?"

"I will show you. But I need your help for that." Laurie pulled him to the storage room and suggested he take gloves and shovel, then walked him outside to the backyard to the rosebush in the corner.

"Here," she said. "Daddy's 'heart and soul' is here. We buried it here. Now I need your help to dig it out. I will keep it in my room until daddy comes home. Then I will put it into his grave with him as I promised. It was our secret."

Absolutely not understanding what she wants, Liam obediently followed her instructions, not to hurt the feelings of the child, suspecting that it was some kind of a game that will bring her closure. First, he dug out the bush and moved it aside; then, dug out some dirt, and finally pulled out the package that was tightly wrapped in plastic. Then the rosebush was returned to its place.

They carried the package inside and cleaned it with paper towels. When Laurie went to bed she put it beside her pillow. "It will stay here with me and wait for daddy," she said to Liam. "Thank you, grandpa."

Liam understood that ethically she had the right for privacy and didn't ask anything, but in reality he was dying from curiosity. He waited until Laurie fell asleep, carefully walked in her bedroom, took the package, brought it into the living room and unwrapped, layer-by-layer. He was astonished to find Rosie's book inside along with a dry pink petunia and three rings – Rosie's diamond engagement ring and both, her and Aaron's, wedding bands.

"This is his heart and soul?" he murmured to himself, barely holding a spasm in his throat. "My God! This is how he loved her! Is there any man in the world who is capable for such mad and deep feelings? Does our kiddo appreciate that? I am sure nobody loved her that much and nobody ever will. Oh, Aaron! Partner, friend, son! Rest in peace, my dear!"

Even not being as religious as Ashot, Liam subconsciously felt an extreme urge to say a prayer for Aaron's soul. He whispered it, covering his face with both palms. Then he carefully wrapped the package making sure that it looked exactly as it was before, brought it back to Laurie's room and placed it beside her pillow.

Two days later Liam got a phone call that Laurie was chosen for the role of Little Maggie in the TV comedy show *Two and a Half Women* which they decided to do in a likeness of the very famous *Two and a Half Men* that has ended.

"Jeez," he said, smiling and hugging the girl. "Congratulations, my sweetheart. You got a job! Your daddy is obviously watching over all of us from Heaven. Look, what's going on: Grandpa Ashot found his daughter, Annush; you became a movie star!"

He didn't tell her that Rosie met her first love, Alex, at the hospital and spent most of her days with him now. It was not related to Laurie in any way. But for himself Liam noticed - it seemed that the time of reunion and success was coming for them. It felt as if Aaron's spirit and soul were inspiring, guiding and protecting the people whom he loved.

CHAPTER 85

About a week later, when Beth, with Levon Ovanesian's help, finished her business with the police and the Funeral Home, she was invited to attend the conference as a special guest – the mother of Dr. Dispenmpre, now perished. But she refused to stay in New York any longer.

"It doesn't matter to me if Aaron wins the competition or not," Beth said. "It will not return him to me. I know his value as an amazing man and great son and I am proud of him anyway. I will cherish his memory for the rest of my life. I have a more important task now – to bring him home to Seattle and organize the celebration of his life.

"There is his university, his family; there are his friends and relatives. There are the graves of his love, Ally, and his father, George, whose ashes I transferred from Atlanta. When my time comes, we will be all buried there together. This is our home."

It was impossible to disagree with that and Ashot saw her at the airport. On the way they only briefly stopped to see Rosie in the hospital. She showed them how active her baby has become these days, moving, turning and kicking pretty strong.

"Did Aaron know that?" Beth asked, making an effort to restrain her tears.

"Yes, he did," Rosie uttered sadly but calmly. "On the last day of his life I let him feel these movements and he said that he is happy. He was incredibly happy that morning, believe me, Mrs. Dispenmore. He died happy."

There was nothing else to do for Beth in New York which became for her the most tragic place on Earth. However, for Ashot and Rosie, their time there was not yet finished.

During the next two weeks of December Ashot and Annush stayed at the conference everyday. After the sessions they usually met Annush's husband, Omid Azad, a manager of a local *Bank of America* branch. All together they were visiting her adoptive parents, their relatives and friends.

The news that Hannah Michelson's birth father was found alive in the USA flew around their Jewish community almost with the speed of light. Especially remarkable for the people was the fact that Hannah's father was proven to be an assistant of the tragically famous Dr. Aaron Dispenmore – everyone saw the story of Aaron's murder on TV News. Now Hannah's father will himself present the cured patient at the competition for the Nobel Prize nomination. This caused a buzzing sensation and everyone craved to see Hannah and her newfound dad and invite them for visits which usually ended up with huge dinners.

A few days after Beth's departure, Rosie was discharged from the hospital – the wound at her upper left arm healed well enough. She should attend the conference where she was registered from the very beginning as the cured patient of Dr. Dispenmore. But all these scientific speeches and debates seemed boring to her. So, Ashot allowed her to appear there only for judges' evaluation in person.

According to the schedule for December 20th, he was supposed to read Aaron's speech and make the presentation of the cure, and then, when the session ended, Rosie would spend several hours with judges in their clinic for tests and personal appointments. Until that time she could be free to do what she wants.

Alex was also discharged from the hospital and Rosie convinced him not to fly to Seattle right away, but stay with her in her hotel room for a week. She introduced Alex to Ashot and he performed a couple of psychiatric hypnosis sessions on the young man to ease, at least for a little bit, his obvious PTSD. Then Ashot promised to continue these sessions in Seattle at the beginning of January to be sure that Alex is in a stable, healthy mental condition for the meeting with President Obama to receive his Medal of Honor.

Rosie decided to take Alex for excursions and to show him New York's attractions. She has some experience here when she came for her poetry concerts a couple of times in 2011. Most of the tours and museums were pretty costly, but Rosie announced that she will pay for everything.

"Are you sure you can afford it?" Alex asked, a bit confused. "I'm sorry, I will only receive my military bonus when I get home."

"You can check on the Internet what the salary is for a government simultaneous translator," she laughed. "I can easily afford everything I want now."

This way the week of fun and entertainment started. At first, Rosie took Alex to Jersey's city *Liberty State* park with a ferry ride to the *Statue of Liberty*. They paid their respects at the *Empty Sky 9/11* memorial; then, the next day they took a buffet dinner cruise on a New York city ferry. Then – walked in *Central Park,* went to the *Empire State* building, visited *St. Patrick's Cathedral*, the *Solomon R. Guggenheim Museum* and finally ended up in *Luna Park* at Coney Island that was full of different amusement thrill rides for children.

The place they loved the most was *Luna park* and they were going there everyday and rode practically on each ride that was available. They laughed, giggled while hugging each other and kissing all the time. It gave them both a chance to relax after their tragedies and sufferings. They were having fun like young kids, in spite of her being a wounded pregnant widow who was almost killed on the street, and him – a handicapped war veteran almost killed in battle. They were recuperating, returning to life, immersing into new experiences, new beginnings and newly found love for which they were probably destined from the very first glance when they saw each other four years ago in high school.

The day before Rosie was needed at the conference, she saw Alex at the airport. He didn't want to stay in a hotel alone while she would be preoccupied with her business, and also he really craved to get home to see his family. It meant a lot for Rosie that he postponed his return to Seattle for her sake.

"Well, see you in a week," he said, hugging and kissing her farewell. "Good luck with your win. I will cross my fingers for you." And she knew he would. In spite of his reserved personality, she could sense his feelings and see sparkles of excitement in his eyes when he looked at her.

As for her own emotions, she was still a bit confused between her intense sexual attraction to Alex - tender nice memories of their first love in her teen years, when she was ill - and the persistent attention of General Simon, who kept texting her several times daily and sent roses twice more during her hospital stay. This high society level of courting that Rosie experienced while traveling with Senator Stephanie Mane seemed very tempting to her; she subconsciously wanted to use it for the benefit of her career in politics.

Could her passion and craving for an advantage be somehow combined in Alex? Yes, she decided, when he will meet the President of the USA and receive his Medal of Honor and a higher ranking in the military. Since doctors said that Alex's leg wouldn't be completely healed and he would always walk with a cane, he won't be able to serve in the army. But Rosie guessed that when she gets her position in the Pentagon, she and her friend, General Simon, together, will convince the Minister of Defense to give Alex office work there as well. She was sure that he really deserved a good job position because of his sacrifice for his country. Rosie also appreciated that Alex did it for his love for her, so it would be worth it to take a serious look at their future together.

December 20th was the most important day of Ashot's life - he read Aaron's report to the conference with a serious scientifically detailed explanation on the process of the Clay Mask cure. For the professional audience Ashot's presentation sounded very impressive. It was obvious that if the nurse-assistant was so deeply knowledgeable and experienced in psychiatry, then Dr. Dispenmore must be a real genius-scientist, even more brilliant. The opinions between judges were formed that he did deserve the recognition and was really worthy of a Nobel Prize because of the huge importance of his discovery.

The personal evaluation of Rosie's condition that should confirm her documented assessment from Seattle's General Psychiatric Hospital went as planned. The judges were absolutely excited that she not only became a mentally stable and completely healthy person, but also developed extremely rare skills – the knowledge of twenty-five foreign languages on the level of the people who were originally born with them.

In their chambers the judges decided unanimously that it would be very beneficial for human society if ill people could be cured and also developed new talents. It could be reached only by using this way of cure in regular psychiatric clinics.

For that reason the decision was made to approve the cure, to permit the use of it in Dr. Dispenmore private clinic **Clay Mask** in Seattle, and in any other clinics of the country who would be ready to accept it and interested in practicing it. This decision allowed the nomination of Dr. Aaron Dispenmore posthumously for the Nobel Prize 2016 in Medicine.

On December 21th the Clay Mask cure was publicly debated at the conference and its outcome was compared to the results of other competition participants. Sadly, none of other patients was completely cured and, at the best case scenario, only stayed in remission which was not constant and potentially could collapse at any moment. Everyone was sure that it was exactly what happened with Dr. Helen Harrison's 'cured teenage patient'.

After this conference session ended, Rosie was checked by judges one more time to establish the final confirmation of the decision made a day before.

On December 22th there was the Closing Ceremony of the conference that went very festive. It began with a minute of silence in the memory of those tragically perished at the conference - Dr. Aaron Dispenmore and Dr. Helen Harrison. Then the American National

Anthem was played. After that many guests and participants held short speeches as their feedback of the whole conference experience. They shared their ideas and suggestions for the future development of psychiatry as a science and medical practice. And, finally, the result of the competition for a scientific personal discovery and invention of the successful cure for schizophrenia was announced.

The winner was Dr. Aaron Adam Dispenmore with his team – the medical assistant, Registered Nurse of psychiatry, Thomas Spencer; the technical assistant, the patented inventor of 4d goggles and the 4D camera used to document the cure, Liam Johnson; and the 100 percent cured patient Rosa Lynn Garcia.

At the end all the guests and participants of the conference were invited to the evening banquet in the restaurant of the hotel where they all were staying. The Closing Ceremony was shorter than a regular session and ended at noon.

Then there was a press-conference where Ashot, Rosie, Liam (on Skype from Seattle), and even Annush, were interviewed for different newspapers, TV shows and radio programs. For them it was a well deserved happy ending of the Psychiatry Scientific Conference in New York.

This morning when Ashot, Rosie and Annush arrived at the Science World building the weather was completely overcast, gray and wet. It was a mist at first but later a strong rain started. However, when they exited the building at about two p.m., they stopped by the door, bewildered. The sky was blue and the sun shone brightly.

"This is the spot where Aaron was shot," the old man said, pointing at the sidewalk in front of them. "We are not coming back here, so let's say something to him now as our farewell."

Rosie took out her phone and found a picture that was taken when she went with Aaron to the fitness club downstairs in Ashot /Liam's condo after her 'Nora' cure session. While Aaron did his workouts, Rosie sat and watched, and took pictures of him with her phone. "I will be looking at them when you are not with me," she laughed then. "For inspiration!"

Now she chose the picture where Aaron was sitting on the stationary bike, riding; his hair was disheveled and dark-brown curly locks fell on his sweaty forehead. He was beaming happily, looking at Rosie with a broad smile that was demonstrating his perfectly white teeth. His eyes shone with love, dreams, and hope. It was the beginning of her cure. If they would only know then what the ending will bring!

This photo was an excellent display of Aaron's personality and character. He was real sunlight.

"I don't know what to say," Rosie whispered looking at his photo. "Just 'Thank you', Aaron. I loved you, and I am sorry. Sorry that I hurt you when I got cured. Sorry that our love disappeared. Sorry that you are not here anymore and won't be able to raise our son. Honestly, I would prefer that you lived, or if I died with you together. I swear to you that I will give your mom a little boy who could probably replace you, although you will always live in her heart. I am sure your mom will bring him up properly because she knows how to do that. She has experience - she raised an amazing son."

"Now it's my turn," Ashot uttered and crossed his hands on his chest. "Aaron, son, friend, partner! I could confess that our relationships with you were pretty rocky. We started with a strict resentment of each other which we both suppressed with difficulty for the sake of my Rosie's cure project. This girl united us and forced us both to comply. We both loved her to death, although in a very different way. For me she was and always will be a daughter; for you she was the love of your life – the woman, then - the bride, then - the wife. I remember, on the first day she said to us, 'you both shake hands in agreement for the project of my cure. If you love me, you both will do that, please.' And we did, nonchalantly and unwillingly, but we did it for her.

"While working together, we fought a lot," the old man went on. "You yelled many times that you hate me. Right, I was a real challenger. The time of our work was extremely tense for both of us, but then, gradually we learned how to tolerate each other, to understand each other, to feel each other's hearts. For you it was unbelievably difficult. There were moments when you were ready to give up but you overcame them.

"Later we came to the point when we became good respectful co-workers, then – friends, loyal, trustworthy and devoted. And then, finally, we developed a sincere deep love as a father and son. I took you in my heart as a real son I never had, and you will stay there forever. I am proud of you not only as a bright scientist that was proven today by recognition at the conference. I am extremely proud of you as a man with a good, kind, deep, spiritual and selfless soul.

"I am really thankful to you, Aaron, for what you did today for me personally and for all ill people who will be cured in your clinic in the future. It will be your legacy. Rest in Heaven, my dear son. Amen."

"I could say something as well," Annush suggested, "although I didn't know Dr. Dispenmore personally. I only know what my dad told me... Aaron, you died as a real hero. You covered Rosie with your own body, saving not only her, not only your child she is bearing; you covered her as a cured patient of your mutual project with my dad. If she had been killed, the cure would be out of the competition because the judges wouldn't be able to determine by themselves the level of her recovery. And if that would be the case, millions of ill people won't receive the cure they so badly need. Aaron, you sacrificed yourself for your love, for your baby and for all of human society at the same time. And this is a really heroic act of selflessness.

"Of course, you weren't thinking about that. You had no time to think, to understand, to realize – it all happened too fast, in a split second. But it was the mission that Fate designed for you and you followed it wholeheartedly. Your death, Aaron, had a profound meaning for humanity and it was not in vain, not for nothing. Subconsciously you did the right thing and I admire you for that. Your legacy will live forever."

They stood for a while silently, deep in thoughts. Then Rosie suddenly lifted her head and exclaimed, astonished, "Look guys, he is answering. He heard us. My God! It's unbelievable."

The clear bright double-rainbow stretched in the blue sky above the street where they stood. They froze on the spot and watched it as if mesmerized, holding their breaths.

"A rainbow in December? ... Is it even possible?" Rosie whispered barely audibly. "It's extremely rare. Right, uncle?"

"Yes," Ashot nodded, making the sign of a cross over his face and chest, and kissing his golden cross on the chain. "Rare... but still could happen. Thank you, Lord, that you let Aaron hear us and gave us the sign. Thank you for the short but deeply purposeful life of this awesome man, Doctor Aaron Dispenmore."

PART 4
EPILOGUE

4 YEARS LATER, DECEMBER 2019

The young woman parked in front of the Dispenmore's house, exited her car, then opened its back door. She unbuckled a little boy, took him out of the car-seat and put him on the ground. He immediately began stomping his tiny rubber boots on a puddle near the porch. She took his hand, pulled him away from the puddle, went to the door, hesitated for a while, and then pressed the doorbell.

The boy freed his hand from her and started jumping around while waiting until the door opened.

"Stop it, please, Arie," she said strictly. "Remember, I told you - you should be polite while meeting your grandma and sister. Okay? I want them to think that you're a good boy."

"I am a good boy," he confirmed heatedly. "It's so booooring, mommy."

The door finally opened, and the woman saw a tall blond man with a young child hiding behind his legs. That was unexpected.

"Good morning, Miss. How can I help you?" the man uttered, looking surprised but smiling politely.

"Good morning, sir," she answered with a confused smile as well. "My name is Jessa Green. I would like to see Mrs. Dispenmore and Laurie. And you are?... Oh, I remember, you're Rosalyn's dad. You probably forgot, but we met once, at City Hall, when Rosalyn was marrying Aaron. I had a summer job at the coffee shop there... Sorry, I didn't expect to see you here. Your name is...?"

"Liam Johnson."

"Nice to see you again, sir," she stretched her hand to him for a handshake which he accepted gladly.

"Wow!... Jessa..." he said bewildered. "It was so long ago, more than four years... I don't remember you personally, but I remember we met some of Rosie's friends from her Poetry Club there. Yeah, it was an awkward moment. She was kind of lost. Okay, Jessa, come in, please."

"Thank you, Mr. Johnson." she stepped over the threshold, pulling her boy by his hand.

"You can call me Liam," he suggested simply. "It is not such an official meeting, I guess. And who is this young fellow?" He squatted in front of Jessa's child and took his tiny hand to shake. "Hi buddy. What is your name?"

"Arie," he answered quietly, confused.

"His name is Aaron Adam Green. After his dad." Jessa said, taking off the boy's boots and unzipping his jacket. "He is my son from Aaron Dispenmore."

"What?!" Liam exclaimed, amused, and stood up taking a step back. "How could it be? I have Aaron's son here," he turned to another boy who was quietly standing beside him still holding his leg. "Here is our Mr. Eric George Dispenmore, right, sweetheart?"

The child nodded silently.

"I can explain, sir," Jessa agreed, taking off her boots and jacket. "Could we talk somewhere?"

"Yes, please, come into the living room," Liam suggested, ushering her with her son in tow from the hallway.

It was warm in the house. The fireplace was on and in front of it was spread a big area rug with a bunch of pillows and toys on it. A wooden railroad was in the middle, unfinished, with a pile of tracks and train cars laying beside it. It was visible that Liam and Eric were busy building the rail road before they were interrupted by the strange unexpected visitors.

"Is Mrs. Dispenmore or Laurie at home?" Jessa asked, settling on a couch while little Aaron pressed his side to her knees holding her hand.

"Just a sec," Liam gestured her to stop, squatted in front of Eric and suggested to him, "Look, buddy, the lady and I will have an adult talk here which is very boring. You don 't want to listen to it. Better you keep building what we started, okay? And then, later, we can all have tea with cupcakes, right?"

"And ice cream," the boy added with a broad smile. "Okay, grandpa?"

Receiving a reassuring nod from Liam, Eric walked to the rug with a pile of toys. He stood there for a while, hesitating about what to do, then took a teddy bear, went back to the couch and silently handed the bear to little Aaron.

Aaron took the bear hugging it to his chest.

"Oh, jeez, they are so cute," Liam laughed.

Then Eric took Aaron's hand and led him toward the rug. Aaron glanced at his mom for an approval and she nodded, chuckling as well. "Yes, yes," she said, "You can go and play with Eric, darling."

The boys walked together to the rug, sat and Eric began jabbering about his railroad while Aaron still held the bear tight by his bosom and listened.

"Gosh," Jessa whispered with tears in her eyes. "His brother accepted him..."

"Yeah," Liam smiled. "Eric has kind of a gut feeling. They actually look very much alike. Definitely Aaron's hair, eyes, and eyebrow line, even chin... They really look like brothers. How old is Arie?"

"Three years and four months."

"Hmm... interesting," Liam smirked. "Eric is three years and eight months old. So, two brothers with only four months difference in age?! Unbelievable! Our friend, Aaron, was obviously very busy not only with science. Jeez! But... yeah... I remember once when Rosie fought with Ashot because he accused her that she forgot Aaron way too fast, she said that Aaron forgot her first and was seeing another woman before leaving for the conference... and he confessed to her the night before he was shot, that he wants to marry this woman."

"That last thing I didn't know," Jessa murmured sadly. "We didn't talk about that yet. We just had one accident and I was a bit worried that I might get pregnant. Aaron promised that we will deal with it after he returns home from New York. But... it never happened. My parents suggested I get an abortion, and, if some guy simply dumped me, I definitely would. But Aaron... He died... And I loved him... I want to keep him with me forever. And that's how I got my new Aaron in flesh and blood. He means the world to me."

"So, you dated Aaron before he left for the conference," Liam established the fact. "What a conspirator! None of us knew about that although we were very close to him."

"Yes, we dated for three months. We met at the university when Aaron returned to work after completing Rosalyn's cure. I approached him only to ask how Rosalyn is doing and... I... I don't know... we just went out. He was still emotionally in pain after their break up, and I simply comforted him... But let's start from the beginning, Liam. I expected to see Mrs. Dispenmore or Laurie. I guessed that Rosalyn's child could be here with them. Aaron told me that he would take the child from her. My son doesn't have a lot of relatives, so I wanted for him to know his extended family. What is your role here now? Are you babysitting Eric?"

"I am sorry to tell you, Jessa, but Mrs. Dispenmore passed away two years ago."

"Oh, I am really sorry to hear that," she uttered sympathetically. "It must be a huge loss for Laurie. Her father... then grandma..."

"Yes, it was," Liam nodded sadly. "And Beth never recuperated after Aaron's death. She suffered a lot with her heart illness but still very bravely flew to Washington DC when Eric was born and took him from Rosie right away. I remember how her face shone when she was holding him in her arms. For her it was her Aaron reborn and returned into her life.

"So, Ashot and I, we adopted Laurie and Eric after her passing," he continued. "There are some distant relatives of the Dispenmore family and they wanted to step in but Laurie strictly refused. She wished to only live with me..." He giggled. "We have love from the first sight with her. And we didn't want to separate her from her little brother. As a result, my husband and I are the couple with two children now, although they call us 'grandpas'."

"And where is the second 'grandpa'?" Jessa asked. "Went shopping or something?"

"Ashot is at work. Didn't you know that Aaron opened a private psychiatric clinic *Clay Mask* with him? We were actually three owners, but when Aaron died, Beth inherited his part. Then she sold it to Ashot's daughter, Annush, who is a Doctor of Psychiatry as well. She moved here from New York. Her husband, Omid, got transferred to work in the *Bank of America* in Seattle and, by the way, he was very happy because some of his relatives live here in the Iranian Baha'i community. Annush and Omid are renting our condo, and we moved to this house for kids' sake. So, now Ashot and his daughter are both working at their clinic as a team. They actually completely cured eighteen people for schizophrenia during the last four years."

"Yes, when in October 2016 it was announced on the TV News that Aaron won the Nobel Prize, they also told about the clinic," Jessa confirmed. "I got curious and drove there one day, just to take a look. I took some photos." She pulled her phone from her pocket and opened it.

"Here," she said then. "I don't have any personal photos of Aaron. I have nothing to show Arie when he starts asking questions about his dad, but I have photos of the clinic. Look... here... The big sign says *Clay Mask*. **The Psychiatry Clinic of Dr. Aaron Dispenmore.** And on one window wall is written in golden letters - *Dr. Hannah A. Michelson, MD, PhD* and *Thomas (Ashot) C. Spencer, psychiatry RN*. On another window wall is a very handsome portrait of Aaron and written with the same golden letters – *Dr.*

Aaron A. Dispenmore, MD, PhD, the Nobel Prize Laureate, and his Diploma and Medal are displayed. This is what my son will know about his father.

"And, of course, Rosalyn as Aaron's widow went to Sweden to receive the Prize," Jessa ended sadly. "Jeez, she is always a winner, even with Aaron dead."

"Don't envy her, Jess," Liam shook his head. "She had an extremely poor and scary upbringing. She survived so much abuse and horrors that not many other people ever had. That made her mentally ill. After the cure, now, yes, she is pretty much a lucky girl," he chuckled. "However, Beth also went with Ashot and Rosie to Stockholm - to attend the ceremony where the King of Sweden handed the Nobel Prize for her son's name. It happened on December 10th, 2016 which is their traditional day for that in Sweden. But after returning home Beth passed away very soon. At least she was happy that Aaron got the recognition and respect. It was her closure - consolation and peace for her soul.

"And I went with all of them to Stockholm as well. We left the nanny and housekeeper to watch the kids at home," Liam continued. "But for the clinic I am just an investor," he lifted his palms and smiled, "sometimes a cameraman, observer, babysitter... I am pretty much happy with my husband, my work and our little ones. They are making our lives full. We are approaching that age when other sorts of entertainment are not interesting, shallow and boring, but to see how the children are developing, growing, thinking, asking questions... It is really 'grandpas' fun. And genuinely, nothing is more rewarding in life than pleasure to watch them. I gladly took my day off at work today because Eric's Montessori School is on Christmas break."

"And where is Laurie now?" Jessa wanted to know. "There is no school because of Christmas break for her too, right?"

"She is starring as Little Maggie in the *Two and Half Women,* the fourth season already. She is on set at the moment, working."

"Oh, I like that show!" Jessa exclaimed. "I watch it all the time. I like that girl. I saw the name, Laura Dispenmore, on the titles, but it didn't come to my mind that it could be Aaron's daughter."

"Yes, she is an actress now," Liam smiled. "And a pretty good one, actually. She is an amazing kid! She will be home in the afternoon. My assistant will drive her here. I am sure Laurie would be happy to know that she now has one more little brother."

Before Jessa had a chance to ask something else, the kids, probably tired of playing quietly, began running around chasing one another, throwing pillows, giggling and shrieking with laughter.

"Okay, okay," Liam followed Eric and grabbed him finally. "Look, guys, what if you go outside to play? You know the rules, Eric – all the active games should be on the playground."

"Yeeah," Eric shouted and ran to the hallway closet to take his jacket and boots. Arie followed him. Liam and Jessa helped the kids get dressed and let them out into the backyard. The boys on the swings could be seen through the big window of the living room.

"I guess they will work up an appetite," Liam laughed. "Let's talk in the kitchen, Jess. I will make some sandwiches for lunch before that tea with cupcakes that I promised. We could continue our conversation there."

"Yes, of course, and I can help you," she suggested readily.

"Would you mind telling me a bit about yourself?" Liam inquired, while taking out from the refrigerator items to prepare lunch. Jessa watched with admiration how good, fast and accurate he was as a cook. Liam gave her some 'what to do' instructions, and she started working with him while talking.

"I am a single mother," she said modestly. "This summer I graduated from the university and since September I have been teaching English literature and poetry at a high school."

"Oh," Liam noted, "Rosie was teaching poetry at her high school as well."

"Yes, they hired her at eighteen and without special education because she was a genius," Jessa commented sarcastically, "but for any other person this job required a university degree."

"I understand," Liam nodded a bit confused.

"My little Arie and I are living with my parents. I decided it is better to save some money for his education, than to have our own place and pay rent. My parents are nice people. I was raised in a happy family without any horrors and abuses. Just a regular normal family. My dad is handicapped now after an accident at a construction site. My mom is a bus driver and works night shifts to take care of dad while I am at work. Alas, my parents are not capable of watching Arie, so he is going to a regular daycare – not a Montessori School. But every evening I am teaching him as well, so he is okay. He knows all the letters, can read, can count to ten, knows some geography - most of the states and big cities," she laughed. "I am trying, as you see."

"It looks like you're doing pretty good," Liam said with an approving smile. "Seeing someone?"

"No," Jessa vigorously shook her head. "And never will."

"Never say never," Liam chuckled.

"No, seriously, I have no time for dating. Plus... nobody could ever replace Aaron. His level of a man simply does not exist. I feel like I still love him, like he is occupying my heart, like he is here. Even to think about another man would be cheating. But how could you cheat on the man you love with someone you don't? It's just impossible!"

"Yes, I understand," Liam nodded. "The grief is still fresh for you but hopefully it passes with time. By the way, you know, something just came to my mind. When Rosie received the Nobel Prize as Aaron's widow, there was a pretty significant amount of money - $ 1,400,000.000. She gave it to Ashot – Aaron told her previously that he would do that. But Ashot decided to save the money for our kids' education. We opened trusts for each of them.

"Before Aaron left for New York, he made a new will because he knew that Rosie was pregnant. So he wrote that in case of his death he wanted his money to be shared equally between all of his children. I remember clearly, it did not say - between the *two of my children* but between *all of my children.* He probably kind of guessed that there could be more than two of them. I am not talking here about all of Dispenmore's family money, of course, but only about that Nobel Prize reward.

"I need to discuss it with Ashot," he continued. "There is probably a legal catch that would allow us to share these two trusts making one more trust for your Arie. It will obviously need to go through the legal procedure in court. The judge will request a DNA test to prove that Aaron is the father – no offense, Jessa, please. I absolutely believe you, but it is just the official way of how it works."

"I didn't come here for money, Liam," Jessa blushed. "We are okay with money. I came here looking for more people who could love my son. Of course, I can do the DNA test if it's needed. That doesn't hurt me at all because I know that my Arie is Aaron's son. I have no problem with that. But I want to be sure that Aaron really said '*all of my children*' in his will. I don't want you to feel pity for me and I don't want to look like a poor relative begging for alms. And I also don't want to steal anything from Aaron's other children."

"We will discuss that with Ashot," Liam repeated. "I don't think you're stealing something here. As for love - to open a trust fund for a child for a little less than a half million dollars – wouldn't it be a sign of our love for your little Arie? You know, we both sincerely loved Aaron, and now we are evidently loving his kids. So... deal?" he giggled.

"Deal," she nodded, blushing, still confused.

At that time the boys burst into the living room, all wet and dirty, jabbering agitated about how they fell into puddles while sliding down the slide. Liam took Eric to change, and Jessa brought a bag with extra clothes from her car and changed Arie. Then all together they had lunch that ended up with tea and cupcakes, and finally the boys settled again on the rug in front of the fireplace with a box of Lego.

"I would like to talk a bit more, Jessa," Liam suggested as they sat on the couch in the living room again. "I am curious... you didn't ask anything about Rosie. Are you still friends with her, or...?"

"My relationship with Rosalyn?" Jessa sadly shook her head. "There is none. She blocked all of us, her former friends, completely. It was hurtful then and it is still a bit hurtful even now. Actually, the main reason why I came here today is that yesterday night I watched Johnny Holiday's followup show about her and Alex. It forced me to come."

"Oh, they repeated it?" Liam wondered. "It was taped this Thanksgiving when Rosie and Alex came to visit us from Washington DC. They usually come every year but in turns – one year for Christmas, one year for Thanksgiving. Yeah, it was a brilliant show as Mr. Holiday always does."

"I wanted to come here many times but I didn't dare," Jessa went on. "I was quite nervous that Aaron's family won't accept me. But when I saw this show, it was the last straw... Johnny Holiday showed on a big screen the beautiful fragments of Rosalyn's 2016 Christmas wedding with Alex. This General Simon walking her down the aisle... Actually, why not you, if you are her dad, Liam?"

"We didn't adopt Rosie officially, so the documents show that she doesn't have a father. For her private wedding with Aaron in church, Ashot was considered her fatherly figure. But, for an official wedding on the government level, sadly, no. It was a requirement of the wedding planners. Ashot and I were sitting in public with Alex's family," he chuckled. "This General Simon was actually like a father for both of them. Alex was his Private while in Afghanistan, and Rosie... She was his protege for a very high position in the Pentagon. Everyone knows that he is 'secretly' in love with her."

"I didn't," Jessa smirked meaningfully, shaking her head, "well..." Then she continued, "Didn't this replacement of you hurt your feelings, Liam? All these guests from the Pentagon and White House... Senator Stephanie Mane was Rosalyn's bridesmaid this time instead of me! It was such a high society! To me it looked kind of alien, distant, and strange. I realized that her world now is not my world. It felt like she is dead for us, her former friends. This is not her, not this humble brightly talented girl who loved poetry and had fun with all of us performing at the teens' concerts and walking on the beach – not the girl who was our loving, caring and devoted friend. It shocked me.

"Only the name of her little daughter, Anastasia, is left from Rosalyn's past," Jessa went on. "And, at the end of the show... when Rosalyn and Alex stood on the stage... she - wearing patriotic colors: white pants, red blouse and a blue blazer, and Alex walking with a cane, wearing his military uniform with the Medal of Honor on his chest... I don't know... when Alex seated their daughter on his shoulders and she was waving the American flag while he hugged Rosalyn... and the band played *God Bless America* again as on their previous show in 2015... it was touching. The people in the audience were tearing up. It looked cute to everyone... but to me... it all seemed staged and artificial."

"It was politically necessary," Liam explained. "The wedding of the Medal of Honor bearer, the hero major from the Pentagon, Alex, and the personal translator of the Minister of Defense, Rosie – it was an important political moment on Christmas in 2016. They live together in Washington DC and worked at the Pentagon since February 2016, but they can't marry earlier because Rosie was supposed to go to Sweden and receive the Nobel Prize for Aaron as his widow. When she returned home in the middle of December, they arranged their Christmas wedding with Alex right away.

"And to follow up this political moment now, three years later, to show that the two young 'all American heroes', white and black, are still happily married and have a charming daughter-toddler, who is a future of our nation – it was needed to unite people... you understand, Jess... in this political situation when a lot of enmity and racial hostility was growing in the country. To stay human we have to be united – and it was the goal of Johnny Holiday in making this show.

"Alex is a very humble and reserved man," Liam commented then. "He didn't want to be on the show this Thanksgiving, even when Rosie begged him that it would be very beneficial for the political career of her dreams. However, Ashot worked with him for a while and explained to him that the unity of the nation is the main point for the future of his daughter and his little siblings. And if this show worked for this goal, it was worth being involved. So, finally, Alex gave up."

"I agree, it's a noble goal," Jessa nodded. "However, in those fragments that Mr. Holiday shows about their two-year-old

Anastasia, there was only Alex or nanny playing with her. Rosalyn didn't even find the time to take one picture with her daughter?"

"Don't be too harsh on her, Jess," Liam objected, smiling. "Rosie is working very hard, sometimes up to fifteen hours a day. And she travels a lot with many different dignitaries around the world."

"Yes, I heard that. She talked with Johnny Holiday about her job excitedly, I noticed."

"She is very special as a simultaneous translator of twenty-five languages," Liam concluded. "I don't think this level of professionalism exists anywhere in the world. She was invited several times to work for the White House, but she strictly refused at that time. However now, with the new president just being elected, she told us that she would probably accept the invitation. At least, she will think about it.

"For her defense," Liam continued. "Rosie has absolutely no time for the family and household. She is practically never at home. They have a live-in nanny for Anastasia and a full time housekeeper. It's like a pendulum swinging in the opposite direction. Rosie was always very poor, weak, sick, helpless, dependent and now she is rich, strong, healthy, self-confident and independent. From one extreme to the opposite. Ashot says that it is psychologically understandable. It will probably settle somewhere in the middle further in her life. At some point he is proud of her, but at some point he is pitying her, and actually me too."

"Yes," Jessa agreed. "I am feeling that as well. Does Rosalyn ever remember Aaron? Does she treasure the memories of their love? Has she ever connected with their little son?"

"Sadly, no. Even when they come for visits, as I said, she never talks to him or hugs him. She behaves like a perfect stranger. But the kids are not interested in her very much either. They consider her some acquaintance-guest of the family. Not to mention Laurie, but even Eric never called her an 'm' word."

"Wow! It's so sad. I absolutely couldn't imagine giving away my child," Jessa shook her head. "And her coldness and indifference to her little daughter that I saw on Holiday's show made me think about Aaron's son. It was that last straw I talked about. It forced me to come here today. For Aaron's sake and memory I decided to check how Eric is doing growing without a mother. Is he missing her?"

"Rosie chose the career," Liam sighed deeply. "It is her choice and she has a right to it. I guess Eric is pretty much okay and is receiving a lot of love from us, 'grandpas', and Laurie. He is a happy child."

"I don't know. I couldn't wrap my mind around it. Every child, even the happiest one, biologically and emotionally needs a mother," Jessa shook her head in disapproval. "Maybe you are right, Liam, maybe Rosalyn is doing important things for the country, for the nation, for unity, for the future. But I knew that Aaron didn't like her new occupation. It was alien and cold for him. He was too sensitive and too kind for that. He loved poetry..."

Then the kids began running around again. Eric got Arie to climb on the stairs to the upper floor and showed him how to slide down on his bum step-by-step. The stairs were covered with a soft carpet and wouldn't hurt kids' bums. They were climbing up on all fours, then sit on the landing and slide down in turns, then together, side-by-side. They were pushing each other, falling on their sides, laughing like crazy, shrieking in excitement and kept playing this way for some time, while Liam and Jessa enjoyed watching them, laughing as well.

"I think we should work out a schedule convenient for everybody and organize play days for them maybe once a week," Liam suggested.

"It would be very nice," Jessa agreed.

"I also would like to invite you, Jess, for Christmas dinner here. Ashot's daughter, Annush, will be here with her husband, some friends from my filming crew and from our Piano Club where Ashot and I met. Usually, Alex's mother comes with her three kids. Her girls are close to Laurie's age, twelve and ten, and they are good together. And Alex's little brother, Dante, is seven already. He usually plays with Eric and Anastasia. So, it will be noisy - a lot of kids, and little Arie will have the possibility to blend with them well.

"However, this year Rosie, Alex and Anastasia won't be here. They already came for Thanksgiving and for that Johnny Holiday show. They stopped here for half an hour and then left – Alex with their daughter went to dinner with his family, and Rosie went to Senator Stephanie Mane, who sent a car for her."

"Did Rosalyn and Alex fight?" Jessa asked, astonished. "Why did they separate for such a family day?"

"No," Liam laughed. "They never fight. They are very good friends and happy together. They just keep their marriage the way that each of them is free to do what they want. Alex wanted to be with his family, Rosie wanted to be with the Senator and her company of guests."

Jessa didn't say anything more, just shook her head in disapproval. She couldn't understand that.

"You can also bring your parents for our Christmas dinner, Jess," Liam continued. "We should meet them, as we are kind of a family now, and you said, you don't have many other relatives. So, let's work it out."

"Thank you so much, Liam. It would be great," Jessa smiled with content. "I am sure my mom and dad would be happy to know Aaron's family. Although it wouldn't be easy – my dad is in a wheelchair."

"Good you said that," Liam noted. "We could build a temporary ramp to our porch beforehand. So, please, pass our invitation to them, Jess."

During that conversation, the boys continued their fun on the stairs until suddenly Arie hit his elbow on the banisters and ran to Jessa, crying. "Ouch, mommy, mommy, it hurts!" he screamed, sobbing loudly while showing his elbow to her.

"It's okay, sweetheart, it's okay," she hugged her child tenderly, comforting him, kissing his injured arm and seated him on her lap. He hugged her neck and snuggled up to her, as she kept kissing his wet cheeks and eyes until his crying subsided.

"What happened?" Liam quietly asked Eric who stood silently, pouted, and watched, mesmerized, as Jessa caressed her son.

"I don't know, grandpa," the boy whispered. "He just hurt himself."

Eric looked very confused and it was noticeable that he also was almost ready to cry. He kept watching for a while, then came to the banister and hit his elbow on it. "Ouch, mommy, mommy, it hurts!" he screamed, repeating exactly after Arie, sobbed loudly, ran to Jessa and hugged her, crying.

"Oh, my God!" she exclaimed. "Sweetheart, what happened? Are you hurting too? Where is it? Show me!"

She kissed his forehead and then, as he lifted his arm and pointed at the same spot where Arie was hurt, Jessa kissed his elbow. Eric hugged her neck on the other side from Arie and held her tight.

"Okay, okay," she said comfortingly, moved Arie on one of her knees and then lifted Eric and seated him on her other knee. This way they both were sitting on her lap and hugging her neck together and she hugged their backs with her arms. "Okay, okay," she repeated, kissing in turns Arie's and Eric's cheeks. "You stop crying, please, guys. It will heal very fast. It's not such a big injury. Let me massage your elbows a little bit, and then you will be okay and can go play again."

"Thank you, mommy," Arie sniffled. "I love you."

"Thank you, mommy," Eric repeated. "I love you."

"Of course, of course," Jessa whispered fondly. "I love you too, I love you too. You see, it's already better. It doesn't hurt anymore, right?" Then, seeing that the boys stopped crying, she let them both stand up, covered her face with her palms and suddenly sobbed herself.

"Why are you crying, mommy?" Arie asked, amazed. "Are you hurt?"

"Why are you crying, mommy?" Eric repeated.

"Please, don't cry, mommy," Arie said and hugged her shoulder.

"Please, don't cry, mommy," Eric stubbornly repeated after him and hugged her other shoulder.

Liam watched this scene literally dropping his jaw until he heard the door open and someone entered the house, talking and laughing. He went to the hall to meet Laurie and his assistant, Nancy, who drove the girl home from the movie set. Laurie, now a nine-and-half-year-old, was a slim girl, and pretty tall for her age. While Liam talked with Nancy for a few minutes, Laurie dropped her boots and jacket off and entered the living room. She saw a woman, dark-haired, chubby, whom she never met before, sitting on the couch, crying, and her little brother with another boy hugging her.

"What's going on here?" the girl exclaimed, astonished.

"Mommy is crying," Arie answered, turning to her.

"Look, Laurie, mommy is crying," Eric repeated.

The girl came closer and stared attentively at Jessa and Arie. Then she took a couple of tissues from the box of Kleenex on the coffee table and gave them to the boys.

Jessa moved her palms away from her face, lifted her head and glanced at Laurie, sniffling.

"Thank you," she uttered with an unsteady voice. "Good afternoon, Laurie. Nice to meet you."

"Nice to meet you too, ma-am," the girl answered, then asked, "Why are you crying, ma-am?"

Arie started wiping his mother's tears from her cheek. Eric repeated after him, wiping her other cheek. It was so touching and cute, that they all laughed.

"Sorry," Jessa said. "Nothing happened. I was just crying from happiness."

"Who is crying from happiness?" Eric made a wry face. "I never cry when I open my Christmas presents."

"Yes," Arie nodded. "I never cry when I open my birthday presents."

Laurie came closer, sat on the couch beside Eric and put her arm on Jessa's shoulder. "No, guys," she said. "I know it's possible to cry from happiness. I worked on this kind of scene a couple of weeks ago. Please, don't cry anymore, mommy. Even from happiness," and she fondly patted the woman's back.

Jessa stretched her arm around Laurie and snuggled all three kids feeling the warmth of their bodies. She closed her eyes and sensed that Aaron was in them, with them, watching them and hugging them all together. *That's how it would be, if he would be alive*, she thought. *We all will be one happy family.*

She now felt his presence and his caring sensation - in kids, in their hands hugging and holding her.

While talking with Liam previously, she was bewildered to find out that during the last hours of his life Aaron admitted that he wanted to marry her. He didn't tell her that. However, at the moment Jessa clearly heard his voice in her mind as he told her after the wild encounter in his car where their little Arie was conceived, "Good news, Jess. We're probably heading there... And if you will read me more poems..."

"I will, if you want to hear them, Aaron," she answered then. "Of course I will. Sadly, I am not even near as talented as Rosalyn. I performed at each concert, but never in five years did I win from her. Ever!"

And now she still heard Aaron's voice whispering in her ears exactly as he said to her then, "Well... you did win from her today."

About The Author

Kate Valery is a professional musician and journalist. She was born and had university education in Russia. While working at the International Moscow Radio as a music editor and correspondent, she authored eleven books.

In 1996, she immigrated to Canada and worked for many years as a pianist and music teacher, and also as the editor of several Russian newspapers in Edmonton, AB.

In Canada she started to write in English and authored five books: **Stolen** and **Deadly Paradise** – 2007, **Curse of Russia** – 2009, **Love Triangle** – 2010, **Love with a Ghost** – 2011, before returning nine years later to the subject of music in her 6th novel - **Midget or Symphony of the Ocean** – 2020.

Clay Mask is her 7th novel in English.

Kate Valery resides in White Rock, BC, Canada where she is the secretary of the local Writers' Club

About The Book

When the young psychiatrist, Dr. Aaron Dispenmore, during his evening walk with his daughter, Laurie, helped a stranger girl on the street to find a bus stop, he couldn't have known that this ordinary event would turn his life upside down, and lead him to the a scientific discovery worthy of a Nobel Prize. But, this discovery could end up potentially deathly ...

Which way had Fate chosen for him then – triumph or death? Or maybe both?

Clay Mask is a deeply psychological story of love, and the tragedy of mental illness; the story that is searching for the meaning and goals of humans' existence, but is also full of dangerous adventure.

It's a novel. However, it is based on a true research study of the secrets of a human brain - its connections to the holographic universe, three-dimensional time, and the endless, mysterious, unbelievable possibilities hidden in 90 percent of its unopened part.

CPSIA information can be obtained
at www.ICGtesting.com
Printed in the USA
BVHW040220010722
641072BV00002B/3